HellFire

Mia Gallagher was born in Dublin where she still lives. Her short stories have been published in Ireland, the UK and the US, and several have been produced as monologues. She also works as a performer, devising original work for the theatre, and occasionally writes for broadcast TV and educational media. *HellFire* is her first novel.

HellFire

A Novel

MIA GALLAGHER

PENGUIN IRELAND

PENGUIN IRELAND

Published by the Penguin Group
Penguin Ireland, 25 St Stephen's Green, Dublin 2, Ireland (a division of Penguin Books Ltd)
Penguin Books Ltd, 80 Strand, London WC2R ORL, England
Penguin Group (USA) Inc., 375 Hudson Street, New York, New York 10014, USA
Penguin Group (Australia), 250 Camberwell Road, Camberwell, Victoria 3124, Australia
(a division of Pearson Australia Group Pty Ltd)
Penguin Group (Canada), 90 Eglinton Avenue East, Suite 700, Toronto, Ontario, Canada M4P 2Y3
(a division of Pearson Penguin Canada Inc.)
Penguin Books India Pvt Ltd, 11 Community Centre, Panchsheel Park, New Delhi – 110 017, India
Penguin Group (NZ), 67 Apollo Drive, Mairangi Bay, Auckland 1310, New Zealand
(a division of Pearson New Zealand Ltd)
Penguin Books (South Africa) (Pty) Ltd, 24 Sturdee Avenue, Rosebank, Johannesburg 2196, South Africa

Penguin Books Ltd, Registered Offices: 80 Strand, London WC2R ORL, England

www.penguin.com

First published 2006
2

Copyright © Mia Gallagher, 2006

The moral right of the author has been asserted

Set in Monotype Dante
Typeset by Palimpsest Book Production Limited, Grangemouth, Stirlingshire
Printed in Great Britain by Clays Ltd, St Ives plc

A CIP catalogue record for this book is available from the British Library

ISBN-13 978-1-844-88081-2
ISBN-10 1-844-88081-8

For Seán

and

my parents, Miriam and Gerhardt

Having during my solitary retirement often revolved in my mind the various scenes of life, in which I have been either a principal actor or merely a spectator; and having always had within myself a secret friend and monitor, who persuaded me to make observations, to draw conclusions and to hoard up for riper years the lessons of experience; I thought that a faithful picture of my youthful eccentricities, drawn with justice and impartiality, would not be unacceptable to my countrymen, and particularly to my younger friends, who will find some few examples which they may follow with advantage, but many more which they ought to avoid . . .

. . . I shall simply give a sketch of my actions and pursuits: I shall unfold the deepest recesses of my heart and unmask the various arts and stratagems that are used to mislead young men of great expectations, and to ruin their health, morals and fortunes.

The Memoirs of Buck Whaley (1797, ed. Sir Edward Sullivan, London)

I've been to hell and back and, let me tell you, it was wonderful.

'Untitled' by Louise Bourgeois (mixed media sewn on fabric, 1996)

Cut

They release me at ten. John Paul's waitin outside in the car.

A coupla cameras, not as many as I thought. Thank Christ. Must be on accounta Big Brother. I'm ready for them any case. Got me hood up and me hand over me gob.

Even so, I stop at the gate. Believe it or not, I stop. But then me foot is over and there's no goin back.

It's a scorcher of a day. Mid-June. Gorgeous. Sun a white ball a fire burstin through a loomin blue sky.

Before goin ta Ma's, I decide ta have a bit of a wander. Not worried or nothin. I just can't stick goin there straightaway.

I head down Capel Street and turn onta the old fruit market at Mary's Abbey where Granny useta buy her stuff. Still the same, if a bit more rundown. Oranges oozin in the corners, crusty paint-work droppin off of the hoardins. Then I walk down the Golden Mile, headin west past the Four Courts and Smithfield and on inta Stoneybatter. I see things I never noticed when I was out on Temporary Release. There's cars everywhere; shiny. And roadworks and niggers and cranes and gangs a Spanish kids takin up the foot-paths and restaurants and big pubs with bigger windas and young trees and Chinese servin coffee in the Spar and junkies goofin out in the open and tourists screamin ta be robbed.

The city is cleaner in some ways; dirtier in others.

Like me great-granda before me, I'm dazed by the noise and the sights of it. And more. By the freedom sittin so unaccustomed on me skin I feel bare, like everyone can see right through me. *Hello, Lucy!*

Some places look familiar even with the changes. But when I get ta Smithfield, I don't hardly recognize it. It's like a ghost of itself. Train tracks over the cobbles. Glass and wood and concrete apartment blocks. Shiny shop fronts, reflectin all the people speedin past, their mobile phones glued ta their ears. Only that church doorway down near the quays where I useta kip is left standin, with bits a grime and dirty papers collectin in the corners a the steps, like memories people can't be arsed thinkin about any more.

In Stoneybatter I walk upta Mary's Place, where Granny was born, and stand outside what I think coulda been her gaff and have a smoke. Then a curtain twitches, some auld lad worryin I'm scopin him for a rob, no doubt, so I turn round and head back inta the city. I walk along the quays, bravin the blue fumes spewin from cars, the rattlin buses, the chainsmokin artic drivers with their stubbly chins and leery eyes.

Hey, pretty.

What you lookin at?

On me right sleazes the Liffey, green and slow.

O'Connell Street is manky and unformed as ever. People runnin round with shoppin, briefcases, kids. They bump me, chatter, ignore me. I keep goin north, up Parnell Square, along by the Garden a Remembrance, under the trees with the drowsy alkies boozin in the shadas. I give a euro ta a lad tappin near the Garden gates. Then I head onta Denmark Street.

When I get ta the Square I stop, and look at the new office block they've built on the place where the squat useta be.

I still can't face Ma, so instead a headin around onta Summerhill and inta the flats, I go down Charles Street. As I'm walkin past one a them little alleyways, I feel ya there, down in the dirt. Just like I felt ya before, all them years ago. Ya fly outta the alleyway and up behind me, perchin for a minute on me shoulder blades; a giant pair a black wings. A guardian angel. Then ya gone. Like that, a passin wind.

After gettin the stuff from the flat I take a bus from Dorset Street. 16A accordin ta the map yer wan from inside gave me.

The bus is full a gigglin girls in tee-shirts with long brown legs and flat pierced bellies. A coupla auld wans tut and look out the winda as I pass. Nothin changes.

I get off at the church after the Castle. There's loads a people millin round. Saturday evenin Mass. I hoist the bag onta me shoulder. Forgot how heavy that yoke was. Then I head south, uphill.

It's an easier walk than the last time, even with the bag. Insects whirrin in the tall grasses beside the road, crows cawin in the trees. The branches move. The leaves sigh. Ssshh. The views are nice. I fall inta rhythm easy. All the boxin trainin. Me feet lift and drop. Heel arch toe.

The wood's deserted. The car park's closed and the tourists and walkers are all gone. Thank Christ. I keep ta the path, only veerin off at that place half-way up. Then I duck through the bushes and the willa trees and when I get ta the big stone where I left her, I stop and scrabble round for a while. There's nothin there. I kick the brambles with me feet, hopin for a sign, dried blood, bone, anythin, and even though I know this is crazy, it was thirteen year ago, I'm still disappointed, and the ghost beside me more so, when I find nothin.

It's a beautiful evenin. The sun's yella rays tickle the brown earth and the dark green needles a the trees. Ta me left I see Dublin creepin its way up the foothills, slinkin its grey octopus arms over the countryside like it's tryin ta cover everythin the world over in a thin skin a concrete.

There's light streamin across the curvy roof, the empty windas. Picks out the roundy bricks. Makes it look nice . . . almost.

I stop at the door.

I hear yer voice slidin up me back. Like oil it slides up me, liquid at the edges like ya got the tail enda the flu, that lazy half-laugh coatin over yer accent that's still got a shred a Manchester in there under the Dublin. Ya laugh, lazy, and I hear ya tell me, *Let it be, Lucy Lu. Put the past away, where it belongs, leave it quiet, don't be rakin up things ya can't be dealin with.*

Then I hear that shushin again. *Ssshh.*

But I've had enough a leavin things quiet. And you know as well as me, old pal, that even if I was the kind ta let things lie, it's gone far too late for that.

I duck me head, step inside.

Ready or not, Nayler.

Shuffle

I

When did it start? Easy. Where it always does, at the beginnin.

Wronnnnggg! Trick question. Granny useta say there's always more than one start ta a story. Ya think ya have it all worked out but then ya dig a little deeper and ya find there's another beginnin underneath, and then another. The truth, said Granny, is like the dance a the seven veils – only there's way more than seven.

Then she'd wink.

When did it start, this whole shebang, this great big fuckin adventure? Me, I see three pictures. A boy throwin a rope a ragged sheets through an open bedroom winda of a Wickla farmhouse. A young wan with bleached blonde hair click-clacketin her hip-swayin way down Dorset Street.

And the third picture, the one that jumps out the most – ya might recognize it, Nayler – it's a black-eyed kid watchin at the stairwell of a block a flats.

The mountain is on the other side a the valley from yer haunt and then on again some. It sticks up inta the sky like a shaken fist, its point a knuckleduster, its grey skin the colour a dead people.

The boy feels it at his back. It crowds him. Everythin in the farmhouse crowds him. The small windas, the shrunken door he hasta bend almost in two ta get through. The pots on the wall, the turf in the stove. And Her.

She's not his real ma. He's known this for a while now, from piecin together the rumours he's thieved off the dairygirls and the workmen on the nearby estate. He's called her Ma for fifteen year, nearly as long as he's been alive, but he's not hers.

She found him on the doorstep and raised him as her own. She has plans for him. She wants him ta look after her in her old age. But she's reckoned without his rovin spirit, the twitchy feet that

9

brung him from his real ma's womb in the first place ta end up on Her doorstep.

In front a him sheets a rain spit and piss on the Wickla hills and valleys. The spire a the Enniskerry church is hazy, half-ghost in the mist. Dusk is comin.

He lifts the rope that's tied round the enda his bed. It's strong; he knotted it together that mornin from some old bedsheets. He doesn't need it really; he could jump easy without hurtin himself, but it feels . . . right. He throws the rope, watches the end as it snakes, rocks, settles.

He backs himself out the winda, holdin the rope, and lets his feet drop.

And so begins the tale a me great-granda, the seventh son of a seventh son, as Granny put it – only how could she ever prove that seein as he never knew who his real da nor ma were? But that was Granny all over, full a stories that kept doublin back on themselves, true one day, false the next. As she said: 'Stories aren't like the world out here, Lucy. They don't hafta match up.'

All the same, she was fulla auld shite, me Granny. She was the one told us W. B. Yeats got all his poems from Zozimus and Buck Whaley was born a Mayo peasant, that the Famine had started in Dublin's inner city and Charles Stewart Parnell was still alive . . . somewhere. And forget about them longboats the Vikings were rumoured ta have come over in; they'd actually swum all the way from Norway because they were so anxious ta get their hands on the monasteries. For years, she claimed she herself was a true Dub, stretchin back generations ta the very same Vikings that had front-crawled their way down the Irish Sea. We swallied her guff, every bit of it, didn't think ta ask how she could claim ta be a real Dub when her own da was a runaway bred in Wickla. She didn't even tell us he was a tinker ta start with neither. A highwayman, she claimed, that travelled the roads robbin from the rich ta give ta the poor. It was only when Marlene, me Uncle Stevo's wife, double-checked the records and called her bluff that we got a glimpse a the real story. But Granny always had an answer for the truth.

'Wickla, Dublin, highwayman, tinker,' she said. 'Does it matter how or where he started? The main thing is how he ended up.'

Then she fixed Marlene with a glare from her one good eye and that shut everyone up.

It was from the runaway – the foundlin, Granny called him when she couldn't get away with callin him a highwayman any more – that we got the gift; Granny, Ma, Samantha and even, I suppose, me. The widda who'd raised him had tried ta beat it outta me great-granda, but once he got on the road he found it was the best way ta make a livin. Palms, tea-leaves, playin cards, a glass ball from a fisherman's net; he used whatever he could find ta poke through the present inta the future, learnin bit by bit ta separate the truth a what he seen from what the punters, rich and poor alike, really wanted ta hear.

'For three year,' says Granny, 'he wanders with the tinkers. Readin hands, mendin pots, sellin the horses. Then one day the King a the Tinkers takes him aside and says he's got a present for him. "A present?" says me da, rubbin his hands at the thought a gettin a fine horse for himself . . .'

'But it's not that!' says me brother Micko, bang on cue.

'No, it's not. Instead of a lovely white horse, the Tinker King wants ta give him –'

'– his ugly yoke of a daughter!'

We all know this story inside out but it's a good one.

'Dried up as an old boot she is,' says Granny, leanin forward in her chair. 'With only two stumpy pegs where her teeth shoulda been. Her breath stinks like a sewer and her hands have no thumbs on accounta the horses ate them. Small wonder me da packs up his stuff that very night and leaves.'

He walks. It takes him two days. They'd camped in Laragh and it's a long stretch over ta the Sally Gap and up inta Glencree.

Amazed at me knowin so much about geography, Nayler? Ya shouldn't. I been studyin it enough lately.

The city crowds inta his eyes, mouth, ears. There's so many

bricks, so little space. The streets are too dirty. The walls too high. The Dublin accent drills itself inta his head. The misty green hills and the songs a the tinkers start ta fade. His heart beats faster. In the grey faces a the factory workers and the dockers me great-granda sees a million futures.

He finds a job tendin horses at the Smithfield market. He knows some a the dealers there from his years on the road. He's made enough pals ta earn a warnin if – no, *when* – the King a the Tinkers is due ta come ta market. But luck is with me great-granda, and instead a runnin inta his old enemy he locks horns with an angel.

She appears on his very first fair day, on the far side a the square, a floatin vision in white, skin pale as the moon, hair long and reddy-blonde trailin down ta her waist. It's a dull April day but what sun there is gets trapped in her curls, sendin reflections like golden fireworks dancin across the cobbles. She looks up. Their eyes meet. And then . . .

'And then the guns started blazin!' says Granny. 'It was pan-deh-MON-ium. People screamin, soldiers marchin, horses goin berserk. Everyone around starts runnin but me da stays where he is, glued ta the spot. If James Connolly himself had come up and grabbed him by the arm, he wouldn'a budged. All round him the Citizen Army and the IRB fight ta free his nation but me da has eyes only for the angel.'

Yeah, ya guessed right. The day me great-granda and great-granny happened ta meet was none other than –

'Easter Monday, 1916.'

Granny made that bit up, a course. Ya couldn'a had a market on Easter Monday, it bein a holiday and all. But so what? As Granny says, a good story isn't the six a clock news, so if rackin gunfire and screamin crowds make a tale a true love more lively, then so be it.

True love?

A stirrin. A flush. Hard tinker eyes scannin through white cloth, drawin lines round the curve and swell of arse and tit. The girl, the only daughter of a Cowtown drover, can't, won't, pull away.

*

They marry – though why the drover would let his only child go off with a pot-mendin foundlin beats me. Maybe me great-granda told him somethin he wanted ta hear, painted his future so bright he couldn't say no. But how and ever, the foundlin wants his angel ta give him babies and she obliges, poppin out sixteen kids one after another. Granny's the seventh, born – if she's to be believed – the very day Mick Collins signed the Treaty in 1921.

'Seventh child of a seventh child,' she brags, though we all know she can't prove it.

Three a the sixteen die at birth, two go under with the pleurisy. And outta eleven that live, some marry, some emigrate and the rest find a vocation, batterin religion inta the masses. But poor Granny, left short on the looks front in spite a the flamin red hair she got from her ma, has no choice but ta stay put, lookin after her parents. Someone had ta pay the price for the agony a pop pop poppin out sixteen children.

Time passes, tick tock, and Granny rots in the tiny cottage in Mary's Place, Stoneybatter, gettin crabby and mean as her parents wither away and the flakin walls creep closer, drippin inta her skin, stiflin her dreams, cloudin her midnight visions and stillin the voices a the dead. Until –

'Until what, Granny?'

Ask a silly question.

It's a filthy day. The clouds are jet, the rain streamin down the gutters and in under the neck of his overcoat. Thunder groans and a fresh loada piss buckets down outta the sky. He scours the street for shelter, spots the post office across the way, and takes a chance, sprintin across like the hurler he useta be, crashin through puddles and dodgin trams. Watch him go – Mick Dolan, Ballina's finest, the only half-decent player on Mayo's miserable excuse for a team.

He reaches the door and squeezes in under the awnin, huffin and puffin like the Big Bad Wolf, regrettin the ten pint from the night before. A vein in his forehead throbs. He knows he's gone purple.

He leans against the glass door, not meanin ta put his weight on it, but with the throbbin in his vein and the rain pissin every-where he doesn't work it out right, and the next minute he's off balance and then the door is openin and he's crashin right inta a young wan on her way out.

The parcels in her arms wobble, tilt, fly.

'Ah, sweet Jesus!' says me Granny.

Mick Dolan bends, tryin ta help her, but she bats him away. Up close he sees she's not that young after all. But she has good features. Her mouth is full, he can tell, only pursed up now on accounta the mess.

'I'm terrible sorry, miss,' he says.

Mick Dolan is from famine stock, reared on salt and stones. He'd never go back there, fuck no. For what? Ta battle with his cousins over the poxy patch a grass the Dolans call a farm? But even though he's been in Dublin five year now, drivin Guinness vans by day, drinkin Guinness bottles by night, he hasn't forgotten everythin the West taught him. Her hips are wide. Promisin. Her jaw is hard and she still has all her teeth. They're white and strong. They're teeth that wouldn't be afraid ta tear grass outta a neighbour's mouth ta save her own child from death.

'And without battin an eyelid,' says Granny, 'he asks me if I'd mind if he walked me home. Love at first sight.'

Love? Not if ya ask me. Granny was twenty-eight by then. She'da jumped at anyone who popped the question. And Dolan's good winter coat and the flash a silver in its pockets musta blinded her ta what was walkin round inside it.

Granny never talked much about what it was like livin with me granda. But once, at a party for Uncle Michael before he went off ta the missions, I heard them – me uncles, Ma, Marlene and all – rabbitin on about the old times. From what I could earwig, hidin under the kitchen table, old Mick Dolan had been a drinker – and bad with it. Uncle Dessie had found him more than once walkin up and down the street at two in the mornin, mumblin away ta himself in Irish, his once-good winter coat moulderin at the edges. He was a gambler as well, bet away all the money he didn't drink, then used his fists ta bet all his disappointment onta Granny's wide shoulders.

When he died, two years after me Ma was born, Granny, expectin a widda's pension, got a not so pleasant surprise.

Three loud knocks came a-knockin on the door. A weelya weelya wawlya.

Three loud knocks came a-knockin on the door. Down by the river –

Camac.

Nine on a Saturday mornin in Inchicore. Granny opens the red door a the railway house; number 15, Ring Street. Three tall men with big red necks and hard grey eyes are standin on the step.

'Sorry, Mrs Dolan, but the rent is months behind. We've no choice but ta—'

The next day, the neighbours have a field day, sniggerin together in the Communion queue.

'Didja see her?'

'Didja see the shock on the tinker's face?'

'That'll show her, thinkin she's goin up in the world!'

Thing is, maybe them bailiffs weren't such a shock for me Granny. She had her foundlin father's gift after all. She musta seen them comin.

Sometimes Ma said it was Granny pushed me granda under that tram in 1958, because she was sick a shovin babies out like her ma before her, even sicker a bein shunted around from one house ta another like an old shoe. Pure viciousness, why Ma started them rumours, the same viciousness that's driven her all her life, especially where I been concerned. Even now, with all that's been said and done between us, there's a black strip in her that would love ta see me brung down lower than I already am. And she was always quick ta slander Granny.

'The auld waggon killed him,' she whispers across the room ta Marlene while Granny dozes in the raggedy sofa. I'm just outside the kitchen door, listenin in.

'She shoved him under that tram when no one was watchin. Took her moment so it would look like an accident.'

'Oh, Jesus, no!' says Marlene. 'Ya don't mean it, Rose. Tell me ya don't.'

I'm only five but I know Marlene is lyin. What she really means is *Tell me ya do*.

All through her life, Granny never said a word about me granda's death. That musta been hard for her, seein as there'da been a great story in it. But she kept her gob shut, no matter how hard we pestered her. It makes me wonder sometimes if Ma was right after all, but I never wonder for long. Murder . . . well, it just wouldn'a been me Granny's style.

She looks at herself in the black-spotted mirror hangin over the fireplace in the front room. It must be the jolt from seein the bailiffs at the door, but she's seein herself fresh now, like she hasn't in a while. Two long lines stretch from her nose ta the corners a her mouth. They're new. He put them there.

Behind her, misty shapes in the mirror, are her six children. She knows if she turns around they won't be there. They'll be gone, vanished! Just like that. But in the mirror they're as real as day.

Inside her belly the seventh turns. The movement makes her feel sick.

She tips the bottle a Gordons ta her lips and swallas. It burns.

She holds out her hand. It's steady. Each finger pulses with life. Each finger is someone she could ask for help. Her ma the angel. Her da the fortune-teller. Her dead husband's three cousins that rule the roost in Ballina. Her other hand holds her five brothers and sisters, the ones left in Ireland, the ones who should help, if they cared enough, but she knows without askin that they won't give her a penny.

Things are awful tight. Ya know how it is.

She closes her eyes, concentratin.

The two middle fingers on her right hand curl. She's left with the cousins.

16

She ignores the twitchin as the three outstretched fingers start ta curl inwards too, and decides ta travel ta Mayo before the week is out.

The cousins said no, a course. Them that weren't dead were emigrated and them that weren't emigrated were too mean ta look after anyone but themselves. But Granny was more than able ta care for herself and her own; Mick Dolan hadn't been wrong about her strong white teeth.

'I want somewhere ta live.'

'Yes, Mrs Dolan, if you put your name on the—'

'I got six kids, another on the way. D'ya think I can afford ta wait? I want ya ta put me inta one a them new flats.'

'I'm afraid, Mrs Dolan, there are no plans to build locally for a while yet.'

'Local? I don't give a curse for local. What about them new places in town?'

'Eh—'

She digs out a crumpled map, unfolds it, points. 'There.'

'But Mrs Dolan—'

'You're givin me one a them new flats.' She speaks slowly, every word nailin her decision inta their brains. Under the table her clenched fists squeeze purply-white. Tiny drops a blood leak from the palm where her fingernails dig inta her skin.

'Stigmata,' she says, holdin the scarred palms up for us ta see. They bleed red tears, she's told us, anytime somethin bad happens ta one a her children. She's not lyin.

Nowadays the flats got such a bad name. I seen the looks on the faces a people when they walk past, like we're dogs or rats or worse, livin in filth, with the graffiti and the smell a piss on the stairway landins, the burnt-out cars and the stunted trees that never got a chance ta grow standin twiggy and dead inside their wire cages. But back then, with the sixties startin ta swing, it musta been different. The stairwells smellin a fresh paint, the windas clean and bright with shiny metal surrounds. And the rooms . . . Me Granny, used ta two rooms and a scullery in Ring Street, suddenly plonked in a four-room gaff with a separate kitchen and bathroom? She musta thought she'd died and gone ta heaven.

Cept I'm forgettin. Granny wouldn't be fooled that easy by the surface a things. She probably seen the future a them bright new spankin buildins, seen how in years ta come they'd be crumblin, reekin not just a piss but all the human blood spilt inta their bricks. She probably even seen them like they are now, with the wreckers' ball crashin inta their peelin skin and metal bones.

'Jesus!'

Ma useta hate the way Granny done that, seen past the surface. Remember?

'Ya auld waggon . . . D'ya never look at the bright side a things?'

Granny never said a word back ta that. What was there ta say when she could see glimpses of all our futures lain out in fronta her?

Granny's stories a what happened once they moved inta the flats were different than the ones that came before. They were more . . . solid, like she couldn't double up on the truth any more. I think it was the straight up and down lines a the flats; they made her stories go in lines too. A ta B ta C. Like a train.

Cause and effect, as Derek says.

The rusty black pram is spillin over with veg. Hairy purple turnips, twisted carrots, earth-black spuds, sprouts like little green shrivelled bollocks. Her hands are cold, the raw bits round her fingernails hurtin. She beats her palms together, willin warmth inta them.

She feels it before she sees it; the glow a light as the door a Gill's Butchers opens, and like a brasser doin herself up for her tricks, Granny brushes down the big black overcoat that useta be his. Then she tightens her headscarf and turns ta face the business.

'Ah, howaya,' she calls as the women step out from Gill's, clutchin their bags a widdas' memories and scrag end a lamb. 'See ya got some tripe there, love. How about some nips and carrots for the stew? Lovely on a cold day like this!'

The women stop, taken by surprise again – though they shouldn't be, this happens all the time, Ma Dolan always knows what they're plannin for the dinner.

'Nips and carrots, so,' she says, not askin this time. 'Pound a each. Here ya go. Dessie, help me load up the lady, will ya?'

Granny useta say the gift passes from the seventh child to the seventh child but in regards ta us she was talkin shite. She mighta been the seventh but Ma was only fifth in line.

Dessie, Violet, Tommy, Michael, Rose, Dan and Stevo. They all grew up in the same place I did, but in the end they all moved out – all except Ma. She claimed she'da gone too if it hadn'a been for us, but I'm not so sure. If she coulda, she woulda. Wouldn't she?

Me Uncle Dessie, first-born, tall and pinched with Mick Dolan's black hair and red cheeks, went off ta work in New York when he was seventeen. He only came back once, that time before Uncle Michael went ta Salvador, and soon as Michael was gone, Des headed back ta the Big Apple. Couldn't stand Ireland any more, he said. Too soft. Dessie sent Granny a cheque every month but when Da went in for the long stretch, that all stopped. Seemed Dessie didn't wanta see his hard-earned cash goin ta waste. Ma flipped.

'That . . . bastard! Sorry, Ma, but he is and all. I'll give him hard-earned. I'll give him a hard-earned bleedin slap!'

In the end she didn't. Me Aunt Violet had a few words with Dessie and them cheques just started rollin again – and kept rollin too up until the day Granny died.

Vi was second. She was hard-lookin, racehorse-thin with brown hair and deep blue eyes. She was Granny's second-in-command, the one who bought the Christmas prezzies for the others, who changed their nappies, who swept and cleaned, who cried at me great-granny's funeral and then a year later, at the foundlin's. She was the one followed Granny onta the street; the one they all thought would carry them till the end. No surprise she was Granny's favourite. Ma always said Vi wormed her way inta favour but I put it down ta the fact that of all a them, she was the one who looked most like me Granny's da.

Third-born was mad Uncle Tom; gingery-coloured and big as a Viking. Like Dessie, he ran away too – but not ta the land a hope and freedom. The sea was his callin. After a stint stowin away in the hold of a Spanish trawler, he went ta work for the Brits – 'God forgive him,' said Granny – in the Royal Marines. But Granny's Brit-bashin bent followed him onta the water and he wasn't there a year when he lost it, jumpin on the captain with a knife, screamin that him and his countrymen should be put down like the evil despots they were. They say that's where it comes from, the stuff in me head. But I don't know if ya can pass madness around like fleas, hand it down from one generation to the next, like black hair or raw bones or fat legs. In anyways, Tom never got better after the fight with the sea captain. Like me Da, he earned himself a set a bars, only his were covered over with flowery curtains and kept nice and secure by men in white coats. Sometimes he'd do well and they'd let him out. But the good times never lasted. He'd always get the heebie-jeebies, start pickin fights and be slammed back for another stretch. I think he felt safer inside.

In the beginnin, Ma brung us in ta see him regular, usually on his birthday. He coulda been let out ta come visit us instead but Granny wouldn't have it.

'Ah no, I couldn't bear ta see him like that, me beautiful boy.'

So she stayed at home, nursin her bleedin palms, while we played chasin in the visitin room and ate all his sweets.

Next in line was Michael, gingery like Tom but thin like Dessie.

'Me brainy one,' says Granny. 'Samantha'll grow up ta be like him, won'tcha, pet?'

Michael had his eye on bein a doctor, done his Leavin and all with the Brothers on Parnell Square. But Granny hadn't the money ta send him ta university, so he had no choice but ta say 'Yeah' when the Jesuits came round press-gangin poor boys for mission-aries. Michael done his seminary, then off ta Salvador. He never seemed very holy ta me. Whenever Granny asked him ta say a rosary, he'd make a face like Granny had told him ta take out his nob and bite it off. He died when I was thirteen, ravin in a jungle hospital, with worms from a dirty glass a water eatin away at his guts and brains, nibble nibble nibble, till there was nothin left.

Child number five, the one with the gift, was me Ma. Rose Dolan, the family beauty. Pretty as a Neapolitan ice-cream. Skin a milk and honey, long long hair a pink gold, eyes a lightest blue, mouth like a film star's. Like that girl Drew Barrymore's, small and perfect, puckered up for a kiss.

Rose was the beauty alright, but Granny couldn't stand her.

'Swannin around like that. What does she think she is – Marilyn Monroe?'

'It woulda been different if me da had lived,' Ma said once ta Marlene. 'He'da loved me. He'da adored me.'

Sad waggon, me Ma. Always imaginin a better life somewhere else.

Me Uncle Dan, second from the end, was heavy-built with dark hair like Elvis. He went on the grift, runnin long firms with the fellas from round about. He'd set up a business, order stock, pay in full for six month, then place a massive order and run off with the goods. Nice. The Don or the Wacker woulda got ta Dan in time I'm sure, only for he skipped outta town just after Sam was born. Dan's excuse for leavin was the Ra. He'd taken up with Dolly, a Belfast girl on the run from her hubby. Unluckily for Dan, hubby was a fully paid-up member a the Green Order who liked beatin his women twice as much as ridin them. Knowin the Ra would waste no time in kneecappin him for stealin a Republican bride, Dan took Dolly over ta Birmingham, and got himself set up legit importin parts for cars. They moved back ta Belfast in the nineties for a white weddin once the Ra-head hubby was outta the picture, courtesy of a pub-bombin on the Falls Road. John Paul brung me in a paper a while ago and shown me the picture: Councillor Dan winnin the local elections, pumpin hands with Gerry Adams.

And last but not least was Stevo, the babby a the family, long and gawky and fair with a soft high voice would make ya think butter wouldn't melt in his mouth. As twitchy as his brothers before him and his granda before them, Stevo got away, just like all the others, only he took more time. Slow and steady, for all his quick wits. Slow and steady like the tortoise.

Stevo: Da ta me cousin Charlie and his five sisters, husband ta Marlene, one a the cleverest women I ever knew.

Granny never liked her. 'Common as muck, that one is. Brung up in the gutter.'

Yeah, well . . . Granny mighta been right about lots a things, but she was wrong about Marlene. Marlene wasn't common at all. She was . . . diamond. She could tell a lie a mile away and had a knack for gettin whatever she wanted outta whoever had it. Plus she was one a the few women that ever got on with Ma. Even now, when I wanta, I can close me eyes and hear Marlene's voice, deep and throaty with that husky laugh a hers, like cat's fur rubbin on the back a me neck.

'Now, Lucy, ya won't tell yer granny I been round, willya?'

'Course not, Auntie Marlene.'

'Auntie? Godsake, darlin, don't make me sound like an auld wan! Marlene. Like the singer. Marlene.'

Mar-lay-ne.

'I don't wanta.'

She cuts the bread on her plate in half. Then she cuts each half in two. Then each quarter. Then she halves each eight. She puts one a the sixteens inta her mouth.

Granny feels like slappin her younger daughter. Feels. Does. She raises her hand –

Rose looks up, stares. Her mouth is a little flowerbud, pursed up. Still starin, she starts chewin. Her lips stay pursed.

'Wanta or not, you're doin it,' says Granny. 'How d'ya think I raised the seven a youse? It wasn't be sittin on me arse waitin for good fortune ta come knockin.'

'Ya don't need me,' says Rose. She's only eleven but she speaks like a young wan twice that. 'Ya got the boys and Violet slavin for ya.'

'The boys has other things ta be doin—' starts Granny, then stops. How does Rose do it, wind her up like that every time? How does she make Granny feel like she's the one should be defendin herself? 'You're comin out with us tomorra, Rose. And that's final.'

Lazy little bitch.

Rotten auld hag.

The thoughts hang between them, clear as day.

Granny breaks the stare first, pours a cup a tea, slurps it. Rose chews, chews, chews. In the magazine it says Audrey Hepburn chews her food a hundred times before swallyin. That's how she stays so beautiful.

'Ya didn't want it spoilin yer complexion,' jeers Granny, wheezin a laugh. 'Imagine that, Marlene love. Little Rose didn't want the dirty weather on the stall turnin her inta an auld boot like her ma.'

Marlene puffs. 'That so?' She makes the question sound like she's bored.

'Jars a potions she had,' says Granny. 'Creams and oils all hidden under the bed. Hidden but I could see them. She got her brothers ta rob them for her from Clerys. What was that in aida, Rose? Ya thought Steve McQueen was gointa ride inta town on his motorbike and sweep ya away?'

Ma says nothin. She doesn't need ta. *Rotten auld hag.*

Delusions. Sad thing, Ma still hasn't grown outta them.

'Howaya, Missus Devlin, see ya got yer bangers this mornin. Makin coddle, are ya? Got some lovely roosters in, fresh they are, good and floury.'

Granny bends, lifts, weighs, parcels. She can tell weight by feel now, the give in her hand of an ounce, a pound, a half a stone.

'Ah, hello there, Mr Price,' says Violet. 'D'ya want yer onions?' She winks.

Mr Price, nineteen, covered in spots, winks back. He's a Carlow lad workin down the GPO and livin with his cousin in a flat in North Great Georges Street. He likes Violet.

'Yeah, Violet, give me me onions,' he says.

Violet roars with laughter and digs inta the brown bag with her just as brown fingers. Rose looks on, her face thundery. She may be the beauty at home but out on the street it's Vi who gets all the attention. As Violet bends over for parsley and thyme, Rose drops the bag a spuds she's been holdin, aimin it for Vi's feet. Vi steps back just in time, grabs her sister's arm, hisses, 'Leave it out, Rose Dolan. I know what you're at.'

Ma twists outta the grab, flickin her long blonde hair over her shoulder.

'Rose!' says Granny, snappin her fingers. 'Missus Devlin hasn't got all day.'

She knows it's only a matter a time. Anyone could see that. The girl has the looks and the brains and she's a hard worker ta boot. If she doesn't watch her step, she'll end up married with kids by the time she's eighteen. Granny knows this is comin. She feels it. Ya can't change the shape a things ta come but it's worth sayin somethin, isn't it?

'D'ya want it, Violet? Ta be tied to a sink with fourteen kids hangin outta ya?'

'Ah no, Ma,' says Violet, seein through what Granny is sayin ta what she really means. 'Ya know I'll never leave ya.'

'It's not about me, Violet.' A lie. 'I'm only . . . worried you'll make yerself a life you'll regret.'

But in the end it's not Mr Price, the post office worker from Carlow.

One mornin, that mornin, Granny wakes up feelin dizzy. She tries to get up, but can't. Her legs aren't workin. *This is the day*, says a voice in her head. She closes her eyes and sees herself reflected in the black-spotted mirror from the front room in Ring Street. Only six a her seven kids are standin behind her reflection. Her palms itch. She can tell they've started bleedin.

'Violet,' she calls, her voice croakin.

Vi comes ta the door, her face still creased from sleep. Granny lifts her red right hand. 'I'm not feelin well,' she says. 'You're ta go down ta the Abbey today instead a me.'

An hour later, down at Mary's Abbey, Vi ladles her pram full a produce. She's tryin ta keep her mind on the job, but her attention keeps wanderin towards the young fella who's helpin her. He's the trader's son, a quiet type. He hasn't smiled once. Somethin about his silence draws her in. She thinks she'd like him ta ask her name.

The pram breaks an axle just as Vi turns outta the market onta Capel Street. The pile a veg wobbles, topples, crashes everywhere.

'Jesus, me ma'll kill me!'

Violet rushes ta rescue what she can. As she reaches for a bunch a carrots, her fingers touch flesh. Male skin, tough from work. She looks up. It's him. He looks up. He smiles. She burns scarlet.

'Here, let me,' he says, pullin Violet up off the street. 'I'm Patrick.'

In the weeks followin the broken axle, Patrick keeps callin up ta the flat with bunches a flowers for Vi, takin her out ta the pictures, walks in the Green, dancin in the Ierne Ballroom. He's always very polite and, even though his people are from Cabra and rich, sorta, he doesn't seem ta mind that Vi lives in the flats.

It was only later, after Vi and Granny's fallin-out, that Vi told Granny the truth.

'Violet,' said Patrick when he proposed. 'I wanta take ya away from this gutter. It's no place for ya. You're a lady.'

A lady. A gutter. No wonder Vi bought it.

Within a year, she was married.

The picture a the weddin shows them all stiff-lookin in sixties' clothes. Granny poker-straight in her good coat and ugly headscarf, her red hair that she was already startin ta dye stickin out in curls over her forehead. Beside her, Vi in a Jackie O dress suit with a mile-high beehive and a little veil balancin on top. Squashed between them is Patrick, solemn, his hair plastered ta his head in a centre partin.

The resta the Dolans crowd around them. Dessie's already flown the coop but Michael is there in seminary black, lookin sour and starin straight inta the camera. Beside him is Tom, gazin off inta the distance, dreamin a the sea that's yet ta madden him. Dan and Stevo are jiggin at the edges a the picture, lookin all wrong in borrowed suits. And kneelin in the front is Ma, plump and juicy and on the verge a thirteen, her long blonde hair spillin down her back. She has her thumb in her mouth but her eyes, lookin right inta the watcher's, are sayin Fuck Me. Even in a picture that old, ya can see the jealousy boilin under her skin.

II

April 1968.

She totters down towards Dorset Street, legs jerkin like a new-born calf, aware a the eyes starin, the mouths ready for whistles before she's even passed. The skin on her head is still stingin from the bleach and every gust a wind that blows against her newly bare neck makes her think someone's gointa run up behind her and cut off her head. She took back the picture a Twiggy – all bob and big eyes – but she said no when Dolores Walsh in Justine's Styles asked her if she wanted ta keep some of her hair. Creepy-lookin, it was, lyin on the ground like somethin dead. Her new high heels click on the footpath. They're a hooer ta walk in. She keeps wobblin, especially when she hasta step down onta the road. Each time she wobbles, she prays she won't fall. So far the prayer's worked and she's stayed upright. She feels ten foot tall.

At the bridge the lights are red. Rose waits, her legs shakin from the strain a balancin on the heels. She tightens the belt on her black plastic mac, licks her white Mary Quant lips. She may only be thirteen goin on fourteen but she's ready for anyone. Across the road, she sees a scooter pull up outside Leo Dillon's Motorcycles. As the rider takes off his helmet, the traffic lights change colour. Rose steps onta the road, wobbles. She prays again, hard. The wobblin stops.

She doesn't dare look over in his direction but she can feel him buzzin in the edges of her sight like a little brown bee. He doesn't come from round the area. That's why they call him the Southsider. He doesn't look like a local lad neither and it's not just on accounta the scooter. He's always well-dressed, in a suit, his hair short and feathered round his dark handsome face like an English rock star. She's never been up close ta him but she's sure he has soft hands and filed fingernails and smells clean, and even from a distance she can tell his eyes are unusual, a mix a every colour under the sun.

As she sways across the road, a tall ship sweepin cunt-first past the traffic, she feels his eyes on her. On her mac, her hips, her swellin legs, her proud tits, her poutin mouth. Someone whistles. She knows she should ignore it but she can't help glancin over.

Bad move.

The Southsider's lookin over at her alright but it's not him that's whistlin. It's his buddy, Artschool Andy the sign-painter's son who works Saturdays in Dillon's Bikes. Rose has never been that keen on Andy; his hair's too long and greasy and his jeans are always in a state. Disappointed, she steps up onta the kerb and forces herself ta walk past the bikes without a second look at the two lads.

As the blonde passes him, he looks down at his hands, pretendin ta check his nails. Even though he can't see her he can still get her smell. It's sweet and harsh in one, a mix a hairspray, perfume, sweat. He looks up once she's passed. The shaved bit on the back of her neck glints silver. He imagines touchin it.

'Hello, Jimmy!'

He turns. 'Ah, Andrew, my man.'

They head inta the shop where Steppenwolf are screamin 'Born To Be Wiiiiiiiild'. Magazine pictures a Rory Gallagher and Mick Jagger throw shapes on the walls. He hates Steppenwolf and Rory even more but Andy's his buddy and Dillon's is the only place that'll service his Lambretta without givin him gyp. At the door, he turns for one last gander at the blonde that looks like Myra Hindley only with the face of an angel.

'Andrew,' he says, 'you wouldn't happen ta know . . . ?'

Andy follas his buddy's glance.

Ah, Jimmy Marconi, the Southsider. Little Jimmy the Eyetie, lone son of a sanctimonious dressmaker and a communist cook from Basin Street near the Jaymo Hospital. Jimmy, with his greeny-bluey-grey eyes, eyes every colour under the sun. Jimmy the part-time stores man for Switzer's; the full-time follower a fashion. Jimmy Marconi; the first and possibly the only Mod in Dublin.

He was introduced ta the scene first by a cousin who was back from London for the Christmas.

'Here,' says the cousin, 'catch a loada this' – and he whacks some vinyls on Jimmy's da's scratchy old record player. 'That's soul, Jimmy.'

The music is good. It feels . . . important. The skippin drums and raw voices take Jimmy's feet and start tappin them.

'Look here.' The cousin flings over a magazine.

Jimmy leafs through. It's a photo special; twelve pages a white-skinned boys in sharp suits and small-hipped girls with shiny bobbed hair hangin round on a pier.

'Brighton,' says the cousin. 'We will fight them on the beaches.'

Their mopeds gleam. The girls pout. The curves a their naked necks will haunt Jimmy for years after.

'See, that's me.'

And so it is. The cousin's posin, staunch, at the enda the pier, a ninety-nine in his knuckledustered paw. He's got his mac pulled back so ya can see the glint of his knife in his belt.

'Cool, yeah?'

'Yeah. Cool,' says Jimmy, stretchin out the word in his mouth.

'Here.' The cousin digs in his pocket. 'Have some dexys.'

Jimmy got his records sent over every month from his cousin in London, his suits made by an auld lad on Francis Street and his pinks and blues over the counter from Byrne's chemist, but findin fella Mods in Dublin proved well-nigh impossible. The scene may be bad now but back then it was way worse. In London they had the Small Faces and the Kinks but over here it was wall-ta-wall trad and showbands. The best we could get was Rory wankin on his guitar and Skid Row beltin out the blues. With no Brighton Pier ta pose on, and the local lads in the Liberties – 'direct descendants a the Animal Gang', as Ma useta put it – jeerin him for bein a fairy, Jimmy found himself at a loss.

Then one Saturday in Dillon's, he meets Artschool Andy from Killarney Parade. Andy's like Jimmy, a fish outta water among the art college poshies, and in spite a their musical differences, the two lads hit it off. They start meetin a coupla evenins a week outside the college on Kildare Street after Jimmy's done his shift in Switzer's. From there they go ta the rockery in Stephen's Green, where Jimmy swallas a blue and Andy smokes a reefer and they argue about music and politics and the purpose a livin. And when Andy comes ta Jimmy with news that an American student on her grand tour wants ta sell on some cannabis resin she'd got in India and thinks he'll be able ta help her, well . . . things get even better.

The door opens. He sets his glass a orange juice on the bar and looks up. It's Andy but he's brung along some fellas Jimmy doesn't recognize. Judgin by the moustaches and the ill-fittin jackets, they're not art students.

'Hey, Jimmy!' says Andy, givin him the peace sign.

'You're late, you scoundrel.'

Back then, he always spoke well; sorta . . . precise. Ma even said he useta have a bit of an Italian accent, though I don't know how much a that is true.

'Jimmy, this is me pal Morsey. Morsey, Jimmy Marconi.'

Morsey, long and gawky, his hair covered in white dust, stretches out his hand. 'Marconi? I'll have a fresh cod, so!'

It's the Italian chipper joke again. 'And a single a chips!'

The other yobs laugh, Andy included.

Jimmy looks at Morsey's outstretched hand. The fingers are strong and blunt. He smiles.

'A pleasure to meet you.'

He leaves his own hand where it is, on the counter.

On Saturday evenins, Jimmy picks up Andy outside Dillon's Bikes, and they do their pub-crawl, droppin off Thai sticks and red Leb ta the punters in Rice's and Synotts and the Toby Jug on South Anne Street. After that they crash a party – in the drunks' house on Leeson Street or the sugar mama's eighth-floor pad in the Jewish flats beside Herbert Park – and hang out, Andy marvellin at the sky fulla diamonds, while Jimmy, up on his jollies, races round outside on his Lambretta like a small fly, buzzin buzzin buzzin.

Sometimes they get off with birds. Sometimes they don't.

On the third Saturday in May, Rose Dolan walks up ta the Drumcondra Bridge. She's been told by Andy's sister ta get there for six. Just as she's about ta cross over ta the lock, the scooter buzzes out in fronta her, makin her lose balance.

'Holy God!' she says.

The scooter brakes. The rider tilts up the visor on his helmet. 'Did I frighten you?'

Ma's thirteen-goin-on-fourteen heart starts ta pound.

Ma let no one in on what was happenin. What with Jimmy bein so much older than her and all, Granny woulda flipped if she'd found out. Course, the secrecy only added ta the thrill – and there's nothin more thrillin than puppy love.

Love? Was it love thrun me Ma and Da together that day on Dorset Street? Even though she always said it was I useta think it was just sex. But now I'm not so sure. Because Da musta been kinda . . . romantic-lookin in them days, with his gentlemanly suits, and his dark Italian hair shapin round his dark Italian face and them soulful, smoulderin eyes a his. But is that enough of a reason ta love someone; two smoulderin eyes and a nice suit? Or was Ma just so determined ta live her life the way she wanted that she made herself believe that's what it was?

He enjoys goin out with her, takin her for rides ta Dollymount Strand. She's his trophy bird, his own little Modette. He likes the way other men look at her: her tits, her legs, her blonde hair. She's young but she's got a sharp tongue and a good sense a humour.

Andy's pal Morsey gets wind of it somehow and jeers him non-stop.

'I've a song for ya, Marconi. Ever hearda "Pal a me Cradle Days"? Get it? *Cradle*?'

He ignores the jeerin. What's Morsey in anyways? Only a pig-ignorant stonemason's apprentice with no plans for the future.

★

They lie on the whitenin grass in the bushes behind the old ware-house. In the distance she can hear Jane Birkin on someone's record player, cooin ta Serge in French. He smooths his hands over her knockers, tuggin at the brown nipples, his tongue dippin in and outta the shaved curve of her underarm. He's shorter than her, by two inches, but on the ground none a that matters. He nibbles her ear and she sighs.

'Ah, Jimmy, no . . . I can't . . . I—'

'Rose, I love ya.'

'No, Jimmy, I . . . ah, Jesus . . .'

Her wet mouth opens, drops a spit like meltin snowflakes on the pink insides of her lips. Sweat collects under her eyebrows, on the tiny hairs over her top lip.

'Ah, Jimmy.'

'Rose, you're beautiful . . . you're a goddess . . . you're so . . .'

He slips in his finger. She moans.

'Ah no, Jimmy, no, Jesus, I can't . . .'

'Sshh,' he says, calmin her like she's a horse. Then he slides himself over her, his cock startin ta search and prod and poke through the pink flaps like a little snake's head.

'Jimmy . . .'

He slides in deeper, easin the way with the finger. She's drippin.

'Oh . . . Jimmy . . . Ya can't . . . I mean . . .'

'Come on, Rosie. Trust me, I know what ta do . . .'

'Will ya . . . are ya sure . . .'

'Yeah, darlin, I'll look after you . . . don't worry . . . trust me.'

And trustin, she curves her back inta the shape of a peacock, her white hair gratin against the dirty ground, her arse pink and swollen as his hands knead inta it.

'Ah . . . ah . . . ah . . . Jimmy . . . ah . . .'

'Jesus fuckin Christ!'

He rolls off her, leavin a pool a sweat in the holla of her belly button, a pool a white juice in her gee.

★

'Try this,' he says.

She looks at the blue pill in his hand.

Later, she lies back against the broken wall, watchin as the scooter races up and down the canal, wishin he'd stay still, even for a few minutes, and hold her hand.

Granny is fuckin *ragin*.

Boo hoo hoo.

'Ya stupid child! Who?'

Boo hoo –

'Who?'

'Answer yer ma, Rose!'

'Quiet, Violet. Mother a divine Jaysus, Rose, *WHO*? – or I'll sendya ta the Magdalenes!'

In the end she caves in. Poor Rose, weepin as she shops her shopfloor Romeo.

The snivellin sets Granny off even more. 'What in God's name were ya thinkin? Lookatcha, three month gone and you're only a chisler! How'm I gointa manage on the stall now, with Violet gone? What kinda life are ya makin for yerself, Rose?'

And on and on. As Granny storms, wavin her bleedin palms in the air, Rose keeps cryin.

'He loves me, Ma! I swear he does.'

Vi, jiggin her baby, shakes her head and looks upta heaven.

Granny took it as a personal insult that Ma was thick enough ta get herself knocked up at fourteen. And ta listen ta Ma years after, you'd think she thought exactly the same.

'Jesus, if I had me life all over again, I wouldn'a been thick enough ta go through with it. I'da stuck a knittin needle up me yoke and got ridda it in one go.'

But she didn't use the knittin needle and she did go through with it. Maybe it wasn't down ta thickness though. Maybe it was because she thought a baby was a way a gettin me Da ta pull her outta that life in them flats, just like Patrick done for Vi, pull her out inta a beautiful Technicolor sunset where she could ride around on a

Lambretta and eat prawn cocktail and strawberry cheesecake like Twiggy all day long.

She looks out the kitchen winda, her hands grippin the frame. Behind her, she hears her youngest daughter, still cryin.

She raises her face and searches the sky for signs. The clouds bundle white and thick over the mountains on the far side a the city. She closes her eyes. In the darkness she feels the sun come out and light up the hills.

A baby on a frosty doorstep of a Wickla farmhouse.

'Have ya decided, Ma?' asks Vi.

Granny turns. The stingin on her palms eases.

'She'll go ta her Auntie Nora's on the Navan Road when she starts showin. She can bring it back here and we'll say it's a nephew that's after bein orphaned.'

'But what about him? We should tell him. Rosie says his da has money—'

Granny silences Vi with a look. 'I can look after me own, Violet. I don't need any handouts.'

'But Ma—'

'I know what I'm doin, Vi.' Granny manages a smile. 'Now, let's see what little Desmond wants for his tea.'

Vi hesitates, wonderin if she should tell her ma the rumours she's heard about Rose's Jimmy.

'I said,' says Granny, 'I know what I'm doin.'

'Shoulda been more careful,' says Morsey, nudgin him.

'You don't know what you're talkin about,' says Jimmy.

'Oh, apologies, Marconi. I forgot, it's not yours, is it? Yeah –' Morsey takes a deep breath. There's a joke on its way '– they say if ya gave Rose Dolan a kick in the arse a bucketa mickeys would fall out.'

Jimmy swallas his orange juice. What's he supposed ta think? He hasn't seen her in months.

*

While Rose is screamin blue murder and squeezin out a small brown head from between her white legs in Auntie Nora's back room, Jimmy Marconi and Artschool Andy travel downta Cork where one a Andy's birds has set up a meetin for them with an Oxford dropout who's plannin ta save the world by turnin it on. Upta now Andy's kept things small, sellin on from students and West Brits, but since the new laws have come in, bannin over-the-counter jollies, Jimmy's started thinkin maybe they should expand their horizons. Breakin inta the local chemist may be all very well for the criminal classes, but it's not what Jimmy and Andy are inta. They're after somethin smoother, slicker.

The dropout fills them in. He knows suppliers in Amsterdam and Geneva and runners that pick up the goods from there and bring them back home. One a the runners is a Scouser, from Bold Moss just outside Liverpool town. Seein as there's a ferry between Dublin and Liverpool . . .

They do a deal. Jimmy will do the travellin while Andy, as ever, supplies the custom. The Oxford dropout raises a toast.

'Peace and love!'

And so Jimmy Marconi starts goin across the Irish Sea on the Liverpool pukebucket every month, returnin with Leb, Moroccan, Paki and his own personal supply a French Blues, all tucked away in the seat a the Lambretta.

On his fourth trip over, the Scouser tells him the Old Bill have been snoopin since the last run from Geneva. Maybe Jimmy should cut loose for a few days till things quieten down. 'Why don't you go down to London, man? That's more your scene, yeah?'

Jimmy's never been ta London before. At first he refuses, not wantin ta leave the goods untended, but in the end the lure a the Big Smoke is too much.

It blows his mind. The girls, the colours, the lights, the traffic. The buildins loom up, cuttin out the sky. There are so many people he feels he's gointa drown. It's the tip enda the Swingin Sixties and Jimmy Marconi falls for it, forgettin all the Brit-bashin stuff his auld fella had drummed inta him since he was a kid.

He goes ta parties in Soho clubs the Scouser recommends,

catches some live music at Ronnie Scott's and rides down ta Brighton the next day with the heads he meets at the gig. There's no Rockers, so they can't pick a fight, but Jimmy's happy enough ta go back ta London where he spends hours on Carnaby Street, buyin clothes and records and watchin the girls; the secretaries in their crotch-high minis, the hippy chicks in their floatin flowery dresses. High on lack a sleep, he tries ta forget the dirty pubs back home, fulla rebel songs and fiddles and smelly old lads without their teeth.

'Stay 'ere, mate, why not, eh?' says one a the heads.

He thinks about it.

No Blacks. No Dogs. No Irish.

He could learn the accent and fit in and have a life for himself.

'Ooh, go on, Jim,' says the head's mot.

But on Sunday afternoon, Jimmy leaves his new buddies and the sweet stink a pigeons in Trafalgar Square and rides all the way back ta Liverpool instead.

He stands at the rail, lookin back as the other island melts inta the sea. Inside the cabin, brown-pin-striped builders are already singin 'Danny Boy' with tears in their eyes. Who knows what's called him back? The lovely Rose Dolan? His mammy with her prayers? Or the smell a them rolls a notes waitin in the pockets of his soon-ta-be-happy customers?

They called him John Paul, after the Popes – John the Twenty-Third and Paul the Sixth – though Ma always claimed later it was for the Beatles. She wanted ta call him Mick, but Granny wouldn't have it.

'Ya won't give yer da's name to a bastard.'

That was the only time she ever spoke ill a any of us.

In the followin months, Jimmy goes back to London as regular as he can, at least twice a month, buyin flashier suits, edgier music, a new Lambretta.

'You should see it,' he tells Andy. He's speakin fast because he's still up from the pills and loud because Andy's got fuckin Zeppelin on and he can hardly hear himself think. 'It's some town. Way ahead of this shitheap.'

'Yeah, man.' Andy wipes his hands on his overalls.

'Yeah, man,' says Jimmy, copyin him. He laughs. 'Like you'd know.'

Andy looks at Jimmy sideways. Jimmy grins, crunchin his teeth together. 'Ah, come on, Andy. Relax.'

Andy burns, crumbles, sprinkles. Jimmy, edgy, glances over his shoulder.

'You lookin ta get us busted?'

Andy shrugs, rolls, lights. 'Cool it, Jimmy. It's fine.'

'Fine for losers. That stuff fucks up your concentration, Andy.'

'What stuff?' Morsey appears at the door a Dillon's.

Bang on cue, Andy lowers the joint where Morsey can't see it and pinches it out.

Jimmy laughs and gets up, pullin on his helmet. 'Goodbye, gentlemen.'

'Little toe-rag,' says Morsey, watchin the scooter rip down the North Circular Road. 'That's the sort gives the workin classes a bad name. I'd love ta stick him in the Royal. That'd be some sight. Watch him go under, him and that bleedin Vespa both.'

'It's a Lambretta,' says Andy, stickin the joint in his jeans pocket.

Nobody knew they were seein each other again. Not his parents, not Granny, not Stevo nor Dan nor Violet – and ya know what, not even me Da himself if ya ask me.

An afternoon here, an evenin there, a Sunday mornin when she was supposed ta be at Mass. Any time she could take an hour away from the baby or the stall or Granny's watchful eyes. Four, five dates in as many months. It wasn't a lot but it was enough ta fool her inta thinkin they were still an item. He had other girls goin besides her: the hairdresser from James's Street, the perfume girl from Switzer's, plus his English birds, the hippie artist from Camden Town and his Scouser Modette. They all loved Jimmy and Jimmy . . . well, Jimmy swore he loved all them.

She tried tellin him about the baby, how much he looked like his da, with his Italian skin and dark hair, but Jimmy wouldn't listen.

'No time for that, Rosie sweetheart. Seize the day.'

He's fallen asleep on her again. She strokes his hair as he grinds his teeth, crunchin imaginary blues.

With the first one she'd roared, but now she's quiet as anythin, her voice so low Rose hasta strain ta catch it.

'After all we done, Rose, all the plannin, ya make the same mistake all over again. Ya stupid little . . .'

Rose stares at the ground, twistin her white fingers round each other.

Mistake?

Sure, Jimmy, we can do it, it's safe. I'm just after me flowers. I'm on that Pill. I got it off me sister. She went ta Belfast last week and . . .

No, Jimmy. I'm sure.

Some mistake. Second time lucky.

Granny takes out the pack her father gave her when he lost his sight and shuffles the cards, takin care not ta get the blood from her stigmata on the pictures. She deals.

Queen a Cups. Two a Cups. Page a Cups. The Fool. The Empress.

The pictures form. A union. A bright child. Herself, lyin on a bed, bein tended.

Somethin's wrong. If they get married, there'll be nobody ta tend her on that bed. It doesn't make sense. She closes her eyes, concentratin.

At last she decides. It's somethin she's not seein; she'll put it downta the Fool. Her palms stop stingin.

'He was never Marconi's lad after all, Marlene. Did ya know that?' says Granny.

Ma sips her tea, keepin quiet.

'He was some greaser's, some Teddy Boy from a showband. Tom Layton or Gerry Gibbons. One a them auld fellas got her drunk and messed her up, leavin her stuck like a pig with her belly out ta Africa.'

Marlene yawns. She's heard this story a thousand times before.

'If Violet was here,' says Granny, 'she'd back me up. She was there when we went down ta Basin Street ta share the good news. She seen the look a shock on that Eyetie's face. Didn't she, Rose?'

Ma takes another sip.

But Granny was wrong. Micko was Da's. Because if ya take away Micko's colourin, the bright hair and eyes which come straight off Ma, ya can see he was the spit a the auld lad. Same height, same fastness.

'I thought you said we were alright,' he said ta her, quiet, when he got a chance ta talk ta her, away from all his ma's noise and sobbin.

'I did, Jimmy darlin,' said Rose, wide-eyed. 'But somethin musta gone wrong.'

And so they got married on a cold January mornin at the dawn a the 1970s in the Francis Xavier church on Gardiner Street.

Nobody took any photos a that one but it's easy to picture Ma, four month gone, dressed in lyin white, Da beside her in a dazzlin suit, small shoes shiny, dark face grim as a chainsaw. Beside Da his best man, Artschool Andy, lookin outta place in his da's Sunday suit. Beside Ma the matron a honour, Violet, smug, with her legal two-year-old clingin ta her stylish crimplene trouser suit. Behind Vi, Patrick, uncomfortable in his white collar, and the brothers, Dan and Stevo, scrubbed up for the day. Uncle Michael's not there; he can't show his face on accounta the scandal.

Granny's at the front, in the same good coat she wore for Vi's weddin, lookin down at the big black pram where John Paul lies, his thick brown paws clutchin a piece a jammy bread.

And behind them all, dyin ta be elsewhere, are Da's parents, The Odd Couple, their scrawny Liberties faces sour with shame.

It was Ma called them The Odd Couple, after she first seen that programme on the telly. And from then on the name stuck. She was Felix because she was so neat, and he was Oscar because if ya had a Felix ya needed an Oscar. He was tiny, though, not like the Oscar on the telly, and he wasn't loud nor messy neither.

Felix had a white face and tiny hands and skin soft and wrinkled like tissue paper. She was like a bird she was so small, all bones and air and fluffy grey hair like feathers. Micko said she had false teeth which she took out at night. He could tell on accounta the lispin sound she made when she talked.

Granny agreed. 'Weak bones them Marconis have. Not like us.' Then she grabbed Micko's jaw between her fingers. 'See! Ya mighta got Marconi's height but ya got Dolan teeth, strong and white and not too big!'

Felix useta be a dressmaker and she still thrun together confirmation suits and shrouds and the odd dress for the wans lived round the area. She always dressed in button-up cardigans and tweed skirts and an apron yoke she called a pinny and even though her clothes were sorta dowdy, she wore nice jewellery all the time – gold rings on her fingers with little stones in them, and pretty earrings that Oscar got for her, and she'd never go without somethin round her neck, a fine gold chain with a locket hangin off it, or a cross, or even a gem.

Oscar had stringy brown hair combed over a bald head, a bushy grey moustache brown at the ends from his fags, and sharp green eyes. Despite a how everyone useta slag off me Da for bein from a chipper family, Oscar hadn't worked behind a fryer since he was a kid. He useta cook for CIE on the trains, makin the dinners and all, but one a his lungs went bad so he got laid off when he was still in his twenties. Oscar was an old-guard Red, big inta the Union, but when they fucked him over with the redundancy, his loyalty went down the tubes.

'I still have my principles, though,' he'd say, glarin at us. 'Me and many others. The Revolution's on its way, just you wait.'

Their house on Basin Street was the neatest gaff I ever been in. Felix even had plastic covers on the sofa and chairs so they wouldn't get dirty. Because Oscar hadta take things easy on accounta his lung, he always just sat there in one a them plastic-covered chairs beside the fire, readin or listenin ta his music, with me Da grinnin down at him from the photos on the mantelpiece. He loved readin, did Oscar, especially the newspapers. They gave him somethin ta get angry about.

'Look at this,' he'd say. 'The rubbish they expect us ta swallow! If James Connolly, the best man this country ever knew, could see—' Then the rage, havin filled his lungs, would spill inta his mouth and force itself out in a deep sore-soundin cough.

I always felt wary round Oscar. The way he read, concentratin like them newspapers were the most important things in the world. I useta think if I said anythin or even moved, he'd round on me and shoot me dead with green fire from them eyes a his. Didn't stop me, though.

She wakes, but she knows from the pains in her legs she won't be able ta stand, let alone work ten hour at the stall. Somethin flickers in her right eye.

'Rose!' she calls.

Ma comes ta the door, Micko hangin off her left tit.

'Will ya—'

The pains shoot up her legs.

Ma moves Micko ta the right one. 'Ya sick again, Ma?'

She can't answer, the pains are at her so bad.

'Don't ask me, Ma,' says Rose.

Two hours later on Parnell Street, Stevo and Dan flash their smiles at the women shoppers and push bags a green spuds inta their hands. 'Lovely floury spuds, there missus, put hair on yer chest!'

After Micko was born, Ma kept hopin she and Da would be able ta move out inta a place a their own. Some hope. Switzer's laid him off in the autumn, sayin money was gettin tight. Tight me arse. That stores manager knew Jimmy Marconi was upta somethin and even though he liked the lad, he was fucked if he was gointa get the blame if somethin happened. Then Ma tried persuadin Da ta use the money from his dealin business ta rent a flat but he told her it wasn't just his money, it was Andy's too; besides, he couldn't get the dole if he done that and the rozzers would come down on them like a tona bricks if they smelt even a hint a somethin dodgy. If she was that desperate ta move out, she should take The Odd Couple up on their offer and move inta Basin Street instead.

Both me parents knew that would never happen, not with things between Felix and Ma bein the way they were. And so they stayed in Granny's flat, humpin under the sheets while their kids bawled in the next room.

Funny. Any time Ma talked about them times, her eyes went misty and she made out it was the best year of her life.

It coulda been. She was still a beauty then and he was still handsome and they were well able ta charm each other inta forgettin their many scraps over where they were livin or how he shouldn't be workin with Andy any more or why he never offered ta take over the stall and find a decent way a pullin in a few bob or if he was hopin ta lead Stevo and Dan astray too or . . .

Yeah. They still had their fun, their scooter-rides ta Dollymount, their Sunday afternoons where they strolled sharp and stinkin a sex down O'Connell Street ta the Savoy Cinema ta watch James Bond lay inta Russian villains. And once Jimmy stopped goin away so regular, lettin Andy travel ta Liverpool in his place while he stayed home ta listen ta his records, Ma fooled herself he was still hers and they would move out, some day soon, and the good times – well, the good times would only get better.

It was a rat. Some Dublin Four acid-head who bought off them but after bein caught on Mount Street with hash in his pocket decided ta shop his dealers ta the Bill. The head arranged ta meet the two lads in their usual spot in the Toby Jug but Andy was comin down from a bad trip so Jimmy went on his own. As soon as the hash changed hands, the Old Bill was on him like flies on shit. Ta make things worse, Andy had originally wanted ta stitch up the head on accounta he was such a prick; give him patchouli-flavoured oxo insteada his usual. But Jimmy decided not ta bother.

'Ah, ya never know when ya might need ta pull in a favour.' Some favour.

He couldn't believe it when he got eight months. He appealed, lookin for a suspended sentence – he hadn't been inside before so he thought it'd be plain sailin – but ta teach him a lesson and warn others about the dangers a dealin, the District stuck another year on instead. All the way past Go without collectin his two hundred pound.

'Here, pretty,' they call down the landin. 'Here, pussy.'

'Want some battered sausage, Pedro?'

Pedro's a fuckin Spanish name, he thinks, not Italian. But he doesn't bother sayin it.

'Here, little girl. Want some lookin after, do ya?'

He studies his reflection in the back of his spoon. He could murder some pills.

'Jesus,' says Ma. 'Whatcha done ta yerself?'

He scratches his chin where the beard is pushin itself out through his dark pores. 'The John Lennon look, Rose. Ever hearda him?'

It was round about then me Da's precise way a speakin started ta fizzle away, like an Alka Seltzer in water. Coulda been the hash he was startin ta smoke. Coulda been just downta survival. When in Rome . . .

'Don't be smart. I didn't marry a bleedin hippie.'

She sets Micko on her lap and jigs him. The jiggin makes a wall between them thicker than any glass.

III

I was born in 1974, under the sign a the Ram. I was born a riddle: five weeks too early, five weeks too late.

By the time Jimmy Marconi was released, the stall on Parnell Street was just a memory. Granny had started readin the occasional fortunes from her bedroom, Dan had got inta his own little scams and me Uncle Stevo was workin with Violet's husband Patrick on the market in Mary's Abbey.

Me first true memories don't include me parents' reunion on the North Circular Road outside the gates a the Joy but that doesn't bother me. I can picture them, her in her bellbottom flares, her waist already startin ta flow out over her belt, her bleached hair, flicked like Agnetha's from ABBA, catchin the sun. And him, little Jimmy Marconi, all growed up with his prison tats, his Jesus Christ Superstar beard and sidies, his Mod feathercut strung out inta a ponytail, the only thing unchanged since he last seen the outside world the razor-sharp Liberty suit he was led away in.

The silence builds between them. She's run outta things ta say. He's actin like he can't be bothered.

'I'll make ya a cup,' she says just as he gets up.

They look at each other. He seems so small and outta place. She sighs.

The movement sends her cleavage tiltin down. He reaches out, touches her left tit.

In the room, they crash over onta the bed, tryin not ta disturb Granny next door. His hair is silky and smells a shampoo. His arms are harder than she remembers.

He pushes against her, feelin her through his trousers. He grabs the folds a flesh over her belt, squeezes. She whimpers.

44

His mouth opens on her neck, bitin. She twists her head.
Her zip pops.

I'm still not sure how they got me. Because Ma woulda been takin the Pill by then, payin a donation every month under the table ta the family plannin clinic on Mountjoy Square. Maybe she was sick that day or maybe she forgot. Maybe I just had ta be born.

While Jimmy Marconi was in jail, his old pal Artschool Andy had got politics the way others get religion and, fired up on Trotsky – and the hairy underarms of a Jewish bird from New York – decided revolution would save the world sooner than hash. Andy went ta Chile first but when things turned sour over there he headed up ta the Glorious North on Jimmy's Lambretta ta give the Cause a much-needed hand. Jimmy missed his weekly visits from his old pal, but – what's that they say? In with the new, out with the old? – far bigger fish were waitin in Andy's place.

Sixteen month inta Da's stretch he was sittin on the landin havin a fag when this tall lad walks upta him.

'Hello,' says the tall man. He's got a lug beside him, thick and scarred.

'Ya got a light?' says the tall man. Jimmy nods, offers his fag.

'Marconi, this is . . .' starts the lug. But Jimmy needs no introductions. Everyone, even gentlemen hash dealers like me Da, knows who the Don is.

Ah yeah, Nayler, ya were probably wonderin when I'd get onta him. Dapper Don Ryan. Lord a the northside, king a the blags, childhood buddy and business partner a Fred Mahon, aka the Wacker. Even though the Don hailed from Ballybough and Wacker from Fontenoy Street they took a real shine ta each other in the borstal, and by the early seventies were runnin the northside together – all the way from Bolton Street ta the Annesley Bridge but steerin clear a the Sheriff Street badlands. They kept the local lads in work but me Da never had much truck with them before goin inside, what with him bein a southsider and them bein strictly

Ordinary Decent Criminals. He'd hearda them though – ya couldn't not. They were the first round us ta get organized and make the big money, though apart from the Don's Copeland suits, they never done anythin flash ta draw attention ta it. Plus they were tops at coverin their tracks.

They'd rules, Lucy Lu, ya said once. Rules is good. They keep things clean. Make sense a stuff. There's a reason why people folla them.

It was because the rozzers could never get them on the blags they tried nailin them on the small charges; parkin fines, drivin with no insurance, that stuff. But the Don and Wacker were well able ta work the courts so they got concurrents, never stayin inside more than a few month at a time. And it was on one a them stretches that Don Ryan ended up on the same landin as me Da and asked him for a light. And strangely enough, sooner or later the conversation got round ta what me Da was in for.

I'm not sure how much the Don planned that little chat. Upta then, the gangs had never been inta the drugs. But soon as he talked ta me Da, I guarantee ya Don Ryan saw a whole new territory open up in fronta him; with his clout and Jimmy's knowledge, they could both be onta a very good thing.

Jimmy was always easy ta persuade and soon as he got out, he set about gettin in touch with his contacts in Cork and Liverpool. The Corkman was slow ta return his calls, slower still ta agree on a deal, and when the Scouser finally got in touch, he told Jimmy he wasn't runnin any more. It was then, when other men mighta given up, that Da got his big idea. What if he bypassed the middle-men, went straight for the suppliers instead?

'One last favour,' Jimmy told the Scouser.

Once he had the names a the contacts in Geneva, he went ta the Don. All they needed now was the Wacker ta come in on it.

A lot a people still go on like the Wacker was always anti-drugs, even back then it woulda taken the Don ages ta make him see the light. And I suppose the paira them was doin well enough from blaggin; why fix somethin if it's not broke? But Don Ryan was nothin if not persuasive, as you often told me. And he musta had some good arguments up his sleeve. Think a the money, he'da told Wacker. Think about our profits that we need ta hide. Think of it as a . . . investment. In the end the Wacker agreed.

Things were startin ta consolidate. The times they were a-changin.

And inside three months of his release Jimmy Marconi had a brand-new job, pyramid-sellin up near the peak.

Oh yes. I was born with a spoon in me mouth.

This I seen. This I remember. Ya might wonder how, because I wasn't popped by then, I was only a hard bump inside Ma's belly, but I remember every word, every beat, every last strike.

The voice sings. I can't make out the words but the rhythm knocks against the thump of her heart, makin me unformed feet tap.

Through the red wall a her womb, I see the door loom closer, her hand knock.

'Jimmy?' Her voice is boomin but that's only because it's comin ta me through her belly. Even then I know it's flat and high and she speaks through her nose.

There's no answer, just the voice and the beat, so she opens the door without knockin again. 'Jimmy, it's late. The kids need ta sleep.'

Ah. Now I hear. It's that boy singin, the one me Da likes.

She looks round, swayin me inside her belly. She can't see him. But I can pick up signals, a red heat comin at me through the backa the sofa.

'Whya listenin ta that, Jimmy? Thoughtcha weren't a Mod any more.'

Uh oh. He won't like that – is this my thought or her wiser self thinkin twice? – but he's okay as long as the boy keeps singin.

'Jimmy—'

'Christ, Rose!' – See? Didn't like that – 'Can I not have a second's peace without auld wans naggin and kids screamin the fuckin roof down?'

His voice is lower than hers, growlin; it goes up and down like the song on the record player. The gills in me transparent head where I take in sound open up. I could listen ta that voice forever.

She touches the bump, smoothin me like I'll protect her. 'Get off me back about the kids, Jimmy. They didn't lick their manners up off the ground. Sides, they hafta scream, with all that racket goin on.'

Don't rile him, Ma.

'Shut yer mouth, Rose.'

'Fuck off!'

Don't rile him –

He springs up from behind the sofa; his eyes are bright and glarin and even through the barrier of her skin and flesh and blood, they keep their colour. Two shots a green, blue, grey, in a red fog. She heaves herself backwards, draggin me with her, sendin a sour taste a fear through the cord.

He lifts his hands.

He's gointa hit her, he's gointa hit her.

Us.

No. Her.

He smiles. His hands soften.

'Know what?' he says. 'You're right, Rose. It *is* a racket.'

He flicks the needle and the boy singer screeches inta silence. Then he lifts the record.

'Jesus, Jimmy!'

He snaps it.

He fecked them all out the winda, 'Itchycoo Park', 'My Generation', 'Who Are You?', 'Sunny Afternoon'; all the singles and albums and specials and live shows he'd collected over the years. I felt them fall, spin outta control as they whirled through the air towards the waitin concrete and the spin made me turn inside her belly. No no no. When they hit the ground, they exploded with a bang and the shock made me kick her.

Your fault, said the kick. *Don't let it happen again.*

He went over ta the radio and turned on a heavy rock station.

When me brothers ran in, yellin, he lit up a joint and sank back inta the sofa. She tried talkin ta him but she knew it wouldn't do any good, so she gathered the lads up and brung them back ta bed. Then she cried herself ta sleep, quiet so he wouldn't hear.

The next bit I don't remember livin through but it happened.

Granny woke later that evenin, roused by Deep Purple and the stinka hash. When she went inta the livin room, Jimmy didn't even pretend he'd seen her. But like me, she caught his heat through the back a the sofa.

She stared at him, at the lines a his body; his bare feet tappin along ta 'Smoke on the Water', his legs and his arms and his small brown fingers holdin his sixth jointa the night. She stared at him, the way she always stared when she read a future in someone's hand, only she was readin it in his whole body.

'Aren'tcha gointa do anythin, Ma?' whispered Rose, creepin up behind her.

Granny shook her head.

When she went back ta bed, she laid her unbleedin hands across her chest and looked up at the ceilin, smilin as the pictures in her head unravelled inta a brand-new future.

Six weeks later Da got caught breakin a red at the junction a Gardiner Street and Dorset Street. Careless. Very very careless. A rozzer pulled him over, done a routine search and found a load a drops stowed in the seat of his Honda 50. The hash was cut, split, wrapped. The pills were in papers. Possession with intent. This time it went all the way ta the Circuit.

Three year and ten month. Fly past Go. Once more do not collect yer two hundred pound. These are the pictures Granny seen on the ceilin. No wonder she was smilin.

Riddle me this and riddle me that. I was born five weeks premature, five weeks too late ta see me Da. They say that's why I got all them things wrong with me but I say I was only hurryin out because I wanted ta get ta him before he got locked up.

It was Irene come up with the theory that I been lookin for me Da ever since I was born and that's why I'm so fucked up because

I could never find him. There's somethin sorta appealin about that notion, and even though I never told her about you, Nayler, it made me think about us; that maybe I put him on you and that's why things been the way they been between us. But then I thought again. People are always lookin for reasons, whether it's the Ten a Swords or the patterns in yer head or the memories a yer da or yer genes or fuckin God, tryin ta point the finger at somethin, but mosta the time there is no reason. Shite just happens, and no reason least of all me Da will make it go away.

People say ya can tell a lot about a person from their dreams. I say ya can tell just as much from what a person remembers; what they choose ta keep in their minds and what they let slip. I remember lots about me Da, but the stuff that sticks with me is the stuff I seen before I hit the air. The movin colours of his eyes and the wiry toucha his hand, the strong curves of his arms and the longin sound of his breath. His voice, like a song. His rage burnin. These are the things a Jimmy Marconi that I seen through me Ma's womb and these are the things that stick.

I don't remember mucha what happened once I got outta the womb. Only bits, some crystal clear, some fuzzy round the edges. The first, the clearest, was the sky.

I was in some park, probably Mountjoy Square, and I was in me pram. Don't ask me what I was wearin or who was with me. Well, Ma musta been because I was only around one. But all that doesn't matter; soft white blanket, Ma, soother, none of it; it's like Derek says, inconsequential. What's important was what was lyin over me; the sky, blue and free and goin on forever. Leaves and their shadas were ripplin grey across the blueness, like little fish swimmin. That's what I remember. Shadas swimmin across a clear blue free forever.

Two years after takin Stevo under their wing, Violet and Patrick discovered that Granny's youngest had been helpin himself to a little extra from the till at their expense. They shoulda guessed. Stevo'd been seen all sortsa places: Copeland's for a white suit, Shelbourne Park for the dogs, boogyin in Zhivago's with a tenner up his nose and a hairdresser from Finglas West called Marlene on his lap. How they thought he coulda done all that on the poxy wages Patrick was givin him beggars belief.

Granny huddles over the kitchen table, huggin her bandaged hands under her arms while outside Micko and John Paul take it in turns ta practise their punches on me.

'They won't,' says Dan.

Ma snorts. 'They will. That bitch always thought she was better than the resta us.'

'Ssshh,' says Granny.

'Choosin her moment,' says Ma. 'Just when you were gointa move in with them, Ma. She's doin it ta keep ya here, ta spite me.'

'Sshh, Rose.'

'And with Marlene in the family way and all—'

'Christ, Rose, wouldya be quiet.'

Ma smiles, seein trouble ahead.

Ma was right ta smile. Insteada puttin the frighteners on Stevo, Vi and Patrick pressed charges and brought him ta court. It went badly and Stevo ended up gettin fined plus a year suspended. For four days Granny locked herself in her room, refusin ta talk ta anyone. When she came out she told us all we were never ta speak ta Violet again.

It musta been round then that Ma started at her games. She always swore she stayed true ta me Da, got Samantha from a hot and sweaty hour in the visitin box, but be that as it may, Sam was born six month before Da's release, and anyone could tell he wasn't the father, even if they couldn't tell who was.

Me, John Paul and Micko, we all had somethin a me Da. John Paul was stocky, but had Da's brown hair and dark skin. I was darker than Micko but we both had Da's build, small and skinny, and his button nose and wide eyes. Granny reckoned we got the jiggin from him too – 'All them drugs, Rose' – but there the similarities ended. With Micko, everythin hung together, like someone said Here, God, make us a model of a good-lookin kid, and God obliged, but with me, well . . . I was a different story. Plain as the day, Ma useta say. Still, of us all, I was the only one that got the colour a me eyes – greeny-bluey-grey – off of Jimmy Marconi.

There wasn't a hinta me Da about Samantha. She was Ma all over, fair and soft with that white skin and goldy hair. The only thing that was different was her dark brown eyes and her long fingers and her big wide smiley mouth like Julia Roberts.

Granny said Ma had three fellas callin on her the time Sam was got. I only remember one, a thick-built lad who rustled me hair when he came past me on the steps. He smelt bad and, even though I was only three, I remember goin, *Ah, don't kiss me, please* . . .

It's pissin wet when we get off of the bus. Ma pulls us past the entrance ta the hospital and on again past Terry's Shop, where the flowers are stacked up like a rainbow. I reach out ta grab the petals but Ma drags me on, grabbin me so tight her rings bite inta me fingers. She's walkin fast in her platforms and I keep fallin, tryin ta stay in pace with her.

Me hood's annoyin me, it's too big because the duffel useta belong ta Micko and John Paul before him, so it keeps fallin over me eyes. I push it off with me free hand. Much better, even though the rain is soakin me neck.

Round me waist I feel me cowboy belt, a cast-off from Micko, the two tarnished guns slappin against me legs.

Someone pushes me in the back. It's Micko. He races past, tossin me a grin, his front teeth gappy and white as Daz. I stick out me tongue, catchin raindrops on it.

'Wait up,' calls John Paul, at the back, pushin Sam.

Their house smells rotten.

'That's Oscar's piss,' Micko whispers.

We're over in The Odd Couple's because Ma's gointa ask them ta the christenin. But she can't do that till we have tea. And we can't do that till Felix brings towels so we can dry off.

'Piss.' Micko nudges me and John Paul laughs. It doesn't smell like piss ta me. But I join in the laughin in anyways because I know Micko's bein funny.

'Behave, will youse!' says Ma, clatterin me on the head.

'Ow!'

John Paul starts ta back me up but before he can say anythin he's got a clatter too.

'As for you . . .' she says, wavin her finger at Micko.

He tosses her the same grin he tossed me earlier on. She licks her finger and smooths his hair flat. I hate her when she does that, lets Micko off the hook. No. I hate them both. And me head hurts from the clatter.

Then Sam starts bawlin, so Ma leaves Micko and bends over the pram ta rock it. 'Don'tcha cry, my little mousie, don'tcha cry.'

A kiss for Micko, a cuddle for the baby, slaps for me and John Paul. I've never bothered tryin ta figure out why; waste a time. So it was in the beginnin and so it will always be, world without end, Amen.

There's music comin from under the closed livin-room door. The fuzziness of it tells me it's on the radio, but I've not heard music like that on any radio playin at home. It's got ins and outs and makes me think a things without wantin ta. It's like a sea, like a dance, like a—

'Lucy!' says Ma, snappin her finger. Felix is back with the towels.

Like a story.

I didn't know a lot at that age, but the second I stepped inta The Odd Couple's I knew it was different to ours. *They* were different. And it wasn't because a what Ma or Granny said, about them bein snobs. The stink a their difference floated inta me nose and ears along with the lavender polish and the music on Oscar's radio, and it still lives there, tormentin me.

One thing that wasn't different was how much Felix hated where she was. That feelin was all over their gaff: in the plastic on the sofas, in the pictures a me Da on the mantelpiece, in the doilies on their shiny table. It made me edgy, that feelin, made me wanta be somewhere bigger, somewhere better. Just like Felix. Poor bitch. Like all the women in me family, she was born ta be disappointed.

Before dinner, she gets Oscar ta turn off his radio. A pity. I like that music.

We eat cold hard-boiled eggs that smell like shite but taste okay. See-through slices a ham that remind me a the flap a skin over the cut on Micko's hand. Bloody slabs a beetroot that stain the eggs pink, white pickled onions like eyeballs, green salad cream that stings the backa the throat, watery tomatas cut in two. The bread is Nimble, round, with grooves in it. It comes in a packet with a picture of a young wan in a balloon, up high in the sky, flyin like a bird.

Blueband margarine.

They've got the good white cloth out, and the nice delph and the silver shakers for the salt and pepper. They shakers have lacy edges ta them and when Felix holds them up she leaves her little finger stickin out like it's got a mind of its own.

She eats with her lips pursed, not makin a sound except when she breathes. Her fingers with their gold rings flash and twist as she cuts, lifts, chews. At the other enda the table, Oscar slurps through his moustache that's already covered with crumbs a yella egg yolk. He's rolled his shirt sleeves up, like he's gointa work, and every so often he lets rip with a big belch and we all giggle, even harder when we see the look on Felix's face.

Just before we start on the cakes, there's a scrabblin sound from outside. Felix hops up. 'Ah, look who's there. Look, it's my little boy. Isn't he lovely? Children, it's Duke. Say hello, Duke. Hello . . .'

She can't remember me name because we haven't been visitin much. Ma steps in.

'Lucy, Mrs Marconi.'

'Yes, of course, Lucy. Now say hello to Lucy, Duke. You like the girls, don't you, my little boy?'

He might normally but he doesn't like me. She holds him up ta herself, cradlin his small brown head, strokin his stringy brown hair, and all the time he wheezes and coughs and farts in me face like he thinks that'll make me go away. But I won't let him scare me. He's only a dog. So I stand there without budgin, keepin me left hand clamped on me cowboy belt while I reach out with me other ta pet his smelly back.

'Good dog,' I say. Across the table I see Micko tryin not ta laugh.

Felix kisses Duke's forehead.

I thought when we were leavin she'd try ta do the same ta us but she didn't bother.

They timed the christenin six month late so Da wouldn't miss it. He stood up at the font beside Ma, spankin clean in his flares and leather jacket, seemin different somehow ta how he was when we visited him in the jail. Ma looked beautiful in her new pink plastic mac with her hair piled on her head. She'd bought me a new coat. It was pink too, but fluffy. The fluff made it way too hot and it scratched me neck and Ma wouldn't let me play in it because I'd only get it dirty.

There were two men waitin for Da outside the church. One a them looked familiar. He was long and skinny and well-dressed, in a suit. The other was short and had an anorak on, with the hood pulled down over his eyes.

Da was happy ta see them but I could tell Ma wasn't because her face went dead ugly all of a sudden, even under the make-up and pretty hairstyle and all.

They didn't stay long, just ta shake Da's hand, and I was sorta relieved because I could tell there'd be trouble otherwise.

'They're Da's brothers,' said Micko as they went.

'But Da doesn't have any—'

'Not that kinda brothers, ya thick.'

While I was still tryin ta work that out, I remembered where I seen the long one before. He'd come ta the flat while Da was inside and after his visit Ma'd taken us ta the cinema and bought us ice-cream in Fortes. Then Micko pushed me, darin me ta race him home, and I didn't think about Da's not-that-kinda-brothers any more.

★

The flat is fulla people. Neighbours, friends, cousins. Oscar stands in a corner, talkin ta me Uncle Stevo, who's smilin a lot. Beside Oscar is Felix, holdin her brown bag tight ta her belly. She keeps lookin round. I know what she's upta. She's lookin for me Da.

Marlene, who's just got married ta Uncle Stevo, sits on the sofa. She looks mad, all thin arms and legs and a big belly which is more kids, so Micko tells me. She's busy tryin ta stop Baby Charlie from runnin off. He's only a few months younger than me but he's still a baby. I'm not, though. I'm a big girl.

Ma comes over ta Marlene, bends, whispers in her ear. Both a them laugh, look round, then laugh louder.

'Sad without Dan here, isn't it?' says Granny, but nobody else seems ta hear.

John Paul, Micko and me play chasin with the Devlin girls from upstairs. I keep fallin down. But every time I fall, I laugh, brushin off Cindy Devlin's kind hands that try ta fix me, and get up again. It's the only way ta win.

Nobody knows where me Da is except me. He's outside, high up, lookin at the stars. He didn't tell me where he was goin but I can see him sittin up on the roof of our block right near the edge, as clear as if I was sittin there beside him, the only thing holdin me safe from the long drop down ta the concrete his hand on mine.

Some men turn up later on with bottles.

'Andy!' Da grabs a long-haired fella in a combat jacket, and hugs him.

Andy says somethin which must be a joke because everyone in the room laughs.

Ma's started tryin ta get us ta bed but she can't talk proper so she just keeps wavin at us instead, like an American on the Paddy's Day parade. Then she pukes up over the carpet and Marlene helps her out ta the jacks.

'That girl. She may be common but . . .' says Granny and winks, noddin at me. I wink and nod back, lettin on I know what she means.

Someone starts singin 'Are Ya Lonesome Tonight?'

'Ah, poor Elvis, God bless his soul.' Missus Devlin crosses herself.

'Hail ta the King!' says Andy. Everyone laughs. 'Elvis has left the buildin!' They laugh louder.

I jig up and down, copyin the rhythm a the song.

'What?' he says, lookin up from his jar.

Someone coughs. 'Eh . . . nothin . . .'

He looks back down.

'. . . just she's got beautiful brown eyes, that's all.'

There's a few laughs but they stop as soon as Jimmy looks up again at Morsey. Marlene shifts around on her seat.

'Whatcha sayin, Morsey?'

'Relax, Jimmy,' says Andy. 'Your kids are watchin, man . . .'

'Whatcha fuckin sayin, Morsey?'

Morsey shrugs.

'Ya sayin what I think ya sayin, ya ignorant cunt?'

'Ignorant?' Morsey laughs.

'Hey, comrades—'

'Leave it out, Andy,' says Morsey. 'So why's it bother you what I'm sayin, Marconi? Shouldn't do if I'm that fuckin . . . ignorant.'

The room buzzes. It's silent but not silent. It's waitin. I've stopped singin but I'm not waitin like the rest. I'm still movin, jiggin me feet, only I'm movin so small nobody can see. The room buzzes and I'm buzzin too. I *am* the buzz, the silence but not silence that's pulsin between me Da and the man in the denim jacket with the dust in his hair.

Jimmy licks his lips, opens his mouth. Then he laughs – a quiet laugh, like he couldn't give a shit – and throws back what's left in the jar down his throat.

The silence holds – breathe in, breathe out, breathe in – then melts back inta chat and laughin and the clink a bottles and Boney M's on the record player and 'Brown Girl's in the Ring' and everythin's like it was before. Except I know different because the silence that's not silence is still buzzin in me underneath the other sounds. It's buzzin through me veins, through me skin, through me sweat, through me bones. I'm puzzled that nobody else feels it and I look round for Micko ta tell him what I'm feelin. But he's nowhere ta be seen and then the feelin starts gettin so strong, I can't help but let it out, quiet at first, singin ta meself, but then buildin me jig up to a full-scale trot, me song into a Red Indian raincall. Nobody else notices. The laughin and the drinkin and the Boney M has got them by their souls. And I keep jiggin and singin, louder and faster, till at last I wear meself out and collapse in a heap.

'Wouldn't back ya up, Rose, would he?' says Granny.

Ma sighs.

'See, Marlene, you were there and all. Ya seen him let her down in fronta everyone. That fella castin aspersions and lover boy said nothin. Good-for-nothin little coward.'

Years after, I heard Da got Morsey on his own and bet the shite outta him. Gave him two black eyes and ruined his nose, not that there was much of a nose ta ruin in the first place. The thick cunt – Da, I mean – musta thought Morsey was Sam's da. Fool. Morsey was ugly as sin. There was no way he coulda got Ma pregnant for him with a baby as beautiful as Samantha.

But the point is, it proved Granny right. Da was brave enough ta do Morsey once there was no one watchin, but he was too much of a fuckin coward ta do it in front of an audience in case it proved all them rumours were true.

You'd think with me Da back from the clink, his not-that-kinda-brothers would be callin round a bit more regular. But they didn't. Musta been Ma kept them away from us – 'No need for ya ta meet them here, Jimmy' – though she hadn't as much luck convincin Da ta stay outta their patch. Maybe – if Andy had hung round Dublin longer before headin off ta Palestine – she mighta had more joy, and the Wacker and Dapper Don woulda had ta look for someone other than Jimmy Marconi ta scam with. But he didn't and she didn't and as long as the Dos Amigos were willin ta show their gratitude ta me Da for not shoppin them for the drugs bust in '74, why on earth would he try ta go straight?

But things didn't pan out quite as easy as he mighta imagined.

It all started in March '78, when the Don moved up a gear, done that hit on the drugs factory and landed himself a quarter mill worth a painkillers in street prices. A quarter mill a profit, a which he shared sweet fuck all with the Wacker. I don't know if me Da was in on the job, but I do know Ma thought he'd been upta somethin. All the bad looks goin round the area, people not talkin ta each other; even kids that age we knew somethin was goin on.

There's still all sortsa rumours about how exactly the Don got inta the gear and why the Wacker didn't come in with him. Some say the Don had been plannin it because he knew there was way bigger money if ya went beyond hash. Others say the Wacker wanted out, and decided ta force the Don's hand. You useta say them stories was bollocks; smart though the Don and Wacker was, neither a them heads was genius enough ta invent the Dublin gear trade single-handed. It was a simple case a the Don makin easy money from the painkillers and wantin ta make more, and the Wacker bein pissed off because he'd lost out. Whatever, nobody was surprised when it turned dirty, and on the next big dope haul from France, shots got fired and a young cousin a the Wacker's got five a them in the chest.

Wacker was ragin – that little fella was like one of his sons. Legend goes he told Don Ryan he better watch out for his own blood, thank his lucky stars he didn't have any kids yet insteada moanin about his wife not gettin pregnant for him, because if she did give him a babby, Wacker'd fuck up its life so bad the Don would wish it was dead. It was then the alliance split for good. Wacker said *No* ta drugs – no hash, no grass, no pills and certainly no smack – and took over all a Dorset Street from the Big Tree downta the Wax Museum, creepin in south from Belvedere Road towards Gardiner Street and Summerhill. Ta rub the salt in, he gave his lot a name and that's why we know them as the Waxboys. The Don bit back, swallyin up Ballybough and the North Strand and spreadin up towards Portland Row. His lads got called the Five Lampers. Lines were drawn, men got armed, and the whole turf from Richmond Place downta Seán MacDermott Street and up as far as Mountjoy Square became a no-man's-land, shiftin from one camp ta the other as each side's fortune ebbed and flowed. They say it's only in recent times we've had wars like that. They're wrong.

With our flats stuck in the middle a no-man's-land, Jimmy Marconi had a choice. And – Jesus knows why because his first loyalty shoulda been ta the Don, and that anoraked little fuck the Wacker was a genuine sociopath if ever there was one – he chose the Waxboys.

They said the Special Branch had been onta them all along, waitin for a chance ta nail the Wacker, but even so, things mighta turned out alright if Frankie Burke hadn't lost his head. They hadn't even got their hands on the cash before the Branch came roarin in. It was then Frankie opened up, straightaway gettin a Branchman in the chest. The Branch needed no excuse and covered the place in bullets. In the end, between both sides, they injured two post office workers and killed one, plus a civilian and two robbers. The Branchman stayed in a coma for weeks before he woke up.

When they asked Da who he was workin for, he said he was the ringleader, in it for the money. They didn't believe him but he still got ten.

Sad, isn't it?

Is it, fuck! Lucky, more like. If they'd had ta switch the Branchman off, he'da got life. And what's sad about a person runnin inta the odd occupational hazard, especially if they decide ta work for some paranoid psycho like Fred Mahon? The only thing that's sad is me Da's hopes that he was on the up – risin ta the top, cream a the crop, gettin matey with Wacker, maybe even one day bein number one himself. Because them hopes were never meant ta come true. Jimmy Marconi was always destined ta fuck things up.

IV

'Come on, come on, come *on*, ya eejits!'

The banjaxed plastic ball lifts, hovers, swoops, falls. We race after it, driven by Micko's yells bouncin like bullets off the walls a the yard.

'Come on!'

The ball lands three strides away from me. I charge. Behind me I hear them –

'Run, Lucy, run!'

'Catch that ball *willya?*'

I'm just gone four, dressed in the pink coat Ma got me for Sam's christenin. It still fits me. It's still fluffy. And it's still scratchy as anythin. But I try not ta think a neither the fluff nor the scratchiness as I duck through set after set a flashin legs, trippin, fallin, pickin meself up.

'Run, Lucy, run!'

'The ball . . . look . . .'

It's alright. It's still ahead a me. I gather me breath, keep goin.

Hunh, hunh, hunh. Me breath in me ears.

Dum, dum, dum. Me heart, poundin in me head.

Someone starts laughin. Me throat and chest are ripped apart with the effort a breathin. But I can't give up, not now.

'Lucy!'

Hunh, hunh, hunh.

Someone raises their foot, kicks – am I too late? Please, no – but the kick is shite and the ball flies clear a the goal and bounces against the wall, liftin over me head. It swoops, a brown and orange curve cuttin through the sky, and as I race ta catch it, it drops again, this time inta the stairwell.

'Get it, Lucy!'

I reach, grab.

A foot, small and neat in a navy runner, lashes out, stoppin the ball.

I look up.

At first, blinded by the sun shinin through him inta me eyes, I see nothin but a transparent ghost. Then the ghost moves, lettin its shada fall over me, and as the sun disappears I see a boy, thin and white with jet-black hair and eyes that are pieces a coal sittin inside bruised navy sockets. He has a fag in his mouth and a twisted stick a willa in his right hand. There's a smile, there, somewhere, lurkin round the corners of his mouth, but his eyes are so hidden, I can't tell if he's bein friendly or not.

'Bloody 'ell. It's a Mikado biscuit.' His voice around the fag sounds different ta ours, under the Dublin drone the edge of an accent I've heard off of the telly. *Coronation Street*.

I ignore the dig at me coat and stick out me hands.

'Give us the ball.'

He laughs. 'Jesus. The Mikado can talk.' He lifts his white fingers.

I still remember the slow way ya moved, the ease of it, like a cat stretchin in the mornin.

'I'm not a Mikado me name's Lucy and ya can't say Jesus because that's a bad word and I want me ball back—'

He takes out the fag and throws it on the ground. It lies there, smoulderin, like he's left some a himself in it.

'What ya say ya name was?'

'Lucy. Lucy Marconi. Give us—'

But as I'm reachin out, he's already threadin his stick inta his s-belt and startin ta bounce the ball with one foot like an English soccer star.

'Here, I'll tell me brother—'

He looks at me, still bouncin. Then he smiles, flips the ball high and with a sudden lunge, slams it with his head back inta the middle a the game.

Catch it, Mikado.

From the scramble in the yard, Micko's blondey head rises, makes contact – and we're on.

*

Things I remember. Yer voice, Irish and English at the same time. The easy way ya slid yerself inta our game, like ya weren't a stranger at all, you'd only stepped out for a few seconds ta let the others pretend they were okay without ya. The way I ran after ya like a dog, goaded by yer unspoken dare, pantin uselessly for the ball that was already gone way beyond me reach. Ya didn't know it then, nor me neither, but lookin back, I think that was the day ya became me master, Nayler.

We musta seen ya round, Joanie Hayes's odd-lookin nephew over from Manchester, but I can't remember noticin ya till that day ya picked up our ball.

Yer Auntie Joan lived in the tower block behind us. Despite all the rumours that her roamin brother, yer da, hid guns for the Ra in the Dublin mountains, and that yer ma was a scarlet woman who'd run off on youse while ya were a nipper, yer auntie kept herself very quiet. Didn't seek out trouble, didn't seek out pals. But you were a different story.

After that first game, ya melted away like you'd done before. But the next day, ya stayed gassin with Micko. And the day after ya stayed even longer. It was as if playin with us gave ya life, made ya more solid, better able ta stick this brand-new country ya'd found yerself in.

It's pushin September and darkness is buildin in the corners a the yard.

'Micko! Micko!' calls Ma from the balcony. 'Tell yer brother and sister ta come up right away. Yer dinner's nearly ready!'

Micko, huddled near a wall with ya, plannin somethin, looks up. He's vexed. I never seen him vexed with Ma before ya came along but that's the main look on his face nowadays. Ya nudge him and say somethin. He grins and leans back in close ta ya and whispers in yer ear and yer face opens up with the sheer delight of it and, before ya can help yerself, ya crackin up laughin and he is too. I wanta get in on the joke, I love Micko's jokes, so I move towards youse. But John Paul grabs me in a headlock – 'Betcha ya can't get outta this, Lucy!' – and I'm down.

'Micko! Are ya comin? Jesus, John Paul, ya leadin yer brother astray again? Get up here or I'll feed yiz nothin!'

John Paul lets me go. 'Come on, Micko.'

Micko ignores him. Ya look down at the ground, twistin yer willa stick in yer hands. Ya might be smilin only I can't see from where I'm standin.

'John *Paul!*' screeches Ma, so loud Missus Devlin on the floor above comes out onta her balcony, *Jesus whatcha at?* written all over her face.

Ya nod at Micko. He stands up. 'Comin, Ma!'

When we get in, Granny's at the table cuttin crusts off of the bread and Samantha's in her high chair, apple muck all over her bib. Ma musta just changed her nappy because soon as I folla youse through the door the smell a shite hits me nose.

Ma sighs. 'John Paul, who said ya could bring yer pal up here?'

'Ma, it wasn't me—'

'Hello, Missus Marconi,' ya say. Yer face looks different all of a sudden ta how it does normal, when ya playin with us; open and younger even and sorta . . . trustin. 'Me name's Nayler. I'm new round here. Miz Hayes is me aunt.'

Ya stick out yer hand. Ma takes it. One of her eyebrows wriggles up her forehead the way it always does when she's surprised.

'Nice ta have somewan with manners round here.' She eyes me and John Paul. 'For a change.'

As ya move ta the table, Granny makes a sudden hissin sound, like a cat.

We all look at her. She shakes her head, wavin her hand like she didn't mean it, and we all start eatin. It's only when she's pourin the tea that I see the sores startin ta bleed on her palms.

She doesn't look at ya once the whole time ya there. But when ya goin, I catch her starin, her bad eye and her good eye both drillin holes in yer back, tiny eye-shaped holes that'll folla ya all the way home.

'Ma!' Ma leans over and clicks her fingers in Granny's face. 'Wouldya give over?'

Granny scrunches up her mouth. 'I can look where I want.'

'Jesus.' Ma sighs. 'If I had me life all over again . . .'

Micko nudges me and we start up: '. . . I'da never have had any a youse!'

She laughs.

She useta say that all the time, ya know. *If I had me life all over again, I wouldn'a had any a youse.* She said it so much, we knew it off by heart. It had nothin ta do with anythin but it always shut Granny up.

Twenty-four. That was how young she was when ya met her first. Hard ta credit, yeah? It's so easy for me ta picture Ma as an auld wan, all puffed out with life and kids and fags and disappointment. Easy ta forget she useta be a beauty; useta be the Rose Dolan that walked like a queen and drove Jimmy Marconi wild.

She liked ya a lot; she liked ya from the start. It was the innocent face, a course, and the polite voice. She was always a sucker for politeness. She even let ya hold Sam the second time ya came up, remember? She had ta go ta the jacks, ta freshen up, as she put it, and Micko was in the bedroom changin so he couldn't mind the baby, and she wouldn't even dream a lettin me hold Sam even though I kept on at her. I was always a problem, far as Ma was concerned: a loud, plain, bothersome problem that would probably drop the baby as soon as touch her.

I remember that day well because 'Tie a Yella Ribbon Round the Old Oak Tree' was on the radio and when I started hummin along, ya stared at me like I was doin somethin wrong. I didn't care. I liked that song.

I told ya as much. 'I like this song.'

You just made a face, like I was stupid, and said somethin like, 'Do ya, Mikado?' – ya hadn't started callin me Lucy Lu yet – and then Sam started cryin. I told ya ta give her ta me, but ya wouldn't listen, kept rockin her, tryin ta shush her. It was then Granny came in, in a state, and whipped Sam away, not even botherin ta give ya the time a day.

But that was Granny all over, wasn't it? Any time ya come up, she done her best ta ignore ya, like ya were a piece a dirt not worthy of her attention. We could never figure out why, because ya were very polite, and at the start in anyways ya never got in that much trouble, but that's how she was right up till the end nearly.

As for me, Jesus, I hung outta you and Micko, remember? Youse were always darin me ta do stuff – chase balls, deliver messages, get in on fights, rob sweets. It irked John Paul no end, mainly because he thought I was way too young ta be a proper pal. Not that it was real pallin, mind. You treated me grand for the most part but there were loadsa times ya didn't even seem ta notice I was there; and as for Micko, even though he looked out for me, and never tormented me the way he done our wimpy cousin Charlie, he was still quick enough ta slag me off. On the whole, though, it didn't bother me. Long as I could join in, I was happy.

'You're our lucky mascot, Lucy Lu,' ya told me once. 'Our errant girl.'

I liked that, errant girl, even though I didn't know what it meant. Made me sound important.

Ya know me, Nayler, I'm not one ta build stuff up, ta say we'd some mad bond as kids when we didn't, but there was things that stick in me mind. Like that Hallowe'en I dressed up as a high-wayman, remember? I made a cloak outta a binbag and a hat from an old cardboard box. The others were bangin on sayin I was Zorro or Superwoman, and Micko said I musta been goin trick-or-treatin dressed as a spa. But you just looked at me and pointed yer two fingers inta me face. 'Stand and deliver, Lucy Lu,' ya said. Then ya pulled yer fingers back and blew on the tips, like Maverick. I know it's not a big thing, but I still remember it.

You'd think with the harassin I got from youse I'da given Sam the same treatment in turn. She was me little sister; that was me birthright, after all, ta push her round. But I never bullied her, no matter how sick she got or how much she cried. It wasn't because she was Ma's pet and I was scareda bein bet. I didn't hurt Sam because there was somethin about her that was precious; that said, *No, back off, leave me alone.*

★

From the livin room I can hear Ma laughin at Ronnie Corbett on the telly and cooin at Sam, but I'm stuck in the kitchen beside Granny, who's drip-feedin me cups a scaldin tea laced with sugar. The wool blanket itches me neck. I hate it. I hate bein hot and I hate bein sore all over and more than that I hate bein sick with the poxy flu. I'm never sick.

Rain slides down the steamed-up windas. Me feet jig. I am *dyin* ta get out.

It's three days after Christmas. We were supposed ta go over ta see Uncle Tom in hospital but Ma says I've got germs and if I go out I'll pass them onta everyone else and the sick people will all die. I wouldn't mind seein that, all them sick people fallin down dead in one go. Anythin would be better than bein stuck inside.

There's a clatter at the door and the Gang a Three pour in, starvin.

'Here, Granny, give us some orange,' says Micko.

'Have one a Missus Devlin's mince pies.'

'No, they're rotten. I want a Toffypop.'

'I want—' I start sayin, but then the coughin sets in.

'What's that?' says Ma, comin ta the door. She sees Micko and reaches over for a kiss. 'Ah, me little troublemaker . . .' Her face is red and her words are runnin together.

Ya laugh softly. Ma doesn't hear it but Micko twists away, scarlet. Ma drops her hand and looks over at me. 'What's that problem doin outta bed, Ma?'

'Ah, Rose, I hadn't the heart ta keep her locked up. She was like a little monkey in the zoo.'

Youse all start laughin. It's not fair. I squirm outta Granny's grip, climb up onta me chair and pull off me blanket. Below me the world tilts but for once I don't mind.

'Lucy!' says Ma.

'I wanta go out.' I fling the blanket away. It hits against the tinsel stars hangin from the ceilin.

'Stop it, Lucy,' says Ma.

'I wanta go *out*!' Inside me I feel the restlessness buildin inta rage. If she doesn't let me go, I'm gointa start shoutin. There's nothin I can do about it. It's startin and like that wave at the start a *Hawaii Five-O* it's gointa keep goin till it stops.

'I'm warnin ya!'

'*I fuckin wanta—*'

'Jesus!' Ma grabs me hand and pulls, landin me with a bang on the chair. Then she smacks me on the face. I'm too hot ta cry so I kick at her instead. She smacks me again. Her breath smells hot and raw.

'Rose!' says Granny. 'Give her here.'

Ma stops, leavin her hand in mid-air, and I see her sizin it up; who has the better chance a keepin me quiet – her or Granny? She decides and lets me go, pushin me across the table.

Granny grabs me wrists. Her hands are hard, strong, bony. 'Easy now, Lucy, stay easy. Sssh.' I kick again but I don't mean it and I know she knows that too.

'Ssshhh.'

I lie on her lap. I'm bakin hot and me breath is so caught up in me chest I think I'm gointa burst.

'Good girl.' Granny strokes me forehead. The touch soothes me, like it always does. Apart from me Da, me Granny's been the only person I don't mind holdin me. I let out me breath, feelin like a balloon. The rage melts inta nothin. 'Good girl.'

Across the table Micko grins and mouths Granny's words, all scornful. *Good girl*. He nudges ya. Ya smile one a yer lazy smiles, sizin me up with yer cat's slitted eyes.

Later on, Ma lights a candle and turns off the light and we get Granny ta tell us a story. Micko wants ta go back outside but you seem easy enough ta stay.

'Starlight,' I beg. 'Tell us the one about Starlight and Jerusalem.'

'Ah, not that stupid horse again,' says Micko. 'It's borin.'

'Please, Granny. Tell us. The jump.'

'Lucy, ya don't wanta hear that one,' says Granny. 'I'll tellya about the boxin ghost instead, the one yer granda saw on Arbour Hill.'

'No, Granny. Please. Starlight.' I cough, tryin ta make it sound as sore as possible, so she'll feel sorry for me and give in.

The story starts. In the flickerin light from the candle I see us like I'm hangin over the table, just like one a them tinsel stars danglin from the ceilin. I see me on Granny's lap, and you and Micko sharin the same seat, and John Paul leanin against Ma's armchair with the ragged hems and the fag burns, and Ma sittin cosy holdin Sam, pattin the hair of her baby that's growin from a mouse to a little girl, listenin and noddin and smokin and sippin her tea and all the time pattin Sam's goldy hair, pat pat pat. She watches us in the candlelight; all four of us – me, Micko, John Paul and you – her eyes slippin over us as if she's tryin ta set her stamp on us, own us all, even me.

Accordin ta Granny, Starlight belonged ta Buck Whaley, one a the legion a ghosties that she called up ta entertain us on the dark winter evenins. Buck – otherwise known as Thomas Whaley – was an Anglo-Irishman and, in Granny's version of events, started off as a highwayman, just like me great-granda. People called him Buck because he was a buck, and some called him Jerusalem because he once flew a magic carpet all the way ta the Holy City, and others called him Lord Thomas because he said he was of royal blood. But if Granny was ta be believed, he was born no lord at all but poor as a churchmouse in the depths a Mayo. On the very first night he came ta Dublin, he bumped inta – guess who? Yes, a course; why would Granny make things complicated when they could be as predictable as one two three? – the Devil. Course it bein late at night, the tail wasn't very obvious, plus they'd met on Leeson Street, where everyone looked like devils, so the upshot was poor Buck didn't recognize Auld Nick for what he was.

'Here,' says the Devil. 'I know a good place ta get some drink.' Parched after the long ride from Mayo, Buck was happy enough ta folla the Devil down to a little coachhouse at the back a the street and there they got drinkin and chattin. The Devil kept pourin out the whiskey and, soon as he was happy his victim was drunk enough, he challenged Buck to a game a cards. The deal was: if the Devil won, he'd get Buck's soul and if Buck won, well . . . he'd get his heart's desire.

Well, they played and played, said Granny, and each was a match for the other. After three days they were proppin their eyes open with matchsticks and there was still no winner. Finally, after another three days, it came ta the crunch. The Devil looked at his cards. Four Kings. That's it! he thought, and risked it all on one last bet. But when they showed the hands, didn't Buck have the Joker and four lovely Aces ta boot! The Devil was ragin – 'As ya can imagine,' said Granny – but he had ta stand by his word. And that was how Buck came by his money and his lordship and his townhouse on Leeson Street and his lodge in the country they useta call the HellFire Club. But best of all his winnins was his heart's desire – Starlight, a huge black stallion, brave and beautiful, with a white star on his forehead.

After his win, Buck gave up the highway – but not because he was afraid. Old Buck Whaley was afraid a nobody – 'Just like Lucy,' said Granny, 'only she was born fearless, while Buck's courage came from havin the Devil on his side.'

Ma useta tut at that bit, like Granny had got it wrong.

Starlight's jump was me favourite story about Buck and it went like this . . .

One night the Devil decides ta test Buck. He's been thinkin; if he can get Buck ta do somethin bad ta Starlight, there's a good chance he'll win back the stuff he lost ta Buck all them years ago. That's because the Devil always wins if he can get someone ta sacrifice somethin for him – that's not like Jesus dyin on the cross ta save the sins a the world, says Granny, it means hurtin somethin good for badness. So he slides upta Buck and says he'll set him a wager – that means bet, says Granny. He'll give him a big reward if he jumps Starlight out the top-floor winda a the house on Leeson Street.

'What kinda reward?' says Buck.

'A place in Hell.'

'Ah, no. Ya wanta do better than that.'

The Devil has a think. 'Why don't I give ya three a me demons ta serve ya forever?'

'Not bad,' says Buck. 'But not good enough.'

The Devil stamps his foot. 'Jaysus!' He thinks again. 'What about this?' And diggin inta his pocket, he hauls out a big pile a jewels.

I always thought that shoulda been the end of it – who wouldn't like jewels? – but accordin ta Granny, Buck just laughed and said he already had all the jewels he needed.

'Jaysus,' says the Devil again, real fed up. 'You're awful hard work. Whatcha want at all, Buck Whaley?'

Buck gives him a smile with his handsome teeth flashin white against his brown skin. Then he whispers somethin in the Devil's ear.

Granny always useta make us guess what Buck was askin for, and we did, but none of us ever got it right. Micko thought it was more money; John Paul said it was an army. I thought he wanted ta live forever. You never said your guess out loud – I suppose on accounta Granny. Whatever it was, the Devil musta liked what he heard because in the story he smiles and sticks out his claw. 'Shake it so, Buck, and we'll seal the wager.'

'Does he do it?' We all look up, surprised at the question. It's you.

'Whatcha think?' says Granny.

For two days and nights they stand at the winda a the big ballroom on the top floor a Buck's townhouse, starin down at the street below. For two days and nights Buck whispers in Starlight's ear, pattin the white star on his forehead, tellin him he'll jump it easy, he'll fly like a bird, and won't it be great ta see the look on Auld Nick's face when they do that? But Starlight doesn't budge. The moon waxes and wanes. Starlight's fine black hooves jitter on the fine polished wood a the ballroom. And as the time passes, Buck starts ta get worried.

'Come on, ya nag!' he says –

'He doesn't!' I say.

'He does, Lucy,' says Granny. 'He's in a terrible state. But he shouldn'a been. Because on the third night as the moon rises, up! Starlight lifts his head and up! he lifts his hooves and then him and Buck go flyin over the sill and out inta the cold night air.'

Me breath catches in me throat. I've heard this story loadsa times before but that fall always makes me shiver. I can feel the windas a the neighbourin houses speedin past Starlight as fast as if I'm on his back meself, rushin past us while we whirl to our death on the spiky railins below. Granny pauses like she always does at this point.

'What happened next? Did he—'

'Well . . . ,' says Granny. 'They fell and they fell. The night air bit inta Buck's skin and his guts lurched in his belly; he looked down and seen the ground comin up ta meet him—'

'And the railins,' I say.

'And the railins. And he closed his eyes, wonderin if it was such a good idea after all ta have gambled with the Devil. For who was he ta think he could best Auld Nick at his own game? Underneath him he could feel Starlight, and he knew then he'd done a very foolish thing, puttin his lovely horse ta the wager. But just as he was givin up hope, he heard a funny sorta rippin sound. What could it be? Buck squinted one eye open, then another, and mother-agod what did he see only . . .'

'What?' I say, even though I know the answer.

'Only wings buddin outta Starlight's back! And outta nowhere came a big yella wind and it lifted up the two a them – Buck and Starlight – and laid them as light as feathers on the ground. No sooner did they land then the wings disappeared and the yella wind melted inta nowhere and Starlight was back ta normal, tossin his lovely mane and whinnyin like if they'd just been out for a walk. Buck jumped down from his back, landin on his feet like a cat, and walked straight upta the Devil ta claim back his prize. And I don't need ta tell ya Auld Nick was as grumpy as bejasus as he passed it over ta Buck and went scuttlin back ta the flames a Hell.'

Me and Sam cheer. Micko sniggers.

'There's a price for everythin, though. Poor auld Starlight got a little cold straight after, just like you, Lucy, because a that night air, freezin it was, but he was right as rain in a coupla days. More than can be said for that Mayo-born brute on his back.'

'Alright,' I say, yawnin, not carin any more.

Ma gets up and turns on the light. 'Shouldn't ya be goin home, son?'

'Sure, Missus Marconi,' ya say. But ya look like ya don't wanta go anywhere.

Musta made ya laugh, Nayler, later on, when ya found out that, like me great-granda, Buck Whaley never was a highwayman. Nor was he a lord, though his da mighta been, and he certainly wasn't born in Mayo, and as for magic carpets and black horses with stars on their foreheads and deals with the Devil . . . well, say no more. Oh yeah, musta made ya piss yerself.

Not that it bothers me. Unlike you, I never cared much for auld Buck, though I was fixated on that horse a his. I useta lie in the bunk below Micko, all them nights I couldn't get ta sleep, and picture meself ridin on that black stallion; sat up high as heaven as I galloped through the night with the wind in me hair, protected from fallin only by Starlight's strong back and the guns at me side. The odd time I did get ta sleep, he was the only thing I'd ever dream about: me and Starlight havin adventures in the desert with Lawrence of Arabia, or in France, savin the beautiful ladies from their heads bein cut off, or up at the North Pole, doin battle with the Abominable Snowman.

You never let on how much ya loved Granny's stories, specially the ones about Buck. Sure why would our quiet Captain Nayler give anyone a chance ta get a dig in? Ya never leaned forward, or opened up yer eyes, or shushed Micko when he was jeerin me for listenin. And exceptin that first story, when ya asked about the wager, and that other time months later, when ya interrupted outta the blue – sayin Starlight was a she, a mare not a stallion like Granny had it, ruinin the story and me dreams for ages after – ya never pestered Granny like me or Micko done; beggin her for more, or What happens next? I suppose ya knew, even then, that though me Granny was a born storyteller, in thrall ta the beginnin middle and end, the bind the story had on her was a fine thing, easily broken – specially as far as you were concerned. Even one word from ya, one hint she was givin ya what ya wanted, woulda cut the whole web down before even the first thread was spun. But I could still feel ya, Nayler, drinkin up her words like they were all ya ever needed.

For ages, I never understood why; why the stories, why especially Buck. Once I asked ya was it because Buck was Irish and English at the same time, like you, but ya just looked at me like I was a kid again, stupid.

I did get a picture once, when I was small. I wasn't there so I can't prove it ever happened but the picture's as clear and sharp as a real-life photo so I can't accept it's a lie. It's of a boy, sittin outside the door of a flat, listenin.

The door opens. The boy jumps up from the step he's been sittin on, but he's too late. She's seen him.

'Oh,' she says. 'Where's Micko?'

He nods towards the yard.

The woman goes ta speak but then a fella comes out the door behind her.

She kisses the fella and takes somethin from him – money, the boy guesses. She counts it and folds it inside the fronta her shiny blue dressin-gown. The fella goes down the steps. The woman pulls the belta the dressin-gown tight. Her skin is white in the sunlight. She turns ta the boy.

'All on yer own, are ya, son? Ya look hungry. D'ya wanta come in, have some orange?'

He shakes his head, puttin on the smile he knows she likes.

'No. I better go, Missus Marconi.'

Like I say, Nayler, I can't prove that picture was real, that any a that happened, even though the fact it's in me mind does mosta the provin for me. But wouldn't it be a laugh if all them times we thought ya were off on business, ya were actually crouched on the landin outside our door, listenin in on Granny's stories like a little fuckin kid?

'What do I hafta wear this for?'

'It's yer school uniform, Lucy.'

'I want me guns.'

'Ya can't have them.'

'But—'

'Jesus! Come on, will ya? Marlene and Charlie are waitin on us.'

I watch, helpless, knowin not even me rage will help me now, as me cowboy belt and guns go flyin inta the bin. Dust ta dust. New rules for a new world.

It's a bright day, too bright for tight shoes and itchy woollen socks. We walk down the canal towpath and I long ta be one a the ducks, dippin free inta the water. School's at the other enda the canal, in a big grey buildin stuck behind tall concrete columns. I know I don't wanta go there but Ma won't hear *No*. She's got me mitt firm in hers and there's no runnin away. In fronta us trots Marlene and me cousin Charlie.

'Jesus, love!' yells Ma, puffin. 'Wait on us, willya! Don't know where ya get yer energy!'

'That's me!' Marlene turns and flashes us a smile. 'Half-greyhound.'

'Wish I'd that problem,' mutters Ma, lookin at Marlene's skinny arse.

Me cousin Charlie was alright. He was a wimp, sure enough, with his Health Board specs – 'That's *her*,' says Granny. 'Ya don't catch Stevo wearin specs, do ya?' – his weedy arms and his slowcoach run. But he was good at numbers and figurin things out and he'd a brilliant collection a Dinky cars. And in a way the wimpiness was a good thing, because it was easy enough for me ta pick on him, makin up for some a the gyp I got from youse.

It was Marlene's idea for us ta start school together. Even though Charlie was younger than me, he was brainy enough for it, and Marlene had some notion that I'd look after him; protect him from the bullies, stave off the slaggin.

At least I was spared havin ta mind his sisters. Marlene's girls were awful cissies, with their ringlets and their cryin, their Irish dancin, their pink-rimmed specs – 'Told ya it was her side!' – and their English names – 'What's she want? The Queen rulin the roost

in Dublin Castle again?' Compared ta them, Charlie was fine. Still
. . . look after him all the time? No thanks.

At break, Sharon Doyle from Pig Lane – funny how ya remember
people's names years after you've forgotten their faces – comes upta
me and pushes me in the back.

'Stay away, ya dirty tinker.'

Stay away? I haven't gone near her. I'm not lookin for trouble,
even though I'm bored sick after sittin down so long in that stuffy
classroom, and with me crips and the fresh air I'm even more
restless and wonderin why we can't stay outside and do runnin
or chasin insteada havin ta go back in. But I'm not lookin for
trouble.

'Yeah, you're a dirty tinker, Lucy Marconi, and so are yer brothers
and yer granny's a witch.'

She pushes me again. Another girl tugs at me hair. Then someone
else comes up behind me and pokes me in the arse.

'Tinker, tinker, ya smell like a stinker!'

That Sharon's the worst. I should do somethin, make her shut
up.

'Tinker, tinker!'

I really should.

'And yer da's in jail and yer ma's a—'

Me fist goes out, decks her in the gob. There's a silence, then
whispers, then, before I know what's happenin, somethin whips
itself across the yard and right at me. It bangs the backa me head;
hard. Ah, here . . .

I go for it; kickin, slappin, bitin any loose bits a skin I can find.
But he – it's a fella, I see now – gets me down on the ground and
forces me on me back. Me uniform is up around me waist and I
know the others is laughin, but I don't care. I go ta bite him but
then he's got me arms in a twist with one hand and he's thumpin
me, hard, with the other.

'Doylo! Doylo!' shout the ring a lads around us.

'Lucy! Lucy!' shouts Charlie, me only supporter.

Shout all Charlie might, even an army a fans woulda been no

use ta me that day. In the end Sister Germaine had ta pull him off me before he murdered me.

Greg Doyle. Sharon's older brother. Doylo for short. A veteran with four years a school already served; a year older and a head and a half higher than everyone else in his class, kept back from the Brothers because he was so thick. After that fight he useta lay in wait for me with his pals when school was over. I was safe on days Marlene brung us home because she was always on time, but if Ma was collectin me and got there late, well . . . Doylo would have his pounda flesh.

They say pain makes ya stronger if it doesn't kill ya. Well, the pain I got from Greg Doyle didn't kill me. It hurt like fuck, but one thing's sure: if he hadn't been such a bully I might nevera learnt the art a millin.

The screw in the navy jumper runs her hands all over Ma's body. Ma looks the other way, a trail a blue smoke easin outta her mouth, fillin the search. On her hip Sam sleeps, her eyes twitchin, her snot silver on her upper lip.

'And what's your name?' says the screw, puttin baby talk over her mucker accent as she pokes at Sam's cheek.

Ma shifts her weight, not so much as ta make it obvious, but enough ta take Sam's face away from the screw's finger. She says nothin. The screw finishes pattin her down, takes Ma's keys and sticks them in a plastic dish.

Inside the first gate we wait, ma's and kids and screws: the ma's all permed hair, lilac jeans and legwarmers; the kids in their best kit; the screws in their navy corrugated jumpers. A lot a the ma's talk different ta us; they sound like Uncle Dan's ladyfriend Dolly, sayin doyne insteada down and hey at the end a every sentence.

They're slow in openin the gates. It's stuffy. I start ta get hot. In the heat, me attention drifts. The women are still talkin round me, but whether it's me jiggin or the heat or not bein able ta breathe proper, somethin funny's happenin ta the sounda their voices. It's like they're mixin up in me head, makin a sorta tune. The tune's not proper music, like Micko's Ska, or me Da's Mod records. It's fulla ups and downs and ins and outs I can only half-folla. I close me eyes. In the blackness I hear it better. The tune's got a story in it, it's leadin me somewhere, a spiral roundin on itself, and as it does it fills me mind with pictures.

I see blue trees in a green haze, and water, and a horse poundin over clouds. The rhythm builds and a castle like the gate we've just come through appears, and in the winda is a beautiful fairytale princess with long blonde hair. There's a lift: the pictures freeze, the music pauses – and then the door a the castle opens and the tune crashes back, swellin for the finish. And I'm swellin too, risin over everyone else at the gate, as I feel it comin, the final crash, and –

'Lucy!' Clatter.

'Ow!'

'Stop makin that noise, for godsake. Jesus, I can't take ya anywhere!'

'Ow!'

Me face stings. Micko looks over at me. I'm expectin him ta take the piss, but he doesn't. Then I suss that he's not really seein me; he's too busy thinkin ahead ta the visit.

The screw turns the key and the heavy grey door slides open. John Paul holds out his arms, takin Sam as Ma tilts the buggy over the metal ledge inside the gate.

They bring us past the rose bushes inta the big grey prefab. Micko rushes ta the table on the right. It's the best one because it's right under the winda.

It's funny, how people that don't know it think a jail. Loadsa bars with hands grippin them, tormented faces lookin out. But when I was a kid, if someone said 'Jail' ta me, I'd thinka grey rooms and brown tables, white prefabs and loadsa other kids goin mental while me Ma and Da shared news and silence. Bars didn't come inta it till way later.

*

78

'Did ya hear a word I said?' says Ma. Her voice is low; she always speaks lower than normal when she's visitin Da. Da shakes his head, says somethin under his breath.

'What was that?' says Ma. She's frownin so hard there's a line all the way down her forehead.

'I said, Rose,' says Da, louder, 'ya can do what ya want with the lad. Boxin, fuckin . . . ballet, I don't care.'

John Paul goes scarlet. Micko laughs. Da gives a half a smile and reaches out ta tousle Micko's hair.

'Da!' Micko jerks away, dodgin the touch.

Da drops his hand and drums a tune on the tabletop with his fingernails.

'I got a Very Good in school, Da,' I say. It's a lie but he's not ta know.

'Yeah?' he says.

'I'm the best at . . . writin.'

'Jimmy—' says Ma. Da keeps drummin.

'Jimmy, he's your child too.'

Da sighs. 'Yeah, yeah. Let him at it.' He smiles at John Paul. 'Good on ya, son.'

And so, when he was nine, John Paul began boxin in the club on Richmond Place, bang in the middle a the no-man's-land that stretched between the turfs a the Waxboys and the Five Lampers. The club was in the basement of a tall Georgian buildin, every inch a which was owned by Dapper Don Ryan.

Story a that club was a real talkin point round us, remember? How the Don took it over ta honour the memory of his dead brother Marty, an international middleweight who'd walked inta the Mississippi one night after a rigged match went wrong, leavin behind a grievin widda and a little lad aged eight, the closest thing Don Ryan ever had ta a son of his own. The auld wans roundabout with sons in the Five Lampers useta get tears in their eyes at that, remember? Poor Don Ryan, losin his brother. No wonder he turned ta the crime. But at least by runnin the club, the auld wans said, he's givin the kids in his area the chance ta succeed where his brother failed.

Robin Hood bollocks, ya always said. Boxin's as crooked as anythin else round here. Just another way a makin money.

Be that as it may, by 1975 the club was the Don's and the nephew was in there, dressed in a stripey coach's jersey ta train in the new generation. Woulda been in gloves only he liked watchin more than hittin, and word was when he did hit he was way too dirty for the ring.

They rented the top floor out ta Billy Fish the barber. Remember him? Billy Fish, renowned for his number one skinheads and cut-throat shaves; Billy Fish, named for the tropical fish in them green aquariums that filled his barbershop and lined every landin a that tall Georgian house.

In the playground on Hill Street, beside the stone tower with the clock on it, they pull at the boy's arms. One each side, pullin him like crows fightin over meat.

Fuck off, ya Brit. Get home, ya English cunt. Fuck back off ta yer Auntie Joan.

He's bein watched again. He looks up and through the blood sees the one that's watchin. One a the crows follas his glance, pauses for a minute in his tuggin.

Here, ease off. D'ya know who that is?

But then the watcher goes and the crows are back tuggin at their meat again.

Fuck off, ya Brit.

Next time he'll be luckier. Next time the watcher will do more than watch.

Me and Charlie are takin turns bouncin a tennis ball against the walla the convent on Portland Row when I see John Paul, Micko and you comin down the road towards us. There's someone else with youse: a tall fella, dressed in a jacket.

John Paul's boxin gloves, strung round his neck, shine red in the afternoon light.

I drop the ball and race up. *Let today be the day*, I think, *please*. Charlie lags behind.

'Here, John Paul,' I say. 'Will ya—'

John Paul cuffs me on the head with one a his gloves. That means be quiet.

'Alright then, me little rascals,' says the tall fella. He's a good few year older than youse, I see now, thirteen or so. He's got pimples and a broad face with a short chin like a cat and a wide mouth that goes wider again when he laughs and longish brown hair that touches the collar of his shirt. His eyes are brown too and sunk deep in his face and when he smiles they sparkle. His jacket is very nice. Fits him. It looks like somethin Uncle Stevo would wear goin ta work. Underneath he's wearin a stripey jumper; grey and red. 'Call round the club later so.' His voice is warm and comfortable-soundin, the same browny colour as his eyes.

Ya nod, swish yer willa stick against the edge a the footpath. 'Okay, Snags.'

'Sure, Snags,' says Micko.

'Keep up the good work, John Paul. Ya doin well.' The pimpled fella does a coupla feints, cuffin John Paul on the head – John Paul grins, a course, delighted with himself – and with one last 'Alright, seeyiz, kiddos,' he strolls away, easy in his good jacket.

'John Paul,' I say, 'can I—'

'Alright, alright,' says John Paul. He looks at you and Micko. 'Are youse stayin?'

'No,' ya say, and spit. The spit lands on Charlie's shoulder. 'See ya later. Come on, Micko.'

And that was me first meetin with Snagglepuss Ryan, favourite nephew a the Don, named after the cartoon cat for his easy voice and wide mouth.

Exit, stage left.

John Paul never admitted it ta you or Micko but he actually liked trainin me. He'd tried with Micko before, but Micko always fought dirty so their fights ended nasty, with John Paul stompin off and you and Micko pissin yerselves laughin. But I was miles better because A, John Paul could boot me around without gettin too much flak and B, unlike anythin else I done, I actually concentrated when I trained with him. Believe it or not, I was able ta pick up the rules that he'd picked up in the club and, believe it or not, I was able ta stick with them. I stuck with the footwork, the boxer's skip, the punches – jab, hook, cross, uppercut. I stuck with the feintin and the duckin, the slippin and the slidin. And all along Charlie – the most brutal fighter in the world on accounta he always lost control and ended up smashin too hard or the wrong direction – cheered me on and John Paul cursed me for not learnin fast enough. I stuck with it all and that's how I learnt when ta keep goin in a mill and when ta bail out.

What John Paul didn't know – what none a youse knew – was that there was a reason for me concentratin. If I could learn ta fight as good as me brother, I reckoned, one day I could batter Greg Doyle inta a pulp and he'd never ever bully me again.

In the end, a course, it didn't work out the way I'd planned.

'Where d'ya get them cuts from, Lucy?'

I look round, me arms achin from the uppercuts I been practisin on the football tied ta the railin. Micko's starin at me legs. 'Them cuts and bruises?'

I look down. Shite. Me socks have fallen down and the cuts are open again, streamin blood downta me ankles.

'Nowhere.' I go back ta the ball. Uppercut. Uppercut. Uppercut. I haven't told anya youse about Greg and I'm not gointa because you'll only laugh at me for bein weak.

'It's that Doylo again, isn't it, Lucy?'

Keep punchin. Uppercut. Uppercut. Uppercut.

Micko grabs the football. 'That fella's a spa, Lucy. He could do with some trainin.'

I lean against the railin, breathin hard.

The last kid goes, runnin upta their ma for a hug, and now it's just me, alone inside the concrete pillars. I head out. Me legs are shakin; not with fear, with somethin else – readiness, maybe. I'm so used ta bein jumped that me legs shake even on days they're not waitin.

I turn onta the towpath. One, two and – fuck! they're on me, boots and fists everywhere, me duckin, tryin ta run past their arms, dodgin smacks, gettin them in me belly, back, knees, head. Try ta punch. No use. All the lessons I've learnt from John Paul are out the winda. I'm dead. But just when I'm crashin ta the ground, three a them kickin me ta make sure I stay down, there's another blur, more bodies rushin inta the fight and . . . Jesus! Micko and John Paul and two others – Dekko Flynn and Paul Cunningham – are on Doylo and his pals like a gang a foxes in the chicken pen.

I crawl out from under the legs and look on. It's mayhem. No neat and tidy rules. Pull hair, stamp on feet, find the arches where the bones give. *Use the force, Luke.* Take the weighta the other bastard and let it knock him ta the ground. Bend fingers, strain wrists, pull hamstrings. Kick the goolies, butt the head, stick yer fingers in his ears, eyes, nose, mouth. Elbow the bollocks, whack the ribs. Bite skin; bite anythin that moves.

Micko looks up at me, wild-eyed as he digs his knuckle inta someone's shoulder. 'Toucha death!' he screams.

Someone lunges at me and I kick them in the bollocks. But then they hit me hard on the face, so hard blood spurts inta me eye. I stagger backwards, wipin the blood away, and see Doylo runnin down the towpath. Me chest's on fire, me heart is thumpin, but suddenly there's a motor in me legs and I'm racin up, catchin up, passin him out.

I jump him just as he gets ta the footbridge and me weight pulls us both ta the ground. His head hits off a piece a concrete and he goes a green colour. But I don't care; I have him where I want him. I start layin inta him, drillin him – uppercut uppercut uppercut – the way I've dreamta for months. He tries kickin back at me, gets me in the chest, but I keep punchin. I can't see, me eyes are red from the blood runnin inta them, but I keep punchin.

'Get off, ya fuckin mentaller!' he screams.

We watch them go, ragged and bleedin. Half-way down the path, Doylo turns and makes a gully. It rises in the air, holds for a bit, then drops back towards us like a green seagull.

'Cunts,' says Micko.

At the enda the towpath we stop at the Black Stores. Micko fishes in his pocket and digs out a coupla raggedy pound notes.

'Here. Lookit what I nicked off of Doylo.'

When we come outta Black's, armed with our penny chews, Cokes and Super Split ice-creams, you're there on the other side a the road, leanin over the bridge. Micko calls ya and runs across the street. I folla, doin me best ta keep up, but it's hard with all the sweets, so John Paul takes pity on me and doubles back, grabbin me by the wrist so I won't get knocked down.

'Here, Nayler. Guess what we done today!'

Ya don't look too bothered but Micko starts the story in anyways, not lettin John Paul get a word in. 'And then we . . . and then she . . .' He doesn't forget ta tell ya how well I fought. I'm thrilled. When he's finished, ya turn and look at me. I've me Super Split in one hand, me schoolbag in the other. I'm covered in scratches and bruises, blood drippin down from the cut in me forehead.

Ya look for ages.

A month later, Doylo and his pals swept inta our flats on their Choppers and cycled in circles in front of our block, whoopin like Red Indians. Micko and John Paul got stuck at the bottom of our stairwell, a cavalry with nowhere ta run but home. I spotted the trouble from the balcony and ran inside ta the back bedroom, where I leant out the winda and whistled.

Within seconds ya were there, with three older fellas I didn't recognize, armed with empty bottles and rocks.

'Lucy!' called Sam, but I paid her no heed as I raced down the stairs, achin ta get stuck in.

They called the rozzers when someone set fire ta Micko's tee-shirt.

Soon as the sirens started, Doylo fled on foot, leavin his brand-new Chopper hostage. His gang raced after him, just in time ta dodge the Old Bill as they swerved inta the yard with their lights a-flashin and mucker faces a-glowin.

The older lads that came in with you were nowhere ta be seen.

Stern words were had. Names were taken. Youse blamed Doylo's gang, a course; after all, they were the ones with the bottles and rocks, weren't they? Micko held his burnt tee-shirt in his bruised arms and cried. Very convincin. Even the pigs looked concerned at that; said youse wouldn't get a caution this time but next time . . . well, there better not be a next time. On the balconies, the auld wans tut-tutted. Ma, thank God, was at the Mater with Granny.

Once the lasta the flashin lights is gone, Micko fucks Doylo's Chopper on the ground and starts dancin up and down on it. It looks like good crack so I join in.

'What's that?' ya say.

We turn, look. Near the back wall away from the windas a figure is standin.

'Holy God, Gay,' says Micko, and we all laugh because he sounds just like the auld wans that ring up Gay Byrne's radio programme ta complain. 'Look who we have here.'

'Spocky Halloran,' ya say.

'So it is, Gay.'

Spocky's one a Doylo's, a big lug with pointy ears like Dr Spock on *Star Trek*. He looks hard but he's never been much good at scrappin. Micko jumps off the bike and starts walkin towards him. Spocky looks around, panickin, but there's nowhere for him ta run, so the thick bastard squeezes himself tighter against the wall. I leave the bike and run after you and the resta the gang as youse folla Micko.

'Come out, come out wherever you are,' sings Micko. We all join in.

Spocky looks left, right, left.

'That's right, Spocky,' calls Dekko Flynn. 'Know the Safe Cross Code!'

'Know the Code!' we all say.

'One, look for a safe place,' sings Micko.

'Two, don't hurry, stop and wait,' sings Dekko.

'Three, look all around and listen before ya cross the road, remember!' we all sing.

Spocky takes a step forward. Ya can see he doesn't wanta but he's no choice.

'Four, walkin straight across, ya –' Micko takes another step '– five, keep watchin left and right and six—'

'Keep walkin,' ya say, not singin, as ya push yer way through the pack. We all stop.

Soon as he sees ya, Spocky panics and tries ta run again, but he stops just as fast, realizin he's stuck. Ya keep walkin, nice and calm. Ya reach for yer belt and I'm sure ya goin for yer willa stick, even though it's got a right batin from the scrap. But instead ya dig in yer pocket and take out somethin bright. I can't see what it is but Micko laughs. 'Go on, ya rascal.'

Spocky whimpers and makes one last burst along the wall, but ya make a sudden sprint and cut him off. He tries ta back away. Useless. Ya take a coupla steps closer ta him, pinnin him against the stairwell. He whimpers again. Still holdin whatever that bright thing is, ya lean across Spocky, puttin yer free hand on the wall behind him like a fella chattin up a bird, and, real gentle, hook yer foot behind his leg. Spocky looks at ya, thick with fright. Ya jerk yer foot sudden. He falls, squealin. Ya kick him in the bollocks; fast and hard.

Micko laughs again. Dekko Flynn joins in but I can tell it's more ta show off than because he thinks it's funny.

Ya crouch down so yer face is close ta Spocky's. The thing in yer hand is shiny.

John Paul begins ta shift about, his runners squeakin off the ground. I can hear Dekko Flynn whisperin, 'What's he gointa do, what's he gointa do?' Micko's lickin his lips. And as for me, I can't take me eyes off yer face as ya bring yer brand-new army knife ta Spocky's throat, tauntin him like a cat with a mouse.

Do ya see me watchin ya? I can't tell.

Ya didn't cut him and I was glad a that. But after ya let him go, I couldn't help wonderin what woulda happened ta the gleam in yer eyes if ya had stuck the blade in.

It was after them scraps that I lost whatever chance I'd ever had a makin friends with the girls in school. Mosta them didn't like me in anyways but after that, Sharo Doyle put the word round that me and the resta the Marconis were mad dogs, in with Snags and the Don ta boot, so we'd go for blood if anyone came near us.

Funny. I thought havin a dangerous reputation would work the other way, earn me respect insteada loathin.

After Charlie left for the boys' school, it got even worse. Charlie wasn't ideal company but any pal is better than none, and with him gone, none is what I got. Sharo had the other girls put me in a boycott. They were too scared ta hit me or laugh at me ta me face. But they were well able ta stop talkin, ta me or anyone else who broke the boycott.

Talk is a small thing, they say. Sticks and stones can break me bones but words will never hurt me. They didn't hurt me; the words, the no words. I was alright on me own.

V

Granny didn't mean ta set up shop. It just sorta happened when Missus Devlin started poppin by ta get her leaves read, and then a coupla other neighbours got in on it, wantin her ta read the cards for them, and by the time I was seven, she was tellin fortunes every Friday night and ya could hardly see the stairs for the people queuin. It got so busy Ma hadta help out, makin tea and takin coats and gassin on ta the customers about the weather while they sat waitin for Granny ta finish up.

'Jesus. Ta think I gave up workin on that manky stall only ta be runnin around after you on accounta that nonsense.'

'Nonsense, Rose? That's rich. You could be makin good use outta the same nonsense if ya weren't such a lazy dose.'

'Lazy? And me slavin for ya in me own home?'

'I wouldn't call it your home. Last time I looked it was my name on the bill, not yours, Rose Dolan.'

'Don't call me that, Ma. I'm married.'

'Hah!'

'Leave it out, Ma.'

'Ah, Rose, you just count yer blessins thatcha not on the street. And if ya hafta make a little cuppa tea for yer ma now and then, it's a small price ta pay for the privilege a havin a roof over yer head. If Violet was in your shoes, she'd be a lot more grateful.'

'Well, she's not.'

'If she was . . .'

'If she – Jesus! If yer precious Violet's so fuckin great, why don'tcha go and live with her? You'd have yer nice stew three times a week and a comfy bed and I'm sure she'd be only too happy ta go traipsin after yer bleedin customers.'

'Ya . . . ya know I can't do that, Rose.'

'Then leave it out, Ma. Jesus! If I had me life all over again . . .'

*

The voices are low. We're squashed behind Granny's bed which stinks a strong tea and mothballs. Sam's eyes are wide and her mouth is open in an 'O' which is the only letter I can make out when the teacher gives us somethin ta read.

'Sssh, Mouse,' I whisper, even though Sam never needs shushin.

'When?' Missus Devlin has got an edge on her voice. I sshh Sam again.

'Ahhh,' sighs Granny, a long sound, the sound of a tree achin in winter.

The room changes.

It's hard ta explain, especially ta you, because ya never got the benefit a Granny's sight; all ya got was Ma and her second-rate scryin. But when Granny started really *lookin*, divin deep inta herself where all the fortunes past and present lay, the world shifted itself round her. Colours brightened, edges sharpened; the space outside got smaller while the space inside got so big there was no room for anythin else.

Me head drums. I can't see Sam any more.

The sound a Granny's sigh comes inta me. It's callin me down ta the bottom a the sea. I follow, tryin ta dive, but I can't go as far as Granny. I'm no fish. I'm only a seagull.

Pictures flash past: Missus Devlin and her ten lovely girls, Ger the eldest in a weddin dress, the twins Avril and Susie turned inta nuns, Cindy the loveliest of all the Devlins with her long long light brown hair swimmin in a river, then babies, the same number as me fingers. The drummin in me head gets louder. Me feet twitch. Somethin grabs me ankles. The pictures are too much; flashin past too fast. I'm fallin, fallin ta the bottom a the ocean. Me seagull brain can't take the pressure; the water's too heavy; I need air. I . . .

Granny's sigh sucks back inta her. Time springs free. I'm outta the future, through the past and –

'Jesus!' says Missus Devlin. 'Who let the cat out?'

I open me eyes.

Missus Devlin is lookin down at me and I realize I'm lyin on the ground, in full view. Somehow I've twisted meself round the bed and out past Granny's chair. Sam's holdin me ankle, tryin ta pull me back. She looks worried.

She needn't be. I can tell from the cold in the room that Granny's still in the ocean. Without lookin down, she waves us away. Then she snaps her fingers at Missus Devlin.

We get outta the room as quiet as we can. Me head's throbbin; Sam tells me later it's from bangin it on the ground while I was outta it. Through the door and in among the throb I hear Granny's low murmur as she continues talkin ta Missus Devlin, but I can't make out the words any more and the pictures – well, they're all gone.

Seven-and-a-half.

Yeah, it's a funny age – neither one thing nor another. As far as she was concerned, though, it was the right one.

'I hafta get ya before ya turn eight, Lucy.'

'But why, Granny?'

'Ya wouldn't understand, pet.'

Maybe I wouldn'a then, but I've a fair idea now. Eight, they say, is the age a reason, and Granny's readins, for all their causes and effects, had nothin ta do with reason.

'But why do I've ta wait so long? Why won't ya do it now?'

'Ya too fresh, Lucy. Ya hafta wait till the half-year is up. Any younger and ya won't have enough choices made.'

But isn't that what a fortune does, Granny – tells ya what's gointa happen so ya can make the right choices?

Over the years there's been many times I've hungered for Granny ta be around so I could ask her things, but there's nothin I've hungered for more than the answer ta that question.

I stand behind her chair and brush her hair. She usually doesn't let me but tonight's different. The boys are off on a boxin trip – Micko isn't fightin but he got a place on the trip from Snags Ryan who's not doin much coachin any more but still has influence – and Sam's asleep.

She asked me ta do it. I didn't hafta ask her. Remember that, Nayler.

'Brush me hair, Lucy,' she said. 'Like a good girl.'

I'm used ta her shoutin me name. It's nice ta hear it soft for a change. It makes me think maybe I am a good girl, after all.

The brush crackles. Her hair is light in colour and feel and so fine it reminds me a feathers.

I lift it up off her neck and smooth the brush through it. I go as gentle as I can. I'm concentratin really hard because if I make even one snag, she'll stop.

She smells a talc and perfume. She had a bath after her fella left this afternoon and in the bathroom is the same smell as from her neck. She smells so nice I wouldn't mind if she hugged me now, even though normally I don't like anyone gettin in close ta me except Granny.

She lifts a piece a Ger Devlin's weddin cake and pops it in her mouth. I can see the sides of her jaws work as she chews. The movement makes a little shada, dimplin in and outta her cheeks.

Lucy.

I look up, thinkin someone's at the door, watchin me. But there's nobody there.

'What's that?' says Ma, turnin. The turn makes the brush snag in her hair, the way I been concentratin so hard on makin not happen.

She stops chewin. I hold me breath and pray.

She turns back. 'Go on, Lucy, like a good girl. That's lovely.'

I let out me breath.

'Lucy,' says Granny. 'It's time.'

The cards are warm in me hands. They're small, much smaller than normal playin cards, and the edges are frayed. The backs are coloured in a pattern a light blue diamonds. I like these cards because the pictures tell me which ones they are without havin ta try and count up like with the normal pack. Granny gestures. I give the pack back to her. She leafs through, picks out one. The Page a Swords.

'That's you, love, that's yer Signifier.'

I nod, lookin at the young fella on the hill with his sword.

She deals the next ten fast, slappin them down in a cruciform.

Number one, the Question card. I get the Lovers. Two naked bodies, bright pink against a bright blue sky. It feels all wrong but –

'That's good,' says Granny, 'means you'll meet someone that'll look after ya the rest a yer life.'

I give her a bad look. She taps the card. 'Lookit, it's not about a fella. You're too young and, besides, a fella will do ya no good. Look what happened ta yer ma, puttin all her trust in a fella.'

'But the picture—'

'Don't mind the picture. The cards have all sortsa meanins. That's a good card for ya, Lucy.'

Number two, the Crossin card. And guess who it is, straddlin the Lovers, only our auld pal, the Devil, with his grey pair a slaves manacled to his hairy legs.

Granny frowns. 'A cross is whatcha bear, Lucy. At least ya know what you'll be dealin with.'

Number three, what's Behind. The Lightnin Struck Tower, a grey castle broke in two by a yella zigzag. 'The end of a way a thinkin.'

Number four, what's Ahead. Seven a Swords, a cheeky young fella runnin away with somethin doesn't belong ta him.

Number five, Beneath. The Nine a Wands. A fight.

Number six, Above. The Knight a Swords, pale and lonely on his white horse.

That was your card, Nayler. I knew it even before Granny turned it, I could feel ya comin up behind me like you were in the room with us. When Granny seen it, she licked her lips and I could tell she was gointa spin me some lies on accounta she didn't wanta waste her breath talkin about ya. But I knew it was you in that picture. Ironic, like Derek would say. Ya always thought ya were the Devil, but ya're not. All ya are is a scrawny white-faced guttie ridin a dirty white nag that's way too big for him.

Seven, eight, nine, ten. Cards for me Head, Place, Fears and Future. Head, The Magician; a man with a bag a tricks. Place, Five a Coins; a family walkin in the snow outside a church winda. Hopes and Fears, the Ten a Swords; a body lyin face-down in a field with ten long daggers stuck in its back. Future, the Hanged Man, a madman hangin upside down by one leg from a gallows.

'Is that me?' I ask, worried.

Granny doesn't hear me. She's gone deep inside herself again. I hold me breath, not wantin her sigh ta pull me in like it done with Missus Devlin.

'Is that me—'

She shakes her head, wavin me ta be quiet. Then she laughs, like someone not in the room has cracked a joke, and leans forward ta place her palm on me forehead.

'That's the best card in the pack, Lucy. That's the mystery card, the card a divine knowledge.'

She takes away her hand. I can feel the mark she's left; a hot red burn bang in the middle a me forehead.

I stare at the pictures, drinkin in the patterns and lines that drag me eye across and back and down and up and inta the centre. The colours meet, clash, fall apart. It makes no sense in the world ta me but inside, somethin's stirrin, a dread, a cold knowin, as Granny starts ta divine for me, reelin off her words and meanins, her seeins and unseeins, pepperin each breath with a 'That's good' or 'Watch that.' I can't take it in.

In the other room, Sam is quiet, huggin all three dollies to her chest.

'Come on,' says Micko. 'We got an errant for ya.'

'What sort?' I say, though I can guess what it is.

'Patience, Lucy Lu,' ya say. 'All good things come ta them that wait.'

'Is Charlie in on it too?'

'That queer?' Youse both laugh.

The sound hits me soon as we go in, batterin me ears like one a Ma's slaps. It's a wall a noise, a battleground a voices and beats and tunes. Politicans and newsreaders and chat-show hosts and Bosco and American DJs welcomin us ta Radeeeeeeo Dublin and men singin fast and women croonin slow and jingles sellin Weetabix and static hissin underneath everythin like rain. I been in this parta Clerys before but it's never been as bad. This time it's like someone's flicked a switch in me skull, pluggin me brain inta all them machines – stereos, amps, turntables, tuners, cassette players, TVs, ghettoblasters, Walkmans. The flashin lights make it even worse, blurrin everythin. I stumble, whackin against a big lad with a beer-belly.

'Easy, Lucy Lu. Keep the head.' Ya grab me arm.

I shake me head, clearin it.

'Alright?' Ya tryin ta make it look like ya not talkin ta me. I nod.

The place is jammed on accounta the sale. Mainly fellas on their own, eyein up the stuff like they wanta ride it. There's auld lads too, though, neat in their tweedy jackets and flat caps, peerin at the radios and the tellies ta see what they're made of, and a coupla what look like tourists, as well as some young wans there ta scope for lads, no doubt. At first I think you've brung me ta do a straight rob, one a yer errants maybe, but when Micko nudges me and points me in her direction I see whatcha after.

She's over near the electric kettles, laden down with plastic bags and fightin, squealin kids that are draggin at her arms, her skirt, her shoppin. She's red-faced, sweaty, fit ta explode. Her bag's twisted round her shoulder and hangin down her back. It's big, navy, plastic. No zippers; button-down flaps instead. The flap on the outside is bulgin.

'Stupid,' ya say. 'Shoulda stuck it in the one nearest her.'

Ah . . .

None a this is new ta me. Other kids grow up learnin ta speak. I grew up knowin when and how ta rob Ma's purse or Granny's stash a coins under her bed. I was four when Micko taught me how ta nick penny sweets from Black's and by seven I was a dab hand at robbin the till a the cornershop on Belvedere.

Alright, I'm not in the same league as you and Micko. I know the stuff ya get upta when John Paul's trainin in the club. Ya got things ta do, errants, ya call them, that Snags sends ya on.

Sometimes you've taken me and – not so often – me cousin Charlie along for the crack, darin us ta rob oil and wheels from Mikey Kinsella's bike shop or comics and toys from Easons while you and Micko lift records or clothes or cash from Dolphin Discs or Dunnes Stores or Boylans Shoes. Charlie's never been a good thief – he's too scared a bein caught or hurtin people, too scared a youse, really – but I've always risen ta the challenge.

By now word's got round about me and sometimes even the Devlin twins bring me on thievin sprees. They got loadsa disguises – nurses and mammies and nuns even, which is the best because they can hide stuff under their habits – and because they're identical they play all sortsa games with the shopkeepers. They usually use me as a decoy, pretendin I'm their kid, or some sick orphan they're takin out for the day. Sometimes they don't go in disguise at all, and work it so while the shopkeepers are eyein them up, I'm busy liftin. And on the days they do the liftin themselves, they always pass me the whack and get me ta run with it if things start ta heat up. Because I'm good at the runnin.

But today's different. Today it's just you and Micko, and ya trustin me, and more, ya trustin me with a dip.

'They know me and Nayler in here,' says Micko, pullin me in behind a screen, outta view a the assistants but unmercifully not outta earshot a them sounds that are still bangin away at me head. 'They think we'll be after the stuff. Ya hafta work fast. Nayler's gointa barge inta them, distract them, I'll do the pickin. You catch and run. Keep an eye out for us and we'll give ya the billy when it's time ta head. Ya right with that?'

I nod.

'Good on ya.' He pushes me away. 'Make it look like ya with someone.'

Already I can see ya headin across ta the kettles. I know Micko's easin up the next aisle so I make a beeline for some youngish-lookin fella who could be me da, or an uncle maybe, and stand beside him while ya do yer stuff.

Ya make it look so easy, knockin inta one of her kids like someone pushed ya.

'Jaysus,' she squalls.

The kid ya crashed inta starts howlin and so does the baby. The two others need no excuse ta let go their ma's hands and start headin down the aisle. You're all apologies – 'Sorry, sorry, missus,' – as ya pretend ta help the kid up, kickin him on the sly so he falls again, this time knockin ya inta her. And while she's fussin over ya as ya moan over yer arm that's suddenly started hurtin, Micko slides in for the kill.

'Jaysus, Anthony,' says the woman. 'Stop it, ya hurtin that little boy. Ah, Martin, Lorna, come back here, willyiz!'

'No, it's okay, missus, sorry, missus,' ya say.

Micko unpops the button on the side a the bag, slides in his hand and grabs the purse. She starts turnin her head just as he's got the whack in his hand, but ya grab her even tighter then and thank her for bein so helpful, yer face gone all innocent, yer eyes big and round like a little toy. She looks down at ya, distracted.

'No problem, son, no problem.'

It's me now –

Except just then the music from the sound system changes, floatin inta somethin high and pure that's like but not like a tune off of Oscar-from-The-Odd-Couple's radio. The pureness takes me over, drownin out everythin else, the DJs, the ads, the newsmen with their stories. The tune builds, it's beautiful. Me hands lift. I'm hummin, I'm off again, forgettin where I'm at –

And then somethin hard flies through the air and hits me in the face and I catch Micko glarin at me through the reflection in the telly and *shit*, I nearly fucked up. And bang on cue, the music changes again, groanin inta Kajagoogoo 'Too Shy Shy' and I'm turnin from me fake da and slippin inta the next aisle and past Micko and he slides me the purse and it's in under me coat and I'm home and dry.

We do a few more, eight or ten maybe, before Micko gives me the billy.

I head out the front, pickin a family ta cling close to so it won't look like I'm on me own. I'm pressed up beside her inside the swingin door and breathin in her stink a fags and sweat before I realize who she is.

'Jaysus, Anthony, if ya took me purse on me, I swear I'll murder ya! Answer me, will ya?'

We went round in that fuckin door three times before she decided ta go back in and tell the store cop and each time we turned I tried ta force meself out past her pram and shoppin and squallin kids but I couldn't. It was like tryin ta get outta hell alive.

The stink of her stayed on me all the way across the street.

After that, ya took me dippin regular when Dekko Flynn couldn't make it. Ya got me on the catch, Micko on the rob and you as the decoy, battin them big black eyes at the mammies and daddies like ya were only born yesterday, sweet-talkin them with that polite voice a yours that was suddenly gone all English again the way it was when we first met ya.

Sometimes it didn't go ta plan. I'd miss the catch, or the store detectives would pick up Micko before he'd even had a chance ta slip them quicksilver fingers in, or sometimes when we opened the purse, we'd find nothin in it. But for the most part, well . . . we were the business. A dream team.

Like any art, there's some that are born to it, and others that are just plain brutal. John Paul, for example. Remember the time he tried ta dip off of the nun on Talbot Street? Poxy idea ta pick her for a start, when he coulda gone for that rake a lads comin outta the bookies with their winnins. In the end he couldn't even get near her, so he just let her go. Micko, on the other hand, was pure brilliance. Quicksilver fast. I never seen anyone dip as smooth as me brother. And as for you, Nayler, well . . . ya were good, especially as a decoy – if ya hadn'a been, Snags would never a kept ya on – but when it came ta actual nickin, ya weren't the prize thief people made ya out ta be. Ya weren't as smooth as Micko and ya were slower than me. Sometimes I even wondered why ya done it. Ya never seemed ta get buzzed up, so it wasn't for the thrill, and when ya weren't workin for Snags ya robbed the maddest things – stuff that wasn't much use for anythin. Even when ya got good whack ya thrun it away.

'See this?' ya said once, holdin up a Rolex you'd dipped off a businessman. 'He never even seen me.' Then ya threw the Rolex up in the air. The gold and silver flashed in the sun, then dropped, tumblin over the brambles ta land on the train tracks. Micko and John Paul went scramblin over the wall ta rescue it. They never found it.

One wet afternoon, Micko asks me ta do the distractin insteada the runnin. I'm well surprised, because botha youse have always told me I'm way too jiggy ta play the innocent, but then youse say it's ta train me in because you were gettin too old ta fool the mammies.

I shoulda known better; I shoulda guessed youse were just takin the piss.

It goes bollocks, a course. The woman I crash inta won't let me go, keeps holdin me, drownin me in her stink a perfume mixed with wet raincoat, askin am I sure I'm alright, am I lost, do I want her ta call the Guards ta bring me home, and by the time I get away, the two a youse are nowhere ta be seen so I end up squelchin home on me own.

It's not hard rain but it's drizzlin non-stop, tricklin down me neck, sleeves, face, gluin me too-thin tee-shirt ta me back. It might be just that, but I keep gettin a pricklin feelin between me shoulder blades that tells me youse aren't far off. But no matter how hard I peel me eyes, I can't see a sign a youse. When I get onta Richmond Place the pricklin gets even stronger, so I look both directions, up the North Circular and down towards the convent on Portland Row. And on me second gawk I see a pair a navy runners splashin in through the front door a Billy Fish's.

There's no time ta even wonder what youse are doin goin inta the boxin club that way insteada through the basement. I race after, runnin up the steps two at a time, and get ta the door just before it clicks shut. But just as me hand's on the plate, the door swings back, and I stumble over the threshold.

'Whatcha want? We're closed.' Standin inside the hallway is Emmet Whelan, the lad the Don's hired ta run the club. He's already renowned for the power of his fists outta the ring as much as in it. I could wonder what Whelan's doin in Billy Fish's parta the buildin when he should be in the club, but, like I say, there's no time ta waste.

I blink the rain outta me eyes. 'I'm lookin for me brothers.'

'They're not here,' says Whelan, and cracks his knuckles. He's got a signet ring on his little finger. Black square in a gold surround. In a tank at the end a the hall, Billy Fish's guppies flash through plastic seaweed, sendin green light ripplin over the stained brown wallpaper.

'But I seen them come in—'

'Ya didn't. Get out.'

And with that, Whelan pushes me, sendin me down the crumblin steps and back onta the wet street. The door bangs shut.

And that, a course, is when I start ta realize things are changin.

'I don't wanta go and play with Charlie,' I say. Ma glares down at me.

'Yer Granny needs ta visit the Mater again, Lucy. I can't be dealin with this.'

'But I'll stay here, with Micko and John Paul.'

Ma cuffs me on the ear. 'You'll do as I say. Marlene's very good ta look after ya.'

'Why can't I stay with Micko?'

I look over at Micko, but he keeps eatin his Frosties.

'He's busy with his own pals. Aren'tcha, pet?'

Munch munch munch.

'He's not. In anyways, Charlie's a queer!'

Ma slaps me again.

'Ow!'

Micko watches as I stamp down the steps, fumin.

Even though Marlene smoked like a chimney and talked like a sewer, her gaff was one a the cleanest places I'd ever seen, second only ta The Odd Couple's. She loved cleanin. Said it was the only exercise she needed. Other people could go on walks, play tennis. All she done was clean.

'It's that keeps me fit, Lucy love,' she says, pattin her stomach. 'Very important. You've gotta look after yerself in this world. Nothin comes ta those that don't.'

She had ashtrays all over the gaff. Plain ones from pubs that she'd lifted after a good night's drinkin; novelty ones from gift and joke shops; the odd few brung back from hollyers in Majorca and the Isle a Man. One, in the shape a Kermit the Frog, I useta dream about havin. Marlene musta read me mind, because she gave it ta me as a present a few weeks after she bought it, savin me the bother a nickin it.

There was lots a light in Marlene's gaff, miles more than ours, which was mad because all the flats in them blocks are identical. She always had fresh flowers because that's what she was doin back then, after the hairdressin and before Stevo got rich from the buildin, sellin flowers outside Arnott's on Henry Street. Whenever I think a Marlene, I think a lilies and tobacco and Mr Sheen, vinegar on the windas and buckets a light streamin in through the net curtains.

Her next two after Charlie were Catherine and Margaret, the twins. They were identical, the same age as Samantha. They ended up havin different jobs when they grew up – one's a nurse and the other's a soldier – but John Paul says they're still real hard ta tell apart. Marlene tried ta get them ta take up with Sam, the way she'd got me and Charlie together, but it didn't work out. Ya mighta thought Sam was bad, the way she lived in a world of her own, but them two were even worse.

'They're scary,' says Sam ta Granny. 'They says things ta each other and their mouths isn't even opened.'

'Oh, I know, love,' says Granny. 'But you're not ta mind them.'

The resta Marlene's brood were all too young and useless ta play anythin, unless it was kidnap victims where ya could stick socks inta their mouths and tie them up and shove them inta a corner for hours. That wasn't bad, especially with the risk a Marlene maybe comin down and losin the rag at us. That was always good for a laugh.

I never got the feelin, though, that Marlene doted on any of her kids the way Ma done on Micko and Sam. Maybe that was because she doted on Stevo instead.

'I got the Jaguar,' says Charlie.

I'm bored. We been playin Top Trumps for ages and Charlie keeps winnin. No surprise seein as I can't read the writin on the cards, only the pictures, but I'm sick a bein dumped with poxy Datsuns; I want the Rolls-Royce. I know I'm not losin just because I can't read; I been distracted thinkin about you and Micko and yer errants. It's been weeks since we went on a rob, even though I know for sure Dekko Flynn hasn't been round, and any time I ask if I can go with youse, youse keep jeerin me. It shouldn't bother me – Micko's always jeered everyone, includin me – but it does. And then I been thinkin about Billy Fish too, and what everyone's sayin, all quiet, like us kids aren't supposed ta hear, how he *started messin with the Wrong Person* and that's why he got *what was comin ta him*, and I don't see how messin, callin names and playin games and havin the crack with a person, even if they're the Wrong one, coulda made that happen, unless they were playin chasin, messin on the stairs, and that's why he fell, poor Billy Fish, tumblin down them stairs with no one ta catch him, head over heels, past all them glowin green fishtanks, ta crash bang inta the ground, endin up a crumpled heap in a barber's coat on the floora the hallway I stood in only weeks before, a white coat *covered in blood* they say, whisperin, *ya could hear the bang from –*

'Yaay!' yells Charlie. 'I got the Beamer, Lucy, twice in a row.'

Fuck this. I've had enough. 'Lookit, Charlie!' I point out the winda.

'What? Where?'

Sap. I grab the cards and I'm off, racin through the hall, out the door and down the steps before he even knows what's hit him.

I got home safe enough without him catchin me, straight inta Ma's bedroom, where I stuck the chair under the door handle ta barricade meself in. Few minutes later, Charlie rolled up, whingin and cryin, Marlene behind him, only she sounded like she was tryin not ta laugh. That woulda been alright except then Ma turned up and she was *rippin*. In the end they stopped shoutin and I just sorta zoned out, got distracted and hungry and forgot why I was barricaded there in the first place, and when I walked out Ma was in the hall waitin. She had ta tear the cards outta me hands, though. No way was I givin them back ta Charlie easy. Fucked if that little bastard was gointa get what I didn't have.

Derek once told me about a book called *The Loneliness a the Long-Distance Runner*. He never read it me, but for some reason it comes inta me head when I think about meself in them weeks I fucked around alone, with neither youse nor Charlie ta keep me company.

Balls bounce. Kids shout. The houses on the Square poke inta the sky like dark red fingers. It's gone September but it's still boilin hot, even though there's black clouds buildin up on the horizon. Through the gate, I see the unbuilt lot beside the college. It looks like an iron skeleton waitin for flesh that'll never come.

'Wouldya like some cake, missus?' Sam's Barbie bends at the waist, stiff as an army sergeant. 'Oh yeah, thanks.' The Cindy hands over a tiny pink plastic plate with a Smartie on it. Barbie's elbow bends as far as a Barbie elbow can go and, with the help a Sam's fingers, takes the plate.

'Mmm, lovely, Cindy. Didja cook it yerself?'

I turn me attention back ta the baby tree I been workin on. It was planted early in the spring. I seen it grow right through the summer; taller than me it is now. It looks pretty with its green leaves just startin ta go red, but I can't resist pullin at the branches ta see how far they'll go before they snap.

'Go on, Charlie,' says a familiar voice. I look up. It's Marlene, with the whole gang in tow. Charlie's standin beside her, lookin extra stupid in his shorts.

Jesus. Why they hafta come ta the Park of all places?

'Go over and play with yer cousin. I'll be back around tea-time. Maybe Lucy would like ta come over then?'

No. Lucy wouldn't. But I say nothin. There's no point arguin with Marlene.

After she leaves, luggin the four blondey girls with her, I go back ta me tree. I don't wanta even look at Charlie, it's been weeks since the fight over the Top Trump and we haven't said a word ta each other since, so why should we now, but from the corner a me eye I can see him sit down beside Sam and take out his *Victor*. I like the *Victor* because the pictures are good – Germans screamin and blood and tanks; Charlie says they're called Pandas, like the bears – but there's no way I'm gointa ask him ta read it ta me.

It's bakin. There's more a them clouds in the sky but they're just makin it hotter. Plus Sam's got her dollies drinkin tea now, and lemonade, only it's not real tea and lemonade, just imaginary, and every time she even says the word 'tea' I feel I'm gointa die with the thirst. Maybe – No. But – No. I shouldn't.

But it's so hot I can't stick it and anyways –

'Got any drinks on ya, Charlie?' I say.

Charlie shakes his head without lookin up from the *Victor*.

'It's very hot.'

'Hmm,' he says.

I try a different tack. 'Is the *Victor* good this week?'

He looks up. 'Okay.'

I can tell from his voice he's still not sure if I'm really bein friendly but . . . 'Charlie, know what? I'm dyin a thirst.'

'Yeah?'

'Aren't you?'

'Hmm . . . sorta.'

'Ya know where they've lovely 7-Up?'

He shakes his head.

'There.' I nod over at Mulvaney's cornershop.

'I don't have any money, Lucy.'

'Who said anythin about money?'

Charlie stares at me.

'Go on, Charlie. I dare ya.'

'I don't know . . .'

'I'll come over ta yours and all after we're done here. Play a game even?'

He thinks. I can tell it's hard for him ta make his mind up. 'Okay,' he says at last.

It feels like ages he's gone. The clouds build, the air gets closer; in the distance, Sam's chattin slows.

'Da-dah!' Charlie unwraps his arms and lets the cans fall out from under his tee-shirt onta the grass.

'Ah, Charlie!' I panic and rush ta catch them. 'Watch it, they'll fizz up.'

'Hwnwatch-ih,' says a voice behind me in spa-language. 'Tnhey'll fihnzz uph.'

I turn. It's Dekko Flynn, standin there with you and Micko. Youse have all got big smiles on. Before I can say hi, Dekko bends down, picks up a 7-Up, and opens it.

'Eh . . . Dekko,' says Charlie. 'That's mine.'

'Thnhath mynthe,' ya say, copyin Charlie the way Dekko done me. Ya grab the can off of Dekko and take a deep slurp. 'Lovely.' Ya hand it ta Micko. He slurps too. 'Thanks, Lucy.'

'They're not Lucy's,' says Charlie, lookin worried. 'They're mine.'

'Yeah, right, ya queer!' Micko grabs Charlie with his free hand and pushes down on his head just as Dekko opens the second can.

'Let me alone!'

'Hnhleh me halonh!' ya say. 'Ya pussy.'

Micko laughs and pulls Charlie's specs off his nose.

'Know what a pussy is, Charlie?' ya say. 'Lucy does.'

Dekko starts pourin the 7-Up over Charlie.

I should laugh, like I normally do when youse slag Charlie, like I always useta before youse ran off and left me on me own, but I don't feel like it.

Charlie, soaked in 7-Up, starts flailin at Micko. Micko dances, easily dodgin the punches. Ya break yer piss laughin. 'It's a woman's gee, ya fuckhead.'

'Catch!' says Dekko, flingin his empty can over at me. He grabs Charlie by the arms. Charlie starts ta cry but I can tell it's not just because he's scared, or sad. He's fumin.

'They *are* mine. Give them back!'

'Ya fuckin—'

'Yeah, lads, lookit,' I say, loud. The three a youse turn, surprised. 'Charlie's right. The cans is his. Well . . . sorta. He blagged them.' I don't want the three a youse laughin at me again, but it's not fair tormentin Charlie when he actually done somethin right for a change. 'Outta Mulvaney's and all.'

Charlie looks over at me, dead grateful.

'He blagged them?' says Micko.

'Yeah,' says Charlie, soundin brave for once. 'I can rob more for youse if ya want.'

'What? Coke?' ya say.

'No. Eh . . . 7-Up?'

Ya look at the can in yer hand. Ya take yer time lookin, like ya never seen one before. I feel us all – me, Charlie, Dekko, even Micko – holdin our breaths for whatcha gointa say.

At last ya look back up. '7-Up.' Ya say it like it's the thickest thing in the world.

'Fuckin queer!' says Micko. The three a youse laugh. Dekko lets Charlie go, sendin him flyin ta the ground.

'Here, Lucy!' Micko throws me Charlie's specs.

'Yeah, here!' Ya feck yer can over at me. 'Comin, Dekko?'

As I watch the three a youse go, somethin cracks in the sky.

'Can I've me specs back, Lucy?' says Charlie.

A raindrop lands on me nose.

'D'ya want me ta get ya a fresh 7-Up and all? I can, ya know.'

I look at the stuff in me hands – the cans, the specs. I am *sick* a 7-Up.

'Here, Micko!' I call, feckin it all at me cousin without even a glance.

'Jesus!' screams Ma Cooper as Micko takes a flyin jump at her pram, knockin it over. 'Little godforsaken bastards!'

At Summerhill we turn, buzzin. Ma Cooper is still wailin as she gathers up her babies – her Crazy Prices shoppin bags – and lays them one by one back in her pram.

★

'Didja not think?' says Ma, whackin me. 'Didja not think about yer little sister, leavin her on her own like that?'

'She wasn't on her own. Charlie was – ow!'

'Ya good for nothin little waggon! Jesus!'

A course I thought I was turnin things back ta the way they useta be. A course I was wrong.

Youse took me out robbin again, sure, coupla places, and other jaunts, and I done alright, but it wasn't the same. It was like youse were just watchin and puttin up with me insteada really lettin me in on it. Then the last time we went ta Peats and I was half-way out the door with a rake a Walkmans bundled under me snorkel when some programme came on, some news story with flashin lights, and I knew I shouldn'a looked at the screen but I did and then everythin went and when I woke up I was sittin in the back a the shop with the store detective and the gonzo from the desk lookin at me like I was dead and you and Micko nowhere ta be seen.

They'da brung the Guards in and all only I lied and told them I was six-and-a-half insteada me real age, well gone eight, and they believed me on accounta me height, but then it all sorta went bollocks because the store dick said he'd hafta bring me home seein as me Ma had no phone. I started bullin, more on accounta what Ma would do ta me than anythin else. I was even cryin by then, and for real nearly, but it was no use.

The dick brung me out ta his Volvo and shoved me in the back seat. We were half-way down Seán MacDermott Street by the time I sussed out what ta do.

'Here,' I say, pointin ta the back entrance.

He pulls in and brakes. I make him walk round the back, keepin an eye out for Ma. I'm gettin braver with every step.

'It's a good idea, bringin me ta me auntie's,' I say, 'because ya wouldn'a wanted ta leave me sittin outside me Ma's gaff on me own. Loadsa things happen round our way. Ya know, a rapist or somethin coulda come up and got me.'

I don't know what a rapist is – Micko says they're headcases that

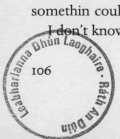

do stuff ta girls but not fellas, though I think he's lyin – but I know they're bad.

The store dick is silent as he walks up the stairs, pullin me after him. He's vexed. Must be on accounta what I said earlier, about him not bein a proper Guard and how he shouldn'a even asked me ta go in the car with him because I wasn't supposed ta get inta cars with strange men and if me Ma found out she'd kill me and –

'Me Ma'll be very grateful when she gets back from the hospital, mister. She's always worryin about me and me little sister because a the lads round here—'

He rings the doorbell.

'Jesus!' says Marlene when she sees us. 'Lucy Marconi!'

'Marconi?' The dick frowns.

'Doyle, mister.' I say the fake name loud so Marlene will cop on. 'Marconi's only a nickname cos we look Italian.'

'Yeah . . . youse Doyles, you're all the same,' says Marlene, puttin on a worried face. I breathe a sigh a relief. 'I'm her aunt, Guard. What's she been upta?'

The dick starts explainin. Behind Marlene I see Charlie, peerin round the sittin-room door.

'Thanks,' says Marlene. 'I'll make sure her ma knows. We can't have this happenin again.'

She closes the door. Inside, she doesn't take off the worried face, just pulls me close. 'Jesus, Lucy,' she says, and sighs. I let her hug me, even though the smell a lilies and tobacco is so close it feels like it's takin me over, and hope ta God she won't tell Ma.

A coupla weeks after that, a proper rozzer called at our door. First I thought Marlene had ratted on me ta Ma after all and they were comin ta bring me ta the station, but it turned out they were lookin for Micko instead, on accounta that fire in the shoeshop off of Henry Street. Not that they were chargin or anythin – them people that said they seen the two a youse hangin round there put it for a good week before the fire, far as I can remember – they just wanted ta ask some questions.

I shoulda known Marlene woulda never ratted on me. Diamond, she was.

Ma stalled the Bill best as she could – 'Are ya sure it's him? Me boy would never do a senseless thing like that' – but he wouldn't go till he seen Micko, so in the end she sent me lookin for him.

'Hmm,' said Granny. 'No need ta look too far.' Then she closed her mouth tight, like she'd said more than she'd wanted ta. We all knew who she was talkin about, but.

I'd only been up at yer Auntie Joan's once or twice before – with Micko, mainly – and them times I never went inside. Yer Aunt Joan wasn't like Missus Devlin or the other wans from roundabout who'd invite us in at the drop of a hat. She wouldn'a had me in that day and all – 'No, sorry, love, he's not in, and I haven't seen sight a yer brother neither,' she said, twistin her miraculous medals on their blue string – only I was burstin for a piss and I suppose she thought I'da gone there and then and ruined her carpet if she hadn'a let me use the jacks.

It was very . . . normal lookin inside. A loada religious pictures, Padre Pio and the Sacred Heart, all that, but not much else.

When I got outta the jacks, yer aunt wasn't around.

I wasn't intendin ta snoop, Nayler, it's just the door was open and it was on me way out and I couldn't help lookin in.

He has things stuck on the wall over his bed. They're organized like in a shop, all in neat rows with writin underneath. That's probably why his aunt doesn't make a fuss; because it's all so neat.

There's a rusted bicycle chain. A kid's teddy bear with a bow round its neck; beside that a Barbie, beside that a gollywog. A line a woolly hats; all colours. A row a watches; cheap, dear, plastic, gold. One Rolex, covered in dirt. There's a board with hooks nailed on it and a set a keys on each hook, each with its own key-ring. Sunglasses; all sorts – Elvis, square, blue, pointy. A set a stamped envelopes holdin letters that peek out like skin from knickers. Scarves – chiffon, wool, silk, lace. Two withered willa branches crossed over each other – not like the church cross; slantywise. Five rings: gold, silver, diamond, barmbrack and plastic. A stack a coins that don't look like normal money. A line a perfume bottles, arranged so the bottle with the most perfume is at the starta the row and the one with the least is at the end. Baby's soothers, hangin off a string. A lone pearl earring. And in the corner, under a tall old-fashioned hat like the one Jiminy Cricket wears in *Pinocchio*, is a pile a wallets that have still got their cards and money and photos in them.

I know these things weren't always his.

He's drawn a picture on the opposite wall. It's of a man's face – red and black – and its eyes folla ya round the room. Underneath the picture is lots a tiny writin – but for eyes like mine, for which nothin stands still, it doesn't mean a thing.

VI

'Fooooor . . .' sings Micko, draggin out the word, twistin his face all directions like the Black Adder.

I'm sick laughin.

'Jesus, son!' says Ma, but she's smilin to herself.

'Get on with it.' John Paul's voice is crackin again the way it does a lot these days.

Micko runs outta breath, takes another one.

'FOOOOOOOOOOOOR . . .'

This one's even louder. Micko lifts his hands, points one of his fingers. I keep me eyes on that finger. That's for conductin. The finger pulls back, slow – 'All together now!' – then shoots forward.

'She's a jolly good fella, she's a jolly good fella, she's a jolly good fe-eh-laaaaaaaa . . .'

Micko holds up his hand and smiles at Ma. She sings. 'And so say all of us!'

Micko waves his hands, bringin us all back in. 'And so say all of us! And so say all of us. For she's a jolly good fe-eh-laaaaaa . . .'

We hold our breaths, knowin the score, waitin for Ma.

'And so say—'

She stops. Somethin prickles up me neck.

Granny's teacup flies ta the ground. Micko flicks his head round and John Paul chokes on a chocolate Rice Crispie. Only Sam stays lost in her own world, gazin at the six candles on her birthday cake.

Ma gets up, bangin against the table and sloshin milk onta the good tablecloth Granny bought for the occasion. 'Jesus, Jimmy . . .' Her voice is hoarse.

I turn me head.

In the doorway, May sunshine linin his body like a halo, stands me Da.

'Howayiz, kids,' he says. He was awful thin on our last visit but he's even worse now. Micko half gets up but I'm there before him, runnin inta Da's arms. Da laughs, a husky sound.

He never once takes his eyes off me Ma.

He'd got out earlier than planned, and as per usual, hadn't bothered tellin Ma. Over the last year we'd all seen things were gettin rough between them. There were more silences, fewer words, and on me Da's side what words there were we couldn't make out. One night before we went ta sleep, I thoughta askin Micko if Ma and Da were breakin up because loadsa the girls in school were sayin that's what everyone's ma and da done nowadays. Then I thought better of it and decided ta keep me mouth shut. Micko'd probably just tell me ta be quiet, like he was always doin.

The last two times we'd gone ta visit, Da hadn't turned up. The flu, the screw said. The other ma's looked over, like they knew somethin we didn't.

'Flu. Oh yeah.' Ma got up, draggin Sam by the hand. 'Well, I'm not goin along with it. He can rot in fuckin hell.'

'Ya know the way Da talks . . .' I say.

Ma bangs dishes down in the sink and starts scrubbin them. She scrubs so hard the fat on her back ripples. Stupid, really. If she wanted me ta stay quiet, she shoulda just kept calm. But between the bangin and the scrubbin it's obvious somethin's up and as long as somethin's up I'm gointa ask her about it.

'He didn't always talk like that, did he?'

Bang. Scrub. Ripple.

'Because . . . ya know . . . I can't understand nearly anythin he says.'

Bang.

'And ya know the way he's in bed in the whole time, Ma . . .'

Bang.

'Is it like that screw said—'

'Guard, Lucy,' says Ma. 'Don't use that word.'

'Well, remember the guard said Da had the flu when he was in jail? But he should be better by now, shouldn't he? That was ages ago.'

I'm testin her. I been hearin things. In the yard, in school at break. *Ya know what's wrong with yer da, Lucy Marconi?* Sly looks and graffiti. Letters scrawled in black paint on the stairwell. Charlie tells me they spell *Pushers Out*.

Ma stops scrubbin and turns around, leanin her arse against the sink. The soapsuds on her yella gloves are all colours in the sunlight.

'Yer da's sick, Lucy.' Her voice is quiet.

'Oh.'

I wasn't expectin this. A clatter, maybe, but not an explanation. I think hard a what I wanta ask her. 'What kinda sick, Ma?'

She looks down at her gloves.

'It's not the flu, sure it's not?' I say.

She looks up. 'No, Lucy, it's not the flu.' She gives me a half-smile. 'Butcha know what, he's gettin better. And ya know what's really helpin him?'

'No.'

'When you and the lads are very good and youse don't get inta trouble.'

'Oh. Like now?' I sorta mean it as a joke because normally when I ask loadsa questions, she gives off ta me for bein even worse of a problem than usual.

She looks at me, puzzled. Then she gets it and smiles. 'Yeah. Like now.'

I've tried ta come up with reasons. He wanted ta go straight. He was sick a the way it was controllin his life. She'd threatened ta leave him unless he made a fresh start. He was too proud not ta give it a shot; he was Jimmy Marconi, after all, the toppermost a the poppermost, not some strung-out waster livin on borrowed time. And her? She was lonely. She couldn't bear the idea a Granny sayin *I told ya so.* She wanted him back. The shame a bein seen ta be left was worse than the shame a havin him round. He swore blind that he'd change, for good, and she believed him.

Some a these reasons stick; some don't. But maybe it's simpler than that. Maybe it's just that he did love her, in his own way, and she loved him, in hers, and that's why he tried ta go clean when he came out and that's why she took him in after sayin she wouldn't. They done it for themselves, sure, for the comfort a havin back what they were useta, but maybe they done it for each other too.

I don't like thinkin a things that way. Ya know me, Nayler, I believe we're all out for ourselves and that love is just sex dressed up so it looks nicer in the mirror, some trick played on us ta knock us off track. Maybe I'm right but still . . . it's a funny thing, love; it's like glue. It binds the maddest people together in the maddest ways.

It's easier ta see why he started on it than why he tried ta give it up. It's always easier ta see that. Last year Derek told me about this book come out, written by some Yank that got his kicks off crack and the gargle. He's cured now but in the book he goes on about his habit, sayin it's not a sickness like them doctors make out; it's a decision. Ya decide ta do it – so ya can't go around givin off, blamin yer bad genes or yer family. I thought about that, loads, and maybe it's true; even though there's times it feels like no decision on earth, feels like the hand's been dealt before ya even know you're playin the game. But it could be easier for some people ta see it's a decision than others. Call it money, call it education, call it back-up in the big blue yonder. The upshot is, some see and some don't.

The important thing is: did Jimmy Marconi see it was a decision? Fuck, I don't know. He decided alright; but I think he stopped seein a long long time before that.

I'd say all the shit with the Wacker woulda been a big reason why. Fred Mahon ditched Da soon as he went inside for the post office job. Jimmy had been a good boy in the courts, stayed shtumm, but ya don't hafta be Sherlock Holmes ta figure out that marriage wasn't gointa last. Jimmy had always been the Don's boy and Wacker probably thought he'd go crawlin back ta the Five Lampers sooner or later. Once Wacker dropped me Da, all the other Waxboys that went inside the same time turned against him too. Meanwhile the Five Lampers, parcelled together on the other side a the landin, were no pals a Jimmy neither, seein as he'd jumped the Don's ship before he got sent down.

It's not hard ta see why Da got edgy, runnin round the exercise yard with bad looks comin at him from left, right and centre. Even the Ra on the upper landins woulda been givin him a hard time, makin bombin sounds if he even yawned durin the nightly recital a the national anthem. No wonder he started moochin over ta the other outcasts like One Eye Hagan, a street dealer originally from Crumlin who'd got on the Quinlan brothers' bad side by stealin a loada their gear. At least One Eye and his pals made Jimmy laugh, cracked him up no end. And that was good, because between the naggin from Ma and the fuck-up with Wacker and the death-threats from the Don's boys, Da hadn't been cracked up no end for ages now.

He knew One Eye's game and he swore he wouldn't folla suit – he was together, he was sharp, he didn't need that shit – but after the sob-story a how it fucked up his life and what a cunt it is, One Eye asked Jimmy the million-dollar question.

'But have ya tried it, Marconi?'

On that rock stronger men have perished.

'There's no words for it. It's better than good, Jimmy.'

All ya need is a reason.

There mighta been more behind his choosin. The Odd Couple's names carved on a bullet. Pictures a me and Micko and Sam and John Paul with our eyes gouged out. I'd like ta think it was somethin like that which drove him there. But a little voice tells me it was just because the timin was right.

The other important thing is: did Jimmy Marconi see goin clean as a decision? Or did he make that choice blind?

Let's get one thing straight. I'm not about ta play Happy Families here, Nayler. Ya were round us enough back then; ya could see what went on. Yeah, we had good times. It was alright goin out with Da or showin him me boxin moves and beggin him ta let me join the club on Richmond Place or chattin ta him about the stuff I'd get upta with Charlie – who I'd made up with again after bein nabbed in Peats, even give him back his stupid Top Trump I done, and it paid off because Charlie turned out a dab hand at plannin the robs – and Charlie's new pal Damo from Ballybough and the Kavanagh brothers from Mary's Mansions. It was good havin Da back too because that way we knew there was someone round who wouldn't scream blue murder if we were caught on the rob – though I can't swear Da ever really sussed us; I just thought he musta, seein as he knew how them things went.

But there was the other side too that no amounta gettin clean could paper over. Granny huffin inta her tea leaves, seein omens everywhere, goin on about what a useless da he was and when exactly was he gointa start lookin for a real job and if he thought he could just waltz back inta our lives he was deludin himself. And Ma startin ta take all that on, and maybe rememberin how things useta be in the bad old days and how even before her Jimmy was off his face on smack he still wasn't the most reliable fella on the block.

Then there was The Odd Couple, who were happy ta have their son back, a course, but equally happy ta send us bad vibes when we went over ta theirs, meanin there'd always be a fight on the way home.

And John Paul, who steered clear a Da from the minute he got back, even after he got clean, like me Da had the plague – or worse. Course we didn't know back then who John Paul's new friends were.

And then there was you and Micko and, more important, yer guardian angel, the Don's nephew Snagglepuss Ryan.

Snags wasn't round when me Da came out, a course, banged up for that fire on the shoeshop on Henry Street, courtesy a three miracle eyewitnesses. Miracle me hole. Everyone knew they were paid for by the Wacker – or should I say, paid outta the compo the shoeshop owner got from the insurance. Don Ryan musta been bullin. All that care he took coverin his tracks, and his nephew gets hauled out with the eyes a the world on him for a simple torchjob. Luckily for him, the witnesses couldn't point the finger further than Snags. So off the Crown Prince went. Two year in St Pat's for malicious damage and arson. Rough, eh, Nayler? But the way some a the auld wans went on – 'Ah, poor Don Ryan. His only kin' – ya'd think it was the baby Jesus himself being sent down.

Story went Wacker Mahon waited outside the court ta watch them lead Snags away. Snags looked at him and the Wacker laughed in his face. Psycho. Mad thing is, Snags just smiled his big cat's smile, as if ta say, *Don't ya worry, sunshine, I'll get ya. Someday.*

Ta start with Micko was alright with Da. It wasn't like when he was a little kid and hung outta Da the whole time, gettin him ta play with him and all. But they got on okay. And as Da got better, they'd have the crack, jokin and messin and slaggin each other off about their music collections.

But then you called upta ours one day and took Micko off and neither a youse said where youse were goin, and when Micko came back that night, things were different.

'Where ya been, son?' calls Da from the sittin-room. It's gone twelve.

Micko walks through the hall straight inta the kitchen.

'Didja hear me?'

Micko pulls out some bread and sticks it under the grill.

Da slopes over ta the kitchen and leans against the door. 'Out with the girls, yeah?'

Micko turns the toast.

'When I was your age . . .' starts Da.

As Micko lifts the toast and butters it, his sleeve catches the light and Da sees the splatters a blood. Then Micko folds the toast in two, sticks it in his mouth, and walks out past Da, not lookin at him and not sayin a word.

It went like that for ages till we guessed why. Not even Ma's bad looks – she never gave Micko bad looks till then – could make him act any different.

'Whya not talkin ta Da any more?' I say, proddin the underside a Micko's bunk with me foot.

'What?'

'Ya know . . .' I hesitate. I don't wanta spell it out too much.

'Go ta sleep, Lucy, or I'll throw ya in the canal.'

'Comin?' says Da.

He looks great. Very fit and all and he's got his beard in a goatee and his face is nearly black from sunbathin on the roof – he takes Sam up there with him sometimes – and the tan makes his eyes even brighter than normal.

'Lucy!' yells Ma.

I scramble inta me runners. 'Wait, Da!'

'Be safe, Jimmy,' she says, kissin him goodbye. It's a long kiss, on the mouth. They hold each other while they kiss, like they wanta suck the other person inside themselves.

I hate it when they do that. The feelin a that sickens me; someone else's body so close ta yer own. But I can't stop watchin them.

When we get ta Dorset Street, which takes ages because we got ta wait for Andy and Paul Kavanagh who are comin with us because they don't have a da, me Uncle Stevo and Charlie are already there, waitin with Charlie's new pal Damo Roche. Charlie and Damo have their colours on, blue and white. Damo looks way too excited for a match.

'Here, Damo,' I say. 'Yer colours are great.'

'Thanks, Lucy.'

Sap. He'd believe anythin anyone would say. 'Ya get them off of Santy?'

Damo laughs. Even more of a sap. Charlie gives me a bad look but I ignore him.

'Hey, Jimmy,' says Stevo. He's gettin fat now. Ma says it's on accounta all the dirty money he's makin off the dead men he has workin his buildin sites. 'Never thought I'd see you at a match.'

'Gotta change with the times, bro.'

The match is good. Our team beat the Rovers three-nil and the roads are swimmin with drink after. On the walk back, Da feeds me Coke and crips and buzzed up, I start pushin Charlie round, gettin Damo ta help me. The Kavs join in too and we act out bits from the game – with Charlie playin the dodgy Rovers' keeper,

Damo his crap defence, the Kavs the wingers and me the star striker – all the way down the North Circular.

'Here, pet,' says Da, distractin me. 'Isn't that Micko?'

I look over. You and Micko are hangin round outside the gates a St Pat's. Beside youse is a big fella that I sorta half-recognize.

'Yeah, Da . . .'

'Son!' yells Da.

Micko looks over, but then away just as quickly. The big fella stares at us.

'Jesus,' says Da. 'What's Emmet Whelan doin with me son? *Micko!*' But then the gate opens and the two a youse and the big fella go inside.

I guess this.

'How's things, kiddo?' he says, smilin his wide cat's smile.

'Good.'

'Yer old man behavin himself?'

'Yeah.'

'Makes a change.' The cat laughs, warm and cosy-soundin. 'Maybe he's tryin ta win his old pals back. It must be lonely for him all on his own. Butcha know what they say, kid – once a rat always a rat. Just remember who yer friends are, Micko, and you'll never lack for them. Yeah?'

Yeah.

As if that pimpled proverb-sayin fuck ever had any friends.

And all the time Emmet Whelan looks on, crackin his knuckles, twistin his signet ring, prayin ta fuck he's not the one who's gointa hafta babysit Snags's little rascals while the Don trains them in as his new generation a footsoldiers.

It was round that time the big gang fight happened outside the Big Tree. Rumour had it was the Don gettin payback on the Wacker for sendin Snags ta Pat's – though the Don was always cautious, so I don't know if he ordered it, or if it was Snags, callin the shots from inside. In anyways, the Waxboys had come outta the pub drunk, and who was waitin for them outside only Emmet Whelan and the Five Lampers, armed with chains, chisels and hatchets. In the mayhem, two a the Wacker's boys got badly beaten and his best gunman bled nearly ta death. A knife-wound, they said. Whelan and two of his pals got picked up by the pigs, but they'd got ridda the weapons by then and the blade was nowhere ta be found.

That night Micko came back even later than usual. Da was watchin the box but Micko went straight past the sittin-room door and inta the jacks. He spent ages there, washin himself. Next day we all seen he had a black eye and a cut on the side a his face.

'Where d'ya get that, son?' said Ma.

'Playin football,' said Micko. 'Gettin very clumsy I am. That right, Lucy?' He didn't even look at Da.

When ya came round later on ta pick him up, ya hadn't a mark on ya. At the time I thought that meant ya hadn't been involved.

A week later the Mass card came through the letterbox. I couldn't read it but Sam told me later that Da's name was on it.

I'm not sayin it was that led me Da from A ta B ta C, Nayler. Like I say, it's easy ta find reasons why. The cold creepin in at the enda the summer, Ma gettin nervous because he still hadn't got a job, Granny's snipin, the jeers from both sides a the battleground any time he went out, bitter memories of what coulda been, the lure a the gear. Reasons abound. What's important is: the choices stopped bein seen, the decision got made.

A shape moves in the winda a the front bedroom, pushin the curtain ta one side. Even without seein proper, I can tell who it is. It's Da. He's got his face tiltin upta heaven and he's happy, the way he always is in that room when he's on his own.

'The . . . what?' ya say ta Micko. Ya sound like ya can't believe it.

'The . . . Zoo.' Micko stretches out the word like it's the thickest thing he's ever said in his life.

Da sniffs, wipin his nose. 'Are yiz comin so?' He looks only half-awake.

'The . . . Zoo, Nayler,' says Micko again, ignorin Da. 'Fancy goin there? We might catch sight of a couple a dogs or maybe even . . . rats.'

Ya laugh but me Da doesn't seem ta have heard. 'Son?' he says
ta John Paul.

Me big brother gets up from the sofa where he's been watchin
Liverpool hammer Man U and pulls his boxin gloves down from
the shelf. As he walks out, slammin the door, Micko winks at ya.

'Mighty Mouse.' The two a youse crack up.

'Micko.' We look around. Ma's in the door. 'Go with yer father,
son.'

Micko hesitates. I can see him thinkin. I can feel it as clear as if
it's in me own head.

'Please,' says Ma.

Ya get up, pushin past us. 'Seeya, Missus Marconi. Thanks for
the tea.'

The Zoo is packed, kids and their da's mainly. After payin in, we
go ta the farm where all the guinea pigs and rabbits are. They don't
get upta much; just sit there, lookin inta space and nibblin on their
grass.

'I want one a them,' says Sam, perched high on Da's shoulders
the way I useta.

'Yeah?' says Da, only he's not really payin attention.

'Me too,' I say.

'Ya can't have one, Sam,' says Micko. He's restless, itchin ta be
gone back ta you or Emmet Whelan or whoever'll have him. 'You'll
forget ta feed it and then it'll die.'

'What about me? I won't forget ta feed mine.'

'Ah, wouldya ever fuck off, Lucy,' says Micko.

'Fuck off yerself.'

'Go on, Da, please,' says Sam.

'Yeah,' says Da, still not payin attention. 'Here, Lucy.'

He passes me the bag a nuts, but before I can start feedin the
rabbits, Micko grabs the bag off of me and starts peltin the guinea
pigs as hard as he can. A woman with shiny hair dressed in a yella
anorak with a camera round her neck leans over.

'You're not allowed to feed the animals.' She's got a foreign accent.

'And you're not allowed ta kill the Jews,' says Micko in the same accent, droppin the resta the nuts in behind the fence. He gives her the finger and heads for the exit.

'Da . . .' I say, but he's not listenin.

As we turn away from the farm, Da reaches out behind him without lookin – a lazy move, like someone who's only half-awake knockin off their alarm clock – and takes me hand. I go ta pull away – I'm way too big ta have me hand held; what's he think I am, some baby? – but then I stop. Even though his skin is slimy with sweat, I can hear the pulsin of his blood in me fingers and I . . . like the feelin a that.

I look down his arm, at the little blue-red marks scattered up his veins, and let him lead me through the Zoo, past the monkeys with their big eyes and thin arms and their gick heaped up behind them like chocolate, past the beautiful black panther swishin through his cage like a shada and the lanky giraffe searchin for leaves and the huge stinkin hippo wallowin in the mud, and the lions with their sad matted manes, roarin for Africa.

'I don't know, Jimmy,' says Ma. 'No. It's not a good idea.'

'Whatcha mean?' He sounds ratty.

'We seen them twice already, Da—' I start sayin, but Ma stops me with a look.

'Quiet, Lucy. We'll be seein them again before the kids go back ta school, Jimmy.'

'That's a long way off, Rose.'

'It's only a coupla weeks.'

'Lot can happen in a coupla weeks.' He starts laughin.

'Oh yes it can,' says Granny, joinin in the laugh, though I can't see why.

Ma turns on her. 'What you on about?'

'I just don't see why ya wanta be disturbin them people.' Granny's never once gone ta Basin Street since me Ma and Da were married but she still hates The Odd Couple with a vengeance. 'The way his health is and all.' She nods in me Da's direction.

'Don't talk about me like I'm not here,' says Da.

'Well, are ya?' says Granny.

'For fucksake!' says Ma. 'Leave it out, Ma. It's none a yer business.' She turns ta Da. 'Yeah. That's a great idea, Jimmy. Let's go see yer parents.'

As it turned out, only Sam went over. Micko and John Paul had no interest and that was the day I got inta trouble for cuttin all me hair off with the kitchen shears. So I ended up stayin in with Granny and eatin Toffypops and watchin *Sale a the Century* while beetroot and hard-boiled eggs and transparent ham got served up on the dinin-table in Basin Street, just like the old days.

They came back at one. I could tell by the bells ringin. The boys were asleep, snorin, but I was awake, high on Toffypops. I'm always awake at that time no matter what I'm high on and over the years I lived at home, I got ta know the sounda that church on North William Street ringin the hours like it was the beat a me own heart.

Someone's gigglin.

'Jimmy, watch it . . . you'll wake Sam.'

'No, I won't.'

There's more giggles and the sittin-room door opens. They go in. I can still hear them. With the buzz from the Toffypops, me ears are sharp as a dog's.

'Come on,' she begs. 'Come on, Jimmy. I'm . . .'

There's a soft heave of a cushion and a little whimper as they lay Sam down on the sofa.

Then . . .

I hear this. I swear I do. Ask me how? Like I say, me ears are sharp as a dog's. The chuckle of a zip bein pulled. The snap of elastic. The tender rustle of hand on cloth, the squelch of hand on tit. The giggles. The giggles a Rose Dolan, giggles that belong to a beautiful fourteen-year-old that knows no better. Breaths risin. *Come on*. Sinkin. Sighin. Risin. Sighin. Calmin.

Calmin?

No, it's too soon. I'm only pushin ten, I've never fucked a man, but I can tell it's too soon.

'Jesus!' whispers Ma. 'Ya fuckin . . .'

'What?'

'Useless.'

'Ah . . . fuck off.'

There's a slither. That's Ma, sittin up. The cushions squeak. Da, turnin onta his side.

There's a silence. Then me Da's breath, harsh, fast. The cushions squeak again. He's restless.

More silence.

There's a gratin sound. That's his shoes slidin along the floor.

'Where ya goin?' says Ma, keepin her voice low.

'Out.'

'Like that?'

There's a pause. The purrin sound of a zip bein pulled up. Ma's voice rises, shocked.

'Jesus, Jimmy. Where d'ya get that?'

'What?'

'That.'

'Ah . . . fuck . . .'

'Ya fuckin . . . !'

'Keep yer voice down, Rose. You'll wake the child.'

There's a squeak as he pushes the door open, footsteps as he walks inta the hall. She gets up and follas him, her high heels sharp and fast. There's a thud as she grabs him.

'Jimmy. Give us—'

'Leave it—'

'Jesus, give—'

A dull smack. That's her, hittin him on the chest. A slap. That's him.

'Jesus, Jimmy!'

'Keep yer voice down and give them back,' says Da.

Another slap. Louder. 'Jesus!' says Ma, her voice shook inta somethin I haven't ever heard in her.

'Give them back,' says Da.

'Whassat?' says Micko in the bunk above me, wakin.

By now there's a limit ta what even the sharpest ears can tell, so I hop outta bed and run ta the door. Through the gap I see Ma standin in the hall, her hands drippin gold. Moonlight shines in through the kitchen door, paintin the back of her head silver. The two metals, gold and silver, turn her inta a picture, one a the pictures from Granny's cards.

'Ya fuckin . . . scumbag.' She lifts her hand. The river a gold sparkles. 'That was why ya wanted us ta visit them? Ta rob off yer own mother? Ya . . .' She starts ta cry. 'Ya fuckin . . . get out, ya fuckin loser. Get out and never come back.'

She sinks onta the floor, sobbin. I hear a creak and see Granny's door open a notch.

Da walks over ta Ma, pushes her away, and takes his ma's jewellery from her fingers. Even from where I'm standin I can tell he's sweatin and his hands are shakin. He stuffs the chains inta his pocket and heads for the door. Ma lifts her head. I think she's gointa say somethin else but she doesn't. As the door closes behind Da, she starts cryin again, loud, like a kid.

Granny's door closes without makin a sound, but her thoughts are loud and clear. *Ya made yer choice, Rose.*

Sam didn't wake up once.

Love. Like all glues, I suppose, it always comes unstuck.

After Da left us that night, Ma made a New Year's Resolution. It was only September, but for her it was the start of a new life.

'I've enough a that man. From this day on, I'm givin him back his name. He can stick it up his arm with all that other shite he does. I don't care. I'm not seein him again. I'm not talkin to him.'

'Jesus, Rose,' says Marlene. 'What about the kids?'

'Better off without him. He can come bangin on our door, he can land up inside. It's all the same. I'm not settin me feet inta the Joy again. Nor that shithole down the country. I'm never goin inta a nick again ta save me life.'

She meant it. But ah . . . life has a funny way of unsettlin the best-made plans.

Da did end up inside again, a course; he was found leggin it down a dark street in the Coombe after some lad did the dirt on him, packed with eight gram a gear and a Special Branchman's Glock 8mm stuffed inta his jeans. That was the time there was all them punishment killins round about. They coppers were achin ta fix the blame on someone; Jimmy Marconi fitted the bill – previous record, contacts, known dealer – so off he went on a lifer. Contrary ta what Ma thought, he never did try ta get in touch with any a us after he left; not while he was on the streets, not banged up, not even when he got out – which he did, accordin ta rumours, in 1998. So only God knows where Jimmy Marconi – me Da, the Southsider, the first, the best, the only Mod in Dublin – is now.

He walks so quiet, I don't hear him till he's on toppa me. I turn round, expectin trouble, but all he does is sit down beside me, take out his army knife and start peelin an apple.

I throw another stone inta the canal, just missin a swan.

Careful, Lucy Lu, he says. Ya wouldn't wanta hit one a them. They're vicious. He hasn't called me Lucy Lu since they stopped bringin me on robs.

Our legs dangle over the bank. He's easy with the knife, workin it round the apple like the blade is just another finger.

Here. He hands me a piece. Tastes okay.

I could ask any number a questions. Whatcha doin here? Where's Micko? Ya plannin somethin on me? But for a change I don't feel like talkin, and neither does he, so we just sit there, in silence, watchin the swans and eatin the apple.

'Ya must be jokin,' says Ma to herself as she reads the card from Basin Street. There's a Holy Mary on the front and a crib. The baby Jesus looks like he's just shat his nappy.

'Hmm,' says Granny. 'At yiz again, are they? You'd think with himself gone they'd leave ya in peace.'

Ma stands lookin at the card for ages, New Year's Resolutions flashin through her head.

It's been tense ever since we got in. Felix is lettin Oscar keep the radio on while we're eatin, but even though the music's lovely and calm it's not easin what's goin on underneath. Felix is on the other side a the table from me, perfect in her grey cardie. I can't help lookin at her bare neck and wonderin what Da done with her gold chains. She's only got one ring left – a weddin band. Without all the gold, her fingers look awful small.

Sam's beside her, starin inta space, fork in the air – it's been there at least two minutes now, I been countin – and Oscar's at the head a the table, chowin down on his turkey curry and tryin ta act like it's all okay.

Beside me is Ma. On her other side John Paul. Micko wouldn't come.

I'm wearin a tartan dress that's two sizes too big, a hand-me-down from the Devlins. The cuffs are danglin inta me plate. Ma's dressed up in a tight yella jumper with fringes and shoulder pads and a diamanté rabbit on the chest. She's got new boots – wine stilettos. They hurt her feet. I've seen the blisters.

On the mantelpiece, starin down at us, is the ghost a Christmas past, neat and clean in his silver frame, his dark Italian hair pulled back inta a ponytail, smilin for the camera as he holds Sam in his arms, pink and white in her christenin gown.

'Well . . .' says Felix. Startin again. 'I can understand if ya don't wanta use it yourself, Rose. After all ya been through.' She makes it sound like whatever Ma's been through, she's done it herself. 'But is it fair on the kids?'

Ma shrugs, stabs at her curry. 'It's done now, Mrs Marconi. Makes things easier if ya ask me.'

'Well, I don't know. School records, all that. Changin children's names like that, it can be very . . .'

She pauses.

'Very what?' says Ma.

'Disruptive,' says Felix, droppin the word inta the silence like she's a priest.

Ma sighs, pushes her fork ta one side.

'Everything alright, Rose?'

'Fine, Mrs Marconi. Just not very hungry lately.'

'Oh? Toucha the flu?'

'No,' says Ma, and stares at Felix. She lifts her hand and pats her belly.

Felix goes scarlet. But what's spoilt Ma's hunger has no bright future; all it'll do is leak outta her gee one cold night the followin month.

On the radio some fella in a low voice talks about the music we just heard. His voice is rich and comfortin, and even though I can't understand him, the sound holds the tension away for a minute; the tension in the room that's cracklin through me body like lightnin through a conductor, like the powder in a Christmas cracker before it gets pulled.

The man on the radio stops talkin and a tinklin tune starts up. Oscar smiles to himself, noddin in time with the music. Me feet start tappin.

Oscar wipes his moustache. 'So how's school goin, John Paul?'

And the cracker gets pulled.

Felix makes a snortin sound and mutters somethin under her breath.

'Pardon?' says Ma.

Felix looks at her.

'Ya said somethin,' says Ma, 'except we couldn't hear it. So maybe ya should say it again.'

'Oh, I don't think so.'

'Sorry, Mrs Marconi, but ya said somethin and it sounded like somethin we should hear.'

'It was nothin.'

Ma laughs.

'Excuse me?' says Felix.

'It wasn't nothin. You were sayin somethin about me boy. That there's no point askin him about school because he'd only be on the streets robbin. That was it, wasn't it?'

'I'm not sayin anythin,' says Felix.

Ma takes out a fag, even though smokin is banned at the table, and lights up. 'Well, sorry ta disappoint ya, but John Paul's a good boy. And yeah, ya should look surprised. It *is* amazin he's so good seein the example he was set.'

Oscar stops drinkin his beer. Felix looks blank for a minute, then she gets it and goes white as a sheet.

'What did you just say?'

'Nothin.' Ma stubs out her fag. 'It wasn't important. Lucy, John Paul, Sam love, time ta go.'

She's been doin good so far, but as she gets up, a fork catches in the fringes of her jumper. Sam tries ta pull it loose, but Ma turns before she gets a chance and the fork yanks at the cloth, draggin it off the table and sendin the whole shebang crashin over, cutlery, delph, plastic salt and pepper shakers, puddin, all.

'Jesus Christ!' says Oscar.

There's a horrible silence and then Felix loses it. She squeals, a high-pitched squeal I've never heard since – except I tell a lie, I heard it once, after, but it's not a sound I care ta remember – then she starts screamin.

'Get out, you little slut! Get out! That's it, Gianni –' meanin Oscar '– that's it. It's not right. You wanted them over, but I can't abide it any more. Get out, ya . . . ya common money-grabbin little tramp, and take yer ragamuffin children with ya!'

Out the back, Duke starts barkin.

Oscar looks over at Ma. His face is tired, the lines chiselled black and deep inside his skin. 'Suppose you'd better go, love.'

It's the only time I ever heard him – either a them – call any a us 'love'.

In the hall Ma tries ta come back to herself, stayin busy by fussin over Sam, doin her buttons and pullin on her scarf so she can calm her shakin hands and melt her temper. But I got a feelin – that tension still hummin in me body – that it's not over yet.

I'm right. Just as we're about ta go, John Paul says, 'Hang on, Ma.'

He opens the livin-room door. Through it I see Oscar, standin with his hands on Felix's shoulders. She's cryin for Ireland now.

'Ya know what?' says John Paul. They look up.

'We always hated youse. You're a pair a snobs. And yer son's nothin but a failed thief that's gointa die in the nick from all them drugs he's been takin.'

The hummin in me body stops.

Oscar leaves Felix and walks towards us, inta the hallway. He opens the front door.

Outside, December rain is washin the dull streets a the Liberties glistenin silver.

'Goodbye,' he says.

Think whatcha want but John Paul was right ta say them things. What else were we supposed ta do? Just take the blame like we were the cause a everythin bad that had happened ta Da? Still, there's times I wonder if it wouldn'a been better ta stay in touch with them. Maybe I'da learnt somethin. Then I come ta me senses. Dream on, Lucy. All I'da learnt was more hatin.

I didn't hear much of Oscar's type a music after we broke away from them. I'd hear a bit of it from time ta time, in a shop, say, or later in school, or leakin outta some fella's car radio, but it was never enough ta pull me in the way Oscar's done. I never really thought about it much till Derek asked me, but I think it was round then that the tunes that useta play in me head dried up too. I said that ta Irene once and she just nodded. Fitted in well, see, with that notion she had about me Da.

At the time I didn't miss me tunes that much. But thinkin back, I wonder if that not missin was real, or just a way a savin meself from more disappointment.

Oscar is long dead now a course. But Felix could still be alive, sittin in her little house down by the brewery, nursin the chalky skeletons of her high, high hopes. After the story about me came out in that shitrag, someone dug up her address and called round for an interview. She shut the door on the reporter – but not till after givin them a blow-by-blow account a every single thing we ever done wrong.

Widda Granny Disowns Scum: 'No Kin a Mine!'

They told me the headline had an explanation mark and all, like what she said was a big surprise.

*

After Da left, Granny's legs got worse and she started havin problems with her good eye.

Mad thing was, the blindness made her even better at the readins. This sorta light would switch on in her face, and she'd start whisperin ta herself, movin her hands over the teacup or cards like she was callin somethin up. Then the words would come, trippin over each other in a stream, while the customer nodded, drinkin it in, hearin meanins beyond the words that me and Sam never could.

By then I'd stopped sneakin in all the time ta listen ta her. The space was too tight behind her bed and, even though I hadn't had another a them fits in a while, I didn't wanta tempt fate. Sam kept pesterin me though, sayin she had ta listen ta them secrets, as she called them, but she couldn't do it on her own. It wasn't like Sam ta pester anyone about anythin but she kept on at that, so much that in the end I gave in. Only every so often, mind. And only for her.

Then Granny had the accident fallin down the steps and the doctor told her she'd hafta stay in bed for a month, and Ma, ever the one ta spot an opportunity, pounced.

'Ya too sick, Ma. Let me do it.'

'You, Rose? Ya couldn't do it if ya tried.'

'I know what they mean, Ma. I understand the signs as much as you. I've got the gift. Haven't I had ta listen ta ya goin on about it all me life?'

'No, Rose.'

'Ya useta give off about me bein too lazy and now ya won't let me do anythin.'

'There was a time when you coulda proved yerself, Rose. That's long gone.'

'Time for plentya things is long gone, if ya ask me.'

'Whatcha mean?'

'Things is rough, Ma. Them kids need food. What with you gettin fuck all from the pension and me with the four a them ta support, there's not much choice left.'

'Rose—'

'I'm younger than you, Ma. I'm stronger and so help me, even if I don't have all the gift, what badness is that? It means I don't hafta wait for the time ta be right. I can have people up here every night a the week, payin as much as I'll charge. But if ya won't have it, there's not much else I can do except hike up ta Mountjoy Square and take me chances with the rest a the girls.'

'Don'tcha dare . . . Rose!'

'No choice, Ma. It's upta you. Is that whatcha want?'

No choice? Hah. There's always a choice.

She lies in bed. The dim shapes in her good eye float and soar. On the ceilin she sees her daughter's future unroll. Her bandaged hands throb. Her leg – the one she's gointa lose in a coupla years' time – hums. A small sound.

'Alright,' says Granny, one sweet May evenin.

And the next day, Ma tells the neighbours that, from now on, she's the one runnin the family business.

At first she was brutal, remember? She'd go through the cards and the meanins, but anyone could tell she was just repeatin stuff she'd heard off of Granny. And she got them mixed up all the time, confusin the Fool with the Hanged Man, the Wheel a Fortune with the World. The customers, specially the young wans, thought she was rotten. I could tell from the way they thanked her when they were leavin that it'd be a long time before they'd come again. She'da ended up tellin nobody's fortunes if she'd kept goin that way.

But one day, when Sam was earwiggin behind the sofa – I wasn't there, fucked if I was gointa listen in on Ma's shite – somethin happened. Sam told me later it was like a light switchin on inside Ma's head, just like the light the Roadrunner gets when he thinks of a masterplan. I asked Sam if the air went cold, like when Granny was zonin out. She said no, but she could still tell Ma was onta somethin real. And from that day on, people started comin back for more.

I still don't know how much of it was real; if she genuine *seen* things or just acted, usin her memory and her skills a fakery ta put one over the clients. Granny wasn't impressed in anyways, kept givin off ta Ma for bein sloppy with her divinin, leavin stuff out or lookin at things from the wrong angle. Like the time she told Martina Kennedy she was gointa be married in six months' time when the cards said the girl would die inside a year from leukaemia.

'Whatcha expect me ta do – tell her the truth?' says Ma.

'No, Rose. Ya know as well as me people can't always take it. But ya can still find ways a preparin them.'

Thing was, Ma probably led on Martina on purpose, outta spite. She didn't like any a the young wans from roundabout, mainly because she seen them as competition. Rose Dolan, pushin thirty and lookin forty, with four kids, two a them nearly grown, thinkin a the likes a pretty Cindy Devlin, with her legs long and lovely as a piece a music, as competition? By then, I suppose, there was reason enough for Ma ta feel threatened. Her men friends, the ones that had come back ta her after Da'd left, began tailin off soon as she started the fortunes. Granny said it was because they were scared a Ma, the way she was all done up like a hippie in her bangles and scarves. Ma wouldn'a paid Granny any heed but then John Paul started gettin at her too.

'Ah, Ma, can ya not do somethin more normal?'

'Some cheek I do be gettin from you, John Paul Dolan. What makes you the expert all of a sudden?'

John Paul shrugs. 'Just sayin . . .'

'Shut up, John Paul,' says Micko. 'Leave her at it.' He says it like she's diggin through rubbish for a livin instead a readin cards.

'Micko, you better watch yer mouth—' starts Ma, sharpish the way she never useta be with him, but then you interrupt, right on time.

'I think ya look great, Missus Dolan. Like the real thing.'

Ma glows, for a minute lookin beautiful again.

Despite a Ma takin over the family business, Granny still read for us. And when Sam turned seven-and-a-half, Granny made her shuffle the cards – the old pack she'd refused ta hand down ta Ma, who'd been made ta go out and buy new cards of her own, even though we all knew ya can only tell a fortune from a pack ya been given – and laid out a cruciform future for her.

'What was in them, Mouse?' I ask.

Sam says nothin, keeps singin a made-up song to her Barbie.

'Sam! D'ya hear me? What did she tell ya?'

'Who?' Sam looks up.

'Granny. Yer fortune.'

'Oh . . .' She drifts, thinks. 'Loads.'

I never asked Granny what it was like for her, and I still regret that. She never once described for me the shapes the future and the past took for her when they crossed over inta the present. Or explained how chance worked; whether everyone's million different futures are like turns in a road that can't be backtracked on – or more like lovers layin on toppa each other, separatin or comin together with every action taken in the visible world. She didn't say if the world a the unseen lay outside ours, linked by mysterious doorways that would open only ta her and her like; or if it soaked inta every moment a the seen, crustin the present like a layer a sleep. It woulda been good ta hear her answer but I was never calm enough ta get the right question together in me head. So I've had ta come up with me own explanation. And here it is.

Ever since that time with Missus Devlin, I've pictured the unseen as a sea, driftin under everythin we do. Some can dive in and others can't. Sometimes the divin brings the underwater world up inta the present and, once it does, there's no pushin it back.

Sam, like Granny, was one a the divers.

When she was six, she told us she'd had a dream. Her best pal Lisa was comin over that afternoon in a new blue duffel coat with her hair all cut off. That day, over pops Lisa, and – surprise surprise – she's identical ta Sam's dream.

'Had ya been plannin the new look, Janice?' says Ma.

'God no, Rose,' says Missus Gough, Lisa's ma. 'She came home from school today sayin there was nits. Well, with all them curls I couldn't take the risk, so I just took the scissors ta her and done it meself. Still, I got her a lovely new coat ta make up for it. That right, pet?'

Lisa glares at her ma, hatin her, while Sam looks out the winda, already forgettin what she foresaw.

Silly, maybe. A little thing. But what's that Derek useta say? Sometimes it's in the little things ya can see God.

And if Granny and Sam were divers, what does that make me?

Easy. I've always been a seagull. Able from time ta time ta slip below the surface a the present, ta hear what people are thinkin, ta feel their wants like they're my own, ta taste possible futures, till the pressure a the ocean forces me up again and I'm back ta normal: Lucy Marconi – sorry, Dolan – jigger.

The . . . ability, I suppose people would call it, was always there a course, but it got stronger that first time I was sent away. Things started comin outta the walls. The monsters a the deep began ta walk alongside me in the wakin world. But one thing's stayed constant. Strong or weak, the sight's never, ever been at me own biddin.

I squawk and fight with the white foam on the crests a the waves. I pick at floatin fish corpses. I drown and sink. I am overwhelmed. I surface, live, breathe again.

Granny and her million ways a seein and whatever happened in me head when I was away may a magicked me, made me dream a other worlds, catch glimpses a past reasons for present doins, but I can say, hand on heart, I never got the full gift. I'm only a chip that cracked off the edge. I may see what's comin, but never seen what's comin next. That's okay. I know the problems magic causes, the trouble brung on by seein the future, and I want nothin of it.

As for Ma, she never loved the sight the way Granny done. It was an inheritance she fought, a tarrin she wouldn't take, but she used what little of it she had ta keep herself off the streets, ta create a show a respect for herself and us, and most of all, ta build a world out from under Granny's thumb, where Rose Dolan could at last be queen a the coop.

VII

At thirteen, ya got yer first stretch, a year in that St Lorcan's shit-hole in Finglas. Ya'd taken a Ford Cortina for a spin, dumped it down by the canal and ripped off the brand-new video recorder the owner had left sittin on the back seat. Micko was pissin on the bonnet just as the rozzers rolled up. Bad move. They hauled youse down to the copshop like two little dogs on a leash. You got the court and the stretch; Micko, still only twelve, got another caution – 'And this will be your last' – and the promise a the Juvenile Liaison Officer breathin down his neck for the next six months.

Granny shook her head and went inta her bedroom, nursin her hands. I heard her thought through her door. *Told ya so. Told ya so.*

In the months that followed, Micko was bullin, ragin, aimless without ya.

Dee-daw! Dee-daw!

Oh, them flashin lights. Oh, them blarin sounds.

'Mrs Dolan?' says the Juvenile Liaison Officer, standin beside the other rozzer that's holdin Micko by the arms.

Ma leans against the doorway, hand on hip, fag smoke curlin up over her head.

'He was caught jumping over the counter of a newsagent's on Liffey Street. You know we've warned him enough times. We're going to have to press charges.'

Micko, tryin ta shrug off the coppers' hands, looks everywhere except at Ma.

'Okay,' says Ma.

When she closes the door, she leans against it a long time, without lookin at anyone. Micko goes ta head inta the kitchen but she grabs him by the arm before he can get away. 'Are ya thick or somethin, Micko?' Her voice is quiet. 'Are ya stupid? Are ya doin this on purpose?' She starts hittin him, soft hits at first, on the side a his head. 'That's it, isn't it? Ya doin this ta wind me up.'

Micko ducks her fists, usin his palms ta ward her off. She grabs him by the collar and shakes him. 'I won't have it, Micko. I fuckin won't.'

He pushes her away, hard, and she loses her balance, crashin inta the doorway.

Timin, ya useta say, is everythin. In the autumn a 1984, three month after Micko was sent away ta Clonmel for the jumpover, you and Snags Ryan got out on exactly the same day; you from Finglas, Snags from Pat's.

By then, a course, all them big changes had been kickin off in the trade. The Quinlans in Crumlin had been brung down, all over the news they were, and everyone was talkin about how the Don would be next ta muscle in on the southside. Accordin ta Charlie's pal Damo – who earwigged the rumour off of his da Tommo Roche who, it turned out, was the Don's favourite mechanic, number one at fixin the plates and sprayin the cars – it was Snags who asked his uncle for an in on the new turf. I'd say that was about right. At nineteen, after two year sat scratchin his hole in that manky den, Snagglepuss Ryan woulda been gummin for a challenge.

Funny the things ya remember. We didn't cop all the ins and outs a the game back then, a course. But Damo was always pickin up bits and pieces and one day he told us he heard the Don had Snags set up as a wholesaler.

I thought it meant somethin rude. 'What's a hole saler?'

Damo looked confused. 'Just somethin I heard.'

'It means ya buy in a lot at a time,' said Charlie. 'Me da does that with bricks. Ya get a good price that way.'

You know better than me, Nayler, but if Damo was right, settin up Snags as a wholesaler insteada just a dealer woulda cost the Don a fair whack. It woulda helped him keep a distance too, though, and that woulda suited that cagey fucker down ta the ground. Ya can correct me on this, but I reckon that's how Emmet Whelan got roped inta the deal, brung in as a minder ta make sure Snags wouldn't lose the head and get wound up in the courts again. The Don musta let Snags have a free rein on how he moved the stuff on, though. Because how else would he a been able ta get away with havin his little rascals do all the work for him? And, how else, at fourteen, would you a got ta be leader a that little pack, answerin only ta Snags himself?

There musta been conditions, though. There's always conditions.

'Lookit, kiddo,' I picture him sayin. 'Do me a favour and keep the black marks off the slate. If I give ya somethin ta do, do it. If I want ya ta carry somethin, carry it. If I give ya somethin ta pass on or pick up, pass it on or pick it up. But keep yer own little ideas to yerself. I want youse outta trouble. Okay?'

You were always so quiet as a kid, I can't imagine ya doin more than just noddin.

Didja nod, though? The Don was already lookin ta get you and Micko and the resta the little rascals under his thumb. By agreein ta work with Snags, you'da been distancin yerself not just from the Don's direct rule but from his protection too. A decision like that is important. Ya musta needed guidance.

Was it then ya first went ta her for help?

Forgive me if this next parta me tale is hazy. But with Micko gone, ya didn't come round as much as ya useta and then mainly when me and John Paul were out, so all I can do is piece together what happened. Some of it I remember. Some I got through Sam and the secrets she heard. Some I got from you, later. Some through the stories Damo heard off of his da. The rest I just made up, graftin me own lifestory onta what I think happened to you. But I don't think you'll mind if I'm missin a few details or buildin others up. Because let's face it, you could never have enough stories, Nayler; especially not with yerself as the hero.

In anyways, who ever said that a storyteller has ta be reliable? Even Granny had her hazy moments.

Frost bites the air; fog lifts off the wide docklands river, meltin warehouses together, dimmin the moon that's only a blurred coin somewhere. Somewhere. Two paces ahead a ya saunters Snags, anorak zipped up against the cold. Ya tag after him, freezin in yer lightweight summer jacket. Snags looks back, cracks a grin with his wide mouth.

'Right there, kiddo?'

As youse get closer, youse hear it. Grandmaster Flash and the Furious Five, rappin and gruntin about that jungle and how they're afraid a goin under.

'Good,' says Snags, noddin in time ta the beat.

Ya shrug. Ya can't hear the notes.

Snags rounds the corner. Light blares out from the top windas a the warehouse. He flashes a torch, lifts barbed wire, doubles under, awkward. You folla, smoother, light on yer toes. His dartin beam catches graffiti. The old favourites. *Drugs Out. No Pushers Here.* Ya laugh.

'What?' says Snags.

'Nothin.' He wouldn't understand if ya told him ya were laughin because it's struck ya as funny, the idea a tryin ta protect a deserted dockland where nobody lives.

'Come on,' says Snags. 'Time the big bad wolf showed up with the basket a goodies.'

Ya make yer way up the wooden stairs, nearly trippin on a loose plank, feelin with yer hands up the wall, yer palms scrapin the damp brick. Someone changes half-way through the song, scrapin the needle across the vinyl, and puts on Lou Reed. 'Vicious'. Ya can't make out the tune, only the words and the beat. At least it's not 'Waitin for The Man'.

The party is anxious. Ya watch them as they huddle round Snags and pay the bill. He hands out the caterin. They're a mixed bunch, half-hippie, half-punk, half-nothin; local boys back for the festive season from London and Berlin, Boston and Amsterdam. They all work on the sites over there, or in bars or warehouses, and they normally buy their drugs off the high-street dealers. But it's too risky bringin back their lunchboxes with all the TV cameras waitin at the airport ta welcome them home – 'The Diaspora Returns! An RTE special' – so they've got Snags on the job instead. Strictly speakin, he should be keepin away from the north docks – that belongs ta one a the Don's other buyers – but some wannabe rock singer from Coolock got his name and passed it on and there ya are.

It's small fry tonight; quarters, tens and twenties, mainly. The Don would never be seen droppin the goods like this in person, but Snags is a different kinda animal. He likes bein hands-on. It gives him the feelin he's in control. In anyways, there's reasons why he's takin a risk. Along with introducin ya ta the scene, he's recruitin some sellers. He has most of his pyramid worked out, but there's some missin links and he doesn't trust Emmet Whelan ta bring the right people on board. Besides, this crowd may be able ta intro-duce him to a few suppliers outside a the Don's golden circle.

They chew, taste, swalla. Ah, acid. The days before E.

Snags pulls a couple a promisin fellas into a corner ta check their availability.

Ya stand there, takin it in, watchin. Across from ya, two punks – one pink-haired, the other bleached – are huddled over a lighter. Brown bubbles in the spoon. The needle dips, sucks. Pinky grips his bootlace with his teeth, pulls, jabs. Brown falls. Blood rises. Pinky's teeth release, the bootlace slumps. Bleached reaches.

A hippie wanders up ta Snags, offers him a joint. Snags shakes his head.

'No thanks, pal, I'm workin. Can't afford to lose me edge.'

'Maybe your chimney sweep then,' says the hippie. He's got a Donegal accent.

'Here,' ya say, and take the joint.

'It's good,' says the hippie. His eyes are half-asleep.

Yeah. It's alright.

God knows how ya kept off it so long. Ya were young I suppose but that wouldn'a made a difference. Everyone knew even with the heighta the epidemic over, the kids were still bein fed it left right and centre. The Quinlans in Crumlin were the worst but it wasn't just the southside that had a reputation. You were always good at knowin yer own mind, a course, and ya wouldn'a just done somethin because it was around. But that argument doesn't always wash well with the gear, so I think it was down ta Snags. He could see the risks. He'da been all fired up back then, hungry ta prove himself ta the Don. He'd got plans for himself beyond the gear and you were parta them. Plus you'd already seen things he didn't want passed on. Small wonder he wouldn'a wanted ya becomin a liability, willin ta sell yer soul ta the highest bidder.

Snags mighta kept ya off the gear but he'd no bother gettin ya ta do the other stuff.

People still go on about his set-up now, don't they? Legend. How, like the Don, Snags never let anyone have stuff on credit. How he split his whack, sellin some in bulk to a few big buyers – less risk – and the rest through a pyramid, with him at the top, creamin off profits every step a the way. How he kept the business out in the open, so none a the merchants that bought from him would ever try a dodgy move, changin his drop-points so the Old Bill never got a decent pattern.

But it was the way he used youse lot that was the real talkin-point. Two or three rascals on each drop; one on the money, one on the gear and sometimes one on security – though more often than not, he'd use a regular enforcer for that. Smart move, usin youse. Back then no rozzer would suspect a kid lollin around eatin ice-cream in the backseat of a Ford Cortina in a shoppin centre car park. Risky too, but by then everyone knew how efficient youse were at defendin yerselves.

First thing I reckon he done was put you and Emmet Whelan workin together. You'da looked after the gear, Whelo woulda been on the gun, and another rascal – Kevin Walsh maybe, or Marky Geoghan, someone who wasn't known by the rozzers – woulda done the money.

They're piebald, owned by the cream crackers, brown and cream with ragged ears and tufts a white hairs fringin down over their hooves. I'm on the mitch, at the low end a the Royal that backs onta Croke Park, makin me way along the railway line runnin alongside to the water. One a them looks over. Big brown eyes, the edges white, streaked with red. He's a white star on his forehead.

Starlight.

'Here, boy,' I say.

The piebald keeps starin at me.

'Whatcha gawkin at, ugly?'

He blinks, swishes his tail. More like a cow than a horse.

When I get up on toppa him, third time lucky, I'm gobsmacked at how slippery his back is. Reminds me a one a the sofas in The Odd Couple's gaff. I grip his mane. Me legs are shakin and me heart is thumpin and me hands are slippy with sweat, but while he's under me I know I'm safe.

'Go on, boy.'

He stands stock-still.

After four tries, I get him ta amble a few feet down the track. Then he stops, shrugs, and throws me. The ground races ta meet me and me stomach lurches but before I can even think a pukin I hit the grass shoulder-first. It jars but it's not that bad. Outta nowhere I start laughin.

When I get home, the front door is a coupla inches open.

'Granny?'

No answer.

A murmur a voices comes from inside the kitchen door. It's open too, only a jot, but enough for me ta hear. I sidle up, close as I can, and peek around the door.

'Ah, Jesus, son. I don't know—'

'Please, Missus Dolan.'

He's sittin at the table, his hand set out in fronta him, palm facin up. She's sittin across from him. I squeeze in closer ta the door, hopin they won't see. From where I am, his hand still looks a kid's, small, white and bruised, the nails bitten down ta the edges. She sighs and takes his fingers. Somethin about the way she does it tells me this isn't the first time. She looks around, guilty sorta – watchin out for Granny, I guess – and bends over his palm.

She frowns, concentratin.

'Whatcha see, Missus Dolan?' His voice is hoarse as it breaks from soft ta deep. 'Anythin new?'

She sighs. 'It's still very full, son.' She's tracin her finger down his lifeline, a silvery snake cuttin across his palm.

'Has it got any shorter? It looks shorter ta me.'

'No. It's still full, son. Ya get ta do lots a things.'

He nods. 'Money?'

She peers, frowns again. She shakes her head, not in a no, but like she's tryin ta get ridda an insect that's climbed inta her hair. 'Oh . . . yeah.' She sounds almost surprised. 'Lots.'

He pushes his black hair off of his forehead. 'Don't sound so shocked, Missus Dolan. I've plans, ya know.' For a minute he's lost the polite innocent voice he always uses with her and somethin different has slipped in – a laughin, teasin edge.

She pulls back from him. 'Oh, I know, son.' She does a half-laugh but she's not teasin him back. She's serious. 'And what about Micko? Have ya plans for him and all?'

He reaches out, take her fingers in his. 'Ya know yer son is like a brother ta me. I'd never let . . .'

He trails off, soundin older all of a sudden.

She smiles. It's a small smile.

The silence hangs between them. He breaks it first.

'So how much money will I make, Missus Dolan?' he asks, a kid again.

She laughs and bends down over his hand. When she starts talkin again, her voice is too low for me ta hear. But he does, noddin away like everythin she's sayin is just what he expected.

Ya turn round at some stage in the readin so I slide out, back inta the hall. Before I go though, I see the colour of yer eyes in the light from the kitchen winda. They're normally black but in the light they look different. Dark green.

Micko got out in the spring, two weeks early for good behaviour. When we collected him, Ma pulled him to her.

'You'll be good for me now, Micko, won'tcha?'

I couldn't hear her but I could see her lips move as she whispered it in his ear.

'Sure,' he said, shruggin her away, lookin round for you.

That was the night Ma and John Paul had their first big fight. John Paul, pissed off with how Ma was moonin over Micko – even though me and Sam didn't mind, we were thrilled ta have him back – said somethin about you and Snags and how Micko'd be hangin round with youse again in no time. Micko said what was the problem with that? John Paul said he didn't hafta spell it out. Then Micko said well, if John Paul didn't like Snags, what was he doin trainin in the Don's boxin club? John Paul said at least he was trainin, not sellin drugs or worse like Micko'd be doin in no time; just like our Da he was goin, only at least our Da wasn't mixed up any more in the Don's dirty business. Micko started sayin somethin then about how little John Paul knew, musta got the dirt on Da off of his new buddies which is why it was all bollocks, everyone knew our Da had been alright with the Don once, and he'd probably still be okay now instead of a class A loser if he hadn't fallen out with him, and then he said maybe John Paul would wanta learn from our Da's mistakes and watch who he was hangin round with – but before he could say any more, Ma lost it, told John Paul ta fuck off if all he wanted ta do was spread dirt, couldn't he see his brother was reformed now, what did he wanta do, drive him inta a life a crime when he should be mindin his own business?

'Fuck off, willyiz!' John Paul was *fumin*. I'd never seen him so wound up before. Then he stormed off, slammin the door.

The pigs brung him home later on that night, for smashin up a phone box on Gardiner Street. It was only the second or third time he'd ever been caught, but they told Ma he was lucky ta get away with a caution. After they'd gone, while she ranted at John Paul for bein a loser, just like his da, Micko snuck off ta hook up with you.

What happens next is the story that went round the Five Lampers after the dust settled. Emmet Whelan, in ta get a fresh seta hubcaps for his Ford Cortina, said it in strict confidence ta Damo's da,

Tommo Roche, and he told his wife and a good while later she told her sister and Damo heard them talkin and that's how it got back ta us. Damo said there was rumours goin on how that wasn't the whole story, there was somethin off about it in a coupla places, the first bit with the car, and the part with the gun too. But it made sense ta us. Suppose that just goes ta show how easy it is ta tell a good story.

'Are we there yet?' says Micko, messin. But you're in no mood for messin. Funny the tricks time plays; the stretch ya got before Micko and the months ya spent workin for Snags have put years between youse. Micko Dolan, who useta be yer best pal, just seems like a little kid these days.

Still, there's work ta be done. No time ta waste fuckin around.

Ya look at yer watch. It's too big, a fake Snags has given ya so ya look the part, and it keeps slidin off of yer wrist, just like yer suit nearly keeps slidin off of yer shoulders – but you're only drivin for a bit today and so far so good.

Course you'll get away with it. Ya look twenty, Nayler.

There's only two a youse on the drop today which is why youse are drivin up together. Whelan's in custody for assault, nothin related ta Snags, just some poor fucker he picked on in a pub. Afterwards Whelan will swear Snags shoulda got a third man in – fuckin *stupid*, sendin two rascals on their own for a job like that, especially when one's barely outta reform school – and Snags in turn will say what did a thick meathead like Whelan know, it woulda been even more fuckin *stupid* if he had sent someone else, seein as how it all worked out. But right now you're not bothered. Two, three men, what difference will it make? – or so ya tell yerself.

Ya have it worked out. You're doin the money because ya reckon that's where the danger is. Micko will handle the gear. Seein as you've no third man on the gun, you've given him the gat Whelan normally carries; a Smith and Wesson .38. Just in case. Ya reckon you'll be alright with yer knife; it's quick and neat and by now ya know where ta stick it if ya need ta silence someone fast.

The car park is packed. Families havin their big dinners, punters celebratin their winnins at the dogs. Ya pray the dealer will know who ta look out for.

Micko fidgets, pattin the gun. 'Alright?' ya say, and head.

Inside, the pub is packed, heavy with smoke and the sound a Elkie Brooks. Shakin the Help the Blind box, yer cover for collectin the money, ya push through the crowds. He looks like Groucho Marx, Snags told ya. Tache, shades, black mullet. Ya look around, peerin through the smoke, but ya can't find him. Then, half-way across the bar, ya sense it. A pricklin in yer shoulders, a burnin in the backa yer head. Ya shift ta one side, easin the box under yer arm, and turn around. Groucho's comin outta the jacks on the other side a the bar, zippin up his fly. Behind him is a burly lad in a brown bomber jacket.

Fee fie fo fum I smell the blood of a . . . rozzer.

First ya freeze. Then ya think, real fast. It only takes a few seconds.

Ya smooth yer hair down and take off yer innocent I'm-only-here-ta-collect-for-charity face, dippin yer neck ta make the shadas under yer eyes deeper. Then ya walk, nice and relaxed, like you are a man a twenty, not a fifteen-year-old kid, all the way back across the bar. Past Groucho, who doesn't give ya a second look. Past the rozzer. There's another pig at the door and ya light up before ya go out, makin sure the smoke's in yer face so he won't see how young ya look in the daylight. Then, still takin yer time, ya wander across the car park, hopin Micko hasn't fucked up.

For a minute ya think the car is gone and ya curse him from a height. Then ya see it, parked behind a coach fulla winda-lickers. Ya duck around the coach and all the spas bang on the windas as ya pass, their Christy Brown tucked-under mouths open in delight. Their minder ignores ya.

'Don't fuckin ask,' ya say ta Micko as ya slide in.

They didn't folla ya out. And youse were nearly there, nearly home and dry; a few looks from other drivers, people crossin the road – ya could see the question, *That kid's too young to be drivin, isn't he?* – but so far so good and then –

The cyclist showed up.

145

Swerve. Too late. Bang. Screams. Blood on the windscreen.

Ya couldn't have chosen a worse place. It was Cathal Brugha Street, for fucksake. People were everywhere. And you?

You were screechin down towards Summerhill with Micko in the backseat tellin ya ta slow down, slow fuckin down, brakin at the mouth a the alleyway, flingin open the doors, screamin, *Run fuckin run . . .*

In court ya tell them youse were just messin, joyridin.

'In the middle of the afternoon?'

Ya smile, actin tough. 'More of a thrill that way. More risk a bein caught.'

The cyclist's in a coma. Back then joyridin was all over the papers; just like the paedo priests these days. You're hopin the court'll buy it. They won't like ya, but they'll believe ya done it for the thrill. Then they won't nab ya for the gear.

'The two of you were on your own?' There's a murmur through the court.

Ya nod, act even tougher.

You've told them ya didn't know what was hid under the front seat, honest. That's when ya put on yer innocent face again and make yer voice shake. Jesus, ya know ya been in trouble but you'd never . . . Ya robbed the car without knowin whose it was, ya never woulda, ya . . .

When they ask ya 'And whose was it?', ya do what the Don's lawyer told ya and shake yer head, lickin yer lips nervous like ya know but ya too fuckin scared ta say.

Ya don't risk glancin over at Micko. But ya trust him. Why wouldn't ya? Youse are best pals. Ya know he won't let ya down.

And he doesn't. 'No, mister,' he says. 'I don't take drugs. Me da had problems that way and I swore ta me ma I wouldn't go near the stuff.'

They took youse aside later on and tried ta get youse ta squeal. Special consideration would be given if youse only talked. Did youse not wanta stop this problem gettin outta hand? Youse had yer futures ta think about.

They picked the wrong lads. Ya mighta mumbled somethin about the Wacker turnin dirty for all his anti-drugs talk, but youse never said a word about Snags. And luckily for him, they'd nothin ta connect youse. Sure, youse hadn't been in sight a the Don's boxin club for years. And they'd never got a squeak from youse back in '81 when they'd hauled youse in ta talk about that shoeshop fire on Henry Street.

They tried ta put a trace on the car but the plates were changed so they didn't get far. They had ta let it lie, be content with the haul. They never found the .38.

That's one a the bits a the story that Damo said was off, the gun goin missin like that. That and the car; not the accident, funny enough, but the part before, near the start, when the two a youse drove upta that pub. Them bits bothered me too, though only after I started thinkin about them. How come everyone knew about the gun when nobody outside you and Micko seen it? How come you drove Micko there, you with yer joyridin convictions, when youse coulda got on a bus with way less risk? Gear or no, knife or no, nobody woulda even looked sideways at youse on a bus.

But at the time I was like everyone else. I believed the story youse told – not the one for the courts but the one that Emmet Whelan bandied about, about Groucho and youse runnin and all that. Granny never swallied it – 'There's more there than meets the eye' – but she never said why neither. And Ma? Well, Ma was like the papers. She bought the whole fuckin thing: hook, line and sinker.

Evil Teens in Cyclist Tragedy Plead Innocence a Drugs Haul: 'We Didn't Know'.

Derek once told me that when the newspapers do that, put marks round whatcha say, it means they don't want people ta believe ya.

'That stupid eejit! That stupid little cunt!'

Her voice is raw. She's been screamin the same thing over and over since Marlene left.

'I'll fuckin kill him! If I had him here, I'd break his head!'

On the narrow bunk, Sam presses close ta me, shakin. She's been like this, shakin, since Ma got in from the court. Her head pushes against me chest, the light bones of her face grindin against me skin.

'Sssh, Mouse, sssh,' I say.

In the other room Ma howls – a sound that makes me thinka animals with their insides bein ripped out. Somethin crashes onta the ground.

'I'll kill him. Don Ryan or no Don Ryan, I'll kill that fuckin Snags. Feedin kids that poison!'

Granny murmurs. Another crash.

Ma's voice rises again. 'That stupid little bastard! I'll fuckin murder him!'

The front door opens. Sam freezes. I grab hold of her arms, prayin she won't fall.

'Oh, look who it is now.'

'Rose—' says Granny.

'Mister good boy himself.' She laughs hoarsely.

I get up, Sam still clingin ta me, and slip over ta the door, openin it just in time ta see John Paul walk inta the kitchen past Ma and over ta the sink. He's wearin his bomber jacket and he's got three green stripes stitched on the sleeve. Haven't seen them before. He turns on the tap.

'Not a word, hah? Mister keep-outta-bleedin-trouble—'

'Leave it, Rose,' says Granny.

'You stay the fuck outta this.'

John Paul finishes drinkin and turns ta leave. Ma gets up.

'Where d'ya think you're goin?'

'Leave off, Ma.'

'Oh no ya don't.' Her voice rises again. 'Tryin ta slip away, yeah? Just like ya always do? Tryin ta –' she puts on a whiney voice '– keep outta trouble, what? I'll give ya what.' Slap. 'I'll give ya fuckin what.' Slap.

'Rose . . .'

'Leave it, Ma,' he growls, holdin up his fists ta protect his face.

'It's all your fault. Ya know that, don'tcha? Your fault yer brother went astray. Ya led him inta trouble, lettin him off like that on his own. Ya shoulda taken care a him. Ya shoulda known he couldn't be trusted!'

John Paul, duckin, turns inta the hall. She lifts her whiskey glass.

'Don't you leave!' She flings the glass and it smashes against the wall over his head. 'Where the fuck ya think ya goin, leavin me like that? Don'tcha dare leave me! I swear, I'll kill ya. Don'tcha fuckin dare—'

She throws her bottle a whiskey, quarter full. This time it gets him. He rushes back at her, fist raised. Ma screams. He grabs her by the throat. They stay like that a moment. Then he drops his fist and goes.

'John Paul?' calls Granny. 'John Paul?' The door closes.

Granny gets up stiffly and walks over ta Ma. She puts her hands on Ma's shoulder. Blood trickles down inta Ma's good white shirt that she wears for court.

'Ya shouldn't be blamin yer boys, Rose. It's not them.'

Ma shakes off Granny's hands and turns. There's no tears in her eyes. Her teeth are gritted so tight, I can feel them squeakin. When she speaks her voice is quiet.

'Why can't ya just keep yer stupid sayins ta yerself? Ya been doin it long enough, Ma. All them things ya see and ya know butcha can't be bothered spellin out ta us because we haven't got the same gift as you. Well, ya know, Ma, all that does is make me wonder what use is that fuckin gift when it hasn't stopped a single bad thing from happenin ta us? I've enough of it, Ma. I've made me own mind up.'

I useta think it was stupidity on her part, not wantin ta see what Granny seen, what we all seen – John Paul, Marlene, even me. That Micko would never a done it without ya. But maybe she thought he woulda; with ya, without ya, it wouldn'a mattered, he'da found someone ta lead him where he was goin. And ya know what? Maybe she was right.

★

I never seen a whole lot a Snags before all that happened – me and Charlie useta spot him roundabout time ta time, a tall smiley fella with an easy-soundin voice – but after you and me brother got sent ta Tristan House he disappeared off the scene completely. Later I found out that was when he went ta Amsterdam, packed off there by his uncle ta keep outta trouble. They say before he went Snags lost the head in fronta everyone, not like him at all, said the Don would regret it, not keepin him on, he'd learn his lesson sooner or later, should know blood was thicker than water, couldn't sacrifice his nephew just ta keep others happy, blah blah blah blah blah. But if ya ask me it was a wise move, and not just for the Don. Seein as Snags'd just lost the mob nearly twenty grand-worth a gear, plus his rascals nearly blowin the whole thing up in the courts, I'm sure there was plenty bayin for his blood. As for Groucho? Well, story goes once the Don had pulled safely outta Crumlin, he sent that little rat hooer a the Quinlans a bullet in the back of his head, courtesy of his number one enforcer Mister Emmet Whelan himself.

It was then things got tough. Because that was the time the so-called People Power was startin up, with that Families and Neighbours Against Drugs shower from the Diamond at the hearta it. Damo told us the FNAD was backed up by Sinn Féin, with Fred Mahon eggin them on with all his anti-drugs this and pushers-out that. The way the auld wans went on, you'd think Wacker was doin that from the goodness of his heart. Gobshites. Wacker still had all his old games – robbin, girls, protection – plus, Damo told us he'd started doin an odd bit a gun-runnin for the paras, thanks ta a new mercenary from the North he'd got workin for him. That fucker woulda never been anti-drugs outta carin. All he wanted ta do was rub the Don's nose in muck and stay on the Shinners' good side.

Though the ones that began the movement meant well – Amanda told me later her da was started with the Youth Action Project up in Ballymun – they ended up splittin the world in two. Inta the ones that thought they were on the side of right and the ones on the side a wrong. It was clear as day which side we were on. If it hadn't been for Granny, I'm sure we'da got graffiti on our windas or shite on our doorstep, even petrol bombs through the letterbox. But people didn't lump Granny in with the rest of us. They blamed Ma for what happened ta the lads; said if she'd reared them better, they'da been okay. But they only felt sorry for Granny, like Ma had done the dirt on her as much as me brothers.

As for me and Sam? Well, ta start with, we got the sympathy vote too. Poor mites, their granny's half-blind with the diabetes, that slut of a mother does nothin for them, that loser of a da – say no more – and the two boys . . . no hope there. All of a sudden we were victims. But I never wanted ta be a victim. I never wanted ta be somebody else's number on a list, held up cryin for people in bigger houses ta shake their heads over. Luckily for me, I didn't stay a victim long. With all the stuff me and the gang got upta, it wasn't long till the sympathy vote passed right over me head, goin straight ta Sam instead.

But things change. Time passes. And soon enough the very bitches that useta cast longways looks at Ma on the street started ta mend their mouths and queue up on our stairs again ta get their fortunes told. Gift or fakery, me darlin Ma had somethin in them readins a hers they all wanted. Self-interest. Wins out every time.

After Micko went, Sam started squirrellin herself inta corners with them comic books she loved. She was only eight but she was good at readin, miles better than the rest a us.

'She's gifted, Mrs Marconi.'

'Dolan.'

'Sorry, Dolan. Yes, gifted.'

The teacher's voice stinks a surprise, like gifted and Dolan are two words should never be said in the same breath.

Sam liked readin her comics out loud as well as to herself. I enjoyed it sometimes but it mostly drove me up the wall because they were so borin, all ballet dancers and schoolgirls and abandoned orphans.

'Lucy?'

'What?' I don't wanta encourage her too much in case she goes back ta readin the one about the ice-skater.

'When I grow up, I'm gointa draw them pictures.' She moves her finger down the page of her comic. Next door, John Paul's got The Wolfe Tones on. 'Boolavogue'.

'I'm gointa be famous.' She says it like it's somethin that's fixed.

'Yeah, well, there's only two ways a bein famous round here, Sam.'

'What?'

I throw a few punches. 'Boxin.' Then I pick up her hairbrush and mime singin to it. 'Or music.'

'Yeah, but you don't play music, Lucy.'

'I can sing.'

'And ya don't box any more. And neither does—'

'I do so box. With the Kavs and Charlie I do.'

The Wolfe Tones grind to a halt. John Paul walks past us and out the door.

'Ya off ta the club again, John Paul?' calls Ma from the kitchen.

The door slams. On our bedroom wall hang John Paul's boxin gloves, empty and sorta blamin-lookin.

I been puttin two and two together for a while after seein them stripes on his jacket, but it's not till Sunday afternoon, messin round after a jaunt with Charlie and his pal Damo – throwin stones at the culchies on their way ta the All-Ireland – that I cop for sure what John Paul's been gettin upta them afternoons Ma thinks he's down at the club.

We see them in the distance first. A bunch a lads at the bottom a Henrietta Street, all wearin bomber jackets with green stripes stitched onta the arms. We're nearly on toppa them before Charlie stops me. 'There's yer brother, Lucy.'

A small and weedy lad with a face like a rat lifts up a plastic bag. Even from a distance I can smell the cider. He hands it to a big lug, who shakes his head. Now I see. The lug's John Paul.

'The Green Strips,' whispers Damo, breathless.

Ah yes, the Green Strips, Wacker Mahon's teenage militia. Far as I could see, all they ever done was hang around soundin off about the Armed Struggle and knockin stuff off of the back a lorries and listenin ta trad on their ghetto-blasters and, in the meantime, bullyin shopkeepers and Snags's little rascals, who were easy targets now their boss had scarpered. Be that as it may, they kept John Paul busy enough.

Six month after you and Micko get sent ta Tristan House, me big brother's earned enough cautions ta sicken the Juvenile Liaison for life, nearly all a them for scrappin and damage. There's not a night when he doesn't come home covered in bruises, his face a patchwork a healin and open cuts.

'Jesus,' says Ma. 'They certainly teach ya how ta scrap in that club, what?' Sounds like a joke now but that's not how she meant it.

After they caught him wreckin a shopfront on Liffey Street they gave him a year in that gaff in Cavan. I know the other borstals were fillin up real fast by then, but parta me still thinks they done it on purpose, ta split him up from Micko.

'Why didja do that?'

I'm fumin. Charlie's spent ages plannin the rob and then Damo goes and wrecks it by moochin inta Nash's Pets way too soon, alertin that steamer Francie Nash and makin us run without gettin in even sniffin distance a the till. Now the Kav brothers are upta ninety and we hafta plan a whole new jaunt for the day.

'Why, Damo?' I say again. But I already know the answer. Damo didn't know any better. He didn't mean ta fuck it up, he's as loyal as a dog. He just can't help bein thick.

'Ya moron. D'ya never listen ta what Charlie said?'

'He's not a moron,' says Charlie.

'He is, Charlie. That's why ya picked him as yer pal.'

The Kavs laugh. Charlie glares at me. But Damo is too thick ta even understand me jibe. And when Charlie jumps me – with the Kavs in like Flynn for good measure – in butts Damo ta protect me.

'Stop it, Charlie. She's only a girl. Ya don't wanta get in trouble with her ma.'

Only a girl? Thick cunt.

But ya know what, Nayler, in spite a Damo's thickness, there was this thing about him that made ya forget his worser points. And it wasn't just his da bein in the know. I was fond a Damo. He was a softie. And he was awful easy ta manage.

Damo was the oldest in our gang, but even with his contacts he was too thick ta be leader, so nobody challenged Charlie when he took over. I tried a few times but there was no way they were gointa take a girl buzzin off them, even with the rep I had from me brothers and the Juvenile Liaison sniffin round me now John Paul and Micko were outta the picture. In anyways, it was fairer that way. I mighta been the one that came up with the ideas for jaunts, whether robbin or raidin or smashin things, but it was always Charlie that done the plannin.

'Yer cousin's a . . . a genius,' says Damo, noddin like he's just invented the wheel.

Charlie a genius? News ta me.

That autumn the Wacker's ma died and there was a huge funeral in the Francis Xavier on Gardiner Street. Everyone turned up. The Don came and all, carried the coffin even. You'da thought Wacker wouldn'a let him within a mile, given the bad blood between them, but accordin ta the auld wans, Ma Mahon herself had asked him ta call a truce for the day she was buried as a mark a respect and Wacker loved his ma so much he went ahead and done it. Woulda suited the Don no end, a course. As Damo said, he needed ta win back the supporta the people; with all the arrests and sickness from the gear, the Families and Neighbours were havin a field day tarnishin his good name in the area. Turnin up at the funeral woulda given him the real human touch.

Ma didn't want us ta go down but I snuck off with Sam and the gang and we hung outside waitin for the procession ta come out.

After the bodyguards came the coffin, all lopsided, slantin down towards the front at the right where Wacker was carryin it, his stubby arms held high. His eyes were red from cryin. I hadn't seen him up so close since Sam's christenin but he hadn't changed much apart from bein a bit balder and packin a few more pound round the gut. He passed us by without a glance. Beside him, his back stooped so as not ta lift the coffin outta Wacker's reach, walked a tall fella, with white hair and a beard like Santy. He had a face like Santy too, kind and jolly, with twinklin eyes. 'That's the Soldier,' said Damo, nudgin me. 'They call him that because he useta be a provo.' Behind him, Wacker's three sons, all stumpy like their da, and at the very back where the coffin slanted up, walked a fella who was long and lean, a black spider in his Armani suit.

Damo nudged me again but I didn't need a nudge ta know who it was. The Don.

His Rolex caught the sun and for a minute I got this mad thought that he'd trapped his own little sun in the metal round his wrist and he was shinin it back at God ta show who was the real boss.

He had the height and the same wide face and short chin as Snags, but not the pimples. His skin was clean, fair, well-kept. As he passed us, he glanced over in our direction and his dark brown eyes stayed there for a while. I guessed he was lookin at me ta check was I me Da's daughter, was I the sister a Micko that had gone down for workin for his nephew. Then he smiled, as if readin me thoughts; a sudden smile, wide and beautiful, like the sun comin out from clouds. Sam shivered.

I held her ta me. 'Don't worry, Sam,' I whispered. 'He won't do any harm ta us.'

She said somethin under her breath, but I couldn't hear what it was.

Then this thing flew through the air and landed on the Don's chest, splatterin yella muck all over his good suit, and a little old woman pushed her way in fronta us and started shoutin: 'Murderer! Don Ryan's a drug-dealin murderer! He kilt me grandson and he'll kill all yours if ya not careful!'

Auntie Walsh, one a the loudest muck-flingin mouthpieces for the Families and Neighbours. The Don acted like he didn't even notice her but the Soldier fella turned ta Wacker and said somethin. Gold glinted in his mouth. Wacker nodded. And at the back, behind the Don, Wacker's honour guard, his Green Strips, nodded too, grinnin at each other, with that little rat-faced fuck I seen drinkin cider with John Paul grinnin the widest of all.

'Come back, Sam. Come on.'

'No, I don't wanta. I'm alright. I'll stay here.'

We're havin a game a football round by the Industrial Centre off of Gardiner Street. Charlie's knocked Sam over. I've told them all to be careful, because she's not like us, she can't take a knockin, but ya know how it is; ya get carried away sometimes and ya can't stop yerself, and before ya know it, someone's hurt. Sam doesn't cry when we hurt her, though, just melts inta the corner, spaced off in her own world.

We go back ta the game. After ten minutes, Damo asks where Sam is.

I look around, breathless. I can't see her anywhere.

'Ya better find her,' says Charlie.

'Fuck that.' I don't wanta go back ta the flats and Ma, who'll probably be in a fouler. Not now in anyways, while we're havin fun.

'Ya better, Lucy.'

The resta them nod. Dogs in a pack.

Once I get inside, I try ta go easy because I can hear Ma in bed with some fella, one a the few local lads who still don't mind givin it to her, even with our bad name. I try ta block me ears but I can hear them, him gruntin, her moanin and wheezin like a bicycle tyre bein pumped up. Makes me skin crawl.

'Where's Samantha?'

I jump. It's Granny, sittin deep inside Ma's raggedy armchair.

'Jesus! Thought ya were asleep, Granny.'

'Ya lost her again, Lucy.' It's not a question. 'Well, what are ya waitin for? Go look for her.'

I run up the stairs, knock on doors. Two landins up Yvonne Bourke – cousin a Sam's best pal Lisa – says no, they haven't seen her. The Devlins, five doors down. No. The Moriartys. No. I'm runnin outta places ta look and gettin worried.

And then I remember where Da useta bring her that last summer he lived with us.

Once I get on the top landin, I go round the electricity box and inta the alcove where they store the ladder. Me legs are already startin ta wobble at the thoughta goin up so high, but they get worse when I see how banjaxed the ladder is. Maybe I should leave it. I'm about ta go when I see the tea-chests. She's built a stairs outta them, leadin right onta the roof. Me legs wobble again.

Come on, Lucy.

I just about manage ta get onta the first chest, and then the second, but then me breath starts ta go. Then I think a the piebald pony down by the canal and how it's not that bad fallin, not really, and besides, it's not that far, only a coupla chests, and the thought gives me enough courage ta force meself up onta the roof.

She's sittin on the edge, readin. Her legs are threaded through the concrete rim at the lipa the roof, danglin over inta nothin, and her comic is spread out before her. Beside her is a plastic bag; filled with sweets or cakes, I guess. Below her is Dublin, laid out like a carpet. The sighta it makes me sick so I press me back in close ta the air-vent chimney.

'Hiya, Lucy,' she says, not lookin up.

'Whatcha doin up here, Mouse? We been worried about ya. Ma'll have a fit if she—'

Sam turns and looks at me. She starts laughin.

'Ah, Samantha, that's bold, ya shouldn't be mouthin off like that, it's not funny.'

She keeps laughin.

Then I start too, don't know why, except it does seem stupid, me that's always so brave standin backed against the chimney terrified a fallin and givin off like Ma, while me fragile little sister's practically hangin off the roof with not a care in the world.

She sticks out her hand.

'I'm not goin over there, Sam.' I press closer ta the chimney.

'No, I know. Just help me up.'

Keepin me arse safe against the chimney, I reach out and take her hand. It's damp and little bits a grit from the doughnuts she's been eatin rub against me skin.

We climb back down the tea-chests and out through the gap onta the landin.

'Why did ya go up there?' I ask, relaxed now I'm on solid ground.

'I like the view,' she says, surprisin me with the word. 'I like bein so high up, seein everythin below. It must be how God feels.'

'Yeah,' I say, not really understandin.

Later that evenin when Granny asked me, I told her Sam had been with her pal Lisa. Granny wouldn'a minded but I knew Sam wanted ta keep it secret.

Chicken and egg. Was it because we ditched Sam so often that she got ta like her own company so much? Or was that always in her, even before I met Amanda and began ta grow up?

She had her own pals, a course. Lisa Gough and her pack a bitches. Lisa Gough whose crewcut Sam had dreamt about, who at age eight knew more about sex than I did at eleven. But whenever I seen Sam sittin dreamy round Lisa and her pals, I couldn't help thinkin of a butterfly hoverin round a swarm a bluebottles. Out on the edges. There but not there. Driftin.

I mightn't a been me sister's keeper but I've always known where Sam went when she spaced off like that. She was in the other world, where comic-book stories came true and the future was hers for the dippin, where feelins and thoughts held as much value as blows or money. And once there, there was no comin back. She had ta be left behind, by us . . . by anyone who knew her.

Small wonder that Lisa hurt her in the end too. But if she hadn'a, if she'd had the savvy ta suss that Sam would be good ta take care a, ta have on her arm when they went out lookin for fellas, well then, maybe . . . What am I sayin?

If if if.

Stupid Lucy. There are no ifs.

'Jesus,' says Ma. The word hisses outta her and beside me I feel her crumple inta a heap.

Across the visitin-room table sits a stranger. Blackened face, turnin purple. Hair shaved so close we can see the scalp, pink underneath. A bandage covers his right ear. He looks up.

'Howayiz.' Somethin like that. Can't make it out. He tries a smile. His front four teeth are broken.

I'm up before I know it, unable ta hold back. Even though in this place we can't do more than hug, I wanta put me arms round me brother and hold him and not let go. Ma's hand grips me arm, drags me down.

'Leave it.'

For the rest a the visit she says nothin, just stares at Micko, accusin. *Ya stupid little bastard*, I hear her think. *Ya stupid little prick.*

Ah, the skeletons a high, high hopes.

On our way out, we pass three lads flanked by screws. One a the lads is you. Ya barely glance at us as ya pass, but Ma notices. She turns and opens her mouth but she doesn't get ta say yer name. As the pack reaches the door, I look back and see ya starin at us. Ya raise yer hand.

'That poor lad,' mutters Ma.

I've thought about it loads and this is the best I can come up with. It was always easier for Ma ta forget what you'd done than ta forgive Micko because you were never a part of her the way Micko was. Not forgivin Micko let Rose Dolan burn her love for him outta her, so she'd never hafta feel disappointed in him again. Burnin love out was the only thing that worked. It had worked with Jimmy Marconi; it would work with Micko.

As for you and what you'd done . . . well, maybe as far as she was concerned, you'd done nothin that needed forgiveness.

That day she read yer hand in our kitchen, she didn't force ya ta finish that promise. '*Ya know yer son is like a brother ta me. I'd never let . . .*' Never let what? She allowed ya trail that promise off inta nothin.

She shoulda made ya finish; she shoulda made ya swear you'd protect me brother, you'd never let anythin bad happen ta him.

Anyone would say that. So why didn't she? Well, here's what I think. Rose Dolan was the type a woman who always had ta keep some sorta hope alive. She didn't make ya swear because she knew that way, ya'd never break yer word ta her. She had ta keep hopin, after all, that she could rely on someone. And in a way, old pal, ya could say ya were the only one of us that never let her down.

Later I found out what happened; from you. Micko told me sweet fuck all.

They split youse up, leavin Micko on his own with no Nayler ta rush ta his rescue. It wasn't long before that fucker and his pals jumped him in the garden, robbin him of his hole and his looks in one go. Ya never told me who it was. A headcase on a four-year stretch who should nevera been let stay after his sixteenth birthday, was all ya said. A headcase and his pals. Micko never pointed them out. If I met that pervert or any of his fuckin pals today, I'd rip their cocks out by the roots and fry their bollocks and stick them all down their scabby stinkin throats.

You'd told him the two a youse would be alright; Snags would make sure a that. But where was Snags when the headcase was around?

Tick tock went the clock.

That Christmas, two weeks after yer Auntie Joan got ya outta Tristan early on good behaviour and the promise that a new life in the country would reform ya for good, three days after takin a phonecall from an Uncle Martin none of us had ever hearda, Micko got a card signed Sasha and postmarked Holland. His pen pal, he told the screws; that girl he'd been writin ta, the one who was helpin him get his head back together. Inside the card, glued inta the golden folds a baby Jesus' crib, hid far far away from the pryin fingers and sharp eyes a security, but exactly where Uncle Martin's phonecall had told Micko ta find it, was a little silver star. And inside the star was a hundred brown grains a heaven.

What had made Snags realize that lowerin the age a consent for his rascals wasn't such a bad thing after all? Foreign customs? The knowledge that, as long as he was the first bidder, it wouldn't matter a jot after all if one of his boys had a soul for sale? Does it matter, the why?

So Snags did look after Micko in the end. He couldn't stop Humpty Dumpty from fallin, but he was well able ta pick up the pieces and put them back together again. Just the way he wanted.

Deal

Pushin nine now and still no sign. But I know you're out there, Nayler, comin over them rusty-red mountains with the orange sun at yer back.

Funny. All these years I been goin round with a picture a this gaff in me head, all black walls and dirty floors, stinkin a smoke, lit by the shreds a moon bleedin in through the arched windas. But when I walked in this evenin, somethin happened. That picture in me head sorta . . . shivered, blurrin over what I was really seein. Like one a them bad photos.

It seems smaller than before. But maybe it was only the darkness made the walls look so high. It's still dirty. Cans and butts lyin around. There's a coupla them alcopop bottles too, smashed in pieces by the fireplace.

It's awful cold outta the sun. I don't remember that. Last time, even though it was freezin outside, once we got the fire goin, it was bakin. And today was so gorgeous – like all the summers in me childhood come together – that I was sorta expectin the stones ta store the warmth for me.

I brung up matches, but I don't wanta make a fire yet. The candles are enough for now.

I'm gettin restless.
Must be the cold. Plus I keep thinkin I'm—
No.
Fuckit, say it, Lucy.
Keep thinkin I'm hearin things, alright? There's this—
No, Lucy, shut it, keep off the subject
La la la la la la la. Remember I useta do that ta annoy Ma? She'd say somethin like 'Jesus, close the door, Lucy, there's a terrible

draught!' and I'd copy her, just ta amuse you and Micko. *Nana, nana naaah, nana, nana nanana naah.* Mushin up the words but keepin the rhythm.

Mad, isn't it, how many things there are ya do as a kid that ya forget? Like all this I'm tryin ta collect for ya, all the memories and thoughts and things that happened, but there's so much I've ta leave out. What's more important? The little things that won't get inta the final story, them shared moments only me and Micko, say, will remember? Or the big events that makes it inta the newspapers? Derek useta have this sayin, *Make little a the big things and big a the little things.*

Maybe I'm concentratin on the wrong stuff.

Ten. Still no sign. But ya comin closer. I can smell ya. Spice and saltwater, liftin on the light wind that's blowin over from across the mountains. Ya just waitin ta make yer appearance; playin games with me, hopin ta throw me off-course, tryin ta make me give up. Stupid, Nayler. Should know I'm not me Granny's granddaughter for nothin. I won't give up now. Not even with the jiggin startin ta make me feet dance.

Besides, if it gets too much, I'll take them.

That's what they're there for. Me little Ritas. I've got the bottle outta sight, tucked in me jacket, but I can feel them callin out for me and with the restlessness in me legs and feet, I'm tempted, sure.

But not right now.

When I was puttin off goin ta Ma's this afternoon, I couldn't help saunterin past Amanda's house off of Summerhill. Stupid, I know. But just ta see, ya know; ta check it out, ta answer the questions been floatin round me head all this time. Such as: is it changed? Does it seem smaller ta me now? Is she still there? The last the thickest of all seein as I know full well she isn't. Still, old habits die hard.

It had changed, a course; like everythin else I seen today. Different but the same. The tree in front of her sittin-room winda was still there, though it looked awful small considerin it was planted nearly twenty year ago. All the other houses had trees in fronta them too, just as small. It took me a while ta cop on that the local kids had probably set fire ta the first trees or ripped them out or done whatever kids do, so the ones I was lookin at were only replacements. In a hundred years, there'll probably be the exact same set a trees in that little square off Summerhill, still as puny as the day they were planted.

I

I was twelve when I met Amanda, on me first day in the new school: St Ita's College for Girls on the Grace Park Road. It was Marlene fixed it for me. Stevo been doin some work for the nuns, buildin a new gym at a good price, and they owed him one. It was a long enough distance ta walk but nobody else roundabout woulda had me.

Amanda and me were a match made in heaven. Small runty tomboy meets big busty brasser. If I'd planned it, it wouldn'a come out better. The only thing is, there was no choosin in that friendship. It was an accident, pure and simple – and if circumstances had been any different, fuck, we mightn'a hit it off at all.

I get there late on purpose. I open the door, knockin me bag against the glass pane. The teacher – not a nun, tall with short brown hair and wearin wojus knee-high wine leather boots – turns. She looks at me, not even botherin ta speak. I hate her on sight. Then again, I hate all teachers.

'And . . . ?' she says.

I look around, behind me, actin thick, like I don't understand what she's sayin.

'Your name, please.'

'Ah,' I say, doin more a the thick act, but exaggeratin it so she'll wonder am I really takin the piss. 'I'm Lucy.' I spell it out. 'Lucy Dolan.'

'All right then, Lucy. Please take a seat.' She turns back ta the board. 'And quietly, okay?'

The minute her back is turned, the resta the girls look up, sussin me out. Narrow eyes, open eyes, curious, judgin. Some a their faces I know. Many more I don't. But even then I can tell who's gointa be me enemies – nearly everyone – and who me pals – nobody. There's a couple a neutral types that I might be able ta call on in a fight. A salla-faced young wan, with thick dark hair cut in a fringe across her forehead, who keeps glancin down at her books when I look at her. Threatened by me? Maybe. Promisin, so. Even more promisin is the fact that the only free seat in class is the one beside her.

The salla girl keeps starin at her books as I sit down, bangin me bag on the ground. The teacher darts a look around and gives me a glare, just like she's meant ta. The other girls laugh, some a bit nervous. I'm glad ta hear the nerves; maybe they'll delay tormentin me so for a bit. I open me pencil case, drawin the zipper down slow as I can, milkin out the sound so the teacher's shoulders, tight ta begin with, stiffen even more.

The salla young wan looks up from under her thick dark fringe, and smiles, tryin ta hide her teeth. A mouth full a metal.

'Hi,' she whispers. Even in the whisper, I can hear her lispin through the brace. 'I'm Amanda.'

I nod, not wantin ta appear too friendly too soon.

Over the mornin she makes a couple more attempts ta start a chat but I hold back. No point gettin in with someone if they're gointa drag ya down. I've learnt that much from me brothers and you. At the lunchbreak she offers me a sandwich. I'm starvin. Ma hasn't given me any money for food – or should I say, there was no money in her purse when I checked for meself – and as usual there was nothin ta eat back home. But I hold back. I don't want the Braces Girl gettin too many ideas.

It's pissin rain outside. I toy with goin out, maybe even mitchin, but there's a nun on guard and in anyways, I owe Marlene for gettin me in. 'Try not ta make a bad impression, Lucy love,' she'd said the day before I started.

So I stay put instead and watch Braces Girl as she eats. She's scarlet, constantly pullin her lips over her teeth, coverin her mouth with her hand while she tries ta dig bits a bread outta the braces. Once she's finished, she hauls herself up off her seat – she's got a fat arse, I see, even though on top she's as flat as me – and wanders over ta the radiator where a gang a girls is clustered.

These young wans look different ta the rest of us; they've all got shinin teeth and hair like honey and creamy-gold skin. They're the poshy set, from the Griffith Avenue enda Drumcondra. Not posh enough ta get outta bein sent ta Class 1D though.

Braces Girl hasn't got the same teeth as them but her skin is the right colour and her hair is almost shiny enough. And, when she gets ta the radiator, the gang shifts like a flocka birds ta make way for her. From where I'm sittin, I can smell she's relieved they didn't turn their backs, and, for no good reason – we're not friends yet, I'm not plannin ta make friends with anyone, am I? – the scent a that relief gets me worried. Then she smiles. Mis-take. There's a flash as the metal brace catches the light from the winda and I get even more worried.

One a the gang leans over to another and whispers in her ear. The one bein whispered ta looks at Braces Girl – whatshername? Amanda – and laughs. She's the prettiest a the bunch – a real Goldilocks. She laughs again, teeth flashin white, and turns ta another young wan. I keep me eyes on her. The chat from the group gets louder, the snobby Glasnevin accents makin music in the echoey classroom. It all sounds friendly enough but I've been around enough scraps ta know this is no idle banter. This is the build-up ta war. Fellas dance round each other, throwin punches. Girls ask each other where they're from and what pop stars they're inta. Foreplay, warcries, call it whatcha want. All that matters is that someone's gointa pounce – and someone else is gointa get hurt.

Goldilocks suddenly turns ta Amanda. Uh oh. Here it comes.

'I saw a James Bond film the other day.'

Amanda smiles again, thrilled. 'Yeah?' she says, tryin ta play it cool.

I'm up outta me desk. I know I shouldn't get involved, but it's not fair. You could say plenty a things isn't fair but I know in me bones I already hate them girls, with their notions a who's better than who, and who's worth talkin ta, and if ya don't look as pretty as them or fit in, ya might as well fuckin die.

'Yeah,' says Goldilocks. 'I can't remember the name but there was this fella in it.'

The whisperer, the one who started the whole thing, laughs. I hate her worst of all. One step, two step. I'm gettin close.

'He had the most ugly-looking mouth I've ever seen.'

The other bitches hush; they know what's comin too. Only Amanda, poor old Braces Girl, can't see the cruise missile headin her way.

'Yeah?' she says, puzzled, still smilin her metal smile.

'Yeah. Full of meta—'

And that's when I punch Goldilocks in the face.

Course, I probably shoulda learnt from me experience with Doylo in the first school, just held me water and not gone near them, because it didn't do Amanda much good in the end. They never hassled her when I was around but when I wasn't, she told me they were on her like flies on shite: copyin her lisp, callin her 'Jaws' after the fella in the Bond films and 'Pancake Tits' on account a she was so flat. If she spoke, even ta answer a question from the teacher, they set up a Chinese whisper that went round the classroom and usually ended with someone sayin, 'Amanda Phelan's as ugly as sin' out loud right in fronta her. I know it sounds stupid, but that's girls for ya. They know where it hurts.

Some a the other young wans that got bullied at least had a brain or two between them but Amanda didn't even have that. She done her homework every day, which is more than can be said for me, but she was wrong more often than not. So she couldn't even get the teachers on side – not that that woulda done her much good.

It got worse when they found out she'd come from the Mun – 'Ballymun bitch', they called her – and her ma and da were separated. They'd rip bits outta her, sayin her ma was a druglord and Amanda was a knacker and a slut and the local bike. Mind you, they went easy on the druglord bit when I was around on accounta the rumours about Micko. And even though they hated me as much as Amanda, especially after punchin Goldilocks, they didn't give me any lashins ta me face. They musta cursed me from a height behind my back, but I couldn't give a toss. Amanda, though, minded everythin. There was times I had ta dig her outta the jacks at break she was cryin so much.

I know ya might find that hard ta believe, Nayler. But you only knew Amanda later on, when she was able ta pretend that she was tough.

We walk down Ballybough Road together. We could go the other way, down Dorset Street – it's shorter and there's more shops for robbin – but Goldilocks and her gang reign over that territory and I couldn't be bothered dealin with that shower a cunts today.

When we get ta Portland Row, I turn down towards the flats.

'Here,' says Amanda, 'd'ya wanta see where I live?'

We're still not proper friends yet. We stick together durin school but we both know it's for Amanda's sake, ta protect her, nothin more. She's tried startin up a few chats with me durin break and I've gone along with it, partways, tellin her a bita this, a bita that, but I don't think we've much in common. Besides, I got me own gang – Charlie and all – even though it's harder gettin time with them these days what with all the homework Charlie gets from his new school.

I hesitate, thinkin of excuses. *Ah, it's a bit outta me way, Amanda. And me Ma . . .*

'It's not that far.' Amanda's blue eyes are hopeful under her fringe.

'Okay,' I say, just as she says, 'Ya won't hafta come in or anythin.'

We laugh. Then there's an awkward silence. I never felt like this before.

'Okay,' I say again, noddin like it's a brilliant idea.

Amanda's gaff is in off Summerhill, in a new square built by the Corpo the year before. The square is red-brick, pretty, real houses with their own front doors. Amanda walks upta number 17. There's a small tree growin in fronta the winda. It's got wire round it ta keep it safe.

Amanda looks over. 'Lovely, isn't it?'

'Yeah.' It is. But I wonder how long it'll last.

'Okay, so. I'd better go,' she says, fast, and before I can think a somethin else ta say she's ringin the doorbell. I can't see the woman who opens the door but I hear her voice.

'Where ya been, love?' she says, but it doesn't sound like she's gointa batter Amanda for bein late.

After that, things were different between us. I didn't mind any more actin the bollocks in front of her. Lettin meself get jiggy after a package a crips or sweets so I'd mess about or talk too much – about music in the charts or the colour a Sister Breda's knickers or even the stuff I got upta with Charlie. Before then I woulda watched it, tryin ta stay cool in fronta the enemy, ya know, but round Amanda it was alright. She laughed at me, but not like them other waggons. Amanda laughed at me like I was bein funny on purpose.

When I get in, it's dead quiet. A fly buzzes round me head. Dirty thing. Ma musta left the milk out again.

I pass Granny's bedroom door and outta habit open it a notch, peek in. She's dozin, snorin lightly. She's taken ta lyin in bed a lot these days. Some days she doesn't get up at all. She useta fight it at first, but now it's like she's given up.

Sam's back. I can tell, even though I can't see her anywhere. It's like her smell is hangin in the air. I stop outside our bedroom door, and peel me ears. At first I hear nothin, just the fly buzzin and the slap slap slap a the cord a the winda blind against the kitchen winda. Then I hear another soft slap, of a different kind.

Ah, thought so. She's lyin under her bed, playin patience with Ma's cards. Or maybe Beggar Me Neighbour, with her dollies lined up in a triangle in front of her like they're playin too.

I leave it. I don't wanta disturb her. So instead I go inta the kitchen and pour meself a glass a milk. It's a bit warm and sweet from bein left out. I sit on a chair and tilt it onta its two back legs till I'm balancin like I'm in a circus act.

The fly buzzes, caught in the slats a the blinds. The cord slaps against the winda. Granny snores.

*

John Paul got outta the Cavan place just after I started secondary school. As Granny said, 'God forgive me but he might as well a stayed there cos we seen more a him inside than out.' The first Saturday after he came back Ma came inta the kitchen and seen a brown envelope lyin on the table. When she opened it, she found a hundred pound in tenners inside. That wasn't bad money back then.

Her face goes white and hard and she scrunches the notes inta a ball.

'Little bastard . . . If he's been . . .'

I slurp me cornflakes loud as I can. Why she always thinkin the worst? Fucksake, he coulda got a job. But I don't say anythin. Don't want a clatter, not on a Saturday mornin.

It's days before she gets a chance ta ask John Paul about the money and all he says then is, 'I'm workin.'

'Where?' She taps her fag against the kitchen table.

'Just a job.'

'If you're upta somethin, son—'

'Don't son me.' He gets up from the table. He's filled out since goin inside; his arms are like lumps a wood, thick and hard, burstin like the Hulk's through his sleeves.

'Where ya off ta?' she says.

He gives her a pityin look.

'He's off ta see his mot,' I say.

The pityin look crumples as he goes scarlet.

'Ah, yeah?' says Ma.

'Yeah.' I know I shouldn't be gangin up with her against him but it's fun. 'Tara O'Keeffe from the Father Scully flats.'

'Much you fuckin know,' says John Paul.

'Oh I know, alright. I've heard things. John Paul's in *looove*, Ma.'

I pin him with me eyes, tryin out the mind-readin trick the fella on the telly showed us. *Hold the thought in your head and send it out.* And the thought I'm thinkin is the sounda Tara O'Keeffe whimperin like a wounded dog behind the bins while me brother rams it inta her. Disgustin.

John Paul musta got the thought. He leaves without sayin anythin else.

'Anytime, anyplace, anywhere, Martini,' I sing as he bangs the door.

Ma slams her cuppa tea on the table.

'Shut it, Lucy. That noise is doin me head in.'

I keep hummin ta meself, not givin a toss what I'm doin to her fuckin head.

Ma had kept to her vow and since Micko had gone ta Tristan House she'd been ta visit him only four or five times. She swore that was only because the authorities made her go so they could get her so-called involvement and feedback on the so-called rehab programme. Each time she went, she just stared at Micko. At first he tried ta charm her back, crackin the odd joke, but she wouldn't budge, so in the end he made do with talkin ta me and Marlene. I worked round it best I could. I'd get Marlene ta take me on visits without tellin Ma – sometimes with Sam, sometimes with Charlie for the crack.

Ma didn't change her tack much when they started sendin him back on visits. She had ta stay round him if the Social was there, but once they trusted him ta do an overnighter on his own, she'd head off soon as she could, leavin me and Sam ta look after him.

I can't say I noticed when he started. It wasn't like he was usin regular or anythin because it wasn't like it is now, when ya can get brown in through the baby's nappy or even in soap. And he never got caught. I don't think the Social even knew about the gear; Ma'da made noises if they had. I think the only reason they kept an eye on him durin them early visits was because they were worried about him gettin back in with the Don.

When he stopped tellin the jokes, I just thought he was gettin all grown up and couldn't be bothered makin a fool of himself any more.

The change I really noticed was how he talked about the future. At the start he was always goin on about what he'd do when he got out; how you and him had plans and how he was gointa make it good, maybe start a business like our Uncle Stevo, buildin or somethin. At them times his eyes would light up and he'd smile his broken smile under his broken nose and it was almost like havin the old Micko back. But after yer Auntie Joan took ya away with her down the bog, he didn't go on like that as much. It was all day-ta-day stuff and yeah, well, he didn't wanta think about things too much and anyway, it would all work out fine. He'd say all that with his eyes dreamin off, like Sam's when she went driftin inta her own little world.

I never thought much about ya and whatcha were upta in yer new life. Coupla times I wondered where ya'd gone, but the thoughts didn't stick for long. Ya were Micko's pal, not mine. So for what would I be thinkin a ya?

Time ta time I asked Micko if he'd heard from ya but he never said.

'See,' says Amanda. 'It's lovely, isn't it?'

She lifts up the eyeshada, dabs some on her finger. The blue sparkles catch the sunlight. It's pretty, alright, but –

'No,' I say as she tries ta smear it on me lids. 'No way, Amanda. Leave it.'

'But ya could look real pretty, Lucy, if ya made an effort. Ya got lovely eyes and skin. If ya done somethin nice with yer hair, ya'd be really . . . go on, please. It'll look gorgeous on ya.'

She's humourin me. Since when have I been anythin other than plain? 'I don't care. Don't wanta look gorgeous.'

Amanda whistles to herself through her braces and squints inta the tiny pocket mirror she robbed off her ma. Light picks up the glitter on her eyelids, the salla swerve of her cheekbones, the buddin swell of her diddies under her lilac tee-shirt. Pancake Tits is fast becomin a thing a the past. Her nipples are hard and without wantin ta I wonder what it would be like ta touch them. Me finger twitches.

'Alright?' She smiles, and dimples that I never noticed come and go in her cheeks.

I push away the thought of her nipples. 'Yeah.'

She *is* alright. She's better than alright. In the eight months I've known her, Amanda Phelan has blossomed inta a princess.

'Ya ready?' I get up, brushin the grass off me jeans.

'Thought ya'd never ask.' She bats her eyelashes.

I punch her in the side. She laughs and grabs me hand. 'Help us up?'

She stuck her arm through mine and we walked like that all the way down there. Funny, I've always hated bein stuck that close ta someone, but with Amanda . . . well, it was different.

They're waitin for us in the Hill Street playground. Against me arm I feel Amanda's tits movin through her top, she's breathin so fast with the excitement. She's been at me ta introduce her ta the gang for ages but it's only now the summer holidays are startin and I don't have the excuses a Charlie havin too much homework or Ma givin off if we stay out too late that I've hadta give in. It's all because a *Jackie* magazine. Amanda never useta bang on about meetin fellas till she started readin that trash.

Charlie looks us up and down. It's just himself and Damo. The Kavs are comin down later, but only if they can make time after football practice.

Under Charlie's gaze I feel meself goin scarlet. I tell meself it's on Amanda's account, not mine. After all, Damo's starin at her too, like he's never seen a young wan in his life. Amanda pulls herself up, stickin out her chest.

'Yeah, in anyways, this is Amanda.' I speak as fast as I can ta get it over with. 'Ya know, me pal from school. And Amanda, this is me cousin Charlie. And Damo.'

'Damo,' she says, purrin the word like a cat. I never heard her do that before. 'What's that short for?'

Damo goes scarlet. Charlie giggles, an awful sound, high-pitched, like a girl.

'Doesn't matter, Amanda,' I say, rougher than I need ta be. 'C'mon. Let's play, yeah?'

It was a disaster. The Kavs came down later and we made a show a bootin the ball around, bouncin it through the net someone had nailed up on the wall a the old tower. But we knew, me most of all, that a show was all it was. Amanda – sittin on a swing, danglin her legs, starin at the sky or her new watch, or pretendin ta read her

Jackie – made it different. She built walls between us: a wall between me and the lads and another wall between the lads who were tryin ta impress her and the ones that weren't. What coulda been a normal game had turned inta a battle for Amanda's attention, and me playin was just a sad way a provin I could fight that battle too.

At four a clock, she gets up, slidin herself off of the swing so slow her skirt gets caught on the edge, showin her big yella legs underneath. The Kavs keep playin. Damo misses a shot. Charlie rushes in, bounces the ball, flings it at me so hard, I hafta duck ta miss gettin me nose broke.

'Ya comin, Lucy?' says Amanda.

Charlie picks up the ball, bounces it a coupla times.

Amanda yawns, stretchin her arms over her head so we can all see the tiny tufts a blonde hair startin ta grow in her pits.

Charlie bounces again.

'Yeah, okay,' I say.

I walk her home. We say nothin. There's nothin ta say. She smells sweet – a sweat and somethin else that I can't make out.

'No,' says Charlie. 'I don't want her comin with us.'

'Ah, Charlie . . .' I say it more for form than anythin else. I'm feelin weird. Half-relieved, half-worried. I don't want her thinkin I don't want her round; even though I don't.

'She's too loud, Lucy. She'll give the game away, get the pigs onta us and all.'

'Loud? Whatcha mean, loud? I'm the one that's loud, Charlie.'

'She's worse. She's the loudest yoke I ever met. And she's always showin off.'

'Charlie, she's not. That's shite! She never joins in the games or nothin—'

I stop, realizin I've just fucked up me own argument.

'That's what I mean!' says Charlie, triumphant, pushin his glasses back on his nose. 'She never joins in when we're playin normal games, so what's the point bringin her down ta a rob, Lucy? In anyways this is the first one we've done in ages and I don't want her messin things up. Which she will.'

'I think she's alright,' says Damo. 'I'd give her one.'

'Did we ask bleedin you?' says Charlie. 'No, Lucy, she's not comin.'

I kick at a loose bit a footpath. I still don't know if I'm relieved or not.

After that, I hadta split me time between them. It felt all wrong, ta be cuttin meself up like that – one piece for Charlie and the lads, one for Amanda – but I hadta do it. I didn't wanta lose either a them; if I lost Charlie and the lads, I'd only be another girl and if I lost Amanda . . . well, I didn't wanta do that.

It was different ta the not-askin-Amanda-home thing. I was happy doin that because I didn't want her comin upta the flat and seein Granny half-asleep in bed or on the sofa or me Ma drinkin or anythin really. Don't get me wrong; I wasn't ashamed or anythin. I just wanted ta keep things separate. Same as when she asked me round ta hers, I always said no; it was enough just seein the outside of her house. I didn't wanta hafta spoil it by gettin ta know her ma or watchin them scrap or seein them gawk at the same telly programmes as we done on a Saturday night. Amanda understood. At least, she knew enough not ta ask me again after I'd said no enough times.

Later on, a course, I found out that she had her own reasons for not askin me back. Her ma had found out about me Da and Micko and warned her.

'She calls ya an element, Lucy,' says Amanda, breakin her hole laughin as she falls back onta the grass. 'You don't wanta hang round with that element, Amanda. That's what she said, I swear!'

I'da sorta liked it if Amanda and Charlie coulda got on better but Amanda didn't give a shit that Charlie didn't want her in the gang. Or so she said.

'Stick round that bunch a kids? No way, Lucy. I thought they were supposed ta be real fellas. They're only babies. That Charlie's the worst, pullin at me bra-strap and all. If ya think I wanta waste me time lookin at his spotty gob' – by now, Amanda, besides blossomin inta a princess, was startin ta get the hang a insultin people – 'ya wrong. I couldn't be bothered watchin their stupid games.'

Ah, Christmastime . . .

'Look.' Amanda grabs me sleeve, points out the winda a McDonald's. I finish slurpin me strawberry shake – lovely it is, thanks ta a cut a Ma's dole, lifted off of her bedside locker where it was lyin beside the stink a vodka first thing that mornin – and look out. Wanderin through the ILAC Shoppin Centre, jostled by the crowds rushin for their last-minute Christmas prezzies, are Charlie, Damo and the two Kavanagh brothers.

'That's yer cousin, isn't it?' says Amanda.

'Yeah.' Is she windin me up? 'And?'

'Yoo-hoo!' She waves out. Damo looks over, puzzled.

Morto, I bury me face in me fries. Through me fingers I see Damo go scarlet. He jogs Charlie, who, soon as he cops it's us, gets the same black look on his face he gets anytime he even hears Amanda's name.

'Jesus, Amanda,' I say. 'Thought ya said ya didn't wanta hang round with kids.'

'Ah well, a bit a company's better than nothin.'

Amanda smiles out at them – a big white perfect grin – and waves. Then I cop it. She wants someone ta share the joy of her new no-brace choppers.

The Kav brothers shake their heads and melt away from me cousin and Damo, who slope in under the golden arches towards us.

'Didn't know youse were on yer hollyers yet,' says Charlie, lookin everywhere except at Amanda.

'We're not, officially.' Amanda winks at him; another tip from the *Jackie*. 'See?' She pulls up her anorak ta show her school jacket underneath.

There's a silence.

'Mine's in me bag,' I say. 'Me uniform, I mean.' I pat the bag. 'I hate wearin that yoke. Give me jeans any day. Specially it's so cold outside. I mean, what do they want us ta do? Die a bleedin . . . eh . . . cold?'

I know I'm talkin shite, but anythin's better than that awful silence.

'We got our hollyers yesterday,' says Damo.

There's another silence. This time I can't be bothered fillin it in, so I just jig me knee up and down.

Amanda smiles at Charlie. He sighs, like he's so bored he could die. I slurp me shake, loud.

'Ya buyin yer prezzies today?' Amanda puckers her mouth round her straw and sucks. It looks like she's waitin for a goozer.

Charlie licks his lips, leans back on the plastic chair. 'If ya call it buyin.'

Amanda stops suckin. 'What?'

'We'll just hafta see what's on offer, eh, Damo?'

'Ah, stop playin the hard chaw, Charlie,' I say. 'They're goin liftin, Amanda.'

'Maybe liftin, maybe somethin a bit different,' says Charlie.

'Youse can't dip ta save yer lives,' I say. 'If me brothers were here . . .'

'Yeah, well, they're not, are they?'

'If they were, they'd show youse a thing or two. Fuckit, *I'd* show youse a thing or two.'

'Yeah?'

Amanda coughs. There's another long silence. Then –

'Them new glasses?' says Amanda, starin at Charlie's bright blue John Lennon frames.

Charlie goes scarlet.

'They're a present from his ma,' says Damo.

'Jesus,' says Amanda. 'Some prezzie. Could she not think a anythin nicer?'

Charlie goes even scarleter. Amanda sighs and sits back, blowin bubbles in her shake. I can't take any more a this.

'Alright then.' I stand up. 'Youse up for it?'

'What?' says Amanda.

'Prezzie-buyin.'

'What? Ya mean—?' She gets it and takes in a breath, all over-the-top shocked. 'But I've got me money with me, we don't need—'

'Doesn't matter.'

'Go on, the Lucy!' says Damo.

Charlie's eyes under his new frames are sharp. I feel them diggin inta me as we leave the McDonald's and go out onta Henry Street.

It's jammed, chock-a-block with mammies and kids, auld wans and nuns. We stop outside Arnotts.

'Happy huntin grounds, what?' says Charlie. 'Member we useta come here with Nayler and Micko and all?'

'We?' I say. 'Don't remember you bein dragged along too many times.'

Charlie glares at me, then turns back ta Amanda. 'Yeah, Nayler, this pal of ours, he useta get us ta rob stuff off the auld wans walkin past. Lucy was great at it, useta make it look like an accident and all.'

'Was? Still am.' It's a lie. Liftin's fine but I haven't dipped in years. I know I'd still be useless at the distractin and I hate the smell a them targets too close ta me, but no way am I gointa lose face in fronta me pal.

Amanda looks disbelievin. 'Oh, yeah?'

'Yeah,' I say. 'I'm a real pro at the dippin. Amn't I, Charlie?'

'Oh, yeah,' says Damo. 'She's the best.'

'Nayler useta call me twinkletoes cos I was so fast on the catch.' Amanda laughs. 'Don't believe ya.'

'What about all them sweets and make-up I rob for us, Amanda?'

'Yeah, well . . . that's different.'

'Ya right there.' I flash her a smile. I'm calm on the surface, so fuckin calm. But underneath, I'm buzzin.

Amanda looks worried all of a sudden. 'Lucy, ya don't hafta . . .'

'Don't mind.' Charlie pats Amanda on the shoulder like he's forgotten how much he hates her. 'She won't get caught.'

'I can't get inta trouble, though.' She's startin ta panic. 'Me ma will kill me and if she tells me da he will too and—'

At least you have a fuckin da, Amanda. I think but I don't say it. Instead I squeeze her arm. 'It'll be grand, don't worry.'

Then I spot her.

She's ancient, up from the country: big wide sunburnt face, bright yella rain mac, see-through plastic hat tied under the chin, brown suede booties with yella fur stickin up over the edges, orange tights half-crumplin down her legs. She's holdin a big stripey mala with everythin stickin out – plastic bags, handbag, specs, brolly, you name it.

'D'ya want me ta—' starts Damo.

'Nah, we'll be grand on our own. Keep sketch, Charlie.'

I slip inta the crowd. In the corner a me eye I see Charlie watchin, all geared up ta catch the bag. I slide up ta her, pushin past the mammies and their kids. She smells sour and rank, a lavender talc and piss, makes me feel sick. But I hold it together, reach for the bag. Ugh. Fake leather. Slimy. Holdin me breath, I tug the strap, real gentle, thinkin she's old, the waggon; I don't even need ta distract her, she won't feel a thing. But boy am I wrong.

Soon as I tug she jerks her head, looks at me and screams – a high horrible scream. It's that throws me off, forces the mistake, so insteada lettin go, I pull harder. She tugs back, screamin louder. I start ta panic.

Give it ta me ya auld bitch.

Charlie's at me elbow, grabbin me arm. 'Come on, Lucy, leg it, come fuckin on.'

The Christmas lights on the tree outside Arnotts are switchin on, switchin off, doin me head in. I know Charlie's right, I should let go, but between the switchin and the panic all I know is that I just want the one thing and that's to get the fuckin bag, wipe that scream off of that auld waggon's face so I can get away from her and her lavender stink, but I can't shift her and she won't stop yellin, and even though I'm pushin the bag at her now, pushin it in and outta her stupid chest, she still won't let go, and now I can't even hear Charlie, just see his mad eyes behind the new specs, glarin at me as the Christmas lights reflected in his lenses switch on and off, on and off.

And then it's too late.

This wasn't like the other times. No chance of a caution. The woman was pressin charges; I was up for assault – 'Ya shouldn'a hit her with that bag, Lucy,' says Charlie later, 'that's what done us in' – and they were already talkin about dates for the court.

The Juvenile Liaison looked on, all regretful like. Too late for regrets. We were in the system now, closed-off far as they were concerned.

We waited in the copshop an hour before Ma and Marlene and Stevo arrived.

The leather bench is hot under me legs. Sticky. I peel me hand away from it, finger by finger. Then I stick it back down. Then I peel it away again. Through the high winda I can see the auld wan. She's sittin outside at the desk holdin her fifty-millionth cuppa tea. She's breathin all funny and her sunburnt face is gone a lovely shade a plum. She keeps pressin her hand ta her chest, like she's tryin ta keep herself from explodin. Watchin her huff and pant and press, I don't feel sorry. I just wish she *would* explode, and that would sort out all our problems. The thought makes me laugh, but I force the laugh back because I don't wanta piss off the pigs, who are givin us the evil eye big-time.

One a them – a plainclothes Corkman with broken veins all over his face – must be psychic, because he looks over at me then. He stops talkin ta his buddy and comes over ta the winda. I starta get nervous on accounta he looks like a right prick, and the nerves make me giggle again, but this time I can't hold it back.

He comes inside and closes the door. Then he stands there, sayin nothin, just lookin at me. I'm gigglin even worse than before.

The Corkman lowers his face till his veined nose is right in fronta me eyes and stares at me. I keep gigglin. He keeps starin. I know what he's tryin ta do. In that stare is a message, a name tag he wants me ta wear the rest a me life. *You are a piece a filth, Lucy Dolan. You are scum.*

A course, I'd been gettin them kinds a looks ever since I could remember, but up till then I'd always been able ta shrug them off. This was different. Maybe it was because it was Christmas, when everyone's sposed ta be happy, or maybe it was just that the weighta all them looks from before had built up so high on me shoulders

184

that I couldn't store them there any more, and there was nowhere else for them ta go except in under me skin. And even though I fought it, sayin to meself under me breath, *I'm not fuckin scum. I'm not the fuckin problem here*, still . . . I couldn't keep that copper's message out. It found its way inta me blood, tellin me brain: *You are a piece a filth, Lucy Dolan. You are scum. I am a piece a filth. I am scum.*

I stop gigglin.

He straightens up.

'Don't let them out of your sight, missus,' says the Corkman.

Marlene smiles a big brave false smile and tosses her head so her earrings dangle like a wind chime. Ma throws her still-lit butt onta the ground.

She built up towards it on the bus home. Like a storm brewin beyond the horizons. I could smell the black clouds buildin up and I knew, fuck, yeah, who the rain would be pissin on.

'Ya little piece a shit!' she says, kickin at me with her muddy white stilettos. 'Nothin but a bleedin problem. You're even worse than yer fuckin brothers! Don't ya *fuckin* do somethin like that on me again, or let me tell ya—'

Kick. I'm down on the ground. Kick. The stiletto digs in me ribs. I start cryin, quiet. I duck me head so she won't see. I'm fucked if I'll let her see. Kick. Gets me on the chest.

'What's that, Rose?' says Granny from inside her room. Her voice is small and dry. 'What's happenin, Lucy?'

Kick. I move me chin away just in time. The white heel lands on thin air. She loses her balance, wobbles, half-falls, gets the balance back again. I grab me chance and scurry on me hands and knees down the hall, fast as I can.

'Lucy pet?'

'Don't you dare call her pet, Ma!'

The stilettos race after me. She grips me by the hair, yanks me head back, slaps me on the face, drops me ta the ground. That one on the face hurts most of all. Somethin snaps inside me and I start laughin, takin up the giggle from where I left off in the copshop, laughin so hard the echoes folla her all the way back ta the kitchen.

'Are ya okay, Lucy?' whispers Sam.

I reach up me hand and grab hers. She squeezes.

I'm sore but I'm not down. The pain's wore off, leavin only a cold knowin that me Ma will never ever break me.

As I lie there, I start wonderin what happened ta Amanda. She musta got away, her and Damo together. I don't mind . . . kinda. She wasn't inta doin it in the first place and she's a lot more ta lose than us, with her Ma bein sorta respectable. Why should she a stuck around, only ta get inta shite? But still, it bothers me.

Over Christmas they run a story in the tabloids, how I'd assaulted the auld doll. Child Mugger Ruins Pensioner's Xmas. I get Sam ta read it for me. I'd heard their lies before but Jesus . . . when they're about you, it's different.

I don't get ta say much in court. Marlene fixes everythin, her and this lawyer pal a Stevo's business partner. It's them get that hippie doctor on board. 'Call me Terence.' He's private, nothin ta do with the Health Board, paid for by Stevo; Ma woulda never a been able ta afford him. It's him does the tests on me and tells the judge I've a hyperactive thing goin on, and that explains why I get inta trouble and why I exert an undue influence over me cousin Charlie but it's not in me nature really and usually these things come down ta nutrition and the right balance a vitamins and minerals and often allergies are involved and there are some courses a treatment I can be put on, and judgin by the family history, ahem ahem, monitorin in the home environment over a significant period may well be more effective than detention and . . .

I look around the courtroom. It's way less excitin than how Micko useta make out. The floor is worn-lookin and the bright-coloured walls do nothin ta cheer it up. As I watch, I half-listen ta the lawyer and the judge, a kind-lookin woman with black hair, who frowns as they tell her about me gettin dizzy and jiggin up and down and not bein able ta stop and the amounta crips I eat and . . . yeah.

They didn't send me away but they put me on probation for a year and told Ma that the Probation Officer and the Social would check in with Dr Terence regular ta see how me treatment was goin and do a report for the court in a coupla months. Plus they'd get onta School Attendance Services and if I kept bunkin off like I done before, they'd definitely think about puttin me somewhere. I'd been half-wishin they woulda and I think Ma wanted it too. But she didn't show it in court – musta been Marlene on her back tellin her ta act all lovey-dovey towards me if she didn't wanta see Sam go next. And Jesus, did Ma act; tellin the judge she was doin her best, she'd always done her best, and with me brothers settin me a bad example, well, what else could she do? She even cried. All done up in her good suit, tears flowin like she'd no tomorra ta live.

Charlie got off because nobody actually seen him do anythin.

Jammy bastard.

That was the Christmas Amanda got sent down ta Cork ta be kept outta me way and came back rabbitin on about this gorgeous young fella she'd met at a funfair. Her first proper fella; a ride, she called him, even though all he done was give her French kisses and feel her tits.

That was the Christmas Ma cut down on the booze for the first time since me Da'd left.

That was the first Christmas was like a prison sentence for me. I stayed in, forced onta good behaviour because a the court loomin. I couldn't go anywhere without someone standin guard over me, watchin, wary, like I was four year old, so all I done in the end was fuck about in the flat and watch telly with Granny and Sam.

And that, Nayler, was the Christmas I became a bleedin woman.

II

'Ah, look, Lucy, look!'

I folla her over. That band A-ha are grinnin out at us from the poster inside the winda a Snips' Hair Salon that useta be Justine's.

'I love him.' Amanda's eyes are misty as she gazes at the lead singer. 'Neil looks like that, ya know, only blond.'

Neil, Neil, fuckin Neil. It's comin up ta summer again and she's still bangin on about the yoke she met in Cork. She's been sendin postcards to him and all, at the address he gave her, but no joy. I coulda told her, I did tell her, not ta waste her time chasin some lad who's probably forgot what she even looks like. He's a good bit older than her, she says – three, four year maybe – so I don't know why she'd even think he'd have any time for her. But Amanda's beyond persuadin. She's set up this Cork fucker as her knight in shinin armour; he's gointa come and get her one day. Every little feelin she has goes back ta him. If I tell her I've a sick stomach from eatin curry, she'll nod and go on about how she feels that way about him, all torn up inside. She thinks about him every night. What she wouldn't do ta hear the sounda his voice. I think deep down Amanda knows she's kiddin herself, he'll never come for her. But she doesn't wanta let go. Sometimes it's like she loves the pain a havin her heart broke more than anythin else in the world.

I feel left out. I can't get excited like her about him; despite a what she says about his lovely eyes and cool clothes and gorgeous strong arms – *like that fella in the 501 laundry ad, Lucy, only thinner* – he's probably rotten-lookin. And Jesus I feel so helpless while she cries to herself and I struggle ta say the right thing.

'Course he loves ya too.'

'Yeah, he's lost yer address, that's it.'

'Course he'll be back for you, don'tcha forget it.'

What I wouldn't give ta have the easy days back, when all I hadta think about was which shop me and Charlie was gointa ta rob next.

I'm not the best at comin out with what she wants ta hear and there's times I can't help lettin me true feelins come through. At them times Amanda goes all cold on me.

'What would you know, Lucy?' she says once. 'Ya never been in love.'

I'd love ta tell her, *Oh but I have*, but I can't. Because maybe she's right. Maybe I never loved anyone. Maybe the feelins I have don't count as love. Especially the feelins that come over me when I see Amanda lyin in front a me, belly on the grass, little red marks on the back of her legs from the creases of her skirt, her blouse opened up so the soft yella swell of her growin boobs peeks out at me.

That's not love, I tell meself. That's sick.

It's sick ta wanta reach out and hold her, stroke her hair, when she's sobbin over her missin Neil; sick ta wanta dive over and kiss her when she's laughin at some stupid joke I've made. Sick ta still wanta protect her when them bitches in school start their endless slaggin.

Sick ta be so happy that first day back in school after Christmas, when Amanda walked over ta me seat and plonked herself down, starin everyone out, includin the teacher, lettin us know, me too, that she wasn't gointa be scared off by what people said.

After school that day, Amanda took me arm and marched me past the rows a starin Goldilocks girls, down the driveway and onta the Drumcondra Road.

'Where are we goin?' I ask.

'Home.'

But this isn't our usual route. This is where the Goldilockses reign.

'Ah Jesus, Amanda. Maybe we should go the other way.'

'We're goin this way today, Lucy,' she says. 'And every day from now on.'

'Alright.' I'm tickled by her new-found courage. Besides, who knows? Might be fun ta take them bitches on in a scrap. God knows I could do with some action.

At Black's sweetshop we go in for some fags and sweets. I'm tempted ta nick a few packs a Marlboro while Johnny Black's back is turned, but Amanda slaps me hand just as I'm reachin out. 'Lucy! Ya lookin for trouble?'

Maybe I am, Amanda. 'No. Course not.'

We stop at Portland Row.

'See ya tomorra so,' I say.

'Lucy—' she says, then stops. She looks nervous. Why?

'Can I come up ta yours for a bit?'

'Mine?' The old anxiety starts. I don't want Amanda seein Ma drinkin cup after cup a tea ta stave off the drink.

'Yeah.'

'What for?'

She shivers. There's a wind blowin in from the east. I can tell it's vicious by the way it's hurlin the rubbish everywhere, but I can't feel the chill. Must be all them vitamins Dr Terence gave me ta help with the allergies.

'I've somethin ta tell ya,' says Amanda.

'Can't ya tell me now?'

She shakes her head.

'What about yer ma?'

'That's alright. I told her I've joined the swimmin club.'

'Swimmin?'

The wind gusts again. Amanda shivers. Her fingers are turnin blue. I start laughin.

'What?'

'Just, swimmin . . . in this cold and all.'

She starts laughin too.

When we get ta the flats, she looks up. 'Which one's yours?'

'There.' I point.

'We were up higher when we were in Ballymun.' She starts walkin.

'Where ya goin, Amanda?'

'Well, if ya not gointa ask me in ta meet yer ma, I'll hafta go on me own.'

★

Once I get her inside me bedroom, she shuts the door behind her and leans against it, her eyes closed. I'm glad a that. I don't want her seein the state a the place, with Sam's dollies everywhere and the sheets and blankets grubby where Ma hasn't bothered her hole takin them ta the wash.

'I'm in love.' She opens her eyes. 'Oh, Lucy, I'm in love.'

I don't think I ever seen Amanda look so beautiful as she done then.

There's a few cars waitin outside the gates. Far as I can make out we're the only ones that've come in a jo-maxi.

'There's Micko!' says Sam, and starts wavin.

He comes out the gate and walks up ta us slowish, like he's not bothered leavin the place. Sam jumps at him for a hug.

'Where's Ma?' says Micko. He sets Sam down on the ground and ruffles her hair.

'She's workin.' John Paul butts in before I can say anythin else. 'Here, bro.' He takes Micko's case off of him.

'Granny's in bed,' Sam tells Micko.

'Still sick? She alright?' Micko's question doesn't sound as worried as it should be.

John Paul shrugs.

A skinny lad same age as Micko – sixteen or so – comes outta the gate, carryin a plastic bag full a stuff. He's got a bright yella shirt on, like a tee-shirt only it's got a collar, and greasy hair slapped down onta his forehead. His arms are crawlin with tattoos.

'Eh, Dolo,' he calls over.

'Eh, Mainser,' calls Micko.

'Keep in touch, yeah, bud?' Mainser winks. John Paul stares at him. Mainser stares back. 'Alright there, pal?'

John Paul turns away and opens the door a the jo.

'Very la-di-dah,' says Micko as we get in. 'Work goin well so, John Paul?'

'Yeah, Micko,' says John Paul, climbin inta the front.

I look out the winda, see Mainser greetin two other lads. The jo takes off.

Sam's chatterin away, tellin Micko all about school and Lisa and some imaginary pal she's just met. Before he knows it, she'll be onta one of her stories from the comics. Micko feels very skinny beside me; like he's almost not there. I look down at his hands, stickin outta his sleeves. They're so small, like a doll's hands, too small for his sleeves. He's bitten his nails down ta the quick and the skin's a bluey-red colour. We go over a bump. The jolt throws us together, Sam on top a Micko, Micko on top a me.

'Wa-ho!' says the taxi driver. 'Sorry about that, folks.'

We slide back inta our seats but Micko stays a bit longer on me.

'So how's me best pal?' he whispers in me ear, and nudges me side.

I don't mind the nudge but I don't like the whisper. It reminds me a Uncle Tom and the way he useta try ta kiss us at Christmas. I shake him off.

'Alright.'

Granny stretches out her hand, feelin all over his scarred face. Her fingers tap, stroke, trace. When they reach his broken mouth, he jerks back.

'Ssssh,' she says. 'Sssssh.'

He quietens. She traces her fingers all over his lips, then between them, inta the gap where she pauses, for a second, before readin the black stumps of his teeth.

That's when he starts cryin.

He'd never let her read him like that before.

After John Paul goes off ta work, I sit up with Micko and we gas a bit. I sorta don't wanta – even though I know someone has ta keep him company – because I'm a bit awkward after seein him cry like that with Granny. But I'm half-thinkin it'll be fine, we'll have loads ta talk about. We haven't before, on the overnighters, but this'll be different. Won't it?

As the minutes tick by, I can see I'm only foolin meself. There's nothin ta say and too much time between us. I try talkin about the allergies and how Dr Terence told me ta stay off the milk and sugar and crips and how good I been feelin in the last coupla weeks. But he keeps driftin off when I start – worse than Sam – like he wants ta be anywhere but home.

I'm not sayin this is a surprise. I'd seen him change over them last two years. But I suppose I didn't suss it, how much I was holdin onta the hope that it wasn't Micko changin, it was only been sent away made him seem different.

I'm in the middle a tellin him yet again how Ma's fortune-tellin's been goin brutal what with all them new horoscope phone lines, when he leans across the table, interruptin.

'How's Nayler?' It's the first question he's asked all night.

I'm surprised. 'Fuck . . . how'd I know?'

'He legged it from his auntie's, ya know. Been roamin round a good while now.'

'Oh . . . okay. He hasn't been back here though.' I shrug like it doesn't matter, but inside I'm thinkin how mad it is that ya haven't crossed me mind in so long.

When I get up for bed, he stays where he is, waitin, the glass a Jameson I've poured for him only barely touched.

He waited a long time. Ma didn't come back till the mornin.

The glasshouse is enormous. Inside, the green frills and spikes a jungle plants poke at the misty windas like they're tryin ta break through.

'Why's it all foggy?' I ask.

'The heat, ya eejit,' says Amanda. 'They hafta keep it warm cos it's tropical trees and all.'

I hate her doin that. Calling me an eejit. How'm I ta know about heat and trees and all when I never been in the Botanical Gardens before in me life?

We're on the mitch, as usual. We hadn't planned ta come upta the Gardens but, after an hour or so lazin round Tolka Park, Amanda thought it'd make a nice change.

In the glasshouse we walk through the trees, starin up at the banana plants. The heat makes me feel sick and the smell is too much; sweet but pukey at the same time, like perfume on a sweaty woman. Amanda says there's an outside garden with bridges and rivers and stuff, so we jaunt round that for a while, then lie down on the grass and watch the water lilies and the flies hummin across the river.

'Hate that!' Amanda slaps her leg.

She shows me the bite. It's huge, the size of a 5p coin.

'Ah, ya poor thing. Poor little Amanda.'

'Leave off.'

The heat's makin her cranky. I like her when she's like that. She's like a big cat, soft but ready ta lash out at the same time.

'Pity I'm not . . . Neil,' I say, still slaggin. She's stopped goin on about lover boy as much, so I reckon it's safe enough ta tease her about him. 'Or I could . . . kiss it better.'

I tickle her leg with a blade a grass.

'Ow! Leave it.'

'Poor little Amanda.' I make me voice go all deep like a fella's. 'D'ya want me ta kiss it better, love?'

I purse me lips and wriggle me fingers, disgustin, like a pervert's.

'Jesus, Lucy! Leave it!'

I tickle her again. She squeals.

'Give us a kissy kiss, Amanda love. Ya know I'm gaggin for ya.' I hoist meself onta her, still ticklin. She pushes me away. I force meself closer, me mouth all pursed up.

'Agh! Get away!'

She grabs me shoulders, still tryin ta shake me off. I force me mouth, still pursed, onta hers. She jerks her face away, scrunchin her eyes shut.

'That's disgustin!'

I roll off her.

She starts gigglin. I feel her gigglin, beside me, soft and warm and heavy, heavin up and down. Her hand is touchin mine. I keep as still as I can, feelin her skin next ta mine, willin the moment ta last.

It starts half-way down the canal. An itchin between me shoulder blades. Like that poem Derek read me:

By the prickin a me thumbs
Somethin wicked this way comes.

Easy ta be wise after the event.

It's very hot. And still. The towpath is bendy with fake pools a water. The scutty trees creak in their cages. Amanda slouches along beside me, but I'm refreshed now I'm on the move again. I'm skippin like a pro.

Easy ta be wise after the event, but I feel it, I swear I feel it, half-way down the canal, and the feelin just grows as we get closer ta the bridge.

Someone's lyin on the grass. No, not one. Two people, both blond. It's the blond takes me by surprise, the blond throws me off. One a the heads lifts, turns. An arm waves.

'Is that yer brother?' says Amanda.

'Yeah. I think.'

Except what's Micko doin out in the sun? Micko's never in the sun. He keeps himself locked up, inside the sittin room where he sleeps on the sofa, or in the kitchen, or in Granny's room, where he talks to her for hours about this and that in a low voice I can't hear, no matter how close I press me ear upta the door. Apart from that, he spends his days watchin telly, starin at the ceilin, countin sheep. He only ever slopes out at night and then I've no idea where he goes.

'Jesus!' says Amanda, under her breath.

Her warm heavy body, still close ta mine, starts tremblin.

'What, Amanda? Is it Micko?' She's never had a problem with Micko before. She hasn't ever talked much ta him any time she's come ta the flat, and she doesn't say much about him ta me, but I know Amanda. She'd tell me if there was a problem.

She shakes her head, unable ta speak.

'What then?'

Tears start inta her eyes. Still confused, I go ta comfort her, and then I realize they're not sad tears but happy ones.

'Neil!' she calls. 'Neil! I'm over here!'

*

Ya may think it's stupid but I've spent years dreamin that it was different. That meetin up with ya after all that time wasn't the normal thing it turned ta be, but somethin wilder, full a the fight that's always been between us.

In me dream, ya don't rise easily ta yer feet, strange in yer new height and widened shoulders; all grown up in yer faded jeans and green combat jacket, yer bleach-job sittin wrong on yer narrow pale face, yer features stretched nearly outta recognition, the bones under yer eyes sharp as knives, and look us both up and down – a smooth approvin gander over Amanda's tits and legs, a quick flick over ta me that stops on me face and holds there, glued, before draggin itself away ta take in the rest a me, then land, only for a second this time, back on me face.

Ya don't break that look with a crooked smile and say, yer voice lazy with the flagons ya been knockin back, 'Well, hello, ladies,' glancin over at Micko, yer mouth still curled, as if ta say, *That's a nice pair a cunts. I could ride them.*

Ya don't twist back, lunge in, go ta dig me in the side like that look, that glance, that curl never happened – only I pull away so ya ruffle me hair instead – and say, 'Hey, Lucy Lu, still the madser, what?', ignorin me blank look as I try ta match up Neil, Amanda's Prince Charmin, the funfair romeo, with me brother's best pal and me own one-time hero.

Ya don't turn, smooth, ta Amanda, and lie through yer teeth – 'Amanda? Course I remember ya, darlin!' – as, unable ta hold back the tears, she steps up ta ya, glowin.

No, in this dream a mine this is how it goes . . .

You step up ta me and I step up ta you. Ya look me in the face, then up and down, then back at me face. That's the only thing the same as that day on the canal; that look and the colours: bleached blond; black; dusty blue; combat green.

Everythin else about ya is gone ugly, rotten-lookin like a night-mare. Yer skin is yella. Red rims round yer eyes. Ya scrawny. Ya stink a sweat and fags and sugar and cheese and onion crips. There's a hole in yer front tooth. Yer hair drips with grease.

I spit at ya. 'Scumbag,' I say. Ya laugh. I say it again, till the air between us grows thick and spiky, darin one of us ta break it.

It's always you that does it. Ya push me on the shoulder.

Then we start shovin, one at the other, forcin ourselves through the spikes between us till horns is locked. Stags in the grass. Dogs in the ring. We push, break, lock again, drivin each other across the ring, darin each other ta break. Until one of us springs sudden, hackin on the other with claw and tooth, drawin blood, and then the fight turns nasty. Snarl knock tear stagger fall gash pounce. We seize and shake each other up against the limits a that ring of ours, rippin ears, slashin muzzles, gnawin at the soft underbellies, usin claw and tooth ta blind, maim, hobble, kill.

It doesn't always folla the same course, this fight of ours. Sometimes Amanda's there, but only ta stop us, run screamin from one ta the other. Sometimes it ends with you the winner, holdin me down with yer manky arms, laughin and dribblin spit inta me eye as I bleed ta death on the grass. Sometimes it's me who wins, and you're the one gaspin on the ground while I kick kick kick the livin daylights outta ya, pulpin yer ugly features inta an even uglier mess.

The things that change don't matter. All that matters is we fight.

But is it back then it takes place, or here, high up in the mountains, Nayler? Because I don't see why I woulda called ya a scumbag back then.

I sit in the shade, watchin Amanda dippin her feet inta the canal. She keeps gaspin and oohin even though she must be well useta the cold by now. It's all for show, a course. Because she's not sure if we should still be hangin round now the initial chat's over but she doesn't want ta head either in case . . . well.

I get that itch again on me back, like someone's lookin at me, but when I take a gander at you and Micko behind me on the ridge the two a youse are deep in chat, low but easy, like me and Amanda aren't even there. Words drift towards me. I get some; not all. That's okay. I can work out what's missin.

'Good behaviour.' Micko laughs. 'Good bleedin behaviour.'

Ya wink. 'Ya hafta know how ta play the game, pal.'

Micko laughs again. It sounds like a cough at first, then trickles off inta nothin.

Ya look at him, yer eyes hidden. Then ya pass him a fag. 'Ya wouldn'a been inta it.'

He takes the fag. 'Yeah?'

'All that muckin about on a fuckin bog. Brutal.'

'Spose.' He lights up. 'But what about, ya know . . . after?'

Ya take a drag off yer own fag. 'After?'

'On yer travels. Ya musta met a few players, learnta few tricks.'

'Yeah, well . . .' Ya shrug. 'Ya wouldn'a been inta it, pal.'

There's a silence. Then he laughs. 'Ya cunt.' He digs ya in the side. 'Bet all ya done was fuck around on them bleedin dodgems.'

Ya laugh, raise the flagon, lift yer face towards the sun.

Was that the closest ya ever came ta tellin him how sorry ya were for leavin him? The closest he came ta acceptin the apology?

Amanda turns round. 'Lucy . . .'

'C'mon, Nayler,' says Micko, and gets up.

Youse leave without a backwards glance. I hafta walk Amanda home and listen ta her gab gab gab all the way.

When I get in youse are sittin round the kitchen table like the Brady Bunch. Ma's even got scones in, on a special blue-pattern plate she musta borrowed off of Missus Devlin.

'And how was – where didja say ya were again, son?'

'Ah, nowhere in particular, Missus Dolan,' ya say. 'Here and there. Hard ta keep track.'

'He was in Cork, Ma,' says Micko, 'livin in Mayfield where they talk mad.' He smiles, jiggin his legs.

I sit down with a bang and grab a scone.

Ma ignores Micko and me both. 'Yeah, I know whatcha mean, son. It *is* hard ta keep track.' She's searchin yer face with her eyes like she's tryin ta find somethin.

'Busy times, Missus Dolan.' You're as polite and innocent as ever.

'Oh, yeah. Tell me about it!'

'Ya still at yer fortunes?'

She laughs. 'Bits and bobs for whoever'll have me.'

'I'm sure there's plenty that'll have ya.' You're serious. Ya don't mean it in a bad way, like with a double meanin.

'Thanks, son.' She smiles. There's a silence. Then –

'Is he still here?' calls Granny from her room, soundin more awake than she has in months.

Ma sighs. 'Jesus, not again.'

Ya start jiggin yer legs in their frayed jeans under the table. You and Micko are like wind-up toys, jiggin together.

'Is he?' roars Granny.

'It's only Nayler, Granny,' I shout. 'Micko's old pal.'

'Oh, I know who it is,' calls Granny. 'Tell him ta go, Rose. There's no room here.'

'D'ya want more tea, son?' says Ma.

'Ah no, Missus Dolan, I'm—'

'Here, Lucy, pass the tea, willya?'

I lift the pot and pour a cupful for meself before pushin it over ta you. Then I take the milk and pour half a the jug in me cup and stick two lumps a sugar in for good measure. Sam kicks me but I ignore her. Ma half-sees what I'm doin, but she's too wrapped up talkin ta ya ta pay any heed ta the fact I've just broken Dr Terence's rules.

Ya say somethin low and Ma laughs.

'Well, like I said ta Therese Devlin, I said, well, I love the boys, Therese. And she says – well, Rose, the boys love you and all!'

She laughs again. Micko scrapes his chair back. Ya glance at him, scrape back too.

'Oh, ya goin already?'

'Yeah, Ma,' says Micko. 'Got some calls ta make.'

She goes ta get up.

'Ah no, Missus Dolan,' ya say, 'it's alright. We can see ourselves out.'

She smiles a small smile. 'Ya shoulda stayed in touch.'

'Is he gone yet?' calls Granny. 'Tell him ta leave. There's no room for him here.'

From the balcony I watch youse head down the stairs. Ya have a willa stick with ya – is it the same willa stick as before, that ya useta wear as a boy? I can't tell – and ya keep lashin it against the railins. Micko's talkin, nineteen ta the dozen. Ya nod. I can't hear what he's sayin but I haven't seen him chat as much ta anyone except Granny since he's come out.

As I walk back inside, past Granny's door, I hear a thump. I go in. She's strugglin up outta bed. Her ma's photo lies on the floor.

'Get back there, Granny. Get back in bed.'

She shakes her head, pushin against me as I try ta force her ta lie down.

'No, no, no. I've done enough lyin around. I should get up now.'

'Sam!' I call. I try ta push her again but there's no use.

'Be easy,' says Granny, like I'm a kid again. 'Lucy, for God's sake stay easy.'

Then she stops strugglin. I let her go. The room is gone awful cold. She sighs and holds tight onta me hand.

'Ah, Lucy, Lucy.'

I normally don't ask her what she sees when she's down there, among the dead fish and the lost villages and the chalkin bones a the ocean, but she's actin so odd, lashin out at ya the way she never done when ya were a kid, and I'm so sure there's somethin real she's seein that I woulda asked her, yes I woulda, except –

Except then Sam came in and the cold melted away, just like that, and all that was left was the blood drainin onta me hand from Granny's stigmata.

Granny sits on her chair. Sam sits on the arm and puts her thumb in her mouth like she's still a baby. Granny puts her hand on Sam's back and nods. Rockabye baby on a tree top.

Funny thing, Nayler; even though Granny had been gettin quiet before then, that day you came back was the last I remember her bein ever so strong or sure in herself.

Question one. Does it make me thick, that I didn't put things together – Amanda's stories and you? Thick that I didn't spot the match between the names, the colour a the eyes?

Question two. Does it make me more thick that when we met, I thought things'd be the same?

Same as what, Lucy? Me bein left out in the cold while you and Micko done yer grown-up jobs for Snags? Cop on. Get real. There was no mad connection between us when we were kids. That's just a dream I been holdin onta ta make sense of everythin.

But there was somethin different in ya when ya came back. Not just on the surface; the way ya talked, teased, swaggered. Somethin deeper. Some might say that was the badness, startin ta take ya over, and maybe it was bein away done that to ya; the borstal, the bogland, the . . . *after*. Granny would probably say ya didn't need an after ta make ya bad because ya were born that way. But I don't know if anyone is born bad, nor good either. I'd like ta think everyone has a choice, whether they know it or not. Ya might think that's mad, seein what I've done: ya might think I'd prefer there was no choosin. But I don't.

So what shaped ya, Nayler, them years ya were away, gettin holda yer heart so the darkness in ya grew bigger than all the rest? Was it the gear? Or did the gear only come after, ta help ya deal with the dark?

In the mirror, we look like Laurel and Hardy. She's been growin non-stop the last year but I'm still runty and with me hair and jeans the way they are, I look more like her little brother than her pal.

'Do I look alright?' She turns, lookin at her arse. In her purple jeans it's stickin out, the way I like it.

'Yeah.'

She runs her tongue round her lips, wettin the lip gloss even more. Strawberry. I can smell it from where I'm standin.

'Lookit, Amanda. I don't think it's such a good idea—'

'Jesus, Lucy!' She's usin that voice that makes her sound more like Ma than herself. 'I'm only bein friendly.'

Yeah, but he doesn't want ya bein friendly, Amanda. He thinks you're just a kid, you and me both. He's got his own pals, probably his own mot even, so why the fuck he'd want some young wan barely on her first jam-rag is beyond understandin. Cop on, Amanda. Don't build yerself up like that.

She pulls at the corner a her eye ta do the eyeliner. Her green eyeshada sparkles. It looks wrong on her yella skin. I know nothin about make-up but I can see that. Her boobs stick up and out under her tee-shirt with the cut-off arms. She got a Madonna crucifix the other day ta look mean and dirty, ta look cool like you with yer bleached punk hair and torn jeans, but on her it looks like somethin from her confirmation.

'Alright?' she says.

She's tremblin. Like the skeleton a that dog we seen the week earlier, in the museum they made us visit with the school. The bones shivered each time anyone went past the box. Ya wouldn't even hafta knock on the glass ta make it happen.

I wanta hold her hand and squeeze it.

'Ya look lovely,' I tell her. 'Like a model.'

On our way up we bump inta Charlie and Damo, dossin round on Charles Street with a football. Charlie goes scarlet when he sees Amanda.

'Look what the cat dragged up,' she says. He goes even scarleter.

'Howaya, Lucy?' says Damo.

'Grand, pal.'

'Ya wanta play some football?' He's clearly not seein that me and Amanda are off somewhere special. Amanda pulls at me arm.

'No, Damo,' I say. 'We're off.'

'Where yiz goin?'

'They're goin on the game,' says Charlie. 'Ta sell their gees.'

I laugh. Amanda drags me harder. 'Jesus, Lucy, we can't hang round all day. We'll be late.'

Charlie throws Damo the ball and saunters up behind us.

'Late for what, Amanda? Late for yer customers?'

Amanda tuts like she's seventy not thirteen. 'Jesus!'

'We're goin up ta Nayler's.'

I say it just ta be rid a him. I know Charlie still hates ya. All that tormentin ya done on him when he was a kid had ta go somewhere.

'Oh yeah?' I can tell from the look in his eyes he's thinkin hard. 'We'll come up too, so.'

'Ya will on yer hole,' says Amanda.

'Leave it, Amanda.' I'm feelin awkward enough as it is but if Amanda slags Charlie off more he'll come deffo, just for spite, and Jesus knows how you'll take that – the Beano Kids all lined up in a row on yer doorstep.

'Comin, Damo?' says Charlie.

Damo nods, up for anythin.

Just as I feared. I feel like punchin Amanda.

There's kids playin outside the Father Scully flats, and in the park on the Square we can hear sounds a more kids, thumpin balls, slaggin each other, chasin. It's not dark yet but the shadas from the west side are already startin ta pour across the park.

'Ya sure he lives in this one?' Amanda's gettin anxious now.

Charlie mumbles somethin under his breath and Damo laughs.

'Course I'm sure.' I'm vexed all of a sudden. With Amanda, even more with the lads. 'He's me brother's best pal, isn't he, and I know where me brother gets ta.'

The tall Georgian door useta be green, but the paint's all flaked off, showin bits a wood underneath, the colour of an auld wan's skin. There's a knocker, brass once but now black with age and half-hangin off the door. The tall windas on the ground floor are boarded up with corrugated iron and the not-so-tall first-floor windas have cardboard on them. The short ones on the second floor are covered with long dirty lace curtains, while the tiny ones on the attic floor have nothin in fronta their broken panes. I bang the knocker. It feels manky – all slimy and cold, like somethin dead.

No reply.

'Try again,' says Amanda.

I try harder.

'There's no one there,' says Charlie.

'Fuck off, Charlie,' I say. I press me ear close ta the door. The flakin paint is warm on me skin. I close me eyes, listenin.

'Why d'youse wanta come up here in anyways?' says Damo ta Amanda.

'Why d'you wanta know?' I can't see Amanda but I know she's talkin ta Charlie, not Damo. And in the same way I know Charlie's goin scarlet again.

'Ssshh,' I say.

Behind the wood, like underwater, is the sound a people laughin and talkin. I bang again with the slimy knocker.

'Call him.' Amanda digs me in the back.

'No way!' I hafta draw the line somewhere. No way am I gointa make a show a meself like that, callin for ya, so the whole bleedin Square will hear.

Amanda kicks the crumblin step.

'Fuck this, let's go play the arcades.' Charlie glances over at Amanda. 'Yeah?'

I wait. I know what I wanta do but this is me pal's call.

Amanda looks up, blinks the tears away, flicks her hair back off her face.

'Yeah, Charlie.' She smiles at him. Must be the first time she's smiled at him in ages. He lights up, scarlet again, but in a different way ta before. 'Come on, Lucy.'

In the arcade we play Mario and pinball. The lights flash red green orange, like traffic signals, all three colours at the same time. It starts doin me head in, so I reach inta me pocket for Dr Terence's vitamins. Amanda's standin wedged close ta Charlie; he's at her side, his hip angled sorta round hers, and the hand that isn't playin the pinball is floatin round her arse, like he wants ta touch her but doesn't dare. Damo's standin at the Mario, his head juttin forward like a bull's, his jaw tight, swearin every time he loses a life. He looks angry. Mad. Damo never looks angry. Charlie lets his hand drift closer ta Amanda. Just then she moves, knockin him in the bollocks with her elbow. Charlie bends over, gaspin. 'Ah, Jesus!'

Amanda stands there, lookin at him. The gap between him bent over and her lookin could be ten miles wide.

I laugh, but only ta meself so the others won't hear, and I leave

Dr Terence's vitamins in me pocket, lettin me mind sail inta the flashin lights ta spin and duck and dive there like a plastic bag caught in the branches of a tree.

Later on, I go back there on me own. No reason, really. Just . . . wanted ta. I look up inta the second-floor winda. Shadas play against the filthy curtains. Light flickers. Candles.

The winda opens.

'Watch it, kiddos,' calls a voice.

Ya pay no heed. Ya stick yer head out the winda and gulp in long breaths a fresh air. A blond skinhead ducks under the sash and up ta meet ya. Micko. His face is light blue, what with the moon and streetlights and all, but yours is a yella rectangle sliced down the middle with the black shada of yer Mohawk. Ya scrunch yer arm out from under the sash, lift a fag butt ta yer mouth. Ya skinny as Micko, but wiry, stronger-lookin. Shadas dance along yer arm, makin the muscles look like steel cables. Ya pass the butt ta Micko. He takes a drag.

'Lads, lads,' calls the voice behind the winda.

Micko hands ya the butt. Ya inhale, drop the butt so it falls, winkin red, ta the ground. Micko ducks back inside. Ya raise yer face sudden, like a dog hearin a whistle in the distance. I push meself closer inta the shadas a the railins. Ya drop yer face, melt back in under the windasash. The winda closes.

The red letters on the corrugated iron covers a the lower windas look black. I only know the S and the O, but I seen them like that enough times to guess what they say – somethinS Out.

Some things happen sudden. They build and build but all under the surface, so when they do happen, it's like a bomb goin off. Other things slip ya by. Me Da's leavin, that last time – that was a bomb. But I couldn't say I noticed when Micko moved out for good. Because he was always stayin over in yer gaff, or somewhere else, or sleepin in so long he might as well not a been home at all. In the end Ma made more a John Paul leavin than she did a Micko.

Sam said there was one night when Micko went out that he

turned round ta face us, and Ma looked at him and he looked at her and, Sam said, that was the time he went for good. She told me it was on accounta John Paul.

'What?' I said.

'They had a fight, see, shoutin at each other. John Paul said Micko was dirt.'

I couldn't remember any fight. 'Stop tellin lies, Mouse.'

But then I got ta thinkin of how moody John Paul useta get when ya came up ta the flat and that maybe Sam wasn't tellin lies after all.

'Ya might wanta think twice about comin up here so often,' says John Paul. He's standin in fronta the doorway, his hand against the frame ta block yer way.

'What?' ya say.

Micko laughs, a weak sound that tails off inta a girly sorta giggle.

'I know we're old pals and all, Nayler,' says John Paul, 'but I don't want that sorta shite round the gaff, yeah?'

'What sorta shite?'

'Whatcha been sellin.'

'I'm not sellin anythin.'

'Don't fuckin . . .' John Paul looks at Micko, trails off.

'I said, I'm not sellin anythin,' ya say. 'In anyways, sorry if I'm talkin outta turn but if yer ma has no problems with me callin up, why should you?'

'Ma knows fuckin nothin.'

'I don't think you do neither.'

'I know enough.'

'C'mon, Nayler.' Micko pulls at ya sleeve. 'Let's leave it, yeah?'

'C'mon, nothin. So what *do* ya know, John Paul? Somethin yer granny mighta heard in her sleep, is it? Or no, let me think, must be yer psycho boss tellin ya lies.'

'At least my boss doesn't set up kids ta take the flak meant for him or his blood.'

A pause; not even a second. Then you're on him again. 'No, John Paul. That's right. He just keeps them bent when they wanta go straight. We all know about that warehouse job a yours, John Paul. So-called security guard. If yer ma only knew . . .'

'Yeah,' says Micko. 'Just because ya not stickin yer fingers in the pie, John Paul, doesn't mean Wacker isn't bakin it right under yer nose.'

'So ya not denyin it then, Nayler?' says John Paul, ignorin Micko. 'Youse were set up that time.'

'C'mon, Nayler,' says Micko. 'Leave it.'

Ya shake him off. 'Know what, John Paul? Ya shouldn't believe everythin ya hear. We made a mistake – me and yer brother here – we paid for it. No big deal.'

'Ah, don't piss me around, Nayler—' says John Paul.

And then youse hear her comin up the steps, lumberin under her bags a shoppin.

Ya look at John Paul, darin him ta take it further. He stares back a minute but in the end he drops his eyes and turns back inta the flat.

'Well, hello, Missus Dolan,' ya say.

'Ah, hello there, son. Will yiz stay for a cuppa tea?'

'No,' says Micko before ya can reply. He spits over the stairwell. 'Better be off.'

So many holes ta patch. So many things ta remember or imagine or – what's that word Derek uses for Sherlock Holmes? – deduce.

'I have it worked out, Missus Dolan,' says Tara O'Keeffe, spread over the sofa like Jabba the Hut, fat ringed hands smoothin the curve of her baby-blue sweatshirted belly. 'Ya see, I can get the unmarried mothers' allowance and they'll give me a flat out by Bayside as long as they don't know about John Paul. But he can stay over mosta the time. And if they double-check, well, we can always say he isn't the father.'

Tara has a mad way a sayin 'father': flat and squashed. It's on account of her ma comes from the Naul, out past Swords.

John Paul nods. He's got one arm round Tara's shoulders, cradlin her. His hand hangs down over her chest, the stubby fingers danglin like a pack a Denny's sausages.

Knocknocknocknocknocknocknocknocknocknocknocknocknoc-
knock. Jesus. Sound's makin me sick. She's drummin her knuckles
together again. It's this thing she's got inta lately; me Granny, who
useta have all the calm a the world inside a her, turnin jiggy in her
old age. Wish she'd stop it. I jog me feet, clack me own teeth
together, tryin ta drown out the sounda the bones.

Sam puts her hand on me arm, shushin me. I feel like tellin her
ta shove her 'sshh' up her hole, I'm so wound up. It's been a while
since I stopped takin Dr Terence's vitamins. I'm not off them altogether – still take a few before he checks up – but I've hidden the
rest inside John Paul's old boxin gloves. I'm more hyper now than
I was before, but I don't care. Way too much hassle takin them
pills and stayin off the sugar and I hated feelin so hot all the time.
Sides, I haven't had a dizzy spell or a fit in months.

The telly flickers. I zap it louder.

'Jesus, Lucy!' Ma knocks the zapper outta me hand. 'We're tryin
ta have a conversation here.' She turns back ta John Paul. 'It's time
you moved out in anyways, son.'

'Ah, no, Ma,' says John Paul. 'I'm not leavin yiz. I'll be fetchin
up here mosta the time what with me workin nights and all.'

Tara nods. Her pursed lips look like a pig's hole. 'Yeah, he's got
the graveyard shifts on at the warehouse so it makes sense.
Overtime, ya know. See, Missus Dolan, we got it all worked out.'

Ma raises her eyebrows. 'Fine,' she says, blowin out blue fag breath.

I zap the telly louder. Some music programme comes on. Talkin
Heads. 'We're on the Road ta Nowhere'.

'Can *some*body tell me what they think the poem means?'

A finger digs in me back.

'*Anybody?*'

I curl me left hand behind me back, grab the note.

'Lucy Dolan, please pay attention.'

I stare back at the teacher, add in some attitude for good measure.
No point actin well-behaved or she'll know somethin's up.

One a the Goldilockses half-way up the front puts their hand up.
'Yes?'

I slip the note under me copy and while the teacher is chattin ta the Goldilocks, unfold it. I sorta recognize Amanda's writin, so I edge it towards Jessie Hegarty and nudge her. She reads it, then goes 'Cool' under her breath.

'What?' I whisper.

She ducks her head down, pretendin ta take notes off of the blackboard. 'Amanda's got a free gaff tomorra night.'

I sneak a glance over at Amanda, over on the honours side a the English class. She makes her face inta a question. I give her the thumbs up.

'Thought ya said they were kids.'

'Yeah, well, they're fellas, aren't they?'

'Charlie and Amanda up a tree, K – I – S – S – I – N – G –'

'Fuck off. Not like that.'

Somethin in her voice makes me stay quiet. We walk a few more steps in silence.

'Me ma has liqueurs left over from Christmas.'

'What's liqueurs?'

'They're lovely. Sweet, ya know, like orange juice, butcha can get knocked off yer head on them real easy.'

'Ah . . . good.'

She flicks her hair over her shoulder. She got it cut the other day, feathery. It's not bad but I preferred it the way it was before.

'You can bring yer brother if ya want.'

'Who – John Paul?'

'No!'

'Micko?'

Swish swish swish goes the sound a her thighs, rubbin against each other under her blue skirt. I can see the lines of her knickers through the skirt.

'Thought ya didn't fancy *him* any more.'

'Jesus, no! Who said I did?'

'It's just why'dya want Micko up if—'

'Jesus, Lucy.' She goes a bit scarlet. 'He can get . . . stuff, can't he?'

I force meself not ta laugh. Since when does Amanda – who rolls up her eyes any time I offer her a joint cobbled together from whatever I can dip from Micko's pockets – care about stuff?

'Yeah, well, maybe he can, but he's not gointa give it out for free.'

'Who said anythin about free?'

She stops swishin and turns, so sudden she gives me no warnin and I crash inta her. We stand like that on top of each other, tryin ta stare each other out. Her lips are at the same level as me eyes so I hafta crook me head back ta really get her.

'*Stuff!*' I say at last, and push her off. She laughs. We play tag all the the way home.

I fuckin hate this. I fuckin hate this. I fuckin hate this.

The dirty black brass flap a the letterbox lifts. I don't look down but I can picture the eyes, lookin out. The flap falls.

The door opens, creakin back on its rusty red hinge.

'Sorry, Micko, but—'

He pushes me inside. 'What the fuck ya doin here?' He's not very steady on his feet and his eyes are pinned. The pinnin makes them look real blue.

'What's the story, Micko?' ya call, from somewhere up in the heights a the house.

'Just Lucy, pal,' says Micko, slurrin.

'Lucy Lu!' ya say, the words bouncin off the high ceilins and flakin walls. 'Me own little errant girl, what?'

'Hiya, Nayler.'

I fuckin hate this. I'm scarlet and I don't wanta be. I wanta be anywhere but this gaff.

Ya come down the stairs ta meet us, slidin down the banisters as we walk up. Micko has me hand tight in his. His skin is wet, slippery. The long winda at the top a the first landin is covered over with green shadas from a tree growin out the back.

The house smells wrong, a mould and rot. Sweet, but not right.

'Thought ya'd never make it,' ya say. Ya got a black tee-shirt on, with red writin on it like drippin candles, and a belt with studs like them old-style punks useta wear. Jesus, who d'ya think ya are, Billy Idol?

I'm just about ta say that except then ya catch me lookin at yer belt and give me a real sly look, like I'm eyein ya up or somethin – as *if* – and then I go even more scarlet. This is fuckin horrible. I feel like Charlie round Amanda. I feel thick.

'So . . .' Yer eyes aren't pinned. They're black as ever. 'Want the guided tour?'

I jut me chin out. 'Yeah, sure.'

Micko raises a hand, as if ta stop us. 'No, I'm fine,' I tell him. 'I been wantin ta look round for ages.' The words give me back some courage. 'Just had ta pick me right moment, what?'

'Course ya did. Perfect timin, Lucy Lu.' Ya smile, real friendly, but then ya look at Micko and wink, in that wink *nice cunt I could ride her*, and I can see youse are gearin up ta take the piss again just like when I was a kid, only worse.

Me skin prickles. Fuck off with yer manky thoughts. I'm a match for either a youse. I jut me chin out even more. 'Ya ready?'

'So that's it, Lucy Lu. Oh. Exceptin . . .'

I folla ya down the hallway.

'We don't go down here much.' Ya open a small door near the back. A bad smell drifts up, worse than the stink in the hall. This smells like somethin dead.

'Go on.' Ya darin me again.

I look down. More steps. Some are broken, some missin. Ya take a candle outta yer pocket and light it. Then ya hold it under ya face and say, all English-soundin, 'After you, madam.'

I start walkin down, half-expectin ya ta blow out the candle and run off, leavin me ta rot away with all the other dead things. I hafta lean against the wall for balance. It feels damp, horrible. When I lift me palm it glows.

'They say there's stuff in them mushrooms. When ya eat it, ya can see inta heaven, Lucy Lu.'

I don't have a bog whatcha on about, so I just say, 'Yeah?'

The bottom a the stairs is the worst. It's so cold.

'Mad, isn't it?' You're very close ta me, so close I can smell yer breath. Warm and sorta spicy. 'When a gaff's as cold as this, they say it means there's somethin up.'

'Like what?' Ya don't reply. I wait a minute, tastin the word on me lips, then I say it. 'Ghosties?'

Ya snort a laugh through yer nose like I'm talkin crap, but the cold gets worse like I'm not. There's a small door at the back. I try it. It stays locked.

'That's a cunt,' ya say. 'We never been able ta get it open.'

I push. It doesn't give. 'Maybe that's where the ghosties are,' I say. Ya laugh again.

'Betcha someone died in that room,' I say on the way back up, while we're still in the dark, where it's safe. You're ahead a me now, the flame a the candle throwin yer shada ta one side. Mine is much smaller; it jumps and flickers, sometimes strong, sometimes weak. It's a jigger, like me.

'Show me a room where someone hasn't died, Lucy Lu, and I'll show you a fuckin miracle.'

Ya turn, smile. The candlelight does all sortsa shit ta yer face, makin ya ugly and beautiful all in one, like one a them fucked-up angels in the horror films. Ya stop smilin, reach out sudden, get the back a me head. I jerk away but yer fingers lock on me skull, hard. I jerk again. Ya ruffle me hair; in the ruffle is a shove. I rip me head away.

'Gerroff, Nayler.'

'So whatcha come up here for in anyways?' ya say.

I take a drag off the joint ya've given me and blow the smoke out. Ya take the joint and inhale. Ya hold yer breath, pushin the smoke down inta yer chest. Could be the draw but I think I see yer heart beatin, through the rips in yer tee-shirt and under yer white skin. Ya got a tattoo on yer left arm, up near the shoulder. It's a horse's head with a star in the forehead. The lines a the mane are done real good. They curve around yer muscles, movin when you do so it looks like the horse is alive.

Ya hand me the joint again. On me next drag I copy how I seen ya toke, forcin the smoke down ta me chest. The cough rises, I push it back. The smoke settles, spreadin through me; warm, comfortin, soothin me jiggin. I look up the stairs, past the overgrown winda with the arched top, but Micko is nowhere ta be seen. Through the dark green light comin in from the winda and the broken fanlight over the door, I hear music, way up high, that reminds me a somethin. A girl laughs. A familiar-soundin voice rumbles.

If I hadn'a been so buzzed, I probably wouldn't a said it. But it just seemed ta make sense at the time.

'Ya know me pal Amanda . . . ?'

Ya hesitate, then laugh, a small laugh like ya just realized ya been thick about somethin. 'Sure.'

'Well, she's got a free house tonight and she's gointa have a party.'

Ya nod. 'Ah, yeah?'

'Yeah.' The words are flowin now. 'Well, she said she wanted Micko over cos he might have some stuff, ya know, but I know she really wants ta see you.'

'Oh yeah?' Ya nod; thoughtful, like what I'm sayin is important.

'She likes ya, Nayler.'

Any other time I'da known better. I'da held me water, shut me trap, stayed fuckin easy, like Granny useta say. And maybe it was just the draw that done it, made it easier ta say it like it was. I seen this film once when I was inside – some detective film, only it was all old-fashioned and in this castle with monks and all in long brown robes. There was one ugly yoke with his hair scalped so it stood up in tufts on his head and he kept sayin to himself, 'Stupido! Stupido!', bangin his head with his hand or the wall, or whatever else that was near, ta knock himself inta reason.

That was me that afternoon, sittin beside ya in the fake twilight a the hallway, propped up against the bannisters, legs stretched out on the rottin wood, buzzed off of me face on a joint that made all the ones I'd ever rustled together from Micko's leavins seem like nothin at all, bangin on about me gorgeous Amanda and how much she loved ya. Stupido! Stupido!

*

As soon as Amanda opens the door, I can tell she's been at the liqueurs. Her face is steamed red and she's staggerin. She's got one a them awful puffball-style minis on and her hair is blow-dried big off her face like Sue Ellen from *Dallas*. But her eyes are sparklin and her lips are fat and moist and, ta me, still mellow from the blow, she looks like a million dollars.

Judgin from the uncomfortable look on Charlie's face, I reckon he thinks so too.

Music's on loud. That shite Amanda loves. The Carpenters. Only, unlike the song, there's no birds appearin, as Amanda can see by cranin round Charlie and Damo.

'They'll be up later,' I say.

'They?' Her eyes slide away from me.

A young wan comes outta the kitchen. She could be Amanda's sister only I know for a fact Amanda doesn't have any sisters.

'Howaya, kids,' she says. She's about sixteen, big and busty with her hair all scraped back off her face.

'Who does she think she is?' I say ta Amanda. 'Sade?'

'Very funny,' says Sade.

'This is me cousin Gloria,' says Amanda. 'She's supposed ta be lookin after us.'

'Yeah,' says Gloria, stickin on a shiny silver jacket, 'but what the eye won't see, the heart won't miss.'

'Gloria's goin out with her fella,' says Amanda. 'Her ma hates him.'

Gloria sprays some perfume on. It stinks the place out. 'See ya, Amanda, right? I'll be back in the mornin. And I'm trustin ya not ta wreck the place.'

She walks out, swayin past us. Damo stares as she goes.

'I love this!' screeches Amanda, and turns up Robert Palmer full whack.

I sit on the edge a the seat, squashed in by two a the Goldilockses and their fellas. We've only been at Amanda's two hours tops and the place is boomin. The note Amanda sent round got read by everyone in the class, it seems. Or else Jessie Hegarty thought it would be fun ta tell them.

I try ta keep the Rizla from fallin off me knee as I scoop out the rest a the hash from the locket I nicked off of Ma's bedside locker. There's barely enough for a joint. That's one a the bad things about Micko not livin at home any more. No more easy pickins.

One a the Goldilockses' fellas leans over towards me. He looks like he's gointa puke. I roll as fast as I can.

'Gis some,' says the fella.

I shake me head, light up and take a drag, real slow. Fuck you, ya dirty weasel.

In the corner, Damo sticks his hand up one a the Goldilockses' tops. I think a him tweakin the nipple like it's a piece a rope. The thought doesn't make me feel sick like it should. Damo's tongue slides over the Goldilocks' mouth; she takes it, her own mouth wide, like a snake about ta eat a rabbit.

In the centre a the room, Amanda, gee-eyed on liqueurs, thrashes her body round like somethin mad. Through the thin material a the mini, I can see the shadas of her strong legs as they move. I push meself up off the couch, holdin the jay safe in me hand, and squash through the crowd till I'm on top of Amanda. I take a drag.

'Here.' I put the lighted tip in her mouth. 'Blowback.'

She takes it, inhales, staggers.

I pat her back and she comes up for air, gaspin, before pukin again. The puke is orange-coloured and smells a sweets. Someone comes upta the bathroom door.

'Go out and piss on the street, willya?' I say without turnin round.

'That's a nice welcome, girls,' ya say.

Amanda's heavin body freezes.

'Here.' Ya crouch down beside Amanda and gently lift her hair outta her eyes. Some of it is covered with puke but ya don't seem ta mind. I step back and watch ya soothe her as she finishes retchin.

Suddenly there's a bangin on the front door. The music screeches to a halt, the needle rippin across the vinyl. In the gap left by the missin beats, the voices at the door sound loud and awkward.

'Fuck!' I leg it downstairs.

A very good-lookin young wan that I don't know is standin inside the front door, talkin ta the Old Bill.

'Of course, officer. Yes. No problem. We're having an engagement party. But of course, yes, we'll turn it down.'

The young wan is older than the rest and sorta Chinesey-lookin and she's got an accent I haven't heard before that's kinda American but foreign at the same time and even has bits a Dublin in it.

Soon as the pigs head off someone puts the music back on. Only this time it's not Whitney Houston wantin ta dance but some old hippie stuff. Lynrd Skynrd.

I think about goin back upstairs ta you and Amanda, but then I think again and go inta the kitchen instead. Micko's sittin at the table, foldin a piece a tinfoil. Two a the Goldilockses huddle by the open back door, watchin him. In the dark Micko looks almost as good as he useta before he got his face kicked in. Ya can't see the scars or his broken teeth, just the light shinin off his number two skinhead. He reaches in his pocket, takes out a small square a paper and opens it. Then he sprinkles what's inside the paper inta the tinfoil. One a the Goldilockses inches her way over ta him, says somethin, but he ignores her. Pissin inta the sink is a fella in a bright yella shirt, with greasy brown hair and tattoos all the way up his arms. He stops pissin and folds his nob back inta his jeans. I recognize him when he turns around; he's one a them lads got outta Tristan the same day as Micko – Mayno, somethin like that. As he comes ta the table the Goldilockses melt away.

Micko rolls another piece a tinfoil inta a tube. He snaps on his lighter.

'Give us,' says Yella Top whatever-his-name-is and takes the first tinfoil, holdin it over the flame.

Whatever's in the foil starts ta burn.

'Jesus, boys, take it easy.' Ya standin behind me, at the door. 'Not when there's kids around, yeah?'

Micko gives ya the finger without lookin up.

'Come on, girls,' ya say ta the Goldilockses, 'have a dance.'

'There's two of us, but,' says one.

Ya laugh. 'No worries. I'll take yiz both on.'

When I go back inta the hall, the good-lookin foreign girl who got rid a the rozzers is leadin a fella by the hand inta the sittin room. He's sorta familiar-lookin but I can't figure out how I know him. He's a proper man in his twenties, older than anyone else here, older than you, or Micko or Yella Top. He's got a wide mouth and marks from healed acne all over his gob that make him look like Ray Liotta, and tufty brown hair that's already goin bald, and deep crinkles round his eyes that give him a sorta smiley look even when he's not.

The good-lookin foreign girl stumbles and curses in what must be her own language. Sounds like someone spittin.

'Oopsie daisie, Sasha!' says Ray Liotta. His voice is a dark-brown colour, and like his face I'm sure I know it but I can't place it. He picks her up, settin her straight. She laughs and presses inta him.

I should go now. Ma'll kill me if I wake her when I get in. I lean forward, meanin ta get up, but I'm so mashed I can hardly move.

'Hey, little boy,' says Yella Top, leerin over at me. 'Who's the pretty boy, then? D'ya need ta relax?' He laughs. He can't keep his eyes open. His hand goes towards me knee. 'I can help ya if ya . . .'

'Leave it, Mainser,' says Micko. He tries ta pull at Yella Top's arm but doesn't get very far. He's even worse; his eyelids are practically glued together.

Ya look over from the couch, and smile at me. 'Little boy,' ya mouth.

I lean back and take another drag from yer joint. Fuck, I am bombed.

Amanda slumps against ya, her wet hair soakin inta yer white shirt. Her mouth's hangin half-open, like a little baby's. Her eyes are closed. The swell of her breath makes her tits heave, slow, like a wave in the sea. Ya playin with her hair, tricklin yer fingertip down the side a her face. Yer hand is just like it was when ya were a kid; thin, white, bruised, nail-bitten.

Mosta the girls from school are long gone, along with their fellas. There's only the hard core left: me, me brother, you, Yella Top Mainser, plus Amanda and the foreign girl and her fella, the Ray Liotta-lookalike who I still can't place. Oh, and Charlie, who's gone missin somewhere.

Bang on cue, Ray Liotta sticks his head round the door. Behind him is his mot, holdin a plastic bag in her tattooed hand, a bag that jingles when she moves.

'Alright, kiddos?' says Ray Liotta.

'Eh?' says Micko.

Ray snaps his fingers. 'Earth callin Micko Dolan. Come in, Micko.'

'Eh . . . sure, Snags,' says Micko, laughin, and gets up, nearly trippin over himself.

Snags. A course.

Micko kicks Mainser in the foot. Mainser shifts his weight onta his toes, winks at me, and unfolds off of the couch like a dirty yella snake.

'Comin, Nayler?' says Micko.

Ya shake yer head.

'Okay, kiddos, be good so. Seeya, sweetheart.' And with a wink at me, Snags follas Micko and Mainser out the door. As I watch them go, I can't help but wonder how much Snags's mot'll get for the jewellery she's nicked off of Amanda's ma.

'Sweetheart?' There's a light in yer eyes, dangerous, like ya sizin me up for a mill.

I'd tell ya ta piss off but I haven't got the energy so I just slouch deeper inta me armchair.

I can hear someone moanin in the back bedroom. Charlie with a bird, maybe, though he's probably just havin a wank. Amanda moans in her sleep, echoin Charlie, and shifts a bit on the sofa so she's closer ta ya. From where I'm sittin, I can see the tops of her legs under her puffball skirt. Yella skin, quiverin like a jelly. I lift me eyes and see you're lookin at me, the tip a yer tongue stickin outta yer mouth like a cat.

I look away. Ya start hummin somethin, outta tune, under yer breath.

When I can't stand it any more I look up. Yer eyes are still on me. Ya start ta stroke Amanda's arm, real soft and smooth. Amanda jerks but doesn't wake. Ya put yer mouth on her arm, at the place ya been strokin. Even from across the room I can see the goosepimples risin on her skin. Ya let the tip a yer tongue slide over the goosepimples. Amanda mumbles somethin.

'Oh yeah, oh yeah!' groans Charlie from the back bedroom. If he's with anyone, they're sayin nothin.

Still lookin at me, ya put yer mouth ta Amanda's and let yer tongue slip over her lips. She moves her head away, gruntin. Ya put yer hand on her right tit. A light touch. Ya stroke down ta the nipple that hardens through the slinky stuff of her top. Then, in a quick easy movement, ya down on yer knees and separatin her legs.

I get up, wobbly on me feet. 'Fuck this.' I can't remember if I said it aloud.

'Why the big rush, Lucy Lu?' Ya move yer hand down Amanda's leg towards her ankle.

'Ma'll kill me.'

Ya shrug, ease off her shoe, and stroke the sole of her foot. The movement is gentle, like ya spellin yer name there. Ya keep lookin at me.

I open the door.

Chicken, I hear ya say in me head. *Bwa bwa bwa, Lucy.*

'Call up again soon, Lucy Lu. Don't be a stranger, yeah?'

Then ya turn back ta Amanda and work her, rollin yer fingers over her feet, her knees, her thighs and up, strokin and teasin while she moans in her sleep like an animal.

I zip up me anorak against the wind and head home, runnin down Summerhill fast as I can given the draw and the drink, keepin me hand up ta shield me eyes from the lights blearin down off of the passin cars. Rain splashes up me legs and down me neck, hisses in puddles around me. As I run I keep hearin yer voice in me head –

'You a chicken, Lucy? You a scaredy little boy?' – and I can't help but wonder if Amanda has woken up yet.

And in between all that I try ta forget the look that was on me brother's face when he chased that smokin dragon up and down that valley a foil.

III

'He's only usin ya,' I tell her. 'He doesn't—' I can't get the word out.

'Doesn't what?' she says, mockin.

Say the word, Lucy. I struggle. I spit it out. 'Love ya, Amanda.'

Flick the feathered fringe, bat the Max Factor Ultra Length mascaraed lashes, pout the strawberry-shimmer lips.

'And what would you know about love, Lucy? Ya never been in love in yer life!'

Try again.

'We're only kids ta him, Amanda . . . Ya don't know him, Amanda . . . You're up yer hole, Amanda . . . You're in too deep . . . He could be dealin, Amanda—'

'So?' That was after the first shock a knowin whatcha were upta was over, a course. 'D'ya think I'm thick, Lucy?'

But

But

But

'In anyways, Lucy, ya should know I'm not goin the whole way with him.'

Goin the whole way? What's that supposed ta mean, Amanda? Why don'tcha say it as it is? Ah, sweet innocent Amanda, protectin that little red cherry of hers like it was a passport to a better world.

So in the end it's better ta leave things – all them buts and ifs and nos and he's onlys – unsaid.

Sasha is truly beautiful. She lies on the rottin oak floor, her long dark hair floatin on the ragged carpet like a sea. The candles dance in each wave and kink and I think a little sailors bobbin in boats, shinin torches ta guide each other through the night. The draw does that ta me. It makes me think a things I normally wouldn't.

Everythin makes sense with the draw. Everythin calms down, mellows, flows.

Snags isn't around. Him and Sasha had a flare-up earlier. They were arguin in her spittin and pukin language – which is Dutch, accordin ta you – then she began cryin and Snags started on at her in English, stuff like she should be glad she's not goin out workin the streets the way she done back home, them risks and all. He said it in his usual easy way, like he was makin a joke, only louder – 'That's so we can all hear,' ya said – and then she started shoutin at him in Dutch. Then he shouted too, real vicious, and we heard a coupla slaps and a smash, like she'd fallen against somethin, and Micko turned the stereo up louder so we wouldn't hear more. That sorta . . . shocked me. I know, it's not like I haven't seen or heard people fightin before. But Snags is usually so comfortable-soundin. It just seemed ta come outta the blue. And there's somethin about Sash, her sheer beauty, that makes a batin from him feel all wrong.

She takes it, though, like she deserves nothin better. And now she lies on the carpet, the red marks from his hand invisible in the glowin candlelight. Pretty mermaid.

Micko and Mainser are in the other room. As far as I can tell, they're the only ones usin. Ya should be. I feel that in me bones. Ya should be joinin them with yer own little bootlace and spoon, but for some reason ya clean. And, far as I can tell, so is Sasha. Snags has got her on somethin, but it's not gear.

But if I go inta the other room, the one at the back that looks out onta the rottin wilderness that useta be a garden for lords and ladies many years ago, I'll see them there. Me brother and his new best pal, huddled together on the floor like Hansel and Gretel gone wrong. Mainser's skinny arm flung like a flag over me brother's tracksuit chest, the rubber band loose, the needle drippin from his fingers. His greasy brown hair liftin off of his forehead, the weasel face relaxed, for once approachin somethin like good looks. While me brother lies beneath him, a shipwreck, dreamin forgotten dreams.

Shouldn't it bother me?

Shouldn't I wanta go?

Shouldn't I remember Jimmy Marconi's shada slumped against the front winda of our flat as he pumps forgetfulness inta his body?

Should I, fuck.

I've come for me own reasons and savin me brother isn't one a them.

So I don't go inta the back room, unless it's ta get somethin – a view a that sprawlin garden, a breath a fresh air, a moment away from you and Amanda and me pals, who take up vinyl after vinyl and put them back on and gas on about the relative merits a Bob Marley versus Television versus Howard bleedin Jones. For the most part I don't go anywhere. I just sit and watch – the watcher on the wall, me – the words and actions that normally shoot outta me silenced by the draw flowin through me body.

The fourth time we called up, we went inta the back room by mistake and walked in on Micko and Mainser like that, off their faces, and Amanda went white and said 'Jesus' in a squeaky voice. Then she legged it outta the room and plumped herself down on the toppa the stairs and started cryin.

I tried ta calm her down – because fuckit, what was the point in gettin so worked up about a fuckin needle for christsake; anyone coulda seen that comin, couldn't they? – and said, 'Lookit, it's okay, doesn't bother me, Amanda, and he's my brother, so come on, just calm down and let's go back in and we'll ignore it, alright, yeah?'

'Lucy, for fucksake, I can't believe ya just said that!'

I could tell she didn't really wanta leave. So I tried again.

'Amanda—'

'Jesus, Lucy. Ya just seen yer own brother like that! It's fuckin *awful*.'

'Ah, Amanda, it's okay.' I was really tryin ta calm her then because I knew you'd laugh at us if ya came out and heard her cryin on like a big baby. 'Everyone's at it, they know what they're—'

'It's awful, that heroin. It's evil, me da says. They're gointa give it ta us when we're not lookin, when we're drunk. They're startin

223

us on hash and then they'll put us on that, turn us inta evil losers just like them. We should tell the Guards.' She stood up. 'Yeah, that's what we'll do. We'll tell the Guards.'

'Lucy,' ya said, appearin at the door. 'Go on in.'

I gave her one last pat on the shoulder and headed back. Ya closed the door.

I don't know whatcha said ta Amanda, or whatcha done, but fifteen minutes later the two a youse walked inta the room, hand in hand, her smilin, rosy-cheeked, you with yer eyes shut down so nobody could read what was goin on there at all.

And after that she never seemed that bothered. Or so she made out.

'Listen ta this,' says Charlie. He puts on some bird caterwaulin in a foreign language. A heavy drumbeat starts a few bars in. Charlie giggles. 'What sorta hippie shite is that?'

Sash stretches her long arms over her head. 'That's Algerian. And fuck off, it's not hippie. Snags knows his music, you little shit.'

Under the dirty gauze curtain at the side a the room, ya break away from whatever ya doin ta Amanda – fingerin her, tweakin her nipples, lickin her gee – ta laugh.

Sash smiles ta herself, dreamy, in a way that reminds me a Sam.

I sink back onta the silky cushions Sash made from materials nicked off of Dempsey's Fabrics on Parnell Street. The Algerian bird caterwauls. In me head rhythms and melodies grow, like ripples made by a stone thrun inta a pond. A tune suggests itself, somethin off of a big brown radio. I hum it under me breath.

'That's nice, Lucy,' says Sasha, her eyes closed. 'You've got a really good voice.'

I break off, laugh. 'Yeah, well, ya can thank me Da for it. Me and Micko, we both got the music off of him. And John Paul got the rhythm. That right, Charlie?'

'Yeah. That's why he's good at the boxin.'

Sasha smiles. 'So what did your sister get from him?'

'Sam? Oh, she's a different story.' That strikes me as funny though I don't know why, and I laugh again. Under me lashes I see ya lookin over at me, an odd expression on yer face. But I don't care. The draw makes it all alright.

'Neil?' says Amanda in a baby voice.

Ya turn back ta her. I start hummin again.

Ya got all sortsa mad shite in yer room. In the corner there's a skull that ya put candles inta. It's not a person's, though. When I asked ya first, ya said it was the Devil.

'Fuck off, Nayler,' I said. 'Go try that on the kids.'

Ya picked up the skull and turned it. 'It's a goat. A mountain goat.'

Hangin on the right-hand wall is a huge poster of a naked bird with a snake wrapped round her. It reminds me a bit a Ma's cards, Number Twenty-Two, the World – meanin freedom and knowledge – only it's not drawn the same style. On Ma's card, the lines are all broken up, and the colours inside are pale and washed out. On this one the colours are glowin and the lines are sorta messy-lookin. Plus the bird in your poster is way more of a slapper than Ma's. She's got a big muscly arse that yells at ya from across the room, *Here, look at me, ride me!* and her hair is drawn so bad it looks like a turban, and the way she's smoochin with that snake you're expectin her ta pop out a scaly baby any day soon.

Near yer bed, where yer books are, ya useta have a deck a cards done the same style as that poster, all glowin colours. One night I picked them up and I was about ta cut and deal them, just for the crack, but ya took them off of me before I'd the chance. Ya musta put them somewhere but I don't know where; I haven't seen them since.

On the wall across from the poster, the same wall yer willa stick leans against, is a rusty sword, hangin up over the huge broken fireplace by a length a red rope with tassels at the end. Charlie asked ya once where the sword came from and ya said ya didn't know, it belonged ta Snags. But later, after we been smokin, ya said ya picked it up in a market in London because the fella owned it said it useta belong ta Buck Whaley. Ya dropped the name idle, like it meant nothin, but soon as ya said it, I remembered Granny's stories about the games he useta play with the Devil and that beautiful horse a his.

'Starlight,' I say, surprisin meself. Must be the hash speakin. 'Buck Whaley from the HellFire Club.'

'Yeah, Lucy Lu.' Ya sound surprised too and sorta . . . amused.

'Thought he was madey-up.'

'Not at all. Real sword so he musta been a real man.' Ya say it teasin, like ya darin me ta believe it. 'In anyways, it's Buck Whaley *and* the HellFire Club. It was a gang as well as a gaff.'

'A gang?'

'Yeah. They useta bring people up there, do mad stuff and all.'

'Mad stuff? Like what?' says Damo.

Ya glance at him, back at me. 'They'd a sayin, Lucy. Do what you will.'

'Do whatcha will,' says Damo. 'Fuck . . . that's cool.'

I laugh, though I'm not sure why. 'A gang. Like us, Nayler?'

Ya smile. 'Yeah. That's good, darlin. Like us. Yeah, we're the New HellFire Club, you and me and Micko and Charlie – oh, and the lovely Amanda a course.' Ya tousle her hair and she snuggles up ta ya. Ya lift yer can. 'Ta the spirit a Buck Whaley!'

'Am I in it too?' says Damo.

'Sorry, bud,' ya say. 'You and Mainser are out. Family members only.'

I lean back, watchin yer tattooed horse's head rear and sink as ya drink yer can and put it down and trickle yer fingers round Amanda's tit, and as I do, I think that old HellFire Club musta been a bit borin if all they done was sit around and smoke draw and drink cans and listen ta music and watch auld Buck ridin his mots.

Yer books are on the floor, near yer mattress. They all look like they been read, and not just once. Most a them are fat, with paper covers with big writin on the front, and mad pictures – masks and knives and deserts and skulls and old-fashioned photos. Tucked behind all them is a smaller book, old and dusty, on its cover a picture of a five-pointed star inside a circle. The cover isn't paper but a pale sorta material, hard and rough ta the touch. The star on the front is dark red, like dried blood.

I picked up that book once, ta look through it. There were some more pictures inside but most of it was just words, printed real close together. I never been the Mae West at readin but I couldn't even make out the Os in that book. Soon as I heard ya come in, I put the book back where I found it, and picked up one a the paper ones instead, a big fat black yoke with purple writin on the front.

'Studyin the occult, are ya, Lucy Lu? Followin yer ma's footsteps, what?'

For a sec I thought ya musta seen me with the hard book but then I copped the fat one I was holdin musta been about magic too.

'Nah.' I went ta put the book down. 'Didn't know ya were a reader, Nayler.'

Ya took the book off of me, started fingerin through it.

'Read us a bit,' said Micko, from over in the corner. 'Read us the stuff about that mad monk and his mind-readin powers.'

Ya gave him the finger. 'You, me pal, know fuck all about anythin.'

'Where's all yer other stuff, Nayler?' I asked once.

Ya looked over at me. 'What?'

'Ya know . . .' I tailed off then, sussin that maybe it wasn't a good thing ta let ya figure out I mighta been in another room a yours once, years earlier, a room that nobody, not even Micko, was supposed ta a seen.

Sasha's room is beside the big one where ya sleep and we all hang round. She showed it ta me and Amanda once without us even askin. She had it done up real nice, with a proper double mattress and clean sheets, plus nice curtains on the winda and a pretty cabinet in the corner. She had two little Dutch dolls on a makeshift shelf and a seta tea-chests with a coupla books and her clothes arranged all neat inside.

'Everyone's like that in Holland,' ya told us. 'Tidy.'

When she isn't in the room, she keeps it locked, with a padlock that's painted bright pink. I haven't bothered askin her why but I guess it's ta keep the lads out.

By now we'd gathered that Snags was back in with the Don. Only this time he wasn't up at the top. Accordin ta Damo, that was all down ta the Don, who'd got even cagier after the last hoo-ha. This time he told his nephew he'd hafta save up till he could afford ta pay for his own stock. In the meantime, he was welcome ta work for his uncle however he could. The upshot, said Damo, was Snagglepuss got left with the oddjobs, bikin cash or buryin stocks for safe-keepin. He worked some girls too, collectin a cut from the houses on the river end a Gardiner Street and the lone traders on the North Strand. Damo said he'da got wages for that, plus a cut from the gear and the cash he ran. But he wouldn'a been makin half the whack he done before, and what with all his debts in Holland – somethin Micko let slip one night – he was fairly skint. That musta been why he shacked up in that mangy squat when he wasn't stayin in his ma's.

None a this was spelt out, a course, not by you, Nayler, and certainly not by Snags. I don't even know how much of it I sussed back then. I was so wound up with you and Amanda, I didn't pay much heed ta Charlie or Damo bangin on about the business. But there were some lines I could read between. And Micko and Mainser useta waffle on an awful lotta shite when they were goofin.

They were on the streets. Snags gave them whatever he creamed off his uncle's stocks and they cut it and done the dirty work for him, holdin batches a Qs in their mouths while money changed hands, gettin their own little percentage in turn.

I couldn't figure out what you were at. Ya weren't usin, ya didn't seem ta be sellin along with the lads, and Damo didn't think ya were back in with the Don; at least, not as parta the regular staff.

'No!' says Amanda. It's only a whisper but ta me it's loud as anythin. I stop hummin and look over at Charlie and Damo ta see if they've heard too. But Damo's bombed on mushrooms, gigglin ta himself, while Charlie's just poxin round with the bricks in the banjaxed fireplace, tryin ta make a house or somethin outta them.

'For Christsake, girl. Make yer mind up.' Yer whisper's louder than Amanda's and the English accent ya had as a kid has come back. This time Charlie hears ya and looks up. Sash catches me eye. She looks awkward.

'No. I said no, Neil.'

'Okay. Fine.'

Zip. Button. Snap.

Ya pull back the gauze curtain that shields yer mattress from the rest a the room. Amanda fumbles with her clothes, zippin up her jeans. Ya walk over ta the stereo, steppin on Sasha's hair as ya go.

'Careful, Nayler!'

'Sorry, darlin.' Ya sound as sorry as Hitler gassin the Jews. Ya pick up the cover a the Algerian record. 'Who put on this shite?'

'Makes no difference,' says Amanda, half under her breath like she only kinda wants ya not ta hear. 'Ya can't hear anythin in anyways.'

Ya start whistlin, tuneless, and stick on a Nick Cave song. 'The Mercy Seat'.

'That's good,' says Charlie brightly. Amanda crosses her arms. Her face is black.

Ya pick up a can and go over ta the fireplace, bootin Charlie outta the way.

'Jesus, Nayler!'

Ya ignore him, kneel down and still whistlin, start takin apart the little house he made outta the bricks.

Nick groans on about burnin chairs and tellin lies. Charlie's right. It *is* good.

'Neil?' says Amanda, in a bossy come-back-and-let's-talk voice.

Ya don't answer. Me and Charlie exchange looks. We seen ya like this before, loadsa times, when we were kids.

I get up and walk across the room. 'Come on, Amanda.' She shakes me off.

'All right there, Lucy Lu?' ya say without lookin up.

'Yeah. Sure, Nayler. Just, we better go. It's gettin late and all.'

Amanda glares at me with a *don't-you-fuckin-dare-try-and-force-me-ta-leave* look, but I haul her up and push her through the door.

This I see, Nayler. Believe me.

When they've all gone and he's calm again, he slides over ta Sasha and pokes her in the ribs with his foot. He pokes delicately, so as not ta hurt her.

Her ribs move in and out under the tips of his bare toes and he soaks the warmth up through his skin. He pokes again.

'Want some cider, Sash?'

Sasha nods. He cradles her head in his hands, tilts back her chin, and pours Strongbow inta her mouth. Sasha swallas, closin her almond eyes. He watches the lump in her throat move up and down, the soft line of her skin, the tiny hairs on her neck glowin gold in the candlelight.

On our way home, we pass the girls, all out in force round the Square. Cindy Devlin, the loveliest a the Devlin clan from upstairs, is on the south-westerly corner, tall and pretty in her short skirt and white tee-shirt. Her legs are long and beautiful, like a race-horse's. Cindy's real . . . professional. The way she dresses, she never looks like a brasser, more like a young wan waitin on a date. She nods ta me as we go past.

'That'll be youse one day, girls.' Damo laughs. 'Sellin yer flaps for the Wacker.'

'Jesus!' says Amanda. 'Watch yer mouth, Damo Roche.'

'They're not the Wacker's girls, Damo.' I say it without thinkin. 'They're Snags's.'

Charlie looks at me. 'Whatcha mean?'

'I dunno. I just . . .' I trail off, not really knowin how ta explain.

'They can't be Snags's,' butts in Damo. He's got his *Mastermind* voice on, like he always does when he talks about this shit. 'The Wacker runs the Square. No shops, no protection, but he has all his hooers here. It's neutral ground, but they got some deal goin. The Don's got his street brassers down the North Strand. Nowhere near here.'

Amanda does a big tut-tut. 'Jesus, the Don, the Wacker, they're all the same. Useless villains. Why we wanta be wastin our time talkin about them I don't know.'

Charlie cracks up at that.

'What?' says Amanda.

He doesn't say but I guess it's on account of us hangin round with Snags and you. Pot, kettles, black.

I think about puttin Damo right, askin him, *Since when are the Don and Snags the same person?* Or, *since when has Snags ever been shy a runnin his own little games?* But then I figure I don't really have anythin ta go on, what I said about them girls and who they may or may not be workin for, just a feelin, and feelins never proved nothin, so maybe I should just keep me trap shut and forget I even said it.

'What sorta secrets, little hen?' says Sam suddenly, wakin me.

'Huh?' I say, the word a blurt from me broken dreams.

'Ya don't hafta tell me. But if ya do ya can have somethin nice . . .'

She tails off and I know she's still sleepin. But somethin about what she's said bothers me. Don't know what it is but I go over ta her bed ta check if she's okay. Her eyes are half-open but I can tell she can't see me.

'It's okay, Sam,' I say. 'Ya still asleep. Go back ta yer dreams.'

'So I take it that's it?' I say. 'You and Nayler. Youse are sorta . . . off now, yeah?'

'Ah, no,' says Amanda, tossin back her hair. 'That was just a tiff, that's all.'

'A what?'

'The *Jackie*. Says it's a lovers' tiff. Happens all the time. It's just layin down rules, that's all. He's a man, and men find that very hard ta deal with.'

Though as things panned out, Amanda was the one that found it hard ta deal with. The next time we called up, ya acted like ya were glad ta see me and the lads but ya didn't make much of a fuss over her. Ya didn't exactly ignore her, ya were friendly enough, but friendly was not what that girl wanted. And it didn't get much better. Some days, especially if we'd mushrooms or good spliff, you'd take her ta bed and fool around – though ya only kissed and cuddled, ya never pushed her ta do more, even though I got the feelin ya wouldn'a hadta by then, she'da given ya whatcha wanted without much askin. But mostly ya left her sittin there, moonin over from the other side a the room, big doe-eyes beggin ya ta take notice. She might as well a been askin the walls ta talk ta her.

It was round then ya started payin me more attention, chattin, sittin beside me, sometimes even puttin yer arm round me if we were havin a laugh, like ya'd forgot, thought I was Micko or some-thin. There was no big deal, I knew ya weren't after me – sure why wouldya a been with Amanda and Sasha around, and in anyways I wouldn'a let ya near if ya had. Besides, we never stayed like that long. Either I'd get itchy and shift away or ya'd cop on I wasn't Micko and lift yer arm, fast as ya'd landed it, and that'd be that. No big deal. Amanda said nothin but I knew she thought ya were usin me ta get at her. Maybe I shoulda thought more about her – but fuckit, it was easier not ta make a fuss. Besides, she was wrong. Ya didn't give a shit about her. Ya sat beside me because I was there, yer errant girl, but we all knew who ya were really after. It was in the way ya looked at her, or laid at her feet, or held her head in yer lap and stroked her long hair.

Funny thing, Sasha never seemed that bothered around you. Any time I looked at youse, I kept seein a dog, fawnin over its mistress while its mistress just . . . well, dreamta her master.

Micko starts it. Him and Mainser had their fix a while ago but they're more awake now, so they've joined us for a chat. The chat's goin on its usual buzz; music, people we know, fellas Micko and Mainser been fightin with, a small detour inta how a deal went wrong – except ya steer it back from that real fast; for all yer talk about our new HellFire Club, there's still things ya wanta keep from the kids – then Micko starts bangin on about the gear and the good it does people.

'Take Lou Reed,' he says. 'Genius.'

'Ya muppet,' ya say. 'Take Marc Almond. Gobshite.'

'Nick Cave.'

'Boy George? Fuckin . . . Dépêche Mode!'

'Boy George's alright.'

'Fuckin shirtlifter. They're all shirtlifters.'

'Iggy Pop. David Bowie.'

'David wasn't on the gear, Micko,' ya say. 'He was inta charlie. That was his buzz.'

'Jesus, you'd think you'da never touched the stuff, Nayler,' says Micko.

'Done and dusted, pal,' ya say. 'All under control.'

There's a silence and the two a youse look at each other. Micko drops his eyes first. 'Jim Morrison.'

'That was the peyote, Micko. Gear done nothin for him.'

'Judy Garland,' says Mainser, outta the blue.

'Who?' ya say.

Damo starts gigglin. Sasha tickles me feet. 'Go on, sing, Lucy.'

I don't wanta; I'd prefer we changed the subject, but she keeps ticklin so I oblige and give youse a coupla bars from 'Somewhere Over the Rainbow'.

Ya give me a slow handclap. 'Bravo, Lucy Lu. Three cheers for Judy . . . whatshername?'

Micko fucks an empty can at ya. 'Ah, fuck . . . leave it out, Nayler, willya. I'm tryin ta think.'

'Don't bother, Micko,' ya say. 'Leave that ta the experts.'

Amanda shifts around, edgy. She's wearin a new top that I lifted for her from Penneys, with slashed sleeves and a deep front so ya can see her knockers, but ya haven't glanced at her all evenin. I'm edgy meself, but for different reasons. I don't wanta listen ta youse talkin like that. Keep the gear in the back room, where it belongs, where Micko and Mainser can do what they want with it, but it shouldn't be brung out here. The rest of us is alright as we are, thanks. *I'm* alright. I catch Amanda's eye.

Wanta head? I ask her without talkin.

Amanda nods and picks herself up, clumsy on accounta the Buckie she's been drinkin. Mainser looks over and says somethin in Micko's ear. He laughs. Ya catch where they're lookin and watch Amanda as she buttons up her coat.

'Where ya goin, Pheelo?' Ya haven't called her Amanda in ages. She stops.

'Home,' she says. But from the way she says it, I can tell she's open ta changin her mind and that pisses me off because now I really wanta go.

'Oh.' Ya sound puzzled. 'It's not because a the company, is it?'

Amanda stares at ya. 'What?'

Ya smile. It's a real innocent smile, like you're only bein friendly, but that's when the buzzin starts in me head.

'Ya know, Pheelo, the company. The lads here. Ya not leavin because ya can't take them havin a little chat about their habit, are ya?'

Like talkin about their habit is normal, somethin even kids wouldn't mind hearin.

'Jesus, Nayler . . .' says Micko, half-laughin.

'Yeah, Nayler, come on.' I can see where this is headin and I wanta get out.

'Oh . . . I see.' Yer eyes widen like ya just copped onta somethin. 'Ya worried about yer daddy, Pheelo. That it?' Ya turn ta Micko. 'Declan Phelan, Micko. You've hearda him. Good old Dekko. Saviour a the workin classes. Very busy man.' Ya glance at Amanda. 'What's that he says, Pheelo? String them scumbags up on a tree with their balls in their mouths. Because that'll solve all the world's problems, yeah?' Ya say it light, friendly, almost like it's true.

Micko looks at ya. There's a light in his eyes I haven't seen in years. It's the same colour as the buzz that's hummin through me, fixin me ta the spot.

'You're the same, Pheelo, aren't ya? Ya think the lads here are losers. Just like Nick and Iggy and Lou. Losers and thicks that deserve ta die.'

Amanda juts out her chin like she's not bothered, but I can tell she's about ta cry.

'Fucksake, Nayler—' I say.

Ya put yer hand up, stoppin me. 'Or maybe they're not thick, Pheelo? That it? Maybe they're evil, like that heroin they take. Because that's what yer daddy says and yer daddy's always right.'

'Nayler,' says Sasha, warnin.

Ya stand up. 'Don't get upset, Pheelo. Just tell me. Is that what me friends are? Evil stupid losers that deserve ta die?'

Amanda looks at you, at me, back at you. I try ta move, can't.

'Come on, girl. Spit it out.' Yer voice is still friendly but gone real quiet. 'We're not good enough for ya, are we? We're scum a the earth, just like yer daddy says. We're born with nothin, we belong nowhere and we're gointa die leavin no trace because that's all we deserve. The only stuff we ever own is filth, poisoned with the stink a other people's misery, and we're too thick ta make even that last. We should be shot on sight, our bollocks ripped off us at birth. No, fuck that; we shouldn't even a been born. Our hooer mothers shoulda flushed us down the plughole and had themselves done so as not ta inflict more like us on the world. Well, why don'tcha get yer daddy in, Amanda? Haul him in with that big long rope of his, so he can string us up and watch us die. Because what loss would we be?'

'I'm not sayin . . . ah, fuck off, would ya.' She's half-cryin now.

Ya walk straight past her and open the door. 'Come on, little girl. Time ta go.'

Amanda stops. 'Ya said . . .' She stops, starts again. 'Ya said ya liked me comin up here, Neil. Ya said . . .' She looks around, lowers her voice. 'Ya said ya . . . ya cared.' She starts blubbin.

God knows what woulda happened next – wouldya a kissed her? kicked her? fecked her out? said ya were only messin – I don't know, because Damo snorts a sudden laugh, real hysterical, tryin ta hold it back like he's at school. Then Sasha gets the giggles, and Charlie too – though he doesn't dare look at Amanda – and then it's Micko and Mainser and me in it too, and we're laughin ourselves sick because it's not funny, we shouldn't be, not after what ya said, serious like that, and especially with Amanda bein so upset and all she wants ta do is make up, but ya shouldn'a said ya cared for her, Nayler, that's not fair because who have ya ever cared for, and I can't help it, none of us can, it's ridiculous, the whole fuckin situation is and . . .

Now even you can't keep yer face straight. 'Jesus, lads.'

'You're right,' says Amanda. 'You are scum.' She spits in yer face and swings her fist. There's a sick thud as she makes contact with yer nose.

We stop. 'Amanda—' I half-get up.

But you've already got her by the shoulders. I'm half-expectin ya ta say somethin like, 'It's alright, lookit, calm down, Amanda, easy' – but she's cryin and won't stop and blood is tricklin from yer nose and she keeps wavin her fists, wild, and then it seems normal that ya slap her across the face; three times, hard.

I feel it in me own face. The rush a blood. The heat.

She stops cryin, drops her fist. Ya grab her by the chin, stare at her.

'Alright. Come on.' Ya take her arm. Even though yer voice is hard, yer touch is gentle, the way it always useta be with her.

Charlie jumps up after youse, his voice breakin. 'Leave her alone, Nayler! Amanda, I'll walk ya home!' but ya turn fast and belt him in the chest, rough enough ta knock him off balance. He staggers backwards. Amanda looks over at me, but ya get her through the door before I can see the expression on her face.

After youse have gone, Micko cracks a joke ta break the tension. Mainser joins in, and Damo laughs, and then the party is back on track. Charlie goes out a few minutes later and I think he's gone after youse but when I go down ta the landin ta use the jacks I hear him inside.

He comes out all scarlet, like he's been cryin.

'Charlie . . .'

He shrugs me off.

There's no soap when I go ta wash me hands. Fuckin disgustin gaff.

When I go back upstairs, Sasha has stuck on Les Négresses Vertes, this French crew that are mad inta the punk scene but do good dance stuff too. And I don't know if it's the music or the fresh air from that hole in the jacks winda that's cleared me mind, but I can't stop the thoughts from swishin around in me head, bouncin off each other like tin cans bobbin in water.

I was right not ta do anythin. Amanda was a thick cunt for provokin ya. She shoulda known there'd be trouble; she shoulda held herself back.

In anyways why should I a had ta rush in? School, here – it's all the same. Why does she always need someone else ta protect her? Jesus knows, if ya don't stand up to a bully you've only yerself ta blame. If it was me, I'da kept at ya. I wouldn'a taken them slaps like I deserved them. I'da slapped ya back – and worse. I'da crucified ya.

But Amanda's not me. It's not fair ta think she could do that.

Ah no, says the second thought. No excuse. Ya always got ta stand up ta a bully.

And ya should know better than ta get a bully started, says the first thought, all reasonable-soundin. Ya can't start a scrap if ya don't know the way out.

But how can I even think she started it? says the third thought. How could she a known there'd be trouble?

Because I warned her! roar the other thoughts all together.

And under them thoughts swishin round is this deep swell a gladness, hot and cold all mixed up. The hot is the same feelin I got that day all them years ago when ya threatened Spocky Halloran with yer brand-new army knife, a sorta sickness and wantin ya ta do it at the same time. And the cold is a fear a what will happen ta Amanda on the way home and is it me fault, but then colder again is this feelin I got that wants somethin ta happen because . . . well, because it serves her right.

Ya can call it spite but it's hard work lookin on at other people warmin each other up without wantin some for yerself.

Even though I know it wasn't, I've often imagined that that was the night ya took Amanda's precious cherry away from her, down some stinkin back alley among the johnny wrappers and the shit-stained babywipes, with the syringes lyin glintin under the streetlights and the sounda the sirens off in the distance screamin for blood.

The next day she put the boycott on me. I kept tryin ta get close ta her all mornin, ta say *lookit I'm sorry but I was so outta it I couldn't* or somethin like that. But she wouldn't let me in, sat beside Carol Keane and all so she wouldn't hafta talk ta me.

I scoured her face for black eyes, her body for Chinese-burn marks, bruises on her knees. But I found nothin, not even a welt from the slaps we'd all seen ya give her.

We didn't call upta yours for a good while after. I half-wanted ta, havin nothin better ta do with me time while Amanda was freezin me out, but the lads weren't keen. Charlie said he just didn't wanta, after the way you'd treated Amanda, and Damo wasn't goin if Charlie wasn't, and I didn't wanta sit there on me tod, watchin ya moonin over Sasha while me brother and that other cunt went off of their heads in the back room. One day, passin by the squat, I stopped at the door for old times' sake. I thought about givin a knock but then I heard the voices from inside; way up the stairs. Sounded like fellas rantin and railin. Coulda been you – though rantin never been yer style – coulda been Snags, coulda been anyone.

The only proper time I seen ya them weeks was the day ya came ta ours. I was on me way ta school. I was dead late and they'd told me the School Attendance was on me case; didn't bother me at first because I was off the probation, but then I heard Jessie Hegarty's sister got sent ta that Overbrook Reformatory kip by them fuckin childcatchers, so I knew I'd hafta smarten up. And that was why I was runnin so fast when I crashed inta ya on the stairs.

At first ya looked confused ta see me, like I shouldn'a been there. Then ya just pushed past me and went on up the stairs. So much for the HellFire Club.

I knew without askin thatcha were gointa see her.

Rose Dolan, fortune-teller: back in business.

*

It starts off as such a beautiful day.

The sun is shinin, the sky is blue and me spirits is up, way upper than they been since the night you and Amanda busted up. I am feelin *fine*. I miss the draw, a course. We're not gettin it regular now we don't have youse. But in a way that's alright. Sometimes it's good ta get the edge back, not just go with things.

I finish me pack a HobNobs and throw the paper on the ground.

The only drawback with havin no hash is I'm gettin bored faster. I say as much.

'I'm bored, Charlie.'

'Hmm?' He looks up from the spybook he's readin.

'Yeah. I'm fuckin slammed bored.' I pick up grass and throw it at him. 'Call down ta Amanda for us, Charlie. She'll talk ta you. Call down ta her and tell her ta come out.'

'She's your friend,' he says, still readin.

'Yeah, but she's not talkin ta me and in anyways she likes you.'

He looks up. 'Yeah?'

'Nah. Only messin.'

An aeroplane flies across the sky, leavin a white mark like slug's piss behind it. I think a the days me and Amanda useta go ta the Tolka Park and I miss her suddenly, rememberin the feelin of her lyin beside me, warm and soft, her yella skin pickin up the light, her skirt ridden up high ta the toppa her legs. The missin fills me.

Jesus . . . can't be dealin with this.

'Ah, Charlie, think a somethin for us ta do, will ya?'

'You're the one that thinks a things, Lucy. I just make them happen.'

'So make somethin happen.'

'Okay.' He puts his book down. 'Tell me what we're ta do and I'll make it happen.'

'I want . . .' I look up at the slug piss. 'I wanta break in some-where. I wanta rob somethin. I want . . . ah, fuckit, I dunno.'

Charlie's gone all quiet.

'What's up – worried I'll lead ya inta temptation?'

He starts tearin grass up and throwin it at me. 'What wouldya say if I let ya inta a secret, Lucy?'

Secret? Charlie? 'Ya must be jokin.'

'I'm not.'

He's been carryin them around for weeks. Two keys. One big and important-lookin with a curvy bit at the top where ya hold it for twistin. The other's a Chubb. He won't tell me where they're for but soon as we step outta the gate a the Square and turn right I know.

'Fucksake, Charlie, how d'ya get them?'

'They keep them in the fireplace, where the bricks are. I found them there one night but I made sure ta cover them up again and I didn't make the copies till he done that on Amanda. Cunt.'

His voice is breakin again. He clears his throat and blinks at me through his specs. 'I just wanted ta have them, Lucy, ya know. Rob somethin off him that he wouldn't even know was gone.' He smiles. 'Stupid bastard. If I was him, I'da moved the keys once I seen someone fuckin around with me hidey-hole. It's a good thing when people think ya thicker than ya are. Remember that, Lucy.'

'What are you, me fuckin da, Charlie?' I bat him on the head.

He used the soap in the jacks. Pressed the keys in, both sides, filled the holes with wax when he got home, and got Stevo's key-cutter ta make them up for him.

The big key opens the front door, which makes sense. The key looks the way the door mighta done before it got all fucked up; magnificent. I'm startin ta feel nervous, not in a bad way, more because we haven't thought this through.

'What if they're here?' I ask Charlie.

'We'll tell them it was left open. Get somebody inta trouble.' He smiles.

As we push the door open, the dampness wafts out, hittin me face. Me back is bakin but inside it's as cold as ever.

Charlie steps inside. 'Come on, Lucy.'

I don't know why I'm holdin back. 'Okay.'

'Leave the door open. Just ta keep our story tight. Here.' He tears off a corner from the cover of his book, folds it in two and passes it ta me. I wedge it between the door and the frame so it won't close the full way. 'Now,' he says. He's awful pleased with himself.

The place is dead quiet. We should really go ta your landin first, on the second floor, ta check if anyone's home, but it's more of a buzz explorin on the risk someone could walk in and catch us any minute. So we go ta the first floor instead and try out the Chubb on the doors – and the other key too, just for the crack – but neither a them work. Then I push the door a the front room and it creaks open all by itself.

'See,' I say. 'Don't need keys after all.'

The room is dark, what with the cardboard over the windas, and empty, apart from a sleepin bag in the corner that looks like it hasn't been slept in in ages. It stinks a piss. There's cans in the fireplace and an auld grey trench coat thrun over a broken chair.

The back room is fallin ta pieces: broken floorboards, more cardboard in the windas. We jump up and down and crack a few boards. In the skirtin we hear rats, scurryin, squeakin, terrified a the noise we're makin. I get the idea a tearin the cardboard off the windas and that's when we see the old chest, covered in dust, at the backa the room.

'Treasure,' says Charlie. 'Fuckit, Lucy, maybe this is where Snags stores the . . . ya know.'

Yeah, Charlie. I know. Gear.

But when we get the chest open, there's only a loada old hats and scarves inside. One catches me eye. It's blue and silky sorta, chiffon.

'Fuck this.' Charlie stands up and brushes the dust off his knees.

When he's at the door, I sneak me hand in under the scarves.

They're there. Twenty or more key rings on hooks nailed inta a board, the same ya had all nice and tidy in yer room as a kid. I'm about ta rummage more, ta see if the wallets and rings and watches ya nicked are there too, but Charlie turns round – 'Come on, Lucy, willya' – so I content meself with takin a set a keys instead. A souvenir.

On the second floor there's no sign of youse, not even Sasha.

Charlie tries the Chubb on her padlock, even though I don't want him ta, but it doesn't work. The back room smells a Micko and I sit down on his mattress for a bit while Charlie's in yer room, tearin pages outta yer books. I can hear him laughin ta himself, sorta manic, but I don't feel like joinin in. I wish Micko was with me, on his own, without that dirty leery Mainser, so I could talk ta him. And a real chat at that, not some stupid half-arsed bollocks about nothin.

'Ah, don't shit on his bed, Charlie.'
  'Why? He won't know it's me.'
  'Yeah, but . . .'
  He hasn't done ya any harm, Charlie.
  Oh, yeah?
  In the end he couldn't. There wasn't a log ready, so he just done a piss instead.

We've nicked some money from under yer hidey-hole in the fireplace – 'I can't believe he's still hidin stuff there, stupid cunt. Still . . .' – and some hash as well, though I warned Charlie not ta rob too much because it won't take a genius ta guess it's us, but we still haven't found what the second key is for. We were gointa try the attic but the steps are banjaxed, so we've left that for another time. I'm hangin out the winda a Micko's room, seein if I can hop out and over ta the tree in the garden, when Charlie calls 'Sketch'.
  'Someone's comin, Lucy.'
  'Ah, fuck.'
  'It's alright, we got our story, come on.'
  'Yeah, but the books and the bricks and all—'
  'It's alright. I got them tidied up. They won't suss it.'
  We leg it down the stairs and we're in the hall when we hear the voices outside; some fella sayin goodbye to another.
  'Shit,' says Charlie. 'It's Snags.'
  'Yeah, well who else didya think it'd be?'
  'I dunno. I just . . .' Charlie's lookin scared for the first time since we started.

'Jesus!' says Snags outside the door. He sounds vexed. 'Who didn't lock up?'

'Fuckit!' says Charlie. He's shittin himself.

For a second I thinka tellin me cousin ta stay cool, we got nothin ta hide –

The front door rattles.

'Jesus, Charlie, we gotta get outta here!'

But Charlie's shakin, fit for nothin, so I push him towards the first door on the landin. It won't open.

'Try the Chubb,' whispers Charlie.

But I can see it's not a Chubb lock and now the front door is creakin open and I look round and I see what I shoulda seen ages ago, that little door at the back that leads down ta the basement, and I shove Charlie towards it and we're through it just as the front door opens fully, and then the two of us are racin inta the darkness on our tiptoes, quiet as we can, down the stairs, hands scrapin against the slimy walls, and I got the Chubb in the lock a the heavy door at the foot a the stairs and it's turnin and then we're in and we're safe and I lock it again just ta be sure and we look at each other and laugh, quiet, so Snags won't hear, shakin with relief and nerves and everythin all at once.

It smells evil.

It musta been the kitchen, or the scullery – somewhere the gentry never visited. There's bars on the windas and a stone floor, deathly cold ta the touch, and towards the back a black iron yoke that looks like an oven. Ta the left is a battered door, half-glass, leanin open a coupla inches. It leads to a passage that's covered with black mould and green slime and has no windas. I can hear water drippin from the ceilin. Near the enda the passage is a fridge, chained and padlocked shut, and down from it on the opposite wall is a little alcove that I can't even see inta.

'Fuck,' whispers Charlie. 'So that's where he keeps it. Ya know, the—'

Gear.

'Yeah, Charlie,' I whisper back. 'I know. Not very safe but.'

'Well . . .' Charlie goes upta the fridge and twiddles with the padlock. 'Ya hafta get in through that door and that's not easy, it's iron and all and nobody would ever . . .'

'Sure.' I go back inta the main room.

'We safe?' calls Charlie after me.

'Long as you keep yer voice down, ya muppet.'

Green light seeps in from the jungly winda onta a pile a manky clothes in the back corner. Somethin about the way the clothes is lyin isn't right.

'Yeah, it's a good lock,' says Charlie, back in the passage. 'Won't be that easy ta break.'

I lift the first layer off of the clothes. It useta be a coat once but it's fallin apart now. Underneath it is an auld wan's housecoat, under that a shiny green dress that some bird in the olden times woulda worn. I can feel fleas scuttlin about but I keep goin.

'Fuck!' A dead rat falls out onta me hands and I drop the bundle. Charlie pokes his head round the door. He starts laughin when he sees the rat.

'Fucksake, keep the noise down, Charlie.' I boot the rat across the room. 'Are ya gointa laugh at me or are ya gointa help?'

'That's only a pile a shite, Lucy.'

'Just help me. Come on.'

He goes ta the other enda the bundle and sticks his arms underneath. I slide me own arms in. The clothes feel disgustin.

'One two—'

We lift up the heap and throw it ta the side.

Underneath where the clothes were is a heavy-duty cardboard box, taped-up closed.

'Jesus, wonder what's . . .' says Charlie as I pick up a bit a broken glass. 'No. Leave it!' He grabs the glass off me. 'Don't be thick. They'll know if ya break the tape. Here.'

He grabs one enda the box and signals me ta lift the other. We turn it upside down. It's brutal heavy and whatever's inside moves as we turn it. Once we got it turned, Charlie takes out his penknife ta prise the staples outta the bottom a the box. Then he lifts the flap.

'Fuck.' I sit down on me hunkers and Charlie makes a small laugh, like the wind's just been punched outta him.

They're rifles. I can tell from the shape. Don't know too much about guns apart from the comics Charlie useta read but I do know the pretty ones with the wooden handles are rifles.

'They're Kalashnikovs,' says Charlie. He sounds like he's comin. 'AK 47s. 7.62 calibre assault rifles. The magazine comes separate. They usually come in a wooden box so they musta . . . fuck.'

The metal is cool ta the touch.

'Go on,' he says, diggin me in the back. 'The Ra uses them, Lucy.'

I lift the gun, put it on me shoulder like in the films. It's way heavier than it looks.

'They're good,' says Charlie. 'Very flexible. They can do automatic or single rounds. Ya just select the fire and then ya squeeze the handle.'

The handle is warm under me skin. I turn ta Charlie and angle the gun so it points at his face.

'Like this?' I squeeze. 'Ack-ack-ack-ack-ack!'

Charlie screams like a girl. I break me shit laughin.

'Fucksake!' He grabs the gun outta me hand. 'Ya spa, Lucy. Makin all that noise.'

Then we hear the footsteps.

For a second we stand there, starin at each other. Then I shove the flap closed and fuck the box back over on its base and Charlie grabs the rotten clothes and flings them back on toppa the box and grabbin each other, we run through the broken door inta the passageway. I pull Charlie down ta the end and we squeeze inta the alcove across from the fridge. It's pitch black.

I put me hand out, feelin for Charlie's arm, and it's only when me fingers come in contact with the metal that I realize he's taken the fuckin rifle with him.

'Whatcha mean, someone's been here?'

'The door was left open, Nayler. And there's piss on yer bed if ya wanta check.'

'Jesus . . .'

Snags sniffs. We can hear him from where we are.

'Whatcha doin that for, Snags? Nobody knows about down here.'

'Yeah, well, nobody was supposed ta leave the door open and all.'

'Don't look at me. I wouldn't do a stupid thing like that.'

There's a silence.

'Fuck,' ya say, like ya realizin somethin.

'Yeah. Fuck is right.' Snags bangs his fist against somethin hard. '*Jesus!* Fuckin *cunt!* Fuck fuck *fuck!*' He's well outta control, nothin left of his normal comfortable self. 'Man, I shoulda listened ta me *poxhead fuckin* uncle. Don't get street junkies involved and keep yer hands fuckin clean!'

'Lookit. Micko wouldn't mess ya round, Snags.' Compared with Snags ya sound like the voice a reason. 'He's sacrificed enough for ya already—'

'Don't give me that sacrifice bollocks, Nayler. That little fairy's weak as the resta them usin pricks when it comes ta his fix and you know that. Fuckin *knew* they were plottin somethin. Moanin they weren't gettin enough gear. Fuckin double-crossin little mary fuckin steamer rats. I'll fuck them up like I done that cunt in Amsterdam. I swear. I'll shred their fuckin ringpieces and feed them that manky virus, I fuckin swear—'

'Jesus, Snags, easy.'

'Easy?' Snags laughs. '*Easy?*'

'Snags—'

'I'll give ya fuckin easy, kiddo. Ya know, I never had you for thick, Nayler. But for a smart lad, sounds like ya not gettin the full scope here. Ya know me, I'm happy ta take me time, watch and wait, that's me, but if them cunts been talkin we can both kiss goodbye ta fuckin time. Ya made yer choice, kid. You're in on this. Yer name will be just as black as mine if me uncle gets even a sniff –'

'Okay, Snags. I get it.'

'– and if our friend finds out we been leakin, he'll bail out and then we'll have *that* fuckin psycho on our backs. And I don't know about you, but I want ta hang onta me hands and me eyes and me big hairy fuckin crigs as long as I fuckin can.'

'Alright.' Ya take a breath. Sounds like ya doin it ta calm Snags as much as yerself. 'So whatcha want me ta do?'

There's a silence. Snags clears his throat. Then – 'Just yer usual magic, Nayler,' he says, back to his normal comfortable self. 'Put a little bit . . . extra on top. Make it . . . ya know . . . look right?'

Ya don't say anythin.

A lighter snaps on and we hear footsteps. 'Oh, and kid,' he says, 'do me a favour, yeah? Check the stuff first.'

Beside me I can feel Charlie startin ta shake. I grab his wrist and push us both as close ta the wall as possible.

The door closes. There's a gruntin sound and we guess ya liftin the clothes off the box. Then there's another grunt and a soft thud and we pray ya've dumped the clothes back on the box without noticin anythin different about the packin. Charlie relaxes.

Ya take a step, then another.

Fuck.

Instead a goin out after Snags, ya comin our direction. Charlie starts shakin again.

The door with the broken glass winda opens. Footsteps; light and calm. You're in the passage. I pull Charlie and meself even tighter against the wall. I know it's only you – you're me pal that's known me since I was a kid, that's known all me family, that's me other brother nearly and like a son ta me Ma – and I shouldn't be shittin it, we're only kids, foolin around, this was just a game, we don't mean any harm, but fuck, all that slides inta nothin because right now we're not just kids, we're trespassers messin with stuff we don't understand and you're no friend now, nor brother, nor son ta me Ma, you're only one thing and that's Snags's little rascal all growed up and all Snags's little rascals do is sort out stuff for Snags and anyone that gets in the way, Charlie, me, Micko, whoever, should get out of it soon as they can or . . .

At the fridge ya stop. I press me face close ta the wall and keep Charlie held tight under me jacket so his hair won't catch any light, tryin ta suck me breath back inta me body so it can't be heard.

Ya take a step towards us. I feel yer breath inches away, hot on me neck, me head, me back.

Then ya flick around on yer heels. Yer Doc Martens creak. I hear the sound of a key turnin. I move me head and take a peek. Ya kneelin down in fronta the fridge. It's open, but there's no light on inside. Ya reach in, feel for somethin. Then ya stand up. I turn around and inta Charlie again and listen as ya close the fridge door and lock it.

And ya gone.

'Fuck,' says Charlie after the basement door has closed, half-cryin as he slides down onta the ground. 'Oh, fuck, Lucy. What the fuck we gointa do?'

I don't know, Charlie. You're the poxy genius.

In the end neither of us had much time ta think of a plan, because a few minutes after ya went, there was more footsteps runnin down the stairs, two sets, fast this time, and then the door burst open again and slammed closed just as fast and there was the sounda someone bein kicked across the floor and gruntin and startin ta whimper and –

'I didn't, I didn't, I swear it wasn't me.'

I can't make out if it's Micko or Mainser and I'm prayin it's not me brother, prayin that whoever ya have up against the wall is that yella-shirted little fuck.

'I swear, Nayler, don't hurt me, man, fuck . . . Jesus . . . it wasn't me . . .'

There's a rippin sound. 'That's gaffer tape,' whispers Charlie in me ear but I jog him ta shut him up. There's a few more rips.

'Ah, man, ah, Nayler, ya know I know how much is ridin on this . . . fuck, I wouldn't squeal ta anyone . . . ah, Jesus, man, not the . . . fuck, Nayler . . . I wouldn't . . . I . . .'

There's a snappin sound, like metal teeth gnashin together. On the wall a the passage somethin glints, light reflectin off a shiny surface. The teeth snap again and then he screams.

He's still tryin ta get out words, 'No it wasn't me, I swear . . . lookit if I was lyin I wouldn't . . .' but then ya do somethin else ta him and then all he can do is howl.

Ya let him go on for ages.

I wish ya wouldn't. I wish ya'd just kill him there and then ta shut him up, even if he is me brother, because I can't bear the sounda him screamin and sobbin and then whimperin like a kid. And I can't bear the stickiness a Charlie sweatin beside me, or the smell of him, or that fuckin gun pressed inta me side, and Jesus knows if I had the strength, I'd kill him too, and you, and that snivellin wreck inside the other room, and leave the lotta youse ta rot in hell.

At last he's silent.

'Okay,' ya say, real calm. 'Let's just leave it at that.'

'I didn't do it . . .'

'I said okay.'

'Sure, Nayler, sure.'

Even though he's talkin different now, lispin sorta, I can make out who he is. But I don't know if I'm glad or not that it's Mainser.

After youse have gone, there's a loud noise outside that sounds like fellas diggin up the road, and when that's finished and we're sure the coast is clear, we go inta the main room as quiet as we can. There's sticky stuff on the floor near the pile a clothes. I don't need ta be Sherlock Holmes ta know it's blood. Charlie bends down and pokes at somethin on the floor. It's small, rubbery, covered in blood. I know it's part a someone's – Mainser's – body. There's another coupla them lyin beside it. When Charlie's not lookin, I pick one up and put it in me pocket, alongside me other souvenir, the keys I took from yer treasure chest. Don't ask me why. I just . . . wanted it, I suppose.

Charlie wipes his hands. He looks like he's gointa get sick.

We listen at the door for a while.

'There's nothin. Let's just go.' Charlie's as white as a sheet.

'Okay,' I say. We might as well. We can't hang round there all night and I don't wanta anyway, not after what's happened.

Charlie turns the key and pushes the door.

He goes even whiter. 'Jesus, Lucy. They've put a bolt on the door.'

★

We tried everythin, startin with the passage. But there was no winda there, only a door at the back, and that was made a metal with not an ounce a give in it. I tried hackin at it with the butt a the gun but it didn't help and it made such a racket that Charlie nearly slit me open. Then we had a go at the bars over the winda, thinkin if we smashed what was left a the glass we could climb out that way. But the bars wouldn't bend, and they were too narrow for even me ta climb through, and even if we coulda, God knows how we'da got through the jungle on the other side. Then I had a look inta the oven yoke because there was a pipe leadin up from it and I thought it might bring us out somewhere open, but Charlie told me ta grow fuckin up, who did I think I was – Nancy fuckin Drew? – and in the end he was right, the pipe led nowhere, only inta the wall.

Neither of us even suggested callin out for help.

'We hafta wait for them ta come back,' says Charlie. It feels like hours later. Outside, the green jungle is dark. I can hardly see Charlie; he's only a white shape lyin beside the pile a rotten clothes.

'Charlie, that could be days.'

'Yeah, but we don't have a choice.'

'What if me Ma or yours starts lookin for us? They'll know . . .'

'They had a break-in.' He's got that cold, steady voice he gets when he's thinkin stuff through. 'They're edgy. They're gointa keep comin back ta check up on their stuff. And when they do, we'd better be ready ta split.'

He has it worked out. We're ta stand beside the door so we'll be hidden behind it when it opens. Then we just hafta wing it.

'Pick the right moment and go,' says Charlie.

I can't stop me knees jiggin. I'm not cold but it's as if I am. I can't concentrate on what Charlie's sayin. 'Yeah,' I say. 'Okay.'

Darkness collapses in on the room. Charlie fades inta the floor. He falls asleep. I wake him. I'm tired and all over the place but I can't sleep. I feel like smashin glass; I feel like breakin the door down. I feel like doin anythin ta get outta this dungeon.

Around midnight – I'm guessin that's what it is because I think I hear a bell somewhere – there's more footsteps. Then a gratin sound as the bolt on the other side pulls. I grab Charlie by the hand and we press ourselves inta the wall beside the door. A key turns. The door swings open. It hasn't swung far enough. If whoever it is looks around, they'll see me and Charlie standin there, holdin our breaths in case we fart.

Torchlight flashes over the room, fixin on the pile a clothes that's hidin the rifles.

'Put it over there,' says Snags.

Whoever's with him grunts and shuffles in through the door, luggin a box. I can't see much in the torchlight, only he's tall and he's not you. Then the other enda the box comes in, with someone else luggin it, and that's you.

Charlie's nails dig inta me palm.

'Lovely wee place, boys,' says whoever's luggin with ya. He's got a Northern accent like me Uncle Dan's ladyfriend Dolly. He places the box and straightens himself up and smiles, and even though I can't make out his face, I see a glint a somethin silver on his chin, somethin gold in his mouth.

'Thanks.' I can tell from Snags's voice he's half-concentratin on youse and half-keepin sketch on the door. 'Alright, lads?'

'Alright.'

Beside me Charlie's shakin, uncontrollable now. I don't blame him. With Snags in the middle a the room, there's no chance a gettin out and any minute you and the Northern fella are gointa turn round and see us and –

Beside me, Charlie bends, then straightens. His hand moves, flingin somethin over Snags's head and across the room where it crashes inta the glassy door ta the passageway.

'The fuck!' says Snags, leggin it over ta the passage. You and the other fella jump after him. Charlie digs me, but I don't need the dig. While yer backs are turned, I'm out around the half-open door and up the stairs, fast as I can. Behind me is Charlie, for once thank God light on his toes. We get ta the door at the toppa the stairs and push it open and we're flyin down the hall, up against the front door and now we can hear voices – 'See who it is, Nayler, fuck-sake!' – and footsteps on the basement stairs behind us, fast but not fast enough, because Charlie's got the door open and it's stuck but it's alright, we're through the gap and down the stairs and onta the street and – 'Split up!' says Charlie – I've legged it ta the right and around inta the alley and I'm like a shot over the wall inta Scully Flats and round the back ta the hidey-hole where they store the rubbish.

I hear someone callin but I burrow meself deeper inta the black sacks full a other people's crap, me heart racin in me chest, and inside I feel fuckin alive, I feel no one can touch me, I feel better than I've felt in months since Dr Terence started on his fuckin vitamins. I am the man, I tell meself as I bend double, gaspin and laughin at the same time because I know I'm not a man, I'm a girl. But I am the fuckin man!

I mitched off the next coupla days, runnin the risk a gettin on the wrong side a the Childcatchers, but it was worth it. No way did I wanta attract attention. Amanda called round – first time in weeks – but I got Sam ta tell her I had the flu and couldn't talk ta anyone.

Maybe I shoulda. Maybe then I coulda shared the load with her and we coulda worked things out and . . .

Oh, grow up, Lucy.

Marlene gives me a bad look when she opens the door.

'What's the matter, Marlene?' I say. Better ta be upfront.

'You're a bad egg, Lucy Dolan,' she says. 'I'm tryin ta keep me son on some sorta straight path but every time he takes one step in the right direction, you're there, leadin him astray.'

I shrug and push past her, ignorin her.

'Alright?' I say ta him.

Charlie's white and sweaty. His eyes are watery and there's snot pourin outta his nose. He gives me the finger and sneezes. There's so many blankets on his bed, ya can hardly see him.

'Whatcha tell her?' I ask.

'Drinkin.' With his cold it sounds like 'dridgid'. 'We were out drinkin and I fell inta the canal and then I ended up stayin over in Damo's. She got mad but . . .'

'She check up on ya?'

He gives me a witherin look and shakes his head.

'What happened? They catch up with ya?'

'Nah. I jumped the railins inta the basement next door. But they hung round outside for ages and then it started rainin.' He sneezes.

'Did they cop?'

'Don't think so. The other fella was suspicious but Nayler told Snags he was gettin too worked up and he was seein things. "Easy, Snags. It was just a rat,"' he says, takin off yer drawl. Then he starts laughin.

'What?'

'It was and all, Lucy. That's what I thrun at them. Only it was dead.'

I light a fag, inhale. I suppose it is funny but I don't feel much like laughin.

'Didja get a look at that other fella, Charlie?'

Charlie shakes his head. 'Nah. He had a cap on and he talked low. But from the way they were goin on, I think he's one a Wacker's. Damo'd know—'

'Fucksake, Charlie, ya not tellin Damo! He can't keep his gob quiet ta save his life.'

'Course, Lucy, I know that.' Then he leans over. 'D'ya wanta see what's under the bed?' Only he's not sayin it like it's a nice surprise.

He got all funny when I went ta pick it up, sayin it was his. He'd found it and he'd taken it out, so I hadn't the right ta touch it. But I reminded him I was the one that thoughta the basement in the first place, and sussed out that pile a clothes, so I'd as much right ta it as him. He was still baulkin and it was only when I said, in passin, not meanin ta get a dig in or anythin, that he'd wanta watch it keepin it there, what with the way Marlene done her Hooverin every two days, that he started gettin edgy. Then it was my turn ta say no, I didn't wanta take it on, but by now he was shittin it and wouldn't take no, so in the end I said yeah.

*

As I walk over ta our block, I'm sure everyone's seein it. They're seein through Charlie's blue sports bag bangin against me legs ta the piece lyin inside. They're seein with their X-ray eyes and they'll tell you and you'll tell Snags and then that'll be it; I'll be like Mainser, screamin in the basement while ya shred me ta pieces, cuttin bits off of me with yer metal teeth. Lucy Lu or no Lucy Lu. HellFire Club or no HellFire Club. You and Snags got business ta do and it doesn't include me.

This is a stupid idea. This is so fuckin stupid.

'Lucy!'

Just me luck. Amanda's in the yard, leanin against our stairwell.

'Where were ya? I called up and all but Sam said ya were sick. Then ya weren't in school, so I didn't know . . .' She trails off. 'Hey, you alright, Lucy?'

'Yeah. I'm grand. Lookit, Amanda, I got somethin ta do, with me Ma and all.'

'Whatcha up ta later on?'

'Nothin,' I say, then regret sayin it. 'Why?'

'I was thinkin we could call over ta Neil's.'

Ah, man.

'I got ta thinkin, see, ya know, after all that happened, well maybe . . . maybe I got carried away thinkin it meant he hated me and I'm . . . yeah, I'm sorry, Lucy, for not talkin ta ya and all but that was really hurtful except . . . in anyways it's alright now, yeah, because I know it's them lads – yer brother and all – they're a bad influence and . . . ya don't know him like me, Lucy. I know he said all them things but in the end he loves me, he just can't say it, he gets . . . ya know, he gets carried away, and all that with Sasha that's just because I wouldn't . . . ya know, but now I haven't been around, he'll probably and . . .'

The bag's hurtin me shoulder now. I'm sick of it, and a Charlie landin it on me, and a stupid Amanda with her stupid ideas about you and love. Maybe if I'd had some draw ta chill me out I wouldn'a said it the way I done. But I hadn't and I didn't and so –

'Amanda, d'ya not get it?'

'What?'

'He doesn't want ya.' Me voice is cold, even ta me. 'You're just a stupid little ignorant kid ta him, Amanda. Like me, like Charlie, like fuckin Damo.'

She stares at me like she's never seen me before.

That was when I learnt there's rules attached ta every friendship, and friendships with girls most of all. Rule number one: never tell the truth.

'You're the one doesn't know him, Amanda. Fucksake!' But she doesn't turn back.

It was only because I had ta get some plastic bags from the kitchen ta wrap the rifle up so it wouldn't rust that I seen it. The door was open so I didn't hafta turn the key or push it. That made a difference too. She'd a heard otherwise. She'd a heard and then I wouldn'a seen anythin.

I'm too fucked off – with the weighta the gun and the bad feelin in me chest after what happened with Amanda – ta call out anythin like I'm home or whatever. So I walk down the hall, after dumpin the bag inside the sittin room door where I can get it on the way out, past Granny's bedroom and upta the kitchen door.

It's a familiar sound but it takes me a step or two ta figure it out. Luckily I get it before I open the door.

'Ugh ugh ugh ugh.'

I can't fuckin believe it. She's always brung her fellas home with her – even though she hasn't been doin a lotta that lately – but up till now she's kept them in her fuckin bedroom where they belong. What the Jaysus is she thinkin a ridin one in the kitchen? Sam could walk in any minute. Or Granny, off on the rampage, lookin for a glass a milk. This is sick. I toy with the idea a knockin on the door, like they do in the films, but then I think twice. Why'd I wanta do that, walk in on her and her ugly fella, give her the privilege a thinkin I'm interested in what goes on between her sorry legs?

'Ugh ugh. Yeah . . . there . . .'

The fella with her laughs; soft, teasin. Dirty prick.

'Jesus . . .' she says. 'Ah, Jesus . . . ya so . . . ah . . . Ji . . .' She makes a stupid sorta sobbin sound.

The lad grunts, raggedy-soundin.

Over and fuckin out. Thank Christ. I turn ta go.

'Ah, come here ta me, son,' I hear her say; soft, sighin, laughin. Son?

I didn't peek round ta see if she had a boy's palm in hers, or if there was cards scattered on the table, or teacups still swirlin with leaves. I didn't need ta see if there was an excuse. I just turned and went, real fast, not seein where I was goin.

I'm sure some people would say that I shoulda seen it comin. *I love the fellas. And the fellas love me. Ya look great, Missus Dolan. Like the real thing. We missed ya, son.*

People would say I shouldn'a been so surprised. With me partial gift from Granny I shoulda *known.* And even if I didn't, it still shouldn'a been that much of a shock.

But . . .

Son. Son? *Son.*

Stupido, Lucy. Stupido.

When I got up on the roof, I crawled over ta Sam's hidey-hole because me legs were wobblin too much ta stand, and gripped both edges a the concrete ledge and heaved. Nothin came out, only spit. It drifted on the wind, floatin, like the insides of a bird. But then the sickness in me stomach lurched and I heaved again. I couldn't stop it.

When the heavin finished, I climbed up onta the ledge and pulled meself up so I was standin. Even though I was still wobblin, I stood as tall as I could, stretchin out me arms on either side while Dublin swooned below me.

That film *Titanic* wasn't out then but that's what I was like. Leo on the bridge, arms out. But sure as fuck I wasn't singin like any Celine Dion. Not me. I was just wonderin what it would be like ta jump, ta folla me spit and float on the risin wind, tumble past every winda in the flats till I touched down – bang! an explosion – on the grey yard.

Me eyes were streamin. I blame it on the wind.

Funny, the things that'll give ya a head for heights. Funnier still, how shock settles the mind, makes even someone like me think clear and cold.

I gave them ten minutes ta finish; clean up, say goodbye, all that.

When I came back down, I picked up Charlie's sports bag that miraculous nobody had stumbled over and, huggin it close ta me chest, went inta the kitchen where I got two black sacks, three Crazy Prices bags and a roll a Sellotape. I didn't look at her. She was sittin at her table, smokin, but I didn't look. She asked somethin thick about school and why I wasn't there today and I should watch it and me pal Amanda was lookin for me again, but I didn't answer. I just grabbed the bags, stuffed them in the holdall, and went.

At the door I bumped inta Granny and Sam, on their way back from the doctor's. Granny had a bad vein in her leg and Sam had had ta bring her down ta the clinic ta check up on it. I said nothin ta them even though they were both lookin at me like I'd got two heads. Didn't matter. Crazy bitches could probably tell what was goin on.

Then I retraced me steps back ta the roof and felt around in the hole I'd spotted earlier and checked that it was the right size. There was some rubbish in there, old sweets or somethin in a paper bag, musta fallen in somehow, so I dug them out first and chucked them over the edge. Then I wrapped the gun in the three Crazy Prices bags, one after another, and sealed them with the Sellotape, then wrapped the two black sacks round it, so it was snug as a bug in a rug, then stuck the whole shebang inta Charlie's sports bag and zipped it up, and stuffed it all inta the hole.

After doin that, I sat on the ledge, with me feet danglin over, lookin down at Dublin, smokin. I smoked one fag after another, throwin the butts away when I'd finished. I watched them fall and willed meself ta forget.

It's all done, Lucy Dolan. Do not think about it.

In the first class, Irish, I see Amanda tryin ta catch me eye, but I avoid her. I don't wanta talk. She's probably lookin for me ta make up and say I'm sorry because after all, what pals does she have only me, but I don't care. I don't wanta talk ta anyone.

Through the open winda I hear one a the Goldilockses play somethin on the piana. She's brutal. I'm no musician but I can tell she's fuckin it up, makin some notes come faster than they should and others slower. The rest she gets wrong altogether, and the music goes haywire then, screamin ugly and outta tune. Each wrong gap, each slippin chorus, each flat note drills inta me body like a five-inch masonry nail. It's a wonder I'm not bleedin.

'Fuck off,' I say.

Sister Agnes stares at me through her round specs. She reminds me a Charlie right now and that makes me hate her even more than usual. I hate everyone: Amanda, Charlie, Sam, Granny; John Paul with his thick mot, Snags with his poxy schemin, Micko with his *stupid* fuckin *loser thick* fuckin habit and that cunt friend a his, Mainser, who shouldn'a left that door open, and you with yer calm voice and calmer footsteps and lyin smile and fucked-up magic and snappin metal teeth. But most of all, more even than that, I hate Her. Me hooerin selfish ignorant sick cunt of a Ma.

'What did you say, Lucy?'

'I said fuck off, ya stupid cunt.'

Any other time I been in trouble I been red hot, I been fire on me feet. Today's different. I'm so cold I'll snap if someone tries ta break me. Agnes knows it, I know it.

'Apologize this instant.'

I get up, walk over ta the blackboard and take the duster outta her hands. I feel her shrink away from me. I like that feelin. That feels alright. I lift the duster, aim.

'Lucy!' she says.

I fuck it straight inta her stupid specky face.

I stay cold as ice in the bee-baw and for a while down at the station, when that stupid cunt from the Social keeps askin me what's up, don't I know what I've done, this is serious, I coulda hurt someone, I should thank me stars I'm the age I am but I should definitely

258

wise up, if I don't cop on now, I'm headin for disaster. All that I can take. Nothin new there. But when she grabs me and tries ta turn me round ta look at her, I go loco. I lash out at her with me fists, flingin her against the wall. I throw chairs. I turn a table upside down. I scream. I am sick. I know this. I am fuckin sick. I am from a sick family. I am sick in the head. I am mad. They want me mad, they'll get mad. I am fuckin mad.

Two nights later I set fire ta me classroom.

The flames rise. I throw the empty petrol can on the heap and scream like a banshee, like mad Buck Whaley on his crazy horse Starlight, like me, Lucy Dolan, Lucy Lu Madser Dolan.

IV

Please don't get me wrong. Please don't think it was all on account a you. Like Granny useta say, the real story is always more complicated than how it seems on the surface.

'Now,' says the doctor, 'following the High Court Order, we've had the opportunity to examine her over the past three weeks while she's been remanded in Overbrook.'

He fiddles with his biro, flippin it back and forwards on the notepad like he's preparin it for the long jump in the Biro Olympics.

'And in my professional opinion, her . . .'

He pauses. Ma says nothin.

'. . . condition – the, em . . . seizures, lack of focus, concentration problems, aggression, etcetera, etcetera – justifies the Department of Education transferring her to the care of the Health Board's Psychiatric Services. The Probation Officer's report has indicated the same, eh . . .'

He clears his throat, shuffles his paper. 'Now, in non-offender circumstances, of course, we would treat someone of your daughter's age on an out-patient basis. But in this case, it's just not possible. Now, of course . . . as you may realize, we don't have any dedicated beds for children, but we can place her in an adult ward where she'll be given the em . . . appropriate treatment.'

He smiles. If ya can call it a smile.

'Our team is very skilled.'

'Do I need ta sign anythin?'

Do it, Ma. Be a good girl. If I concentrate hard enough, I can make ya do it.

'No, Mrs Dolan. The court order has established that she's in statutory care so—'

She gets up and walks out without lettin him finish.

There was a big fuss in the papers about it at the time. Some took me side, others didn't.

Child Sent ta Mental Hospital – Are We Livin in the Dark Ages?

'Youse'll All Burn!' Threatens Psycho Teen.

Ya might think I'm spinnin here but I can understand why they done it. They thought I was a danger ta society.

There's six of us to a room. The colours on the walls remind me a school. Piss green. Pus yella. Battleship grey. Cunt pink. They've tried ta jazz it up with pictures but by the time ya make yer way once round the corridors, ya realize they got the same eight pictures all over the gaff. Sunset. Sailin boats. Flowers. Kittens. If I see another kitten, I'll throttle it.

'This will sort you out,' says the nurse, a friendly type with curly hair. I like her because she doesn't call me 'love', like the others. 'It'll calm you down.'

Calm me down.

Fuck. Who says I want calm?

It's called XYZsomethin. It's on the chart at the base a me bed but I can only barely make out the letters. It sorta does what it says on the tin. It doesn't so much calm me as slow me; but only me body and me surface thoughts, coverin them in a thick blanket a clouds, makin everythin outside very far away. Underneath the slowness, I still feel the deeper parts a me brain, edgy and jumpin, hummin away like a fly at a winda pane.

'There, now,' says the nurse. 'All better.' It's the one thing she says that drives me nuts. Like I'm sick or somethin.

Dr Terence has been irresponsible. He shouldn'a tried out his new ideas on me. Guinea-pig, they call me. Allergies! they tut-tut, shakin their heads.

'We got you just in the nick of time,' says the new doctor. 'There's been a breakthrough in medication for your condition and with any luck . . .'

I wanta laugh, mainly for him sayin the word 'nick'. I don't. The new doctor has eyes like a fish – cold and blue and stickin out – under round milk-bottle glasses, and thick hair that's brown but grey at the edges. No stranger ta Grecian 2000. After the first chat, he doesn't talk ta me again. He's sorted out his XYZ; let it sort out me.

On me fifth day I meet Betty.

'I heard you burnt down your school –'

She has a loud voice that goes up and down and curly black hair and freckles and she's dressed in red. Socks, pyjamas, dressin-gown, slippers. They're six different reds and each red clashes with the next, flashin strobes in fronta me eyes that haven't stopped itchin since they gave me them pills. She keeps talkin but I ignore her and concentrate on me dinner. It tastes like muck but I shovel it in in anyways. She digs me in the side.

'– and you beat up a Garda but they'd have let you away with it if you hadn't burnt down the school I'm Betty I'm an anarchist I'm from Cork I'm sure you can tell from my accent everyone can –'

She's talkin too fast. I can't folla her.

'– three months but I'm leaving soon I'm getting better they're all saying I'm –'

Wrong. She said somethin wrong.

'– very young to be here I'm eighteen I signed myself in you know you can do that do you know that jeez you're very good-looking you know actually very exotic like Audrey Hepburn and you've great arms they're very strong –'

If I can only concentrate, I can remember what she said and put her right. If I can –

'– but if you try hard enough and if you don't get on their nerves they'll let you –'

Got it.

'I didn't burn it down,' I say.

Betty stops for a moment. Then she nods and continues like I said nothin. 'Okay, okay, that's good you know it's tough some-times when you want to do things—'

'I'd a loven ta burn it down,' I say. 'But I only torched one room. I didn't beat up a pig neither. It was a Social worker and I only pushed her against a wall.'

'Oh,' she says, like she heard this time. 'Okay.'

She spears a spud with her fork and holds it up. Under the neon light it looks greeny-grey, like snot. I wonder if she sees what I'm seein.

'Ya can't light up here, Ma,' says Charlie. 'That right, Lucy?'

Marlene looks over at the notice on the wall, and puts away the fag with a sigh.

'How long am I gointa be in here?' With the pills it's hard gettin the words out, so hard sometimes I just think me questions instead a askin them. But not this one. This one I can't stand not knowin the answer ta.

Marlene glances over at Ma, who's sittin on a stool, her arms folded tight under her tits. Christ, me darlin mother looks pig ugly. Her tits are burstin all over the place and her arms under them are like rolls a sausages. Plus her arse is only balancin on the stool, because she's so short she has ta stretch her legs ta reach the ground and that looks thick. And her legs have too many veins in anyways and her feet are gone purple because she's wearin the wrong shoes – white high heels insteada proper boots for the rain. And her hair is horrible. Dry and yella and it looks like it would break if ya combed it which is why she hasn't, dirty bitch. Why have I not seen these things before? Why has it taken me till now ta see what an ugly cunt me Ma really is?

'Well,' says Marlene, 'it won't be that long, Lucy. Coupla . . . months, maybe? They hafta be seen ta be doin somethin. And because them pills is new they hafta, ya know, keep an eye on ya. But it's not too bad in here, is it?'

She keeps lookin me up and down while she's talkin and I know she's tryin ta work out am I really alright and at the same time tryin ta pretend that she's not shocked ta see me the way I am.

'They feedin ya alright?'

I nod. Ma sighs, loudly.

The friendly nurse brings us down ta the smokin-room and when we're in there she tells Marlene ta be sure ta keep an eye on me. She looks at Ma when she's talkin but I know she's really tellin Marlene. The pills are helpin me see this. All slowed down, I can read under the surface, dip inta thoughts or meanins just like—

'Where's Granny?' I say, suddenly.

Marlene glances at Ma. 'She's, eh . . . she's not great, pet. That vein in her leg has got very bad. Hasn't it, Rose?'

Ma says nothin.

'They think it's diabetes. They're even thinking a operatin. Very hard, at her age. Isn't that right, Charlie?'

'Yeah,' says Charlie.

'But Sam'll be inta see ya soon. John Paul's gointa bring her later in the week. And if he doesn't, Charlie will. Won'tcha, pet?'

'Yeah.'

When they're not lookin, I sneak a glance over at Charlie and give him the finger. He jerks back, like I've slapped him. Then he smiles and gives me the finger back.

While the nurses weren't lookin and Ma was in the jacks, Marlene sneaked me a fag and got Charlie ta stand in front a me so nobody would see me puffin away. The smoke hit me lungs and I got a sudden yearnin for the draw and ta be back in the squat listenin ta records with you and Amanda and the lads. But I pushed the yearnin back in the past where it belonged and when Ma came back I turned me attention on her instead.

I could tell she was itchin ta be gone, so I stretched out the chat as long as I could just ta spite her. It was a struggle talkin, but I came up with loadsa questions for Marlene – How are the twins? Whose birthday is next? Blah blah blah. I didn't care about the answers. I just wanted ta watch Ma get edgier and edgier. Just before they left I stuck me hand out and asked her ta read me fortune. She was so shocked she actually spoke ta me.

'Jesus! Whatcha want that for?'

I said nothin. I wasn't sure meself why I'd asked, only I had the feelin it would test her in some way, rock her off her ugly little perch.

She looked at me and I could see she was confused and I was glad I'd shaken her, even if it was only a bit. But then Marlene butted in, tryin ta act all normal, though I could tell she thought I'd lost it, sayin Ma couldn't do me fortune that visit, but she would next time, won'tcha, Rose?

The way she talked ta me, ya'd swear I was four year old again.

'– burn down the government I know you can do it you can do anything you want I –'

It's a bakin hot day, so they've let us go inta the garden for an hour. It's a reward for doin all that thick Occupational Therapy lark. Still, any reward's better than none, so I squash meself behind the tree and light up a fag from the pack Charlie snuck me.

'– anarchy everywhere did I tell you I'm a shopsteward? Karl Marx is great you know he writes very well very intelligent I'd love to buy *Vogue* you know in *Vogue* –'

There's squeakin footsteps, rubber on pebbles. Shite. Gestapo alert. I duck round the other side a the tree fast as I can, which on the pills isn't very.

'– help me burn down the Dáil I'll take you to Paris Paris is wonderful they have shops you know –'

Double shite. The new nurse is on. Last time she caught me smokin, she took the fags off of me and I almost lost the head, even with the pills, but I was so slowed down I couldn't swear at her the way I normally woulda, much less give her a dig, so they jabbed me with a needle and I was out for the count the resta the afternoon. Afterwards I heard the Fish-eye doctor say somethin about ECT and that night Betty sneaked over and said I had ta be careful, I didn't want the ECT, she got it and that's why she was the way she was, they wired her up like on the electric chair and fried her head, so now she can't think proper. I don't know how much a that is lies, Betty lies about everythin, but still . . . no harm in bein careful.

The Gestapo passes without stoppin.

'– this book? you'll like it it's very interesting and it's funny as well –'

I finish the fag and grind it out. Then I hide the butt under the yellowin leaves beside the tree. 'Sure, Betty.' I lie down beside her.

She starts readin out loud. She's been readin me the same book for two weeks now. It's about this bunch a pigs on a farm that are tryin ta take over from the farmers. She never gets far because she's always goin off on her own bat, thinkin about make-up or anarchy or space exploration or just fuckin anythin. She's not like me, a danger ta society. She just goes off the beam every so often, ends up scootin round Dublin or Cork in the nip. They feed her stuff ta keep her quiet, but whatever it is it's not enough.

'– you know what happens to the pigs in the end oh yes all animals are born equal but some are more equal than others –'

That's when I started thinkin, Nayler. Not because a the story, which I couldn't folla, certainly not the way Betty read it, but because a what she said, about bein equal, and the way it made me think a what ya said ta Amanda that last night we went up ta yours.

We're born with nothin, we belong nowhere and we're gointa die leavin no trace because that's all we deserve.

Are some animals born more equal than others? That day in the hospital garden the first thing came inta me head was school. Secondary school, not the first one. Soon as them teachers read me address, they had me sorted – put me straightaway in the worst class possible. They didn't even check ta see was I good at anythin. Yeah, sure, I had an attitude, but they had me sorted before they even met me.

Ya know me, Nayler: I'm not sittin here feelin sorry for meself, thinkin, Oh God, I coulda been a brain surgeon only they put me in the wrong class. And maybe I am a good learner after all, like Derek says, and them teachers mighta been wrong, but outside will that really mean jack? Can I bring meself outta the life I been born ta? Some people do, they haul them up all the time in the papers or on the telly, sayin ya don't hafta end up an addict or a robber or a stupid cunt just because ya grew up in the inner city or wherever, but if ya ask me the ones that make it good are the lucky ones.

'Historical material,' Betty useta say. Meanin, far as I could make out, that money and the past make yer luck for ya. But isn't that just like Granny's fortunes – a handy way a sayin, *Don't fight because ya can never change things*?

What I think now is: if ya believe somethin's gointa happen, it might. And because I believed for so long that I was no good, ya could say I played a part in makin me own misfortune. But where did that belief come from? Me Ma and her *Lucy's a problem* bollocks? The school that lost faith in me before I'd even a chance ta try? Or somethin else, somethin I came ta the earth with, like the colour a me eyes or the shape a me nose?

Derek says it's real tough ta look beyond blamin. But it can help sometimes, make ya feel more in control. But then ya could say it's easy enough ta do that when you've got money and an education behind ya. Which brings us back ta Betty's historical material.

Jesus, Nayler, I don't fuckin know.

'Lucy Dolan!' calls the Gestapo. I look up.

'Visitor.'

As I leave the garden, Betty flips the book back ta the start and begins readin ta the tree.

She's sittin on me bed but she gets up as soon as I walk inta the ward.

'Hiya,' she says.

I suddenly hate the look and feel a meself. I'm bloated out like a water balloon on them pills and me skin is in shite, covered with zits all over me chin and forehead. I'm like a leper I'm that ugly. She hands me over a brown paper bag and for a minute I think about stickin it over me head.

'Me Ma said I should bring ya somethin.'

That bothers me but I don't know why. I open the bag. It's grapes.

'I'm not sick,' I try ta say. But I only get as far as 'I'm not' before she starts talkin, rushin over me words.

'Loadsa them are askin for ya – Jessie Hegarty and Carol Keane and—'

Then I get what's botherin me. 'Yer Ma let ya come in?'

She looks blank.

'Yeah. So?' Then she gets it. 'No, she thinks you're alright now thatcha in here.'

'Safe, is it?'

'Safe?' She looks blank again. Then she laughs. 'Yeah. I suppose so.'

I laugh too and hand her the bag a grapes. 'Here, have one.'

She picks up a grape, starts peelin the skin off of it.

'We're back together, ya know,' she says, tryin ta be casual. Her face is gone bright pink and she's lookin down at the grape like it's the only thing in the world.

I get an awful cold feelin in me gut but I don't know what ta say so I squash me grape between me fingers.

'I was in the ILAC Centre and I bumped inta him.'

Yeah, sure. Betcha that was an accident. She looks up, readin me mind, and comes clean. 'Alright, I seen him go in and I went in after him. I was with Jessie Hegarty.'

Jessie Hegarty?

'I'm only pallin round with her because ya not in school. Ya still me best pal, Lucy.'

She puts the grape in her mouth and bites. The juice spurts out onta her lips. 'I didn't tell Jessie it was him. She knew I was after some fella but I didn't tell her who. I seen him go inta the café near the fountain. Jessie wanted ta go winda-shoppin in Dunnes but I told her I'd forgotten somethin for me Ma and I'd meet up with her in a bit.'

She swallas, picks up another grape. I keep squashin mine. Squash squash squash.

'Oh, he looked gorgeous, Lucy . . . I know ya don't see it . . . ya know, but . . . and he was real nice. Told me he was sorry and all. Said he'd take me ta the pictures, like a normal fella.' She looks up again. 'Ah, Lucy, I toldya he loved me. Ya just don't understand him the way I do.'

★

After she went, I asked the friendly nurse if I could have a bath because it was me period and I wasn't feelin well. I stayed in the tub for ages, turnin the water on hot as it could go and let it scald through me skin, burnin the thoughts I didn't wanta have outta me. When after an hour they got sick a bangin on the door ta get me out and unlocked it themselves, I stood up naked in fronta them, burnt red from tip ta toe, not carin if they were gointa do the ECT on me because at least that would fry everythin outta me so I wouldn't hafta think any more.

It was hard gettin a chance ta talk ta Charlie. Ma and Marlene were always standin guard, watchin us like we were plottin ta take over the world. But one day Marlene went ta the jacks on the way back from the smokin-room, and just after that a nurse came up and asked Ma for a word, so at last we got a coupla minutes on our own.

'Did anythin . . .' I started sayin but Charlie shook his head before I was even half-way through the question.

'I haven't been up there. And they haven't come lookin for it, so I reckon—'

'Jesus, Charlie Dolan, hold me bag, will ya?' said Ma, buttin in.

Just before he went, I grabbed his arm and mouthed one word that Ma or Marlene couldn't see.

Amanda.

'– just wondered if you want to because sometimes do you want to see something?'

I look up, surprised. Betty's stopped at the enda the question the way she never does normally.

She's standin by me bed. Her eyes are brighter than usual and her skin is flushed nearly the colour of her jammies. Before I can answer, she grabs me by the arm, drags me ta her bed and starts rummagin under the bedclothes.

'Okay okay okay okay okay okay okay here –'

She picks up her book. I'm about ta tell her not ta bother, I don't wanta hear about them stupid pigs right now, but then she puts the book on me lap, open half-way through.

'– good, isn't it? Karl Marx would approve you know anarchy –'

She's glued all the pages in the second half a the book together and cut out a hole in the middle. In the hole are pills, loadsa pills – green and pink and orange and blue.

'– you can you know –'

She opens her mouth and lifts her tongue, pointin underneath it.

'– hide them.'

In the followin weeks, I started doin the same, siphonin me pills inta whatever I could; me porridge, Amanda's grapes, the dregs a me tea. Sometimes the nurses would come around and stick their fingers in our mouths ta test us so I had ta be careful. I made sure ta take them before blood tests, all that, but they done that regular enough so it was easy ta plan ahead. Over a coupla weeks I started feelin more like meself. Me body and me brain began talkin ta each other; I started thinkin quick again, movin fast, sayin things without havin ta struggle. But I was careful ta stay quiet and dopey when they were around, so it looked like I was still on them.

Cheatin them doctors gave me a reason ta behave meself. If it wasn't for that, I mighta gone off the rails for real. It paid off. They started treatin me like I was doin great. The friendly nurse said they might even bring me dosage down and, with luck, I could be lookin at a full day out in the next month.

Soon after, Amanda told me that Charlie had started callin up for her. She said it was a pain, she'da much rather just had her dates with you, but I could tell she liked the attention and that made me feel . . . well, nearly better.

He's doin me head in. He was alright the first few visits, makin small-talk and actin all concerned, like he was me da insteada me bleedin brother, but since he's started on the pep talks he's been drivin me spare. Goin on how I don't wanta end up like Micko – meanin the gear, though he doesn't say that – how I need ta get me act together, and if I try hard, I might even make somethin outta me life. Bangin on about the new school I'll be gointa in

September and how I can do sport there, maybe even boxin, because there's plenty a other ways a doin well, Lucy, than lessons. Then he starts sayin stuff like We only have one life and It's upta us ta make the mosta it and Ta give in ta bad influences just because a boredom is stupid. I tell him I'm not stupid, I've a condition, that's what the doctors say.

Then he comes out with this Bible-thumpin lark, like it's my fault if I go down the wrong road and I'd wanta be careful because once ya go down the wrong road ya damn yerself for life. Jesus, I say, who sent *you* ta Bible classes, John Paul? He goes scarlet at that, because everyone knows Wacker Mahon's well inta the born-again business, and then he guffs on how, since gettin outta jail, he hasn't looked back, got himself a family now, and a nice place ta live, and a decent job that doesn't involve robbin or drugs. Some decent job, I think. Like Micko once said, *Just because ya don't stick yer finger in the pie, John Paul, doesn't mean Wacker's not bakin it right under yer nose.* I'm about ta say as much, only Sam speaks up – quiet as a mouse till then, just dreamin out the winda – with some message about Granny missin me and how she woulda come visit only Ma said she was too sick.

As they're leavin, John Paul says, 'Don't worry, Lucy. I'm not givin up on ya.'

As if he has the right. Fuckin . . . dick.

Then, after they've gone, Betty starts on *her* buzz, talkin about this and that and the class struggle and aspirations, and people buyin washin machines insteada gettin angry, and—

Jesus, girl! I think. Can't ya see it's fuckin hard enough? Can ya not fuckin put a lid on it for one fuckin minute?

Then she blinks and I realize I've said it out loud. With no pills ta hold them back me thoughts are slippin outta me mouth again, like rain through a sieve.

The place doesn't look bad. Bit cleaner than normal. Smells cleaner too. Must be Sam. I can't picture *Her* puttin in the effort. Dirty bitch.

Feels weird, though. All wrong, like I don't belong any more.

271

We're in the sittin room. We had dinner earlier, decent food and all it was, and a bit of a chat, but then I vexed Ma by askin her ta read me fortune again – because I was fucked if I was gointa make it easy on her, seein as she was the one tellin the Social she didn't want me back on an overnight – and she got narked because she knew it wasn't an innocent question, knew I was tryin ta get a dig in, even though even I don't know what kinda dig I was tryin ta get, just wanted ta make her fuckin itch, I did, and then she walked out in a stinker. She's in the kitchen now, so it's just the two of us, me and Sam.

'How's Micko?' I ask.

Sam shrugs. 'Okay. We haven't seen him in ages. He . . .' She trails off.

'What, Mouse?'

'Nothin.' She looks up at the ceilin. Somethin bright around her neck catches me eye.

'Show us,' I say.

She leans forward so I can look at it. 'Ya gettin skinny again, Lucy.'

I lift up the chain. Tiny silver daisies are hangin off it. 'Nice. Where d'ya get it?'

She pulls away.

'Come on. Where?'

'Secret.'

'Ah, Mouse. Ya can tell me.'

'Can't tell anyone. I promised.'

I get a cold feelin down me back. 'Didja nick it?'

'No!' she says like I'm stupid. The feelin gets colder.

The doorbell rings. Sam sticks the chain away under her jumper.

'Ah, Marlene,' says Ma in the hallway. 'Thanks a million, love, for comin up.'

'I thoughtya were goin out with Charlie?' says Sam.

I shrug and get up. 'Yeah . . . and Marlene, and the twins, and the fuckin baby and all. Bowlin. Fucksake.'

'It'll be good fun,' says Sam hopefully, but I don't believe her.

'Here, Mouse, give us a hug.'

She does. Through her jumper I feel them little silver daisies, bitin at me skin.

'Lucy.' Ma's standin at the door, deliberately not lookin at me.

In the car, Marlene gives me a can a Coke. The bubbles slide down me neck and as they do, I feel me old jigginess start ta hum away under the cold feelin. Rush in, jiggin, I tell it, rush in and wash everythin else away.

There was only so much watch-keepin Charlie could do and it wasn't long before ya started playin yer games with Amanda again. Makin dates, standin her up, not answerin the door, runnin inta her and tellin her lies, then backtrackin, askin her out again. She told me ya brung her on a walk ta the Phoenix Park and I shivered, thinking of whatcha could do ta her with nobody watchin, but it turned out ya hadn't any johnnies with ya and she was too scared ta go all the way – *all the way* again, Amanda? Fucksake – so ya left her ta make her own way home through the tall grasses.

Nothin changed. Ya told her she meant somethin ta ya then ya said she didn't then ya said she did. And all through the highs and lows of her stories, I wanted ta ask her: How's me Ma, Amanda? Didja ask him how me Ma was?

Slap slap slap slap slap slap slap slap slap slap. She brung them in at last, whacked them on the table before I even asked. This time it was my turn ta be shook and I was. So much I let her start dealin before I remembered I needed ta shuffle them first.

There's somethin up. It's in the sideways looks Sam keeps givin me, the worry on her face. The worry makes her seem miles older than she is; it fights with the fairy wings and the pink gauzy dress she's put on for her pal Lisa's fancy-dress party. But why isn't she at the party now? Why is she come visitin me instead?

It's not just Sam. It's in the way Marlene keeps tappin one fag on the canteen tabletop, puffin away at the other in her mouth; in the way Charlie keeps starin at me.

Please don't let it be the gun, I say ta meself. Please don't let them a found it.

Eight a Swords. Five a Coins. Magician. Empress. Seven a Swords. Fool. Pope. Three a Cups. Eight a Wands. Hanged Man.

'Doubt.' Ma rattles them off like a shoppin list. 'Starvin. Playin tricks with yer mind. A pregnant woman. Gettin away with somethin. Madness. Power. A love triangle. Buildin a business. And the mystery card.'

'Nothin more, Ma?' I can tell there's more and I'm fucked if I'm gointa let her get away with her usual palaver.

'No.'

'What's it mean, the mystery card?' I know the answer, I'm only testin but . . .

'Well, if we were supposed ta know what it meant, it wouldn't be called a mystery, would it?'

Jesus, I hate her. I wanta make her squirm.

'Been doin much readins lately?' I haven't planned it, I swear. The question pops out before I've even thought it.

She looks at me, surprised.

Too late ta stop now. 'Just ya very good at them, Ma. Loadsa special customers and all.' I put a little load on the *special*, but not too much. 'Remember them Fridays when the young wans useta—'

'Yeah,' she says, ridin over me, tryin ta act normal. 'Now ya ask, I have been doin a few. Only the odd person, mind, here or there.'

'Ah, yeah. The odd person.' And I stare hard at her, even though I haven't planned that neither, me stare sayin, *I know whatcha been upta, ya hooer.*

She stares back, and her cheeks flush two little spots a pink, and for a minute I think she's gointa crack, she's gointa ask me in fronta everyone, *What do ya fuckin know, Lucy? Whatcha fuckin gettin at?* But instead she cops herself on – I see the thought as clear as if it's me own, *Don't get inta this, Rose,* and in a way I'm glad because I don't know if I wanta get inta it either – and breaks away from me ta look down at the spread.

And it's then, suddenly, that I get the vision.

It's not the same as them fits I got as a kid. I'm awake. I can tell where I am. But I've got that same giddy feelin a bein sucked outta

the present and inta another world, and in fronta me eyes the cards
and their meanins have risen up off of the table and are dancin
towards me, blankin out Ma's greasy white face.

The Empress turns and smiles. The eight kids with their sticks
start a dance, smashin their sticks inta each other's faces, flowin
blood inta the brown ground. The Magician hides pills under his
twisty hat in the shape of a lyin-on-its-side number eight. I run
away from the Pope, me swords under me arm. I sip from the cup.
I sip from the cup. The Fool steps off the mountain. I hang, waitin
for the mystery ta unfold.

'Jesus!' says Marlene, breakin it. 'Are ya gointa tell her or not,
Rose?'

Ma looks up, startled. 'Ah, Marlene—'

'It's Micko.' Sam's voice sounds like it's comin from a long way
away. 'He's in trouble again, Lucy.'

I don't dare look at Charlie.

'They're sayin he was in a robbery, pet.' Marlene takes over,
smooth. 'That gang been doin all the post offices in Kildare. There
was another one last week and a woman got killed. Brutal, it was.
They're sayin Micko's one a them. He got caught with guns – him
and another lad.'

'Who?' The minute I say it, I wish I hadn't.

'Nobody we know,' says Ma, fast.

After they've gone, Charlie comes back, speedin inta the ward.

'How did ya get away from them?'

'I told them I'd forgotten me schoolbag.' He digs under me bed,
gets the bag and as he does starts talkin, fast. 'It was Mainser with
him. They took off their ballies for a smoke in the car and a witness
seen them. Then the Guards got a tip-off and they found them in
a safehouse in Cabra with the money and the bang-bangs, all . . .
outta it, ya know. Damo says it wasn't the Kildare gang, though.
They'd never fuck up like that.'

'Did they . . .'

'They didn't squeal on anyone else. But Damo says everyone
knows the Old Bill didn't find all the whack though they're not

sayin that ta the papers. Fifty grand went missin but they only found twenty. Do the maths, Lucy. Damo says they musta been doin the dirt on the Don so's they could get more gear and set up on their own. He says everyone reckons they went runnin with one a the Wacker's lads, the gee-face one from the north they call the Soldier.'

I think of a soft Northern accent in a basement, of a fella seen at Wacker's ma's funeral, a fella with a silvery beard and twinklin eyes and a gold tooth.

'How did—'

Charlie shakes his head. 'See, Mainser's ears been cut inta points with a scissors, like a rat, and the tip of his tongue been forked, like a snake, and Damo says the Soldier musta done that because that's what they do ta rats up north.'

Charlie stops, looks at me, bitin his lip.

Yer usual magic, Nayler. With a little extra on top. Make it . . . ya know . . . look right?

He starts up again. 'Damo says the Soldier musta used Micko and Mainser as patsies, ratted on them ta the Bill and made off with the resta the whack, and they're too scared a him ta squeal. See, the Soldier hasn't been seen around since, so they reckon he must be up north again gettin in with the RA – and if Micko or Mainser squeal on him, get sent ta Portlaoise for the blag, they won't survive three days there because the Soldier'll have the Ra after their blood. They can work awful fast on them landins.'

We look at each other. 'Didja—'

'Fucksake, Lucy, will ya believe me? I told Damo nothin.'

Later that evenin, I spot the picture on the newspaper stand on me way down ta the smokin-room. A shopfront with the windas shot in under big black letters. When the nurse isn't lookin, I grab the paper and stuff it under me dressin-gown.

I sneak the paper over ta Betty and ask her what it says. She's not in good form. She looks at it, dull.

'Horror in Kildare,' she says.

'Any more?'

'Woman beaten, then brutally shot in head.'

Beaten.

In me vision, eight kids dance and fight, swishin their sticks –
what sorta sticks? bamboo, oak, willa; the butts of AK 47s? – through
the air and inta each other's soft flesh. Blood flows, makin the
brown ground browner.

Do the maths. I never been good at countin but even this one's
easy for me because I can do it on me fingers. Twenty is for two.
Ya take it from fifty leaves thirty. Thirty gets split inta three real
easy. It was a five man-job.

Micko, Mainser, the Soldier. And Snags. And you.

And a missin thirty grand that's made somebody somewhere a
whole lot richer. Rich enough ta set up shop on their own and
learn their poxhead uncle a lesson, maybe?

The routine. Fuck. The routine. Get up, get pill, get rid of it, get
fed, do somethin, anythin, doesn't matter, pretend ta do literacy
lesson, listen ta radio, talk ta someone, get fed again, have visit, go
ta garden, sneak smoke, listen ta Betty – except Betty's not talkin
much any more, Betty's sunk deep inside a herself and it's hard ta
get her out, Betty's started wanderin round in her bra and knickers
instead of her red pyjamas but that's not my problem so leave well
alone – sneak smoke, get fed again, go ta bed. Try ta sleep.

Have day visit. Behave meself. Listen ta Amanda. Try not ta say
anythin I'd regret. About you. About anyone. Believe her when she
says she'll miss me next year in school but we'll still pal around,
we'll still be friends. Behave meself. Stay glued ta Sam or Granny
or Marlene like I'm some fuckin baby. Do not look for trouble. Be
good.

Plenty a time for thinkin. Too much time.

It was Charlie and what he told me that triggered it off. Up till
then I was fine. But his story made everythin different. I couldn't
shove the thoughts away the way I useta, the way I wanted ta. Back
they came, boom boom, stompin inta me head. You and Ma and
Amanda and even Sam, and what I heard from that kitchen and
what I didn't, and Snags and you in the basement and Mainser

howlin with his forked tongue, and that fella the Soldier, and me brother banged up, and did I imagine it and did I imagine her and how could you and how could she and what was goin on and why was I so wound up in anyways and shouldn't I forget it, yeah I should, I should forget everythin but fuck . . .

Them were the days where I craved for people – ta come in, take me away, do anything – so I wouldn't be left on me own with nothin but me head for company.

And then . . . Well.

Then Amanda told me her news.

Correction: she didn't exactly tell me; I'd ta dig it outta her – and it didn't exactly make things easy that Marlene had come in ta the Burger King ta keep an eye on me. She was no interferer, Marlene, she'd made sure ta sit two tables away and read a paper and all, but still . . .

That's why I had ta ask in code.

'So ya still shoppin in the ILAC Centre, Amanda? Any bargains there lately?'

Amanda nibbles her burger, leavin a pink lipstick stain round the bitemark. 'Well, actually . . . no.'

It takes me a coupla seconds ta cop.

'No? Thought ya loved that place.'

She makes a face and sucks at her Coke. 'Nah, I'm dog-tired of it. Way too much hassle. Anytime I go there the place is closed. I been tryin somewhere new. Miles nicer.'

She glances at Marlene, who's still got her head stuck in her paper.

'Oh?' I say, coppin on. Then I raise me eyebrows and sorta half-look in Marlene's direction. Meanin: Does *she* know?

Amanda smiles, a real pouty smile that's upta no good, and shakes her head.

I know she only half-believes it, what she says about bein tired a ya and preferrin Charlie, but the fact that she's lyin ta herself as well as me gives me some sorta hope.

*

278

'Ya alright there, pal?'

She's sobbin again; long, slow, endless sobs. I creep over ta her bed and take her hand. 'Hey now, Betty.'

She sobs louder. I stroke her hand. Her skin is cold.

'Hey, pal, don't worry, I'm here. It's alright, darlin.'

She freezes. Her head turns, real slow, ta look at me. Her face is wet, her eyes ringed in red. 'What the fuck do you know about being alright?' She says it slow, slower than I've ever heard her speak, linin up the words so they come out one at a time.

'Jesus, Betty—'

She laughs. 'You haven't a clue. You're as fucked up as I am.' She keeps laughin only the way her breath is breakin it sounds just like her cryin earlier on.

They moved her the next day when they found her in the jacks tryin ta take her eye out with a scissors. 'I'm Betty!' she screamed as they pulled her away. 'Don't you know anything about anything, you fucking eejits? I'm Betty fucking Blue!'

It's a small world. I met a woman years later who said she'd known Betty. Told me she ended up jumpin inta the Lee and never swam out. I see her, like I see all the other lost girls, floatin down that river, her black hair minglin with the rushes.

Some might say that jump was Betty's last desperate go at makin order outta the mess in her head. Not me. I like ta think it was a final stab at anarchy.

'Good,' says Fish-eyes, lookin at me chart. He doesn't bother his hole lookin at me. 'Very good.'

I took the pills earlier on – mainly because I was bored, what with Betty gone, and the way they cancelled me day out because it was too much of a risk, and because I don't wanta hafta think about Betty, cryin or laughin or with that scissors in her hand, and because I'm stuck in this place and there's nobody else ta talk ta and me thoughts are risin again with no conversation ta steer them off, and because I'm gettin out for good soon and I don't wanta think about that neither, what's waitin ahead a me – and right now they're washin over me, a heavy blanket, warm but itchy underneath. In the bed opposite, the yoke with the moustache who's taken Betty's place is snifflin in her sleep.

Hey, Lucy. I feel ya before ya speak. Ya standin at the end a the bed, a long black shada, but I'm feelin ya on me too, like ya pressin down on me chest. How can ya do that? Stand at the end and sit on me chest at the same time? Maybe it's magic; you're the Magician in Ma's spread, able ta do ten things at once.

Scumbag, I say, or think I say. Me teeth are gritted so hard I'm not sure if I'm speakin. Ya laugh.

Go away.

Ya lean closer. *Lookit, Lucy, this is just ta say we been keepin an eye on ya and we're very happy with how ya doin.*

Now it's my turn ta laugh. *Yeah, right.*

Hidin the gun, keepin quiet about Mainser, the post office job, it's all been noticed. We'll look after ya when you get out, me little errant girl.

Ya wink. Yer pupils are tiny, tiny, tiny in yer black eyes.

What about me Ma? I say. *What's all that about?*

Ah, Lucy, never woulda had ya for a sap. Yer Ma's nothin.

Nothin?

Nothin.

I don't know if I believe ya. *What about Amanda?*

Don't worry about Amanda, Lucy Lu. She's just a kid. Don't worry. You're one of us now. Keep in with me and you'll be fine. We got things worked out.

Get off of me. I don't need ya, I tell ya, and it almost sounds true.

Ah, Lucy. Lucy. Lucy.

Yer breath is hot and smells of oranges. Me name in yer mouth is the sounda the wind in the trees, the sea on the shore, the sun as it rises, grows, falls.

I'm not me brother. I – Don't – Need . . .

Course ya don't, Lucy. But I need you.

Yer pupils are tiny. The weight a you on me chest bears down

so much I think me heart will explode. I feel like I'm gointa puke.
Ya smile.

I'll come for ya, ya say. *I'll look after ya.*

I don't need . . .

Ya slide yer mouth ta me ear so I feel yer breath against it. One.
Two. Ya lift yer head, smile and then ya disappear.

That was the first visit, as far as I can remember. That was when
I started knowin what it might be like ta be Granny.

'Congratulations,' says Charlie. He slides his hand along the ground
onta mine.

'Jesus, get off!'

Charlie gives me a warnin look and opens his hand. I shut up.
Somethin drops onta me palm. I close me fingers round it. Over
at the far side a the garden, Ma and Marlene talk in low voices.
Sam's readin a comic.

'Yeah,' says Charlie, loud. 'It's great ya comin out.'

Marlene looks over and smiles, pleased as punch. 'Keep up the
good work, Lucy.'

'It was nothin ta do with Lucy.' Sam doesn't look up from her
comic. 'It was Micko.'

'Jesus, love!' says Ma.

But we all know it's true. The hospital are dyin ta be shot a me
since he was put away.

'We're movin out ta Malahide next year,' says Marlene brightly,
tryin ta change the subject. 'Soon as the plannin comes through.
Oh, it'll be lovely – sea views and all.'

When they went, I opened up me hand. A jay was restin there,
white and innocent as the day. I kept it inside a Betty's book that
she left me, tucked it up with all the pills she never took, and I
didn't smoke it till the day I came out for good.

I still don't know where Charlie got it.

V

When I first told Derek about the hospital and bein there when I was fourteen he went very quiet. I made a joke of it but he didn't laugh so I asked him what was up.

'Was that legal? I mean – Jesus. You were so young,' he said.

I hated that look that came inta his eyes sometimes when I told him about me past, so I felt I had ta put him straight.

'I asked for it.'

'What, as a punishment? I thought you didn't believe in that sort of absolute morality.' Then he said, like ta explain, 'Good and bad—'

'I know what it means, Derek, and that's not what I'm sayin. I didn't go there because I thought I was bad. I wanted ta be there. I wanted ta get away.' Then I sussed I mighta gone a bit far, so I pulled back. 'Typical. Ya read about it all the time in the papers. Broken home. Bad family. Ya know the score.'

'It must have been pretty bad if you chose that.'

I shrugged. I hadn't told him about you and nor was I gointa, ever. We done a few scales and then he stopped.

'I know this might sound . . .'

Say it, Derek.

'Did you get what you wanted in there?'

'What sorta question is that?'

'You said . . . Forget it.'

I went back ta the scale; E, chromatic.

'It must have changed you,' he blurts out, breakin me concentration. 'How did it change you, Lucy? What were you like before?'

I laughed. 'Jesus, Derek, people change all the time.'

The scrapin a the knives and forks is wreckin me head. Ma's eatin like she's on the telly, all small mouthfuls, holdin her fork up with her little finger stickin out. Who's she tryin ta impress? John Paul and Tara are side by side, both shovellin the grub in. Tara's in bits. She's up the pole again and little Jimmy is teethin – as she's been tellin us for the last two hours – so between him screamin at nights and her mornin sickness, she's gettin no sleep at all. John Paul puts his arm round her shoulders. Moral support.

I'm not hungry. I push me mash round me plate. In the corner a me eye I see Granny chewin a bit a meat. It looks like the same meat she's been chewin since the dinner started. On Sam's plate, the carrots and peas and mash are arranged inta a smilin face.

'So ya lookin forward ta the new school, Lucy?' says Tara.

What's she fuckin think?

'Yeah,' I say, playin it safe. 'Ma, can I go now, please?'

She shakes her head without lookin over. 'Finish up there, Lucy.'

'It's great John Paul sorted it out, isn't it?' says Tara. 'St Mary's is a very good place. Very understandin.' She smiles up at John Paul. He squeezes her hand in his big fingers.

'Ya know, Ma,' he says. 'We should do this more often. Real Sunday dinner like a proper family.'

Ma smiles tightly. 'Yeah. Sure.'

Only if it keeps the Social off yer back, Ma. Isn't that it?

Baby Jimmy starts bawlin.

'Sorry, Rose,' says Tara, gettin up. While she's gone inta the bedroom, Ma leans over ta John Paul. 'Tell her ta call me Missus Dolan.'

John Paul's fork stays lifted in the air.

Workin as quietly as I can, I scrape me mash onta Granny's plate.

'Can I go now, Ma?' She looks over at me. I show her me plate. 'I'm all finished.'

'Take yer pill!' she yells at me as I leave. 'Hear me, Lucy? Ya still hafta do what I say!'

I'm enjoyin the air, the damp September feel of it on me skin. I'm enjoyin the space, the fact me eyes can go as far as they want without bein stopped by a pus-green wall or a wire-covered winda. That I can walk where I want without someone watchin or callin me back. That this is not just for a day or a night or even two, but for good.

I lift me arms and flap them. It feels like they're ten foot long and when I flap them, like they're sendin gusts a wind everywhere. I'm makin a sandstorm in Africa, I think, a hurricane in America, I'm changin the look and feel a the world every time I flap.

I lift me feet up and set them down, and I do it without willin ta go anywhere in particular. Me feet are walkin; I'm not walkin them. They're takin me somewhere I've never gone before.

The houses stretch up either side, the dirty sycamore trees shadin them from the sun. Colours are bright. A Coke can, an empty crip package, a piece a broken plastic. The sun dances on raindrops on a bench, and I feel the light and heat as if it's dancin right inside a me.

The blue a the sky looks like I could touch it.

I feel every inch a me feet on the ground as they curl from the heel through the arches to the toes.

I am free.

Here, Lucy! calls the canal. Over here!

Soon as me feet hit the concrete a the towpath, it changes. All that airy wet sense a freedom around me dries out. I scuttle towards a hedge, feelin way too visible against the raggy grass and the burnt-out cars. It's more a bush than a hedge, really, with dark green leaves yella at the edges, and the ground underneath is littered with used johnnies and old fag butts. But there's enough space for me ta crawl under. Once there, I feel safe. I can look out at the world as it passes and nobody will know. I can make me changes on the earth and its people but nobody will know it's me doin the changin. I squash close as I can ta the dried-out, prickly trunk, and watch.

Limits. The canal is limited by the bank. The bank limited by the wall. The wall by the road. The road by the houses. The houses by their roofs, their bricks, the walls behind them, roads behind that. The city hems itself in, stops itself from goin anywhere. I am stuck. A fly on a pin. It makes me wanta cry, like Betty, *whatcha fuckin know what is ta be alright*, but I don't want anyone hearin. It's not safe.

I curl in on meself and pray ta sleep.

When I wake up, it's touchin dark and I've a pain in me neck from twistin meself round that fuckin bush. The first thing I feel is stupid, so I take a quick gander ta see if anyone's there. It's alright. Coast is clear. Then I slide meself out and dust meself off. The freedom is back, hummin in the brightenin lights a the city and the evenin buzz a the traffic. I stretch out, feelin me muscles pull like a prizefighter's, and head off.

The light comes on in the glassy bit a the front door. I toy with throwin some stones at the upstairs winda where her bedroom is, but then I think twice. I really don't wanta face her Ma, lookin down at me with all that hate and pity. In that fuckin hospital I had all the pity I needed for a lifetime. So I wait instead.

One hour. Two hours. No luck. I marvel at me patience. Six month ago I wouldn'a been able ta wait five minutes, let alone two hours. It's gettin cold. I can't feel the chill but I can see the goose-pimples risin on me arms. I turn ta go.

As I'm walkin past the alleyway off of Charles Street, I feel ya. You're down there, Nayler, in the dirt. You *are* the alleyway. I stop, waitin for ya ta come out. But ya don't. Too cosy down in the dirt. When I start walkin again, I feel ya creep up and lodge yerself between me shoulder blades. I carry ya through the streets. You're a giant pair a black wings growin outta me back. You're me guardian angel.

'Didja take it?' says Ma when I come in.

'Course I did,' I say. 'I'm not lookin for trouble.'

I lie in me unfamiliar bed, lookin up at the glow-in-the dark stars Sam's stuck on the ceilin. In me hands are the souvenirs I've dug out from under me mattress: the keys I took from yer trunk and the piece a Mainser's ears that I picked off the basement floor before I officially turned from bold ta bad. I hold them, lettin dried flesh warm cold metal, and wonder if Ma has a chain I can rob ta hang them off of.

Across from me, me little sister snores gently, like a cat.

'I still feel it there.' Granny takes me hand and puts it on her stump. 'Me leg, ya know.' Her voice is light and wonderin, like a little girl's. 'It hurts in bed at night.'

'It's fine, Granny. Healin up nicely.' I'm lyin. The wound still looks bad; red and raw. But who'm I ta say what's healin and what's not?

'Lucy, isn't it?'

'Yeah, Granny.' I lift her hand ta me face and let her feel me. Her fingers trickle inta me eye sockets and rest there, pushin against me closed lids.

'You're a terrible child.' She sighs.

'Yeah, yeah. Didn't lick it up off the ground.'

She laughs, coughin up snot. I put a hanky to her mouth and wipe her clean.

'Ya know what I mean, Lucy.' Her fingers brush me lips. She sighs again.

'Ya see somethin, Granny?' I'm surprised by how much I need her ta say yeah.

She lets go me face and laughs. 'I'm gone beyond tellin it, pet. There's a time where ya think it helps but not at my age. At my age ya know it won't make a blind bit a difference.'

'Ya should say that ta Ma.'

She shakes her head. 'Where's me tea?' She's a little girl again. 'Make it milky, Rose, will ya? Plenty a milk.'

I make it just as she wants and hold it ta her lips as she swallas. 'You're a good girl, Rose. Ya have ideas beyond yerself but ya alright.'

'Fuckin cunt!' I scream at him. He shakes his head, sneerin that way bus drivers always sneer, and the number 19 pulls away, leavin me in the rain. Fuck this. I kick at the bus stop. The auld wans standin there look me up and down. I can hear the whispers in the back a their heads. I slam me bag on the ground and kick it too. The new schoolbooks slide out inta the rain, under the wheels of a jo-maxi. The jo screeches to a halt and I scramble in the gutter, tryin ta rescue me books.

'For fuck's sake!' yells the jo driver. 'Get on with it!'

'Fuck yerself!' I yell back. 'Fuck you and yer ma!'

The back winda rolls down. 'Well, who's in a bad mood then?' A girl giggles.

I look over and see Snags, leanin outta the winda. Behind him is Sasha, eyes slitted, draped over the seat like she's melted onta it.

'Lucy, isn't it?' says Snags. 'Lucy Dolan?'

The whispers in the auld wans' heads get louder. 'Get in,' says Snags. 'Ya look like ya need ta dry off.'

There's a new lock on the front door a the squat, dirtied up so it looks old. The doors on the ground floor have new locks too and I wonder whatcha keepin there. The money from the post office job? The gear ya bought with it? More guns? I hear noises behind the doors and picture the Soldier hidin away, outta the sight a the Wacker and the Ra, happy as he trains in the new recruits, the ones that have taken the place a me brother and Mainser. The gaff smells worse than I remember, like shite and damp mixed together.

Yer room is different. It's neat and tidy and you've taken down the picture a the bird with the muscly arse and yer books aren't around and neither is the goat skull nor yer stick nor Buck's sword. There's a new stereo on toppa the cabinet that useta be in Sash's room, but apart from that, I can't see any hint a the money youse blagged from the post office. Are ya gone, Nayler?

Snags snaps his fingers in fronta me face. 'Wake up and smell the coffee, Lucy.'

'What?'

'Literally.' He's holdin out a mug. I know it's a bad joke but I laugh in anyways.

The coffee smell seeps through the room, rich and brown. Snags takes a bottle from his rucksack, and opens it. Glug glug glug goes the whiskey inta the coffee.

'There's a present for ya, me darlin,' he says ta Sash, handin her a coupla pills. She swallas them, then sniffs at the coffee.

'Mmm, good.'

'Course it is, sweetheart.'

Sasha laughs. The trackmarks inside her arm are blue and red, like the Union Jack blew up right beside her and scattered her with its dust. She sits on Snags's knee and he hugs her. I look away.

'I take it ya haven't been up here for a while,' he says.

'I was away.'

'Oh, yeah, I heard about that. I meant since ya came back. Sash says she hasn't seen sight nor sound a ya. Have ya, Sasha?'

Sasha shakes her head, her almond eyes half-closed.

I sip the coffee. It jolts right through me. Very good.

'Shame about yer brother,' says Snags. His face looks even wider now his head is shaved, and his crinklin brown eyes are wide too. They look like the sorta eyes that wouldn't hide anythin.

'Yeah. Youse all on yer own here now?'

Snags laughs, a comfortable sound. 'D'ya think a gent like me would live in a kip like this?'

I shrug.

'She means is Nayler still here,' says Sasha.

He laughs again. 'Ah, yer good pal Nayler . . . course he is, Lucy. Wouldn't leave this place for the world. We go back a long time, ya know. Like that.' He crosses two fingers.

I'm dyin for a waz. The coffee. I get up. 'Thanks for the coffee and the towel and all,' I say. I don't know what ta call him. Nobody ever calls him by his other name and Snags feels too familiar. 'Better go.' Then I add, 'The Social's keepin an eye on me,' like I need ta explain.

'No problem, Lucy.' Snags flashes me his wide smile. 'Stay in touch, yeah?' He grabs me hand as I push past. 'I mean it.' His hand is big and warm and dry. I pull mine out, tryin not ta make a fuss about it.

'Sure,' I say.

★

When I get back home, a woman I don't know is plonked on the couch in the sittin-room.

'Ah, hello, love,' she says, and moves over, pattin the space next ta her. I stay standin.

'Oh, you next?' Her face sours and she checks her watch. 'Gas. Coulda sworn she said six-thirty for me.' She looks me up and down. 'You're very young for it, aren't ya? Though I spose it's never too young ta have yer heart broke.'

The kitchen door is closed. Behind it I hear voices: Ma, murmurin, and some other wan who doesn't say much. I take a gander in our bedroom, but Sam's nowhere around.

When the kitchen door opens, I peek round from the hall, tryin ta keep meself outta eyeshot. She's got it all done up like an Aladdin's cave. Coverin the table is a big cloth, with fringes hangin down ta the floor, and on top is a small lamp, old-fashionedy, with a red scarf draped over it so the light shines like a brasser's winda. Ma steps inta the doorway. She hasn't all her Mystic Meg stuff on, just a shawl round her shoulders, but even I hafta say she looks the part.

'Goodbye, love,' she says.

A girl steps outta the kitchen, diggin in her bag. For a minute I think it's Sash, mainly because a the long hair and the longer legs – and I think, fucksake, how did she get up here before me? – but then she turns and I see it's Cindy Devlin, the prettiest brasser in town. It's funny seein her like that, with Ma, lookin for advice on her lovelife like any other young wan. Still, what do I know about hooers? Who's ta say even the most professional ones can't mix business with pleasure?

She presses coins in me Ma's paw. 'Thanks, Missus Dolan. That was a real help.'

I whistle again, low. The curtain twitches. I signal. She gives me the thumbs-up.

'Hey,' she says. 'Good ta see ya.' The air sits between us, sharp edges.

'You too. Here.'

I open me arms. She steps in. Her hair smells beautiful.

Round by the Square, fellas from the Father Scully flats whistle at us. Amanda pulls herself straight, stickin out her tits so the rain soaks inta them, makin the nipples stand up.

'Go on, ya slut!'

I turn, ready ta lash the fellas outta it, but she grabs me and pulls me ta the safety a the trees on the park side. Mosta them have lost their leaves but there's still some with needles where we can shelter. We've just about got there when I see a tall, familiar shape lopin across the road. 'Lookit,' I say ta Amanda, pointin at a plastic bag that's caught in a tree, hopin ta distract her.

While she's puzzlin over the bag I watch Snags round the corner past the brassers. They're standin in huddled clumps, hunchin over their fags, shiverin in their short skirts and lowcut tops as the autumn air bites at their skin, but he doesn't give them a second look, not even Cindy Devlin in her pride a place at the south-westerly corner.

So why have I suddenly got that feelin again, that hunch I had months ago when we were walkin back from the squat with Charlie and Damo, that the girls on the Square were workin for him? *They're not the Wacker's, they're Snags's*. And why this time am I so sure I'm right?

Maybe it's the ease of his walk as he passes. Or maybe it's the way they look at him. It's not a here-mister look, they don't shift their stance, juttin out tits and cunts ta tempt him ta buy. But they're not actin casual either, like he's just another lad. There's somethin wary and searchin and hungry in their faces that follas him all the way across the street. But surely not even Snags Ryan would be fool enough ta rob that sorta merchandise from under the Wacker's nose? Anyways, there's miles easier ways a makin a few bob than runnin hooers.

I pull at Amanda's arm. 'Come on, willya. It's easin off.'

We peel ourselves out from the railins and saunter past the girls.

'Hiya, Lucy,' says Cindy.

I hear the rumours ripple through them: *Rose Dolan's daughter. The fortune-teller's kid. The one that went mad and tried ta burn down her school.*

'Lovely evenin, ladies,' I say, ta break the ripple.

Amanda tugs at me – 'Jesus, Lucy!' – and as we head down towards Summer Street I feel the hooers' laughter folla us, light as a wind blowin through heather on a hilltop.

Amanda couldn't stay out too late that night, on accounta her Ma. Seems like Missus Phelan only thought I was safe if I was behind a nice big hospital door. But we made a plan ta hook up the next week. She'd tell Charlie, he'd bring Damo. Old times, all that.

Seems loadsa people get sick on a Tuesday. With all them wheel-chairs and crutches and ambulances whizzin round the Mater, it's like Croke Park at a mucksavage final.

Amanda's still in her uniform and hasn't brung a change a clothes.

'Me Ma was lookin,' she says. 'Asked all sortsa questions the other night.'

I can't be bothered talkin about her Ma and her stupid opinions, so I nip inta the jacks and change inta me tracksuit. When I come out, Charlie and Damo are there. Charlie's got his glasses off. He's smokin a fag and lookin very pleased with himself.

I dig him. 'Ya look very gnick without the specs, Charlie. Almost like a real fella.'

'Yeah, suits him,' says Amanda. 'I always useta say ya shouldn't wear specs, that right Charlie?'

'Hear that, Charlie? Amanda says ya look better without them too.' I dig him again.

He digs me back. 'Fuck off, Lucy.'

'Howayiz,' says Damo.

'I'm not talkin ta you,' I say. 'Where were you when I was slammed up?'

'I . . .'

'No thought for yer pal, eh?'

'Ah, fucksake, Lucy, I'm sorry.' Damo goes scarlet. 'I didn't know . . . I thought it was just . . . ya know, family.'

I shake me head, real sad. He goes even more scarlet.

'Damo, ya thick!' says Amanda. 'She's only messin!'

The number 10 is empty. Just some drunk lad down the back singin a rebel song and a coupla auld birds that remind me a Felix, all tight grey curls and tighter mouths, shakin their heads every time we say anythin.

Amanda takes out her make-up bag and roots round. A rake a lipsticks and eyeshadas fall onta her lap. She lifts up one, squints at it, twists off the cap and starts smearin blue on her eyelids. It's hard work with the bus movin, but she does alright.

'Ya don't need that muck,' says Charlie. 'Ya gorgeous enough as ya are.'

'Yeah, right,' she says. Then, in a different voice – 'Jesus, Charlie Dolan! Are ya mad?'

He's rollin a jay.

'Charlie—' says Amanda again but I dig her in the side before she can say any more. I can see the bus driver lookin at us in his mirror. She giggles.

Once we get ta the Phoeno, we race down the bowl ta the kids' playground. There's one Ma there, with a little boy barely outta nappies who's swingin on a baby swing. She goes over ta him the minute we get there.

'Jesus!' shrieks Amanda as Charlie digs his feet inta the wooden step. The four-person swing goes higher. The chain drops and I bend over Amanda and she bends over the wooden bar. Charlie's hands grip the bar either side a hers. He leans back inta Damo, pushin him against the chain their side. He whoops.

'I'm gointa get sick! Lucy!'

Our turn now. I push hard, enjoyin the effort as it travels up me feet inta me legs, burnin out all the laziness I built up in the hospital. Amanda falls back on me. Her body is soft and sweaty. Through her hair I see Charlie's wild eyes.

★

'Ya know what they're sayin now?' says Damo.

'What?' says Charlie, lazily passin the joint.

'That fella that was blown away the other night in Dolphin's Barn – it was a professional job.'

'Ah, yeah?' I say, but I'm not really that bothered.

'Bollocks,' says Charlie. 'He was a pusher. It was vigilantes done it. Some fella whose kids is dyin with that new virus. Everyone knows that, Damo.'

Damo shakes his head. 'That's what the papers say. But me da says the lad that was killed useta be a Green Strip, in with the Wacker before he went on the gear. And there was two different sets a knife wounds in him. The ones that killed him don't match up with the vigilantes'. They're not givin it ta the papers but the rozzers been askin round who does knife-jobs for the Don.'

'Here, Amanda.' I pass the joint. 'It's good, this.'

'What's the Don gotta do with it?' says Charlie. 'That killin was on the southside. Don Ryan's got nothin over there any more.'

'Exactly. Now, me da thinks it's the Wacker, tryin ta put it on the Don, but –' Damo lowers his voice, looks around '– I got other ideas.'

'Great,' says Charlie. 'Good for you, Damo.'

'I think it's Snags.'

'What? That's bollocks,' I say, and glance at Charlie.

'No,' says Damo. 'Think about it. All them rascals he had, they were deadly at the knife work, remember? And Snags useta run the Barn in the old days. He could be tryin ta muscle in there again, set up shop – only behind the Don's back. He'd hafta a got the money from somewhere ta buy the stuff but once that was sorted, say no more. First step, get rid a the competition.'

I don't wanta think about this shite. 'Fucksake, Damo, that's thick. Snags is sorted now, isn't he?'

'That's what everyone thinks, he's happy back with the Don, but I reckon not. He's been dirt-poor since he come back from Amsterdam. Livin in that squat and all.'

'He's not livin—' I start ta say, then shut meself up, just in time.

'The only thing is, who's he got sellin for him? Because the Don woulda sussed it if he'd taken any a his dealers.'

'Jesus, Damo,' says Charlie. 'I think ya onta somethin.'

What? I stare at Charlie, willin him ta stop now before he blows his big mouth and lets off about everythin we seen, because that's none of our fuckin business, right?

He ignores me. 'If I was Snags, I'd be doin the same thing.'

'Yeah,' says Damo, meanin *See, Lucy?*

'It's normal,' says Charlie. 'Everyone needs ta, ya know . . . shunt their da outta the way ta move on. And with Snags all he has is his uncle so, ya know . . .'

'That's bollocks,' I say. I'm vexed now. I don't like where this is goin.

'Ah, no, listen—' says Damo.

'He has his ma,' says Amanda outta the blue.

Charlie turns like what she said means somethin. 'But he's nothin ta gain from shuntin her. Think about it, Amanda. If you had ta choose, which one would it be?'

'I wouldn't choose neither. That's horrible!'

'But ya hate yer Da. You're always sayin he's a bastard.'

'Yeah, but that's sick,' says Amanda. 'Which one wouldya kill?'

'I didn't say *kill*,' says Charlie. 'I said *shunt*.'

'Doesn't matter,' says Amanda. 'It's wrong. Besides, I don't hate him. He's me Da. I love him.'

I laugh. She glares at me. 'Leave off, you. I mean it. Why'd I hafta . . . shunt him ta . . . what . . . move on?'

'You'd shunt yer Ma, then,' says Charlie.

'No! I swear, Charlie Dolan, if ya don't shut up I'll smack ya. I wouldn't shunt neither. It's wrong.'

'No, no,' says Damo, like he's just got another brainwave. 'It's not wrong. It's – whatcha say it was, Charlie?'

'Normal.'

'Yeah. Because I'd shunt me Da. No contest. He's always on at me for bein stupid. Me Ma's alright, though.'

'Ah,' I say, jumpin in. 'Yer ma's alright. Isn't that nice, Charlie? Damo's a mammy's boy.'

'Fucksake,' says Damo. 'Ya know what I mean.'

'It's all them lovely dinners she makes, Damo. Isn't that it? Keeps ya full a good ideas, so ya'll never shunt her. Shunt, that's a good word, rhymes with . . .'

'I said, fuck off.' Damo throws a stick at me. 'Jesus! Last time I'll tell youse one a me ideas when all youse do is rip the piss.'

I don't look at Charlie then but when he's passin me the joint I say 'Thanks', puttin an extra load on the word so he'll know I mean it's not just for the joint but for changin the subject so none of us hafta think a any a that stuff more than we need.

Later we lie on the bandstand, in the shade. The trees are gold and red and yella. The leaves drop slow, one at a time. Amanda lies between me and Charlie. Charlie's got his legs up so his feet are flat on the ground, and his arms are folded under his head. His Walkman is playin somethin only him and Amanda can hear because she's got the other earphone. Her arms are under her head too, but her legs are crossed at the ankle and she rocks them in time ta the music. On the other side a me is Damo. I can feel his hand itchin ta touch me leg but I summon up all the power I can in me head ta warn him away. Keep off the grass, fuckface.

A wind starts up. I turn on me side, snuggle inta Amanda.

Hello, kids.

I'm awake – lyin down but able ta see everythin. Ya standin at one a the pillars a the bandstand. As I watch, ya unzip yer jeans and and take out yer nob. Ya piss. A golden arc that breaks, flyin ragged in the wind.

D'ya like this? ya say. *D'ya like ta watch, Lucy Lu?*

Ya turn around but I can't see yer face. Ya holdin yer knife in yer right hand. Ya twist the knife, sudden, and it comes flyin towards me and without any effort, I catch it. The blade digs inta me hand, releasin blood. The feel a the blood is warm, comfortin, but when I look down at me hand there's no sign of it.

When I look back up, ya kneelin down and writin somethin on the ground. I'm still lyin down but I'm hoverin over ya too, like I'm flyin, and this is what I see:

A five-pointed star with a name at each point. Yer name is at the top. I know it by the N. In the middle a the star is a drawin of a horse's head with another star on its forehead. The horse moves an eye. The eye winks.

Come up and see me.

Every evenin, the women's voices leak out from under the sittin-room door.

The auld wans mutter about fluke tips on the gee-gees, bad tins a salmon predicted in Duffy's Nite'n'Day, a freak bus accident foretold outside Teasy Maguire's front door.

The young wans giggle about their fellas.

And over in a corner sit the silent lot, Wacker's girls from the Square – Bernie Cooke and Lily Lawlor, Yvonne Kehoe and Christine Bourke. Makes me edgy ta see them, though I don't know why. Brassers have a right to a fortune like anyone else, right?

The door closes but before it does I see the fringes at the bottom a the tablecloth move, like someone's brushed against it. Someone who's crouchin there, under the table, drawn ta the precious secrets like a magpie ta gold.

Hey, Mouse. I smile ta meself, thinkin of her still so innocent.

D'ya like that, Lucy Lu? D'ya like ta watch?

I dream a you ridin Amanda in the long grasses a the Phoeno Park. On me belly I creep forward, watchin while yer bodies sing. I squeeze closer, squashin meself smaller, so small I can slide onta yer skin, down yer white chest, yer hard belly, onta yer nob. And there I dance, right on the tip, as ya lunge in and outta Amanda's giant drippin cunt.

Amanda sits up. She's got me Ma's face on insteada her own.

'Lucy!' says Sam, shakin me awake. 'Lucy, stop yellin.'

296

I lie there in me sweat till Sam's asleep again. Then I get up and go ta the kitchen and pour meself a glass a milk. I sip it, one warm mouthful at a time.

Ya been around. I know it. I don't need ta fool meself, like Ma, that I can read hands or cards or a crystal ball ta sense ya. Little things give ya away: scents, sounds, sights. A bleached blond hair with a two-inch black root, caught in the ragged plastic edge a the kitchen table. Doc Marten footprints leadin a trail a mud ta Ma's bedroom. I try not ta give it heed, I try ta push it back, but I can't.

Any visits? I ask Sam, but she's too lost in her own world ta pay any attention ta what goes on in ours. So I'm never surprised when she shakes her head.

Any fellas? No.

Any strangers? No.

Anyone we know? No.

I come home early, tryin ta catch youse at it. I don't wanta see but I'm desperate for proof, ta tell meself I'm not imaginin things. I'm always too late. The door slams and ya down the stairs, out the back, runnin through alleyways as I reach the yard.

One day, as I'm brushin me teeth, I think I see ya in the corner a the mirror and I stop, like a cat with a bird. Any movement I make will scare ya away.

Whatcha want with her? I think but don't say.

Ya lean back against the door and smile yer lazy smile. *Can't ya guess, Lucy Lu?*

When I turn round, you're gone.

He sits by her knee as she reads his future, showin with a flick of her wrist who ta avoid and who ta pal up with.

Tell us about Billy the Bowl, he says.

Tell us about Buck Whaley. Scaldbrother. Arbour Tom. Ironeye Flanagan.

Tell us tell us tell us.

*

It's late, way too late ta be up, let alone out, but I can't sleep. Can't watch telly neither, nor play records, on accounta it'll wake everyone up. And me Walkman's fucked.

The Devil, goes the sayin, makes work for idle hands. Well, fuck the Devil and fuck bein idle. I just can't sleep. That's all.

The Square is empty, bleached grey by lamplight and the shreds a moon leakin out from the clouds. There's a wind up, sendin scraps a paper and crip bags flyin across the street, makin the skinny arms a the trees sway. Even the girls are gone.

The moon slips free. She's got a woman's face – smooth, like Sasha's – and hair streamin out in mist. I tilt me own face upta hers, soak up the light.

There's still a candle on in yer winda. Are ya there, Nayler? Or are ya hid in me Ma's bed, hid so deep I can't see ya even though I stand in the doorway and stare and stare? Are ya swappin stories with her now, or are ya up there with Snags, and his soldiers and his girls and his bloodstained presents for his darlin?

I'm starvin. Mad how just the memory a somethin can make ya feel it. Well, Granny's got her missin leg wakin her up in the night, so why shouldn't I get imaginary munchies from the memory a draw?

It was as I turned I seen her. I was too far away ta make out who she was, and she'd an anorak on and trackie bottoms, which didn't help, plus she was all hunched up, huggin herself against the cold, but there was no mistakin the fast trot of an off-duty brasser.

I still don't know why I done it – after what we seen and knew and with Micko banged up and and me own hunches and Damo blatherin on in the Park, I'd no real hankerin for more trouble; like I say, it was none a me business. But –

I followed her.

The brasser took me all the way inta the hearta Wacker's territory, up Eccles Street, down Nelson Street and across ta Blessington Street. Then round by Paradise Place, Long Lane and down inta Dominick Street. She doubled up a coupla times, like she knew she was bein followed, and when she got ta the Dominick Street flats, she went along the balconies, knockin on a few doors each one. Each time someone answered, she'd go in, but only a few minutes. Then she'd come out and move onta the next one, just like an auld wan givin out parish papers.

No. Like a tinker tryin ta sell carpets.

The only thing is, who's Snags got sellin for him?

Fuck.

Shoulda listened ta me, Damo, back in the old days when I wasn't watchin me mouth. I knew them girls were Snags's.

I lost her in the Lower Flats, at the statue a the Holy Mary behind the meat factory.

'I had a word with the sports teacher,' says John Paul. 'They're willin ta give ya a go on the boxin team, long as ya keep gointa school.'

'Fucksake. I don't—'

'Ya hafta get it together, Lucy. I told ya once. I'm not gointa tell ya—'

'I – Don't – Want – Ta – Do – Boxin,' I say, real slow. 'Ya deaf or somethin?'

'Ah . . .' He takes a real impatient-soundin breath. 'It's for yer own good, ya know. I'm tryin ta look after ya, Lucy. Ma's behind it and all.' He nods, like that makes it great.

'I'm not inta it, John Paul. Got me own things goin on.'

'Oh yeah? Like what exactly?'

We shiver under the awnin. The rain is at us horizontal almost, drenchin our school coats.

Amanda's face is blue. 'I can't stay long, Lucy,' she says. 'G-g-gotta study.'

'Study?'

'Christmas tests.' She checks her watch, a new one someone got her for her birthday – only she won't say who, and I'm thinkin maybe it's you but she wouldn't keep that from me, would she?

'Fuck. Gotta go.'

I head inta the Deluxe on me own and huddle over a big cup a milky coffee till the rain clears.

'Stick out your tongue, please.'

I do as they say, too stoned ta fight back.

Last time I forgot ta take the pills and I was high as a kite. They asked me and Ma if I was bein cooperative – in other words, was I still takin them? – and we both said 'Yeah'. But I could tell they had their suspicions. They'd hafta be thick not ta.

The nurse folds her lips together while she measures me temperature. Then she looks up and smiles. Good.

'That's great, Lucy. Doctor may consider bringing the dosage down once he's had a chat with you. However, we noticed you missed your last counselling session. Now . . .'

Blah blah blah. Consider. Dosage. Counselling.

Fuck you, ya thick bitch, I say in me head. Fuck whatever cloud ya came down on. Ya can't pull one over me.

I sorta hate meself when I'm like this, hatin everyone, but it's not me. It's the . . . dosage, as they call it. Or maybe it's the counsellin. Useless talk about sweet fuck all.

Once we're outta the Health Centre, I expect Ma ta do her usual – stop pretendin ta be the World's Best Ma, and leave me to it. But instead she grabs me by the arm and marches me ta the bus stop.

'Leave off.'

'Oh no, madam. I'm comin with ya today. Ya can play all the games ya like with the Health Board but them yokes from the School Attendance knows what's what. And I'm not bringin down any more shite on me head, not if I can help it.'

We sit on the top deck. I look out as the trees on Botanic Avenue whiz past, grey and brown in the golden winter light. Ma's smokin. The smell drives me nuts.

'Give us one,' I say.

She slaps me hand. 'Buy yer own.'

I laugh.

'What?'

'It's just . . . it's funny,' I say, still laughin. She stares at me, like I really am mad. Then she starts laughin too. She still doesn't give me a fag but it feels alright, laughin with her on the top deck a the bus, as if there's nothin bad between us after all.

'Pay attention, Miss Dolan, please.'

I jerk me head up. The teacher's starin down at me. 'Have you any idea what was said in the last five minutes?'

The class sniggers.

'Detention, Miss Dolan – and today we'll try not to get caught sneaking out the front gate, shall we?'

They snigger again.

As soon I come in, I hear the wailin, so I drop me bag and race inta the kitchen, bumpin inta the door on accounta still bein a bit zoned out on the pills. And when I make it –

'Jesus!' screams Ma. 'I never asked for this!'

Granny's lyin on the kitchen floor, her head in Sam's lap. Blood is oozin out from a cut on her forehead.

'I never wanted this!' Ma's swingin her fists. She's grippin a glass in one hand and vodka's flyin everywhere. 'I had plans for me life. I had things I wanted ta do! Ta end up – Jesus!' The glass smashes inta the drainin board. Ma lifts up the bit she's still holdin, looks at it. 'Ah, Mother a—'

And then she's down on the ground, shovin the glass towards Granny's face.

'No, Ma!' screams Sam, pushin her away. 'She only tripped, that's all. She forgot she couldn't walk. Ma!'

'Shut up!' screams Ma. 'Shut up, ya useless little—'

I walk over ta Ma and slap her hard on the face. She staggers back. I grab the hand that's holdin the glass.

'Leave off, ya fuckin lunatic,' she says, spittin the words in me face. Her breath stinks. She jerks, tryin ta tug the glass back off me. There's a stingin in me hand. I look down and see that both our hands are covered in red, just like Granny's useta be when she felt somethin bad comin. Ma tugs again. This time I lose me grip and jolt forwards, slippin on the ground – piss, Granny's piss. I stagger, catch me balance.

There's a smash as Ma fecks the glass inta the bin.

Sam grabs me and shoves me towards the door. 'Get out, Lucy!'

'No.' Marlene frowns. 'Charlie's not here. He said he was meetin you.'

'Ah, yeah,' I lie. Marlene glares at me.

'Lucy, are you—?'

'No, that's right, Marlene. Sorry. I forgot. We were sposed ta be goin off for a game in the park or somethin. It's the pills, ya know. Have me head melted.'

Marlene's mouth tightens as I go.

I throw another stone at her winda, knowin it's useless. She's gone too. Gone wherever they've planned. Without me. I toy with the thought a callin round ta Roche's garage, where Damo's probably hangin out, tryin ta learn ta fix bikes, but then I think better of it.

There's no answer for ages, and I think, Okay, I'm off the hook, better make tracks, but then the door slides open. I'm sorta wishin it's Sash or even Snags, but no such luck.

'Ah, Jesus.' Ya seem a bit confused ta see me. 'Lucy Lu.'

Ya got yerself a different look. Less a the Billy Idol. Yer hair's still in spikes but ya've let the bleach half-grow out, makin it look like ya got little yella flames dancin round yer head. Funny. In me visions ya were just a black shada, a ghost almost. But ya not black now. Even though the shadas round yer eyes and cheekbones is darker than before, yer skin looks paler, lit up almost. Kinda like how ya were as a kid. Kinda not. And though ya thin as a cat, ya no ghost. Ya wearin a dark tee-shirt with a ragged neck and sleeves and under the rips I can see the muscles in yer arms is real, hard and knotted as ever.

'Hiya, Nayler. Long time no see.'

'Yeah.' Ya don't open the door any wider.

'Eh . . . Snags said ta call up.'

'Snags?' Ya frown.

'Yeah. I met him and Sash a few weeks gone and they said . . .'

For a second I think ya gointa close the door in me face. But instead ya pull it open.

'Okay. Come on in.'

Inside, it's darker than usual. Ya snap on yer lighter and light a candle. Our shadas grow wings. I look up between the curlin seashell a the twistin bannisters and watch our wingtips fightin ta burst through the roof.

It smells way worse than it did the mornin I came up with Snags.

'Ugh,' I say, nerves forcin the words out. 'Too many bodies down in the basement, what?'

Ya pause a minute, look at me.

'Only jokin,' I say.

I can't hear any rumblins behind the locked doors, but climbin up the first flight a stairs, I see the big winda in the back wall is covered over with a piece a cardboard.

'What's that in aida?' I ask despite meself.

'Ah, we'd trouble with kids a while back. A break-in.'

'Can't have that. No squatters in the squat, what?'

Ya grunt neither a yes nor a no.

I think a the gun and wonder if you've ever thought—

Ya look at me. 'What?'

'Nothin.'

At the top landin, ya open the door on the right that useta be Sasha's.

'We done a bit a movin round since ya came here last.'

'Yeah.'

I'm wary, followin ya in, rememberin Mainser's screams, aware there's nobody else in the gaff; not Snags, not Sasha. It's gone past the time ta feel wary, a course, but I'm feelin it.

'Jesus!'

Ya grin. 'Good, isn't it?'

Ya got the room done up like yer old one next door, only more. All yer stuff is on the walls: yer stick, yer sword, yer poster, new posters, a drawin of a man with red eyes that keeps lookin at me.

But it's not that takes me breath away. It's the skulls. The goat's one has pride a place on the mantelpiece, but there's others everywhere. The windasills, the fireplace, the floor. Some's got horns, some not, some are whole, others broken.

'Whatcha do, Nayler? Rob a graveyard?'

Ya laugh. 'Nah. Pal a mine works in the abattoir off of Meath Street.'

'On the southside?'

'Yeah. Why? Ya wanta arrest me for that?'

I laugh – it sounds holla, even ta me – and touch me souvenirs, hidden under me school shirt.

Ya flick yer finger against one a the skulls. 'One thing we can't run from, Lucy Lu. Death. Comin for us all. Here.'

Ya fling a cushion over. It's got mirrors on it, and magic signs, like the ones Ma has on the scarf she puts over her fortune-tellin table. I sit down on it. The mirrors dig inta me arse, so I move around, tryin ta get comfortable.

Ya slouch down onta yer mattress, stretchin out yer legs, hard in their dusty jeans. Ya hook one arm up against the wall, leanin inta the other so yer tattoo bunches up inta yer shoulder. Ya look at me. Yer eyes are hidden but there's somethin in that look makes me feel real itchy. I scratch me neck.

'So. Why ya up here, Lucy Lu?'

Answers flash through me head. Because I keep dreamin a ya, Nayler. Because in a dream ya told me ta come up and see ya. Because you and that invitation a yours is there in the signs, the small things that happen every day: the walk of a neighbour, the trail a leaves in me cup, the tunes that play on a radio each time I go past, the snatches a chat I hear on the bus, the pictures that come inta me head when I drowse off durin class, in the shape clouds make in the sky, in the big 'N's, the letter I know now better than any, even than 'O', that I see everywhere.

Because I need ta ask ya about me Ma.

Because I wanta hear from yer own mouth that ya helped Snags stitch me brother up on that post office job.

Because I need ta be close ta someone and you're all I've got.

But I know ya won't like any a them answers, so I give ya the other one, the easy one, the one I've prepared.

'Got any draw?'

Ya go blank, then laugh, soft. 'Oh, it's like that, is it?'

I make a face. 'Suppose so.'

'There was me thinkin ya'd come up ta share the wisdom a yer time in the slammer.'

'Not exactly the slammer, Nayler.'

'Near enough.'

I shrug.

'Okay.' Ya twist yerself up, pull the gauze curtain in front a the mattress so I can't see and start rummagin round. As you're there, I think about all the things I could tell ya, about Dr Terence and the Fish-eye cunt in the bin, and Betty, and the friendly nurse and the Gestapo and the headcases droolin on their pillas, and the noises people make when they send the electricity through them. But instead I say, 'Me Ma's askin for ya.'

Ya stop rummagin. 'Yeah? She's been like me own ta me, Lucy.' Ya sound innocent, like ya mean it.

'Oh, I'll bet,' I say, not thinkin.

Ya stop. Stock-still. Then ya pour yerself out from under the curtain and walk towards me. Ya movin easy, but prepared. I seen ya move like that when ya were a kid, gearin up for somethin bad. Are ya gointa slap me for makin that dig about Ma? I shift around. For the first time, I'm vexed I didn't take John Paul up on his offer and join that boxin club.

'Sure ya came here for the draw, Lucy?'

I jut out me chin. 'Yeah. What else?'

'You tell me.' Ya less than a foot from me. Yer fist is bunched. Close-up ya look real strong, like ya could deck me easy if ya wanted.

'Tell ya what?' Me knee starts jiggin. I laugh. 'Jesus, Nayler. Relax. I just want some calmin. What's the crime in that?'

Ya don't laugh back. Me knee keeps jiggin.

Fuck this. I'd get up and go only ya blockin me way. 'So d'ya have some or—'

'Can't do it, Lucy.'

'What?'

Ya shrug. Yer fist releases. 'I'm all out.'

Relief first then – Ah, *fuck*.

'But if calmin's whatcha've come for, I've somethin else might help.'

We look at each other.

'Like what?'

Ya crouch down in fronta me, open yer hand and show me what's lyin there, bang in the middle a yer lifeline.

'Only if ya sure, Lucy Lu.'

Not much expression. Just one black eyebrow lifted. The low light makes it hard ta see yer eyes, even this close, but I can tell ya darin me, like you've always dared me. *Scaredy little girl, Lucy Lu. Or are ya a little . . . boy?*

Along with the dare is somethin else.

Yer nostrils are open, only a touch wider than usual, but enough ta remind me of a horse sniffin with excitement at the startin line. Ya calm on the surface, but underneath there's a twitchin comin from ya, streamin like heat outta yer angel-white chalky skin. I know that twitchin. It's the same buzz I get anytime a fight's brewin.

How much I'm actually seein I don't know. But I'm more aware than ever there's nobody else in the squat, only us, and that's tellin me lines is bein drawn, lines I'm readin between, and they're tellin me thatcha doin somethin ya shouldn't. This offer ya makin me is secret, not somethin anyone else should know about; not me pals, not Sash, not Snags, especially not Snags, though God knows why if he's back in business again.

Decision time.

Tick.

Tock.

Me mind's already goin inta overload. Fuckin Micko hadn't a clue. Lad was always weak in anyways, just like me Da, always had ta folla someone. I'm not like them. I'm me own person. I know when ta stop. Fucksake, *you* knew when ta stop, and how. Ya said as much ta Micko. Ya have it under control. And I will too. It's easy ta take control. All ya gotta do is be strong. And that's me. I'm strong. And this is our secret. Our secret, Nayler. Nothin ta do with Ma nor nobody fuckin else. With you in this alongside me, I'm even stronger. I'm queen a the fuckin castle.

'Course I'm sure, Nayler,' I say, dead cas. Then I say it again – 'Course' – quickly, just in case ya change yer mind.

Folla me inta the wood, says the Big Bad Wolf. Because there has ta be a wolf. God forbid Little Red Ridin Hood would just decide ta wander off the track off of her own bat.

'Ya gointa smoke this,' ya say after lockin the door. Ya businesslike, efficient, like Doctor Fish-eyes givin me the XYZs. 'If ya inject on yer first go, you'll be done for.'

Ya fold the foil, lengthways, widthways, click yer lighter on, hold the foil over it.

'Burns the lead out,' ya say, conversational.

Ya roll another foil inta a toot. 'Here.' Ya gesture ta yer mouth. I hold the toot in mine. It's cold and warm, all in one. The tin burns me lips. It tastes like blood. I'm startin ta feel like a spa.

Ya tip the powder inta the foil and click on the lighter again.

Bubble, bubble, toil and trouble.

I look over at ya. The hunger in yer eyes nearly makes me faint.

'Go on.' Yer voice is dead rough all of a sudden.

A thought strikes me. Is this why ya makin such a big deal, Nayler? Is this why Snags isn't supposed ta know? *Keep yer hands clean, kiddo?*

'What about you, Nayler? Ya not havin any?'

I dare ya.

Hunger fights with somethin else. An iron will.

'Go the fuck on.'

I inhale, darin ya with every inch a smoke that fucks itself inta me body.

Everythin goes.

*

'Ya askin me about inside,' I say – hours after? minutes? – when I'm capable a speakin.

'Yeah?'

'I met this . . .' I stop, searchin for the word. 'This young wan. She was mad.'

Ya laugh.

'No, not like me. Really mad. She was up all the time but when she crashed, fuck, she fell. You'da liked her.'

'Yeah?'

The plasterwork on the ceilin is smooth cream where the damp and spiderswebs aren't at it. I can hear a fly buzzin in the park. If I concentrate, I can hear Ma at home, givin off ta Granny. If I concentrate even more, I can hear me Da's heart beatin, some-where.

'Well?' ya say as we walk down the stairs.

'Well,' I say.

At the door, ya put yer arm round me shoulders. Ya don't squeeze or grab, just rest on me, barely touchin. Between us buzzes a line a hot white space. For once neither of us pulls away.

'Don't be a stranger, Lucy.'

I nod, in me invincibility not needin ta say anythin, not even, It's okay, Nayler, our secret's safe with me.

I got the freedom now, that's for sure. I got the freedom now but none a the limits. The air has never felt so fresh, the sky so blue, the ground so firm. Forgive me for speakin shite, like somethin off of a greetin card, but what words can ever do justice ta the feelin a blessed relief?

VI

Everythin has a price. Currency, ya call it. Bring me this, bring me that. Bring me a set a china dogs made in 1795, with floppy brown ears on them and white bellies. Bring me a crystal wine jug with a carved silver top. Bring me a velvet coat, old-fashioned, and a lace shirt.

'Why?' I make the mistake a askin.

Ya look down at yer combat jacket – still no shellsuits for you, ya hate all that – and pull somethin off it. It's a hair, brittle and bleached. Hers. Ya stretch it between yer fingers and watch it snap.

Why? Easy, stupid. Because everythin has a price.

Oh, yes, whatcha give me I hafta pay for. But I'm okay, I got it under control. I'm not desperate like whatever sad junkies you and Snags got workin for youse on the streets, sellin and runnin and buyin and payin and catchin and fetchin and dodgin and scammin. I'm not sellin me body ta buy off ya. Nor queuein outside manky drop-offs under the coppers' cold gaze ta pay over the odds for shite gear cut with glucose and polyfilla ten times over. Nor am I runnin from pillar ta post, from the Square ta the Don's snooker hall on the quays and back just because someone says supplies are short.

I got it easy. I roll up whenever it's safe – meanin, whenever Snags and Sash aren't round – and with whatever you've asked me ta bring. And then I smoke with ya watchin and I dream and chill and maybe we chat and then I go home and wait for the next nod.

I'm sorted. I hafta be. I've given up the mental tests but the Social is still callin up regular so I can't let stuff show. I'm not like Micko, dyin for his visits from the Ice-Cream Man, uppin his fix from a ten ta a forty, his daily from once ta five times. No everyday pangs a hunger for Lucy Dolan – though I think about it sometimes, sure I do, but that's natural, isn't it? lookin forward ta it? – I'm a weekend user, me. That slaggin term, I'm happy ta own it. Though I wouldn't call meself a user . . . no. In anyways, I'm only smokin it. I got it under control.

So what does it matter if I catch ya comin outta her room, yer smile hidden in the shadas under yer eyes, zippin up yer tattered jeans with yer hard white fingers? What does it matter if I smell her on yer neck, in the skin a yer elbow, under the black crescents of yer fingernails? What does it matter if ya drop her name in chat – Rose says this, yer Ma says that – without even lookin over ta see if I'm wise, if I'm ragin, if I'm under?

Bring me a paintin of a man. A good one with a goldy frame.
 By now I should know better than ta ask but –
 'A who?'
 Ya curl yer lip. Anyone. Long as it's a fella and from the right time.
 I cop it then, when ya stick the paintin on the wall, what you're after with all them antiques. And it makes me laugh. For all yer guff ya still just a kid, Nayler, lookin ta build a shrine ta yer auld hero Buck Whaley.

I'm learnin from the master. He who knows, wins. That's what it says in yer books, so ya tell me. *Knowledge is the only thing makes us powerful, Lucy*. And in return for me tribute, ya share what ya know, handin it out grain by grain along with yer goods.
 The gear's not as bad as they make out, ya say. By itself it doesn't fuck ya up, it's the stuff they put in it. Once ya keep things clean and don't get greedy, it's okay. Easy enough ta get off it too. A few days is all it takes for the body, even if ya been on it years. The withdrawals can be hell but that's the price. The phy is way worse butcha can kick that too. Wean yerself off it and back on the gear then ya just got the seventy-two ta get through.
 'Seventy-two what?'
 'Hours, Lucy. That's when it peaks. After that it gets better. It's okay once ya know how.'

Ya take me through yer Smack Addict Survival Handbook. Rule One: Can ya afford it?

'Well, Lucy Lu, can ya?'

Sure, I think but don't say. Sure.

'When ya start not bein able ta pay for it, get off it.'

Rule Two: Never rat on yer dealer and be very careful when ya change shop.

'No chance a that happenin, Nayler, what?'

'Maybe not. But if ya do, check the stuff out. Always taste first, shoot later.'

Three: Keep yer works clean and don't share them. Unless ya want ta get sick, or worse, catch yerself an ugly livin death courtesy a the virus. 'But you won't be usin works, Lucy, because a . . .'

Rule Four: Always smoke or snort insteada shootin, way easier on the body. Five: Never shoot with tap water, always boil it first. Six: Watch when ya goof. Ya can do it at night butcha just attract attention staggerin round in the daylight.

Seven: Don't mix with the gargle or you'll OD.

And Eight: If ya can, keep somethin on ya in case ya do OD and be sure ta tell yer buddy what it is.

Ya give me the name a one: naxy-somethin. It's good, ya say. Gets ta the nervous system and reefs the smack away from the bits that love it. Usually works in a flash if ya get it inta a vein or a muscle. If ya been mixin, though, it'll take longer. If ya been mixin lots it mightn't work at all.

'It's a deal,' ya say one night. 'We both get somethin outta it. She does. I do. There's a price for everythin. You understand that, Lucy.'

Oh, I understand, Nayler, only too well. I sink back in me understandin and I enjoy it. Because like ya say, he who knows, wins. And I know youse are kiddin yerselves, you and Ma both. Youse both think youse are gettin somethin for nothin but she's only sellin ya lies ta make ya believe yer future's secure, yer bogeyman Death's still centuries off comin for ya, and you're only sellin her the illusion a love because ya don't have the real thing ta give, because ya never were Jimmy Marconi nor never will be. And as long as I know that, I got one over youse both and specially you, Nayler.

I know, therefore I win.

Prices go up. Prices go down.

Bring me jewellery for me lady friends. Cheap silver, fool's gold, glass drops the colours a plums and apricots and goosegogs, precious stones like tiny tears, that disappear if ya stare too hard. Bring me rings and bracelets, chains and beads. Stuff ya'd never wear, Lucy Lu, around yer brown little neck, not in a million years.

Bring me black lace knickers, the ugly, scratchy sort, and bras in matchin scratchin black, 38 double D, a million sizes too big for you, Lucy Lu, with yer little boy's flat chest. Hang them up on the wall and touch them, like ya touchin a girl. Because ya like that, don'tcha, Lucy? Ya like the girlies, you.

And in return ya invade me sleep ta tell me other things, slips a knowledge I'm not lookin for because they're none a me business.

We're makin inroads, Lucy Lu. We got the southside sorted out, like Damo said, we got kids in the Barn, and the local bosses are goin berserk but they think we're the Don so they don't dare cause trouble.

Ya guessed right, Lucy Lu. The girls on the Square are ours. We stole them from the Wacker with the helpa the Soldier. He's one a the Wacker's, only not any more. He got us them sluts and now he's gone and they're dealin for us, scattered like sores through the Wacker's territory. And if ya don't bring me what I want, you'll be one a them sluts too, and I'll fuck you like I fuck them, like I fuck her.

Nah, ya say, laughin. Only messin! I'd never fuck me little errant girl like that. It'd be like stickin it in me brother.

Ya play me, spin me lies. I'm tellin ya all this because I owe it ta you, ta Micko, ta yer Ma, that's why I'm lettin ya in on it. But it's our little secret, right? Don't let on, Lucy.

And while ya play me I play ya right back. I never once let slip what I heard in that basement. I never once ask ya, not even in me sleep or goofin, where that Soldier's gone. I might say other things but I never once ask ya about that. Because everythin has a price and knowledge costs the most of all.

I Don't Need You, I remind meself, every day. If anyone's the needer, Nayler, it's you. Because who knows what shit would fly if I let on ta Snags whatcha were at? *Keep yer hands fuckin clean.* It's not like I seen ya do anythin that would piss him off. Yet. But that hunger in yer eyes each time ya watch me score is a terrible thing, and it's growin by the week.

And that's why it doesn't matter, not one jot, why I don't care, not one bit, that you're fuckin me Ma, Rose Dolan who useta walk like a queen.

'Nine a clock.' Ya stretch yerself out on yer mattress. Yer tee-shirt is rucked up so I can see yer nipples, pokin soft and pink through the tight welterweight muscles a yer chest. Yer skin is so white it looks like it'll melt in the sun. Yer gut scoops in under yer ribs, hard and knotted as the rest a ya. There's a big ugly white scar across yer left ribs; old-lookin. Seein me glance at it, ya give me a sly smile, stretch out yer foot. Dirty bastard.

'Fuck off, Nayler.' I kick, hard as I can.

I'm itchin. Come on come on come on.

'Didja hear me?'

Sure. I nod.

'Nine a clock. There'll be a door left partways open so ya can see. Ya like that, don'tcha, Lucy? Watchin.'

I nod. Come on, Nayler.

Ya fold the foil.

Ah yes, everythin costs, and the best currency is the blood that binds ya to another. So bring yer good self ta the door a yer ma's bedroom and watch me fuck her, ridin her like a dog, slappin her big white arse till the blood rushes ta her cheeks. Watch me make her come with me tongue, with me clever fingers, with me willa stick, with the unbroken end of a shattered whiskey bottle. Just watch me –

'– if ya not too much of a chicken?'

'Fuck, no.' I grab the toot.

Poor little Red Ridin Hood. Never knew that jaunt in the woods would cost so much.

If I wasn't so scared a ya not payin me the next time, I'da burst out laughin. Yer arms thrustin inta the mattress. Yer face screwed up, yer front drenched in sweat. And her like a blow-up pig, red-faced, eyes closed in concentration. Her mouth opened when she was nearly there. 'Ah . . . Jesus . . . ah . . . yeah . . . that's it . . . ah . . . Ji . . .'

Ya looked at me. A smile lurkin round yer mouth.

He shoots. He –

The broken ribbon a sound stopped. She froze, her face scrunched up in surprise. Ya didn't see that, though. Ya were still watchin me. Yer dirty smile had faded. Not gone, no. Just faded.

The laughin inside me held. Didn't stop, no. Just . . . held.

She sighed, disappointed, and slid off ya. Turned onta her back, her tits floppin out either side like burst party balloons. 'Y'alright, son?' All concerned. She stroked yer forearm. Ya flinched like a cat, glancin down like ya only just remembered she was there.

'Come here.'

Ya lay down on her front. She smoothed yer hair. 'Much better with all that dye out,' she said. 'Such a beautiful-lookin boy.' She kissed yer forehead. Ya closed yer eyes, sank inta her tits.

The laughin inside me withered away. I went inta the jacks, thinkin I'd heave, but I didn't. So I just grabbed the sink instead and looked hard inta me reflection, willin meself ta be other than what I was.

I call up on Saturday, like we've arranged, but a big foreign-lookin cunt with a shaved head that I don't know from Adam answers the door and when I go upstairs the door a yer room is wide open and Snags is sittin on yer mattress, tottin up sums on a pocket calculator.

Fuck.

'Nayler,' he calls. 'Company.'

Ya come ta the door, lookin all surprised. 'Jesus. Lucy Dolan.' Ya make it sound like ya haven't seen me in weeks.

'Howaya there, Lucy.' Snags smiles over. He's lookin well, wearin a new shellsuit and expensive-lookin rings on his fingers, like a white version a Run-DMC, but I don't give a shit. All I care about's how'm I gointa get me smoke in with him around. Fuck. This is *vexin*. Ya could at leasta warned me they were gointa be here. Then I wouldn'a got me hopes –

Ya peer behind me like ya expectin ta see someone else there.

Oh, ya cunt. If ya've set this up on purpose, I swear I'll—

'What?' I say. Fuck you if ya think I'm gointa hang around playin one a yer poxy games. 'Ya lookin for a present, Nayler?'

Ya dart me a look – 'Say what?' – then do a puzzled laugh like I'm thick and, all innocent – 'Nah. Just thought yer little buddies would be up with ya. Charlie, Damo, what's that girl's name . . . ?'

'Amanda,' says Sash, comin up behind me. 'Hey, nice to see you again, Lucy.' She kisses me once on both cheeks.

'Look what I got.' She holds up a doll. It's poxy, all white shirt and red skirt and windmill plaits.

Ya smile. 'Snags is been on holidays, Lucy. Berlin.'

Sasha laughs. 'Nayler, I hate to contradict you but it was Amsterdam.'

'You're both wrong,' says Snags. 'It was gay Paree.'

Yer eyes flick up, same time as mine. On *gay*? Don't you dare—

Ya look away, yawn. 'Well for some. I'd love a change meself.'

'Wait yer turn, kiddo,' says Snags. 'It's all ahead a ya. Soon's me and Sash get our flat sorted, you'll be a free agent.'

'Yeah, still. Gets borin eatin off of the same menu.' Ya wink at him.

He laughs and goes back ta the calculator. Looks like he'll be there all day and from the way ya lollin at the door, looks like you're in no hurry ta get rid a him neither.

I turn ta go. 'Here, I'm off. Things ta do.'

'That's it!' ya say suddenly. 'Phelan! Little Amanda Phelan . . . Jesus, I haven't seen her in ages.'

Snags laughs his easy laugh.

'I sorta miss her, ya know,' ya say. 'Very sweet girl.' Ya look at me. 'Lovely tits.'

Ya prick.

'Bring her up sometime, Lucy, yeah?'

I look at ya. Ya give me nothin back but I'm already readin between the lines.

Bring me the head a yer best pal on a plate.

Jesus, this is horrible.

'I don't know whatcha expectin off of me, Micko,' I wanta say. 'I don't know why ya look up with all that hope every time I come ta see ya. Why'm I the one ya expect ta fill ya in on the truth, what happened, what's still goin on? Why wouldya think that I know? Why don'tcha ask *him* if ya need so bad ta find out?'

'Stop pretendin,' I wanta say. 'Stop makin out thatcha fine, ya can handle it. Because ya can't, Micko. Get real, Micko. Stop deludin yerself ya got it under control. Grow up for fucksake. Be a decent brother ta me. Guard me in me hour a need. Stop lookin at me like that. Stop lookin at me like that.'

'Things is good,' I say, willin the words ta fill the space between us.

'Nnh. Heard any good tunes lately?'

'Yeah, sure. Sash turned me onta this one Nina Simone. Sings like a fella but she's deadly. I got a tape for ya and all. Sent it through security so it'll be with ya tonight.'

'Good.'

Fill up the fuckin silence, Micko.

'Heard Ma's back at the cards again.'

Good man.

'Yeah. Doin well. She's tellin people stuff and it's actually comin true.'

'How's Granny?'

'Well . . .'

Whatcha expect me ta say, Micko? Whatcha want me ta say?

Why does it matter when ya don't give a shit any more for anythin that isn't the gear?

'Here,' ya said, handin me a cassette tape. 'Yer brother will like this.'

Seven little pyramids, so small ya can hardly see them, little black liquorices stuck inside the top edge a the Nina Simone cassette. Premium acid, brung over by Snags from Dam Square, so small that when ya press Play, Nina sounds just like she always does. A fella. And taped ta the walls a the cassette, flat plastic squares a brown powder; so thin them flat packs a powder, but fat where it matters, in the takin.

Thank You! Get Well Soon! Sorry I'm Late!

'Didja tell Snags?' I said before I bent over the foil.

'About what?'

'The tape.'

Ya said nothin.

Me? Did ya tell him about me?

'Are ya gointa smoke it or fuckin sneeze it, Lucy?'

And fuck you. I bent, sucked, swooned.

It was me second that week; I blamed it on Snags bein there, messin with me rhythm.

'When can I come up again?' I said when I was goin. I didn't mean ta but it slipped out and soon as it did, I wish it hadn't.

'How's Amanda?' ya said.

She ignores me but I race up ta her and grab her arm.

'Hey, stranger, where ya been?'

'Some stranger I am,' she says, lookin down at me.

'Don't look at me like that, Amanda. I'm still yer pal.'

'Hmm.' She tosses her hair over her shoulder and keeps walkin.

'I like that colour ya put in. Chestnut, is it?'

She turns. 'Lucy, whatcha at?'

'I wanta catch up, that's all. Haven't seen ya in ages.' The Goldilockses brush by. I can hear the taunts, feel the sneers, but I just stare them down.

Amanda shifts around.

'They still givin ya a hard time?'

'No,' she says. 'It was never me they hated.' She starts walkin again.

'Hang on, Amanda, wait. Amanda!'

She has ta stop at the traffic light. 'Lookit, Amanda, I just wanta pal out, that's all.'

'Ya took yer time, Lucy.'

'Ah here, ya know how it's been. Home's been fuckin brutal and—'

'Lucy, yer home is always fuckin brutal.'

The red man changes ta green. Beep beep beep goes the lights, helpin all the blind people ta cross. I grab her so she can't go.

'Leave off, Lucy!'

'Jesus, Amanda! Okay, if ya wanta know, it was you and Charlie. I couldn't find youse any time I called round. He tells Marlene he's meetin me and when I try ta root ya out, ya gone too. Whatcha want me ta do? Ring yer ma's door? Ah, hiya, Miz Phelan, I'm that headcase pal a yer daughter's, oh Jaysus I'm sorry, I forgot ya hate me . . . then chase down the canal so I can sit in on yer pettin sessions?'

'Jesus, Lucy!' She looks around. 'Quiet, will ya?'

'Ya know what I mean, Amanda. It's not nice.'

'Well, where've you been then? Any time I called round ya were out.'

'Like when?'

'Last Saturday, yeah?'

'Well . . . fuck, whatcha expect me ta do . . . stay in scratchin me hole?'

'Okay, okay.' She sighs. She puts a hand out, touches me arm, smiles. 'I'm sorry.'

'Okay.' I'm feelin a bit guilty for what I'm about ta do but fuckit – it's her choice at the end a the day, isn't it?

'I been pallin out with Nayler some,' I say, slurpin up the resta me milkshake.

318

Amanda stops messin with her straw. Just a second. Then she starts again.

'Oh yeah?'

'It's alright. Nothin goin on.'

Go the fuck on, Lucy. Say it.

'Not that you'd be too pushed though now, what, Amanda?'

The minute I say it, she smiles a small secret smile that makes the dimples in her cheeks come and go. Somethin about the way them dimples soak up the light, leavin more ta bounce off her cheekbones, makes me wanta just stop now, forget it all, go back ta bein normal and just pals with her and Charlie and Damo and fuck everythin else.

'Ah . . . I dunno . . .' She trails off, leavin a space for me ta fill.

Shite. Why did I start this? I slurp again and get the watery enda the shake, warm and weak as mother's milk, and spit it back down the straw inta the carton.

Amanda drums on the counter top with her nails. 'Charlie's alright. But that's all.'

'Ah, don't be talkin me cousin down, Amanda. He's a great catch.'

'It's not the same.'

In the jacks mirror, waitin for Amanda ta finish her piss, I catch sight a meself. I haven't looked at meself proper in ages but under them blue lights with all that glass, I can't avoid it. I look like someone I know but can't place who. I'm gone skinnier than before, more like a boy than ever; even me face is thin, the bones standin out, me eyes bigger than I remember. Me hair is brutal, longish on the neck and scraggy-lookin, but the spots from the XYZs is gone, faded away under me tan. I cock me head ta one side, then the other, twistin round till I get the view I'm happiest with. Then I cop it. With the tan and the hair and the build and the new cheek-bones and all I look like a smaller version a me Da when he was a lad. Not so plain as the day any more, Ma, what?

Who's a pretty boy, then? I wink at me reflection.

Suddenly ya there behind me in the mirror, yer hands hoverin over me shoulders. I'm expectin ya ta laugh, start jeerin. But ya don't. Instead, ya drop yer mouth ta the crown a me head and hold it there. Ya not touchin me but I can feel the heat between us scream and as it burns, blood starts tricklin down me face.

'Whatcha doin, Lucy?' Amanda's in the jacks door, lookin at me.

'Fuck, nothin.'

As she bends over ta touch up her eyeshada, the school skirt rises at the back, showin the red creases in her legs from where she was sittin. I've a sudden urge ta kiss the back a her knees.

At the door a McDonald's, we both start speakin at the same time.

'D'ya want—'

'Can I—'

'Go ahead,' I say.

'No, you.'

'No, go on.'

'D'ya mind if I come up with ya one a these days?' She doesn't look me in the eye.

I laugh, relieved it wasn't me who done the askin – 'Still burnin a torch then?' – and dig her in the side.

There's some story on the news when I come in, and they're showin pictures a the Dominick Street flats and that politician who does all the agitatin is talkin ta the camera sayin we can't get compla-cent there's another epidemic waitin ta break out and we all know who's responsible and the government has a duty ta nab them or there'll be more innocent victims. Then they show a picture of a young wan I know from somewhere, and then an auld wan, must be her Ma, is sobbin ta the reporter sayin things is changin, never useta be problems like that round here and then the Drug Squad lad comes on, noddin, sayin there'll be an end ta all this, heads will roll, the people behind it will pay, and then Ma kicks the sittin-room door shut, closin me out, so I go inta the bedroom instead.

Soon as I open the door, Sam scrambles inta her trackie bottoms, pullin them up round her waist like she's scared a bein seen. It strikes me how tall she's growin. Even her boobs are startin ta poke out a bit and that makes me feel a bit sad, really, that she's growin up so fast.

'Ya don't hafta be shy,' I tell her. 'Nothin I haven't seen on meself.'
She ignores me, slips past me ta wherever she's goin.

Sasha lets us in. I tell meself ta stay cool; just because she's there doesn't mean . . . She looks a bit bothered, but she does the hug-kiss thing with Amanda like they been best pals forever.

As we climb the spiral, voices float down. I get yours first, but I can't make out whatcha sayin, only ya not as calm as normal, and then I cop the other one's Snags, all wound up, vicious, rippin along. I try ta blank it out and I'm glad when Sasha starts talkin loud ta distract us, tellin Amanda how lovely she looks in her new miniskirt.

A door bangs. Footsteps. Snags comes rushin down the stairs, his face black. He's got a suitcase with him. Sasha tries ta stop him – 'Snags . . . wait, please' – but he barges past.

'Are you guys okay going up on your own?' says Sasha.

'Sure,' I say.

'Snags, wait . . . Martin!'

Funny. That was the only time I ever heard anyone use that name on him.

We stop on the landin a minute before goin in.

Amanda's hands flutter as she fixes her hair. Her feet in their new heels shift, throwin her hips out wide and sexy. Her lips smack together, grindin in the lip gloss. I smell the sourness of her fear and longin under the stink a the squat and for a second wish I hadn't done it, enticed her up here without fillin her in on what's been goin on; I even wonder what would happen if I told her now, came clean. But then I think a what's waitin for me and that takes over any regret, and I poke her in the back, at her waist where her arse starts ta swell out majestic like the prow of a ship, and she steps inta the room.

You're at the winda, starin out. I think it's the first time I seen ya so . . . bare. For once them eyes in the backa yer head aren't workin. I cough ta let ya know we're here. Ya turn, and yer face is blank and sorta . . . lost-lookin. Then ya clock Amanda and snap! ya put yer Neil-face on, smooth, admirin and happy – but not too happy – ta see her.

'Jesus.' Ya make it sound like it's a surprise. 'Amanda. Howya been?'

She shifts her weight, tosses her hair so the highlights catch in the sunshine.

'Good,' she says. 'Never better.'

Ya look at me, back at her. 'Heard you and Charlie been upta stuff.'

She makes a face. 'Maybe.'

'Ya wanta do somethin, go somewhere?'

I feel like I shouldn't be here watchin, but there's nowhere else for me ta go.

'We could go ta the movies. Make up for all them times I left ya standin.'

Amanda goes scarlet.

'What times is that, Nayler?' I say. 'How d'ya know Amanda didn't leave you?'

'Leave it,' says Amanda, glarin, but ya act like I haven't said a thing.

'Wouldya like that, Amanda?'

She nods.

'We can have a little chat on the way. Catch up on old times.' Ya smile at her. She smiles back. 'Wait for me downstairs, darlin.'

She goes, and for a minute I think about followin but then I remember why I'm here.

'Here.' Ya throw me a Q. 'Hold off till the coast is clear, yeah?'

I stuff the Q inta me jeans and watch ya wash yerself. Ya pull on a fresh tee-shirt, ruffle me hair as ya pass.

I jerk away. 'I'm not yer fuckin dog, Nayler.'

Ya stop, look at me, sizin me up with yer cat's eyes.

When ya gone, I open the Q. There's only hash inside.

I chased youse down all the way ta the Garden a Remembrance. I could see Amanda lookin up at ya, gooey-eyed, laughin. Ya musta been tellin her jokes.

Ya take her hand and lift it, pointin ta the sky. Ya smile at her. She's alive under yer glance, alive and well, and even though I can tell from the swagger a yer shoulders that ya know I'm there, watchin, and ya darin me ta folla ya further, I don't wanta this time. So I wander up ta Blessington Street instead and sit in the little park at the border a the Wacker's patch and smoke one joint after another till the darkness sinks over the city.

It was nowhere near the gear but it musta done somethin because as I was comin up the stairs ta the flat I thought I seen Cindy Devlin walkin towards me, fast, dressed in a big jumper, with her hair tucked inta a cap and a pair a huge don't-look-at-me-I'm-a-filmstar-tryin-ta-hide-from-the-papers sunglasses. She had her street make-up on, kohl two inches deep and fake lashes which I could see through the shades, musta been because I was so stoned, and big juicy red lips.

Hey Cindy, I was gointa say, ya shouldn't wear that muck, ya gorgeous enough as ya are. But she had her eyes down and was huggin her chest like she didn't wanta talk ta anyone so I let it be, and when I seen her disappear at the bottom a the stairwell, I told meself I musta just imagined her.

When I got in, Ma was clearin her cards and cloths and all off of the kitchen table.

'I'll help,' I said, or somethin like that. She didn't give off like normal. She looked folded in on herself, quiet and sad sorta.

I felt like sayin, 'Ma, I know why ya sad, butcha got ta admit ya had it comin, ya knew he wouldn't love ya forever, if he did at all, and in anyways you're not half as gorgeous as Sash or even Amanda,' but in the nick a time I remembered I was stoned and had the sense ta keep me trap shut.

After she went ta the pub, I stayed in the kitchen playin with her cards, makin spreads in cruciforms and spears and circles till I got the fortune I wanted. I done it ta keep me mind off the itchin thoughts a the smoke I didn't get and how I'd get me next and how I didn't need it, I was okay, and even though the cards reminded me a you and Ma, and then Amanda and that made me a bit edgy, it was better than thinkin a the smoke so it worked. In a way.

About an hour in I got the munchies and raided the biscuit tin. I knew I'd be in luck because Ma always kept it stocked up on a

Friday on accounta her customers, and sure enough, she had Jaffa Cakes and Rich Teas and Mikados. I amused meself peelin the coconut strips off of the Mikados with me tongue, then suckin the jam off, then bendin the shite biscuity part in two and crumblin it over the table. When the Mikados were done I went onta the Jaffa Cakes and flaked the chocolate off with me fingernail, suckin it out from there, then peeled the jam off of the sponge with me tongue, then popped in the sponge in one go and tried ta swalla it whole. When I'd finished with them, there was nothin left ta do only stamp on the Rich Teas.

I looked at the table, covered in patterns and weaves a cards, all sprinkled over with Mikado crumbs. Somethin came over me then and I lifted me hand, preparin ta knock it all ta the ground. But just before me hand hit the table, I caught a glimpse of a face, white-cold in mornin light, and it came so sudden and unexpected it stopped the movement dead in its tracks.

Creepy.

Call me stupid but I wiped every last crumb off of them cards and made sure they were in their suits and all before stickin them back in Ma's little Chinese box.

'Sam?' I called, but she wasn't there.

I stayed sittin on her bed till she came in.

I could tell she'd been cryin. It wasn't her face – the light was off, so I couldn't see her – just the way she was holdin herself, huddled over and stiff.

'Where ya been, Mouse?' I said. 'I been worried sick.'

'Nowhere.' She sniffed.

'Ah, baby,' I said, and held out me arms.

She pushed past me and climbed inta bed, pullin a sheet over her legs.

I called upta the squat the next day but there was nobody in. So I headed over ta Charlie's, and we picked up Damo and went down town and I tried ta distract meself from thinkin about stuff like when ya'd be back with me smoke by listenin ta them rabbit on about the latest, how that girl from the news that OD'd useta live in the Dominick Street flats, and she was one a Wacker's brassers – and I copped it then, she was that girl I seen walkin ages ago along the balconies dead a night, though I didn't tell them that a course, just tried ta change the subject onta somethin more cheerful . . . But Damo kept on, sayin the brasser was found with enough ta supply, and Wacker was fumin, because none of his pimps sussed she was dealin, and he'd started snoopin round the Don's lieutenants, seein if one a them was responsible for robbin his girls and poisonin his turf. But everyone knew Don Ryan was way too antsy ta stir up strife with the Wacker, what with tryin ta figure out who was behind that new ring in the Barn, not ta mention havin ta deal with the Old Bill that was startin ta harass him big time on accounta all them politicians bangin their drums so's they could get more votes in the election. Far from expandin, the Dapper Don was pullin back, said Damo, droppin staff, movin others, and all the time lookin ta see who was doin the dirt behind *his* back.

By now I was wonderin if this was such a great way ta distract meself. I tried ta stay cool, zone out, thinka other things, acid house music, MTV, only then Damo said he'd a brainwave as ta what was goin on, and I didn't want ta hear him bangin on about Snags again, and have Charlie lookin at me ta see if maybe we should tell Damo what we seen and heard in that basement, or even ta check how much I knew about stuff now, stupid prick, when he shoulda sussed none a that shite never had anythin ta do with us and specially not me any more. So I just got up and went.

'Ya shouldn'a brung up all that, Damo,' said Charlie in a low voice. He was yards behind me but with me nerves so jumpy I could hear everythin. 'Makes her thinka Micko.'

Micko? Fuck. Leasta me worries.

On me way back home I went down by Seán MacDermott Street. I'd smoked all the fags in me pack, so I headed inta the little café across from the swimmin pool ta buy some. I usually never go in there but I needed somethin ta calm me nerves.

I was payin up when I seen her.

Cindy Devlin, sittin in the shadas at the back, talkin to a man with broad shoulders and a thick neck. Cindy Devlin, Wacker's prize tart – Wacker's? Fuck, no; Snags's, just like the rest a them – all dressed down in sunglasses and a big jumper, her long brown hair piled inta a cap, sittin right across from Emmet Whelan, knuckle-crackin number one enforcer a the Don.

Should I say anythin?

Should I stay or should I go?

In the end I go. It's none a me business. Besides, everyone knows Cindy's a professional. She's not the kind ta jump ship, and certainly not sell her soul; no matter what the price, no matter who the buyer – Wacker, Snags or even the Don.

Anyways, like I say, it has nothin ta do with me.

There's a jo-maxi waitin outside and just as I roll up, Sasha comes out, wearin a big coat and holdin a suitcase. Ya behind her and it looks like ya tryin ta persuade her ta do somethin but she keeps shakin her head. I stick close ta the railins a the house two doors up, and only leggit up towards ya when she's in the jo and gone.

Ya got that lost look again but that just turns ta vexation when ya see me.

'Whatcha want?'

I look around. It's risky talkin ta ya out here but I want me payment. Now. 'Where's me stuff, Nayler?'

I see ya about ta play me with some 'What stuff is that?' shite, so I nip it in the bud. 'Leave it out. I brung ya Amanda, didn't I? So why'm I gettin five joints worth a hash instead a me usual?'

Ya look around. 'Jesus, I don't know whatcha talkin about—'

'Fucksake!' I bang me fist against the door.

Ya grab me wrist. 'Hey. Easy, there, darlin.'

I shake free. 'Don't you fuckin darlin me, Nayler. I'm not one a yer brassers. Ya told me ta do stuff and I done it. I brung ya everythin ya wanted, I got the coppers watchin me in all them poxy antique shops so many times I lost count, I watched *her* like ya said, and then I brung ya Amanda, so why ya stringin me out like some street user? I'm not—'

'Lucy. Easy. Remember where we are.' Yer eyes are lookin everywhere.

'Nayler—'

'Jesus, Lucy.' Ya lower yer voice. 'Things is bad. I'm serious here.'
Ya look at me again and the vexation is gone, nearly, and the lost
look back, and I see how exhausted ya are, how deep blue them
shadas under yer eyes. 'We're out. Won't be for long but the next
coupla weeks is gointa be slow. Snags has stuff ta sort out. Ya don't
wanta know.'

'Where's Sasha gone?'

'I said ya don't wanta know.'

'What about me gear?'

Ya think. 'Okay. Look, I can give ya an address . . . if ya want it
bad enough.'

The gap before the 'if ya want' is enough ta make me wonder,
but fuckit, I want it. I want it now. 'Okay.'

'They'll want more than what ya pay me, Lucy.'

'I said, okay.'

I'm half-way down the street, racin, repeatin the southside address
in the back a me mind like a chant, but it doesn't stop the thoughts.

Remember the rules, Lucy. One: Can ya afford it? Two: Careful
when ya change shop. I'm tryin not ta dwell on what they'll want
that I can afford. Me body? Don't think about it. Sides, they won't.
I'm not that good a catch. Maybe they'll just get me ta deal. That's
alright. I can handle that. I won't make the mistakes me brother
or them others done. I'll be loyal, I won't rat, I won't fuck up. And
if they want payment now, well, fuckit, I'll think a somethin. In
anyways, I'm not goin there because I'm desperate, because I'm
not, I don't even really want a smoke, or if I do it's just one, but
I'm not hooked, I'm just goin along with this because I'm showin
ya I don't need ya, I'm showin ya I can look after meself.

I'm turnin the corner onta Parnell Street when I hear ya behind
me, yellin.

'Lucy. Lucy!'

I ignore ya.

Ya yell louder. 'Lucy Dolan, come here! *Fucksake!* Come fuckin here, Lucy!'

I turn. 'Whatcha fuckin want?'

Ya storm towards me, ragin, like I never seen ya rage before, but man, am I ragin too and if ya even so much as *think* a playin games with me I'll fuck ya over for good. I swear, Nayler. Threaten me with the army knife ya used years ago on that Waxboy outside the Big Tree, with the blade ya used ta kill that Green Strip in Dolphin's Barn, with the scissors ya used on Mainser, even with that gun youse used on the poor yoke in that post office, I don't care. I'll rip ya apart, so don't even fuckin think it. But ya got me by the arm, grabbin hard, and somehow ya got yer other arm round me, pinnin me side, and fuck, ya strong, way stronger than I thought, and ya turnin me and pushin me back up the hill towards the Square, and even though I'm punchin at ya and kickin ya, so hard I know I'm raisin bruises, ya won't let go.

'Fucksake, Lucy, fuckin calm down!'

But I keep kickin even as we reach the squat and, holdin me fast, ya dig a hand inside yer pocket and take out a key and unlock the door and push me in, and it's only when we're both inside and the key is turned in the lock that ya let me go and I stop kickin, both at the same time, like there's nothin else ta do.

'*Fuck!*' ya say, smashin yer fist inta the wall hard as ya can.

Then ya sigh, lean back against the bannisters, look at me. I can hear yer thought. *Jesus, Lucy.*

Ya told me if I said a word I was dead. Ya said it in an okay way, calm, not vexed or anythin, but ya said it like I could be anyone and I knew ya meant it.

Ya made me wait on the second-floor landin so I couldn't see whose door ya opened. But I heard the lock turn and turn again and then another one too. Me ears were sharp with hunger. Plus that house was awful echoey.

When ya called me up, ya were standin inside yer door, holdin three little white pills in yer palm.

'Phy,' ya said. Then, like ya needed ta explain: 'Methadone.'

I was about ta get smart and ask what about rule whatever and the phy bein worse than the gear but the look on yer face stopped me before I could get a word out.

Dare ya, I say ta ya.
Hunger rises in ya, battles with yer will.
Which wins? Ya turn yer head so I can't tell if ya swalla or not.
In me mind's eye, the pills melt, joinin our tongues.

After pukin, I lie on the mattress ta settle me stomach and wait ta come up. Ya sink down on the floor beside me, stretch out. Sunlight streams in through the big winda. A breeze blows the tattered muslin curtain this way, that way. There's a foot a empty space between us and it hums like somethin alive.
When the sickness has passed I turn me head ta ya. Ya turn at the same time. Slow motion.
The shada a the curtain washes over yer face. The dark patches under yer eyes are bruised, sore-lookin.
I lift.
I stretch across, over the empty space, reach out me finger, and touch the darkness under yer right eye. Yer skin is soft. I trace the shada along yer cheekbone, over the curve a yer nose and under yer other eye.
Thanks, I say.
Ya breathe, yer mouth openin and closin in a small movement, like a baby's. The breath makes yer nostrils wider, innocent sorta, but not in a fake way. I put me finger on yer lips. They feel softer than I woulda thought. I push in. They give way. The star in the forehead a yer tattoo horse twinkles.
Starlight, I say. Or think I do.
Ya smile against me fingertip. It's a kid's smile, nice. It makes me wanta smile back.
Did I ever tell ya about the time me da brung me up the Dublin mountains, Lucy?
Ya twist yer willa stick in yer hands. *Go on, ya daisy. That's what he useta say when he bet on the gee-gees. Go on, ya daisy.*

Then ya start tellin me a story about when you were a kid and yer da scared the shite outta ya in the dark, and as I listen, half-closin me eyes, the wind blows the tattered curtain this way, that way, and I sink inta heaven.

Oh, the beauty a seein someone fall, Nayler. Even if ya only half-see it, it's still beautiful.

He hugged me after, cried, told me he loved me. Lyin cunt, ya said, droney. Call that love?

She's waitin for me in the kitchen.

'Ah, Lucy, look who called by,' says Ma. 'D'ya want another cup a tea, Amanda?'

'No, Missus Dolan, I'm grand, thanks.'

We open the bedroom winda and puff out blue clouds a smoke.

'So?' With the phy and all that happened earlier, I'm not really that bothered about her and her feelins about ya but it seems like the right thing ta say.

She shrugs.

'What's that sposed ta mean?'

She turns ta me, a big grin on her face. 'I got him, Lucy. I got him twisted round me finger.'

She told me ya'd said ya only stayed away from her because ya were scared a hurtin her. I asked her if she was gointa break it off with Charlie, and she laughed.

'Ah, no, Lucy. After everythin he put me through? I'm gointa make him sweat.'

I look out the winda, watch the smoke from me fag rise. Seems awful far away.

I've noticed it before but this is the third day in a row, and it just feels . . . wrong.

'Sam, why ya wearin them trackie bottoms under yer uniform?'

'Because I'm cold. Can I've some money for lunch, Ma?'

'Sure, darlin,' says Ma, diggin in her pocket. Sam slings the heavy bag over her shoulder – it looks way too big for her, that bag – and opens the door.

'Darlin?' calls Ma, and pushes out her face for a kiss. Sam kisses her. Ma hugs her back like she can't bear ta let her go. 'Have a good day, sweetheart, yeah?'

When Ma sits down, she's got that sad look on her face again.

'Y'alright?' I can't help askin.

The sad look melts straightaway. 'Get yer schoolbag, willya, and stop bein such a fuckin problem.'

Over the weeks I told meself ta keep alert; that way I'd be able ta catch ya usin again. Again? For sure, then. But between the urgency a me hunger risin and the care ya took never ta show and the fact that I was always gone before ya, lyin back and already wafflin while ya looked on, slouchin against the wall, half-smilin, there was no sure tellin, only a feelin ya were at it.

Ya didn't wait too long ta put me back on the smoke. Ya told me it was for me own good. I was buildin up a tolerance ta the phy, even though I was only takin it a coupla times a week, but if I kept at it, it'd be brutal ta wean off. When I asked ya where ya got the new gear ya told me ta stop askin questions.

'Is Snags sorted things out so?'

'D'ya ever listen ta what people tell ya, Lucy Dolan? Mind yer own business.'

The new stuff's okay, but it doesn't give me half the buzz that Snags's useta.

I get a feelin somethin's up just as I'm turnin onta the Square. Somethin about the girls and the way they're standin. Then I see him. He's a big lad, and he's walkin away from the squat with a strut, like he's showin everyone his muscles. The girls get even edgier as he passes, pressin close together like horses bein rounded up.

He's not from round here. Makes no odds. I can still recognize him. He's one a the Wacker's.

I wait one whole hour till I'm sure he's gone before cuttin free a the bushes, walkin past the hooers who've no greetins for me tonight, not even Cindy, and knockin on yer door.

Tell me that story, again, Lucy Lu, ya say. Ya know I love the stories.

I start on some ramble, forgettin it as soon as it's outta me mouth. The waffle seeps inta the cracked walls a yer room. All bollocks. All shite. Means nothin. But fuck, is it nice; fuck, is it easy.

'Hi.'

'Hi yerself.'

'Haven't seen ya round much, Lucy.'

'Yeah, well.' I wipe me nose. It's startin ta run all the time since spring started. 'So what's the story, Charlie?'

He throws a pebble, hits a moorhen on the beak. The moorhen squawks, soundin like one a them paper whistles ya get at kids' parties.

'Amanda . . .'

Surprise surprise. 'Yeah? She broke it off with ya?'

'Fuck! No. Lucy, she's pregnant for me.'

A second's silence, though it feels longer. Then it kicks in. Why didn't she tell me? Why am I always the last ta find out?

'I don't know how it coulda happened,' says Charlie.

'Ya mean ya weren't—'

'No! We were. But I was real careful. I only . . . ya know . . . once or twice and when we didn't have johnnies I . . . ya know . . . pulled out . . .'

'Jesus, Charlie.'

He throws another pebble. The moorhen squawks again. 'It's not the way it's sposed ta happen. I'm not like Damo or all. I don't want this. I got plans. I'm gettin me Inter this year, and movin home and . . . fuck!'

Another pebble. Another squawk. I say the only thing I can think of.

'Have ya told yer Ma yet?'

★

'I won't,' says Amanda. 'Youse must be mad.'

Her eyes are red from cryin and she's wringin her hands on her lap. I grab one a the hands. 'Lookit, Amanda, if yer Ma finds out about Charlie—'

'She knows about Charlie, Lucy. He's been up ta me gaff and all.'

'Oh,' I say.

Charlie looks away, awkward.

'She likes Charlie. Thinks he's reliable.' She starts bawlin again.

'Jesus, that's nice,' says Charlie. 'Reliable.'

'Well, ya are.' Boo hoo hoo.

Her squawlin is makin me edgy. If I'd a smoke I'd be alright, I'd be calm, but ya told me yesterday I'd hafta stay away for a few days, it wasn't safe, and besides, ya were feelin sick, somethin ya ate, and then ya made me smoke on me own, without watchin like normal, and . . . I see they're lookin at me, so I snap back ta the present best I can.

'Lookit. All I'm sayin is if ya tell Marlene, she'll come up with somethin. She's great at fixin stuff, got me outta enough jams already. Trust me, Amanda.'

I squeeze her hand. She looks down at the ground.

Marlene is smilin when she opens the door but soon as she sees Amanda there all red-eyed, the smile melts inta nothin, and she pushes us all inside.

'Jesus, Mary and Joseph.' She sighs. 'Okay. Amanda, isn't it? Lucy's pal?'

Amanda sniffles and nods.

'Okay. Come on inta the kitchen.'

The twins are at the kitchen table doin their homework, their identical specky faces bent over their identical flower-wallpapered copies.

'Out,' says Marlene. They scram. 'Here.' Marlene pushes over a mug a tea, sweet and milky, and lights a fag. Amanda sips. Marlene looks at Charlie, sizin him up. He twitches under her look.

'Ma, I—' Marlene raises her hand. Charlie stops.

'Okay, love. How long are ya gone?'

'Eh . . .' Amanda's lip starts quiverin again. 'Five, six weeks?'

'Ya sure?'

'I'm four weeks over. I'm never late.'

Marlene hands her a tissue and Amanda blows her nose with a big trumpety sound.

'Jesus, Charlie,' says Marlene.

'Ma, I was careful. I—'

'Lookit son, get out for a second, willya, while we talk.'

When he's gone, Marlene stubs out the butt and lights another fag. 'I don't know why he didn't tell me about ya, love. It's not as if I'm the type a Ma wouldn't . . .' She sighs. 'Have ya thought about whatcha gointa do?'

Amanda shakes her head, snifflin.

'Well, you've two options, ya know. Ya either have it – which means tellin yer Ma and yer da and goin through all that – or ya don't.'

Amanda looks up, surprised. I am too. I thought Marlene would tell Amanda ta keep it, say it's not that bad, loadsa young wans from the area have kids now. And it's not like Charlie himself's one hundred per cent legitimate.

'I can fix it,' says Marlene. 'It's easier ta get ta London now. Butcha got talk ta someone first. There's women in them centres and they can talk ya through the whole thing. Because ya gotta make up yer own mind. Yeah?'

'Okay.'

Marlene tips the ash from her fag inta the ashtray. 'Lucy'll take ya ta the centre. Won't ya, Lucy?' She smiles over at Amanda. 'Lucy's a good pal ta have.'

On the way out, she pulls me back. 'Lucy Dolan, I'm trustin ya with this one. I know ya been upta no good lately. I'm not gointa ask any questions. Yer Ma has her own way a handlin things and I don't wanta interfere. But Jesus . . .' Her fingers bite inta me arm. 'I know ya got yer own life, but I'd like ta see ya do alright. If ya can stand by yer pal through this one, it'll be good for ya, I swear . . .'

Two things. Two feelins.

One. Fuck you, ya interferin cow.

Two. Okay, Marlene. Almost.

We turn onta Cathal Brugha Street and Amanda stops.

'Lucy, I'm not goin in.'

'Why not? Marlene said—'

'She's not me Ma. In anyways I know what I want.' She smiles a bitter little smile. 'It's not Charlie's baby, Lucy.'

Oh.

'It only happened the once, Lucy. I swear. Down the Garden a Remembrance. And he wasn't even that . . . nice ta me or anythin. It was like he was . . . I dunno. Somewhere else. But I can't have his baby. And I don't want ya tellin him.'

'Why not? If he . . . if he loves ya . . .'

'Promise ya won't tell him.'

She takes me hand. Her skin is covered in goosepimples. 'Please, Lucy. You're me only friend. I trust ya. Promise?'

'Okay.' I sit down and pull her close ta me. 'I promise.'

We sit like that for ages, her snuggled inta me, me with me arm round her. I stroke her hair and tell her lies. It's gointa be alright, Amanda. It's gointa be alright.

Why –

The feelins rise but I push them down. They have no place in me.

Why them, Nayler? Why Ma? Why Amanda? Why Sasha? Why not me, Nayler?

Push them down. These are not the thoughts a Lucy Dolan. They belong ta someone else. A weak sap, a girly-wirly-woo that's too scared ta stand on her own two feet. A fool that can't see the lie a the land, the wood from the trees. I am not that, Nayler. I am somethin else.

I don't want, repeat, *Don't Want*, whatcha give them. We got our own deal goin and I don't want anythin else.

Still . . . why d'ya never act with me the way ya act with them, Nayler? I'm not that fuckin –

Ugly.

Push it down. Push it down. I am bigger than this.

'Sshh,' I say, smellin in the sweet cleanness of her hair. 'It's okay, Amanda. I'm here for ya.'

The big deal was what we were gointa tell Rose. Fuckin Rose. In the end Marlene came over and told Ma she had ta go over ta London for a business trip with Stevo, and she thought why not bring the twins with her, do a bit a shoppin for the new house in Malahide, and then she thought maybe I'd like ta come too, see a few sights. We'd hafta take the boat over, what with Marlene bein afraid a the flyin and all, but it could be a nice little break.

Ma wasn't inta it at first, but then Marlene took her aside and told her she'd look after me, meanin the XYZs. Probably said I'd be better off outta the flat too, that way she'd be able ta give me a good talkin ta and sort me outta whatever mess I was in.

Ma went for it, relieved ta have me off her hands.

Sam didn't say anythin, but I could tell she felt bad about not bein included. Marlene musta picked it up too because she told Sam she could come over next time they went ta London. She might even bring her ta see *Cats*. Sam gave a grin and all at that but the shada didn't lift off her face.

On the day before we went, headin down ta Clerys ta get stuff for the journey, I passed Missus Devlin, gabbin on ta Doris Dwyer on the second landin. She lowered her voice as I went by so I only heard a bit.

'. . . hasn't been around for days. Awful worryin. I coulda called the Guards butcha know the way they are . . .'

Somethin about what she said rang a bell but the bell wasn't ringin clear enough for me ta pay any heed and by the time I got around the Square, it had stopped.

I wasn't lookin ta go over ta yours. The last time I'd called up, after I told ya about London, ya didn't even open the door, just pushed stuff out through the letterbox. Ya said ya were still sick, that food-poisonin lark, and when I opened the Q there was only half me usual and I had ta find somewhere safe ta smoke where nobody would find me.

It wasn't like I needed more. It'd been only two days since me last. I was fine. I just wanted . . . ta walk round the Square, that's all.

You were on top a me, meltin outta the buddin trees, before I even knew it.

'Payback time.' Ya look more wideawake, sharper than ya been in ages. Ya tap the packet. 'Lookit, keep clean on the way over. I can't risk ya gettin caught. And ya know what ta do when you're there?'

'Yeah. Nayler—'

'Ya wanta keep this quiet, Lucy Lu. Not a word ta anyone.'

'Does Snags—'

Somethin flickers in yer eyes. 'Jesus, Lucy, enough a the questions already.' Then ya grin. 'Hey, chin up. After all this time ya got yerself a real life errant.'

I shouldn'a but I can't help laughin.

The sea floats up ta meet me. It's all colours. Greeny-bluey-grey. It's the colours a me eyes, the eyes a me long-gone Da. I lean over the rail, feelin it press inta me trackie top that presses inta me waistband that presses inta the notes that press inta me skin. The edges a the notes tickle me, scratchin.

Even with the itchin under me skin, somethin in me soars.

'Jesus, Lucy, get away from that, will ya?' I look back at Amanda, who's sittin shiverin on one a the white plastic benches. I bend over further, just ta annoy her. The notes dig deeper inta me skin. Then I turn round and bend backward, so me head is danglin over the rail and me chest is high up, tilted towards the sky.

'I'm a seagull,' I shout. The wind whips me words away, flingin them ta the clouds.

'What?' yells Amanda.

I lift me head up. 'I'm a seagull.'

'Ya mad bitch!' she laughs.

Marlene comes outta the roundy-topped door. She's wearin a new suit, with big shoulder pads, and she's got her hair done special for the trip, flicked over ta one side. Very Princess Di. I can tell she's gearin up for more chat. She's been talkin non-stop since we got on the boat, fillin us in on all the news.

Their plans is goin great. The new house in Malahide is nearly built. They're movin out there next month. She'll miss the flats herself, she says – 'Nothin like havin family round, is there, Lucy?' – but I don't believe her. Stevo's just won a big government contract, and she's been lookin after the money, puttin it inta the bank and all. She's had a coupla investments goin but she's pullin them out soon. Everyone says a war in the Middle East is brewin and what with the trouble over in Eastern Europe, all them revolutions and what, stocks and shares, blah blah blah . . .

Most a what she says goes over me head, but I'm happy ta sit back and listen. Keeps me mind off the other.

'Thanks for comin along,' she says, after Amanda's gone down ta hurl yet again. 'She needs ya with her.'

Off the spur a the moment I ask: 'Why didn't ya want her ta have it, Marlene? Was it the cost or somethin?'

She stops puffin and gives me a real searchin look. 'The cost?' She takes a drag, then smiles. 'Well, actually, yeah, Lucy. It was.' She says it serious, like I'm her age, not mine. I know she's not just talkin about money. 'We got . . .' She shrugs, leaves it unsaid.

I know, Marlene. Plans.

'Anyway . . .' She looks down at her fag, twists it in her finger. 'Suppose I'm not ready ta be a granny. Plenty a life in me yet!' Then she laughs her throaty laugh like it's a joke, and I join in.

But I suddenly want Charlie ta be with us too, even though I know it's not right, this is not the sorta thing lily-livered boys get inta.

We got in at lunchtime. Holyhead a mean strip a warehouses on the edge a the sea, stinkin a fish and seaweed. Amanda got sick twice on the train. Second time round I thought I was gointa join her, feelin crap I was, all pukey and hot. We hit London in the evenin. Rows and rows a little brown houses set high on the railway sidin, packed tight together and spiked with TV aerials. Welcome ta the Empire.

The river crawls beneath me, wide and slow. Does the slowness make it wide or the other way round? I look through the bars a the footbridge and wonder what it's like ta climb up onta the high beam and cross the Thames that way. On the bank ta me left is the station I've left behind, where all the homeless kids and auld lads and wans lie in sleepin bags and cardboard boxes all day long, paper McDonald's cups gapin for money. On the one ta me right a big white bulge that Marlene tells me is some sorta centre.

'They do all kindsa things there, love. Music and concerts.'

As if I'm interested.

There's another station on the right bank. That's where I'm supposed ta catch the Tube.

Behind me, the cars rush past on their way ta make more money.

The city is purple and grey in the evenin clouds. Somewhere up the river are the dusty peaks a Westminster. I can't see them through the bridge but I can imagine them from all the postcards. Thinkin a Westminster makes me think a The Odd Couple and Oscar, and how he useta bang on about colonial oppressors and all that, and that makes me think a me own Da, Jimmy Marconi, whose dark reflection I keep seein more and more in the mirror. Did he perch, like me, over this city, wonderin what fate was lyin in store for him? Or thinkin, This Is It, I'm Made? And if he had a stayed here, instead a racin back ta me Ma's white legs, would it a been better? I might never a been born then. Would that a been better?

Then the car headlights streakin through the April fog make me think a Granny's stories, and the one about when Jack the Ripper ran away from London and came ta live in Dublin, and how he murdered all the huzzies, dumpin their bodies in the canals ta be washed up in the mornin rain. And that makes me think a you. And then I see how everythin is the same, every city has its own ghosts, its own half-deserted streets and foggy killers and strangled huzzies lyin in pools a saltwater down by the docks.

What if I stop time?

What if I don't go onta the other station, but instead walk back ta the hotel on Tottenham Court Road? Marlene won't be there yet – she's still at the clinic waitin for Amanda – but both a them will be back soon. And I haven't done anythin yet ta spoil their trust. I told Marlene I had ta get outta the clinic because all the bright lights were givin me the shakes.

'You'll be alright on yer own?' she said, distracted by Amanda's weepin.

I told her I'd stay round Oxford Street; she took us there yesterday ta buy some clothes so she thinks it's safe. And then I'd walk back ta the hotel.

There is time. I could still do this.

I think of Amanda cryin, 'Ah, Jesus, Lucy, I'm terrified. I'm gointa bleed ta death without ya, I swear!' and Marlene sighin and comfortin her and me slippin out soon as I could.

I think a the wax statues we seen in Madame Tussauds the day before, and the mad pastries and coffee in Covent Garden where Marlene brought us for breakfast, and Hyde Park with the dogs and the walkers, and all the raver gear on the King's Road. There was somethin normal in all that; that felt like a holiday should. I don't have much experience a hollyers but that felt like the holidays on telly programmes, all laughin and sunshine and gawpin up at strange buildins.

If ya hadn't got lost on us, Jimmy Marconi, wouldya have ever a brought Ma and us on hollyers ta swingin London, or is that just wishful thinkin?

The wad a English notes tickles me waist.

I cross the river.

Take the Bakerloo line ta Elephant. Change ta the Northern, headin north. At Moorgate change ta the Metropolitan, headin east. Change at Whitechapel ta the East London, headin south. Get off at Rotherhithe. There'll be a lad at the station wearin a green scarf. Let him go, then folla him, keepin thirty yards behind. He's gointa turn left outta the Tube station and go on straight. He'll cross through the tunnel, and walk on for a while and then he'll come to a block a council flats. Brown brick with yella lines goin through them, boarded-up windas. Number 75 Acorn House. Leave the lad go up first, five minutes. Then when ya see a white hanky at the winda, folla him in.

It was a bitch ta remember, even with ya tellin me ta look out for the colours and ta count the stations so I wouldn't hafta read, and if I was really lost, ask people directions. I missed a few stops here or there but when I got out at Rotherhithe the lad was waitin just like you'd said.

He was tall in a familiar way but he had a peaked cap pulled over his eyes and his green scarf up round his mouth, so I couldn't make out his face.

We run the gauntlet, a long strip a road with grey walls climbin either side, shuttin out the empty docklands. Danglin off the barbed wire on top a the walls are scraps a material, paper, a kid's shoe. From ages away I see a bunch a skinheads walkin towards me. I prepare meself, grittin me teeth and fixin me stare so I can give them as good as I get, hopin the fucker up ahead doesn't do anythin stupid ta start them off.

In the end, they walk past us both without a second glance. The notes around me waist burn. I feel at home.

Jesus fuckin Christ. Ya said a block a council flats but there's fuckin millions. Makes home look like Beverly Hills. The fella I'm trailin doesn't seem ta know his way either. He stops twice, once on the street ta talk ta a black bird in a tiny mini; the second time he goes inta a Paki shop and doubles back on himself. I cross the road and look over at an empty lot so it won't seem obvious ta anyone lookin on. Then, when I've given him enough space, I turn round and folla him.

Zillions a kids race around the yard. At least they got a gate in front a their blocks. Not like us. Our gaffs are easy access. Anyone can walk in or out. Fuck, they do things better here. After ten minutes, the white hanky waves at a winda.

*

341

It's on a third-floor landin, and there's a smell a orange peel everywhere. I knock on the door. The letterbox flap lifts. A pair a eyes stares out.

'Rayo,' I say.

The door opens; behind it is a skinhead with Nazi symbols tattooed on his arms. The smell a oranges drifts away, replaced by the stink a dryin spunk and stale sweat.

'Come in,' says the Nazi. He's got a black moustache that doesn't go with his skinhead and he doesn't sound Irish. Nor London neither, nor even Dutch like Sasha.

In the corner is a hippyish-lookin fella, long red hair, smokin grass in a bong. 'So this is Nayler's little pal, eh?' he says in a Cork lilt.

And sittin beside a roarin fire, rubbin his hands and unwindin his long green scarf, is our mutual pal Snagglepuss Ryan.

For a minute I panicked, thinkin I'd fucked up. I'd walked inta a trap and I was bringin ya down with me. Then I copped on. Foolish Lucy. Shoulda known me darlin Nayler would never keep secrets from his guardian angel.

Little things came inta focus. That day Snags came back from his holiday in gay Paree. Was it then ya told him ya were danglin me off yer line, testin me ta see if I could hold me water better than me brother? The treats for Micko in the cassette. A course Snags was in on it. What better way ta check if I could carry without fuckin up? And the big deal about not lettin me buy on me own – there was me thinkin ya . . . cared or somethin, but all along ya were only takin out insurance ta stop me gettin in with another shower a fucks.

But it didn't all add up.

Like yer first offer. Ta this day I don't believe that was planned. And the first time ya gave me Sasha's phy; call me thick but that wasn't just insurance, was it? Because ya nearly lost yer head there, shoutin at me on the street in fronta everyone. And even if all that palaver was just you lookin after business, takin that phy alongside a me wasn't. Because ya did; ya took that phy with me – turned head or not, I swear I seen ya take it; even if I didn't see ya swalla I seen ya goof and nod.

And what about the new gear, Nayler, the stuff ya said ya bought ta get me off the phy? Get me off it, me hole. Ya got it for yerself because ya wanted back on the real thing. Done and dusted, bollocks. But ya didn't keep on it long. Soon after – how soon? I don't know, when supplies ran short, when Snags said youse could start sellin again, when ya decided off yer own bat, I don't *fuckin* know because ya didn't *fuckin* tell me – ya learnt the error of yer ways. And – food-poisonin me arse – ya got yerself clean.

In and outta the seventy-two with flyin colours. It's easy once ya know, Lucy Lu. Only it wouldn't be so easy if *he* knew, would it?

I'd love ta be able ta tell ya that after the shock I was cold as ice as I totted it up, the pros and cons a betrayin ya just like you done me. But I didn't, Nayler. The thoughta leakin out yer secret never crossed me mind.

In anyways, it all started movin too fast.

'Okay,' says Snags. 'Cook it up.'

The Cork boy does the cookin.

'Where is your works?' says the Nazi ta me.

'I don't—'

'Ya don't think she'd risk carryin them, Vassily?' says Snags. 'Ya Greek gobshite.'

The Nazi doesn't understand what gobshite means but he does understand Greek and he gives Snags an evil look like he wants ta kill him.

'Give her yours,' says Snags.

'I only smoke,' I say ta Snags. 'I don't bang up.'

The fuck. He looks real pissed off. 'Okay, smoke it so.'

It hits and hit, I fall.

Ya couldn't call me an expert back then but I knew that stuff was good, better than the phy, better than any you'd given me in the squat. This was pure.

Under the haze I hear this and that. The business is okay? says the Greek Nazi like he doesn't believe it.

Snags easy: Course it is, Vassily, as always.

I thought you were having the plumbing problem?

All sorted, Vassily. Watertight. That's Nayler for ya. Great way with the ladies.

They wait till I can stand, then Snags takes the money off of me and they give me the stuff and I tape meself up – wouldn't let them fucks touch me, wouldn't let them see the knife ya gave me tucked inta me waistband – and then Snags pushes me out back inta the compound and I'm walkin down the street again, only this time on me own, and I stagger from time ta time, but not badly. I am floatin on air, and behind me the Don's nephew watches ta see do I take a false step, but I don't. I've me knife and me nerves and me eyes peeled. I am ready for anyone.

When I got in, Marlene and Amanda were out; at a restaurant, said the clerk. Thank fuckin Christ.

I'm countin on bein able ta blame it on seasickness. Most a the jacks are bunged up, full a puke and shite and all sorts; one more locked cubicle won't make a difference. When I'm fit enough, I can stagger onta deck, blame it on the weather.

'Alright?' says Marlene.

I let me half-shut eyes close fully and slump against her.

'I'm proud a you, Lucy.' Her voice is soft. 'I was sure ya weren't gointa be there when we came back last night. Very proud a you.'

Amanda's standin at the rail, lookin out. She hasn't said much since comin back.

I look through Amanda, towards the horizon, and picture the look that'll be on yer face when I unstrap the gear from under me shirt.

I passed, Nayler. I passed, ya usin fuck.

Sam told me after it was the twins done it. Ma called over – ta check up on Charlie, she told Sam, 'poor lad, all on his own mindin the fort', but if ya ask me she knew somethin was up – and a course who answered the door but Catherine, the oldest twin. Marlene had told them ta lie low, but would they? No. Little bitches always hated me.

'Oh?' says Ma. 'I thought you'd be away with yer Ma and da.'

'No,' says Catherine. 'In anyways Da's not gone away this time.'

She coulda played it safe. But she didn't. Little bitch.

Ma does her puzzled look. 'That's strange, Catherine. Cos yer Ma told me she was takin youse off ta London with her on accounta doin some shoppin.'

By now, Margaret, the other twin, has sidled up ta the door.

'No,' she says. 'She only took Lucy.'

Bitches, both. Makin it worse, they said nothin about Amanda.

'That little hooer,' says Ma.

Did the twins look at each other and smile behind Ma's back as she went stompin off back home? I like ta think they did.

Sam told me that woulda been bad enough except then the Social called up outta the blue, concerned about me health, and ate Ma outta it when she saw I wasn't there. Ma had started on the Jameson so she wasn't the most articulate when the Social asked where I was, sayin how the fuck should she know and what business was it a the poxy Health Board in anyways any more? Then the Social started pryin, checkin the kitchen and the bathroom – which were both manky dirty, in spite a Sam's best efforts. The Social even looked inta Granny, woke her up and inspected her leg, and when she seen that, she told Ma Granny needed serious medical attention. Ma went ballistic, told her Granny was gettin all the attention she needed – who else washed her wound or bathed her or brung her down the stairs? – so the Social could shove her fancy ideas up her hole. It was then the Social told Ma that if things didn't look up, the Health Board would hafta start thinkin about gettin other arrangements together for me and Granny and Sam.

I asked Sam what happened then and she said Ma started cryin.

'Course she did,' I said. 'Bet she said she'd die before she'd let them take ya.'

Sam said nothin at that.

'I love ya, Sam,' she says, holdin her to her. 'I'll never hurt ya again. I promise.'

'Jesus, is that Rose?' says Marlene, as we walk down the pier towards the gate. 'I wasn't expectin her ta meet us.'

Still mellow on me fix, I only half-hear what she's sayin.

Ma marches up, grabs me.

'Ah, hiya there, Rose—'

She rounds on Marlene. 'What is it, Marlene, thatcha hafta keep interferin in other people's business? D'ya think I can't look after me own? Get outta me fuckin way.'

She doesn't see Amanda, who's laggin behind us, gazin back at the sea.

'Rose—'

'I said, get outta me way.'

She pulls me and I float with her, out inta the fresh air, where, for some reason, pictures a Cindy Devlin are decoratin every single lamp-post from Dun Laoghaire pier ta Liberty Hall.

I was expectin her ta hit me but instead she just stood me beside the gas fire in the sittin-room and talked at me. She didn't yell, just asked question after question in a low voice.

Did I wanta ruin me life?

Did I wanta end up like her, laden down with four kids before I was old enough ta tie me shoelaces?

What did I think I was: better than anyone else? Thinkin I could hide off ta London and get rid of it like some huzzy on the streets?

What was I playin at?

I don't know whatcha on about, Ma, I said, only half-lyin.

Don't lie ta me, Lucy. I know ya went over for no shoppin.

Honest, Ma, I don't.

Bit by bit I resurfaced. The edges a things got sharper. I felt meself risin ta the top.

Why didn't I tell her? Why'd I hafta go ta Marlene?

I didn't bother answerin that one.

We were there about an hour before I got it. She let somethin slip – I know where ya go every Saturday, Lucy. Don't think I don't – and then I started laughin because it was so stupid and so bleedin obvious and so fuckin wrong.

'Ya think I got pregnant for him, don'tcha?'

She stops pacin and her face goes ashy white.

'Ya think I went over ta London to kill his fuckin baby.'

'I knew it.' Her voice is hoarse. 'I knew he was seein someone else.'

I know I shouldn't but I can't resist. 'What d'ya think he was, Ma? The Virgin Mary? Ya could be his own Ma, for fucksake. Whatcha expect him ta do, keep it stacked away in his jocks and lash it out just when he comes visitin you, ya ugly old waggon?'

She grabs whatever's nearest ta her, a china pig Micko brung back from Funderland when we were kids, and hurls it at me. I duck, but not quick enough, and it hits me on the forehead, knockin out whatever easiness was left over from me fix. I stagger ta me feet.

'Ya cunt!' I scream. 'Ya pig ignorant ugly waggon of a perverted hooer!' I grab the biggest bit a the china pig and feck it back at her. Then I feel round for somethin harder, pick up a brass horse Stevo gave her one Christmas, and feck that at her too.

She's screamin. I'm screamin.

I take out yer knife.

Fuck off with yer rages and yer hatred a me. Fuck off with you and yer boyfriends, except they're not yours any more, are they, ya sad cow. Fuck off the schools with their poxy Inter. Fuck off the Social and the Health Board and the Psychiatric fuckin Services and the courts. Fuck off the lot a youse. I don't need youse any more. I can look after meself.

I put the knife back in me belt. Ma is breathin hard, starin at me. I get the feelin she'll jump on me and bite me face off if I don't move.

*

'Where ya goin?' says Sam.

'Away.'

I start throwin clothes inta me bag. I feel like I'm sweatin blood. I go ta take off me sweatshirt because it's drippin wet but then I remember the gear strapped ta me skin so I leave it on instead.

'Don't go, Lucy.'

'You'll be alright, Mouse. You're the only one she doesn't hurt.'

'Lucy, please . . . can I come too?'

'No, ya can't. It's not safe. Stay here with Granny. She'll look after ya.'

We both know it's a lie. I turn ta her and grab her hands.

'Sam, you'll be alright. Lookit – next time the Social come round and I'm not there, they'll take ya away, setcha up somewhere nice. And that'll be good, won't it?'

'I don't wanta go to another home. I wanta stay here.'

'Ya said ya wanted ta come with me.'

'Yeah, but not on me own ta some stranger's.'

'Ya can't come, Sam. It's not safe. Believe me.'

I take her by the shoulders and hold her tight. She's soft and peachy, a little girl on the verge a bein a woman. The gold off her hoops throws reflections onta her face.

'Lookit, I'll be back regular for the Social, okay? Send a message and I'll stay a day or two. Then ya won't hafta go live in any stranger's house.'

'Lucy—'

'Please, Sam. Trust me. You'll be alright. I'll be back ta look after ya. I promise.'

'Oh . . . kay.'

'Good.' I smile and she smiles back. It's not her usual wide smile, I can tell she doesn't really mean it, but it's the best I can do. I can't take her with me, not where I'm goin, and I hafta get out. The rage is still risin in me, seepin through me pores. If I don't go now, I'll kill Ma.

Behind me, Ma slaps cards on the table. Every one laid down the sound of a face bein hit. And no prizes for guessin whose.

'Watch it with Sam,' I say.

She ignores me.

'Any messin round with her, treatin her like ya done the rest of us, I won't come back next month and then you'll lose her.'

Slap slap slap.

Granny's door is open, so I peek inside. She's sittin at the winda, starin out. I'm half-expectin her ta notice me, ta say Goodbye, Lucy, or even give me a warnin, but she doesn't. I wonder if I should go in and give her a hug, like I normally would, but then I think no, it'll confuse her. She'll start bangin on, thinkin I'm someone else entirely and then I'll never get away.

So I blow her a kiss instead, sendin it like a jimmy joe through the open door and across the room, where it rests on her pink scalp under her thin dyed hair like a blessin.

The way ahead is clear, as clear as if little elves are lightin it for me with magic lanterns. If only, I think once, if only Ma hadn't fucked things up with Marlene, I could stay in theirs. But then I think no, not such a good idea. Because Marlene would have me rumbled fast as anythin and then I'd be fucked. And John Paul's no better. In anyways, why would that do-goodin shite want me livin with his lovely Tara and cryin baby?

Amanda's Ma never found out what happened, ya know. I thought Amanda woulda cracked real easy, but she never let on. She told me afterwards she'd almost gone ta confession ta tell the priest because she felt so guilty. But as she was sittin there in the pew, waitin her turn with the auld wans, she seen how it would end up. With the priest tellin her Ma and then that would be the end a that; a Charlie, a fellas, of ever goin out, ever gettin the chance ta see you again. Because despite a whatcha might think, with the abortion and all, she still wanted ya.

It starts rainin as I round the corner. The rain is cool, April showers, and it soaks inta me collar and hair, runnin down me back and me chest. I stick out me tongue and taste it. The drops glisten like jewels.

The flakin green paint a the door beckons. I look round, makin sure I'm not seen, because it doesn't matter what Snags said back in Rotherhithe about things bein watertight, I know it's still dangerous, and I knock.

Home sweet home.

VII

Don't mess me around, Nayler.

Don't treat me like I'm me brother. I understand how ya used me, you and Snags both, and why ya tested me, settin me up for the errant, all that, but ya don't need ta play that game on me any more. I'm up for stuff. Tell me things, not just the shite everyone knows. Tell me the important stuff. I'm better use for ya that way.

Would it a been different if I'd said that? Would ya a lain the ground between us open, told me everythin I wanted ta know? Or would ya a just laughed and ruffled me head and said, *Ya should know that's not how it works, Lucy Lu. Ya should know everyone has ta hold somethin back.*

Stupid ta even wonder.

Ah, happy days. The summer a love. I'd be a liar if I said it didn't start out okay. It always starts out okay.

I lie on the mattress but I can't sleep. The whole house is stinkin and everywhere I look I see Micko. On the pilla beside me, floatin from the ceilin, dancin outside the winda like that vampire brother in *Salem's Lot*. The room is so full of him I feel it's gointa burst.

Sasha's door is locked, like it's been since she went, so I knock on yours.

You're wide awake. Before ya can say even 'Oh', let alone some thick slaggin comment, I tell ya it's not like that, I don't want ya near me, I just don't wanta sleep in there on me own.

Ya tell me I'll hafta have the floor so.

In the end I sleep on them mirrored cushions. They dig inta me skin and the smell is no better and I can hear ya breathin six feet from me on that mattress but at least Micko stays away.

*

'He's expectin payment in twenty days,' says the delivery boy. He's from down the country, Kerry, somewhere like that. Ya weigh the pack in yer hand.

'This all?'

The delivery boy shrugs. 'Take it or leave it, Nayler.'

'Alright.' Ya take out yer scales.

Ya bolt the ten locks as soon as the delivery boy leaves. One two three four five once I caught a fish alive.

'Can I help?' I say.

'Later.'

We're in the shop on Hill Street, the flat at the back a the playground. It's not in great shape but it's way cleaner than the squat. Plus there's proper furniture and all: a comfy armchair and a good table. If ya didn't look too close, ya might think it was someone's auntie's gaff. Plus it's outta view and safe from the rozzers and it's off the Wacker's beat but still too close ta him for the Don ta touch and we don't use it ta sell direct from in anyways and, better than all that, it's got them ten locks on the door.

I watch ya weigh, cut, weigh again, pack. Ya frown as ya concentrate on the scales. Light from the winda catches the edges a bone and muscle in yer lower arm. There's a rhythm in yer movements that's easy on the eye. I don't care, for now, that there's nothin ta do.

'Here, Lucy.' Ya throw me over a bag a tablets. 'Sort these for me.'

They got little birds on them, like swans. I sort them inta bags a ten.

Storm clouds build up in the sky beyond the city. The wire grille on the winda shakes with the electricity, hummin ta the tune a that Doors song. 'Riders on the Storm.' I feel it rushin through me veins, like someone's standin behind me, strokin me skin.

I look up, catch yer eye. I can't read yer expression.

Ya turn back ta the scales.

Weigh, cut, weigh, pack.

When the weighin's done, ya cook up.

I know about you, Nayler, whatcha been hidin from yer boss, I wanta say, but me teeth grippin the bootlace as ya lift the needle give me no space ta speak. Then I crumple against the wall.

As I fall I see you fall too; cook, spike, slump. I know full well ya whistle-clean, still standin at the winda, watchin me, but I've wanted ta see that picture so long it's burnt itself inta me eyes – like they say pictures a murderers do on the eyes a the people they kill.

Many places I've lived in, locked and unlocked, and what's mad is the way life . . . settles. Ya get inta routines whether ya free or chained and the routine manages yer time for ya. It was no different livin with ya. I got useta it. You'd think I'd remember that time as the best buzza me life, but as ya know, Nayler, I'm no romantic. In some ways, them days were the most everyday of all I've lived.

We used; I say we but a course I mean I. Far as I could see, you had it under control, hadn't slipped up since I'd come back from London. But in another way I do mean we because you were part and parcel a me usin as much as if we were sharin the same blood. Ya watched, ya sank with me, ya talked and listened and ya fed off the diminishin highs and so we both done it.

Ya went away sometimes for days at a time, and came back smellin a strange cities or, every so often, somethin different; fresh, outdoors-sorta. But them were the good times and while ya were gone ya never let me go short. And I went home whenever Sam sent word, bringin her presents a gold and silver ta buy off me guilt – though at the time I wouldn'a said that's what it was – and done me meetins with the Social, armed with uppers ta open me pupils, and played normal for a few hours till it was safe ta skip off again. And I helped ya in the shop and got in on the odd rob – but mercifully went uncaught by the rozzers – and hopped across the water on Snags's account and bought CDs with me pay that was mountin up note on note under our floorboards.

One day ya took me aside and told me ya'd hafta teach me stuff so I could look after meself better on the job; and we done it then, workin tricks with bits a wood shaped like knives and later on the real thing. Ya showed me what blade ta use, and, on yer body, where the weak points were, and how much was enough for a warnin, a counter-attack, a damagin or a . . . as you called it . . . incapacitation. *Always keep the head, Lucy Lu. Only hurt as much as ya need. And always do a good job. Keep it clean.* Then ya said somethin I didn't understand. *Ya can be kind.* But I didn't dwell too much on all that, just focused on the task in hand, shuttin down pictures a people screamin in basements – how could that be kind? – so I could concentrate better.

And between times ya packed me off ta school in the mornins with me bag on me shoulder and g-g's in me pocket – *they won't fix ya, Lucy, but they'll keep the withdrawals at bay* – and that way I stayed outta the grasp a the Childcatchers, and finished school and all, even managed ta fail the Inter. But apart from that, in them two months before Sasha came back, nothin, as Amanda would say, happened.

We ate, sometimes, and drank, but not much alcohol, and played cards with that gammy deck a yours. Ya told me a fella called Crowley had made them, and they were as good as Ma's for showin what things meant, but in a different way. This lad knew his stuff, he was a magician a sorts, ya said, had ways a makin things happen – power, ya said, Lucy Lu, it's all about harnessin power – though there was a price a course, there's always a price. He had a rule, ya told me; do what you will – I nearly said, *Nayler, didn't someone else have that rule?* only ya were gettin serious and I didn't feel like interruptin – it doesn't mean do whatcha want, Lucy, means find out what ya supposed ta do, what yer purpose in life is, yeah, because everyone has a purpose, and just do it. But I wasn't inta his shite pictures nor his scary voodoo bollocks, and in anyways, readin between the lines he just seemed like some sorta mixed-up smackhead steamer, so on the whole I zoned out when ya started on about him. We never told each other's fortunes with them cards. I wasn't inta it and even if I had been, I knew ya wouldn'a let me. But I spied ya buildin a spread for yerself once or twice when ya thought ya were on yer own and it made me laugh, ta see ya mad inta that hocus-pocus like ya were still a kid.

And besides that I played me radio and CDs and listened ta tunes ya couldn't hear, and ya read ta me from yer books I couldn't read stuff I couldn't understand and some stuff I could. Every man loves the thing he kills, went one poem, set in a jail and all it was, or maybe it was the other way around; everyone kills what they love; somethin like that. Only I laughed then, for what did you know about love, ya twisted fuck, nor me neither?

Cymbals, ya said ta me once, everythin is ruled by cymbals, Lucy Lu – for a minute I thought ya meant the drum yokes, till I copped on it was signs ya were talkin about – that's the only way a makin sense a the big things, ya said, life and death and all, and that's why people get confused, because what's a good sign for one person can be bad ta another. And we shared some memories, but not all, and ya gave me history lessons about the trade, but ya never spoke much about the goins on at the top of our own little business; what Snags was upta, what grounds was bein lost, what new ones won, what measures was bein taken ta keep it all tickin over in them troubled times. I was there ta take orders, ta run and catch, not ta be a hands-on partner, and ya know what, Nayler, I was happy enough with that.

Sometimes ya brung up girls, free a charge on accounta yer looks or reputation or whatever. They came from the street but never the Square – none a them came near us any more, least of all Cindy Devlin, prettiest brasser in town, Cindy Devlin who'd been missin since April, though I didn't wanta think about that – and, sometimes on yer invitation, sometimes not, I hid in the shadas a yer room and watched as ya teased them on the juice-stinkin mattress a yer bed, makin them laugh and sigh and moan and sometimes even sing. For the most part they looked happy enough, though that coulda been just manners, but there was times when ya seemed ta give up sooner than I'da expected, leavin both them and yerself unsatisfied, like yer heart wasn't really in it.

Yer back. Yer shoulder blades like the buds a wings pokin through the muscles stretchin taut under yer white skin. The nuggets a yer spine like keys on some fucked-up flute, each an eye watchin me ta see if I'm watchin you. The swoopin ridges under the bony swell a yer ribs. The twistin strength a yer arms. The sharp lines a yer

355

hips. The triangle a bone at the base a yer spine, powerin ya as ya lift, slide, shudder.

Yer white shape after, draped on the mattress.

For the most part, though, we lived in silence, with a foot a space hangin between us, singin with potential from pole ta pole. We. . . fitted. Like hands in glove; like monks, or brothers, or cats. Cats do that, see, if there's more than one in a gaff. They keep equal space between each other and the owner.

As for our owner . . . well. He stayed safe on the other island, away from his uncle, sendin mules and couriers over with packs in their socks, their holes, their mouths, their bellies. I done five runs before the Inter, each time goin over with a Cork bird, a sister a yer pal Rayo's who pretended she was me aunt – she didn't use herself, but she was handy with a shooter and was paid well enough ta cover me. We stayed in a dive in Camberwell and I travelled ta Vassily the Nazi Greek in Rotherhithe again, twice, and went once to a black crew in Brixton and two other times picked up from some Irish geezer in the Peckham flats. Snags was there on each run ta handle the transfer but I was nothin far as he was concerned. All I was good for was ta test and carry, test and carry.

Still, it was alright. It was a buzz, a sorts. And I learnt things from the small-talk they shared when they thought I was outta it. Understand, though, I didn't wanta learn much. I was happy with things as they were; I didn't want stories a necessary incapacitations or hooers missin from the Square or deals gone wrong interferin with me buzz.

On me fourth run I banged up insteada smokin. No comparison. Ya got real vexed when I told ya, started naggin on how I shouldn'a and I shoulda kept smokin or I'd really fuck meself up, even started givin off about Snags and did he make me do it and how and did he get upta any funny business while I because if he . . . As if ya cared, ya prick.

I stopped runnin in May. I was gettin too visible. Or maybe too careless. Or maybe it wasn't ta do with me at all but everythin else that was happenin around us. The Don bein pulled up by the Old Bill for anythin they could stick on him; speedin fines, parkin, TV licence. They brung him in for interviews on any blag that happened in the area, started crackin down on his girls, hauled his men in at the drop of a hat, asked about his bank accounts, even tailed his wife when she went shoppin. Small things ta start with, mosta which he shrugged off, but they kept him busy, and worse, got him mad.

He mighta been goin down but he was fucked if he was goin down on his own.

And that, as they say, was when the good times started ta turn, though we didn't suss how bad they were turnin ta for quite some time.

The knock came early, round ten, just as ya were about ta give me me mornin fix.

Christ, I heard ya say. Sasha, what he do ta ya?

Not him, she said. I went home.

Only with her accent, it sounded like *I want home*.

I sat on the stairs and through the rods a the bannisters watched her fall inta yer arms.

Ya stroked the cuts on her forehead, the bruises round her neck, her swollen eyes.

That night she slept next door. She didn't say why, and neither did you, but I knew it was because she was keepin that room for Snags. She was waitin for him ta come back. All night long she stayed awake listenin for his steps and you stayed awake listenin out for hers and I stayed listenin out for yours, and the gear moaned through our bodies and the cracked walls of our stinkin home.

The bass booms at us from half-way down the street. I got me hood pulled over me head so I look more like a fella than normal. You're in a long coat, black, with a velvet collar. Ya got an earring in yer right ear. I think ya look like a queer with that but Sasha gave it to ya and says it looks good, so ya been wearin it non-stop.

The wind rises.

At the door, the bouncer we've bought turns away when I walk past.

Get in and out, fast, ya said. The Don's fellas come down at two. I want ya ta work the place solid before then. Stay away from his customers, remember. Ya know who ta spot.

Inside, the bodies twist and turn. The music pounds through me feet, snakin its way up me legs. Two fellas in a corner maul each other, stickin long pink tongues down each other's throats. Faggots. Downstairs, girls in short skirts with long legs weave themselves through fellas with tight hair and tighter tee-shirts. Donna Summer wails. 'I Feel Love'.

Someone grabs me. A sweaty-faced fella with a curly half-mohawk and a raggy black tee-shirt. He whispers in me ear. I palm him the Es, take the cash. I work through the crowds. The fella we call the Student appears in a corner and gives me the nod. I squeeze through the bodies and while the Student fiddles with his big black-rimmed specs and slides the cash inta me arse pocket, I give him the acid and hash. The Student sells on, mainly to his buddies, all college kids. I don't care. He could sell onta the Queen for all it matters ta me.

Prince bumps and grinds. 'Sign a the Times'. Just as he's meltin inta James Brown's 'Sex Machine', I see the Don's dealers roundin the spiral staircase onta the dance floor. I race down the other stairs, the ones at the back, and out through the kitchen where the chefs toss steamin baskets a chips and force burgers face-down on greasy fryers.

Ya waitin in the door a the Stag's Head. I give ya the cash, minus the 10 per cent I've peeled off for meself.

'Shite,' ya say, fingerin through the notes.

A week or so later they jump us on Gardiner Street, just past the IDA Industrial Centre. I'm alert, thanks ta the uppers ya made me take, so I get an itchin down me back that tells me somethin's up. A second later they're outta the shadas and on us. Three lugs, the biggest one with a familiar strut and a knife-scar itchin down the side of his nose. He grabs me. In the corner a me eye, I see ya dig in yer belt.

Time jumps back and I'm five again, millin Greg Doyle with

Micko and John Paul. Yer knife flashes out and inta the middle fella's face. He lifts his hands ta protect himself and stumbles back, cursin. I squirm in the scarred lug's grasp, reach for me own blade and in one motion flick it open and draw it across his ribs. He squeals, he's down and you're on him, workin him. A slash across the back a one ankle ta hobble him. A twist in his right shoulder ta fuck up the weapon arm. In out, quick. The small fella swears and grabs at me, tryin ta catch me hair, only he can't get a grip, I have it too short, and even though I feel his chain scrapin against me forehead, I remember what John Paul taught me about the martial arts and give way, droppin like a sack a spuds. The small fella teeters, thrun off-balance. I smash me fist inta his bollocks. The chain drops with a clatter. I hear somethin behind me and turn. It's the middle fella – he's comin at me, eyes drippin blood, haulin somethin outta his coat – but I duck just in time, barely missin the mason's hammer as it swings past me face, a flash a dull white glintin at the edges. It swoops back up and I see the glint's from pointy things stuck on the head. Nails? Welded? Fuck. I try ta scrabble away along the fence, keepin low as I can, but me trouser leg catches on barb wire, and I can't get it off, and he's got that hammer peakin and it's already startin ta drop again and I'm sure it's gointa get me this time, but suddenly ya there in fronta me – 'Stay fuckin down, Lucy!' – come outta nowhere, yer arm liftin ta take the weight a the hammer's handle, yer knife hand out, yer blade a sixth finger curvin down ta slash at the gouger's neck. The handle connects. Ya sink, twist, slash. Yer knife bites in, the gouger goes white, grabs his neck, jerks his arm up one last belt, the hammer jerks too and crashes inta yer side, nailed head first. Ya grunt, an animal sound I never heard from ya before. The gouger drops his hammer, staggers back. Ya crumple onta the ground. I rip me trouser leg free from the barb wire, reach over, grab yer hand. Yer side is wet with blood. I can see the biggest lug staggerin up on his good foot now, scrabblin with his good arm under his coat and it's an axe-head he has there, I know from the curvin shape, and on me right I know the middle gouger's swayin forwards again, hand still clamped ta his blood-drenched neck, yellin

yellin somethin at the big lad, and that small cunt is on us too and without knowin what I'm doin, I push ya behind me so ya safe, shovin ya up the road, but that big lug is lurchin up too, way faster than he should, raisin that axe, and as I turn ta face him down it comes, swoopin towards me.

Someone says somethin.

The axe stops, inches from me head.

The small one, groanin, reaches out again. I can see the razor blade in his fingers.

'Come fuckin on!' I yell at ya, and we're harin up the road, me pullin at ya, you limpin, while the small cunt start ta rage at the big one who's crumplin in a heap onta his knees as the middle one shakes his head, wavin his free hand like he's tryin ta explain somethin.

I coulda sworn he said, *No, don't touch her*, but why, I don't know.

'That Don's losin the plot, gettin soft on girls,' I tell ya after, when we're home.

Ya say nothin.

I thought them lugs woulda tried jumpin us again, real soon after. But they didn't. Hung around, sure, specially near the shop, but for ages all they done was watch us.

Was it then ya went back on it? After the batin, ta soften down the pain a havin that old scar across yer rib opened up? Was it Nurse Sasha that gave it ya ta speed yer recovery? Or had ya begun before that – only a pinch, mind; nothin regular – ta celebrate her return from Amsterdam?

In them months I seen Damo the odd time, mainly hangin round his da's garage where he'd started an apprenticeship. He'd taken ta wearin a bandanna round his head. Probably thought it made him look like Bruce Springsteen. Sap. Once or twice I thought about sayin hello but as things heated up with the Don that seemed like a bad idea. His da was a true-blue Five Lamper, and them lot were gettin so paranoid I'da probably ended up in that self-same carshop with a Ford Fiesta rollin over me knees.

It was Sam told me when Marlene and Stevo moved out ta Malahide. Marlene seemed ta have taken Ma's threats serious and didn't call round any more. Sam bumped inta her one day in town, though, and Marlene gave her their phone number, told her ta ring if there was an emergency. 'This is just for you, pet,' she said.

'Meanin I'm not ta have it?' I asked Sam.

'Meanin Ma.'

I played with the idea a askin her for it, but then I thought no. For what would I need their charity?

And Amanda . . . ah, her I didn't see at all.

Ya come in while me and Sash are chattin. She's dead easy ta chat ta. Different ta Amanda. Real . . . interested. Makes me blather on a bit sometimes, like one a them heads on the telly tryin ta sound all deep. In anyways we been gassin on about families and the shite goes on in them. But when ya come in she switches ta tellin me all about the tattoo parlour she worked in where she met Snags. Savin yer feelins, I spose.

After ya fix us up, she tells us a story.

Ten years ago, we all lived in a hotel near the Vondelpark, she says, dreamy, rubbin at the tiny sores dottin the roots of her lashes, the sores that still haven't healed from the beatin she got in Amsterdam. There were fifty rooms and the people who'd been there the longest each had a room to sleep in. Everybody else slept in the ballroom. When someone left, the person who was in the ballroom the longest got the new room. It was beautiful, that ballroom. There were chandeliers, long windows which we boarded up. Except for the ones at the back. We used them as doors. The floor was beautiful too, once upon a time, white carpet, but by the time I lived there it was ruined. Cigarette burns.

She leans her head on yer chest, still rubbin her eyes. Ya wince; them nail wounds haven't healed yet.

Everyone was doing it, she says. We didn't know then what it could do.

Regrets? ya say in her ear.

No, she says, and starts singin that French song she loves.

I don't know the words but I join in. Better that than be left out in the cold.

'Jesus!' ya say, lookin at the pack. The delivery boy shrugs. He's new, Spanish I'm guessin from the dark face.

Three loud knocks come a-knockin on the door.

Ya tear off the cardboard over the back winda and grip the metal hooks with yer fingers. Ya lift the sash, yer body strainin with the effort.

Hi-de-hi, campers, he says in his familiar dark-brown voice as he steps over the sill. He's wearin a long blonde wig and high heels and even with the acne scars and all he looks like a proper bird.

They're fightin. His voice is low but vicious like it always is when he loses the head. She's cryin like a baby. Across the room I can feel ya on yer mattress, tense and sweatin.

This isn't my problem, I tell meself. This is between them and maybe you.

They been at it since he's come back. Yesterday he walked off once it got dark, still dressed as a bird, and she came inta our room and lay down beside ya. Ya told me ta get out so I did. But I peeked in the keyhole and seen ya hold her like she was one a yer precious china dogs that I useta blag for ya outta the antiques shop on Francis Street, strokin her long hair and whisperin in her ear. Youse looked picture-perfect, the two a youse, like some dark angel had matched youse up in heaven or hell.

Things is not good. Sasha wants ta go back ta London with him but Snags says it's too risky. The Don's got spies over there, he says, fuckin up his deals, tailin him. He was lucky he was able ta get on the plane without bein followed. And now he's got ta keep movin; he's headin off ta Europe which means she can't go with him; she'd only run inta old friends that she doesn't wanta see. In anyways he needs us ta stay, keep things tickin over. We're safe; they don't want us, they want him. *What about that hidin we got?* I wanta ask. *What about our supplies?* But this is not my time for talkin, this is not my argument, and you don't say nothin because it's not yer argument neither, and neither does Sasha, and even if we all brung it up, it wouldn't make a jot a difference because he has his answers all prepared.

We're not ta worry, he says. It'll ease off. It won't be long. Them Fundercover Drug Squad cunts are buildin up their evidence on the Don and it's only a matter a time before they catch him. Then he'll be packed away and we'll get our hands on the serious money. No problem. And forget about the Wacker; that dick's days are numbered; we'll find a way ta blow him outta the water too. Oh yeah, both them cunts, we'll sort them, learn them a lesson, find every last chink in their armour and use it against them, take our time if we hafta but we'll rip the fuckers apart. The coppers want a sacrifice and it's not gointa be us. And as for their lackeys, them no-brain Waxboys and them snivellin Five Lampers, they'll be crawlin ta us soon as their main men are fucked. And then Snags will be king a the coop, north and south, and he can buy that flat in Ranelagh they always been talkin about, and Sasha can clean up for good, won't need that shit any more, and they can get married and start a family a their own. But in the meantime, she's gotta keep goin.

She sobs.

Stay staunch, Sasha, he tells her. I need you and Nayler; I really do, now I don't have them cunts on the Square dealin for me any more. Lookit, it's only a few more weeks. We're all makin sacrifices. Nayler'll help ya. He's a good kid, me number one. Make it last, darlin.

I push me fingers in me ears, not wantin ta hear about any a this – business or plans, sacrifices or cunts on the Square, some a who been missin eight long weeks – and under the blood thumpin through me head I can feel ya in yer bed across the six foot a space. Ya sweatin bad, like ya been sweatin ever since Snags came back, and in me mouth stings the copper taste a yer fear.

Up at the seventy-two again, Nayler?

How ya hid the withdrawals from him is anyone's guess. Then again, pal, ya were always tops at hidin.

*

Make it last, he said. And so began the other summer, the summer when the river started runnin dry.

At first we managed. Sasha's phy had run out a while before so we'd no pills, but ya were able ta buy us the liquid stuff off of a street junkie still in Snags's pocket. Then this graphic artist from Phibsboro – some small-time user owed ya a few favours – turned up trumps and done ya up a fake prescription for pills. The scrip came in handy, more than handy, vital. Three hundred tablet a phy every two week that ya collected off a little auld wan in a chemist in Kilmainham, wearin yer neatest threads with yer hair slicked back like a college boy and speakin in yer best English accent. It was way cheaper than the gear, three pound fifty for a ton when they were three quid each on the street, and the buzz lasted alright and we could drink with them and even when they ran short, ya could get us dikes through the artist on another fake scrip.

The dikes were pretty in pink and Sash and me crushed them and banged them up even though ya told us not ta, said we should just swalla them instead, and it was good . . . for a while.

Sash sits on yer mattress, starin inta the empty fireplace and pickin at her eyes. Them scabs growin along the edges are gettin bigger now, but she won't leave them be.

Stop it, I try ta tell her. You're only makin it worse. She doesn't listen. Maybe she doesn't hear. Maybe I'm not speakin loud enough. Pick pick pick.

You appear at the door.

Sasha looks up, but ya shake yer head. Ya make ya way over and sit down on the mattress beside her. Ya strip off yer tee-shirt. Ya still welterweight hard but scrawnier, like there's less a ya there. The scar that got opened up from the nails is startin ta heal but it's still real ugly-lookin; purple and raised. Ya lie down beside her. Yer face is awful relaxed, and I'm wonderin if ya been back at the cookie jar again without our knowin.

Sasha moves ta get up. Ya grab her ankle. 'Stay,' ya say.

She stops, haltin in the movement. At last she shuffles up and out ta the landin. No sound for ages.

'He's gone a month, Sash,' ya call after her. 'He won't be back.'

I picture her standin outside Snags's door, fist raised ta knock. At last, without knockin, she shuffles back in and sits down beside ya again.

I wake in the middle a the night because I get that feelin again, a someone leanin on me chest. But there's nobody there. You're asleep on yer mattress and Sasha's with ya, lyin in yer arms. Yer lips are on her hair.

On the ground beside me is a spike. But we had no gear last night, only phy ta put us ta sleep, and even though it was pills I don't remember neither me nor Sasha bangin them up. I lie back, wonderin why, if ya been tempted again, ya were so careless as ta leave yer needle out like that insteada hidin yer tracks like ya usually do.

In the mornin, she's still out for the count. Her right hand is curled under her cheek, like a little kid. You're nowhere. I hang round for a bit till it's time, then head out.

The sun cracks open the fanlight over the door. I brace meself, swalla the happy pills you've given me, half-dreadin the buzz, and step out. Heat hits me, a fist in the face, belly, chest.

Ma answers the door. She's got her hair done and all, is even wearin an apron.

'Ya took yer time.'

I don't bother risin to it. 'They here yet?'

'No.'

Sam's at the kitchen table doin a drawin. She's got a pretty gold chain around her wrist and a silver ring with a green stone on her middle finger.

'That's a lovely chain, Sam.'

'Yeah.' She doesn't look up. 'Ya gave it me last time ya came.'

Did I? 'Oh, yeah. Didn't give ya the ring, though.'

'What ring?' says Ma.

Sam glares at me – why? Fucksake, I didn't say anythin – and pulls the ring off before Ma can look at it.

'D'ya want a cup a tea?' says Ma.

'No.' The stuff is startin ta work, twitchin inta me feet and me fingers. I remind meself ta keep me mouth shut. Don't talk, Lucy. Just smile and act like ya grand. I pull the sleeves a me trackie top down over me palms.

'D'ya hear the news?' says Ma when Sam's gone out ta the jacks. I shake me head.

'Poor Cindy Devlin. They found her by the Ringsend Docks this mornin.'

'Yeah?' I'm buzzin all of a sudden. Fuck I'm high.

'They could hardly recognize her she was that far gone. Only a chain she was wearin gave it away. Poor Therese, God bless her. Ten weeks searchin and now this.'

'Ah.' The happy pills rush inta me, pushin out me pupils so they fill me eyes. No pinnin here.

'Awful hard ta find out what happened but they say her throat coulda been slit. That line a work, though. I mean, she had it comin.' She takes a drag and looks at me.

Don't even go there, Ma. I'm happy happy happy.

Sam comes back in. I tip her with me foot. 'Alright, Mouse?' She nods.

'So according to the School Attendance Office, you finished your Inter Cert,' says the Social.

I nod. Don't talk, Lucy.

'How did it go?' She's tryin ta be friendly but it's not really workin.

'Oh, grand,' says Ma.

'Your health is still a concern, Lucy.'

I glance at Ma.

'Oh, we'll be goin back ta the Psychiatric shortly. Just wanted Lucy ta finish school without any stress, ya know.'

'Well . . .' The Social frowns and looks around, sizin up the gaff, Sam sittin quiet at the kitchen table, Granny wizened in the raggedy armchair, her two hands tremblin on her good leg, Ma's gleamin kitchen surfaces, her spotless floor. 'Okay.'

'Lucy!' she calls me just as I'm goin.

'Mouse, I can't take ya with me—' I start.

'No. I got somethin for ya.' She digs in her pocket, takes out a postcard.

'Fuck, who's that from?'

'Doesn't say much, Lucy,' she says. 'Just a date and Wish You Two Were Here.' There's a picture of a windmill on the other side.

Sasha is still outta it when I get back. The hand under her face has gone white. I wonder if I should turn her round, but soon as I touch her, ya standin in the doorway.

'Leave her.'

'Fucksake, Nayler. I'm only tryin ta—'

'What's that?' Ya pick up the postcard.

I grab it off ya. 'Here, that's mine.'

Ya grab it back. Ya stare at it. Then ya smile. I get it.

'What's it mean?' I say. 'Is he back?'

Voices echo through the flats. I can hear kids playin in the playground nearby, swingin and seesawin and all them things kids do when they don't hafta worry about anythin. Across the road, someone is watchin us. I don't know who it is, but it's someone.

Ya glance round, like ya sense them too, catch me eye, laugh. 'Relax, Lucy. It's okay.'

Then ya open the ten locks, quick as ya can.

Ya check yer watch. 'It's a new system,' ya told me. 'He puts a date on the top. That's delivery day. He puts a number in the middle a the words, that's the time.'

At two a clock, the courier comes. It's a girl this time, black, with an English accent.

Ya give her what's owin on the last batch and crack open the pack.

Ya sit back. 'Fuck this. Where's the gear?'

'What gear?' she says.

★

'He doesn't know ya need it, Nayler,' I say, after she's gone. I don't plan ta say it; it just sorta . . . comes out.

Ya look at me. I bite me tongue.

'He knows Sasha does. The . . . fuck!' Ya kick at the door. Then ten locks rattle, mockin us.

'We can get by on the phy but—'

'Yeah. Okay.' Meanin *Shut the fuck up, Lucy.*

But when ya ring the auld wan in Kilmainham about renewin the prescription, she tells ya she had the Drug Squad in the week before.

'I'm sorry, Mister Wilson. I don't want to see you stuck or anything. You've always been a good customer but you see, they told me I couldn't . . .'

Thank fuck ya rang before callin down.

'Okay.' Ya dig in yer pocket. 'G-g time.'

I take them and start crunchin.

'Now . . . ya know Pearse Street?'

And that was the night ya sent me down ta enemy territory across the river, me pocket stuffed with a wad a notes ya peeled outta nowhere. Better you than me, Lucy, ya told me. They don't know ya so they won't have it in for ya. Remember ta keep yer knife ready, and don't lose the head.

Fuck, ya snarled. Snags is a stupid cunt. Anyone would think he was tryin ta put himself outta business, hand it back to the Don like it never was his in the first place.

The prices were shite and it wasn't the best, but what's a little low quality between pals?

When I brung the gear home, ya took it off me before I could say anythin, and real slow, like one a them birds on a cookery programme showin everyone else how it's done, ya shot up in front of us while we waited our turn.

Ya used a vein in yer upper arm, close ta yer horse tattoo. The blood swelled at the tipa the spike, blazin purple against yer white skin.

Ya didn't look at us once.

I watched yer mouth slacken as ya collapsed onta the pilla. Sasha was already searchin for a vein. It won't surprise ya if I tell ya that it gladdened me a bit, Nayler, though it saddened me too, to at last see ya fail out in the open, not even pretendin ta hide, just as weak as anyone else.

That night I got me first dream a her. Floatin in the water. All green and swollen in the light from the city. Little fish swimmin in her hair. The tip of her tongue stickin out like a cat's. A chain round her neck and above it, a gash. Number Twenty-two. Ma's card. The World.

Ssshh, ladies, said the gash in her throat.

'Ahahaahahahah.'

'Jesus, what's that?'

'Sshh,' ya say, rockin her as she moans. 'Go back ta sleep, Lucy.'

I try, but it's not easy, her moanin, you shushin.

In the mornin I see what it is. Her right hand is bent over. 'I can't move it,' she says, as ya inject her. 'The feeling is gone.'

'Them fuckin dikes,' ya say. 'It's the chalk. I told youse not ta bang them up.'

'Why don'tcha go to a doctor, Sash?' I ask.

'Jesus, Lucy,' ya say, lookin at me like I'm thick. 'Whatcha think this is? Fuckin Toytown?'

It was round then the attacks started on the squat: rocks at the winda, wreaths on the door, shots from a passin car. I thought it was the Don's lads but you said it was the Waxboys; too fuckin crude ta be Don Ryan's work.

We moved a coupla nights after they shot the windas out, shiftin everythin – skulls, candles, cushions, furniture and Sasha – inta the back room, the one that useta be Micko's.

That was when Sasha started workin. Ya told her she shouldn't, she didn't hafta, we were still doin okay with the stuff we were sellin for Snags, but she wouldn't listen. Now I think she done it as much ta punish him as anythin else.

It still amazes me why we stayed in that house. One time I asked ya why we couldn't just go. Ya said nothin but yer thought was clear as day: over my dead body.

I suppose it makes sense. It was our turf, wasn't it, all the home we had? Besides, like Sasha, ya believed Snags when he said he'd be back.

She sits at the mirror and tries ta brush her long dark hair. The hand makes it harder. It's got no feelin in it, so the brush just whacks against her hair. Whack whack whack.

Use the other one, I wanta tell her. But she's got the brush twisted in the bad hand like they're one and the same, and from the way she keeps whackin, I see she's doin it on purpose. She's tryin ta prove it's alright.

When she's finished, she looks up at ya and ya nod.

Ya look beautiful, ya say ta her with yer eyes.

She does. She looks like a queen.

She leans closer ta the mirror, goes ta pick at the scabs round her eyes. Ya grab her hand, stop her. She tries ta move forward but ya take her hand and raise it to yer lips.

I watch youse in the mirror but this time, you're not checkin ta see if I'm watchin.

Forgive me if I'm wrong, Nayler, but for all ya mighta wanted it, ya never done it with her. Ya mighta seen yerself on her, with her long hair stretched out on the pilla like a stormcloud, them goldy legs wrapped around yer back. Or the other way round, you moanin like a girl while Sasha sat on top, tattoos spirallin down her good arm onta her hand where the blue ink on her skin melted inta yours. Her face goin red when she came, that little laugh at the end, gaspin; you moanin her name. Ah, Sasha, Sasha.

But ya never done it. In the good times, youse were both far too gone ta be ridin. She lay on ya with her clothes off, long and gold and still beautiful even with her sore eyes and crooked wrist, and you lay below her, soft and useless, and the sweat mingled and ya moved, maybe, up ta meet her, but there was no in-out. Not as far as I could tell.

And even if there had a been, who's ta say it woulda been so fuckin great after all, Nayler, for you or for her? Maybe she'da just lain there, pale yella like a plastic bag a washed spuds, her eyes somewhere else, driftin, thinkin a him as she serviced ya like ya were just another trick, while you rammed it inta her, uncarin, all yer great way with the ladies wastin away along with yer fine hard body, all yer pride in havin Snags's woman spoilt by the disappointment that she was just another empty cunt ta fill. I don't mean any offence, Nayler. Youse looked awful well together, sure, and youse had yer moments, but judgin by what went on between youse I'd say that woulda been more like it. Her driftin; you rammin.

So much for the good times. In the bad times, none of us could bear ta be touched.

The packages are gettin smaller. Some weeks there's gear, some weeks not. Me paypack under the floorboards is gone. The business is eatin up our profits. We'll be fine once Snags is back but till then . . .

We make what little Snags gives us last and I go back ta robbin so we can pay for extra from the southsiders; sometimes we go ta the Barn and buy off of the kids that useta run for youse but mainly we stick with that shower from the Pearse flats. I'm gettin clumsy, me that useta pride meself on me fastness. Nearly got nabbed by this young fella I dipped off of on Dame Street. He followed me inta the Castle and I had ta whack him in the bollocks so he'd leave off. Sash is workin the streets regular now, huggin close ta the canal so she won't be picked up by the Waxboys. And you, well, ya doin whatcha can ta keep things tickin over for yer boss.

The net's closin and openin like the jaws of a fish. Emmet Whelan was in the club on Dame Street last time I went down. I scarpered before he seen me and ran up towards the bridge. I could feel him on me heels up till Liffey Street when I ducked inta a derelict house. That's not the worst. The Don's three lugs from Gardiner Street have taken ta standin guard permanent in the playground on Hill Street. God knows how they can get away with not bein attacked by the Wacker, but last time we were expectin a drop, they got ta the courier before we done and bet the shite outta him, leavin him for dead and robbin him a the gear. Ya said once when ya were goofin that they weren't the Don's lads and that's why Wacker wasn't touchin them. But they're not local Waxboys, and if they're outside mercenaries then why the Wacker would get them ta mess with our couriers but not us I don't know.

Since the shootin, the squat's been stoned a few times but the three of us haven't been touched. Don't know why: both crews know where we are, they could jump us any time. So why don't they?

Ya say the Five Lampers don't dare make a move with the rozzers watchin them – and maybe they are only lookin ta hurt Snags. Besides, ya tell me, the Don was always cautious about open aggression, never too quick ta order a disposal unless he had ta. But I don't know about that. I remember Billy Fish from when I was a kid, and that Groucho rat that set up you and Micko when youse were kids, and the fact that you, the fastest knife in the west, came back ta Dublin way before Snags started runnin on his own. Could it be we're not worth disposin any more?

Still doesn't explain why the Wacker's lads are holdin off. That anoraked fuck never fought shy of a good batin and we know they could shoot the door down in the mornin.

As for the Old Bill, every time I even go out there's one lookin over. We been picked up a coupla times and brung down the shop but so far so good they haven't been able ta pin anythin on us. We keep our Qs in our mouths and anythin else in our jackets and our jackets over our arms so we can swalla or chuck as needed. Ya tell me they're not after us; we're too small fry. They got their eyes on the Don. But still . . .

We hear there's another dealer runnin the streets round by the meatpackers on Parnell Square. His prices are good and his stuff is clean, way better than ours by the time we got it cut for the street, and we're all wonderin who's put him in business.

It's him, ya say one night. He's playin us. But when I look over at ya, ya have yer mouth closed like ya never said it at all.

'Where is it, Nayler?' says Sasha.

'Yeah,' I say. 'It's been two days.'

'Ah, fuck off, Lucy,' ya say. 'Get yer own if ya that hungry.'

Fuck you. I'm gointa show ya. I'm gointa get off this muck and get back ta livin a normal life and fuck, fuck you.

'It was never like this with Snags.' There's a whinin edge ta Sasha's voice. 'He was always able ta get good stuff for me.'

Ya get up, stride across the room and hit her.

Wishful thinkin.

Ya stare at her, and I see the longin under yer skin, but ya bite it back. Ya reach out behind ya, take out yer deck and shuffle them. Ya lay out a spread and stare at the pictures.

'What's it say?' I ask.

Ya sweep the spread away with yer hand. 'Jesus. How'm I supposed ta know?'

'Is she in?' I ask Sam.

'No. Lucy—'

I push past, inta Ma's room, head ta the dressin-room table, rifle through what's there. A coupla bangles, not much, some earrings, good, 14-carat they are, a silver chain.

'Here, Sam?' I say, cuttin through whatever she's been tryin ta tell me.

'Yeah?'

'Thought this was yours.' I hold up the little silver daisies.

'No. Yeah. I mean, that's what I'm tryin ta say, Lucy—'

'The bitch. She rob it off ya?' I bite the chain. 'Shit. Fuckin brass.'

'Take this. Here.' She holds out the gold chain I gave her.

'Ah, Sam, I can't.'

'Take it. It's not gointa last.'

'Huh?' I'm through with Ma's, inta Granny's room. She's so quiet now, and so small, she might as well not be there. Only her breathin is loud. I open her bedside locker. Nothin there, a coupla rosary beads – Jesus, Granny gettin religion in her old age? – and a photo a me granda. There's a silver frame round the photo. Could be worth—

'No,' says Sam.

I look at the photo, put it back, even though parta me is screamin Go On, Take the Fuckin Thing.

'Lucy—'

'Jesus, Sam.' I wipe the sweat from me face. 'Can't ya see I'm busy?'

'John Paul's been askin for ya.'

'Yeah.'

I open the kitchen presses, one at a time. Nothin. Then I see the biscuit tin.

'And Micko.'

'Good, good.'

'Micko's not great, Lucy.'

Tell me a fuckin other, Sam. I shake the biscuit tin and open it. Kimberleys. Nice. Mariettas. I dig under the packs, find what I'm lookin for.

'Lucy—'

I can hear she's on the verge a blubbin. I stuff the notes inta me pocket. 'You're okay, sweetheart,' I tell her. 'It's not gointa last. I just gotta look after meself this week because Nayler's not feelin too well. But once I'm through this, I'm finished. Alright, Mouse? And then I can come back home ta ya.'

I kiss her on the forehead. In the kiss I feel how me lips must be on her forehead. Slimy and wet and full a the salt a me sweat and the g-g's crumblin in me mouth.

On the way out, I think, *I've forgotten somethin, there's somethin else I could sell*. But it trips outta me head soon as I think it.

I avoided youse that night. No point turnin up lookin like the cat who ate the cream. So I slipped over ta Hill Street instead, after checkin the three lugs weren't around, and shored meself up in the back room. And in the mornin I wrapped me stash up good-oh and taped it ta me body, safe there because ya never touched

374

me, neither you nor Sash, and so you'd never find out what emergency rations I got hid under me skin.

A glimpse a somethin in a passin winda.

Sasha leans back in the plastic chair a the café. Emmet Whelan taps the edge of his fag inta an ashtray. His signet ring gleams.

Am I makin things up? I ask meself. Are things comin outta the walls again?

Sshh, ladies, says a voice in me ear.

I unpack in the room where ya keep yer treasure chest. I'm sweatin. Beads a wet stick ta the clingfilm, tiny raindrops a saltwater. Won't do. I root around till I find a loose board; not the one where I useta store me pay; that's the first place you'll look if ya think I'm fixed. Then I slide me knife in and lift up the board. I take out what I need, wrap the rest in chewin-gum foil and stick it under the board.

I've ta work quickly. You're out, tryin ta score off of some cunt in Whitefriar Street. Ya could be gone an hour, or longer. Or shorter.

Sash's on the game.

Talkin ta Emmet Whelan?

Don't wanta know. None a me business. She's on the game.

I slap me arm, tense, slap again, cook, shoot. Even outta it, I keep it together enough ta shove the works under the board with the gear when I'm done.

Then I stagger upstairs and lie down on yer mattress and look up at the broken ceilin.

Thanks, Micko, says Snags. He's lyin on me right. His voice is pleasant. Thanks for takin the flak.

Whatcha mean? I ask.

Micko, lyin on me left, jogs me in the ribs. Don't be a fool, Lucy. Sure ya knew it wasn't just me nor Nayler in that car.

Say what?

The first time. When we were fifteen. That hit-and-run, Lucy, the one I got sent ta Tristan for. The cyclist, remember? Bang crash coma. Ya wondered about it. *How come they drove ta that pub, them with joyridin convictions and all, when they coulda got on a bus with way less risk?* Well, we didn't.

He grins. Worms writhe among the black stumps of his teeth. What?

Drive there. That was Snags. Nayler was at the wheel on the way back, but only because Snagglepuss –

Snags wobbles his face and makes a shiverin sound. Too scared ta drive, kiddo!

He lost the plot, Lucy. Too scared the rozzers would see him leavin the car park so he hid in the back seat and got us ta front for him.

Thanks, kids, says Snags.

And the gun, Lucy. Remember the gun. Where d'ya think it came from?

Emmet Whelan, I say.

Wrong, Lucy.

Never left me hand, says Snags. Where d'ya think it went?

Oh, Snagglepuss. Micko laughs. Never seen ya run as fast as ya done that day, leggin it down that alleyway off of Summerhill.

I was hands-on, kiddo, says Snags. Big mistake.

Specially leavin that gear in the car. Ya shoulda taken it with ya.

Specially that, kiddo. Big mistake. Someone had ta pay.

Ya pig, I wanta say. Ya sick selfish pimpled pig.

No, says Micko, and touches me, smoothin me hair down on me forehead. It was all part a the game, Lucy. We hafta make sacrifices. Didn't ya hear what the man said?

Sacrifices, says Snags, laughin, and puts his finger to his mouth. *Sssh, ladies.* Don't be talkin.

Above me Cindy Devlin floats, turnin over invisible waves like a chicken on a spit, her long hair seaweed, the knife wound in her throat a black smile drippin saltwater inta me eyes.

Sssh? I say.

People, says Snags, have awful big mouths when they're off their heads. Waffle on about everythin. Ya hafta be careful. All walls have ears, Lucy, even cracked ones. That right, Micko?

Oh yeah, Snags.

Yeah. He puts his finger on his lips, winks, and disappears, leavin only his wink on the pilla beside me.

When ya come in, I see I've nothin ta worry about. You've already scored so all ya do is float over ta the winda and sit there, lookin out.

There's a funny smell about ya and it takes a while for me ta suss it's funny because it's that smell ya useta get when ya went away before, in the good times; outdoors and sorta Christmassy. Ya got bits a yella flowers stuck in yer hair. Gorse.

'Any for me?' I say it more for form's sake than anythin else.

Ya shake yer head. 'Sorry, Lucy. Next time, yeah?'

'Didja keep some for Sash?'

Ya move yer head again. It's a little movement, half-way between a nod yeah and a shake no. I notice ya got a scrape on the inside of yer arm and it's bleedin, and in yer other hand ya got a new willa stick, fresh-cut and still smellin a sap. Ya swish it from side ta side. 'Been upta anythin?'

I shake me head and close me eyes, soothed by the sounda yer stick swishin, and beside me I feel Micko and Cindy Devlin, protectin me, tapin me mouth shut *sshh* so I won't tell ya about seein Sasha with Emmet Whelan the way I mighta told ya about seein Cindy with him all them months ago. Without wantin ta, or meanin ta, a course, because I was off me face.

Stupid cunt, ya say. Stupid cunt.

On the front page a the newspaper is the Kerry boy Snags useta send us stock through.

Is he dead? says Sasha.

Near enough. Cunt.

It wasn't his fault, I say.

Don't be a dick, Lucy. Nobody gets hurt without good reason. That's the shop fucked. Stupid bloody cunt.

Ya not talkin about the boy in the picture.

★

'Don't go.' Ya nervous. Fuck, we're all nervous. I got one fix left under me floorboard, but as far as I can make out, you and Sash have nothin.

'I hafta,' I say. 'It's part a the deal.'

'I don't have any uppers, Lucy. It's gointa do yer head in. They'll see you're withdrawin.'

'I'll take the g-g's. We got some left.'

'Lucy—'

'I hafta fuckin go, Nayler. They'll take Sam away from Ma if I don't show up.'

'So what? It's not like yer auld wan's any good for her.'

I shake me head, tryin ta dislodge pictures that keep creepin inta me mind, Sam flinchin anytime she's touched. 'She treats her okay once I turn up. In anyways, that's no way ta be talkin about yer lady friend.'

'Would you fuck off, Lucy. Haven't been there in ages as ya well know.'

I drum me fingers on the floor. 'I'm goin.' I get up.

Ya grab me. I try ta shake ya off but yer grip is like iron and ya won't let go. 'Jesus, Lucy Dolan, willya ever fuckin listen ta me—'

'Get yer fuckin hands off me, Nayler!' Me voice comes out way sharper than I thought it woulda.

'Don't be a fool, Nayler,' says Sasha. 'If she doesn't show up, they'll get the pigs.'

Ya release me.

The Social stares at me. I wish I could stop sweatin but I can't. It's weepin inta me eyes. Plus I'm freezin cold and startin ta cramp. I think a the gear in its safe little chewin-gum wrapper under the floorboards and I steady meself.

Scratch scratch scratch goes the Social's pen.

Drug Addict. Heroin User. Can I fool meself any more I'm not a user, me?

Ma's starin out the winda. She hasn't bothered with the apron this time.

Before she goes, the bitch makes an appointment for next week.

'Ya useless ugly little loser,' says Ma, without turnin ta look at me. 'I know what ya been upta. Whatcha want? Send us all down where you're goin?'

'Ya know what I been upta, Ma?' I stay in me bubble as best I can. 'So who's been upta it with me?'

'Don't talk ta me like that, ya—'

Hooer is what she wants ta say but she can't. If she says it, she involves you. And she can't do that. You're still her shinin prince, even though ya been absent months. If she says it, she strips ya of yer armour and makes what she done ta Micko a lie.

Coward, I think, sendin the thought out ta her as strong as I can.

'Ya nothin but a fuckin – Jesus, ya know, if I'd me life all over again I'da had none a youse. Except Sam.'

I get up ta go.

'Don't go robbin me children's allowance or I'll—'

'It's my bleedin allowance in anyways. So you keep yer hair on, where it belongs – on yer manky cunt.'

Sam follas me out. I don't look back at her till I'm down at the next landin. Then somethin makes me look up. She's rollin up the trouser legs of her tracksuit. It's the first time I've seen her legs in ages.

There's somethin on them. Brown marks.

She looks up, catches me eye. She's callin ta me.

But I got other things on me mind. I blink sweat outta me eyes. When I look back, she's gone.

By the time I get in, I'm weak with sweatin and the heat. I check you're not there. Then I go downstairs and inta the room, open me knife and slide it between the floorboards. The loose board gives, rises. I drop me hand in, feel past the slime. Me hand brushes nothin.

I sit back on me hunkers.

Ya dirty fuck.

Without the gear ta calm me, I buzz. Bright lights flash, pushin me towards madness. I think a Betty and resolve. I swear I'll get clean, get out, do anythin, anythin, if only – if only I could have one more. One more and then I'll go. The nerves eat at me legs, drivin them ta move. I run upstairs, lie down, get up, pace. I tap endless tunes on the windasill. I walk. Walk. Walk. Half-runnin, racin against meself.

Is there not somethin else I can sell? Somethin I've forgotten? Jesus. Fuck. I hafta get off this. Yeah. Fuck it. Fuck it all.

Then Ma comes inta me head unbidden and all I can hear is, *I toldya so think ya so smart ya useless ugly little loser*, and that just makes it worse because is that cunt right no fuckin way and then I see Sam again, beggin me like for what as if I can and—

Then I hear the door open behind me, and not carin if ya hear me or not, not even knowin what I'm sayin, start rantin.

A soft laugh. I turn. It's not you but Sasha. She's leanin against the door, lookin at me. She's grey, sweatin. Her hands are shakin.

I ask where ya are, and she shakes her head.

She laughs again.

Whatcha laughin at?

She goes ta lie on the bed.

She gets up a minute later.

Where is he? I ask her. I imagine shakin her so her teeth, bones, skin fly loose. Where the fuck is he?

It came ta me half-way through the next day. Ya might think I was thick, that it took so long, but I was findin it hard ta think and with the pukin and all I was so fucked I knew I'd make a mess of a rob or a deal. And in the end it was only after chewin the lasta the g-g's and hearin somethin downstairs that Sasha thought was a rat that I remembered what it was could be sold, down the basement, except it didn't need sellin, it could be used straightaway, and more ta the point, by me.

Yeah. I know. I wasn't thinkin straight. Because if that gear was still there, you'da used it already, wouldn't ya? But like I say, I was fucked.

I went back ta the flats and hung around till Sam came out.

Then I told her I needed her ta get a key from Charlie, and what ta tell him if he started gettin antsy. I got this feelin she was tryin ta keep me there, and then I started thinkin it must be a trap; she didn't mean ta set them on me but someone had put her upta it, and if I stayed hangin round in full view, they'd be on me, the Waxboys and the Five Lampers and them three lugs and all, like flies on shit, and I'd be made a sacrifice of for the sake a you and Snags and the business, just like me brother was not once but twice before.

I went inta the arcade place on O'Connell Street and even though the flashin lights were doin me head in, and the noises worse, it felt sorta safe there.

When it was time, I met her down at Connolly station, like we'd arranged. All the sunbathers poured out, happy from their jaunts in Portmarnock and Malahide and Dollymount. She was at the back.

'Did Charlie give ya gyp?' I said.

She shook her head and held out her hand. The Chubb lay there, gleamin.

I jimmy the padlock key open with the knife ya gave me. It takes me three tries with two blades and I snap the first one, but in the end I use the little scissors, and that seems ta work and, even with the sweat and all, I get it open and the key in the Chubb and turnin and I'm through.

The stink I'd thought I'd got useta hits me in the face. It's bad, it's worse than bad, but I ignore it and push past the heap a rottin clothes that's lyin in me way and inta the passageway.

The fridge is wide open. And there's nothin inside.

I search it, tear it open with the knife, stab freezer and rubber and plastic through and through, but there's nothin.

Ha ha ha laughs a voice over me head. It's a girl's voice but when I look up I see the dead thing hangin nailed ta the wall is a man. Meat rottin off of his bones. Big nine inchers through his shoulders, elbows, hips; pinnin his hands either side of his head like a soldier in surrender. There's an AK47 strung round his neck and a hole in his forehead. The bottom half a his face is a broken mess. On his chin the leftovers of a silver beard are sprinkled with tooth-chippins, stained dark brown with blood.

Hahahahaha laughs the girl.

Get away from me, ya stupid vision, I scream, grabbin an iron bar that's leanin against the fridge. Get fuckin away.

The bar crashes inta the man's mouth. Plaster crumbles. Face, beard, nailed hands, gun, all melt back inta the wall. Black mould. Green moss. Brown rust. I stop bashin, drop the bar.

It knocks against the floor, makin a clangin sound, sendin somethin rollin along the ground. The rollin thing gleams. Gold. Money?

I bend down, pick it up.

I think I locked the door behind me. I think I got it together enough ta do that.

We waited hours. It was touchin the sixtieth I think – though I can't swear ta it, all I remember is sickness and pain and sheer fuckin wantin – when ya came in.

We were both up on our feet in no time.

Ya had a cut on yer forehead and a black eye and there was somethin else different in yer face that wasn't just from the batin. When ya smiled, I seen they'd knocked out one a yer side teeth. It made yer smile look more crooked than usual, like it wasn't even pretendin ta reach yer eyes.

'Good news.' I could see ya were holdin yer hand behind yer back.

'Give us.'

'Hold off, Lucy. I got somethin ta tell youse.'

I didn't care about whatcha got ta tell. I only cared about what ya had behind yer back.

'It's all over the papers.' Yer eyes stayed on us, hidden. 'The Fakeys set the Don up and got him unpackin in a safe house. They say he won't get bail.'

Then Sasha took a step back and yer eyes flicked over ta her and that somethin different in yer face got stronger, but then ya opened yer hand and she was jumpin on the Qs like a cat and so was I, like nothin else mattered in the whole wide world, not ever.

So many times. Still it never fails ta amaze me, how blessed the relief, how all the agony from before melts inta nothin, inta the sheer feelin of It's okay now, for now.

Ya watch us but ya don't use.

Through me half-closed eyes I see ya take off yer shirt. Ya covered in bruises and cuts. There's a bandage round yer arm over yer tattoo. I watch as ya unpeel it.

They've destroyed yer horse. Ugly slash-marks runnin through its eyes and mane. Long red sores that look like burns. Black stitch marks like a scarecrow's mouth. Some places it's so bad there's no skin left ta stitch.

Ya touch the cuts and sores one by one, real gentle. Then ya put on some cream and a fresh bandage. Ya walk over ta the winda, push the curtain back. It's nice outside. Ya lift yer arms up in a V and stretch them. Looks painful with them bruises. But ya tilt yer head back, arc yer chest, stay stretched. The sun comes out from a cloud. Ya close yer eyes, smile, drink in the heat. Yer body pulses, blazin like white fire, so bright it hurts ta watch. I slit me eyes, but ya keep burnin, white against the red a me eyelids.

The sun goes back in. All of a sudden ya look real bare. Ya drop yer arms, turn from the winda. Ya pick up a fag, light it, smoke it. Yer fingers is shakin. Only a bit, but still . . .

When the fag is done ya throw it out the winda, sit down, take out yer cards and start ta shuffle.

Later, when we were fit enough ta walk, we took a hike down ta the canal. It was my idea. It was a scorcher, too warm ta waste it hidin behind the curtains, especially with the threat gone and Dublin openin up like a hooer's snatch for us ta ride under Snags's guidance.

You and Sash walked in front a me. Sasha hung off of yer good arm, slippin, jelly legs. Ya strode easy, like she wasn't there at all, only the odd flinch as she knocked inta ya ta show how bad ya'd been bet. I was slippin too but I didn't care. Fuck the world if it sees me noddy.

We lay in the shade under a hedge and ya opened a bottle a 7-Up. The sugar soaked inta me, soothin.

'Here. Lucy.' Ya sit up, knockin Sasha off-balance. She laughs ta herself and slips back down on the ground.

I folla yer gaze. One a the pavees' ponies is loose.

Ya look at me. *Dare ya.*

I know I'm gone but it still surprises me, how hard it is ta stay on while the nag goes jumpin and kickin all over the gaff. I should be better than this, I say ta meself, I should be ridin this beauty like a bronco cowboy. But he keeps throwin me. One, two and I'm down, crashin inta the ground. Even with the vexation, I keep laughin because I'm so soft with the gear, I melt back together like I'm not hurt at all.

'He's a fucker,' I call.

'She, Lucy,' ya call back. 'It's a mare.'

After the tenth or twelfth throw, the mare bends her face down over mine and breathes on me, snufflin Hunh hunh hunh.

The breath is hot and full a hay and sunshine. She looks inta me eyes and all of a sudden I get it. Respect.

Can I? I ask her. Is it okay?

It works. Next time she lets me stay on and we mess around on the bank a bit before I jump her inta the canal. The cool water climbs up me trouser legs. She moves beneath me, beautiful, strong, her black and white piebald coat drenchin grey with the water.

Dim in the distance I hear ya laugh.

Can I? I ask her. The muscles in her back twitch. I pull meself up. Under me feet her back ripples. I drink in the ripples, letting them travel up me, inta every corner a me body. I'm shiftin and settlin, constant motion, jiggin like I always jig, only she's jiggin too so it all balances out. I turn me head, see ya watchin. Yer face is too far away ta read but I give ya a grin in anyways.

Ya grin back, sudden, one a them wide open grins ya useta give

Micko when youse were kids and he was crackin ya up with the jokes. 'Go for it, Lucy!'

I smile, stretch out me arms. The sun bakes me neck. I look down at the water. It's dirty green. Fulla cans and fluffy sick-lookin seaweed stuff floatin like snot on top. I tense, spring, dive.

Underwater the world is dark green. The piebald's legs tread and I swim between them. I am a fish. I am unstoppable.

I surface, gaspin for air.

Ya lift yer 7-Up, cheer me on.

I go down again, deeper this time. The water grows colder. There's somethin glintin near the bed. I push meself deeper again, even though the pain in me chest is tellin me No, Don't do it, Come back.

A gold chain, big enough ta fit on a kid's wrist. I pull at it and it comes loose. As I peel meself up from the bottom, up towards the piebald's legs that are movin above me, blockin out the sun that shimmers around her body in spears a light, a hand grabs me ankle and pulls.

Help me, she says.

If I'd been less outta it, I'da started thrashin. But the gear was still calmin me so I reached down and unpicked her bony fingers one by one, sayin No, Cindy Devlin. There's no need for ya any more. Ya were made a sacrifice of because ya talked and we needed blood ta pay for a victory. But it's all paid off. The war with the Don's nearly over, we've won, almost. Go back ta sleep now.

I didn't look down at her, though. I didn't wanta see the little fish swimmin in her hair.

'Ya okay?'

I nod, shiverin.

'Come here.' Ya hold out an arm, the one with the tattoo on it.

I curl inta ya, careful not ta knock inta yer cuts and bruises. Ya keep yer arm tense, a little bit off of me skin, then, as I move closer, ya let it go, meltin onta me. I sink in, lettin the sun and the heat a yer skin take the chill outta me body. It's the closest we ever been. Ya smell real clean; no old sweat nor manky breath stinkin a crips and fag smoke. Just saltwater and, somewhere underneath, spices.

'Sing somethin, Lucy,' says Sasha, her eyes still closed.

I oblige. Some song Granny useta do at parties, about a girl called Jeannie with light brown hair.

We ran inta her on our way back, me on the horse, you and Sash walkin behind like me servants.

Her face lit up at first, then shut down.

'Amanda—' I went ta call but she'd turned, walkin quickly across the road and back up towards Drumcondra.

'Pheelo,' ya said, snortin a laugh ta yerself. 'Jesus!'

I wondered what it would be like if they were all there now, her and Charlie and Damo as well as me and you and Sash, and for a minute longed ta turn back time. But Amanda kept walkin, her big arse swayin under her white jeans, her back stubborn against us, her newly permed hair springin out from her head like coils of electricity, and the longin faded quick as it had been born.

'Go the fuck on!' ya say. 'Get her up the stairs! Jump the fuckin thing!'

'I can't! She won't go!'

'For fucksake, Lucy! Go on!' Yer eyes are mad.

Around us, windas open, heads peer out, people shout.

'Leave it!'

'I'm callin the Guards!'

'Will yiz be quiet!'

'Get out with yer drugs, yiz troublemakers!'

I feel the horse's fear as she resists me. Sash slumps on the doorstep, not carin.

'Go on, Lucy! Ya scared?'

Scared? Ya fuck. I'm never scared. I kick the horse in the side, willin her ta go up the steps and inta the house. She rears, throwin me. I grab onta the mane but it's no good. I'm over her back and the ground is flyin up ta meet me. I land badly, twistin me ankle.

'Get her, Nayler! Fuckin get her!'

But she's gone, trottin down the street, and you're standin there, doubled over, pissin yerself laughin like a kid, watchin her go while I ache in the gutter. The onlookers mumble and turn away, disgusted.

Ya stretch out yer hand. I take it and ya hoist me up. Me ankle is in bits.

'Hey.' Ya slip yer arm round me. 'Not one a yer lucky days, is it?'

'Leave off.'

'I knew ya wouldn't do it. I knew you'd be too scared a hurtin the lovely horse.'

'Fuck off. I'da brung her up only she thrun me.'

'That's me girl.' Ya squeeze me shoulder.

'What's that?' says Sasha.

'What?' I look down and ya folla me gaze.

'That charm?'

The feel a yer arm around me changes.

The buttons in me top musta opened durin the fall and it musta slipped out that way because now it's lyin there in full view across the flat curve a me breast. Me silver chain with the souvenirs hangin off of it. There's the keyring I stole from yer treasure chest, still holdin its tarnished old keys, and the Chubb for the basement that Charlie made for me, and Mainser's ears that I picked up off the basement floor, and that gold-filled tooth I found beside the fridge, and they're all there, winkin in the sunlight.

It's just rubbish, I wanta say, only me throat is too dry ta talk, and for no good reason – because ya wouldn't recognize the keys, wouldya, not when ya had so many in that trunk, and the other stuff, fuck, what's that only shite means nothin? – I don't wanta look at ya.

Ya pick them up, yer fingers tensin as they brush me chest, and ya feel them, one by one; the keys first, the tooth last. Ya rub them between yer fingers and yer touch is soft but pryin, like ya fingerin a bird for the first time, and I start buzzin, not for whatcha might think, rememberin ya ridin, no way, nor even that I'm scared, thinkin a that stuff in the basement, because I'm not, I never been scared a ya, but . . .

We lift our heads at the same time. Our eyes meet.

I should say somethin. I can't.

The difference in ya that I seen earlier is back and I can see it better now, and it's definitely not the batin. Ya look . . . lost. Bare. Sick sorta. I seen ya lost and bare before, but never like this. It's like somethin's peeled yer skin off, leavin ya raw and quiverin like a lump a bloodied meat, and ya not even tryin ta hide it. Yer eyes are stuck ta mine and burnin, bleedin with feelins, mad feelins I never thought ya had, all mixed up together – rage and hate and even fear I think – and it's not right, Nayler, this is not . . . I want ta say somethin but I can't because yer stare is pinnin me ta the spot, like I'm some piece a shit and you're some black torch searchin inside me, through everythin I ever said or done, for somethin ya despise. I wanta rage, scream, *Fuck off*. But I can't.

Ya take the chain and twist it so the links bite inta me neck. Yer fingers are tremblin. Me hands are sweatin. I wish I'd taken me knife with me insteada leavin it upstairs.

We stand like that, eyes locked, chain bitin me neck, for what feels like hours.

Then ya smile a little smile that only touches the corners a yer mouth. Ya tug and the chain snaps loose, and yer face goes smooth again and yer eyes go back ta their normal hidden selves.

Ya let go me shoulder and I wobble on the step. I try ta put me weight on me ankle but it won't take it and I crash down, second time that day.

Ya watch me land, then ya turn away.

Wait, Nayler, I wanta shout. Wait for me. But me ankle hurts too much and even if it didn't, fuck you if ya think I'm gointa run after ya like yer dog. And although I can feel the hunger longin ta rear its ugly head and growl for its next fix, still I stay staunch. Fuck you, Nayler. I'm gointa get clean, and off this stuff, and away from ya, just ya wait, Nayler, then you'll be comin lookin for me, I swear, ya won't be turnin yer back on me for no good reason, leavin me ta rot on the side a the road, because ya need me; for what I am, for the understandin I have a ya, for the past that's between us, for me skills in the streets and the shop, and more, much more than that; oh yes, I'm not some piece a shit, ya need me more than anyone else in the world, more than I need you, and even if ya leave that door open, I won't folla ya, I swear I won't.

Ya turn the key. Sasha picks herself up and follas ya inside.

I meant ta get up and go, just walk, somewhere, anywhere. But I couldn't. Me ankle was too sore. That's what I told meself in anyways and I've told it so often it must be true.

I'm not thick, Nayler. I only thought that for a while, that it was me. That ya flipped just because I'd taken that stuff a yours – that ya recognized straightaway, who was I foolin? – and that's why ya showed more a yerself ta me than ya ever done before, and that's why ya turned yer back.

I'm not sayin it meant nothin, seein them souvenirs a mine out in the open. It was a betrayal a sorts. But in itself would it a been enough ta open ya up like that? A betrayal from yer poxy little lapdog, yer little errant girl?

Cop on, Lucy.

Stupid me for not coppin on sooner. Stupid stupid me.

I dream and in me dream I ride the mare up the stairs a the squat and inta yer room, just like ya wanted, goadin her loud so ya can hear the courage in me voice.

The winda beckons, tall and black and full a glass.

She hesitates, but then I whisper in her ear, Go on, Starlight, and she obeys.

I close me eyes. We jump. She screams. I look. She's stuck. Half in, half out. Her belly pierced by ten swords a broken glass, leakin blood and white guts. Her front legs claw air, seekin ground. Her head thrashes. Blood runs down her legs, down the walls a the house, through the streets a Dublin, and I sit, stuck, high above the city, while behind me, stretched against the wall, yer stick and sword crossin under ya like an insect's arms, ya laugh yerself senseless.

Between me and you is another you, sittin on the mare's back, yer arms clasped round me waist, chained ta me by silver and skin. This you isn't laughin. This you is whisperin, *I'll come back for ya I'll come back for ya I'll come back for ya*, and its breath is hot in me ear, hot and smellin a salt and spices.

'Lucy, Lucy.'

I open me eyes, wincin at the pain. It's early mornin. Sam's crouchin beside me on the doorstep. She's in bits, snot runnin down her face, eyes red with tears.

'Jesus, Sam, whatcha doin here?' Me first instinct is ta push her away, back home where she'd be safer. She grabs me hands.

'Lucy, it's Granny.'

That day it seemed like I chose. I resolved. But now it feels like all I done was give in, because I was too tired ta fight back; because there was nowhere else ta go. Is not fightin back the same as choosin? Sometimes that's how it seems.

We walked through the dawn and I told meself I was resolved.

'It was a heart attack,' says Marlene. 'She went in her sleep. Quiet as a mouse.'

Ma barely looks up, just keeps smokin like her life depends on it.

'Are ya goin in?' says Marlene.

'Yeah,' I say. I'm startin ta shake.

Granny is lyin on the bed. Her face is sorta restful but sorta not at the same time. Then I see I'm wrong. It's not Granny lyin there. It's just a face and a poor old body that useta be hers. I touch her. Her lips are grey, her skin is grey, even her reddy dyed hair has a grey sheen ta it. I can feel her everywhere in this room: her smell, her presence, like she's just outta sight, just round the corner, waitin ta surprise me. I keep thinkin she's gointa wake up, tap me on the shoulder when I'm not lookin. But when I look at that putty face, I know she isn't comin back.

'Here,' says Sam, from behind me. She takes me hand and lays it over Granny's. Me fingers are shakin like mad.

'Sssh. It's okay.' Sam presses me hand closer onta the dead thing beneath it.

I feel Granny then, not in the meat I'm holdin but very close ta me, almost inside a me. I can't help it. I close me eyes and I dive. I folla her, right down inta me body and beyond and I can still feel her, almost see her, through me closed eyes.

It's okay, says Granny.

She's right. It is okay. A course it's okay. Why wouldn't it be okay for her – or any of us – ta get off of this fuckin kip?

I start cryin. I feel Sam's hand, warm and soft; Granny's, cold and dead and havin nothin ta do with the feelin a *her* that's all around me, and between them both me own, with the pulse beatin in it, loud and clear tappin out that old rhythm. *Bom* ba bom. *Bom* ba bom. I'm a-live. I'm a-live. I'm a-live.

VIII

Easy enough ta get clean of, ya told me, once ya know how.

Maybe for you, maybe for others, but for me, fuck no. It was hard. Nothin is as hard. I've been through it five times willinly – and God knows how many not a me own accord – and each time it's got harder. It's not the pain – the cramps and sweats and chills and pukin and sheer cravin – as much as the fear and the wantin and the feelin that if I can't do it this time I'm useless.

Ma stayed over in Malahide. Sam told me later that was Marlene's doin. 'If anyone's gointa put the kibosh on Lucy, it'll be Rose.'

Marlene came over herself the first night ta make sure things were okay. But Sam told her ta go. Marlene argued a bit, said I should go somewhere proper, like Coolmine or Jervis Street, but Sam held fast; told her they were only takin people who had the virus or were up the pole – though God knows how she knew that. She'd be fine, she said ta Marlene, she'd be able ta handle me on her own. And believe it or not, she did, and it *was* okay with just the two of us – and Granny a course, Granny in the air, in the sweat pourin off of me, in me head, in me blood, urgin me on.

Come on, Lucy, get on with it.

I was a demon. Like I say, I been through this four times since a me own choosin, and each time was harder than the last, but nothin is ever like the first.

The desperation came crawlin outta me skin like maggots. I was dead, deader than Granny on her bed in the next room. Even though by that time she'd been buried, in me head her body was still there, rottin away like all the other corpses, mine included, while her spirit kept urgin me on. *Come on, Lucy, get on with it.* Death and life, fightin over me.

Ya think once ya done it once, you'll never hafta do it again. Some hope.

The funeral was awful. I could feel every set of eyes in that church, even Charlie's, glarin at me, knowin, seein right through me inta the poison leavin me body.

The whole brood was there – apart from Michael, who'd died two year before, and Dessie, who'd telegrammed ta say he couldn't make it over from New York on account a work. But the others – Dan and Dolly, Ma, Vi and Patrick, Marlene and Stevo, even Uncle Tom, who they'd dug out from the loony bin and looked like a big dog with all its teeth taken out – were there, linin the pews like a family a skittles.

Sick and all as I was, I could see straightaway there was no love lost between Vi and the others. The minute she came inta the church, she raced upta Ma and flung her arms round her. Ma took a step back, but Vi wouldn't let go. She kept claspin Ma's hands, sobbin, 'Ah, Rose, wasn't she the best Ma we could have?'

Ma, poured inta in the nylon suit she'd got from Penneys, stared at Vi, the mix a feelins runnin across her face as clear as if she was statin them aloud.

Ya two-faced cunt, says one feelin. *Ya hypocritical bitch only turnin up now.*

And the other was, *Jesus, look at her cryin. I could never cry like that. After all this time, she's still the favourite.*

Then she turned away and I swear I seen her poke her eye just ta get it goin.

They brung her out ta Glasnevin graveyard, and Marlene said Vi flung herself on the coffin as they were stickin it inta the ground. She lay there for ages, beggin forgiveness. Ma wouldn't be outdone, though. Shed a fair few crocodile tears herself and threw in a long-stemmed red carnation like it was a jewel.

'That's for you, Ma,' she said. And they all applauded. Like she was the best daughter in the world and Granny should be hoppin in her grave for the pure joy a bein honoured by her.

But I seen none a that. By the time Mass was over, I was startin ta get the pictures: tiny cartoon horses flickin in fronta me eyes, dancin through hoops like at a circus. Sam took me hand and, once the service was over, got the nod from Marlene ta stick me in a jo and bring me back ta the flat.

After the funeral, Marlene said they went back ta Moran's Hotel for a jar and some sambos. Dan and Stevo paid for the whole thing – apart from the few bob put towards it by the savins Granny had built up in the post office. Even in the state I was I couldn't help thinkin, *Post office savins? How come I never found the book?*

'Drink this, Lucy.'

Jesus, Sam, how didja get so wise?

'I thought ya just lived in yer dreamland,' I say – or think I say.

'Ssshh,' says Sam, soothin me forehead, soakin up the sweat with a soft cloth.

'Ya too young ta be mindin me. Ya can't hold the fort. Ah . . . fuck, keep them away, Sam, will ya.'

And on. And on. Yes, keep them away – them pictures a dancin horses and golden rings, of hands at the bottom a the sea and men nailed to a wall and giant scissors cuttin out holes in people's faces and horses shredded on windapanes, and worse than any a that, the sight a yer eyes, Nayler, bleedin feelins like black fire – keep them away.

That's why I asked her so many questions.

How long did ya know, Sam?

Did Granny know?

How d'ya know what ta do, Sam? Are ya sure –

Ma knew, didn't she?

'Ssshh,' says Sam, holdin out the bucket while I puke yet again.

Where's Amanda, Sam? Does she know I'm gettin clean? Will ya tell her? Will ya ask her ta come up?

And on. And on.

'How long did ya know, Sam?'

She sits back on her hunkers. 'Ages, Lucy.'

She smiles, her big wide lovely smile that makes everythin okay again. For a second. Until the pictures come back again.

Did Ma know, Sam? How long did she know? Would she evera done anythin?

'Sshh.'

A course Ma knew. But she blinded herself to it, closed her eyes ta the tracks on me arms as much as she closed her ears ta all the talk about how I'd got on it in the first place, the rumours a you and the Don's nephew that were by then common knowledge.

I useta think she blinded herself just because she couldn't admit seein anythin wrong with ya. She'd fooled herself inta thinkin ya were special and ya loved her and she wasn't gointa let that go, not if it killed her. But now I think there was other stuff too, that she never liked me enough ta really care what happened ta me. She was probably even glad I was fuckin meself up. Then I'd be off her hands forever. That sounds over the top – *Jesus, what Ma would ever think that about her own kid?* – but it happens. Trust me.

If it was Sam in trouble, she wouldn'a blinded herself. She'da done somethin, killed you or locked Sam up; she'da tried ta stop it.

Then again, maybe not. They say in the telly wildlife programmes a mother will do anythin ta protect its cubs, even tear off its own foot in a snare, but they musta made another programme for Ma. Far as she was concerned, she had no choice; she had ta blame us. If ya believe that most babies are born good or even sorta . . . neutral, then ya hafta accept that if they turn bad somethin else is involved; it's not because they have it in them. But if ya don't think that, if ya think people can be born evil or trouble or even a problem, then it's easy ta say it's their own fault if somethin bad happens. And that's what Ma done. Because if she hadn'a blamed us, she'da had ta take a good look at who or what had turned us bad – and for once I'm not talkin about you here, Nayler.

'That's lovely, Mouse.'

She's drawn a house on a hill with people havin a party. The colours are beautiful, reds and golds and oranges and the sky is a big blue bowl over the people's heads, fadin ta a sorta purply haze near the hill.

'I got more.'

'Show us.'

She hesitates.

'Come on, Sam.'

She crawls in under her bed and slides out a big wide book. There's pictures on each page. Some a them are people I know. Granny sleepin, lookin exactly like she useta. Lisa, Sam's best friend, starin at herself in the mirror. Me, curled on the lino, grabbin me belly. Them ones are done so exact I expect the person ta turn out from the picture and start talkin ta me. I don't know anythin about drawins or that lark but I can tell they're way better than ya'd expect a twelve-year-old kid ta do.

She's got other drawins too that are just colours and shapes. Messy sorta, like what ya see in High Babies.

'I like these the best,' says Sam, pointin ta the messy ones.

I like the others. Jesus, they're good.

He tiptoes around the question like it'll bite. At last –

'Are ya okay?'

Phew. 'Yeah.' I'm dyin ta say somethin smart, like yeah, Charlie, all them nasty drugs is outta me system now. But I'm too tired and weak and, in anyways, I don't think he'll get it. So –

'How's Amanda?'

He shrugs.

'Ya not seein her any more?' I don't mean ta sound worried, but it comes out in me voice and he looks up, surprised.

'Now and again. It's been . . .'

He doesn't hafta finish the sentence.

Different.

'Bring her up here,' I say.

'Bring her up yerself,' he says, firin it back on me just like the old Charlie.

I can't tell him I'm terrified a leavin the flat, just like I can't ask him ta own up that it was Marlene who got him ta come over on his mercy visit.

'D'ya want a cuppa tea?' I ask for want a anythin else ta say.

'Sure.'

When I come back, he's rootin through Micko's old record collection. He turns round, guilty. 'This is shite.' He lifts up Grace Jones's *Nightclubbin*.

'Yeah. Here's yer tea.'

We sit on separate ends a the sofa and drink our tea and smoke. When the silence gets too much, I start ta speak, but he does too, at the exact same time.

'Go on,' I say.

'Did ya ever tell him?' he says. 'About us and the gun and—'

'Fuck no, Charlie!' I say, tryin not ta think a me souvenirs and where they might be now. Then, because I don't wanta think about that stuff any more, I say what I was gointa say before he interrupted me.

'Got any hash?'

'That bird,' I say, tokin. 'She looks like a fella, she sings like a fella. Well, it's only natural ya wonder . . .'

Charlie, jivin awkward in the middle a the room, giggles his high giggle.

'Go on, the Charlo!'

He takes me hands and pulls me up and now we're both shufflin away, hands in fists, all elbows and shoulders.

Someone opens the front door.

'Fuck!' Charlie races over ta open the winda while I stub out the joint. 'It's yer ma!'

Luckily for us, she doesn't bother comin in ta check up, goes straight ta her room instead and bangs the door shut.

'Come on out, Lucy. We're goin on the piss next Tuesday. Amanda'll be there and all. She's been askin for ya.'

'Ah no,' I say. 'Come up here, instead.'

As he's goin, I call him back. 'Tell her I'm alright, willya? Tell her I'm . . . over it.'

We're avoidin each other. We've agreed – without talkin about it, a course – it's the easiest thing ta do. When she's in the kitchen, I stay in me room or the sittin-room, playin records. When she's in the sittin-room, I go inta the kitchen.

Marlene hasn't been over in a while. Words have been said, I suppose. Stay outta me business and I'll stay outta yours. Nothin too angry, just enough ta keep interference away.

I've only asked her for one thing since she came back, and that was if I could sleep in Granny's room.

'No,' she said. 'I'm usin that for me readins.'

There was lots a questions I coulda asked ta push her inta givin in ta me. Like, are ya not worried I'll be a bad influence on Sam? Or, are ya sure ya wanta use it that way with Granny's spirit hangin round there ta jinx ya? But there's an agreement between us not ta go there, so I don't.

I can bide me time.

Every so often she says somethin. 'Are ya stayin in bed again today?' 'Have ya nothin ta do?' 'Wouldya not think a gettin a job? Oh no, I'm forgettin. You'll probably feck that up and all.'

I hold meself back from risin ta her. I'm weary from cleanin up and I know once we start we'll never stop, and right now I need the flat and the space it gives more than anythin else, so I pay the price.

'That's you all over. Studyin. Ya know –' she directs this ta everyone in the room, me, Damo, Damo's bird Cecile, Charlie himself '– it's awful, comin second place ta books.'

'Ya swot,' says Damo, mainly for Cecile's benefit. She laughs, bang on cue.

'Youse are gettin me wrong.' Jesus, Charlie's smooth. Fuck me if he isn't turnin inta Stevo right before our eyes.

'Swot,' says Damo again. 'Doin whatcha Ma and Da tell ya. Ya turnin inta a snob, Charlie, out there in Malahide with the resta them poshies.'

Charlie drapes his arm round Amanda's shoulder. She snuggles inta him but he doesn't seem ta notice her. 'I have a plan,' he says, givin me a sly wink.

'And what's that, Charlie?' Even though I know it already.

'I know the way forward. And it's computers.'

Cecile laughs, but this time she's the only one. Amanda's got a bright smile on which means she doesn't have a clue what Charlie's on about, even though she's pretendin she does. Damo just looks confused. 'Jesus, Charlie. I thought you'da been all for The Dole Is Me Leader, I Shall Not Work.'

Now we all laugh.

'Seriously, lads,' says Charlie. 'In two or three years' time, the whole world's gointa be talkin to each other through computers. Wired up like a bomb. It's already started ta happen. And ya know what they'll be passin ta each other along them wires?'

He pauses for effect.

'Money.'

Damo laughs. 'Charlie, ya been watchin too many movies.'

'No, Damo. It's gointa be shiftin around from one terminal to the next and all you'll need is a coupla ins on software programs ta find out how ta tap inta it.'

'Yeah, right.' Amanda starts laughin.

Charlie's arm slides off her shoulder as he starts wavin his hands around. 'I got plans. I'm gointa crack it, lads. I'm gointa get sussed at the computers, do me Leavin and all, maybe even go ta college, but only ta get more of a suss and only if I need it. Once I know me way round, I'll start scammin. It'll all be set up by the time I'm outta college; ripe for the pickin. Fraud on a level nobody's ever seen before.'

'Ah, Charlie,' says Amanda. 'I don't know. I mean, I thought ya weren't gointa get inta any funny business. It'll break yer ma's heart.'

Charlie looks over at me with a real See what I mean? look and I give him back a Yeah, I do look but Amanda catches us at it and glares like she wants ta kill us.

'But he isn't in any funny business, Amanda,' says Damo. 'Fucksake, d'ya see him doin blags or runnin for the Wacker or shootin up or . . .'

He tails off as Amanda goes scarlet.

Stupid bastard. Only one way ta deal with him. I get up, slow as I can, and walk over ta him. Then I say, real pleasant, 'Damo, thought ya knew I was sorted. Ya sayin I'm not?'

'Eh . . .'

'Ya got problems with me? Or is that yer da talkin?'

For a minute nobody knows what ta say. I feel like you in that minute, the way ya useta stop and start a room by sayin or doin just one thing. Then I grin at Damo, and do a fake lunge, and he jumps ta one side, nearly crushin Cecile, and then we all start laughin.

In the kitchen I hear Sinead O'Connor moanin about 'Nothin Comparin ta You' and I picture Sam, sittin feet tucked under on Granny's old armchair, listenin in on us and sketchin what she thinks is happenin.

'I'm sorry,' says Charlie later, when the rest a them have gone.

'It's alright. Ta be expected.'

'Ya know, I didn't ask Damo over. I don't really pal out with him these days. That was Amanda's idea.'

'Oh? Didn't think she ever had much time for Damo.'

Only later I sussed she brung him over because A, she wanted ta keep things the way they were in the old days and B, with so many people round we wouldn't have the chance ta be on our own and hafta face that silence.

I try ta block me ears, do a Ma, but some rumours don't stay where they're supposed ta. They trickle outta doors and down landins and off the telly inta me ears. Word is you've gone off ta the other enda the world. Word is the Don's gointa get ten, twenty, life. Word is Snags is back, set up in a lovely apartment in Ranelagh, runnin a new ring. Word is Sasha's with him, and they're gointa get married, just like they planned, start a family and all.

Word is ya back home, in the squat, workin for Snags. Word is – big surprise – Snags and the Don are patchin things up before the Don gets banged up. Transfer funds. Big money. Keep it in the family. May happen yet. Word is Emmet Whelan's missin. The

Wacker, they say, tryin ta rub the Don's nose in it. Word is someone wrecked the Wacker's ma's grave. One last retaliation from the Don, they say. Real vicious, considerin how good Ma Mahon always was ta him. Not really his style. Then again, Whelan was his number one. Wacker, they say, is rippin.

Word on you is ya clean, ya usin, ya straight, ya fightin. Word is the Waxboys are after ya, determined ta run ya off the Square. Word is Snags isn't protectin ya, though nobody's sure why. Maybe he's backin off from Wacker's turf, they say, leavin ya twist like a maggot on a hook, because unlike his uncle, he doesn't want any more wars.

And here, despite me best intentions, I can't but picture ya. Lyin on yer bed, a spike in yer arm. Standin at the winda, arms up in a V. Crouched in a corner, shufflin yer cards. While all the time the hounds outside howl for yer blood. But then I hafta stop, because it's got nothin ta do with me any more, you or where the fuck you're at.

I block me ears. I go out as little as I can. I sleep till late. I watch the box, play records, chat ta Sam.

Ma is out most nights, drinkin. Lookin for somethin? I don't dare wonder. I watch the box, play records, chat ta Sam.

I get bored.

I feel like I'm four year old again, twistin against Ma's grip as she brings me ta school. John Paul strides ahead. What's he fuckin know, the do-goodin cunt? Where was he when I was gettin straight? When I was sweatin and cryin in Sam's arms? Why the fuck should he care now?

I hate the feel a the air on me skin. The world is too big for me. I don't wanta run inta anyone.

John Paul turns, calls me forward. Like I'm some dog he's takin on a walk.

Bastard. What gives him the right ta know what's best for me? I should just leave, split now.

I hate this. I got me hood pulled up over me face but I still feel everyone can see me. I long ta run away, back ta the safety a the flat, but in me head I hear Sam, eggin me on. *Do it, Lucy. Go on.*

'You're fifteen?' says the woman in the Health Centre. She's new.

I nod.

She sighs. 'I'm afraid we can't offer you anything here. The Resource Centre in Baggot Street may be able to help you, or the National Drug Treatment Centre in Pearse Street. They provide harm-reduction schemes.'

'What's that?' I ask.

'Syringe exchange, disinfectant tablets . . .'

John Paul nods.

Fuck this. I wanta split.

'There are detox facilities there too, but as you may be aware the waiting list is very long, what with the current situation, AIDS and—'

'Lookit, missus, ya got the wrong enda the stick. I don't have a problem any more. I'm clean.'

She looks at me like she doesn't believe me. In the corner a me eye I can feel John Paul starin at me like he doesn't believe me neither.

'It's true,' I say. 'I'm clean. I done it off me own bat.'

I get up but John Paul grabs me arm and pushes me back inta the seat.

'Let's just hear what the woman hasta say, Lucy, alright?'

She sighs. 'So you're looking for a support group?'

I throw me eyes upta heaven.

'Yeah,' says John Paul, eager.

'Well, we don't have anything here. There is a Narcotics Anonymous group in Ballymun Youth Action Project –'

Bally fuckin Mun?

'– or you could apply for treatment in a psychiatric hospital. But apart from that . . .'

John Paul's got his stubborn face on, the one he useta wear in the ring when he didn't know he was bein milled ta death.

Give up, ya fucker, I tell him. *I made an effort just like ya wanted but they can't do fuck all. So do yerself and me a favour and give the fuck up.*

I leave him at the bus stop.

'Comin up?'

He checks his watch. 'No. Gotta collect the baby from her nan's.'

'Say hello ta Tara.'

'Lucy?' he calls as I turn.

'Yeah?'

'Ya know I always held out for ya, yeah? Well, I'm really proud. Ya doin great. And we'll find somewhere ta help ya, never mind what that wan said. Let's go visit Micko soon, yeah? Show him how ya are.'

Like yer own little puppet-show? Fuck you, John Paul.

'Sure,' I say.

Bye. Bye.

As I watch him go, I push away the thoughts a Micko that are risin and head inta the greasy spoon on Seán MacDermott Street across from the swimmin pool.

I order a big cuppa coffee and drink it, leanin back inta the plastic seat Emmet Whelan useta sit in. It tastes good; milky and strong and bouncin off every nerve endin.

I'm half-way through me second cup when it hits me.

Ya know I always held out for ya, yeah?

He couldn'a.

I think a the big lug on Gardiner Street swingin his hatchet and stoppin just before the blade hit me face. *Don't touch her,* said the middle lug. That's what he said.

I'm not givin up on ya, Lucy.

He couldn't.

I thinka the big struttin lug I scoped outside the squat, that time before I went ta London. He wasn't local but made no odds. I knew he was a Waxboy. Not struttin so much any more since he been hobbled?

Ya told me once them three that jumped us weren't the Don's, they were the Wacker's. Mercenaries after all, then, workin for Fred Mahon on the sly?

But . . .

He couldn'a. John Paul put in a good word and kept them fucks off of our backs for my sake?

Nah. I push that thought ta one side too but the coffee doesn't taste so good any more so I get up and go, leavin me cup unfinished.

When I come home, it's the smell gets me first. Somethin familiar and then somethin else over it. Like roast pork.

I drop me coat in the hall.

The radio is blarin. Gay Byrne bullshittin on like an auld ninny about parkin fines or joyridin or some other shite.

The smell teases me nose.

A whimperin sound. Like a dog bein kicked.

Roast pork. When was the last time Ma cooked a dinner? Two, three month ago.

Not a dog.

I pause at the door, me hand hoverin over the handle.

'What did I tell ya? I told ya not ta go around like that.'

Whimper whimper.

'Ya look like a tart, done up like that.'

A sizzlin. Sausages.

Whimper.

'You're a good girl, Samantha. Ya shouldn't—'

I turn the handle.

I need a minute ta take it in: the burnin red tip scorchin inta Sam's white knee, Ma's head bent over, Sam shakin hers, no no no, whimperin. A minute for me stomach ta churn, for Sam ta look up, guilty, like she's the one doin wrong, for Ma ta turn, eyes blank, and stare at me before seein I'm there. A minute. And then there's no more time for thinkin because me rage rises, sendin me flyin across the kitchen, shoutin, 'What the fuck ya think ya at?' as I push her against the oven, knockin the fag butt outta her hand. 'I'll report ya!'

I smack at her head with both hands. She ducks. I slap her ear. She grabs a pot, brings it down on the side a me head. It connects but I feel no pain. I grab her throat and squeeze. 'I'll kill ya!'

'Lucy! Lucy!' screams Sam.

Ma cries, great heavin sobs that come from nowhere, and collapses against me. I push her off.

'Get off me, ya sick cunt.'

She slides down the side a the oven onta the ground, sobbin. 'Sam, I'm sorry. I love ya. Come ta yer Ma. I love ya. I didn't mean ta hurt ya.'

I kick her in the side.

'Lucy!' screams Sam again.

'Come on.' I grab her by the hand. 'We're gettin out.'

She pulls back against me like she doesn't wanta but I keep draggin till we're out and down the stairs. And all the time she fights me, the burns on her legs leak hot red, hospital yella, healin white.

As we pass the mouth a the flats a gang a young fellas turn and stare.

Little fuckin rascals.

'Ignore them,' I tell her.

'Where we goin, Lucy?'

We walk and the choices race through me head.

Marlene's, says Choice Number One. She'll sort us out. We can stay with her and she'll look after Sam and make sure this doesn't happen again and Ma can be locked up where she belongs.

But what about me? asks a small voice in the back a me head. A sly voice this, sly, but Jesus, it makes sense. Do I wanta be tidied away in Marlene's little house, packaged inta a box along with her plans and the used clothes for the St Vincent de Paul, not free ta do what I want, see who I want, go where I want?

Fuck me. This is not about me. This is about Sam. Sam will be safe there. And Marlene's relaxed a lot; she won't –

'Where we goin, Lucy?'

Up around Parnell Square. East. South. West. North. And again.

Relaxed, bollocks. Think about it. She'll make me get a job, go on a course, do the right thing. No *freedom*.

She'll help Sam.

But what if Ma comes chasin after her, after both of us? This happens. Then we might as well stay where we are.

'Where we goin?'

Dorset Street. Whitworth Road. Phibsboro. Back again.

John Paul. I'll bring her ta John Paul's. He'll –

Fuckin hypocrite. Fuckin bullyboy for the Wacker. He's just as bad.

Vi?

No way.

The Social? Fuck no. Fuck fuck fuck no. They'll think I'm mad and stick me in that bin again with that Fish-eye doctor feedin me stuff and Sam worse off than before –

Then the thought strikes me. I got one over the cunt now. Which means the ball's in my court. I stop.

Sam stares at me. She hasn't cried since I dragged her out, but she's shiverin.

'Are we goin home now, Lucy?'

'Yeah.'

As we walk back me head pounds.

'Why didn't ya tell me, Sam?' I ask. Only it's not really a question; it's a way a distractin us both from the fact that I'm takin her back. 'If ya'd told me, I'da come back. I'da been back in no time.'

Me head pounds. Christ, I need somethin ta give it rest.

'Lay one finger on her ever again and I'll report ya,' I tell her. 'I'll bring Sam down ta the Social and show them the scars and that'll be it. They'll put her in a foster home and they'll lock ya up.'

Ma puffs, not darin ta look at me.

'I'm usin Granny's room from now on,' I say. 'I'm runnin the show here. And if you even think a sayin anythin different or givin me grief, I'll report ya.'

I don't wait for her ta agree. I just go inta Granny's and move all me stuff there.

'You'll be okay from now on, Mouse. I'm here ta protect ya. I'm wise to her now, I can see what's goin on. Tell me if she even tries.'

It's the best I can do.

Now the flat is mine. She scatters when I move from one room inta another, fleein from me like a rat from a dog. She hasn't touched Sam since.

She can't stand her little baby growin up. That's what it is, a course. The minute Sam started buddin, growin breasts and hair, emergin inta what Rose Dolan coulda been, fuck, it made her sick. That's why she done it.

I got it all worked out.

I wake late, watch the box, eat, play records, talk ta Charlie. I rule the flat with an iron fist. She flees when I come near.

I am in charge.

Some days I even dare ta go out – but only for shoppin or ta see the Social or go inta that Centre or such. The courage is risin in me the more time passes. The fear is dwindlin. I am in control. I am gettin ready ta face the world again. Almost but not quite.

I hear rumours. Ya went away again – sent or fled? Nothin ta do with me – but came back, though nobody's seen ya round our way. Snags has a new mot, they say, not from round here. Sasha's gone. Sick, apparently. She had a fight with Snags while ya were away – bad, they say, though nobody knows why – and he thrun her out and off she went. Disappeared one night and never been seen since.

Snags has been seen, though. Back on the Square. Visitin you. And since his visit the Waxboys have eased up, meltin away from the squat like butter in the sun. A truce with Snags his uncle doesn't know about or just . . . manners?

And what about you, Nayler? Still a maggot on a hook or back in business?

None a me business.

I zap from one TV channel ta the next. I play records, skippin tracks, startin again. I've played every fuckin record in the collection and I am gettin bored.

Ma cowers from me. I am in control. Sam is safe.

So much control and safety bores me. With too much time, ya start ta think, and I've no interest in thinkin. I seen what happened ta Betty when she started thinkin too much. I am clean. I am sorted. I am bored a bein sorted.

I am gettin hungry.

The night before Hallowe'en, ya came ta me. Ya hadn't come since I'd got clean. I hadn't seen much since then. No visions, nothin comin outta the walls. I told meself maybe goin through the seventy-two had sorted out whatever was wrong in me head.

I'd been up half the night watchin music videos on MTV. Sam had been up too, on accounta her not havin any school that week, and the two of us gassed a bit about the videos and I slagged her off about the stars she fancied and that scarf she been wearin non-stop round her neck the last two days and she tried ta slag me off too but she couldn't, or not well, in anyways. She had crips and sweets – Mars and Rolos and some awful boiled ones – and I ate four packages a crips while she polished off the Mars. I'd no hash on me but I rolled up a coupla fags and we smoked them – she'd been gettin inta smokin since I'd come back, and after I showed Ma who was boss, we done it in front a her without any bother.

An ad for some Hallowe'en party came on the telly.

'Here, Sam. Whatcha gointa do tomorra night? Trick or treat?'

She went scarlet. 'I'm not a kid any more, Lucy.'

'Oh no?'

'No.' She went even more scarlet.

'Alright. Only messin.'

She glared at me.

'Ya goin out with yer pals then? That Lisa Gough – I'm sure she's dyin ta have some fun.'

She took a long drag. 'Hmnh.'

'What's that supposed ta mean?'

She shrugged, turned away. The shrug was sayin *I don't mind*, but the tight set a her mouth wasn't, and then I remembered – fuck! Sam had come back upset the other day after goin out ta the cinema with Lisa. Lisa's Ma said they'd be grand, they'd be with Lisa's big sister who's over from England on holidays, and some pal a hers doesn't live round here, but Sam was white in the face when she got in so I reckoned the little bitch had been at her, makin a dig or somethin.

'Ah, don't mind her, Sam,' I said, tryin ta make it better. 'Ya better off without her. She's a waggon on wheels.'

Sam turned the volume up. Some shower a cunts with big hair started whackin away on their guitars. 'So how was the film?' I had ta raise me voice ta top Big Hair and his gang. 'Action or lovey-dovey?'

Sam shrugged again.

Somethin about the shrug vexed me. Turn round, Sam. Look up from the book and talk ta me. Why can't ya talk ta me? What am I, Ma or somethin?

Me head started poundin again, so I rolled up another fag and smoked it while Sam kept starin at the telly. After a while, she asked me for another smoke. I rolled one and threw it over at her.

'Thanks.' She took a puff. 'So where are you goin tomorra night then?'

'Where d'ya think?'

She stared at me. 'Don't be like that, Lucy.'

'Like what?'

'You know.'

'You started it.'

'Started what?'

'Ah, fuck this!' I said.

'Yeah,' she said. 'Fuck this.' Then she picked up a cushion and flung it at me. I lifted me hand, caught it just in time, without even lookin.

'Lucy—'

'What?' I said, meanin *Don't say anythin*. She read me and stopped.

She rustled round in her bag a goodies. 'D'ya want a sweet?' she said.

I held the cushion ta me belly, thinkin, *I haven't a breeze what I'm doin. Not tomorra night. Not ever.*

Sam conked out about one, after moanin about feelin sick. I told her it was from eatin too much sweets and probably not bein used ta the fags but she toddled off ta bed, still moanin. I'da nodded off sooner if I'd had some cans on me. But I didn't, so I ended up stayin there, on the couch, till the wee hours a the mornin.

I wake up. The usual thing. You're at the end a me bed. Except I went ta sleep on the sofa, so what am I doin in me bed? And what's me bed doin on the roof insteada in me room? I try ta move me head but can't. It's dark. I strain me eyes, tryin ta see, and then I realize ya not on my bed at all, but on Sam's.

Ya crouchin on her chest like a bird a prey, a long black shada suckin at her throat.

Hey! I try ta say. Get away. No words come. As usual.

There's a funny sound. Like bees. It's you. Ya hummin a song inta Sam's ear. Some nursery song askin a little hen when it'll have an egg ready for yer tea.

Sam opens her eyes. Have ya got presents for me, Nayler? She sounds real small.

Presents? ya say. Well, let me see. Ya dip inta yer pocket and haul out a rustin metal chain.

That's nice, says Sam.

Ya put it round her neck. Thorns spike out from it, metal daisies, barb-wire roses, diggin inta her skin.

D'ya like it, little hen?

Mmm . . . She looks away, dreamy.

Maybe ya want some more, ya say. Then ya reach inta the ground beside her bed and the carpet – yeah, the carpet, there is a carpet even though we're on the roof – the carpet peels away and ya lift up a chain, and then another, and bracelets too, and rings, silver rings with green stones, and earrings and golden watches and baby's soothers and old men's wallets and sets a keys, and ya cover Sam with them till her bed creaks.

Ya can have them all if ya want them, little hen. Ya can keep them.

She nods, and the nod is sorta sad. Ya want somethin back, though. I'll hafta give ya one a me secrets.

Ah no, little hen. Only if ya want. Yer voice is soft, carin. Ya liar.

I want the presents, says Sam.

Well . . . ya nod, thoughtful. There's a price for everythin.

Sam's head swivels. Without movin her neck. Just like *The Exorcist.*

Will I tell ya about the pretty girl with the long hair? What she got told—

Yeah.

Then Sam's mouth opens and outta it all these pictures fly. They're identical some ta the pictures she showed me, her drawins and all, colours and lines and shapes, but as they whirl outta her mouth and dance in the space between us, they twist, formin other pictures, and these ones I know well.

Queen a Wands. A lovely woman.

Number Eighteen, the Moon. Madness. Water by moonlight.

Number Twenty-two, the World. Freedom. Things women know. A young wan with streamin hair.

The Ace a Swords. A knife. The start a somethin bad.

King a Coins. A man in a dark coat. Power. Business.

Four a Cups, upside-down. Normally an offer a love; upside-down, refused.

Three a Cups, upside-down. A triangle. Normally love; upside-down, business.

Knight a Swords. A pale man ridin a white horse. A headfucker.

What's it mean, little hen? ya ask.

She said, says Sam, the pretty girl with the long hair is gointa be offered somethin by a man. She said it's down by the water, at night. A full moon. The pretty girl is a lover, she said. The offer's ta do with that. But she'll turn it down. She's waitin for another, her true love. When the other comes the girl will be floatin, free.

Good, ya say. Anythin else?

Me heart beats and as if youse have heard it, youse both turn ta look at me. But youse see nothin. I'm not there.

No, says Sam.

Don't hold off on me, little hen. There's two pictures missin. What did they mean?

Sam twists and turns in yer grasp. Nothin. The other pictures meant nothin.

Above me, Cindy Devlin twists and turns too. She's got blonde hair now and her skin is blue from the cold and that gash in her throat is gone but she's still drippin wet.

Tell me, little hen. Ya start singin yer tune again. I've never heard ya sing in tune before, Nayler, but ya doin it now. And then I see why – ya got Snags's face on ya, though I don't know what he's doin there. I start ta speak but soon as I do ya turn back ta yerself. The song stops.

Ya drop her on the bed and rise up and go ta the winda where yer white horse is waitin. And then ya gallop away, me Knight a Swords, ya gallop outta me bed and me room and me life, with yer lone knife, the Ace, held high in yer hand.

I shouldn'a but I sneaked inta Sam's room after I woke up. I couldn't sleep. I didn't wanta see ya in me dreams again that night. And I couldn't help wonderin if there was somethin in that vision that was the truth; that maybe it wasn't just from me wafflin that ya'd learnt about Cindy Devlin rattin on youse ta Emmet Whelan. Because if Cindy'd been talkin ta Ma, gettin advice maybe, without sayin what she needed the advice for, and if word got out on that, and if ya'd seen enough tablecloths twitchin over the years ta know Sam liked listenin in, and if ya found a way ta get ta her somehow, and . . . then . . .

It wasn't obvious. If I hadn't been lookin, I wouldn'a seen it. But on the floor under her drawins a square a carpet had been sliced away, and when I lifted it, I found a hole in the concrete, neat round the edges like bricks had been taken away. There was no jewellery there, though; no gold chains nor silver ones with daisies on them, nor a pretty ring with a green stone, only a top or skirt or somethin made a sparkly white stuff, and a paira red shoes with platform heels that I never seen her wear, all bundled up together in a plastic bag. Dressin-up clothes for a makey-up game, probably.

I dropped the carpet back where it had been and watched her, me beautiful little sister, her yella hair mermaidy on the pilla, as she slept the sleep a the innocent.

I didn't know if I felt relieved or disappointed.

The next day, All Hallows' Eve, dawns clear and blue with golden light spreadin over the city like a fire.

I wake up with no dreams a you. Covered in sweat, dyin with thirst.

I look out the winda. There musta been a big wind up durin the night. Beyond the roofs, all the trees on the North Circular are bare, the leaves tumbled ta the ground, leavin the branches sharp and bright at the edges.

I ache. There's a hole in the base a me that won't go away.

Call

Do I wanta stop it here? Ask a stupid question.

a course a course a course a course a course a course a course

Stop now. Halt the story. Tell it ta pack up its bags and turn back the way it came. But how can I, while the ghosts are still racin over me head upstairs, scratchin at the ground and walls ta be let out, playin tag and laughin themselves sick at me? While them women are shushin me, *ssshh*, ssshh? While I keep gettin them odd jolts a pictures and sounds that don't, no matter how much I beg them, slow down enough ta make sense.

Come on, Lucy. Get up and go. Leave now while the goin's good.

I been through all this before

No I haven't

Have too

I been through it. What's the point in rakin over this shit, rakin it over again and again?

Go.

Go.

Go.

Go.

I'm on me feet, risin, half-shovellin me cans and fags back inta their plastic bags.

This is about comin clean. This is about facin up.

But I've faced it. Haven't I? Through the stories a the whys and wherefores I've done it, I've seen the role I've played. So *why keep bangin in the fuckin nails?*

I bend down ta blow out the first candle so I can end this lark. But then, outta nowhere, the urge rises, ragin in me, and I think a you and where ya might be and I grab me weapon and run ta the black hole that opens up inta the stairs thinkin I'll go up there now, ta put ya ta sleep —

Except . . .

Ya not there yet, are ya?

Ya still somewhere else, on some other mountain, hidin till the wind eases and ya can make yer way over here.

I drop the weapon, sink back down and wait.

I

When I get inta the kitchen, Sam's sittin there, spoonin cornflakes inta her mouth and readin a book.

Ma's at the other end a the table, hummin ta herself. Somethin from the seventies. *Where's your momma gone, where's your momma gone?* She looks like crap. *Far far away*, says the song. Wish Ma was and all. She stops hummin and turns away soon's I come in like she can't bear ta face me.

I make tea and roll up a fag. Outta tobacco. Shite.

Silence strains between us, a dog on a leash. The ache inside a me won't go away.

Outside the sun lifts in the sky. The day calls ta me.

'Where ya goin?' says Ma as I get up. The shock gels our eyes together. It's been a long time since she's challenged me. Two weeks, maybe. There's somethin satisfied in her eyes that I don't like but she can fuck off if she thinks I'm weakenin.

'Where's it look like?' I say. 'Out.'

I nip inta her room on the way and peel off a few notes from her purse. Then I let meself out the front door, pullin me anorak up around me neck but leavin the hood off.

I perch on the top a the stairs and feel the hugeness a the world outside.

Time ta go, Lucy, I tell meself. Time ta meet it head on.

I am okay, I tell meself. I can deal with whatever the world throws at me.

I head down the stairs, ta the stairwell and the grey yard, gleamin gold in the new autumn light.

I go a bit outta me way, down onta Dorset Street instead a the usual cornershop. No reason. Just . . .

'Ten Major,' I say, countin the change. I buy a pack a Tayto too, and a new lighter. Near the door I see a picture a the Don on the front page a the paper. He's got a bag over his head as the rozzers push him inta the van but there's no mistakin them long spidery legs a his. There's mugshots on the bottom a the page. Emmet Whelan, Kevin Walsh, Headcase Flatley. There's a big black question mark over Whelo's gob. There's no pictures a you nor Snags.

Because I'm lookin at the paper I don't watch where I'm headin when I go through the door and that's why I crash inta the fella that's standin outside. I lose me footin. Me head jerks back. He grabs me arms just above the elbows, steadyin me. His hands burn me skin through me anorak.

Me head comes up. I meet his eyes.

I feel sick. We stay like that one, two, three seconds too long. Then, even though it feels like the worst effort in the world, I step back and ya drop me arms. Same time. Ya shift on yer heels like ya goin ta go, and for a minute I think a runnin too, doin a two-step sideways, pretendin I haven't even seen ya – but it's too late.

Ya wearin a darkish jacket like somethin a soldier would have and ya got a canvas bag on yer shoulder. Ya look okay. A bit tired. The shadas under yer eyes are jet. Ya seem . . . taller. Could be the jacket. A bit edgier than normal. Otherwise fine. Ya not gone any skinnier. Yer hair's longish now, like mine. Looks alright. There's somethin else different about ya but I don't know what it is.

Are ya usin, Nayler, like the rumours said? You're edgy but ya not sweatin nor grey like ya sick. Or noddy and smiley like ya fixed. And yer pupils are black as ever. No pinnin as ya take me in, head ta toe, comin back ta rest on me face. Oh yeah, yer eyes are their normal hidden selves, no black torchbeam today, but still I feel me skin burn.

What gives *you* the right ta look at me like that? I lift me chin, stare back.

Ya smile. It's yer old smile; lazy as ever, only for the tooth missin from that time before –

I should go –

'So how's tricks, Lucy?' Yer voice is the same as ever. Nearly.

I haven't took a step. I should –

I smile back, cool as I can. 'Never better.'

'Ya back in yer ma's?'

'Yeah.'

'She treatin ya okay?'

'Fine.'

'And Sam?'

What business is it of yours? 'Whatcha want, Nayler?'

Ya start ta speak but, suddenly afraid a whatcha gointa say, I interrupt. 'Lookit, ya should know I'm gone beyond all that—'

Oh, yeah? says yer eyes. 'Okay.'

It's only now I realize how much I'm shakin.

'Here, d'ya want a fag?' Ya take a pack from yer jacket, offer me one. Yer fingers are hard and white and nail-bitten as ever. Yer sleeve rides up and I see ya got a new tattoo round yer wrist; a barb-wire bracelet.

I can feel me box a Major in me anorak pocket. I should go.

I shrug, take the fag. Ya lean in, light it. I can feel heat from yer face that isn't just the match. Yer fingers aren't shakin like mine but they're not the steadiest neither.

'I came lookin for ya, Lucy, ya know. The next mornin.'

'Yeah?' I don't ask why. I remember ya that last day outside the squat, sick and ragin as ya twisted that chain a souvenirs round me neck. I should go.

I take a drag, laugh, real cas. 'Well, took ya long enough ta find me.'

Ya laugh too like you're in on the joke but yer eyes go even more hidden. 'Yeah . . . well . . .'

Under the frayed collar a yer jacket I can see the glinta somethin silver. Is that me chain? Ya tryin ta scare me, Nayler? Ya should know ya can't scare me any more. I'm clean now, outta yer grasp.

'How's Sasha?'

Does yer fag stop for a sec on its way ta yer mouth? I can't tell. Ya shrug, smile. 'No idea.'

I shift on me feet. I really should go.

Ya flick yer ash on the ground. Ya run yer hand through yer hair, rumplin it up.

'So . . . whatcha upta tonight, Lucy Lu?' Ya say it idle, like ya just makin conversation.

I should say nothin. I should stub out the fag and go.

Nothin, I said. Then there was a gap and then we started talkin at the same time. Well, d'ya wanta – Why –? And I said, fast again so ya couldn't answer, Lookit, Nayler, told ya I'm gone beyond – I know, ya said, interruptin me, vexed sorta. I heard ya, Lucy. Then we both took a drag.

We stayed like that a bit, not talkin. Ya looked round, distracted, nervy almost. I could feel ya itchin ta go as much as me.

Okay then, so. Forget it.

Seeya –

Nod. Nod. We both turned.

Then turned back at the same time and started talkin again.

Whatcha plannin— It's just—

We both laughed. Nervous.

Go on, I said.

The set a yer head as ya sized me up. That glint again.

Well, I'm just thinkin . . . why don't we do somethin . . . different tonight? Somethin special?

Special? I said. Thinkin: *Why do we need somethin special? Whatcha mean by special, Nayler, didja not hear what I—*

Yeah – ya say it like I know what ya mean – yeah. Special. Different . . . Fun?

Fun? I said like it was the thickest thing in the world. Fun for fuckin what?

I dunno. For fuckin – ya looked around, nodded yer fag at the masks in the shop winda. Grinned. For fuckin Hallowe'en, Lucy. That's for.

Ah, Nayler I—

Just fun. Ya smiled. That's all. Like we useta have in the old days, yeah?

The old days? Thinkin: *Whatcha mean, the old days?*

Yeah. Remember? When we were . . . Yer face softened. When we were kids.

Kids?

Yeah. Ya nodded. Remember? Youse useta call round and we'd have the laugh and all and—

Youse?

Oh, ya mean Charlie and Amanda and Damo and all? That old fuckin . . . HellFire Club lark?

Ya stopped, puzzled. Laughed, surprised. Yeah. Ya nodded. Yeah. That's it. That's it. The old HellFire Club.

I laughed too – even though I shouldn'a, I shoulda gone then, I know that – I laughed like a stupid fuckin girl, and stayed put, even got another fag from ya, and let ya light it up for me and all, like I was too cool ta be standin round, not bothered at all.

Some fuckin HellFire Club, I said. Far as I can remember all we ever done was sit around and smoke dope and talk about music.

And cut people up in basements.

Ya laughed again. Yeah, I know. But what if we done somethin different tonight, Lucy? Somethin real?

Then ya touched me. It was a light touch, just yer fingers on me arm, but it burnt like a match. I could feel yer pulse. I wanted, I swear I *wanted* ta pull away from ya.

Real? I said. What the fuck's real, Nayler?

Ya smiled.

In yer smile somethin starts ta hum. A needle explodes, a vein bursts, silver flies through blood and sweat and all's right with the world.

Ya nodded. Okay, so. Said it like there was no arguin. One last lash. Tonight in the squat. Ya up for it, Lucy Lu? That glint back in yer eyes, darin me.

Dare ya right back.

Yeah. I'll bring the gang.

The gang? A pause, then – Yeah, yeah. Ya smiled, nodded. Yeah. A course. Great plan. Last get-together a the HellFire Club, what?

I stepped back. Ya dropped yer hand. I turned away.

I shoulda said it again: I'm beyond all that, Nayler. Get the fuck outta me life.

But I didn't.

Go straight home, Lucy. Go back ta the flat and Ma and Sam and watch TV and smoke the Major and forget about him, and maybe even phone up Marlene for a chat, and get straight onta that fuckin programme the Social are pushin, and force him out and never look back.

But instead I walk down the canal, ta the place you and Micko met up with me and Amanda that day ya came back ta Dublin, and I remember.

I let me body fill with the memories, of the buzz and the calm and the heaven, and I ache. And all the time I ache, gazin at the swans on the canal dippin their orange beaks inta glintin blue water, I busy meself with me mind, pretendin there's nothin goin on underneath, castin for reasons, good solid reasons, why I should accept yer offer.

What harm can it do? I tell meself. I'm clean now. And besides, it's only gointa be the once. One last lash.

Last? Why? Are ya goin somewhere, Nayler? Goin for –

Don't think about it. A get-together. That's all. Old times' sake. For when we were –

Kids.

Kids? Were we ever kids? *Clean* is whatcha meant. Were we ever clean?

I watch the swans, wishin I'd bread ta throw at them. Anythin ta keep me hands and mind busy, anythin ta stop the jitters from risin.

Fucksake, I tell meself. I'm buildin all this way too big. It's only gointa be one night. And I haven't seen the others in ages. It's probably be the last time we'll all pal round, what with Damo and Charlie goin their separate ways and Amanda more or less off the scene. A shame ta let that pass without somethin . . .

Special, croon the memories. Somethin special for Lucy.

A taste a heaven. Dark shadas under yer eyes in a white room.

424

And what about everythin else, Nayler? What about Sasha? What about—

Fucksake. All that shite's over now, isn't it? All that hurtin and . . . dyin and stuff. The Don's banged up. The Wacker's backed off. The war is over. Tonight will be different. Ya said as much. Tonight we'll just be . . . goin back, ta the way things were before they got sticky. Ta how it was in the beginnin, when we were—

But what about Snags? Are ya out or are ya back workin for him, Nayler? Are ya still—

Dealin?

I didn't ask ya that.

I get up from the ridge, dust meself down. Bye bye, swans.

Fuckit. It'll be fine. I'm on top a things. I've sorted out Ma and Sam and the Social and I'm goin on that programme. Soon. So what the fuck do I hafta worry for? I'm in control. And I'll fuckin stay there.

Come on, nudges the buzz. Somethin real.

'Hey,' I say, pressin meself as tight ta the phone box as I can. I got me hood pulled up so neither Ma nor Sam will see me if they walk past.

'Hey,' says Charlie.

He's the toughest one. If I can get past him, the others will be a piece a cake.

'Whatcha up ta tonight?'

'No plans. I was supposed ta be goin out with some lads from school but they called it off.'

'Good,' I say. 'Because how wouldya like ta do somethin mad?'

'Mad what way?' he says.

'Mad sounds, mad blow, mad gargle.'

'Sounds alright ta me.'

'We could have a bit of an old get-together, ya know. Bring Amanda and Damo.'

'I'm not seein Amanda now, Lucy.'

425

'I'm not sayin ya hafta ride her, Charlie. Just, ya know . . . a get-together.'

He pauses, thinkin. 'Ah, fuck. Why not?'

Here's the why not, Charlie.

'I met an old pal today.'

'Yeah?' He hasn't copped.

'He says we can call by his and all later on.'

'Yeah, sure.' He's distracted. In the background I hear Marlene callin him.

'He says he's got some great acid in.' A lie. But Charlie's been bangin on about wantin ta do good acid ever since readin this book on Jim Morrison.

'Yeah . . .' Still distracted. Then he starts ta cop. 'Hang on. Who?'

'Nayler,' I say, tryin ta get it across real smooth before Charlie can interrupt. 'Bumped inta him today. He's clean and all and workin off his own bat. No complications. Just sellin on acid and hash now. Nothin ta do with, ya know, the other. Says he's got some great stuff in.'

'Jesus, Lucy,' says Charlie. 'I don't know. I mean . . .'

Here we go. 'Ah, not ta worry. He was sayin ya probably wouldn't be bothered. Probably too busy with yer studies, he said, ta be havin fun. I told him ta fuck off, ya had plans. That's the only reason ya were studyin. Some plans, he says. Specky's always been a swot. Cunt, yeah?' I laugh.

'The fucker!' says Charlie.

'Never mind, Charlie. I can go up on me own after youse have gone home.'

'But—'

'No, really, Charlie. It's grand. Just thought ya might – nah, fuckit, leave it. I'll sort meself out, fill ya in later.'

'But Lucy—' He's flustered now.

'See youse at mine round eight, what?'

'Wait . . . Lucy!'

'What?' I act impatient.

'What sorta acid?'

*

One down, two ta go.

'Alright, Charlie, better go . . . here, has Amanda's Ma got that phone in yet?'

'Yeah. D'ya want her number?'

'Yeah.'

He gives it me.

'Great . . .'

Two ta go.

'Actually . . . wait a minute, Charlie. Maybe it's better if you ask her instead.'

'Me? Why?'

'Well . . . it'll sound better. Me and Amanda haven't exactly been palsy the last while. And ya know, if we're plannin ta head over ta Nayler's and . . .'

'Ah, yeah . . .'

'Not that we hafta. Like I said, we can just pal out round the flat or the canal—'

'Fuck, we sorted this, Lucy. Let's go see that fucker, fleece him for what we can.'

'If ya sure . . .'

'Yeah. I'm sure.'

'Butcha know the way Amanda's round him, she mightn't want . . .' I leave a gap.

'I'll sort it out,' says Charlie, his pride risin. He mightn't want much outta Amanda now but he still remembers how he was never number one in her eyes while you were around. 'Leave it ta me. Okay?'

Once I've hung up, I give her a bell. Luckily, it's her that answers, not her ma.

'Hi.' She sounds surprised. 'Where d'ya get me number?'

'Charlie. He been onta ya yet?'

'No.' She's wary. 'Why?'

'Fuck, gobshite called upta me the other day and was goin on about ya for ages. Sayin how much he misses ya blah blah blah and he's dyin ta see ya, but he doesn't know if you're inta him any more. Thought he'da called ya by now.'

'Charlie?' she says. 'Fuck off.'

'Fuck off yerself.' Then I move on so it won't seem important. 'In anyways he's comin up ta mine tonight so if ya wanta patch things up, feel free.'

'Yeah . . . I don't know.'

'Suit yerself. Wouldn't blame ya for wantin ta torment him.'

'Yeah.'

'He's mad about ya, though—'

She butts in, not lettin me finish. 'Here, why ya ringin me, Lucy?'

'I told ya . . . Charlie.'

'It's not that. There's somethin else.'

Fuck. Think on yer feet, Lucy Dolan. I think. I think. I—
can't

'Okay.' I'm relieved in a funny way that I can't fool her. 'It's him.'

I say no more but she doesn't ask who. I feel exhausted all of a sudden.

'I met him today, Amanda. First time in ages, since I . . . since I came home. He wants me ta go over ta his tonight.'

'Jesus.'

'Come with me,' I say, beggin. 'Please, Amanda. Keep an eye on me, willya?'

'Ya don't hafta go and see him,' she says, but I can tell she's lyin.

'If I can do it, Amanda. If I can prove I'm past it . . .'

There's a silence as she mulls it over. Then –

'Does he know I'd be comin too?'

'Yeah, yeah.' I think fast, lie. 'He's the one that asked ya ta come. Please, Amanda.'

She says nothin. I feel sick.

Two down.

'And lookit,' I say, 'don't tell Charlie. He thinks I'm settin this up so the two a youse can get back together. Ya know how he hates Nayler. He wouldn't go near him if he was paid.'

'Sure,' she says. 'Sure.'

Did I mean it? Did I really want her there, ta protect me, or was it just another lie? Jesus fuckin Christ, how I've agonized over that.

Now I think it was a bit a both; the Devil on one shoulder and the angel on the other sayin the exact same thing at the exact same time.

'Great,' says Damo, wipin oil off his hands and onta his overalls. 'Can I bring Cecile?'

I shake me head. 'Lookit, it's just the old gang for now, yeah? Don't think Cecile would be inta what we're plannin.'

He winks. 'Sounds good, Lucy.'

Sap.

Sam's hummin that song Ma was at earlier but she stops when I come in and stares at me.

'What?' I say, vexed. She knows, I think.

'Nothin.' She starts hummin again.

Yeah, Lucy. Nothin.

Doubts rise. I jitter. There's minutes where I think about it, seriously think about harin back down the stairs and ringin them and callin it off. But then the other voice surfaces, real reasonable. We don't hafta go up there, says the other voice. The lads can come over and we can party away here – no need ta go anywhere else. No need ta ring up and cancel just because I'm gettin cold feet. Sort it out later on.

Yeah? ask the doubts. Ya sure?

Course I'm sure. No pressure.

Okay, say the doubts. That's fine.

Around six a clock it gets dark. I go out, quiet so Sam won't hear – why would that bother me? Doesn't matter, no reason, I'm just quiet, that's all – and go up the stairs. Lights gleam from Missus Devlin's front winda; a pumpkin head, a candle. Funny; wouldn'a thought she'd a been inta partyin what with Cindy gone and all. But I suppose she's got all her other daughters, and their kids. Ya can't put yer whole life on hold for just one person. The pumpkin grins at me as I walk past and I think a the story a Missus Devlin's hair goin grey overnight. All because a Cindy, said Ma. *And what do you know about Cindy?* I nearly asked her, surprisin meself, but didn't, a course, because what does it hafta do with us any more, what happened there?

The Goughs' gaff is dark but I can hear the telly on through their door. For a minute I send bad thoughts Lisa's way. Fuck you for the way ya been treatin me sister and you pretendin ta be her one good friend, say the thoughts. Die, ya bitch. Then I catch meself on and give it up, rememberin what Granny useta say about what goes around comes around.

It's cold but clear. The moon is half-full, hazy at the edges. A coupla scraps a clouds are floatin across it. Fuck off, ya auld bastard, I say ta the Man in the Moon. Getcha nose outta me business. Stop spyin.

I give the moon the finger and step out onta the ledge. The cold bites at me arms and legs. I can feel goosebumps risin, and under them a pulsin in me veins, the cool rush of excitement.

Is this it? Are all lives made up a small bits a time where choices is made? One choice leads ta another ta another. Is this where meanin rests or is it in the current that flows underneath, forcin the choices ta happen? I stand on the edge like I stood on it before, like I stood on a bridge in London, and spread me arms and prepare ta fly.

The old fear surfaces in me, mixes with the excitement, soars. Below me the city twinkles, twitchin like a brasser with crabs. Come on now. Go for it.

I waver, totter, jump.

No goin back.

I dust off me knees and – don't know why, just got this urge – go ta me hidey-hole and check that the gun is still there. I stick me hand in, but there's a thorny branch near the openin that musta fallen in durin a storm and got stuck there and it's blockin me way. I can't pull it out, but I rummage past it and grope, and the bulk a the long hard barrel through the canvas and plastic reassures me.

Coulda sold it when I was strung out. Fuck. Why didn't I think a that then? Easy, Lucy. Because ya *were* strung out. Thick.

The stupidness of it makes me laugh.

I hold the barrel and for a sec think about bringin it with me. The sec passes. I leave the gun where it is.

Another parcel a time. Another choice.

When I'm pullin me hand out, the branch scratches at me, leavin deep red marks that bleed in the moonlight. Some thorns.

Hallowe'en. Fancy dress.

I open her wardrobe, poke in the back where she's kept it. Twenty year old it is, but still in good nick. Five years she's kept it after throwin everythin else a his out.

It's a bit big for me, but not much. If I turn up the sleeves and wear the hoodie under, it'll fit perfect.

I push me hair off me face, scrape it back inta a ponytail. The bits at the front flop loose but on the whole it does the biz.

I point at me Da's reflection, smile his Italian smile.

Behind me, I hear ya breathin, slow and harsh.

Me guts start ta wrench.

They arrive at eight. Charlie first, luggin a bag a cans, then Damo with the flagons, then Amanda, carryin two bottles a vodka inside her jacket. I don't have any gargle on me mainly on account a Mahon's won't serve me because they know I'm only fifteen, but I've a few tenners I robbed from Ma that I'm keepin for later. Charlie's left the specs at home and has put gel in his hair so he looks cool – he thinks. Amanda is in a short skirt that clings to her arse and a top that's hardly there. She looks ripe, ready ta be touched. Her skin is gorgeous, glowin, probably some new blusher she got, her eyes are wide, rimmed in purple kohl, her lips wet. I've forgotten how good she can look and I do me best not ta stare. Makes no odds. She keeps lookin over at Charlie. He does his best ta ignore her, but I can tell her outfit's workin for him too because he hasn't taken his hands off his lap once since sittin down.

Ma's gone, off for a session down the Big Tree with the local auld wans. She was in the bath for ages earlier, soapin herself like she thought she was some Hollywood queen. Good riddance.

Charlie digs in his pocket, hauls out some tapes. 'Here, Lucy. Put this on.'

It's some American band, dark and thumpin with wailin guitars and a fella and a bird switchin the vocal. Pixies, they're called. The first tune sounds like it's about a basement.

We start on the madman's soup. Between the cider and the nerves, the three of us in the know start ta talk too much, me too, me the most, about nothin in particular; Charlie's exams and his plans, these yokes called email and EFT, Amanda's new pals in school, Damo's apprenticeship, the Kav brothers bein sent ta Pat's for joyridin. The conversation skitters over us and apart from Damo, we keep missin what the others are sayin. Sam's hoppin round the edges of our chat, tryin ta join in and not gettin very far. Charlie keeps feedin her cider when he thinks I'm not lookin and she starts gigglin.

Amanda tosses her hair, pouts her lips. She's on edge, waitin.

I take sly glances at Charlie's watch. *Come on come on.* But the time isn't right.

A track comes on, about some monkey gone ta heaven, and Sam stands up ta dance. But she's hardly up when she goes white in the face and staggers ta one side before fallin back onta the couch. Charlie tries ta get her up, 'Bedtime, Sam,' but he can't budge her. She's out cold, heavy as a rock.

Amanda fusses, tuckin a blanket round her. 'Put her on her side,' says Damo. 'That way she won't puke in her sleep and die like Hendrix.'

'Ya dick,' says Charlie, lookin over all anxious at me.

'It's true,' says Damo. 'Don't scoff.'

At last the fussin is done and we got Sam sorted, lyin under the blanket with a bucket beside the couch in case she pukes. The screamin lad stops singin. There's a silence in the room; the first that night.

'Well?' I say, lookin at Amanda, then Charlie.

Sam'll be fine, I tell meself as I step out inta the air that's bitin cold, fizzy with the sounds a bangers. She'll be AOK. Her colour's not too bad and she's sleepin. In anyways I'll be back soon, one, two a.m. at the max. Way before Ma comes in and can do her any harm.

What happens if somethin goes wrong? say the doubts.

Stop worryin, I tell meself. Jesus! What am I supposed ta do? Stay in the rest a me life just on account a me baby sister? Sam's a big girl now. She'll know what ta do. She can go ta the Devlins or even Lisa Gough if somethin happens. She'll be fine.

'Ya ready, Lucy?' says Amanda. She's itchin ta see ya. I can smell the heat off her.

'Yeah.' I close the door, turn.

We wait outside Mahon's while Amanda gets the Buckie and cans. The fella inside is droolin over her. She leans on the counter so her tits are in his face and blows smoke at him and laughs.

I catch Charlie starin in and nudge him. 'Second thoughts?'

He shakes his head, still lookin at her.

'This is great crack,' Damo keeps sayin. 'Great crack.'

Amanda comes out and Mahon's door closes behind her, the little bell ringin.

'Come on,' she says. 'Or we'll be late.'

They had a choice too, ya know. They didn't hafta come if they didn't want. It wasn't just me.

'Jesus,' says Charlie real loud, as we pass three young fellas from the Sheridan Court flats. 'Look at *that*. I can see why they say it's a zoo round here. It's all them gorillas.'

Damo looks at him, confused.

'And as for the young wans, no wonder they say—'

Amanda, walkin ahead of us, stiffens.

'Who say?' I ask, interruptin Charlie. 'Yer snobby pals in Malahide, is it? Them shirtlifters wouldn't know a box if it hit them in the gob.'

Amanda turns. 'Yeah, Charlie Dolan. Ya wanta be careful thatcha don't get asked ta pick up a penny in the jacks.'

Damo laughs. Charlie goes tense but I grab his arm and whisper in his ear. 'She's only edgy on accounta him.'

'I know.' Charlie shakes me off and quickens his step ta catch up with Amanda. He puts his arm round her shoulders. She stiffens again but she doesn't try ta get rid a him.

There's corrugated iron over the bottom part a the door and the windas upstairs been broken. It looks like nobody's lived there in ages. Have ya been havin me on?

Me heart pounds. I raise the knocker.

Stop.

Go.

I drop it.

You've opened the door before the brass has hit the wood. Ya look well. Ya wearin one a them big old-fashioned shirts I robbed for ya and that earrin Sasha gave ya. Ya seem even edgier than this mornin, but in a more . . . ready way. Like a boxer psychin up for the ring.

'Hiya.'

'Hiya.'

Yer eyes glance over me, take in me jacket. Ya give me a grin. Yer teeth look real sharp in the light from the street.

'It's me Da's,' I say. 'From when he was a Mod.' I don't hafta say anythin but it's the nerves. I can't help it.

Yer grin sharpens more. 'Cool.' Ya spot the others behind me, put yer Neil-face on.

Ya may be actin all smooth in fronta them, but as ya lean back inta the door ta let me past, I see yer forehead is slick with sweat. And there's a twitchin goin on under yer angel-white skin, a twitchin only I can see.

Sweat? Jitters? Have ya been usin after all, Nayler? Are ya withdrawin? Does that mean there's none around? Fuck. *Fuck*.

Stay chilled, Lucy. Ya don't need it, remember. Ya clean now.

'Hey, hello there, Amanda darlin. Come on in.' I hear the soft squeak as ya kiss her on the cheek but I know yer eyes are still on me, sendin a pricklin between me shoulders.

434

I try ta ignore it.

The place has rotted even more since I left. The floorboards squelch under our feet and the candles in the hallway do nothin ta cheer it up. Lookin up inta the seashell curve a the staircase I wonder how I ever thought this was somewhere special.

It stinks.

Drums beat upstairs. Some nigger goin on about fightin the power.

'Thought ya didn't like the music, Nayler,' says Damo. Everyone looks at him.

'It's the drums,' I say, though I shouldn't speak, there's no need for me ta fill the gap, except I can't help it, just bein back is sendin the shakes through me. 'He gets the beat. Ya don't need tunin ta get rhythm.'

Ya laugh. 'Right as always, Lucy. We head up, so?'

Ya got candles lit in all the skulls in yer room.

Amanda takes a step back when she sees them, and I remember she hasn't been up here at night for ages, but ya take her hand like there's been no time since ya last touched her. 'It's alright, sweetheart. It's nothin human and it's all clean.' Ya look over at me.

Ya makin a dig, Nayler? Tryin ta scare me? Don't ya know we're over all that now? Bones, blood, guns, bodies: over. None a me business any more, not that it ever was.

I walk over ta the stereo, start rootin round the CDs. Ya still got loadsa mine that I bought in the summer.

As I root through the CDs I start ta figure out what's wrong. Even with the candles and music, the place feels empty, sorta. Like ya not supposed ta be livin here any more. Like ya pretendin, somehow. I watch ya throw a can over ta Charlie and josh with Damo and flirt with Amanda, touchin her knee real light, and even though they're all buyin it, laughin and gabbin, ya don't look like ya pretendin any less and that just makes it feel even more wrong.

I sink inta yer mattress, feelin like a ghost a meself, brung inta another time.

Wherever Sasha went, it's not here. I peer inta the dark corners, lookin for traces of her. But there's nothin left. She might as well a never lived here.

'Lucy?'

Ya lean over, hand me a joint.

For a sec I think a askin ya, *What happened, Nayler? What happened our beautiful Dutch mermaid?*

But I don't.

'Ta.' I take the joint, drag, let it hit me. Fuck, it's good.

We drink two cans each and the Buckie Amanda got in Mahon's. Ya don't drink much. That's a good sign, says the ache in me body that's risin by the minute. Nobody ever drinks much if they're usin.

Good?

But ya restless too. Ya keep gettin distracted, goin in and outta the room that useta be Micko's, rustlin around, lookin for stuff. And that's not good.

It's normal, I tell meself, watchin ya jump up and head out and then come back in again. Comin off the gear makes ya jiggy. Don't ya remember?

Somethin sours in me mouth. Not disappointment. Fuck no. I'm not disappointed. I didn't come up for any a that. I'm clean, remember? A party, bit a booze, bit a hash. One last get-together. That's all.

So why do I wanta ask ya them questions? Like . . . *Are ya still workin for Snags? Are ya still dealin? Are ya usin? Do ya have some? Can ya tell me? Please.*

There's no space ta speak, though. The music's too loud and ya don't stay still enough for me ta grab ya and talk ta ya. So I drink more Buckie ta calm meself and then ya come in with vallies and we have them and that calms me more till I'm almost okay.

'Let's tell ghost stories!' says Amanda, loud, stretchin her legs out on the mattress so we can all see up her jacksy.

Ya lean over her and say somethin. I can't make out the words from where I'm sittin. She looks puzzled, then makes a face, like she doesn't give a fuck, and swigs more from her naggin. Ya pat her on the shoulder, head out the room again. She watches ya go.

Damo plumps himself down beside her and starts barfin on about shite. Amanda takes another sup and brushes her legs against his hand. Damo looks round then, real sly, moves his hand till it's on her knee. Amanda throws her head back, laughs a messy laugh.

The Buckie and the vallies are givin me a headache. The room is too bright. Too many candles. Charlie pokes me in the side. 'Ask him.'

'Not now.'

'Fuckin ask him, Lucy.'

'Later.'

'Lucy, I'm not hangin round this tip unless—'

'Okay,' I say, and get up.

I stand outside the door a the room that useta be Micko's. I stand there for ages. Then I push it open. It doesn't make a noise. There's only one candle lit, near the winda. Ya crouchin in the corner, huddled over somethin.

Ya lyin usin cunt. I knew it. I should pack it in now. Go.

I step on a loose board and it squeaks. Ya turn, jumpy, rubbin yer nose.

Ah. The bitter taste in me mouth sweetens, dries. And there was me thinkin—

'Speed?' I ask.

Ya laugh. 'Speed? Fucksake, Lucy. Give me some credit. It's coke.'

Shadows from the garden outside move across the winda. Is this what's real? This all?

I hafta say somethin –

'Give us some.'

'Jesus, Lucy. Ya just had the vallies. D'ya not want ta wait—'

'I'm sick waitin, Nayler.'

I step inta the room. Ya stand up.

Ya got somethin in yer right hand. I lunge in, go for it. Ya step away, twist yer fist behind yer back. I grab at yer arm, miss. I grab again, close me fingers round yer wrist.

Ya sink against the rottin wall, trappin me arm behind yer body. The nuggets a yer spine press like chisel-heads inta me skin;

I can feel the mess a scars on yer shoulder from where they destroyed yer horse gratin against me upper arm. Our legs hold against each other. Ready, tense, shakin a bit. Stags in the grass. Dogs in a ring.

Yer eyes are black slits. 'Sick, Lucy? I thought ya were all better.'

I pull at me arm, tryin ta free it, but ya press further inta the wall. I think a Sasha's twisted hand. Under yer shirt me chain glitters silver on yer white skin. The round curve of a key catches the light.

I look inta yer eyes.

Ya lift yer free hand sudden and I go ta duck, thinkin it's a slap. But instead ya catch me jaw with yer fingertips, real light. Ya lift a finger, stroke me face up ta me hairline, real careful, and then ya stroke me hair.

'Suits ya long.'

'Yeah, right.'

Are ya sick, Lucy? Or are ya better? Are ya in control, Lucy?

'Nayler, I . . .'

Somethin flashes in yer eyes and yer hand stops strokin. I change whatever I was gointa say.

'I *am* all better.' I laugh like I'm cool. 'Done and dusted. But I want some coke. Never done it before, ya know.'

I'm expectin ya ta drop yer hand but ya leave it there, touchin me.

'Will ya come with me tonight, Lucy?'

I start ta say 'Where?' but ya drop yer fingers ta me lips.

'No questions?'

Yer fingers are pulsin. Between each beat I feel the throbbin a me own veins.

I feel sick.

Yer fingers are soft. I could kiss them if I wanted.

I feel like cryin.

Fuck this.

'What about the others?' Yer fingers move against me lips as I talk. 'Ya know Charlie only came round cos he thinks ya got some acid.'

438

Ya smile. Then ya drop yer hand, move away from the wall, freein me. 'Ya sick puppy, Lucy Dolan.'

Before givin me the note ya ask me if I'm sure. It doesn't do ta mix, ya say. Bad shit. Mix what? I say, and snort.

Everythin feels good with the coke. Not as good as gear, it's way different, but it's good. Sharp and clean in a smooth way; pushin away the Buckie mist and vallie clouds. Maybe it's only on accounta that but ya seem smoother yerself, still alert and movin round a lot but not as jumpy as before.

'Ready, Lucy?' Ya pull a canvas bag out from under the table. Same one ya had this mornin outside the shop.

For some reason I think a the Magician card from me Ma's deck when I picture what's inside. A cup. A coin. A knife. A wand. A lyin-on-its-side number eight. And a book with a hard pale cover and red writin on the front.

Amanda looks up all worried when we come in, but ya go over ta her and squeeze her waist just like ya woulda in the old days, pushin Damo outta the way, and then ya kiss her on the neck and she seems alright with that.

From the door I give Charlie the thumbs-up sign and he sits up straight. Ya turn from Amanda and crouch down beside Charlie, palm it. He brings his hand up ta his mouth, slips it in.

Ya pull on yer soldier's jacket. Looks good over the shirt, I hafta admit. Amanda glances up at ya. The candlelight gleams off her hair. Ya whistle at me, throw me somethin. It's yer willa stick, the one ya cut just before the shop on Hill Street got smashed up and that Kerry boy with it. Ya take Buck's sword off the wall and buckle it on around yer waist.

'Here, Damo, hold this a while.' Ya give him yer canvas bag.

Then ya kick the stereo off.

'Alright?'

Alright, Lucy? is whatcha mean.

'Yeah,' I say. I need some air.

*

Did I know then where ya were takin us? In me head, the answer is No, a course I didn't. How would I?

'Where we goin?' says Amanda. She's slurrin.

I look up at the broken windas a the squat. They're dark but I picture the one at the back, lit, the candles still on, sendin shadas flickerin against the curtains. Ya call me, loud – 'Lucy, ya plannin ta camp out there all night?' – and Amanda giggles.

I turn and folla youse down Gardiner Street towards the city. Amanda's waverin all over the gaff, knockin inta you on one side, Damo on the other. Ya keep grabbin at her ta keep her steady but that makes her giggle harder. It's freezin.

Amanda stops suddenly. 'I *said*, where the *fuck* are we goin?'

'Surprise, Amanda.' Ya say it teasin, put yer arm round her waist. 'Come on, darlin. D'ya wanta be left behind?'

'Surprise? I don't want no . . .' She turns, looks at me. I stare back.

Remember what I asked ya, Amanda? Remember why I begged ya ta come? Keep an eye on me, please.

She winks a messy wink and puts her finger ta the side of her nose.

'Jesus,' says Charlie, starin at the traffic cone in the middle a the road. 'The colours . . . they're . . .'

As we pass the cars and the drunks and the party-goers, pissed in their witches' hats and white faces, fairy wands and clowns' wigs, I start ta fight it. What the fuck am I doin? I got me charlie, I'm happy now, I don't need anythin more. Why the fuck should I keep goin with you, of all people, and this shower a stupid cunts useta be me pals? Why shouldn't I just turn round and go home, back ta Sam? I don't want anythin more. This is thick. But ya haven't told me where we're goin and the edge the charlie's given me is makin me curious, and wantin more, and besides, I can fuckin handle it.

I can handle anythin.

I pull me hoodie out from under me Da's jacket and up over me head.

I swish the stick. Me legs keep walkin.

★

On Cathal Brugha Street, a gang a slappers dressed in fishnet tights and white stilettos yell abuse at ya. 'Ah, lookit! It's Adam Ant back from the dead!'

'Go on, Adam! Stand and deliver!'

'Deliver yer mickey!'

'Fuck youse!' shouts Amanda, turnin ta give them the finger.

The slappers call her names and she starts gigglin, crumplin over on herself.

'Go on, Amanda!' I shout.

She looks back at me, still gigglin.

'Look.' Charlie kneels down ta stare at the little weeds growin up through the cracks in the footpath. I put the willa stick through me belt and grab his arm, tryin ta lift him.

Damo lumbers up. 'This is fuckin mad. Mad!'

Ya grab Charlie's other arm. 'Okay, Charlie boy, everythin's real normal now.'

Charlie nods, lookin serious. We hoist him up together and drag him forward between us.

'You alright, Lucy?' ya say as we drag.

'Sure. Swimmin. Never been better.'

As we turn onta the road, somethin behind ya catches me eye. A glimpse of a card, Number Twenty-two, the World, a young wan with flowin hair, standin below a streetlight. Cindy Devlin, I think first. Then . . . no. She's dead. Sasha? But she moves then, outta the light, like she was never there at all.

I race up the stairs, clingin close ta the tall cunt dressed as a skeleton that I sneaked in behind ta get off payin me ticket. Behind me is Amanda. She stumbles as she climbs upta the top deck, but Damo catches her just in time. She giggles, fallin back inta his arms.

'Ah, Damo, you're a real gentleman. Not like the resta them.'

I laugh, but Charlie's too far inta the stripes on the bus seats ta pay any attention. I folla Amanda up towards the front and sit down across the aisle from her. Amanda leans over Damo's knee.

'Are you alright, Lucy?' She's still pissed but serious all of a sudden.

'Yeah.' I pat her hand. 'I'm grand.'

Am I? I stop pattin.

Then Amanda's face sobers, and in the soberin I see the real her again, me best pal that I led ta you and worse and – fuck! I think, let's get outta here. Let's forget this stupid game that I can't handle in anyways and go –

I move ta get up and she moves at the same time, but then Damo pulls at her – 'Ah . . . Manda . . . where ya goin?' – and she slumps down beside him, gigglin.

'Move over.'

I squash meself close ta the winda as ya slide yerself inta the seat next ta me.

'Ya okay?'

Fucksake. Fuckin *sick* a people askin me if I'm okay.

'Why wouldn't I be?' I say, not lookin at ya. Me feet jig; me fingers tap me knee.

'Hey.' Ya touch me hand, hold it. I stop tappin.

'Thanks for goin along with this.' Ya say it low, close ta me ear. 'I mean it.'

I keep starin out the winda but I leave me hand where it is, under yours. Weakness? No. Ya got somethin up and it's not just where ya takin us. I can tell it from the buzzin that's goin on under yer skin. And I am fucked if I'm gointa let ya think ya can best me, scare me off without even showin yer hand. Ya think ya testin me now, with them light fingers a yours restin on me knuckles? Ya not. I, Lucy Dolan, am sorted. I'm the one runnin this game.

'Jesus,' says Charlie. 'The moon.'

It peers over the buildins and through the branches like a big white eye.

I'm beginnin ta sweat. The charlie is good but it's not good enough.

A test? Fuck tests. I am in control.

Trees fly past. Houses. Neat gardens. Clean roads. More trees. We are leavin what we know.

★

'Okay.' Ya uncoil from the seat, press the bell.

We stagger down after ya, jolted as the bus rounds one corner, then another. There's a gang a boozed-up noisy lads already queuin up ta get out and on the seats down the back there's a party a young wans, all long legs and high platform shoes, their faces hidden by their hair.

The bus shudders, spits us out, takes off. The gang a lads surrounds us, then splits, headin down a cul-de-sac. Ya lead us across the road, dodgin the southside Volvos. In the corner a me eye I see the bus stop again, let someone else off. Then it's gone, little red lights and foggy yella windas winkin off inta the distance.

'Hoo hoo hoo,' says Charlie, comin up, breathin in me ear. 'They're everywhere.'

Fucksake. 'Yeah, Charlie,' I say. Then, real spooky, 'Ghosties.'

'Ghosts?' He looks worried.

I push him away. 'Not ta worry, Charlie. They're friendly ones.' I look over at ya. Ya still lookin back the direction we came in. 'That right, Nayler?'

Ya turn, grin. 'Yeah. Sure. Lucy's right, Charlie. Only real pleasant ghosts round here. Here, Damo, give us me bag. Youse on?'

You on, Lucy? is what ya mean.

Then ya stride past us inta the darkness, only the gleam from the streetlights on yer sword showin us where ya are.

I'm startin ta get it.

We walk fast, followin yer pace. Seems like ages but with the charlie I can't keep track a time. Our breath puffs white in the freezin air. It's pitch black; the streetlights ran out a good while ago and the moon's nearly vanished behind a growin bank a black clouds. We've left all the houses behind and we're on a narrow road that twists uphill in hairpin bends. I never been here before but it smells awful familiar: fresh, outdoors, Christmassy, sorta.

No streetlights. Just the odd glimpse a yella from farmhouse windas in the distance, the odd weak flicker a moonlight through the clouds. It's the first time I been in the country since visitin me

Da in Portlaoise. I don't mind it. Even the noises don't bother me; the rustlins and cooins and hootins – and the other stuff Amanda keeps hearin.

'Jesus!' she says for the fifteen-millionth time. 'What was that?' She squints back at the road behind us.

'We're bein followed,' she says. 'D'ya not hear it? I swear I hear it. It's footsteps back down the road. Can ya not—?'

'Jesus, Amanda,' you say for the fifteen-millionth time. Ya sound vexed. Ya turn round and flash yer torch. 'There's nothin there, alright?'

She shakes her head and walks on.

I know what she means. I've heard the footsteps too, and once, when I looked, I seen a white shape flit under a hedge, but I'm so used ta hearin and seein things that aren't there that I keep me mouth shut.

I'm gettin it.

'Me da brung me up there once,' ya told me once. 'Frightened the life outta me. Then, when it got dark, he . . .'

Yeah. I'm gettin it.

In the dancin light a the torch I see ya reach out suddenly and pull somethin off of a hedge on the side a the road.

'Whatcha at?' says Amanda, curious. She's still pissed.

'Nothin.' Ya slide over ta her, squeeze her side. She giggles. I see me own hand there, feel the warm flesh. Me stomach churns. I stop and turn back, take a breath.

'Miaow,' says a voice right behind me.

'Fuck!' I jump.

'Jesus, Lucy. Easy!' Ya grab me waist.

'Fucksake, Nayler! Leave off!' I elbow ya in the chest, try ta wriggle free. Ya laugh, don't let go. I've forgot how strong ya are. Yer arms feel like iron round me, smotherin me.

'Ssh. Ssh. Easy, Lucy. Look.' Ya flash yer torch past me and over ta the right. A cat's archin back appears, black on a white gable. It's a paintin.

'They say that pub's haunted. There's a dwarf buried in the cellar.' Yer breath is hot as it passes me ear. 'Yer granny woulda known the story.' Yer torch dances more. Under the cat I see writin. 'Kill a Key, it's called. And see that cat? She was a woman once.'

A wind starts ta rise, pullin at me hair.

'Fucksake, Nayler. If ya believe that—'

'What was that?' says Amanda, turnin. 'I heard a—'

Ya snap the torch off.

Amanda squeals.

'Sshh,' ya whisper. 'Everyone real quiet.' Ahead of us I hear Charlie and Damo's chat melt ta nothin.

'Know where we're goin now, Lucy Lu?' ya say, real soft, in me ear.

Oh, I do. I fuckin do.

'Race ya.' Ya let me waist go, melt from me side.

Yer tread is so light I can't hear where ya've gone at first under the sounda the risin wind. Then I get a sudden feelin – *this way* – and – 'Come on, Amanda!' – I'm runnin too, no time ta think. I'm guided only by a half-seen shada, a pricklin in me shoulders, light steps. *This way, Lucy. No, here.* Behind me I can hear Charlie and Damo on the bockety road, Damo thuddin, heavy, Charlie light but clumsier, both takin it in turns ta grunt or shout as they trip or veer off inta the ditch. Behind them is Amanda, cloppin in her heels, pantin and moanin for us ta wait up, wait up.

Uphill. Twist. Turn. Right. Left. *This way, Lucy. No, here.* Where?

I stop, pantin. The wind gusts, suckin our breath away, freein up the moon so it lights up the road. I see we're on a sharp bend, an ancient wall one side with trees behind it, more trees, no wall in front, loomin up on the other. There's no sign a ya anywhere. Fuck. The moon goes again. The wind eases. Where ya gone?

Somethin snaps in the darkness, ta me right, the side without the wall.

A twig?

I turn. Take a chance. Run. The surface under me feet changes and I stumble. Gravel, mud. A path? I feel ahead with me hands,

445

take out the willa stick, swish it. The branch finds trees ta me left, but none straight ahead.

'Lucy,' says Charlie, creepin up behind me, 'I'm seein God everywhere in the blackness.'

'Yeah, yeah, Charlie.'

The wind gusts, worse than before. Then – 'Ah, for fucksake!' screams Amanda – there's a sudden crash and the rain starts, outta nowhere, big hard freezin needles drummin our heads and bodies.

There's a whoop ahead of us, thin under the drillin rain. I sprint forwards. Behind me I hear Amanda screechin, 'Jesus, can we not go inside somewhere?' and Damo bangin inta a rock and Charlie shoutin we can't go inside because we're in hell, that's where we are, but I don't give a shit for any a that. All I want is ta catch you, ya fucker. The trees sigh. Ya whoop again, changin direction. I folla, veerin ta me right so I won't lose ya, but I misjudge; me foot comes down on air, and I tumble forwards, crashin onta somethin wet that rips at me skin. Above me looms a mass a black. Trees. Fuck.

'Jesus!' yells Amanda behind me. 'I seen a fuckin rat!'

Ya scream – a weak sound ripped inta nothin by the wind.

This way. And – 'Comin, Nayler!' – I scream back, sing-song, not carin if ya can hear or not. I scrabble for the willa branch but can't find it. No time ta lose. I pull meself up outta the ditch and inta the trees and scramble uphill through the wood.

Sprint, crawl, tumble, fall. Me hands and face are numb from the cold, me knees are achin and me front is soaked, but I am *buzzin.* I fight through brambles and pine needles, low branches and rottin trunks, ditches and juttin rocks. Overhead the wind rips and the rain drums, soakin up any sound ya might be makin – branches crackin, stones fallin, water splashin. Makes no odds. I know where ya are, Nayler. Ya yell and yer yell is the wind groanin too. Ya call me name in a high voice, like a mot's, and the echo throws it way off in the wrong direction, behind us. Ya almost fool me; I'm about ta stop, turn back, check if ya been behind us all along. But then I see a glimpse a light ahead – a torch? – and I keep goin.

Charlie races past, his face shinin. 'I am a tree, Lucy. Look at me grow!'

'Me shoes is ruined,' calls Amanda, pantin. 'Lucy, wait for us, will ya?'

'It's alright, Manda,' says Damo. 'I gotcha.'

The rain begins ta ease, the wind ta calm.

I stop, search for me bearins. The light flickers again, up ahead in the distance. Not enough ta be sure, still . . . I step towards it, pushin through branches, thorns, gorse.

'Ow!'

'What's up, Lucy?' says Damo.

'Watch it, there's a rock.' I rub me shin, then feel me way round the rock that's nearly as big as meself. Willa branches pull at me too-long hair, rip at me face. I come out from the trees.

I am half-way up a hill. Black waves a countryside, dotted with a few faint lights, fall towards the city below that's blinkin amber and hazy through the thinnin rain.

I squint upwards. Far as I can make out, the ground swells to a peak. I see a light flash on and off at the top.

'Je-Jesus.' The run has sobered Amanda up. She's so outta breath she's sobbin.

I put me arm round her. 'Alright?' I mean it not just as a question.

'Lucy . . .'

'We'll be fine, Amanda. Only a bit left. We'll have a few more scoops and relax once we get ta the top and then we'll be grand.'

She doesn't look convinced but I take her arm. 'Come on.'

It's a steep enough climb and, even though the rain and the wind are easin, the ground is so loose we hafta take extra care. Our breathin is rough and broken. Nobody says anythin, not even Charlie. I suppose the acid is tellin him ta be *really quiet now*. The climb steepens, the summit comes inta view. There's a dark shape on it, stickin out against the sky, a witch's nipple on the mountain's tit. Yer torch flashes again.

Nearly there.

The slope levels. The rain drizzles its last few spits. The air's so cold the wet on me face feels like it's gointa freeze solid.

447

The moon creeps out from the last remainin clouds. The hilltop and the house on it shine grey. Me blood thumps in me ears, a horse's hooves. Go on, Starlight.

I let go Amanda's hand and walk forward. 'Ready or not, Buck Whaley!' I call, loud.

Ya laugh.

The light flashes on, straight inta me eyes, blindin me. I put me hand up.

'Ah, fucksake . . .' whimpers Amanda.

'Jesus!' says Damo.

Yer face is hangin, upside down, inside a winda.

'Number Twenty!' I call. 'The mystery card. The Hanged Fuckin Man!'

'Right as ever, Lucy!'

Ya jump down, flash the light in our eyes again.

'Welcome ta the Club,' ya say in a souped-up scary voice.

Ya madman.

The moon shines off the wet bricks a the house on the summit, makin it look like someone's taken up a brush with silver paint and scattered it all over the walls. It's like an igloo, only bigger and not as roundy. There's a gable one end, with a winda. Another winda underneath that. From the side I can see a row a windas on the top storey, and more on the bottom one as well as a coupla doors. All the windas and doors are curved at the edges, softened by time, empty a glass. They are eyes and nostrils and ears and mouth. The moon disappears again. The house on the hill breathes in. The rain stops.

Should I stay or should I go?

Too late for them type a questions. I duck me head under the blackened door and enter.

II

Inside, our shadas are boxers, duckin and curvin, Ali stingin like a bee, Sugar Ray Leonard pullin back for a hook. The ceilins are high, blackened with smoke and age. We're in a hallway a sorts. There's two stairways leadin off it: one goin upstairs, the other down ta the right.

'Here,' ya say, guidin us down the second one.

The room at the bottom is bigger again than the hallway. It's got a fireplace – a scooped-out holla in the wall, fulla old cans and fag ends and ash – and two windas. The winda on the right is chest-high and through it I see the black sky and the blacker slope a the ground. The winda on the left is higher, nearly at the roof. It's got bars and reminds me a some film I seen once about a prisoner in a dungeon. Across from the entrance is another doorway, smaller, empty like all the doorways in the gaff. Ya got a candle or somethin lit in there. I move towards it.

'Hold off, Lucy.' Ya grab me arm, pull me back. Ya sweatin from the run. Ya smell a the forest, and underneath, a sweet scent, like roses. 'Later, yeah?'

Ya get Charlie ta light the fire, tellin him he's brilliant at fire-lightin, the best in the world, and believin everythin the acid tells him, he obliges, buildin a little house a sticks and rolled-up papers and lightin it carefully, one paper edge at a time, till the whole thing is in flames.

'Lucy! Catch!' Ya throw over a bottle a stuff I haven't seen before.

'Fuck!' It's disgustin. 'Whatcha put in this, Nayler? Paint-stripper?'

'Hooch. They make it on the landins, from porridge flakes. That'll heat ya up.'

Amanda hovers round the edges a the room, pullin at her skirt, rufflin the rain outta her hair. I can tell all them small movements mean one thing – she doesn't wanta stay – but it's too late for turnin back.

'Here.' Damo pulls at her arm. She flops down on the ground beside him and looks over at me.

Lucy Dolan, this is your fault, says the look.

'Fucksake, Amanda. What?' I stare back at her.

'Nothin.' Her mouth tightens. 'Here, give me that.'

I pass her the bottle.

'Jesus!' Damo rubs his hands. 'Some chase that!'

'Yeah,' ya say, comin back in with more wood. 'Catch, Charlie!' And then ya start banterin with Damo, and Amanda joins in, tryin ta act cool, while Charlie sits back, grinnin at his fire and the steam risin from our jackets like it's his own little movie show, and as for me, I hoist meself up on the windasill and look out at the hill and the spiky forest loomin behind it, and think, What d'ya mean by *later*, Nayler?

'Okay.' Ya reach for Amanda's hand. 'The guided tour.'

She hesitates a minute before takin it but then she's yours, her fingers locked inside yer palm as she staggers to her feet.

'Here.' I jump down from the windasill. Fucked if I'm gointa be left behind like some fuckin kid that's in the way, seein as without me ya wouldn'a got any a the others ta come and, more ta the point, I'm the only one that sussed where we were goin. 'Wait for me.'

Ya look round.

'Comin, Damo?' Amanda throws a look back at Damo and bats her lashes.

Ya let go her hand.

Ya bring us out ta the hallway and up the main stairs. There's about fifteen steps leadin up and they're all soft at the edges, like everythin else in the place. Yer torch picks out corners, bends, missin stones, loose bricks. At the top a the landin is a small room, dark and low with a winda at the back. The floor is clean-lookin, like someone's just swept it.

450

I get a bad feelin there. Real bad. Funny, the whole place is rottin, fallin apart, spooky as fuck out in the middle a nowhere, but this is the first time it hits me.

'Alright, Lucy?'

I don't say anythin. I can see faces in the bricks at the back, cryin faces and long wet hair, and the smell a blood is in me nose and I just wanta go.

'Alright?' ya ask again.

Is this what ya mean by *real*, Nayler? I nearly say. Is this the stuff old Buck Whaley got upta in his club with his gang; blood and cryin and hurtin, stuff me Granny would never a dreamt a tellin us? Is that why ya like him so much? Only I feel his ghost behind me now, auld Buck, breathin on me neck, his breath smellin a wine and oranges and the heat of his brown skin, and I don't wanta think anythin more in case he hears, let alone say it, so I laugh, like it's all okay, because what is he, only an auld wan's fairytale, and what have I ta be scared of in anyways, me that's seen all I've seen?

'Course I fuckin am, Nayler.'

It's better on the next floor. There's two more rooms there, wide and long but lower than the ones downstairs. One looks out towards the tiny yella necklace that's the city. The other gives a view a blackness.

'Wickla,' ya say. 'Loadsa forests there.'

'Gorgeous,' says Amanda. 'Real fairytale.'

Fairytale! laughs Buck, nudgin inta me.

'Where's me can?' says Damo, soundin a bit bleary. 'Had it here a minute ago.'

'Ya gave it me,' says Amanda. 'D'ya not remember?'

'Where?' Damo's cut-out shada in fronta the winda bends and Amanda squeals.

'Get away from me, ya dirty bastard!'

She backs off towards the door, movin slow so he'll catch up, then speedin up again just as he's about ta grab her. He lunges. Squealin, she races down the stairs and he follas.

Ya lean against the doorway. I walk over ta the winda that looks out onta Wickla and breathe in the air from outside. It's freezin but nice, sorta.

Behind me I can feel ya, calmin down after all the hoo-ha, and I realize that for the first time that day nearly, I feel calm too. It's not just on the surface; it's like I'm not buzzed up on the charlie any more, not itchin ta be anywhere but where I am, and I wonder if that's what you're feelin too, and if ya are, if it's just the change a location that's eased us.

We stay a while, not sayin anythin, just breathin in the fresh air and lookin out at the unseen view a the Wickla mountains.

At last ya speak. 'Ya . . .' Ya pause. 'Ya wanta stay here all night, Lucy?' Ya nearly sound like ya askin for real, not just hintin ta go back down.

'No. No, ya grand. I'm comin in a sec.' I turn around. But ya right. I don't wanta leave. I don't wanta go back down, past the little room on the stairs where the bad things happened, and risk pickin up his ghost again.

Go now, says a voice in me head. Get the fuck out now.

'So when did ya guess?' ya ask on the stairs. Below us I hear Amanda squealin, no doubt on accounta Damo again.

'Guess?' I laugh. 'Jesus, Nayler. Ages. You've always been so fuckin obvious.'

'Obvious, Lucy?' Ya give me a sideways look.

'Yeah, with yer –' I stop. He's waitin for me ta say his name. Ah, cop on, Lucy. He's only a figment, some stupid mixed-up vision that I'm havin on accounta the charlie, so say it, go on, just say it, '– yer Buck Whaley this and yer Buck Whaley that.'

Ya smile. 'So whatcha make of it? How's it live up ta yer granny's stories?'

'Alright, I suppose. Bit dirty.'

'It wasn't his gaff, Lucy, ya know.'

We're passin the dark room. I speed up.

'Oh yeah?' I say, meanin *I don't give a shit*.

'Nor did he win it off of the Devil like yer granny said. A pal of his da built it, for the huntin. They say he made it outta a cairn. That's a pile a rocks. The Celts woulda used them ta mark an altar or a burial ground, yeah?'

'Ah, yeah.'

'It was Buck's da started off the Club, later on. There was loadsa them all over England back then. They done things, brung people there—'

'I know. Here.' Enough a this shite. 'Give me more a that hooch.'

Ya wipe the mouth a the bottle with the edge a yer shirt and hand it over.

'Sure ya can handle it, Lucy?' Ya got a soft mockin smile on yer mouth but I can't see if it's reachin yer eyes.

'This?' I take the bottle. 'Yeah. Course I can.' I swig.

The hooch burns, buzzes, hazes.

'Who Whaley what?' says Amanda, gigglin over at Charlie while Damo feels her leg.

'Jerusalem.' Charlie's eyes are as wide as saucers. 'He was a mad Englishman and our granny was in love with him.'

'Fucksake, Charlie, ya muppet. Ya mixin him up with our grandda.'

'Oh.' Charlie looks confused. He starts countin somethin on his fingers.

I feel safer now that we're beside the fire. 'He's Nayler's hero, Amanda. D'ya not remember? That sword he's carryin tonight that he useta put up on his wall? That was Buck's, so Nayler says.'

'Oh, yeah,' says Amanda.

'Oh, yeah,' says Charlie, copyin Amanda's voice and starin at her like she's just found the Holy Grail.

'He brung people up here, Nayler says. *Done* things.'

Maybe it's the lasta the charlie still actin on me, or the hooch, or that vision on the stairs that's rattled me, but I'm feelin reckless now. Who are *you* ta ask me if I can handle it, ya pathetic loser cunt so down on yer luck ya need ta haul a gang a kids upta some dump in the mountains on fuckin Hallowe'en for no good reason, only ta make ya feel good about yerself one last time before ya

453

fuckin leg it ta wherever ya goin? In anyways, after all yer talk, ya not actin like ya got somethin special for me outside of a dirty gaff and manky hooch and one poxy line a coke, so what's there ta lose in vexin ya?

'All spooky wooky things. That right, pal?'

Ya lean against the door and say nothin. The slow angle a the lean tells me I should shut up now, if I know what's good for me, but ya can fuck off. Think I'm scared a ya? Grow up.

'Devil-worshippin and all they done here. If ya believe in that kinda thing. Nayler does, ya know. Loves all that stuff. The spells and the magic. Hundreds a books about it, he has. Helps him make sense a things. That's why he loves the fortunes. They give him *meanin*, ya know. Useta go ta me Ma for them, Amanda, didja know that? Just like a little auld wan. Went there a lot, specially when he was feelin lonely. Very kind she was ta him. Like his own Ma. Useta treat him *real* good.'

I stretch out the real, lettin what I'm not sayin hang between the sounds. Amanda glances up, worried.

'Ya gettin restless, Lucy?' ya say from the doorway.

'No.' I take another swig a the hooch.

'Lucy gets terrible restless.' Ya say it like I'm not there. 'It's a problem she has. An affliction, winds her up, makes her think she can do anythin. Makes her think she's brave when she's not. She's had it since she was a kid, ya know. She can't keep still even when she's supposed ta. Gets very distracted lookin for her kicks. Makes her very loud too so she can't shut her mouth. Sometimes, man . . .' ya shoot a glance over at me, '. . . the stuff she comes out with. Takes a lot ta keep her quiet. Though from the way she goes on at times ya'd think she'd do anythin ta calm down. That right, Lucy?'

Ya cunt. I jut out me chin. 'Sometimes, yeah. But Jesus, everyone here knows that.'

I can feel them all starin at me.

'Times, though, I can be very quiet, Nayler. Don't let a word out a things I know or seen.'

I think a Sasha, sittin in that café with Emmet Whelan. I think a Micko. I think a that chain a mine ya wearin under yer shirt.

'In fact, I'm nearly as good at hidin things as you, pal.'

Ya look over. *Yeah?* says yer eyes.

I say nothin.

Ya shrug. 'Yeah, well. This isn't one a them times, though, is it, Lucy? Right now I wouldn't say ya quiet at all. Right now ya gettin very loud.'

'Loud? Me? Fuck no, Nayler. If I was loud you'd hear me singin all the way ta . . . except . . . sorry.' I make a face for the benefit a the others. 'He wouldn't, would he? Hear me singin? Because auld Nayler can't hear a tune even if someone's beltin it down his fuckin ear.'

Ya raise an eyebrow. 'Jesus, Lucy. Sounds like ya need some calmin right now. Here, give us yer lighter.'

Me heart starts poundin. 'Why?' Ya not gointa bring it out now, in fronta everyone?

'What's this, the third degree?' Ya click yer fingers. 'Come on. I need a fag.'

I throw it over, sick for some reason ta me stomach. But I am not sick. I am better. All better.

We sit at opposite ends a the room. I watch ya banter with Damo and flirt with Amanda, and when she gets up ta walk over ta me, I watch ya whisper things in Charlie's ear and his face light up like he's seein all the mysteries in the world come together.

Amanda's messy again with drink and she's tellin me she thinks I'm doin great, holdin off like this, she wouldn'a thought I'd be able ta handle it – that fuckin *handle it* again – but it's alright here, isn't it, almost like the old days? And she's really glad she came after all, she's been havin fun, and she knows I need her there, and she knows I know she . . . loves me, really she does, I'm her best pal, she'd never let me down . . . and she looks down at her hands at that and clears her throat and looks up again and tells me: Okay, she *was* worried a bit, when we started on like that, me and you, because she hadn't heard us snappin at each other like that, ever, and with your . . . ya know . . . moods and my temper she was worried, but it's fine now, isn't it? All over in a flash, and in anyways it shows how much I've grown up, that I don't swalla everythin ya say . . . and while she's talkin I'm pullin meself back from sayin: Holdin off, Amanda? There's nothin ta hold off from, sweetheart, he hasn't got any gear ta even tempt me so don't be fooled, darlin, I'm not doin any magic, I'm just danglin, a fish on a hook . . . and while she's talkin and I'm pullin back, I'm half-glancin over at ya, and ya lookin at me, and there's this sorta amused look on yer face, like ya can hear everythin she's sayin and everythin I'm not, and somethin darker and more considerin, and at times ya even seem ta be gettin twitchy again, and that makes me feel restless too, and as we look at each other across that space I'm itchin ta tell ya ta fuck off, Nayler, for all that, sayin I'm not brave, but at the same time not, just in case, when –

'Jesus, d'ya hear that?' Amanda jumps.

We all strain our ears. A second later, there's a crash from upstairs, like somethin landin on the floor, and we all jump, even you.

Amanda staggers ta her feet, pullin on her coat. 'I'm goin. I swear I am. Come on, Lucy. This is way outta order.'

'Ah, Jesus, Amanda, cop on. It's alright. It's only a . . .' I pat the ground beside me, look over at you ta see if you can sort her out, but fuck me if ya not standin starin up at the ceilin lookin worried too. Jesus. Am I the only one? –

'Lookit, Amanda, don't be gettin inta a state. There's no ghosties here.'

'Jesus, scarlet! I didn't say there was, Lucy.' But she's upset now, wellin up.

'Fucksake, Amanda!'

'She's right, Lucy,' says Charlie, lookin round behind him. 'I can feel somethin too.'

Damo nods. 'Yeah.'

'Yeah,' says Charlie. 'Like a monster or a . . . a zombie. Musta come in through an upstairs winda. Nayler was sayin—'

'Charlie, shut *up*! Amanda lookit, it's fine. It's only a—'

Then there's a scrabblin sound, like little feet runnin over our heads.

'Some monster,' ya say, real dry.

And that's all it takes.

We all crack up laughin, even Amanda.

After we've settled back and we're chattin about this and that, loud and laughin and mellowed on the hooch, Damo tells us a story about this lad in the Dominick Street flats: '. . . and his Ma had a baby for some other fella than the lad's da when the lad was goin on fifteen. But the baby died in the cot and the Ma was in bits, and the lad always felt, ya know . . . sorta jealous. In anyways, he hears this bawlin one night from the room next door and he goes in ta see but there's no baby there.'

'And?' I say, meanin *Go on*.

'And that's it,' says Damo.

'Ooh, that's scary,' says Amanda, slurpin back more gargle.

I look at ya. Ya tryin ta look serious but I can tell ya pissin yerself.

'That's crap,' I say.

'Yeah,' ya agree. 'Dyin babies. Not very cosy-makin, is it, Amanda darlin?'

Ya bastard. Amanda starts ta look puzzled and so does Charlie, and then Amanda's face starts ta darken and she looks over at me, real vexed, but I get in there, headin it off before it gets nasty. 'Damo, ya shouldn'a fucked up the punchline like that.'

'Don't blame me. I didn't make it up. Happened ta one a Andy Kav's pals.'

'Alright,' I say, 'who's for the next story. Amanda?'

She shrugs. 'I don't know any.'

Ya touch her knee. 'It's easy. Just make one up. Go on.'

'I can't.' She lights another fag. 'You tell us one, Neil.'

'No,' I say despite meself.

'Why not?' Ya got yer innocent face on all of a sudden. 'Ya not scared a ghosties, are ya, Lucy?'

Behind me faces come outta the bricks again, cryin faces with long wet hair.

'Fuck, no. Go on, so.' I get up and walk over ta the winda.

'Okay, kids. My story is about how the magnificent HellFire Club got its name.' Ya say it with a dry voice, like ya couldn't think of anywhere less magnificent in ya life, and I'm surprised at that because I never thought you'd take the piss outta stuff that meant somethin ta ya, so I turn around ta see whatcha gettin at. But yer face is as dry as yer voice, hidden way back behind yer eyes.

'Well, one night Buck brung some people up here –' ya flick a glance over at me '– ta have a party, just like us. Knock back some gargle, tell tales, get up ta all sorts. There was girls there, a course,' ya cast a sly look at Amanda, 'all gorgeous-lookin. And helpin out with the drinks was Buck Whaley's favourite servant, an old geezer called . . . Manfred.'

Everyone laughs, includin me – even though somethin's botherin me and I don't know why.

'Now, the reason Manfred was Buck's favourite was because—'

'He'd won him off of the Devil,' I say, makin it sound real obvious.

Ya raise the hooch. 'Cheers, Lucy. Nah. Auld wives' tales. Manfred been in the family for years. He was a good lad, very efficient, woulda done anythin for Buck, no questions asked, but as the years went by, well, he started ta fall apart, didn't he. The legs went first, then the eyes, then he twisted his back when Buck's mare went on the rampage. He stayed on top of it best he could, kept his head, and for a while he fooled Buck he was still up for the game. But by the time the party came along even Buck hadta admit the cunt was a write-off. Pure raspberry ripple. Knockin inta things, fallin down, spillin wine all over the ladies' dresses.'

Ya pretend ta spill some hooch on Amanda. She squeals and the lads laugh harder. What is it? What's not right?

'Now, Buck had always had a lotta respect for Manfred, but Jesus, this was embarrassin, and when the auld bollocks dropped the brandy bottle inta the fire it was the final straw. There was the fine lords and ladies pissin themselves laughin, and Buck feelin like a real dick, and all Manfred could do was say sorry, sorry.'

They laugh even harder at the gormless look on yer face.

'"I say, Sir Thomas," says one a Buck's pals –' and yer voice is pure English now, like off the telly '"– are you intending to keep this buffoon on?" "Well," says Buck, thinkin fast, "Maybe . . . but only if he entertains us!" Then he grabs a candle and fecks it over at Manfred's wig. Manfred's not that thick, tries not ta panic, worst thing ya could do in a situation like that, right, Charlie? but all a Buck's friends join in on the act, start pushin him round the room, whackin him inta the furniture, and all the time his wig's blazin higher and higher. "Good lord," says Buck's pal, "look at what the idiot is doing! He's set the tables on fire!" The lords and ladies are breakin their holes laughin, but when the stupid bastard sets the chairs alight, and then the carpets and then the tapestries – that's carpets on the wall, Amanda – the laughs turn ta screams, and soon everyone's panickin and the whole place is blazin.' Ya pause. 'The locals say they screamed for hours.'

'Ah, Jesus,' says Amanda. 'That's horrible.'

Ya lift a hand. 'That's not all. The next day when the constabu-lary – that's yer pals the pigs, Lucy – when they went searchin in the ashes, the only thing they found was a wig, with not a hair on it burnt, and a single set a hoof-prints leadin off inta the forest. Ta this day they say them hooves belong ta Buck's horse and he was the only one got away. But I think it was Manfred ridin that mare.'

Ya stop.

I got what's been botherin me. Not just because one minute ya sayin there's HellFire Clubs all over England and the next gabbin on about some stupid fire. It's because ya never talk like this, tellin long stories in fronta people. The only time I've ever heard ya like that is either one ta one or when ya goofin, and it's neither a that now.

There's a silence. Then everyone claps except me. Ya flick a fag butt at me.

'D'ya not like it, Lucy?'

I say nothin.

'Funny. Ya were always a great one for the stories.'

Waffle seeps inta cracked walls.

Ya bollocks. I know yer game. Ya tryin ta get a rise outta me.

I light up, real cas. 'Nah. The only stories I know are the usual ones, Nayler. Youse'll have heard them before.'

'Yeah?'

'Yeah. People dyin and gettin hurt and . . .'

'Ah, no,' says Amanda. 'Let's not—'

Ya take a drag, real cas too. 'Oh, sad stories, is it, Lucy? But ya know there's a lot worse things than dyin. And people don't get hurt without good reason.'

'So you've always said, Nayler. Rules a the game.'

'Shit happens, Lucy.' Yer voice sharpens. 'Ya need rules ta keep it clean. People mess with stuff they shouldn't. People get hurt. That's how it goes. Can't run away from it. Thought you of anyone would know that.'

'Shit happens? Jesus, Nayler, ya sound just like Granny, with her fate this and destiny that.'

'Fuck yer Granny and her fuckin destiny. I'm just tellin ya how things work.'

'Price for everythin, Nayler? Sacrifices, all that?'

Ya stop, surprised. Then laugh, real disbelievin, like I'm the thickest person ya met in yer life. 'Ah, fuck off, Lucy. You don't even know what a sacrifice is.'

'Oh, I do, Nayler. I know plenty—'

'Yeah. What then?'

I look at the others. Damo's gone green, swallowin like he's afraid a pukin. Charlie's listenin, eager, but on the acid he'd be eager no matter what we were talkin about. Amanda's lookin worried but she's still pissed as a fart.

I could do it now. I could tell ya what I've kept so quiet; the stuff I know on ya, about Mainser and Cindy Devlin and me brother and that gold tooth I found in the basement beside the vision a the dead man, and the Soldier I think that dead man was. And I could ask ya ta confirm what ya done ta them, you and Snags, but specially you; and if I played a part in any of it, through wafflin stories or by leavin a door open one summer afternoon – or is that just fears talkin? Then I could ask if that's what a sacrifice is ta you, Nayler – hurtin people; not just because they deserve it, but because anytime ya spill their blood ya get something back. Money, power, silence; for you, the business, Snags. Doesn't matter long as there's a pay-off. Then I could ask, if ya so sure all that hurtin is stuff ya can't run away from, nor none a them people, nor me neither, then why the fuck do ya need yer poxy so-called magic for guidance? And finally I could ask what really matters; why ya brung me out here tonight, and if that's somethin I can't run away from, or if there is some choosin in it after all, for me and you both.

Oh, yes. I coulda asked all that and got clear, and then I coulda walked out and that woulda been the enda that.

But that was just what ya wanted, wasn't it? Ya wanted me ta rise ta yer bait, ta spill me secrets. But who says you'da spilt yours in turn? And even if ya had, would that a made anythin better? I'd got by up till then, not knowin. Besides, I didn't want us speakin like that, open and all for the first time, in fronta everyone else.

So I leave the questions unasked and – 'Nothin, Nayler' – laugh like I really do mean it. 'Jesus. If I'd known we were gointa fuck around tellin fairytales and havin deep chats about bollocks I wouldn'a come. Thought we were gointa do somethin real.'

I didn't mean ta say it. Honest.

'Real?' Ya smile.

Mis-take.

'Ya right as ever, Lucy Lu. This storytellin is shite.' Ya kick Damo in the side, wakin him. 'Hey, playtime.'

When ya stuck yer hand in yer pocket, I thought ya were takin it out then, and I hated meself for wantin, and hated meself even more for feelin so bad when I saw it wasn't it after all, only yer gammy pack a cards.

'Who's for poker?'

I swear the air went cold then. I felt it and it was tellin me ta go and I coulda. Even then I coulda gone and it woulda been okay. I coulda taken Amanda and Charlie, and left Damo ta fuck around talkin shite with ya. Because that cold air told me ya'd somethin up yer sleeve, somethin ya'd been plannin all night maybe, and by doin and sayin all I done I'd brung you and me both closer ta where ya wanted us ta be.

But I didn't leave. Why should I when there was nothin happenin I couldn't handle?

As ya shuffle, pullin out the Major Arcana but leavin in the four Pages as wild cards – except they're poxy Princesses in your deck – ya give us directions. Sit there, Lucy, ya say, furthest from the fire. And Damo – over there. Charlie, Charlie, Charlie – tryin ta pull him away from the pretty flames – you here. And Amanda, sweetheart, you here, facin me. And then, before we know it, we're sittin in a circle – me, Damo, Amanda, Charlie and you.

No. Not a circle. Five points of a star. I shrug off the cold feelin that's got colder. Spooky bollocks.

Amanda laughs. 'Jesus, I never played poker before. Help me out, willyiz?'

Ya deal. I look at me cards. A King, a Knight, and a Ten, all Cups, plus two Queens: Coins and Swords.

'What'll we play for?' I say.

There's a silence.

'Blood,' says Charlie in a deep voice.

'Jesus, Charlie!' says Amanda.

'Christ, no,' ya say. Ya pull out a Mars Bar a hash from ya pocket. 'Somethin a bit easier.' Ya cut the hash in ten and place each bit beside yer hand a cards. 'Alright?'

It's very easy ta distract yerself. Take it from the expert.

We start off the pot by puttin a coupla quid in each but when it comes ta the bets, Amanda and Damo run outta cash before the rest of us, so she sticks in her Rimmel Purple Haze lip gloss and Damo puts in a coupla cans. Charlie wins the first two rounds, though how he can do that and still be off his face I don't know.

Round three starts good. I get two Fours, two Eights and a Queen. We do swapsies. I get another Four for the Queen. Very nice. We bet. Everyone's in but it's harder this time on accounta it's not just Amanda and Damo bein outta stuff but me too, and now I'm the one that wants ta raise.

'Ya could put in that jacket,' says Amanda. 'I mean, it's a fella's anyway . . .'

'No.' I wrap me arms round me chest. Try ta ignore yer mockin smile. 'Lookit, I'll stick in a bike I'll rob next week off Trinity College.'

'But how—'

'Here.' Charlie takes out a notebook and tears out a sheet a paper. Then he writes down the IOU for me and sticks it in the pot.

'Alright.' Damo frowns and belches, loud. 'I'll put in twenty quid from me da's till.'

'Ah, no.' Charlie taps his pen against his teeth. His voice is gone real cold, like them numbers are leakin outta his head and addin themselves up right in front of his eyes, and in that moment I see how he's been winnin. He's not just playin the game. In his mind, he *is* the game. 'You'll want more than twenty, Damo. Ya know how much them mountain bikes are worth.'

'Okay,' says Damo, too sick ta fight back. 'Seventy quid then.'

Charlie sticks in Damo's IOU and you put in the five remainin bits a yer Mars Bar.

'I don't have anythin,' says Amanda.

'Think a somethin you can rob,' I say.

'Yer ma's weddin ring,' says Charlie. 'That'd do it. Here we go,' and writes an IOU for her too. Then he sticks in everythin he won in the last round for himself. He looks chuffed.

'So who's gointa raise then?' I look at ya. 'Fuckin . . . Manfred here? Or would that be too much of a fuckin sacrifice?'

Ya stare at me. The others laugh, Charlie the loudest.

Then ya smile one a them smiles that doesn't reach yer eyes and ya take somethin outta yer jeans pocket.

It's a – is it?

'What's that?' says Amanda.

Three things.

One. Yes! I knew it. I fuckin knew it.

Two. It's charlie. That's all it is. Cop on. It doesn't do ta mix, ya said. Charlie wrapped up so it looks like a Q.

Three. Ya dirty usin cunt, Nayler, tryin ta rope me in again. Go, Lucy. If you've any sense, *go*.

And thumpin in time with me heart are Buck Whaley's footsteps as he makes his way down them creepy stairs.

'It's gear,' says Charlie ta Amanda, like he's talkin ta a kid. 'That's what they put it in. A cellophane wrap and then the corner of a plastic bag. It's called a Q cos it looks like one. Have ya not seen one before?'

'It's not, it's coke,' I say, or maybe I only think I hear meself say it because you're in then, smooth –

'Very good, Charlie. Well spotted.'

Amanda starts – 'Ah, no. Lucy?' Then she panics, starts breathin real harsh.

Me vision is got awful small. All I can see is me cards and that Q burnin red inta the edges a me eyes.

'Meet ya, Nayler.' Charlie sounds like he's a long way away. 'I'll stick in . . . what is it, a twenty?'

'Forty ta some, Charlie, priceless ta others.'

'How about I split the difference? I'll stick in me da's credit card.'

There's a scribblin as he writes another IOU.

Damo groans. 'What happens if ya don't wanta bet any more, Nayler?'

'Ya fold.'

'Alright. I'll do that.' There's a slap as he lays his cards down. 'Unnh, Jesus—'

'I'm not bettin,' says Amanda. I don't look up. 'I don't want that shit and neither does Lucy—'

'Fucksake, don't show yer cards, Amanda!' says Charlie.

'Ya can't call for someone else, Amanda,' ya say. You're calm. So calm.

'You'll lose yer ma's weddin ring,' says Charlie.

'I don't care. I don't want any of it. Lucy—'

'Leave it, Amanda,' ya say. 'Let her make her own mind up.'

Me hand is good. Very good. A full house. Okay, it's only low cards, Fours and Eights, but still . . .

Hunger swells and aches, the curve a music on the radio, the high-ta-low flow of a boxer's winnin jab.

Just Say No.

In anyways, ya could still be messin me round. It could just be charlie for all I know.

In the small moments are choices made.

'I'll meet ya, Nayler.' I look up, ignorin Amanda's stare. 'I'll stick in a favour.' I keep me voice relaxed as I can. 'Next job ya doin, I'll come on board, scot-free. No expenses, no shares, no nothin. I'm all yours.'

Yer eyes stay hidden.

'Sounds fair,' says Charlie. Then he stops scribblin. 'What if I win, though?'

'I'll do whatever you want, Charlie.'

We lay the cards down. You have two Kings – Coins and Cups. Charlie's got nothin, a shite hand: Two a Swords, Three a Wands, Knight a Swords, Five a Coins, King a Cups.

Ya push the pot over ta me.

'Jesus, Lucy—' says Amanda.

I pick up the Q. Me hands are shakin.

So small it is, in the palm a me hand. Inside the ache growls, grows, owns me. I'm sweatin. I wipe me hands and open the plastic, unfold the wrap.

The powder's brown.

Somethin inside a me lets go. I remember. Jesus, I remember. Heaven in a white room.

Now now now now now now now

I feel in me pockets.

'Lucy, remember what—'

'Sshh, Amanda, darlin. Ya lookin for this, Lucy?' I look over. In yer hand ya holdin yer works.

I hesitate. How long's it been? Two month? More? If I bang up now after bein clean so long, I could OD. Not if I only use a bit, though. If I—

'Please, Neil, leave her be. Lucy—'

Ya open yer other hand. There's two bits a foil there, gleamin. 'Lucy—'

Yeah. Safer ta smoke it. I reach for the foil.

Ya close yer hand and smile. 'Sorry.'

It takes me a second ta cop on. Then – 'What? Give us the fuckin thing, Nayler.'

'Sorry, Lucy. Can't just give it away.' Ya stick the works and yer foil in ya pocket. Ya tap the cards, start shufflin.

Ya fucker. A price for everythin. Ya want me ta play for it.

It dawns and I sit there like a moron, starin at ya, flickin through the options in me mind. I could snort it. Yeah, that's what I could do. It'd be safer in anyways, safer even than smokin. Yeah, I could roll up a note or one a them cards even, and then I wouldn't hafta –

'Jesus, Lucy, let's go.' Amanda pulls at me. 'Give that filth back ta him. Come on!'

Or I could use tomorra, I could bring it home with me and not touch it. I could.

Ya cut the deck. 'D'ya not wanta play any more, Lucy? This not real enough for ya?'

'Lucy, come on, don't fuckin listen ta him, come—'

Wait. That's the cleverest thing ta do. Or snort it, right now. Don't play, don't –

'Thought ya said ya could handle it, Lucy.'

'Fuck off, Amanda.' I shake her off. 'Sure, Nayler. I'm in.'

'Ah Jesus!' Amanda starts ta cry. 'I've had enough a this—'

She stands up but ya say 'Charlie' real soft, and, bang on cue, Charlie yanks her back onta the ground with a thump. She starts blubbin, slumpin against him like a sick kid. I think I hate her right now, though I don't know why, but it doesn't matter; nothin matters now except the game.

Ya smile at me, calm. Oh so calm on the surface.

But beneath the calm that twitchin is up full force, stronger than earlier on, stronger even than the very first time ya offered me the gear, and even though I'm sure you've set all this up, even though I can hear the warnin bells goin, tellin me I should get out now, I know there's a fight goin on under that angel-white chalky skin a yours, and I am fucked if I am gointa leave without callin yer bluff.

Ya deal. I pick up. Two, Three, Five, Seven a Wands. King a Swords.

Ya throw down two. I throw down the King and the Two. Ya pick up. I pick up. Four a Wands, Princess a Swords. Wild card. Fuckin A. Straight flush. Nearly there. Me heart starts poundin but I keep me face straight. Do not fuck this one up.

'Okay.' Ya put the works and the foil inta the pot. I put in the stuff I got off Charlie in the last round.

'That's not enough. Right, Charlie?'

'Right. See, it's value, Lucy – forty ta some and priceless ta others – ya gotta match—'

'Shut up.' I add everythin else I won in the last round except the Q.

Ya shake yer head. 'Nah.'

'Jesus, fuck off, Nayler.'

'It doesn't match up. Sure it doesn't, Charlie?'

'Yeah. Nayler's right. Ya need ta balance it out, Lucy.'

'Fucksake—'

I'm on a winner. I've got a straight flush and next ta nothin can beat that. Stay calm. Do not fuck up.

I stick in the Q, hatin the feel of it leavin me hand.

'Nice one,' ya say. 'I'll raise ya.' Then ya dig in yer pocket and pull out another Q.

I can't believe this. Ya can't be doin better than me. Only a royal flush or fives and the chances a that are few. Ya could be winnin, though. There's the other Pages or Princesses or whatever they are, three a them, wild cards and . . . No. Fuck, I'm too close now. I'm fucked if I'm walkin away without gettin what I came for.

I do me best ta close down me face and yawn like I'm bored. Takes an effort. 'Okay. I'll rob ya anythin ya want, Nayler. Write it down, Charlie.'

Ya shake yer head again. 'I don't think so, Charlie. Stakes still don't match.'

Charlie stops, puzzled.

'This one's a eighty. Well . . . ta some. Meanin it's even more priceless ta others. I wouldn't say Lucy's an eighty. What would you say, Charlie?'

Charlie stares at me.

'Jesus fuckin Christ, Nayler! It's only a coupla fixes. What the fuck d'ya expect me ta stick in?'

And then I get it – or so I think – whatcha been settin me up for. Fool I am, thinkin ya'd wiped it under the carpet, what I seen opened up in ya that day ya found me souvenirs. Ya been savin it up, haven't ya? Ya want ta punish me. Ya want me head on a plate.

The air freezes. Flames flicker. Wood cracks. Damo moans in the corner. Upstairs, the rat scurries along the floor. And across the room, in the doorway leadin ta the little room where the candles are, stands yer hero, fannin himself with his hand a cards.

'Okay.' I laugh but it's a holla sound, even ta me.

'Okay what?' ya say.

I look at ya. 'So this is what yer hero done, Nayler, when he brung people up here?' I'm guessin here. Anythin ta buy time, ta see if you'll let that mask slip so I can see if I'm right in thinkin what ya really want from me.

Ya say nothin. Behind ya the faces in the bricks moan and cry.

Me back is freezin but I force meself not ta shiver. 'Oh, yeah, fuck games with the Devil when auld Buck had real people ta play with. Because let's not forget, he was a real man with a real sword.' I look at the manky hilt stickin outta yer belt. 'Only he liked ta have a bit a fun, didn't he, before he brung out the blade.'

Amanda stops cryin. 'Lucy, what . . . ?'

'I don't know whatcha on about, Lucy.' Ya look straight through me, like I'm thick. Like I'm not there, like I could be anyone; most of all big-eared, nine-year-old Spocky Halloran cryin in a heap on the ground while ya taunt him with yer brand-new knife.

'Did auld Buck just give them a warnin with the sword, Nayler? Or did he . . . eh . . . what's that word . . . incapacitate them?'

Ya say nothin.

'Did they do stuff on him, Nayler, them people he brung up here? They musta if he hurt them like that. Because nobody gets hurt without a reason. So ya say.'

Ya shrug, like I'm way off the point. But yer fingers have started creepin up yer shirt towards that chain that useta be mine.

For a minute I wish I'd brung the gun after all. I'm sweatin bad. I stare at the chain, at the hard tips a yer fingers pullin at the links, at the sharp bones in yer wrist between the barb-wire tattoo, and I remember that sick hatin black look ya scorched me with the day ya found what I been hidin. 'So what was the reason? Did them people mess with his head, Nayler? Did they find stuff out about him? Little . . . secrets? Things that meant somethin? Did they keep them from him? Is that why he got them ta play?'

'Ya don't hafta keep playin, Lucy.' Yer voice is calm. 'Ya can back out any time. I'll respect ya if ya fold.'

Liar.

It's only a Q. I can get a Q anywhere, anytime. I don't need it now.

Liar. Two Qs and one's an eighty, and if I walk away I'll have lost the one I won. A forty and an eighty and it could be pure, and I could have it now, soon.

I shoulda fuckin snorted when I had the chance. Thick cunt I am.

In the doorway he laughs. The women's faces are outta the bricks now, slidin along the ground towards me.

'Well, Lucy?' D'ya want me ta back down? Ya starin through me and I can see the will holdin yer face hidden, but yer fingers are twistin round that silver chain, only now I can see there's other stuff on it that I didn't put there – a lock a dark brown hair coiled inta a figure a eight and a piece a gold, bashed, sorta, with a black square in the middle.

Damo's still moanin. Amanda and Charlie are silent. Three onlookers, on three points a yer magic star. Why all the hoo-ha,

Nayler; why d'ya agree ta let me bring them along if ya wanted ta punish me, you that does most a yer hurtin in secret, in the dark?

I reach across and touch the lock a hair. It's warm, alive-feelin. Yer skin goosepimples under me touch. Yer fingers tense.

Ya cunt. Think ya can frighten me like ya frighten everyone else, with yer trophies and yer skulls and yer killer's eyes? Think ya can lower me inta a snivellin cryin heap a shit beggin ta be saved? Think ya so fuckin powerful, pal, with Buck and the Devil on yer side ya can win every game we play? Ya fuckin . . . kid.

I let go the chain. 'Okay.' It's funny but now I don't need ta work ta keep me voice calm. 'Reckon I'll take me chances, Nayler. Charlie?'

Charlie looks up.

'Write an IOU ta Nayler for me life, for him ta take however he wants.' I say it light like it means nothin.

Dare ya.

Amanda makes a whimperin sound, but Charlie has his hand on her mouth, shushin her before she can get the scream out.

We look at each other, you and me, and I swear in that moment I keep me face as poker-straight as yours has ever been.

We turn up.

My straight flush to your four Aces and a black figure on a red ground – is it a girl or a fella? – holdin a sword.

'Jesus, no, Lucy!' screams Amanda. 'It's a wild card! Ah, Jesus! Ah, fuckin no!'

Ya round on her, snarlin, raise yer hand. 'Jesus, shut up, ya stupid little bitch! Ya don't even know the rules.'

She cowers back. Charlie jumps up, fist out ta punch ya, but ya jerk yer foot, sendin him reelin back and onta the ground. Behind us, Damo pukes, sprayin chunks inta the fire.

On yer card, the figure with the sword sharpens inta focus. Some muscles it has. That's no fuckin Princess. That's a fella. Hard ta tell at first without the white horse but yeah, it's the card I've always known was yours. Knight a Swords. I'd laugh at the joke only I can't. A bluff.

Yer face is frozen.

'Tough shit.' I scoop up the pot. 'Ya won't get this one after all, Nayler. Amanda –' I fling over the IOU '– keep yer ma's weddin ring. Don't think I'll have much use for it.'

I look at ya. I'm smilin, broad, like it's all been a big gag, but at the same time I'm searchin ya, tryin ta see if ya'd meant it, if ya woulda gone through with it, killed or hurt me for – fucksake, Nayler, for what? For pryin and stealin? For darin ta think I'd the right ta know what was goin on in yer head? For knowin more than I should about the business? Or just for bein a . . . problem? Some fucked-up little boy-chested plain runty gee-less imaginary-lezzer outta-control hindrance of a street junkie that was always more trouble than she was worth?

But ya still hidin from me, and that makes me feel sick and disappointed, and even the Qs in me hand feel like nothin, and I'm angry at meself for feelin this way because I shouldn't; I should be up on cloud nine, I've took ya on without needin ta, I've beat ya at yer own poxy game, I've won and –

Everythin stops. A sick emptiness.

Somethin shifts in yer face. The curtains lift.

And then there's nothin in yer eyes but pure gladness, alive and laughin, and somethin else I've never seen in ya before, and the shock a that cuts through me like a torch. Ya jump up, reach out, only I'm up too, a split second later, fist liftin, ready for the mill. Ya lunge in, seize the back a me head. I jerk away, thinkin *Don't ya dare laugh at me ya cunt*, but ya hold fast, grabbin me fist, twistin it down and behind ya so me arm is trapped round yer waist. Ya try ta pull me closer. I reef yer hair with me free hand, tuggin it outta the scalp nearly as I try and push ya away, but ya fight back, forcin yer face closer ta me neck. Yer body is hard and tensed, pulsin, like mine. A thin white line screams between us. Dogs in the ring. Then ya push through that line – how I don't know – and drop yer face, breathin in the scenta me hair, and then ya kiss me throat with a kiss that's got more care in it than anythin else I've felt in me life, and then I can't do anythin only reach me skin upta yours. Ya lift yer mouth onta mine. I open up, drink ya in. Yer tongue tastes a salt and spice. Me fingers loosen on yer hair, cradle yer skull. Ya drag me inta ya. Yer arms are fierce as they close round me and yer hands are burnin and yer body is alive on mine, every inch, as ya press me to ya, careful and shakin and hard and hungry in one, and I melt inta ya, drinkin ya up. And as ya pull me, still wrapped around ya, away from the others and towards the little room at the side, between us on their chain our souvenirs grind inta our skins, crumblin dust and bone and hair and metal inta our blood and sweat as yer fingers twist through mine, sendin me winnins fallin ta the floor.

Then there's a knock at the doorway even though there's no door and we jump, and pull apart from each other, and ya down on the ground fast grabbin yer torch, and ya flash it at the door and then the winda, and the gladness in yer eyes melts away and ya make a sick sound, like someone's punched ya, and say somethin under yer breath that I can't hear, and that other feelin I couldn't recognize flies outta yer body, and ya push me away as I grab yer arm, pushin me off like I'm an ugly piece a shit, so hard I fall on the ground, and then you're up at the winda and Charlie's there too, lookin out, and Amanda's followin, and I'm back on me feet too, and even before I get ta the winda I can see her, grey in the moonlight that's free now of all clouds, totterin across the grass from the far side a the hill, not the side we came up, her long hair dark with wet, her long legs on their too-big platform shoes, kohl two inches deep runnin down her face like black tears. Number Twenty-two. The World.

   Ya close yer eyes, sink back against the wall.
   'Oh, God,' says Amanda. 'Oh, Jesus. Where did she come from?'
   I start ta shake.

None of us went outside ta meet her. We let her make her way across that grass alone. Do you remember that, Nayler? Because I certainly do.

She steps over the threshold and the firelight sends shadas racin up the scarred muddy skin of her legs.

She smiles, awkward, through chatterin teeth.

'Ah, Jesus,' says Amanda again. 'How did ya get here, Sam?'

Ya open yer eyes. Ya got them curtains up again. 'Hey, little hen,' ya say, unpeelin yerself off the wall. Ya smile yer lazy smile, put yer arm around her shoulders.

It falls on me, red-hot and blazin, so I can hardly see. It's bitter and it bites at me ears, chokin me, and I've no control over it. The stupid little – What the *fuck* is she thinkin, comin up here? Doesn't she know it's dangerous? – The stupid little – Go away. Go fuckin home, Sam. Get the fuck out.

'I . . . I . . . g-got lost in the woods.' She's shiverin. She looks over at me, pleadin. 'I f-f-followed youse from town.'

'Followed?' ya say.

A figure under a streetlight. Long legs in the back a the bus. A shape bein spat out at the stop. A white shape flittin under a hedge.

Ya stupid little bitch. Ya stupid stupid stupid . . .

I try ta speak but can't. Me throat is boilin with rage.

'That's fuckin . . . good!' Charlie laughs, like it *is* good, like it's the funniest thing in the world.

Sam smiles, real nervous. 'Yeah,' she says. 'I knew youse were upta s-s-somethin.'

'Knew?' ya say.

'I g-got one a me f-feelins. So I p-p-planned it early on this evenin before youse came over.'

'Ya planned it? All on yer own?'

'Yeah?' she says, worried almost.

Ya start laughin then, like it is a big joke, and Charlie joins in, louder than before. Then Amanda's laughin too, and I'm sure Damo would as well only he's outta it and then even Sam starts gigglin, nervous-like, holdin her hand up in fronta her mouth.

'I c-c-couldn't find youse. I heard youse yellin but I couldn't see . . . the rain and . . . I called and all but youse didn't hear . . .'

a high voice like a mot's callin me name from the wrong direction

'. . . and when the wind stopped I . . . I heard nothin. Nobody round for miles. So I just kept walkin, for ages. Then I found a path and . . .' She laughs again, still nervous.

I start jiggin me foot.

'Ya need ta warm yerself up, little hen.' Ya pull her towards the fire. She goes, still lookin at me, still waitin for me ta laugh with the others.

Ya pick up the hooch. 'This'll do the trick. Won't it, Lucy?'

I open me mouth but I can't say anythin. I staked me life for ya, ya weak cunt, I wanta say it, but I don't.

Ya pull Sam's hair away from her face and tilt the hooch up ta her mouth. Her top slides down her shoulder and I see she's got a little black bruise near the neck. She swallas, goes for more. Ya pull it away. 'Hey now. A sip's all ya need.'

Charlie's still laughin. He's lookin at Sam's hair – the light dancin on it, a course, probably looks like elves – and pissin himself.

Damo pukes once, silently, then stops. Out cold.

Who's stupid now, Lucy? Who's weak?

The foil and works wink in the firelight. The Qs are white eyes in the dark.

I reach down.

One last lash. Do it now, Lucy. Get it over with. Then ya can put it behind ya and start again. Without any a them.

I get up, takin a candle. Amanda glances at me, but I ignore her as I go past her out inta the hall.

'Hang on a sec . . . Lucy! Where ya goin? Fucksake! Lucy Dolan, come back here!' Ya run after me, reach for me arm.

Don't you fuckin *dare*.

Yer hand stops above me skin.

I turn, look at ya.

'No sharin, Nayler. I won, fair and square. Sides, you're over all that, aren't ya?'

'Lucy . . .'

'Fuck off, ya sad cunt.' I keep me voice light.

Ya drop yer hand.

*

Yes. I know. Rage has been me friend but it's a terrible thing. And mixed up with blindness even more terrible. No excuses any more.

Me hands are shakin as I get everythin together. I've never been so nervous, not even the first time in London with Snags and all watchin.

'Do yerself a favour, Lucy,' I hear ya sayin, like ya right behind me. 'Smoke it, for Christ's sake.'

Fuck you, ya stupid bastard.

I open the first Q, slap me arm for a vein. Find one, pinch it, tie the lace. The works is clean, as per usual. Ya been kind enough ta supply a plastic bottle a water so I add some a that for the cookin. Work up. Pull the lace, tight. Just as I'm about ta shoot, I feel someone behind me and look around, expectin it ta be Sam.

'See,' I wanta tell her. 'This is how it works, darlin. And with all the best will in the world, there's nothin you can do ta stop me. No amounta lovin or carin or readin or knowin or even fuckin followin can stop it. See?'

But there's nobody there.

The room smells bad.

Fuck ghosts. Fuck the past. The faces in the bricks melt away, like snow in rain. Buck Whaley's orange breath vanishes.

I shoot. I score.

I fall in the bad room as the sounds – birds, trees, laughin, singin, whispers from the bricks – collapse in on toppa me.

Me eyes close and the sickness rears, and the fears, and a cold voice tells me, *This is it, Lucy, ya stupid cow, you've OD'd now for good, shouldn'a mixed it with the gargle, shouldn'a gone near the charlie, stupid cunt ya deserve it.*

I try ta push back the terrors but it's no good; I'm fallin inta a black pool and me breath is slowin, huunnnnnh hunnnnnh, and even me heartbeat feels further away and I try ta stay awake but I can't and –

Raise

It's twelve hours since I left John Paul, seven, more or less, since I got here. Seven hours, touchin two in the mornin.

Jesus.

Anyone else woulda given up the ghost by now.

Ya can't say I haven't made good use a the time. I've had a chance ta look things over, wind through the past, make sense of it, be sure again, so when ya do turn up, smilin yer crooked smile, I can destroy ya with a steady hand and clear mind.

Ya might wonder how I remember everythin so clear; every last conversation, every fleetin look. Well, I've hadta. Otherwise, how else could I be sure? It's the only proof I have. If even one detail goes, the whole picture falls apart.

Though, in this tellin, things are bein said that aren't the way I've held them all this time. Me memory is catchin me sideways, colourin itself over with other truths, things I don't remember . . . well, not that way.

By the way, I'm sorry about the gargle, Nayler. I know I shoulda waited till ya got here. Then we coulda had a coupla scoops and that woulda made things easier. We coulda swapped a bit a chat – How ya been doin, pal? Whatcha been upta? – before gettin onta the big questions. Like Why, Nayler? And – because me memory is playin games again, not just in the tellin but in them flashin signals a sound and vision it's sendin me even faster now – it *was* you, wasn't it?

Yeah. I shoulda waited, but it was either the pills or the other or the beer and I thought it was better ta go for the lesser a the three evils.

I've figured out where the rustlin is comin from. It's upstairs, that room I OD'd in. I haven't gone up ta check it out yet. It's not because I'm afraid, Nayler. I could take me courage in me hands and climb them dark stairs, and I'd say I'd even find yer stuff up there, yer sleepin bag and all. But I'm not goin. Because it's only a rat makin them sounds and in anyways, what happens if ya come back sudden and surprise me and mess up me own little surprise I've got lined up for you? We couldn't have that, could we?

No. I'll just stay here and drink the resta the cans and wait for you ta show yerself, and while I'm waitin I'll keep unravellin me memories, spinnin me lies – even though I'm sick a this tale, Nayler, sick like you must be ta hear it – till ya come.

I

I hear me name. Then –

Cold. Lonely and high up, driftin further.

– somethin I. Then –

Stops.

Last bit a warmth rips away from me.

Nothin now.

Nothin.

Nothin.

Thank God . . .

– except then somethin with a giant's strength grabs me, lifts me and shakes me, thrashin me against the nothin. I resist but the thing's too strong, and as it shakes and racks the nothin starts ta crack, fill up, get colder, harder. I start ta feel me head, me hands, me feet. And now the thing is draggin me, still thrashin, down through the coldness that's so sharp now it's cuttin, through the hardness that's like brick, smashin me through layers a glass and ice. I fall, screamin as I start ta burn, as the cuttin ice turns ta fire, makin every cell in me blood match-lit petrol, and just when I think I've got used ta that, the real pain kicks in, stabbin me, jerkin, ta consciousness.

For a second – a second only – I don't know where I am.

It's almost mornin. Not long past dawn. I can tell by the birds startin ta sing outside, the cold blue light eekin up from below. Despite the burnin in me blood, I'm cold. Frozen. Shakin. Sick. Through the tremors still rackin me body and the waves a nausea I can see blood on the floor near me face and all down the fronta me Da's jacket. I musta puked it up when I was out. Lucky I wasn't lyin on me back or I'da choked on it.

Me right arm is sore and the sleeve's rolled up, though I coulda sworn I shot up in the left one.

Me mouth tastes a salt and blood. I'm shiverin. Rivers a shivers runnin up me legs me arms me back, sendin out the flesh in tiny bumps, like what's happened the night before, the OD – except it wasn't a proper OD, was it? I'd be dead if it was – whatever screamin horrors I heard in the blackness, is pushin itself out through me skin, sayin: *come on Lucy, wake up, come on, wake up, tell me, remember what* –

But I can't remember, can't get it together in me head, all I'm feelin is sick ta me soul and even though I try ta close me eyes and go back ta sleep, I can't.

In fronta me lies me spike, empty. It's so close it looks like a mountain. An enormous mountaina glass.

I lie there for . . . what? Half an hour. Forty minutes. I can't tell. The dull light through the winda grows brighter, but only just. I keep hopin the sickness will ease. That I'll warm up. That someone will come and find me and look after me.

I hafta move when the cramps start.

They creep up on me, a twinge here, an ache there. I think they're just the last dregs a the OD so I grit me teeth, willin them ta end. But instead a easin they get worse. Then I start sweatin and it's only then that I cop on.

I'm withdrawin. I'm fuckin withdrawin like I never been clean at all.

Me nerves start at me, itchin at the edges a me bein. I try callin out for help but nobody answers.

Lazy fucks. Must still be asleep. Cunts. Leavin me alone like that. Bet they didn't even bother their holes checkin up on me.

Me stomach spasms and I retch white goo spotted with slimy bits a black blood.

The sweatin gets worse. I can't lie here any more. Maybe if I get up –

I stagger up ta me feet, lungin at the wall for support.

Somethin crunches under me shoe. I look down. It's plastic or glass; must be me spike. Somethin feels wrong about that thought

482

but I can't fix what it is. A curse on the fuckin thing.

Through the winda I can see nothin but whiteness, big fat blankets a fog billowin everywhere. The ground is just a shimmer a green and brown underneath and that only beside the house. I can't see the edge a the hill, let alone the forest or the slopes or the city below.

I force meself downstairs. Every coupla steps I call out, tryin ta wake youse. Nobody answers. Half-way down I stumble, bashin me foot against a loose brick. I reach out, clingin ta the cold wall so's I don't lose me balance. Ugh. Wet. Mould.

At the bottom a the stairs I double over, retch, then stagger inta the big room where we lit the fire.

It takes a while for me eyes to adjust ta the light, and even so, I think I'm hallucinatin for a minute or two.

Nobody's there. No thing. No person. Just the cans and the fag ends, stickin outta the ground like weird flowers someone's planted. I'm startin ta shake uncontrollable now, but I keep it together enough ta pull meself over ta the small doorway on the left, thinkin youse must all a crashed out there. But there's nothin in that little room neither, only damp earth and a heap a heather and bracken in one corner with red bits a colouredy paper scattered over it, and that white fog pushin in through the winda. I turn ta go but as I do, sickness takes me and I double over again, pukin. The stuff is blacker now and burns me throat on the way out.

I'm achin with thirst, sweatin so much now I can't see.

When the retchin eases I make me way outside, callin yer names, even though I'm finally startin ta believe there's no point.

Outside it's deadly cold and white like nothin on earth. The fog is everywhere, smotherin the sunlight, blankin out the mountain, the house, the sky. Through me shakin I can see me own body below me – bloody jacket, manky jeans, ragged runners – and the ground at me feet with its shabby scraps a grass. For a dazed minute I think ya musta won that poxy game after all; that I am dead and this is some poxed-up version a heaven, all fluffy clouds only no angels – so no, not heaven but purgatory instead, where I gotta wait till fuckin God with his long white beard comes out ta give off ta me like the worst rozzer ever lived. But then another cramp seizes me, and I puke again. There's a wrench in me chest like I'm pukin out me lungs, not whatever's left in me gut.

A soft wind starts up, rufflin me hair and sendin cool drops a mist down me cheeks. The coolness feels good, even though I know it won't last. I lean against the wall, prayin the pain ta keep itself at bay.

Then the clouds, pulled by the wind, drift open. A finger a sunshine leaks down on the wet black ground, and at the tip a the finger is –

no

– and I wish I was dead after all.

They'd – they? Who's they? You? The others? Fuck, answer me! – they'd stuck ten needles in her. At first I couldn't tell whether they were just stuck in the flesh. But when I forced meself closer ta her, I could see they'd been plugged inta the surface veins, with black bruises kissin the metal where the blood had gone bad.

Her clothes were gone. She looked cold. So cold, but there was no little bumps pushin outta her skin, no memories tryin ta force themselves outta her any more.

I searched, but this wasn't like Granny. I couldn't feel her anywhere.

Ten a Swords. Body lyin face down on a battlefield, ten long swords stickin inta its back. Meanin: death, desolation. Ruin.

The needles weren't the worst thing. The worst thing was her face. They – fuck they; you; you, you, *you*, ya sick cunt – had broken it inta a mess a purple, gold and black.

And on the ground, lain round her head like a halo, was a silver chain, drippin with memories a the dead.

Without thinkin I scramble over ta her – it – her – and grab the chain and throw it away from me, far as I can. Then I get another cramp and that buckles me legs, sendin me collapsin in a heap beside her. I lie there, shiverin. Two inches between us; between her mangled face and mine. Might as well be an eternity.

That little bruise near her neck that I noticed the night before is clearer now, and I see it's not a bruise after all, but a tattoo, small and delicate. A daisy.

Ah, Jesus . . .

Somethin inside a me takes over, and I curl meself round her, as close as I can get, and hold her, cradlin her ta me like a doll, me arms around her, me face in her hair, smellin her, huggin her much as I can without makin any more damage. I'm not tryin ta ease me pain. I'm not tryin ta warm her up. I'm not thick. I know when someone's gone.

But do I hafta explain what it meant – after everythin, after what I'd done, what I shouldn'a what I shoulda, although I knew yes *it was too fuckin late* – ta hold her in me arms one last time?

After a while me brain started ta wake up. I knew I didn't want someone comin up and findin us like that. But I didn't know what else ta do and I was too sick to move, so I just kept lyin there, holdin her. Then – I dunno, ten, fifteen minutes maybe, two hours, fuck, I dunno – it came ta me. That maybe the best thing would be ta move her, but where, I didn't know, just somewhere more private, and maybe . . . yeah, I could get help and . . .

Me body lurched inta action. Find her clothes. Dress her first, then move her. But there wasn't a stitch of hers left, not even in the house – which I forced meself ta go back and search, even though the very smell of it made me puke again. They'd – fuck they, *you* – you'd got rid a every last thing belongin ta her.

Before I lifted her, I tried ta pull out the spikes. Understand: I didn't want her ta be left like that, marked, used, like someone's sick idea of a joke. The spikes were blue and I cursed ya for that, usin fat blues when an orange gauge woulda done the job, and they were plugged in deep, and with me hands shakin so bad and slippy with sweat, I ended up snappin mosta them in two, leavin the ends stuck in her skin. I tried ta dig in under the metal but it was no use; me nails kept flakin and I even pushed some deeper by accident. So in the end I left them as they were, and put the snapped ends inta me pocket, for throwin away later.

I think it was round then, when the needles broke, that I started cryin.

Then I lifted her cold arm around me neck and dragged her down the hill.

'You shouldn'a come, Sam,' I said ta her as we stumbled over rocks and skidded down the frosty ground. 'Ya shoulda known better. Ya shoulda stayed away. This was none a yer business. This had nothin ta do with you. It was my pals, my party, my—'

Nayler

'Ya had no business comin.'

I'm not thick. I knew she couldn't hear. But it was sorta comfortin sayin it, like it took some a the fault from me.

Yeah. Sick. I know. But can ya understand? She chose it. She chose ta fool us inta thinkin she was passed out on the cider earlier that night when she wasn't. She chose ta dress up like that ta folla us – no, not us; God knows why but she followed you, Nayler, don't kid yerself she was after anyone else – she chose ta keep goin, even after she lost us and coulda backed off, she—

Ahem, says the Judge in the sky, interruptin me. Backed off, Lucy Dolan? She was lost in the woods, on the other side a the mountain. She couldn'a backed off anywhere.

Yeah but she still chose ta—

Ahem. *Chose?*

Yeah—

No child would choose a death like that.

Maybe they would, though, Judge. The Zen stuff says ya make yer own destiny, Judge. Nothin happens only ya choose it.

Already I feel meself graspin at straws, hear the invisible jury booin and hissin.

Don't pass the blame onta her, Lucy. It was your fault. Don't forget. Y-O-U-R. It was upta you ta take care of her and ya didn't. Ya walked away and—

Okay, ladies and gents a the jury, you're right. *O-kay.* But it doesn't change the fact that she chose ta come up after us in the first place.

Boo, hiss. Ya sayin she was askin for it, Lucy? Ya sayin she deserved it?

486

No, I—

Ya sayin anyone leaves bloody handprints at the scene a their murder deserves ta die?

No.

She's heavy. Her arms keep slippin off me neck. I know I won't be able ta bring her down all the way like that. But I don't wanta hurt her by draggin her legs. So I hold her under the armpits and let her feet skid down the hill in front of us. Her shoulders are cold and stiff and her feet keep gettin caught in clumps a heather, or loose rocks, and I hafta keep lettin her down so I can untangle them. She'd put some a Ma's nail polish on her toenails before goin out, bright red, and the red jars with the grey purple of her skin and that makes me cry even harder.

After a while I start prayin. Mad, because I haven't prayed since I was a little kid, and then it was always for somethin thick like toys. I can barely make out me own words, me voice seems so far away.

'Jesus Jesus Jesus Come on Tell me Jesus Help me Help me Fuckin Help Me.'

Jesus isn't much use. The fog splits open but only seconds at a time, and blinded, I keep trippin, landin on me knees, me front, me side.

When we get ta the big rock by the willa trees that we'd passed the night before, I hafta stop. Me strength is gone and I know once I've let her down, I won't be able get her up again. But as luck would have it, there's a holla beside the rock and her head fits nicely there. I push her legs and arms close ta the rock so she's lyin in a sorta crescent.

I wasn't intendin ta leave her there for good. Just till I got help or . . .

It takes a while ta cover her up. Between the pukin and the cramps I can only work a coupla minutes at a time, and me vision is flecked with little red dots so I can't see what I'm doin. Through the fog I can hear the cows mooin. But I get it done and by the time I'm finished, ya wouldn't know anyone was there at all, under the brambles and the dead leaves, guarded by the tall shape a the rock and the twisted branches a the willas. Voices rise, a man and a woman, some couple down the path on a Bank Hollyer walk.

'Stay there, Sam. Don't move.'

Then I take the spikes outta me pocket and I throw them as far away as I can.

What happens in that space between seein somethin and knowin it? How come I was able ta work, ta function like that? Okay, anyone else, the invisible jury for example, they'd say that wasn't functionin; they'd say that was all wrong, their word, disfunction, but ta me it was a function, I . . . worked. But how come? How was I, even in that state, able ta get it together enough ta bring her down that hill and cover her and hide her?

I can see the reasons the tabloids would give.

Inhuman. Drug-Crazed. Brute. Cold-Blooded. Heartless. Animal.

Is there truth in that? Was I – that mass a blood and bones and cravin called Lucy Dolan – in that time took over by somethin other than human because a the sheer horror a what I'd seen? Or in the bottom of ourselves are we all this other yoke, this Inhuman Cold-Blooded Heartless Animal that can flee and hide and cover their tracks like that's all that matters?

In the bottom of our souls are we all you, Nayler?

I force meself ta leave her. I don't wanta. I wanta stay there, ta guard her, but somethin in me is forcin me up, and I know if I don't go now, I won't ever, and then I'll never be able ta help her, so I tug me hoodie up so it hides me face and stagger away from the rock, through the trees and over the little barbed-wire fence we crossed last night.

Through the thinnin fog I can see that couple I heard comin up towards me – some long fair-haired cunt with a skinny woman, him wearin a rucksack, both walkin real brisk, runnin almost. Bit fast for a Bank Hollyer walk, but there ya go. I keep me eyes down even though I can feel them stoppin and starin at me, like they know me, the cunts, like they can see right through me ta what's happened, and leggit past them without once glancin up.

Even messed up like that, I was clear on one thing. Get Charlie. Get fuckin Charlie and ask him what the fuck's goin on.

They looked at me funny when I came in. Then the lad behind the bar leant over ta his buddy and said somethin. I made out the word 'scumbag'.

'Yeah,' I said, out loud. 'I am a fuckin scumbag. I look like a scumbag and I sound like a scumbag so that's what I fuckin am.'

They backed off at that and I was glad ta see I hadn't lost it. But then I had ta ask him for change for the phone and that made me feel thick.

One a the twins answered.

'Catherine?'

'No, Margaret.'

'It's Lucy,' I said, me teeth chatterin. 'Get me Charlie.'

She put the phone down with a clatter and I heard her yell for Charlie, and him answer, and then the phone picked up again.

'Jesus, Charlie,' I said, tryin ta force me teeth ta be still.

'He's not there,' said Catherine or Margaret or whoever the fuck it was on the other end.

'The – ya liar,' I said. I didn't care what she thought. 'I heard him. Get him for me.'

'No. Sorry. He's not there.' She sounded so smug I wanted ta burst her, and that wasn't a bad feelin, that clean rage risin up in me, breakin through the sickness. 'Give me yer fuckin Ma then,' I said.

'She's not there either. She's gone for a walk.'

'Ya fuckin liar!' I screamed. 'She never goes on walks! Give her ta me! Fuckin give her!'

But the little bitch hung up without sayin any more. I smashed the phone against the wooden counter and sank down on the ground. Behind me I could hear the barman talkin low ta someone but I didn't give a shit.

Think, Lucy, think.

Jesus.

If only I had somethin ta take away the fuckin pain.

Another cramp. I doubled over and dug me hands inta me jeans pockets, clawin at the cloth, bitin me lips against the sickness. In me pocket, me fingers clutched fabric, fluff, the crumpled folds of a tiny piece a knotted plastic.

Plastic?

Fuck.

It was—

Fuck. It was a Q. The second one. Because I'd won two and I'd only used one, hadn't I? But I'd forgotten, and here it was, and yeah, I could use it now, that would sort out the pain. Then I'd be able ta work it out, what ta do with Sam, what next.

I was already lookin around for somewhere ta use – could I risk snortin it straightaway, in the booth? – me fingernails pullin at the knot, when I remembered Amanda. I wrestled with it for a few seconds, but it was no use. I *had* ta ring her first – she was the only one who'd know anythin, what happened, what ta do. Once I talked ta her I could take me medicine, and wait for her, and then we could both sort out Sam. So I picked up the phone and tried diallin. But the number that Charlie had given me the night before kept slippin outta me head, and with the shakes I couldn't get me fingers ta push the buttons proper, even though I kept beggin them ta *work ya cunts, work ya fuckin cunts.* Then I dropped the phone, and I couldn't get hold of it again for ages because me hands were too far away, and when at last I did, it vexed me so much the way it kept slippin outta me hand, that I tugged it and somethin gave, and then I kicked the wall so hard I felt the bones in me feet crack, the same foot I'd twisted that day I fell off the horse outside yours. I turned round, sick a the place, sick, sick, and was on me way ta limp out, anywhere, to a ditch, back ta the Club, just anywhere I could lie down and snort that Q, when the door a the pub opened and the Old Bill walked in.

'I believe you're having some trouble,' they said ta the barman.

I tried ta run, but me foot was killin me and they grabbed me before I reached the door. I kept pushin against them as they dragged me towards the car, tellin them they'd no right, what had

I done, only lose the head on the phone, that wasn't a crime, what did they think I was, some fuckin murderer or somethin? But they pushed me onta the back seat, meaty culchie hands on me head, forcin me down like a kitten they wanted ta drown. And because I had the Q in me hand, like a fool, insteada in me mouth, there was no hidin it even though I tried ta drop it onta the floor a the car. But the one holdin me down saw it and picked it up, no problem, cool as anythin, and then the barman got in on it, runnin out after me and holdin up the broken phone where I'd ripped it outta the wall and yellin names after the cop car: 'You're a useless piece a scum, ya troublemaker, ya scumbag, we'll have none a your type round here,' and the cops told me ta shut up, behave meself if I knew what was good for me, and the one that hadn't picked up the Q grabbed me wrists and cuffed me, holdin me arms tight ta me sides while I sat there, slumped against the back seat, shakin.

I coulda told them. I shoulda told them, some would say. But the Old Bill have never been on side. So why would I trust them with that?

It's taken me years ta figure it out but I've almost got there. Almost. It's still missin holes. But of all me ideas it's still the best, the one that convinces me the most.

It was a sacrifice, wasn't it? That's why ya done it like that, the needles, layin her out on the grass, on yer hero's altar. Only it wasn't the usual sacrifices – the cuttins, stabbins, maimins ya done for the business; the killins ya done, professional, for Snags.

Was it?

No. This was somethin – you said it, remember? – *special*. Real. A full-blown proper order black magic ritual killin. That was what ya were plannin all night. Wasn't it? Why ya let me bring the lads up? Why ya had that creepy little book in yer bag? Ya were plannin somethin. I could feel it. But the thing was, it was never her ya planned ta use. It was me ya wanted ta sacrifice. Wasn't it? Only then I went and won that poxy poker.

When did ya get the idea, Nayler? Playin with it for a while, were ya, readin yer magic books, mullin over it? Did ya start thinkin about it that day ya found me souvenirs, or did it only come ta ya that Hallowe'en mornin? When did it harden inta certainty – in the squat? The Club? With the stories? The game? The gear? When did ya know for sure ya could walk me inta a corner and get me ta stake me life in fronta three witnesses and not back out?

I knew ya'd somethin up. I knew it. But I didn't cop what. If I had I'da never—

See, at the time I thought it was all about me. That ya wanted ta punish me for . . . whatever. Takin them souvenirs, seein them feelins in ya; walkin off on you and Sash, knowin too much about you and Snags. Fucksake, for even just bein a thing ya . . . despised. A nuisance, a pain in the arse, an itch wouldn't go away, a pawn beyond its use. Stupid me. Shoulda seen what was goin on. If ya wanted ta punish me, ya coulda done it real easy; one stab down a dark lane. Instead ya brung us all up ta some spooky gaff on a mountain, sat us round in a five-point star and got me ta stake me life in a game a poker. Couldn'a stuck more magic in it if ya tried. And don't tell me it was all coincidence.

Ya even let it slip, didn't ya, when I brung it up without knowin? That sly laugh. *Ah, fuck off, Lucy. You don't even know what a sacrifice is.*

I shoulda got out then.

Sacrifices. Hurtin people ta make things go yer way. Money, power, safety, silence. Never mattered what as long as there was a pay-off. Best currency is blood, ya always said. So what did ya want in exchange for mine, Nayler? Am I right?

Was it . . . him?

Oh, I shoulda paid more attention ta that story ya told about that poxy servant runnin outta favour with his master. I shoulda listened more ta them rumours that time I was gettin clean, a you and Snags and what was goin on. I shoulda thought more about that bare look on yer face the day ya came back after that batin. I shoulda sussed who had the power ta make ya so bare. And oh oh oh, I shoulda figured out who of all people knew what it meant ta cut and burn that precious tattoo a yours inta an ugly mess.

It started with the gear, didn't it? Ya went after Snags ta challenge him, ta find out why he wasn't sendin it, and he sussed ya were usin. So he broke ya up ta teach ya a lesson. A slap here, slap there. Wouldn't blame him; with the way things were anyone woulda got paranoid and Snags – *easy, Snags* – was never the best at keepin his head under pressure. You'da taken that batin as yer just deserts. You'd broken his rules. Ya knew how he stood on the gear. But then he went too far. Didn't he?

There was a rat. That's why he'd stopped sendin it. Even after Cindy Devlin was disposed a, someone was still leakin the Five Lampers info. And he thought it was you. Ya'd been the Don's hired knife, after all, and it wasn't like ya'd any other ideas a who it could be, did ya?

Wrong. Oh, ya had an idea, alright. But ya didn't tell him. Because ya . . . yeah, let's spit it out, Nayler . . . because ya idolized her, our beautiful Dutch mermaid. Made it easier for ya that ya'd no proof on her, what with me holdin me tongue for a change, never once tellin ya about seein her chattin away with Emmet Whelan. So ya kept yer mouth shut, and Snags, knowin ya were hidin somethin, turned on ya and then it got bad. Oh, I can picture him, Nayler, screamin he'd fuck you up for good, teach ya a lesson, show ya who really owned ya, as he set his Dutch thugs on ya ta work their own little magic.

That musta fucked with yer head. Because ya never thought yer guardian angel would treat his right hand, his smart kid, his number one like just another piece a street scum.

I shoulda remembered her too, how she took in the news a Snags's victory, that step back; shocked. I shoulda copped what that look on yer face seein her do that meant. Betrayed, were ya, seein all yer gallantry had been for nothin?

Ya shouldn'a thought ya meant somethin ta them, Nayler. Ya shoulda kept yerself hid round them like ya done round everyone else. Ya only got yerself ta blame ya got yer mammy and daddy pissin all over ya again. No wonder ya opened up and let it all out when ya seen them souvenirs on me chain. Straw. Camel's back. Nothin more.

You and Snags patched things up after, a course. When the good news about the Don came through, yer owner looked at ya hangin maimed from the wall of his Amsterdam dungeon and decided ta let it be. Then he dressed yer wounds and tended ya through the seventy-two and sent ya back ta us with the news of his victory.

But ya didn't patch it fully. He'd lost his trust in ya and there was no winnin it back.

Them rumours. You fallin outta favour, him leavin ya danglin, a maggot on a hook. Stupid a me not ta ask, straight out that mornin. *So ya not still workin for him, Nayler?*

That jaunt was all about goin back ta bein kids? One last lash in honour a the old days? Me hole. One last try, more like, at winnin back yer place at yer master's table. That was why ya planned ta spike me body with ten smack-filled needles and lay me out on that grass. A big bloody gesture ta win back Snags. Wouldn't matter if he knew or not . . .

Would it?

No. Just as long as whatever god ya serve – the Devil? Buck Whaley? Yer own warped fallen angel a killin – seen whatcha done and smiled on it. Symbols. They mean things, ya always said. Magic. Makes things happen. Blood gets spilt. Snags wakes up the next day and all of a sudden finds himself regrettin the bad things he done ta his rascal.

I know. There's holes. Like, why just . . . *do it*, somethin so whacked-out, risky like that? Why leave the body on show, you that was always so good at hidin yer tracks? And if ya really needed a death, why leave it ta chance? It was always fifty-fifty ya'd lose the poker. Other things bother me. Somethin in how ya were that night. Somethin in that servant story. Somethin in the rumours while I was gettin clean about ya headin off and comin back. Somethin else, in the way ya were after the batin. And stuff I don't wanta even think a . . .

But Jesus, Nayler, them holes are nothin compared with the big one. Why *her*?

Ya coulda still taken me. Ya shoulda. I deserved it. I'd stolen, spied, seen too much. Them smack-filled needles were my death. I'd earned them. And okay, even if ya felt ya couldn't take me life because ya'd lost it in the poker, ya coulda still – Fucksake. If ya needed a body that bad ya coulda taken one a the others, even. Charlie, for bein a smartarse; or Damo, for bein thick or in with the Five Lampers; or even Amanda, for, Jesus, killin yer baby. But ya didn't hafta go after me sister. Scratch that. Ya *shouldn'a*. That wasn't in yer rules, yer *People only get hurt because they deserve it, Lucy* . . .

Anyone else would say: psycho cunt, he didn't need a reason for killin Sam, anyone woulda done for that sacrifice, her included, and I'm worse for thinkin otherwise. But I know ya, Nayler. You always needed reasons. Some people might say her comin up after us gave ya all the reason ya needed. Others would point ta what I seen today and say that was enough. But . . . no. Fuck, no. No no no. She was still innocent. A kid, for Christsake, twelve year old, a baby ya useta hold in yer arms, a child not fully able ta make the right choices. She didn't deserve that. Don't tell me she did. And I was there for the takin. Me, the easy target, the nuisance. So what was the *fuckin point* in takin her – and don't dream a tellin me there wasn't.

Come on. Tell me. Come *on*.

Ya looked sick when ya seen her through the winda. Sick, like ya'd seen a ghost, and then ya said somethin I didn't catch. What was that about? Could that tell me Why?

The station is freezin. Through the glass winda I can see the rozzers arguin with the doctor from the Health Board. The barman's pressin charges for what I done on his phone and the rozzers are chargin me for possession with intent because a the size a the Q, but they still haven't managed ta get holda Ma. They wanta wait for her and soon as she's arrived, bring me ta the district judge's house for an emergency hearin. But far as the doctor's concerned, he's the only responsible adult they have for me at the moment, and he's sayin I'm real sick, it's a wonder I'm even on me feet, and I need medical care.

The rozzer shakes his head. Don't blame him. They think I'm gointa do a runner once I'm in sniffin distance of any hospital bed.

Blackness crawls up me back and inta me eyes.

The Old Bill wins, a course.

We're on our way out, the doctor holdin an anxious hand on me shoulder, when Ma turns up.

I see her first through the one-way winda behind the desk. Her hair's in a state and her eyes are wild and there's a woman copper with her that's tryin ta hold her back. But Ma rushes upta the No Entry door and the copper has no choice but ta folla her through.

Her heels clack up the corridor like little nails bein hammered inta wood.

The rozzer and the doctor exchange a look.

Ma rounds the corner. Her face is white and her mouth is open and there's a light in her eyes I don't remember seein before.

'Oh . . .' She stops, takes in me face, me scrawny build, me Da's bloodstained jacket. The light in her eyes goes out. She looks brutal disappointed. 'That one?'

'You said your daughter was missing,' says the woman copper, tryin ta sound all enthusiastic.

Ma shakes her head. 'Oh no. No. Not this one. It's me other girl I'm lookin for. Me baby. Samantha. She went out last night and she hasn't been back.'

There's a pleadin in her voice that saws at me mind.

The coppers from the station look at each other.

'Well?' says the woman rozzer ta me.

Me stomach cramps and I double over again.

'Lucy. Lucy, come on. Do you know where your sister is?'

I raise me head. Ma stares, chewin her lip, twistin her hands, eyes fillin with tears, willin me ta die.

Even now I can't fully explain what happened. Ya might think I'm only sayin that ta get meself off the hook but I'm not. All I know is the cravins stopped, suddenly, and the hole inside a me screamin ta be filled closed over. Everythin felt calm, and in the right place. I sorta lifted outta meself, just like I done when Ma read me fortune in the bin, and it was like I was in the middle of a three-way cross, with the bones a me future and past lyin either side; right and left, front and back, above and below.

I see the things I'm cursed ta do. The streets, the sickness, the sin, everythin. And it looks ta me there's dots a light in that darkness, but what they are I can't tell. And bang in the centre a this, I see a point where they come together, where some truth is told.

'Do you know where she is?'

I do as the future tells me I'll do.

'How . . . the . . . fuck . . . should . . . I?' I say, spellin out the words.

Later, when they'd put me away where I'd be so-called safe, I cried for that. Not for me. I stick ta that, Nayler, I never cried for me. I cried because although I hadta do it, sayin them words was the same as spittin on me sister's dead body.

The judge's house is nice. Nice wooden floors, nice carpets, nice pictures on the wall. The judge is nice too but he's not happy about the gear. When he asked where I'd got it, I told him I'd found it on the bus. Rule Number Two: Never rat on yer dealer.

There's a lotta people talkin. The Social's turned up, and that Fish-eye doctor cunt from the bin. The judge is quizzin the rozzers about the intent charge, and they're tellin him I been suspected a mixin with criminal elements. The Social looks pissed off with that, because clearly she's on the hook for not doin her job proper over the summer while I was in the squat, and even more pissed off that the rozzers didn't pass the info onta her in the first place, but I don't have it in me ta feel sorry for the little bitch. Meanwhile, old Fish-eyes is bangin on about psychiatric evaluation and the judge is listenin, but he looks a bit wary when Fish-eyes says he can put me in one a his beds straightaway, and I'm guessin even through the state I'm in, that what with Sam bein gone and nobody findin her they don't want to attract any bad guff from the papers.

Then the Health Board doctor chips in, sayin whatever about me mental health I need immediate if not emergency medical supervision as I claimed I'd OD'd the night before, even though I'm withdrawin now, and I feel like kickin meself for lettin that one slip.

At that the judge started ta wrap it up, sayin he agreed, noddin over at the Health Board doctor, the immediate priority was ta take care a me physical symptoms. In the longer term however, he said, there was several issues involved and it was important ta be sensitive ta the case and the family circumstances – lookin over at Ma – so he'd assign someone from Probation and Welfare on me and once I was back on me feet I'd be remanded in Overbrook House. The rozzers nodded away good-oh, chuffed at that. At that stage, the judge went on, givin the nod ta Fish-eyes, I'd receive me psychiatric evaluations in Overbrook and, dependin on the results, I could continue ta get counsellin and psychiatric treatment there while I served me sentence, or, if it was deemed more serious, well, they'd hafta consider sendin me ta the bin again.

'Well,' said Ma, 'she's not comin back ta me.'

Before we left, the woman copper who'd brung Ma took me aside and asked me about Sam again. When was the last time I'd seen her? Where had I brung her? Did she come up with me to the mountain? What was I doin up there in that neck a the woods in anyways? I could feel her playin games with me, twistin the words round ta fool me, but I kept me head, kept the truth ta meself.

I am amazed, lookin back, that I didn't give somethin away. It woulda been easy. The withdrawals, all them people, all that fuckin chat. But I stayed brand-new and told her nothin. I knew this wasn't gointa be the end of it but somethin in me had made a choice when I'd lied ta Ma and there was no goin back on it.

Ya probably think I was thick. Because they were gointa find her, weren't they? And if they didn't, some tourist or hill-walker would, even that couple I seen earlier. But like I say, I'd made me choice. Besides, what good would it do the rozzers ta know me story? They probably wouldn't believe me, headcase that I was in their eyes. They'd probably even think I done it. And even if they didn't, even if they did take me story on board and went after ya, would they get ya? The law is a hooer. Justice is a joke. Would they nail ya, pal, really, for what ya done?

I don't think so.

Call it habit, but once ya start lyin ta the Authorities, it's very hard ta stop. At the time it seemed . . . not easy, but crystal fuckin clear.

Because it's been so hard ta find a reason I sometimes useta tell meself it was an accident. Maybe that's only because I knew *I* wouldn't do it like that, I'd only kill if I was pushed –

and we all know about that

– though the invisible jury would say that was bollocks, I been just as capable of intent as you. I planned bringin Charlie and Amanda up, after all. I said the right things ta push their buttons, and what's the difference between that and you plannin yer sacrifice?

There is a difference. There *is*.

Enough. Get back ta the point.

Okay. I useta tell meself if it had been an accident, whatcha done ta me sister, then it explained why ya ran off. Ya freaked out because ya didn't mean it. Ya lost the poker game and decided ta leave the sacrifice idea, chill out, have some gargle, use me ta . . . fuckit . . . whatever. When she came up the Club like that, appearin outta the darkness like a ghost, it was a shock, but that was all. All ya said at the winda was *Ah, Jesus*, or somethin. With the long hair and all she might even a reminded ya a one a the women ya killed, Cindy or . . . It was only later, when ya went ta fuck her, boozed up, maybe even thinkin she was Sasha, and she said No – after sayin Yeah before – when she began ta fight back, cryin and all, that ya copped on she wasn't Sasha, that Sash was dead too, like Cindy, long gone, disappeared inta thin air, leavin nothin only a coila brown hair on yer chain. But Sam wouldn't stop cryin, so ya hit her ta make her shut up, but it made no difference ta me little sister because she was so used ta bein hit, and worse, so she kept screamin and ya had no choice but ta hit her more.

I useta thank God that ya hit her. It sounds sick but it's not. If ya hadn't hit her so bad I mighta thought it was me and that . . .

Jesus.

Could anyone stand that?

There was times when I dreamt – come on, Lucy; it's not 'there was times'. That makes it sound like once in a blue moon. Say it as it was.

Alright. For the first five years I dreamt a her every night. I dreamta comin down the stairs, goin out and findin her. In some dreams she wasn't there. There was just empty grass, or the mark where a body useta be, or rose petals. Odd, them rose petals –

Keep on track. Other times, she was lyin there, but only sleepin. Still others she was dead, but not battered. Them last dreams were the worst because they meant anyone coulda done it. Includin me. Especially me.

I'd wake, sweatin, terrified I'd screamed out loud, not wantin the others in the ward or the cell or the street ta share it.

But them dreams were wrong. She *was* battered. And not by me. And that's what made me think ya mightn'a planned it – because it showed ya were outta control. Them needles were just a cover, ta pretend ya still knew whatcha were doin.

Except . . . I never seen ya force yerself on a woman. Not once. Nor beat one in a rage; not Sasha, not yer brassers, not me Ma, not even me when I dared ya. Ya slapped Amanda, yeah. But only once and then it was ta knock her inta sense. Besides, Sam's teeth were all smashed up. Everyone knows ya can't tell someone who's dead if their teeth are gone.

And in anyways, if it had been an accident, there'da been no reason ta leave them souvenirs at her head like that ta taunt me.

From the back a the copcar I see Ma, standin sunk and grey beside the woman rozzer. She doesn't look up at me. She's just starin down at her shoes. For that moment she reminds me a Granny and I think *Maybe I should*, but then I remember the bones a me destiny. I sit back against the seat and wait for it ta unfold.

★

I know what they're thinkin, that invisible jury a mine.

Cruel. Barbaric. Malicious.

No daughter in her right mind, they tell me, would inflict a punishment like that on her own mother; leave her in the dark all them years, wanderin around the city with them Missin posters pinned ta her coat, flappin in the wind like bats' wings, others in heaps under her arm waitin ta be plastered up over every lamppost, every shop winda, every post office noticeboard, so nobody could take two steps without bein asked *Have ya seen Sam?* No daughter would torment her mother like that, let her live a half-life lie a hope when the truth woulda at least . . . settled somethin in her.

Yeah, right. Rose Dolan lived off hope and its twin sister regret. She couldn't face the present if it walked up ta her and pissed on her face. I was doin her a favour by givin her somethin ta live for.

Wrong answer, Lucy Dolan! says the invisible jury, shakin its heads.

Okay, then. She was always willin ta believe the worst a me so why give her more rope? Just like the rozzers, she'da pinned it on me.

Beep! Wrong again!

Fuck youse, ladies and gentlemen. Alright, I admit it. Here's the reason you're lookin for. Simple.

I wanted ta punish her. She was a useless mother and I don't just mean ta me. The things she done on Sam. She had no right ta know what happened. If she'd cared about us – Sam, Micko, me – when it mattered, not just after everythin went ta shit, then maybe –

Ah, fuck. If, bollocks.

Hate me for sayin it, ladies and gents a the jury, but far as I'm concerned that's the truth.

In the car the doctor – not Fish-eyes, the other lad – gives me a shot in the arm. 'Hopefully this will ease the discomfort somewhat.' His voice is dry. Somewhat is right.

I starta hear the sirens when we cross O'Connell Bridge and then a fire engine rushes past, squashin us onta the kerb. We head up O'Connell Street and round Parnell Square. The sirens get louder. I can see a big blanket a smoke billowin down from Denmark Street and onta Parnell Square. We turn at the Wax Museum, onta Dorset Street. North-bound. Outta habit I glance up the corner a Gardiner Street towards the Square. It's gone dark two hours since but there's somethin bright searin the sky, along with the sirens blarin and the horns beepin. People are pointin south, towards the Square.

A picture comes inta me head. Flames leapin over the squat, sendin yella fingers ta grab the sky; every winda and door an eye alight. And in the back garden ya throw yer petrol can away and wipe down yer sooty hands and laugh like a madman while Snags slaps ya on the shoulder, delighted ta have his number one rascal back on track.

Seven a Swords. A cheeky knave braves danger and gets away with it, scot-free. Winner takes all.

I start shakin again.

They bring me ta the hospital and stick a drip in me arm. Rehydration, they say. They take me blood. Tests, they say. Ta see what I took. I coulda died, they say later. All that stuff in me system. I'm lucky, they say. Such a slight chance a me recoverin, even with –

I zone out.

The next day they move me.

Feels different ta the last time I was here, before the bin. The walls seem higher; greyer. The railins spikier. The gates bigger. It's still warm inside but it smells all wrong.

I'm in a dormitory with five other girls, all me own age.

A week in, a detective comes visitin me ta probe me on Sam. They still haven't found her. I smell it off of him. The glinta desperation in his eyes. The twitchin hands. The weariness.

I can't understand. I hadn't buried her that well. Fuck, a dog woulda found her by now. A kid, even, messin on that rock. Jesus, I'd a found her if I was goin for a walk, even if I wasn't lookin.

I keep me head, sedated by Fish-eyes' pills, and don't stray from me official line. I don't know how I got ta that mountain, I say, musta gone up there while I was off me head, and when I woke up it was mornin. The detective doesn't believe me, keeps quizzin me what time did I get there, and when exactly did I OD and was I on me own or did someone help me? I tell him I can't remember times and places. I say I musta blacked out in the night but I came back spontaneous – happens sometimes. And when he asks me again if I'd someone there ta help me recover because – I know what he's gettin at, if I'd someone ta help me kill Sam, so I cut him off, fire it back at him. No no no.

Over the month, Fish-eyes does his mind tests. Even though I'm too tired ta struggle, I can feel the wrong actions burstin outta me, the wrong words itchin ta speak. I am doomed, I think, and me stomach crawls at the thoughta pus-yella walls and withered women in beds waitin ta die. But on the day a reckonin he surprises me.

'The tests have indicated a change in your condition. And as a em . . . result, we suggest that you stay here for the rest of your sentence. Your new medication will be supervised, of course, and we will organize counselling and occupational activities . . .'

blah blah blah

Irene told me later that was when they decided they'd got the first diagnosis wrong and I was clinically depressed insteada hyper.

Depressed? After what I been through? I hafta laugh.

Six ta eight months. Then they would reconsider me accommodation situation.

'Ya heard about Nayler,' says John Paul on his first visit. It's half a question.

I try not ta look like I'm thinkin of anythin.

'He died in that fire on the Square the day after Hallowe'en. They found a body in the basement. Burnt ta cinders. They say he was tied ta a chair and had his hands and feet cut off. They reckon it might be more than him. Emmet Whelan went missin, ya know, and that Dutch girl, and there's other bones lyin around the basement.'

His voice is calm like he's readin the news and he doesn't take his eyes off me once. He's never before talked ta me like this, like I know as much as him, like I'm grown-up, not some stupid little kid hangin outta his arms.

I get the same picture as before; yer house blazin. Only this time you're in the basement, workin fast ta hack up the body – whose body, Nayler? – before runnin back inta Snags's welcomin arms.

'Why ya tellin me all this, John Paul?'

He says nothin.

'It's not because ya know somethin nobody else does?'

'Jesus, Lucy—'

'I know ya know stuff, John Paul. I know ya called them three lugs off us when I was livin in the squat.'

'What's that gotta do with anythin?'

'What I'm sayin is –' I raise me voice, enough ta get him edgy '– settin someone on fire after cuttin them up, that's not the sorta thing psycho Fred Mahon would do, is it?'

He looks around. 'Fucksake, Lucy, keep it down . . . Okay, lookit, they think someone done it ta try and pin it on the Wacker. Could even a been one a the Don's crew. Jesus . . . Snags even? See, Nayler been seen callin upta Wacker. Rumour was he was lookin for protection. Cleaned-up, seeminly. Now, I'm not sayin for sure, but the way things been, it's . . . And Whelan was nothin ta do with Wacker. I can swear ta that. This could be . . . ya know. Dirt. Get the MO right, piece a cake ta land it on Fred Mahon. Course, the Don's sayin nothin, but why would he . . .'

It's the first time me brother's even half-way admitted he's in on all that but I hafta say, it doesn't feel like a special occasion. I can feel his eyes on me, searchin for what I know. But I'm fucked if I—

'Were there teeth?' I surprise meself with the question.

'No.' John Paul looks at me, still searchin. 'Smashed.'

I think of a coila brown hair on a silver chain and picture how ya mighta kept Sasha starvin in that basement, waitin till it was time ta use her. I picture how ya mighta killed her then, tyin her ta that chair, sawin through her while she was still alive, The cards have a picture like that, Eight a Swords. A woman in a red dress, blindfolded, with her hands behind her back, surrounded by eight swords. I useta think that woman had no hands when I was a kid. Doubt, it means. Undecidin. Not knowin.

'And spikes? Were there spikes?' I say, seein eighta them stuck inta the ground round her like a forest.

'Jesus, Lucy, how'd I know? The place was a shell.'

It coulda been Sam's body tied ta that chair.

'They're practically a hundred per cent sure it's him,' says John Paul.

Practically. A lovely word. Never, for a minute, do I believe ya gone.

'Why ya tellin me all this, John Paul?'

He looks at me for a second, thinkin. Then he takes a breath. 'Lookit, I been askin round, Lucy. That's how I found out about Nayler. Called up ta check if he seen anythin of her that night. Maybe if he seen anythin a you . . .'

He leaves a pause, like he's waitin for me ta deny it. I say nothin.

'. . . ya know, somethin ya mightn'a remembered, bein gone off yer head like that.'

I keep quiet.

'But there was no one there, only coppers. So then I asked yer pals.'

'Which pals is that, John Paul?' Me voice surprises me, it's so calm.

'Charlie and that girl Amanda, and that other fella, Damo Roche. Missus Devlin said she heard voices that night round the flats but couldn't recognize them. She said it coulda been anyone, havin a party, but I thought ya mighta had them round ours before ya went out, only you'd forgotten because ya were so outta it.'

Inspector bleedin Morse. I say nothin.

'Well?' he says.

I shrug, meanin *Don't ask me*. 'What did they say?'

'Same thing. They were in Damo's all night. He'd a free house.

And they didn't see sight nor sound a you. Nor Sam neither.'

I stare at the ceilin. He dares me ta contradict him. 'Marlene said the same when I asked her.'

'Well, there ya go.'

I feel relieved at that, in a funny way. Marlene woulda been the first person I coulda run ta. Do I blame her for not sayin more? That doesn't make much sense. Who's ta say how much she knows a what went on? I think a Charlie, mental on acid. What the fuck would he remember seein or not seein? What the fuck would he a told her?

And so one lie feeds another feeds another feeds another till they weave themselves up inta somethin ya tell yerself is the truth.

John Paul rolls up the posters under his arm. He's got them rolled so Sam's smilin face looks out at the world. I know he's done it on purpose, ta make me crack, but it's no use.

'Oh,' I ask, just as he's goin. 'Did ya get the Old Bill on me pals too?'

'The fuck good would that do?'

Ya can take a bullyboy outta a gang but ya can't take the gang outta the bullyboy.

I get a memory that night. It's you and Sasha, lyin together in bed with me. We're runnin low. That's clear on accounta we're all sweatin.

I'm leaving, says Sasha. I'm sick of this. I'll pack up and find Snags. At least he can look after me.

Fine, ya say. Go on if ya want.

She gets outta the bed and stops. Then she gets back in. Then she gets out. Ya watch her, yer jill in the box, gettin out, gettin in, gettin out, gettin in.

Should I stay or should I go? Bom bom bom. Undecidin.

Didja kill her just ta cover yer tracks, Nayler? Or did ya want ta punish her for what Emmet Whelan told ya while ya tortured him ta death – Whelo, missin five long weeks with a big black question mark hangin over his head, whose signet ring ya cut off his finger and bashed flat and tied as a trophy on yer chain? After ya found out from him ya were right, she was the rat, did ya go crawlin ta yer master with the information, Nayler? Is that why he thrun her out?

In them months they searched for her, hot at first, then coolin off as fresher stories grabbed the headlines, I kept waitin.

I waited for you ta come back and tell me why.

I waited for her ta show up – on a beach, in a river, in a field near Buck's gaff.

I waited for someone ta come forward.

I thought Damo would crack first. Once he knew Sam was missin, I was sure he'd tell. Then I remembered he was out cold when she arrived, sick in the corner from too much hooch and vallies. But even if he didn't remember her bein there, he musta come to at some stage. He couldn'a still been outta it when they left, could he? He musta seen her then, dead or alive.

I could understand him not wantin ta say anythin if he'd seen the body. But if all he knew was that Sam was missin – if that was all they all knew – then he'd say somethin. Wouldn't he? Wouldn't they?

I rang Charlie once, twice – how many times? I forget – and every time I rang they hung up. One day I thought I seen him come inta the visitin room, but when I looked again, he'd vanished, and it was only John Paul.

I waited for the bus driver ta come forward. He'd recognize me picture when the Old Bill made their enquiries; he'd remember me gettin on with the resta youse, remember us gettin off at the round-about. I waited for him ta cop on and recognize Sam. Ta say Yeah, he'd let on a young wan who matched the description a the girl on the poster. For passers-by ta remember seein her walk down Gardiner Street after a gang a kids led by a fella dressed as Adam Ant. For anyone ta have seen her.

It took me ages ta suss that the driver wouldn'a remembered me gettin on because A, I had me hoodie up over me face and B, I'd sneaked on behind that skeleton cunt so's I wouldn't hafta pay me ticket. And he wouldn't remember me nor the rest of us gettin off because we were all mixed up with that big bunch a noisy boozin lads. It took me ages more ta suss that the picture on Ma's poster looked nothin like the Sam who chased after us that night, made up like a tart and dressed ta the nines in that sparklin white miniskirt and cheapo red platforms she'd hoarded under her bed. Not even Ma knew what Sam looked like that night. Only us and now us was only me.

I kept waitin for that couple ta turn up, the pair I'd seen on the path after I left the body. Hopin they'd recognize me, or even a found her, even though I was prayin they hadn't—

They didn't.

And Amanda? Well . . .

I thought she mighta come see me after the fuss died down. But she didn't.

They didn't find anythin of her, ya know. Fuck, what am I sayin? Course ya know.

They searched the gaff after knowin I been up there, but they didn't find a single hair. She musta left hairs there, somewhere, but they didn't find one they could say was hers. Sometimes I think that was because ya scoured the gaff after, gettin rid a every trace. But then I think no, that's bollocks, nobody coulda done that, got rid a everythin, so it musta been negligence on the parta the Old Bill. Fucksake, how many other blondes musta visited that gaff? Besides, they musta been sick a Ma and her problem brood by then, and who gives a shit about a juvenile delinquent junkie's family in anyways when there's other crimes, more appealin missin girls, demandin attention?

They found blood – O and full a smack and coke and somethin else, only I can't remember the name, musta been a fancy word for the vallies – but it wasn't any good because that was mine. They found a coupla spikes in the meadow but they were all rustin by the time they got them and only two weren't snapped near the points, and they had me prints and me smack-filled O blood on them too. When the papers got holda the info they said I'd been playin a sick game all by meself up on the hill. Shootin up and tellin meself stories.

Drug-Crazed Frenzy.

'I went up lookin round them woods,' says John Paul.

And? Didja find what the rozzers couldn't, Inspector Morse?

'HellFire Wood, they call it.' He pauses. 'Didn't Granny useta tell stories about there?'

He's waitin for me ta answer as much as I'm waitin for him ta tell. Why ya searchin so hard for her, John Paul? I wanta say. It still won't make Ma love ya.

'Didn't she?' he asks again.

I shrug.

What did ya do ta her, Nayler?

Did ya watch me bury her?

Did ya get rid a her body in one of the hundreds a ways ya knew how? Under water? In concrete? In pieces all over the mountains? Or did yer sacrifice work its magic? Did Snags come ta yer aid yet again?

Were ya sane when ya done it?

Were ya crazed?

Were ya an animal, doin only what an animal does for survival?

How the fuck did ya do it, destroy what was left of her so well even I started thinkin, like Ma, that maybe she was still alive after all? That she'd come to, she'd hooked up with you, somehow, somewhy, I don't know, and run off somewhere, and that's where she is now, happy, alive, with you?

What didja do with her, Nayler?

That year I was in Over brook I behaved meself. Say it was the pills or Fish-eyes poppin in regular ta keep an eye on me; say it was the activities that distracted me, the poxy groups with everyone sittin round cryin, or the readin classes that never amounted ta much; or the way I kept meself apart from the others, because I didn't want another pal, not ever, and so kept apart from trouble too. Say it was the thinkin and the waitin that occupied me so fully there was no space for nothin else. Say it was the answers I gave them when they interrogated me, me promises not ta go back on the gear, ta learn me lessons, ta support me Ma when – not if – I moved back home.

And all the time I looked at Ma's manky coat dotted with the posters a Sam and felt her hatred towards me sharpen.

Why couldn't it a been you, ya ugly little tomboy runt, instead a her?

I can hear me jury booin and hissin already, but I've often wondered if Ma was mournin Sam or if it was really you she cried and grew shrunk and withered over.

I waited. She'll turn up, I, kept thinkin. But she didn't.

John Paul helps me pack. Tara's waitin in the car outside, up the pole again.

'We'd love ta look after ya,' she says. Liar. 'Butcha know, Lucy, with the Social and all needin ta keep an eye on ya and yer Ma thinks it's the best and . . .'

'Yeah, Tara,' I say. 'I know.'

I'm still gobsmacked she's takin me back.

The place smelt like shite, with Ma's spirit breath and sour sweat linin the walls. I couldn't sleep. I could smell Sam in me pilla and I kept thinkin she'd walk in through the door – Hey Lucy, it was a joke, I'm here after all – and when I wasn't seein her I was seein you, climbin in through me winda, gone old and skinny, ugly and stinkin, damp and rotten and red-eyed like somethin been left out in the rain, yer teeth a mess, yer face on fire, callin, *wake up, lucy, wake up I'm comin for ya* –

Just before dawn I conked out and had me usual nightmare. Wakin up sick, comin down the stairs out onta the grass, findin her, and I was just about ta turn her head over ta see if her face was battered or not, when the fog around me thickened and somethin pressed down on me neck. Then I couldn't see Sam any more, only the fog, and it was in me mouth and eyes and tighter round me neck, chokin me. I struggled but it got stronger and me breath was goin and then me eyes forced themselves open, only the fog was still there, black like the OD, suffocatin me. I don't know how I done it, but somehow I pulled whatever strength I had together, and forced her hands off me neck and the pilla off me face, and when I could breathe again I got together me last bit a strength and swung at her with me arm clenched like iron, sendin her flyin across the room.

'What did ya do with her?' she screams.

I open me mouth ta scream back but no sound comes out.

She holds the pilla to her chest and starts sobbin. 'I was a good mother. Jesus Christ. I didn't mean ta hurt her.' She looks at me, her eyes streamin. 'Lucy, love, tell me . . . did she go with ya that night?'

I stare at her, unable ta speak.

First time I remember her callin me love.

That time was the hardest.

In one way it woulda been easy. But if I'd done it, if I'd let pity weaken me, then I'd a lost any chance a reclaimin me own life. Because if she'd believed me, I'da had ta let her go after you. And it crucifies me ta think a that happenin. Yer blood belongs ta only one person, Nayler, and that's not Snags, not the Waxboys, not the Don, and certainly not me Ma.

When ya take yer last breath I'm gointa be the one spittin in yer eyes.

She walked out, the posters on her grey coat flappin in the early mornin light, and went inta her room. I could still hear her at it when I was leavin. She was mutterin prayers ta herself, clickin through the thousand crucifixes danglin like Madonna's round her neck. Every so often she stopped the mutterin ta cry. Fuck that any more.

II

Word on the street for the most part copies what John Paul told me, that ya dead, burnt alive, butchered by some loose cannon or set up by Snags, or what was left a the Don's crew, or even by the Wacker himself. But I didn't believe it when me brother told me and I don't believe it now. Ya not gone, ya too clever ta be taken like that, so obvious. Ya set it up yerself ta hide yer tracks. That was Sasha in the basement, or Whelan, or the Soldier – yes, it was one or all a them, like it was Cindy in the docks and Sam on the mountain – and ya roamin free, Seven a Swords, with nobody ta touch ya.

I sleep in the doorway of an old church down by Smithfield, where the ghosts a me Granny and great-grandda come ta keep me company, and I know ya not gone.

I get other reports too. They whisper knowledge ta me in the rain, in the dribblin gutters, the loose slates a demolishin buildings, in wet concrete, in dead branches. They tell me you're in London, in Australia. Ya racin down by the Liverpool docklands, fleein from the cops. You've a ring a girls walkin the streets a Hamburg, a ring a pushers in Chile, you're a ganglord in Colombia, São Paulo, Buenos Aires, New Mexico. You're in with Gotti in New York, takin bribes and heads in Nigeria, puttin boys out ta ransom in Bangkok.

You're everywhere.

I cover meself with newspapers and hunt for ya in the bins and rubbish tips, lookin for pictures of other bodies killed in other ways. A man turned upside down, danglin from one leg, his mouth scissored inta a shark's wide smile. A woman strung up by catgut between two pillars, S for slut engraved on her naked tits. A child sittin in a bed, its chest nailed ta the wall by nine smack-filled spikes.

I can't read but I hear stories from others on the street. We gather round the trees outside the Garden a Remembrance, round the stone garden in Stephen's Green, under the square arch on Molesworth Street, and they tell me, yes, this body was found, that body was found, yes, the needles were there, yes, the teeth were gone, smashed, useless.

I knew it, I tell them.

Mad Lucy, they call me. Mad Lucy, patron saint a fire and dancin.

I've been on the streets four, five year now, off and on. When I left Ma's I went lookin for Charlie, and Amanda, and Damo too, just ta check, ta see if it happened and why they never came ta me and what should I do, but I'd no luck. Amanda's neighbours told me she didn't live there any more, but they didn't tell me where she'd gone so I knew they were lyin. I still wait for her whenever I can, hangin round her gaff in the hope she'll appear, but she never does. I seen her on the street a few times but she's always walked past, lookin through me like I wasn't there. Once I grabbed her.

'Amanda,' I said, but she just shook me off.

'Jesus fuckin Christ!' she said. 'Who ya callin Amanda?'

Tryin ta fool me, she was. 'You fuck off!' I yelled after her. 'You in yer blonde wig pretendin ya not who ya are. I got ya worked out, ya bitch!'

She didn't turn back ta me then ta explain. Nor did Damo when I went down ta his da's car shop. He didn't even talk ta me, just got one a the lads there ta thrun me out like I was some piece a rubbish. 'Tell us, Damo, tell us,' I called at him. 'What happened that night? What did ya see?' He went bright scarlet but kept actin like he didn't know me.

And Charlie, Charlie, me sweet cousin Charlie . . . I heard from somewhere – John Paul maybe, last time I seen him? Only I can't remember when; never mind – Charlie was sent down the country ta boardin school ta do his Leavin Cert. When he came back Marlene had a gate put up outside their gaff, with a code and high walls spiked with glass that ripped me knees when I tried ta climb over, and a cleaner who caught me as I broke in and called the Old Bill ta take me away so I couldn't even get ta see me cousin's face.

John Paul says he's in college in England now, Bristol or some-where, doin computers.

I've tried goin back there. I've got on any number a buses – 14, 16, 12, 13; the numbers get mixed up in me eyes but I've got on them nonetheless – but I never been able ta find me way back ta the mountain where Buck Whaley useta live.

'Where is it?' I ask shopkeepers, bus drivers. 'Where's the HellFire Club?' They point me in one direction or another, but they're trickin me. The bus is wrong; the lane bricked up; the forest looks different. I am lost.

'Ya don't understand,' I tell the bus driver as he fecks me off onta the side a the road. 'I'm lookin for someone.'

Someone who's gone. Someone who might still be there, lyin under the brambles.

I got close, once. I got as far as the cat painted on the wall. But then a car came speedin round the corner and I flattened meself against the hedges ta keep outta the way. And after the car passed, I seen a gate across the road I hadn't seen before and I went over there, thinkin this is it, this is Jerusalem's forest. But the gate led ta some other wood, and I got lost in a valley beside an ancient wall and started ta withdraw, and only for some German lad helpin me out, I mighta conked out there and then and never come back ta the land a the livin.

Never mind. I'll get there soon. I got new pals now that under-stand, that can help me. I got other places ta search. I am queen a the arches, the goddess a cardboard. I got a new second name. NFA it is; stands for No Fixed Abode Never Forgettin Again Naylers Fleet Assassin. I'm the spirit a revenge, I tell me pals. I got a mission, a man ta track down.

I look twelve, they tell me, me pals on the streets. Even with the hard livin I could pass for a kid. It's the gear does that, I say. Relaxes all the muscles in me face. Nice gear, lovely gear, shit gear that eats inta the roots a me teeth, nibbles at me gums and me veins, bites sores inta me legs and arms. I use it ta slow me down when I get too wound up. I use it ta fill the hole. I use it because I hafta.

Oh, nobody hasta do anythin, Lucy, don'tcha know that?

No. No, I don't know. I hafta. I hafta.

I love the gear and the phy too when I can get it. Oh, Lou Reed was right, sayin it was his life, his wife. It's mine too. I hate it too. But only when I can't get it because it's the only thing keeps me sane. And oh boy, I feel ya closer when I use; even though I've abandoned mosta the rules ya taught me outside a keepin me works clean I haven't OD'd since that night on the mountain, not me, and oh when I use, I feel ya, in me blood in me flesh in me skin in me bones I feel ya, Nayler, and that makes me think the search is comin to an end. The gear calls ya to me, lightin the way, showin me where ta search, where ta find.

'You could use somethin else,' says Barbara Cantwell, the do-gooder lezzer that works the night shifts on the Simon. 'If you want to relax. What about your medication?'

Sure, Barbara. Sure.

She's alright that one, but fuck, she hasn't a clue.

'Now, now, Lucy,' she says every time I turn up at the Simon lookin for a bed – which isn't much, let me tellya, because I can't stand the smell a them other fuckin losers close ta me, no way – 'Have you gone ta the Social yet? Have you sorted out your accommodation? Have you been to NA?'

'Yeah, yeah, yeah, Barbara.' Anythin for a quiet life.

She tuts, not believin me. Now, now. Like I'm a kid, or thick, or worse. Like she knows better. Like her gettin me ta do somethin will change things, make all animals equal.

I been inside what – three, four, eight times? Can't remember. It's like most things nowadays, most numbers. They get all fucked up in me head. Days is months is years so what. I been inside. That's all that matters and even then it doesn't. Nothin matters outta findin Sam again and you and makin ya pay for whatcha done. But yeah. I been inside. Small jobs mainly; robbin, dippin, dealin and the other D; drunk and disorderly. A few assaults. Inside doesn't bother me – not on the gear front in anyways. Security's so lax in the Joy ya might as well land there for life if ya wanta keep usin. Hup, the packet's over the wall; hup, the string's down;

hup, it's in me pocket. But because I got other things ta do – the search, remember, the mission – I mind me manners when I'm inside so I can get out sooner. Oh, I'm a good girl. I take whatever pills they feed me – or pretend ta, haha, hate them pills, they just slow me – and soon as I'm out I head back on the trail.

I think, can't remember but think, they'd nowhere ta put me before I turned eighteen, can't remember when that was, but yeah, they'd nowhere ta put me so they sent me ta the bin. Got shocked there – once, twice – and stoned with them pills, and they took me gear away from me and wouldn't give me none, no matter how hard I screamed. After the second shockin, I got wise, sussed if I didn't watch it, I'd be there for life, wastin what was left a me days droolin in the corner. So I boxed clever, took the pills, turned up for the therapy, got John Paul ta put a word in and they had ta let me go. Haven't been back since. There's been a coupla near misses; the dippin and the dealin are no problem, but twice when I been up for assault the court shrinks have done their tests. Evaluation they call it. Evaluation be fucked. I know what that means: Dundrum. But ya see, Nayler, I can switch it on when I want, the sanity. Little do they know, but I got me mind powers developed from me years on the streets. I know what they're thinkin, what they want, and I can play them fucks against each other and the system like nobody's business. It's a thin line between bad and mad but I got it worked out. And shithole as the Joy is, it's ten times better than them bins. I am fucked, F, U, C, whatever, if I'm goin back in there.

Everythin's easy when ya know how ta play the game. Or nearly everythin –

I see John Paul when he collects me from the Joy. Sometimes I see him when I go back home ta rob somethin for the gear. I wait till Ma's gone out or outta her head in her bed – ask me how I know, Nayler, go on, but it's easy, I can smell the whiskey way across the city – and then I slip back in and nick what I can. Anytime John Paul catches me robbin, he makes me give it back. Once he tried ta fool me, the cunt. Told me he wanted ta bring me away ta live with him and Tara, but I could see right through that lie.

He only wanted ta lock me up so I wouldn't find Sam again. So I ran.

Micko I seen only a coupla times, the last six month ago. He'd only just found about the virus but he looked like he'd been sick for ever. Shufflin, shamblin, his blond hair out in clumps, what was left shaved close ta his skull.

I'd just been let out and I was clean – not intentionally and I wasn't plannin ta stay that way – but still I wouldn'a gone ta him. He always brings me down, me brother, like seein him is . . . but John Paul told me the news so I felt I had ta. Duty, ya know, and besides, last time I'd got a feelin he maybe knew somethin about ya I didn't, and maybe he'd tell me . . .

His hands were shakin and covered with scabs. Reminded me a Sam. I nearly started cryin at that, but then I remembered I'd work ta do; had ta dig, find out.

'Have ya seen our pal?' I winked so he'd know what I meant.

He thought about it. Then he looked straight inta me eyes and his own were clear as the summer sky as the sea as anythin as anythin.

'Yeah,' he said, reachin for me hand.

His skin was dry, the crusts a the scabs standin up like little ridges. He rubbed the tips a me fingers. I leant closer, disregardin the frownin face a the screw.

Where is he? I said, usin no words, only me mind powers, but he said nothin, just kept rubbin. I felt his fingernails dig under me own, scrabble at the webbed bits a skin between me fingers, root around under the cuff a me trackie top.

Then I sussed it. He was lookin for gear.

Somethin jolted me – blame it on bein clean or the poxy white lights they have in them visitors' rooms – and for a minute I forgot about me errant, about you and even Sam and why I was visitin him in the first place.

'Jesus, Micko. What happened ta ya?'

He stopped rubbin.

His downturned face me own, our shared reflection's, our Da's, only old and blond. His fingers on mine cold and quiverin. His eyes like –

But before I could say anythin else, he started scrabblin again for the gear, whistlin through his broken teeth. And his whistlin took on a new shape and in it words. *You'll find him, Lucy. Keep searchin.* And I remembered everythin – you, Sam, me mission – and the urgency of it all forced me up and out and away from him.

I haven't gone back since. What's the point? He's helped me all he can. Otherwise, what is he, only some fucked-up mirror tellin me nothin I don't already know?

I've kept quiet about Sam, Nayler, and what I seen that mornin, and what I done. All these years I've kept it quiet. I may be forgettin things; words, names, whatever, but I know better than ta admit I ever seen her dead with them ten spikes stuck inta her. That's my secret, Nayler – mine and yours – and I won't let it slip till I got yer severed head bleedin in me grip. Which I will, ya fuck, because I am still Lucy Dolan, fast as lightnin, able ta catch anythin she wants. Yes, I am the empress a the doorsteps, angel a the gutters, hard and fast and dyin for vengeance. Some days I am so quick and there and with it, it would make ya cry; it's like me pals are right, I *am* twelve again. On them days nobody can touch me for blaggin. I'm in and outta a shop like lightnin, I'm onta a woman's bag – ignorin the smell a the body too close ta mine – and off it in jig time.

Jig time is three-four, one a me new pals tells me. He useta be a shrink and now he plays the recorder for money, buskin on Grafton Street while I sit a few yards up, tappin for quids off of tourists at the bank machine, listenin ta his notes rise and sink, lettin me feet do their own soft-shoe shuffle even as I sit there. His name is Andrew and he has a long black beard and drinks meths straight from the bottle. I told him about the drugs they give me inside and Fish-eyes' pills and he shook his head.

'All drugs are shit,' Andrew said. 'They fuck you up more than they sort you out.'

'Tell me about it,' I said, and laughed.

518

At night he plays a jig and I dance ta it. Then I box against me own dark shada on the walla the arch across from the Pink Elephant, frightenin the good-time party girls in their stacked heels and short dresses.

Whoo hoo, Lucy, call me pals. Go, go, go.

I float like a butterfly, sting like a bee. I pretend I'm one a the black boys. Tyson and Ali and Leonard and Robinson all mixed up inta one. Die, white scum, I yell at me shada. Die, Jake La Motta, ya white wife-beatin piece a shit.

Whoo hoo, Lucy. Whoo hoo, Mad Lucy.

Later on, when Derek asked me how it started – the decline, he called it – I said it felt like I'd always been that way. The walkin and sleepin in the rain and thinkin and searchin and shit street gear and nice street gear and the phy and meths and not washin any more and me pals and the dancin and the rest just sorta grew on me until it became . . . normal. He asked if it was the pills; stoppin and startin them like that. But I said no. Pills had nothin ta do with it. There wasn't one moment when I slipped from bein one thing ta another. It was almost like I'd always been that way, under the surface, and all I needed was the opportunity – the right time, place, people – ta turn inside-out.

It's rainin. I curl up close ta the metal shutter and the Saturday night drinkers walk past, their heels clackin, their umbrellas givin me second-ta-second breaks from the drizzle. I got a fix earlier that afternoon and I'm alright now. I'm brand-new shampoo, cool as –

I hear a snatch a music, somethin from the seventies. Then a couple stop beside me.

'Come on, darlin,' says a familiar dark-brown voice.

I can't believe it but then the familiar voice coughs and I know I'm not hallucinatin.

I hold me breath. For months I wandered the streets where I grew up lookin for that voice. I searched Drumcondra, Eccles Street, Phibsboro, North Strand, Mountjoy Square, Portland Row,

Seán MacDermott Street, Dorset Street, Ballybough. I searched them all but couldn't find it. And now, on the other side a the city, under the metal awnin a the old burnt-out buildin on South Great Georges Street, I hear it.

'Wait!' says the voice's girlfriend, vexed. I squint open me eyes and see her lift her foot and adjust the strap on her killer heels.

She's a blonde. Long curly hair, tossed and tweaked the way they do it nowadays, wearin a catsuit and a tight denim jacket. Snags flicks his butt over at me without seein, but with the rain the edge a me cardboard is too damp ta catch fire.

'I got a plane ta catch in the mornin, Imelda. Get a move on, will ya.'

'Jesus,' she says. 'I don't see whatcha so worried about. It's not like ya need yer beauty sleep or nothin.'

'Come on, sweetheart.'

She fixes her shoe and they head off, under their umbrella.

I can't sleep now. I get up, foldin me cardboard and tuckin it under me arm, and I walk the streets, lookin for inspiration.

What plane is he catchin? I ask the drizzlin rain and the dim moon.

I think and muse and wait for the signs ta come.

A tattered beermat with a picture of a windmill floats in the gutter. I know that windmill and the name it heralds. Amstel beer.

Two buses pass by, splashin me. The number is one-one. Eleven.

I stare inta the puddles in the buildin site near St Pat's Cathedral and see a sailor's tattoo reflected there. A knife in a heart. Ace a Swords. On a lamp-post *Have You Seen Sam?* smiles at me. There's a hoardin across the road with a big ad for runners. Can't read the words but I recognize the symbol. It's a swish.

Nike. Andrew told me they've a sayin: *Just Do It*.

First thing in the mornin after robbin the money – a mucker builder stompin down Westmoreland Street on his way ta the sites, wallet stickin outta his back pocket – I nip inta McDonald's on O'Connell Street and clean up. I'm not thick. I know I hafta look presentable or they won't let me on the bus, much less sell me a ticket ta Amsterdam. I robbed a comb off one a the madsers last night and I drag it through me hair that's down past me shoulders and scrape it inta a ponytail. I wash under me arms and around me neck and straighten out me tracksuit, ignorin the looks a the secretaries and the spic students in for their EggMcMuffins.

While the young wan beside me is dryin her hands, I slip me hand inta her bag and rob her perfume. I store it under me sleeve till she's gone, then I spray it on.

I look alright. Clean. I smell okay. I reef through me pockets, makin sure the money's still safe. I smile. Me Da smiles back, lookin exactly the way he done just before he walked out on us. *Do it.*

They shift away from me when I sit down. A heavy dark-lookin fella on me right, a frizzy redhead nosy type with specs on me left. The dark-lookin fella has a suitcase with him.

'Goin back ta the jungle, yeah, bud?' I'm tryin ta be friendly. He looks lonely.

He stares at me. The specky one sniffs.

'Here, I'm only bein friendly, missus,' I tell her. 'There's no crime in that.' Then I laugh out loud, thinkin a what I'm gointa do ta you when I get ta Amsterdam and how that might be seen as a crime in some quarters. The specky one shifts away. With me X-ray eyes I see the bus driver look at me in his mirror.

I'm onta you, pal, I think, and wink at him.

He doesn't wink back.

I have a nice chat on the way up with the dark lad. He doesn't have much English so I hafta speak dead slow with him. I tell him about you, that I'm goin ta find an old pal and settle some scores. I start ta show the darkie me knife in me belt but with me X-ray eyes I feel the driver jottin down everythin I do, and who knows, he might be one a Snags's spies, so I think again and pull me tee-shirt back down. I don't want Snags coppin on what I'm upta and –

No way, jose. No sirree, bob dixie.

So I wink at the darkie and tell him telepathically what I mean instead a spellin it out. He nods at me, dead slow.

'Maybe you'd like ta come with me ta Amsterdam,' I suggest. 'You're a grand big fella. Ya can hold him down while I slit his throat.'

The darkie nods, slow.

The redhead gets up and moves ta another seat.

Shit, I think. Now the bus driver has heard. But he doesn't seem ta mind. Maybe he's on our side after all.

'Last stop!' roars the driver.

'This is us, bud,' I tell me dark pal. I help him pull his suitcase off of the bus. He grabs tight onta it, like he's afraid it'll run away from him.

'There ya go.' I pat his shoulder. 'All grand. Have a good time back home with the resta the jungle bunnies, yeah?'

He stares at me. His dark brown eyes are like pools a shit.

I scour the board. The numbers dance, swappin places. The lights are doin me head in and I'm hopin I won't pass out, have one a them fits like when I was a kid, end up thrashin on the floor before I get within even sniffin distance a ya. I turn round. A young skinny fella is comin me way. He's got a long fringe and a uniform that looks half-way official. I can tell he's a steamer even from a distance but maybe he can help. I grab him.

'Here, where do I get a ticket for the eleven o'clock ta Amsterdam?'

He looks down on me hand on his arm like I've got a disease. 'Do you know which airline it is?'

Airline?

He shakes his arm loose. 'All the information is on the board.'

'Yeah, I know.' I'm tryin ta stay calm, but I'm gettin nervous because around me the loudspeakers are sayin Flight AE102 11.45 to London is boarding now and maybe I've missed it even though I timed meself right, got the right bus from town – didn't I?

'I got an eye problem. I can't read. Go on, be a pal.' I smile ta calm him down.

Somethin goes through his face at me smile and he takes a step back, says somethin ta his walkie talkie.

'Ya don't hafta ask yer pal, bud. Ya can read it yerself. It's all there. Just read it for me, yeah?' Me feet start jiggin and I scratch me head, feelin somethin crawl there.

He stares at me. 'There is no flight to Amsterdam at eleven.'

'Ah, here.' I start laughin. 'Don't be messin with me.'

His walkie-talkie crackles. He mutters somethin else inta it that I can't understand. Like Tiger Bay Prawns ta Alabama Spot Check.

I grab his arm again. 'Come on, son. Just tell me where I can get a ticket.'

'Take your hand off me.' He pulls away.

He's not hearin me. 'Ya not hearin me, pal. I need ta get this flight. I've a friend I hafta catch. See?' I lift up me trackie top with me free hand and show him me knife handle above me belt.

He freezes. His eyes are glitterin. His mouth twists and he reaches for his walkie-talkie again. Then I understand. Fuck . . . how could I a been so stupid?

'What the fuck have ya done, ya stupid cunt?' I grab him by the face, pushin his lips together so he can't speak, and knock the walkie-talkie onta the ground. 'I don't want him ta fuckin know!' With me other hand I grab his throat.

People gasp around us, clearin space—

Under me hand his Adam's apple wobbles. Feels disgustin. I squeeze a bit.

'Unngghha!' He's kickin, flailin, bitin at me hand that's holdin his mouth. The kicks madden me. I duck, stamp on the arch of his foot, bring me knee up, whack him in the bollocks. He slumps. His spit lines me fingers. I shake him by the throat like he's a dog.

'Where is he? He's here somewhere! Stop hidin! Tell me, ya fuck! I know ya workin for him—'

'Unnnggha!' His face turns purple and shifts sideways, becomin yours the moment ya seen Sam through the winda.

I let go yer mouth, feel in me belt for me knife as ya scream. I lift the blade. Slash.

Funny; sounds like it went real slow the way I'm tellin it now. It wasn't slow. It was fast, and what came next faster still.

Afterwards, when I realized how bad I'd fucked up, I wondered if he'd been strugglin only because he wanted ta tell me that poxy flight number after all. If I'd let him go, he'd a been able ta speak before he turned inta ya and fooled me, and then I'da got ta ya, the real you, sooner.

Oh, I can feel ya out there, itchin ta know. So, go on, ask me, Nayler.

What the fuck have ya done ya –

No. That's not for me. Ask the other. Am I –

Junkie Slasher in Airport Bloodbath

Okay. Lookit. There's reasons and complications and there's any amounta things I could say. That he panicked me by panickin. That he shoulda been calmer. That I was outta control, over-wrought, maddened by me time on the streets, didn't know what I was at. That I was goin after someone else, not him, and he was gettin in the way. That I didn't mean ta kill him, that the fuckin plastic knife from McDonald's was proof enough a that, that it snapped for godsake, and even though it went inta the jugular I wasn't expectin it, that the blood squirtin inta me face shocked me as much as him, that I didn't mean ta push him, that I didn't push him, he fell, because the ground was slippy with his blood, that I didn't mean ta kick him, it was only because I lost me balance with him fallin, that the crack of his head against the trolley was a shock, that the looka him, neck twisted, eyes starin at the ceilin, will be with me forever, that that that that that that that that that that that that *that*

Oh yes.

I could say all them things ta ya now, just like I done back then; ta the solicitor, the court, the gicknaw journalists with their pens scratchin away like beaks as they searched for stories, not carin which was true and which false as long as it captured the

524

public's imagination. But I know it won't wash with you, Nayler.

So why not tell ya the other stuff – the reasons and complications that I thought at the time and after; the stuff I only ever let slip ta Irene and even then not fully?

That he was a patronisin little fuck and he was askin for it.

That there's harsher ways a killin people than breakin their necks. Did ya know that, ladies and gentlemen a the jury? Ya can poison someone just by lookin at them like all they deserve is ta die. Ya can leach the spirt outta them by strippin them of hope and beauty, by stickin them in a barracks a grey concrete, by leadin them ta expect nothin from their lives only failure. Who would say a life lived in failure, in yearnin and wantin and hatin and fearin and cryin and seekin, is any kinder than death? Death – Christjesus, we all hafta die; but sometimes I wonder if it's the only real peace any of us will get.

Ya said somethin once, about bein kind. Is that what ya meant?

But that's not what ya wanta hear from me, old pal, is it? What you want is the truth, the whole truth, and nothin but the truth – so fuck you anyway, here it is:

Yes, I am guilty. I did mean ta kill. In the moment he fell he was you and yes, I wanted a death. But not *his*. He was a stranger, for fucksake. What good would his blood ever do me?

Hah. And there's the rub, as Derek would say, meanin problem or sick joke or thing ya don't wanta face. Because no matter what way ya look at it, his blood did do me good. That sacrifice paid for me sanity, for more; for me life. Without it I'da never got normal again – real normal, I mean, not the inside-out kind. I'da died on the streets without ever gettin it together ta find you. I'da gone, just like that, snap!, another invisible number.

Many would hold that's how it shoulda been; that his life was too high a price for mine, that I shoulda just snapped out and the world woulda been a better place for it.

Do I believe that too?

I don't know how ta answer that question.

Ah, come on, Lucy Dolan. Stop avoidin. Own up.

Okay, then. There's times I do believe it, yeah, that I shoulda

gone. But there's other times, Christ . . . no. Them times I'm glad
– I am, even in the middle a this shit cycle a breath and sleep –
that it's me who's alive.

Ya not satisfied, though, are ya? Ya got that other question for me,
the one I hate.

Am I—

Are ya sorry, Lucy Lu?

Sorry. There's a song goes like that, about words not comin
easily. Boyzone. Not my sorta music but—

Jesus. Stick ta the fuckin point, Lucy Lu.

I'm.

Yeah. Okay then. I'm sorry. I'm sorry it wasn't you, ya cunt.

No. No. *Really . . .*

Oh, Jesus. God. Fuck—

Lookit, if I'd the chance ta tell this story the way I want, as
opposed ta the way it is, yes, Jesus, I'd change it. There's been times,
many, where I've prayed for a different endin. For him ta recover
and me ta get away with a GBH, five year max. That woulda made
lots a things easier, not least the rightness in what I'm doin now.
But that's not how it went. I killed. And it was the wrong person.
And given everythin, the circumstances, meself, I don't know if I'da
ever done – if I coulda ever done – things different.

Back ta the question. Am I—

Let's leave it at this, okay? If I hadn'a been sorry, I wouldn'a
pleaded the way I done. Would I?

Words don't come easily.

The solicitor said there was no way they'd be able ta prove intent
– even with the darkie from the bus sayin I was talkin violent and
showin him me plastic knife – but they'd probably push for
manslaughter. That left us a coupla options. I could plead not guilty,
diminished responsibility on accounta me mental state. The minute
he said that I seen it, me future – years and years of hospital wards,
gettin old and withered in a room fulla ancient bearded biddies
with eggyolks down their fronts; years a bein fed with shocks and

drugs and shite therapy that would never make a blind bit a difference. So I told him No.

I could tell he wasn't expectin that but he tried not ta show it. 'Okay.' He thought for a moment. 'Well. We can plead not guilty to the manslaughter charge but guilty to assault. Try to win it on the medical evidence. Death as a result of the blow to the head which you didn't instigate.' He paused. 'It could be tough. There may be witnesses who'll say you pushed him deliberately and you will be cross-examined. But—'

I pleaded manslaughter.

Four ta five for Grievous Bodily Harm, normally. Six ta eight for manslaughter.

In the end they gave me nine, in the women's wing of a new medium-ta-high-security gaff down the country.

'I can't understand,' said the solicitor after. 'Even the McIntyre case a few years back . . . well, he got nine but they knew that was planned, except they couldn't prove it. And they're usually easier on women. Maybe we could appeal—'

No, I said. I'd enough.

Even then I think I knew I needed the time.

After the trial I zoned out again. Livin became a set a pictures that crowded in on me, whirred past, makin no sense. You'da thought the shock a what I'd done – and not done – woulda jolted me inta takin a fresh look at things.

Wake up, Lucy! Come on! Come on!

The sinner repents. The bad girl makes good. Lucy Dolan examines her life and determines ta get it back in order.

Reformed Slasher: I've Learnt Me Lesson the Hard Way

Sad ta say, though, most things don't turn themselves around overnight.

Inside again. I'm home from home. This time it's for real. I'm a head honcho. People avoid me eyes on the landin. I've a serious reputation.

Mad Lucy. Killer Lucy. Whoo hoo.

I'm back on the gear soon as I can. Business as usual. Buy, sell, exchange.

I pay with stories and visions. I read their hands, read their cards, pay attention ta the small creatures hoverin round the edges a me visions and tell me fellow travellers what lies in store.

Some ladies aren't happy with tales. They want satisfaction, so that's what I give them. Oh, I know it's all wrong; against jailhouse rules. If ya top dog ya not supposed ta groom anyone else. You get the groomin, they get protection. But I don't want groomin, and I've no hankerin ta protect anyone, least of all them.

I've imagined it so many times but in the end, it's different. I use the lessons ya gave me on me Ma, on Sasha, on them hooers in the squat; lick, chew, spit, finger. They tell me what they want. They moan as they come. I feel nothin. I try puttin Amanda's face on one or two, but that just makes me feel sick and rage rises and I go ta hit them, and I don't wanta risk gettin another year or two, so for the most part I switch off, let me fingers do the talkin. I feel nothin.

There's fights, time ta time. Even outta it, even strung out, I'm still good with me fists, and for the most part I know ta strike when nobody's lookin.

I'm trouble and the screws know it. The law says losin yer liberty is punishment enough, ya don't need ta scrub floors or be lashed with the cat. Not me. I get visits cancelled, sly kicks, solitary confinement in the Cellar. I probably deserve it.

Nine years sounds a lot, but there's a part in yer head that screens it out, zip, like that. How can I think a nine years when it's day ta day, one step at a time?

Buy, sell, exchange. Sterilize, shoot, score.

Rumours spread on the landins like oilspill. Did ya hear the Wacker's bought a stud farm and gone respectable? Did ya hear that peace deal between Snags and the Don went sour a few years back, ta do with Emmet Whelan, they say, though nobody knows why? Did ya hear there's a new boy, the Bishop, and he's gunned down the Dempseys in Ballyfermot? Did ya hear Snags has got his hands on every pie south a the Liffey? Six years he's not been on the northside, they say, what's more kept himself so clean the rozzers will never pin a thing on him. Nobody mentions your name, though, except as somethin belongin ta the past. Nayler, fastest milkman in the west.

I probe sometimes, when I hear a rumour there's a new runner in Marseilles, or a fresh pimp on the Square, but when the looks get too enquirin I back down. Don't wanta raise any suspicions.

Questions rise. What am I doin here? What the fuck did I do? What in Christsname am I gointa do next?

But I push them down. I got no use for that kinda askin. And I sink back onta the other questions, the familiar ones, the ones so long in me head they've grooved a track for easy access. Did ya beat her before or after ya killed her? Did ya watch me, Nayler, as I took her down the hill? What did ya do with her body? Where the fuck are ya?

And then even these get too much too, too heavy, because I see meself stabbin that lad again and I can't tell the pictures apart – me goin ta kill him and you killin Sam – so I push them down too.

Brawl, buy, sell.

Daylight creeps away from me. I see everythin through thirty small square panes a glass. Me skin whitens, me chest flattens, me cheekbones jut, me eyes shada, me muscles harden inta steel ropes. I work out, do weights. Use, get sick, get clean, use, get sick. Me resolution dissolves.

The routine grabs me by the ankles, draggin me down. A shrink comes in regular and does the rounds. He's a busy man. There's a lotta people ta see. He doesn't have much time. When I'm called up he spends five minutes askin me questions I don't answer. Then he hmms, reads me hospital reports and ends up prescribin a new set a pills. Most a them I don't take. I find ways a hidin them in me mouth, under me arms, anywhere. Fucksake, things are bleary enough as they are.

He ignores me habit; all the habits oozin out under the cell doors. Everyone knows what's goin on but officially there is No Problem Here.

On the landin they call me names: Madman – even though I'm a woman – and CopKiller – even though he wasn't a cop – but McSlasher's their favourite.

'Here, Slasher,' says Lola Byrne over lunchtime, passin me a Q her fella gave her in a kiss. 'I heard you're the one killed yer sister, only ya buried her so good nobody ever found out.'

The rumour seeps inta the gear that night as I shoot it inta a vein near me cunt.

Relief hits me. It's not heaven any more; stopped bein heaven a long time ago. The gear I use now only soothes the cravin, addin no extra value in itself. Tolerance is a terrible thing.

That night me nightmare isn't its usual self. This time you've come back from the dead and ya shakin me, callin me a stupid bitch, beggin somethin I can't make out. I hate ya – not for havin done what ya done but for havin come back from the dead, for havin been dead in the first place so ya could come back from it, because in me soul I know ya not dead, never were, so does this mean me soul is wrong and all the other rumours are right and ya are dead, and if so where does that leave me, have I imagined have I imagined have I fuckin imagined have I done what I done for nothin? – and I rise outta bed ta kill ya again, ta make ya dead for sure this time, but ya melt away at me touch, and when I wake someone is screamin and I've got me hands round Sharon Stokes's throat.

The Borstal Strangler, they call me now.

Sharo didn't report it. She went so far as ta laugh it off after; she's a tough nut. But even less a them on the landin meet me eyes now.

I can't understand why time is draggin. I keep lookin at the clock and it's always twelve, them two hands lifted up at the top like they're terrified a fallin down. Come on, come on, I yell at them, at life, at time, at you. Let me out.

I can talk ta people now without openin me mouth. I can read minds. People walk past me and their history walks with them. I see their futures, their unborn children, their certain deaths. Some days the visions come and go like ads on the telly. Bam bam bam, one after another. Other days, weeks, nothin happens.

It doesn't worry me. But it's distractin. It has nothin ta do with you or Sam or why I am where I am so why should I see any a it?

I work out, pushin the veins and muscles in me body ta breakin point. I see red when I sleep. Rivers a blood. *Come on come on come on come on.*

Irene told me I was in denial all that time. That's why I was so fucked up. I looked at her.

'It's not a river in Egypt.' She laughed, but I didn't get it. 'Our minds are very good at playing tricks with us,' she said, serious again. 'Yours wasn't acknowledging what you'd done. It needed something big to wake you up.'

'How are ya?' asks John Paul, leakin sympathy like pus from a sore.

Come on come on. I jig me feet, stare at the ceilin, at the flakin paint, at his meaty face gettin fat on Tara's home cookin, at Tara behind him with her new baby clamped to her tit. Only she's not with us, is she? She never visits. She's back in their gaff in Phibsboro feedin their baby.

'I said, how are ya, Lucy?' His voice is louder, snappin me back ta the moment.

Whatcha think? I ask him telepathically, curlin me lip in a crooked lazy smile so he'll be one hundred per cent sure a me meanin.

He's got a security firm of his own now, on the Navan Road. He says it's his own, but everyone knows it's just another front for the Wacker. On the surface that little psycho cunt Fred Mahon has pulled out, but deep down, stud farm aside, he's the same type a businessman as he ever was. And his profits hafta go somewhere. The knowledge a what me bro is upta splits the landin down the middle. Some give me more respect on account of it; others shun me. In the yard it's important ta know what pack ta run with.

Front or not, it's doin well for John Paul. I can tell by the love handles.

He hasn't searched for Sam in years. He thinks she's dead but he doesn't dare say it ta Ma. He tells me, though, sometimes, when he's not on his guard. 'She's gone, Lucy, isn't she?' I never say anythin. It could be he's not off-guard after all. It could be he's probin. Best ta keep shtum.

'That girl useta be pals with Sam . . . Lisa whatshername. Missus Devlin told Ma—'

There's a flicker a light ta John Paul's left, and I see Tara kneelin there, buck naked with her brown tits bouncin up and down, gettin fucked up the gary by their milkman.

John Paul breaks off, distracted. 'Whatcha lookin at, Lucy?'

I can't help smilin. Tara looks so outta place, what with everyone else sittin at their tables, talkin dead earnest about this and that. Tara stretches her long neck and pretends ta come. The milkman grunts like a pig and shoots his muck up her arse.

Ah, Jesus, lads. Too much. I look away.

'Ya got three a them now, don'tcha, John Paul?'

He looks startled.

'Three nippers, I mean. One a them's like me. Can't take the flashin lights. Be careful a the bath, John Paul. Twelve year old. Drownin's a horrible death.'

John Paul looks afraid at first, then disgusted. 'Fuck off, Lucy.'

I laugh, but more on accounta he thinks I'm takin the piss than because it's funny seein that poor dead kid drippin water from the ceilin above us. That's not funny at all.

Lola Byrne's visit looks over at us.

Fuck off, ya cunt, I tell him telepathically. Then Lola starts talkin, and he switches his attention back ta her.

'Charlie's got his degree,' says John Paul.

I start singin 'Baby Love'.

He tries talkin over me. 'Yeah, he's in London now, workin in a big computer firm.'

'Not surprised. That boy always had plans.'

'Sure.'

'Was he askin for me?' Dangerous water, but still . . .

'No,' says John Paul. 'I wasn't talkin ta him, ya know. Only Marlene.'

I laugh again, this time thinkin a Marlene and how she's managed ta hold onta the secret for so long. Five, six year it's been and she still hasn't let slip a thing. But then maybe I have her worked out wrong. Maybe she never knew what happened. Maybe Charlie said, 'Ma, somethin awful's happened,' and she told him ta shut up, she didn't wanta know. I don't hold it against her. Marlene's a good woman. She fixed things for me when nobody else done—

'What?' John Paul's frownin like I've said somethin.

'Nothin.' I stare at him. Fuck, now I've lost me train a thought. I've—

'Ma's fucked it up,' says John Paul. 'She made me drive her out ta Malahide the other night but she had a few scoops on, ya know the way she gets . . .'

I jig. Don't wanta talk about me fuckin Ma. Shut up, John Paul.

'But I had ta bring her out. Jesus, she gets little enough . . .'

Am I imaginin things again or is that pity in me brother's eyes? I jig harder.

'In anyways, she screamed at them – Marlene, Stevo, the whole gang – sayin they're all a shower a bastards, don't understand her, abandonin her in her hour a need, abusin her trust, interferin where they're not wanted. They'da called the Old Bill out if I hadn'a been there.'

'Yeah, yeah, yeah.' I'm only half-listenin. I can't believe Marlene knows but hasn't said anythin. She wouldn't string Ma along like that, that's for sure, even ta protect Charlie. She wouldn't let on ta Ma that Sam was still alive if she wasn't. Marlene's a good woman. She's got principles. She—

'That's not what I've come here ta tell ya,' says John Paul.

The door a the visit room swings open, sendin bright light in. A screw rushes ta close it, but it's too late. Someone's got in. I can only see a shada from where I'm sittin, thin and fit, its face hidden by a hoodie, but as John Paul coughs and ahems, tryin ta get the words together, the shada walks up behind John Paul and throws back his hoodie. It's Micko. He's got his two hands open, stretched out in fronta him. There's little black spots in the middle a each palm. He smiles and his teeth are alright.

Somethin big.

*

'Ma drank solid for five hours,' says John Paul when the room has stopped spinnin. 'I had ta batter the door open. She was lyin in the kitchen. She was after cuttin herself on one a the bottles. Guess what she said ta me?'

I shake me head. He sucks his cheeks in, takes her off. 'Jesus, if I had me life all over again, I wouldn'a had any a youse!'

I hafta laugh. Behind John Paul, Micko's ghost laughs too, but it's a laugh with no real joy in it.

On the way back ta the landin, things come at me through the air. *Go away*, I try ta tell them telepathically, but I can't use me mind powers any more. They are useless against the strength a the dead. The kid from the airport is jumpin in fronta me like a dolly on a string, laughin at me, jeerin, his twisted neck gushin blood inta me eyes as he screams, *wake up Lucy wake up wake fuckin UP*. Women's faces hang on the walls as I pass; strangled, slashed, drowned, battered, burnt. Goin, goin, gone. And on me shoulder me brother's invisible hand weighs a ton the way Sam's has never done.

The screws lead me through the gates. The wire cage hemmin the stairs is wet with sweat and tears and blood and boredom. Someone starts singin 'Baby Love' in me head.

I lie on me bed. I kid meself I'm thinkin things through. But I'm not. All I can feel is the weight a everythin on me mind and it's drivin me mad.

I am goin mad, I whisper ta meself, low so the others won't hear. I have been goin mad for seven whole years and I am not gettin any better. If I don't wake up soon I will try ta kill again and once more it will be the wrong person.

Please help me. Somebody, anybody, please help.

That was the night I died. I prayed, I begged, and nobody heard. I fell inta a black hole where heaven and hell twisted round each other, eatin each other's tails. The madness owned me, thrashin me body, forcin me ta leak sweat and steam. I fell inta the black hole and stayed there; wept and begged ta be released. I did not know what ta do. I did not know what I believed any more or what

534

I knew. I did not know the real from the false. I prayed and wept and begged, and when I breathed, me breath stank a sulphur like the Devil's farts. The ghosts a the livin and the dead tormented me and I let them because what did I know any more? And who was I any more only nothin? The least equal a the animals.

It took me another two goes before I got clean again for good, but that was the night the work really started.

A catalyst, said Irene.

'I always knew he was gointa die, but. Since forever. It was obvious. So it wasn't like it was a big shock or anythin. Not like—'

I stop.

'Some years ago my pet cat died under the wheels of a car,' says Irene. 'She was real cute and I cried for three weeks afterwards.' She pauses. 'Two months before that my mom had died but I hadn't shed a tear. See, Lucy, you were ready.'

She smiles one of her brief smiles.

I feel bad about the truths I'm hidin from her but I smile back. Sides, it's not like it's all lies, is it?

'Here,' says Lola, passin me the daily dose. I shake me head.

'Slasher!' says Lola, louder, nudgin Sharo Stokes ta nudge me. I shake me head again.

I don't know what I'm doin, exactly, but this has ta be a start.

I must get clean. I must get clean. I must get clean.

I focus. I work out. I avoid the glances. I snatch me hand back from the daily communion plate. I work out. I start boxin again.

I get sick, cramp up, puke, feel like dyin. But when I'm on the verge a fallin again, the angel a madness catches me and reminds me what I hafta do.

I shave me head. I smash me red-gloved iron fist inta the big black bag hangin like a body from the ceilin a the gym.

I must get clean. I must get clean. I must get clean so – enough.

I am not yet okay enough ta add 'so in the end I can find ya'. For the moment, any thought a you will mess with the programme.

For the moment, you're banished, Nayler. Sent ta oblivion. Off limits.

I must get clean.

It was round then I started grapplin with that lad from the airport, wrestlin with his accusations, constructin me defences and then blowin them up, one at a time, because the dishonesty a them sickened me so. It was round then I started wonderin about rights and wrongs and payments and choices and if again what then and . . .

I hadn't met Derek yet then, or hearda the Zen stuff, but I started tryin ta work out some of it, get me head straight.

I must work it out. I must work it out. I must work it out so –

I wasn't yet okay enough ta add 'so the next one I kill will deserve it'. But that jeerin boy could finish me thoughts for me and Christ, they made him laugh.

I asked them for Temporary Release so I could get out for the funeral. I'd already started ta do the work so I was ready ta face Micko for the last time, look his eyes in their dead sockets and answer any questions he might have a me.

The bastards wouldn't let me go. I even asked John Paul ta get Ma ta put in a word, but they still wouldn't back down.

Mad, isn't it, Nayler, how he kept goin all that time? I seen him just after he found out and I'd have put him for two year at the most. But he lasted three-and-a-half, till the pneumonia got him. Three-and-a-half year. Fuck, what kinda half-life is that, slow and seepin, watchin yer body crumple ta nothin while yer spirit struggles ta stay livin? Did he wanta hang on that long just ta be alive, or was it fate, laughin at him? Or did he only stay so he could pay Ma back, give her three-and-a-half extra years a disappointment?

There weren't many at the funeral. Just Ma and John Paul, Tara and the babies, and Violet, of all people.

John Paul said it was after Ma took Micko's hand when he was lyin in the coffin that she got better. Her eyes cleared, he said. One minute foggy; the next clear.

536

A course, it wasn't a total recovery. She stayed on the booze and she still had her religious mania. But she was better than before. Even started visitin me and all.

She treated him like a fuckin saint once he was in the ground, a course.

'She said he was too good for this world,' said John Paul. 'A beautiful boy.'

Oh yeah, beautiful. Now he was outta sight and she didn't hafta look at his marked body and ruined face she could have him back like he useta be, her bonny blue-eyed boy. She could put him where he belonged, in a goldy frame in her heart alongside her Missin posters a Sam. A hero ta worship, a Jesus to adore. First it made me think, *Fuckit, maybe she'll do the same for me when I'm gone*, but then I saw sense. I was never her favourite and I was never beautiful. When I'm gone, she'll sweep me dust under the carpet where she won't hafta explain me ta anyone any more.

I consolidate.

The world around me sharpens. The ghosts retreat inta the walls. They only bother me at night, and even then, apart from him, they're not as loud as they useta be.

I'm gettin used ta bein clean. In this new hummin in me blood and strength in me muscles, I feel ya flee from me too, ta some other limboland where ya could be livin or dead, it doesn't matter which.

Around me business goes as usual. Banter, buyin, sellin, brawlin. I play cards with the quieter ones. People meet me eyes now, and I start ta tell them apart. Girls from the streets, mainly; brassers, robbers, users, dippers, dealers. There's a few killers and maimers beside me. Not many, and I stay clear.

Girls from Cork, Limerick, Donegal. Some become pals, a sorts, start askin for me Ma, John Paul; tell me they're sorry about Micko and – they pause before sayin it but still they say it – me sister. They don't ask if there's any news of her.

I still see her, frozen white on misty brown ground. But she's got flatter over time, not as real somehow, like one a them drawins in that book she useta keep. There's times I can't even see her face the way it was before ya beat her; not even with the Missin posters still pinned ta Ma's coat that mock me each time she visits. I can't remember the feel of her nose in me eyes, the curve of her cheek, the jut of her chin. She's dissolvin at the edges, like old glue eaten by the rain.

I haven't seen Micko at all since he came ta tell me of his death. I just feel him, like a gust a wind, a hole in me belly. It's a missin feelin, like he died years ago. And over that a sense a bitter disappointment. That's partly his, the look he left me with the last time I went ta see him when he sussed I'd no gear on me. It's more too; it's the shada of all the disappointment Ma lumped onta him for wreckin her hopes.

Bitter bitter bitter.

And the lad from the airport? The boy with his jibes, his *Oh come on Lucy, ya gointa just do it again like ya just done it with me, aren't ya, just do it, fuck up again* –

Him I'm still grapplin with, but there's times his jeerin seems – almost – ta quieten to a whisper.

'Ya know what?' she says, laughin her wheezin laugh. 'Ya useless, Lucy.' She curls her mouth just like she done when she useta say the same thing about me Da. 'You're a shame on yer family.'

'Ah, fuck this.' I get up.

'That's right. Walk away from me, why don'tcha?'

Sharo Stokes glances at me under her over-mascaraed lashes. Fuck off, Sharo, if ya know what's good for ya.

'Walk away because ya can't—'

I turn. 'Ya fuckin—' I lean over, about ta spit at her, spit on her stupid cross, but Sam stares out at me from the tattered poster on her sleeve and the look in her faded eyes forces me back.

I slump onta me chair, hold me head. Jesus Fuckin Christ. How long?

Ma nods, delighted with herself. 'Look at ya, ya look like a fella shavin yer head like that and the state a whatcha wearin. Ya can betcha life Sam isn't goin round like that.'

Don't rise. Lucy. Stop.

'That right, Lucy, yeah?'

I nod. I still can't bring meself ta say 'Yeah' because that would mean I'm agreein with her and her deluded notions. I mightn't have much morals ta speak a but I can't bear sayin 'Yeah' when I don't mean it. Noddin isn't lyin. It's just avoidin a scrap.

Ma sits back, swallas, knits her hands together. She's nervous now she's won. She's expectin me ta get a dig in sideways.

'I seen a young wan in the *Hello!*, Lucy.'

I say nothin.

'Gettin married. A model, she was. Gorgeous. Long blonde hair, and a smashin figure. Like mine when I was a girl.'

Her voice has that same pleadin edge it had when she came ta the copshop that mornin after Hallowe'en.

'Ya know, with all that make-up and all it was hard ta tell, but . . .'

I dig in me pockets.

'I'd swear it was her . . . the way the light hit her face.'

I roll up.

'Gorgeous, she was. And the lad was dark, with pale skin. Thinnish. Beautiful-lookin. The image a . . .' She takes a little breath, lets it out; smiles, fond. 'A gorgeous couple they made.' I take a drag. She stops smilin, snorts. 'The state a ya, Lucy, the way ya holdin that fag and all. Are ya inta the girls? Is that it?'

Are ya readin me, Ma a mine, with whatever tattered scrap is left of yer second sight? Is that why ya baitin me, hopin I'll leak, split at the seams like an old water bottle, tell ya what's happened ta yer baby?

She leans closer. 'They say ya can never get off of that stuff. Not for real.'

I've had enough. I get up.

'Yeah, go on!' she calls after me. 'Ya useless!'

Why don'tcha tell her, Lucy? Why don't ya put the old waggon outta her misery?

Told ya already, members a the jury. She won't believe me. In anyways it's gone too late. 'You're only tormentin me,' she'll say. 'Ya murderin bitch. Puttin lies in me head after all these years so I can forget me little mouse.'

Funny that. While my picture a Sam's got blurred over time, Ma's is clearer, hardened inta pure diamond that nothin will crack, least of all the truth, least of all pictures in the *Hello!* that anyone can tell bear no fuckin resemblance ta either you nor Sam. No. The only time for the truth is in the future, when I come ta her holdin yer head in me hands. Till then, she won't believe me. And she certainly won't thank me.

Besides, if I tell her now, she'll fuck it up on me. I've got work ta do. I got ta find some way a gettin out with me mind safe from the madness and me hands clean a more blood. Because I might never be able ta loosen that dead boy's grip on me neck, but at least I can hope ta prove his tauntin wrong.

I'm a model prisoner. I work. I box. I start art classes. I'm useless at it but it's somethin ta do while I watch the two hands creep around the face a the clock.

I'm four year inside. Hard ta believe but time flies when ya lurch from bein lost ta livin moment by moment.

Times they are a changin. A new shrink is comin ta work the gaff ta take the pressure off the other fella. If ya get yer solicitor on her good side, say the others, she can help ya get out early. It's all part a the programme.

Jails at Burstin Point

I pummel the bag, uppercut after uppercut, and wonder if such a thing as hope exists.

III

Irene Ryan. Chicago. Tall and skinny with long arms that go every-where when she talks, long legs that wrap themselves round each other under the table like ivy on a tree trunk.

'I'm a forensic psychologist,' she tells me on our first meetin. 'I specialize in behavioural change, including anger management and substance abuse.'

Substance abuse? Thought there was No Problem Here.

She stops, lookin at me like I've spoken, then when I say nothin, continues: 'I'm not a psychiatrist. That means I won't be prescribing medication for you. Dr Greene will continue to look after that. However, I'll work with him in evaluating your profile, assessing your needs, and in our sessions together I can help you address particular issues.' She flashes a smile, briefly. 'This way you get the best of both worlds.'

She talks careful like a book, all long words. She is bright-eyed behind her red-rimmed specs. Her skin is yella, her nose sharp, her mouth full. When she speaks the top lip curls away from her teeth, makin her pout. She's wearin a black poloneck with a big clunky necklace over it, and a long multicoloured skirt. Gold bangles on both arms. Very hippie.

A sucker, I think on our first meetin. A piece a cake.

She asks me a rake a questions. The standard ones: school, family, relationships. I start off holdin back the usual way, but she raps her pencil on the table.

'Okay.' She pushes her hair back. 'We can do this one of two ways. You can say nothing and I can make assumptions based on your behaviour and history, and make some recommendations to Dr Greene based on that. Or you can tell me about yourself and we can work out a strategy that might actually help.'

She smiles, but the smile doesn't reach her eyes. 'It doesn't matter to me. I get paid either way.'

'She's alright,' Avril Meagher told me the other day. 'Me sister was in Cork and she helped get her out two years early, good behaviour, all that.'

I weigh it up. 'Alright.' I lean back in me chair so she'll know who's boss. 'Shoot.'

She asks me where I am in the family, about me brothers and sisters. Reminds me a Sasha. I hesitate when she asks me about Sam, then tell her as much as I can.

'I don't know where she is. She went missin ten year ago and never came back.'

'Ah.' She taps her pencil against her teeth, looks through me papers. 'You were detained at that time.'

Every sentence she says is like a question.

I think about sayin, Actually Miz Clinical Behaviour I been detained so many times I can't fuckin remember, but somethin in the look on her face makes me think twice.

'Yeah. Well. I got arrested the day she went missin. Went on a bender. Done some damage. They sent me away for safety as much as anythin else. Ma couldn't cope with me livin back home. The shock, all that.'

'Okay.' She scribbles somethin down. 'You miss her?' she says, still scribblin.

What sorta question is that? 'Me Ma?'

'Your sister.'

She looks up, reads me face. 'We assume that when somebody goes missing it's a source of grief. It's less acceptable to admit that we might be angry about it.'

I can't help laughin, thinkin a what she doesn't know, what nobody knows only me.

'You agree?' she says.

'Anger is me middle name,' I say, without thinkin. Then I bite me tongue because I shouldn'a said that at all.

'Okay.' She puts down her pen. 'I'm going to have a word with Dr Greene and we'll take it from there.'

That it?

'I'll inform you when our next appointment will be.'

She gets up ta leave me out, clankin from all the gold she's wearin.

It bothered me, that chat. It shouldn'a. She was only a shrink, for fucksake, not even a proper doctor, and a Yank at that. What the fuck should she know?

Anger is *not* me middle name, I told meself as I lay in bed, restless as fuck, urgin meself ta go back ta sleep. Or if it is, it's not for the reasons she'd have me believe.

'Coupla people been sick, ya know,' says Ma, tappin out the butt of her fag.

Am I mistaken or do I see the gleam a satisfaction underneath the laid-on sadness?

'Oh, yeah?' I lean back in me chair. Me top rides up over me belly.

Ma tuts. Me belly probably. Well, fuck her and her tuts. Me belly is nothin ta be sneezed at. I got a six-pack comin up there so hard Steve Collins would break his fist tryin ta hit me.

'That little Lisa Gough's real bad with the virus. Coupla years now since she found out. Funny. They've no idea how she got it. It's not like she's ever had any problems with . . .' She pauses. 'That stuff.'

Meanin: why don't you have the virus, ya little drug addict bitch?

'Yeah, well,' I say. 'There's other ways—'

She cuts me off. 'Musta been some bad yoke gave it her. And Marlene's not good either.' The gleam gets brighter. 'Cancer.' She rummages around, digs out another fag.

I tilt the chair forward. 'I'm havin a test on Friday.'

Ma stops, looks at me. In the look, *What's it ta me?*

'The shrink set it up. It's a neuro somethin evaluation. Thought ya should know.'

She snorts, lights up. I reach out, grab one a her fags, light up too.

'It might help me get out earlier. If they can figure out what's wrong, ya know, for real this time, might help . . .'

'For real?' She snorts again.

You're a killer, ya little bitch, the snort says. Ya pleaded guilty. Ya don't deserve ta get out at all, let alone early.

I wonder why I'm doin this. I haven't tried ta tell her anythin in ages, so why now?

We smoke in silence.

'They're gointa give her the chemotherapy,' says Ma.

'What?'

'Marlene,' she says, like I'm thick. 'If ya ask me, I'd say it was him.'

'Who d'ya mean by him?' I know the answer but I can't be bothered playin along.

'That Charlie.' She tuts again. 'Jesus, he's gone ta the bad.'

'Yeah.'

She ignores me. 'Jail in England of all places. Who'da thought, what? Him with his college degree and all. Just goes ta show.'

She looks me in the eyes, first time since she's come in. She looks like she's waitin for me ta say somethin. Me hands feel hot, itchy. The anger boils in me. Let it out.

'Show what, Ma?' I keep me voice as calm as I can. 'Show ya not the only one fucked up yer kids, what?'

She stubs the fag end out. 'There's no talkin ta you, Lucy Dolan.'

Under me breath I take her off – *na na nananana nana nana* – and watch her lumber out, her rosary beads clickin like little teeth.

Poor old Charlie. Seven year in the Scrubs for fraud, diddlin one a them big computer companies through sellin chips on the sly. See how ya like it, Charlie, bein rammed up the hole by National Front bruisers that think all Paddies are cunts.

That Wheel a Fortune goes round, so it does.

When I get ta the artroom for the paintin class the door is closed. Some music is playin, somethin familiar, oozin around the metal lock and under the door and inta me head.

'What's goin on?' I ask the screw standin outside. It's the red-headed one with the purple cheeks. She's a psycho. Normally I try not ta talk ta her but today is different.

'Music class,' she says.

The music emerges, tricklin from the dark, leaps inta white nothin.

'It's art today, but.'

She looks straight through me. The other screw, Marion with the dark ponytail, pipes up, 'The art class has moved. If you put in a request, we can get an officer to bring you over now.'

I go up ta the door and look in through the glass spyhole.

Two tattooed hands lift over black and white keys. Fall. The sound is horrible. A shape moves in fronta the spyhole, blockin it off, then moves again. Two other hands, thin, lift the tattooed paws, settin them on the notes. Much better.

'Are you going over?' says Marion.

'Nah, I'm grand.' I lean against the wall, lettin the sounds creep in through me skin, calmin me, teasin me inta their story, down a green path where the sun is always shinin through thick leaves and where, high above in a mountain castle, a beautiful woman is lettin her gold hair down through an arched winda.

That night, Marlene comes visitin. Apart from the lad, she's the first visit I've had in ages but she doesn't do or say anythin. Maybe that's because she's not dead yet.

She's lyin in her bed. A winda's open and a curtain's flappin in it, white and long. Marlene's face, like the picture a Sleepin Beauty in a book she shown me once, is white too. Her bones stick out like edges a coral. Beside her, kneelin on the ground, is Stevo. Behind the curtain, the sea rises and falls.

Flowers are everywhere. Lilies, violets, roses, geraniums.

I love ya, Marlene, I tell her. I'm sorry for what happened and I wish ya hadn't turned yer back on me but I still love ya. She doesn't wake up but I can still tell she's not dead.

*

The screws keep so close I can make out every smell comin from their bodies. One a them stinks a Chanel and talcum powder. The other a bacon. I wish they'd move.

He's old, with glasses and a beaked nose. He's got an English accent.

I realize I'm nervous. Why? This might help me. So she said at our last meetin. *Dr Greene is bringing in a specialist to run some tests. We'd like you to attend. It might help your appeal.* Dr Greene, bollocks. Five-and-a-half year in the gaff and he'd organized nothin like this, ever. The minute she told me I knew only one person was responsible, lesser shrink or no, and that was Irene Ryan from Chicago.

'Ahem.'

I look up.

'When you're ready. Please arrange these pictures in the order you think they should be.'

The pictures are like outta a fairy story, somethin about a farmer and a fox. I arrange them best I can. He takes notes.

He asks me ta read from a piece a paper. I try and fail. I try and fail again.

Whatcha lookin at? I ask the screws telepathically. *So what if I can't read? Fuck off with yer superior fuckin attitudes.*

He takes notes. He asks me ta put different-shaped blocks inta different-coloured boxes.

'These tests are for kids, yeah?' I tell him. 'I should do alright so.'

He says nothin, just takes notes.

'Is this light flickering?' he asks me, pointin ta the fluorescent strip in the ceilin.

Stupid question. 'Course it is.'

'Are there . . .' he pauses, makes a movement with his hand like rain fallin, 'white stripes coming from it?'

'Yeah.'

Do words jump around on the page? Yeah. Do letters swap places? Yeah. Do I like people bein near ta me? The talcum powder, perfume and bacon press closer. Fuck, no.

He takes notes.

'Double vision?' he says.

I shrug.

He holds up somethin in front a me. It's Mickey Mouse. 'How many do you see?'

Mickey and his twin slide apart, gel together.

Just before I go he asks me if I have any other unusual experiences. I think I know what he's gettin at but I play thick and ask him ta explain.

'Do you see things?' he asks, a bit vexed. 'Such as . . . perhaps . . . people who aren't there?'

I thinka insanity pleas and lines a hospital beds. I choose. 'No.' I act puzzled. 'Only the lights and the readin and all.'

I will pass the results on to Dr Greene, he said.

And that's it?

Two weeks till the next appointment. Time has started creepin again, painful slow. I get booted outta the art class for distractin the others. I keep pickin fights, tearin up pictures, talkin when they wanta concentrate. The teacher doesn't boot me out. It's the others. They're sick a me.

Everyone's sick a me, includin meself.

I'm feelin bothered. It's not like the madness. It's a hot, vexed feelin.

Me arms and legs have started itchin at night. I scratch and scratch but get no relief. I put on some cream but that doesn't help either.

Marlene keeps comin back ta visit me. Some nights she turns inta Sam. Makes no difference. She still doesn't hear me when I tell her I love her. It's because a the airport boy; he's laughin so loud it's a miracle anyone can hear anythin. I'm vergin on goin back on the gear. I can feel it, the hunger, just as I can feel you in the base a me bein pushin ta be let out, but I won't let ya. It's not time yet. I am not free yet.

The landin is quiet, apart from the music.

I pass a poker game. They shush as I come closer.

'Got any fortunes for us, Slasher?' jeers Lola Byrne.

'Got the clap yet, Lola?' I jeer back.

The other yokes laugh. Lola spits.

The door a the old artroom is closed again. Behind it, notes climb up a hill, one after another, then back down again. I lean against the wall, and the itchin in me body calms.

Up the hill they climb. I think a Jack and Jill.

The notes aren't goin in the right rhythm. They should be bam bam bam bam like footsteps, but whoever's playin keeps trippin themselves up. I'm relieved when they stop.

There's a bit a chat. I can hear it through the door. Then other notes start, a tune this time. It's someone else playin, the teacher probably. She's stretchin the tune out then pullin it back together, like an accordion. Then the rhythm changes, a sudden jab I didn't see comin. I start ta concentrate, followin the notes, and the concentratin soothes me somehow, helps me forget everythin else that's crowdin in on me head. I forget I'm locked up, dyin ta be out. I forget you, gnawin at me belly. I forget me itchin.

I hang in the moment, like a bird on a wave of hot air, and listen.

When they're finished I scoot off inta the cell Ger Roche shares with Lindsey McHugh. I don't know why; it's just a panic that takes over me. The door opens. Margo Clarke comes out, followed by a tall fella with light hair.

A fella? Thought it would be a girl. Knowin it's not makes me feel . . . disappointed, sorta.

He's wearin a tweedy jacket and poxy beige trousers, which makes me think he's old, plus the fair hair which looks grey under the lights. But then he turns his face and I see he's young, my age or roundabout. Margo heads off down the landin. The young fella shifts his weight, organizin himself round the long cardboard box he's holdin under one arm. There's somethin heavy in the box. I can tell from the way he's standin. A leather bag with bits a paper peekin out from it swings off his other shoulder. He tucks a lock a hair behind his ear and walks towards the cage.

*

548

I try ta sleep. The rash is even worse than before. I burn, try ta hold back, scratch, burn, try ta hold back.

Underneath the rash, I feel ya bangin at the door a me soul, beggin ta be let out.

Wake up, Lucy. Can't ya hear it? Are ya ready ta fuck up again? says the boy grippin me neck. *Ready ta take someone else who doesn't deserve it?*

Not yet, ya fucker, I hiss. Not fuckin yet.

The music Margo Clarke was tryin ta play echoes through me head, on and on, bad timin, wrong notes. I scorch. Ya drum at me gates.

I get a ringin in me ears, like radio fuzz, like the sound a waves crashin on the shore. *Any minute now*, says the airport boy. *Any minute now and you'll be wakin and Nayler will be standin at yer feet, Lucy Lu, and I know, oh I bet, I bet me life, you'll –*

'Sharo!' I whisper.

Sharo Stokes turns, mumbles in her sleep. I reach down, grab her toe. She jumps awake, gruntin. Outta habit I put me hand on her mouth ta shut her up.

'Got any?' I say.

I've learnt me lesson and snort this one. When it hits, ya hit me too. Everythin – livin and dead – melts ta nothin, leavin only us. Oh, dance with me, old pal. Dance with me and take me away somewhere the sun don't shine.

I missed Irene's next visit. And the one after that. And the one and the one and the one . . .

How long? Search me. Time lifted two hands at midday and held them there. Time ate at me. I lost tone. I used. But, believe it or not, there was no joy in it. I wasn't – what's the word? – committed ta what I was doin any more. I could see meself doin it, like me, the see-er, was at the bottom of a well and her, Lucy Dolan, the do-er, was at the top, out in the everyday world, a tiny doll that I watched while she used, got sick, wasted away, missed appointments.

Oh, it's borin, isn't it, Nayler? Every user's life is borin when ya look at it that way. A round a usin and clearin out and usin and clearin. Dead fuckin borin.

I sat outside the piana room and watched Margo stagger through dancin lines a notes, one after the other.

I can do better than that, I thought through the haze.

At me elbow ya laughed yer lazy laugh.

I can, Nayler, I said, too spaced out ta even hate ya.

Ma and John Paul visited and I either seen them or I didn't. I could feel Ma's *Told ya so* in every glance, every puff a every fag, and I could see her, Lucy Dolan the do-er, rise ta it, rage unheard and beaten.

The only good thing about it was it kept *him* away.

In the end I got clean because I had ta. Sharo ran out and I couldn't score off anyone else. And even as I raced round the landin, seekin out friend from foe, seller from buyer, offerin anythin – the future, the past, me hands, me head on a pike – the see-er at the bottom a the well tut-tutted like Ma, like anyone who's ever looked down on me, tutted and in the end thought, Thank Fuckin God.

Through the grinder again as the posion leaves me. Jesus. How many more times?

Oh, come on, Lucy Lu, ya whisper. Ya so fuckin borin. So fuckin predictable.

'I suppose ya thought I'd lost it,' I tell her.

'Is that what you think?' She's wearin a pink fluffy jumper. And a deep purple velvet skirt. She looks like somethin in fancy dress.

'Ya look like somethin in fancy dress,' I say.

She pushes her finger against her eyebrow, pullin the skin up so it crumples. 'Okay. You've been to see Dr Greene and he's given you the results of your tests?'

'Yeah.'

ADHD. Attention Deficit Hyperactive Disorder.

'I've heard the name before,' I tell her. 'Loadsa the wans have it.'

She looks at her notes. 'He's prescribed Ritalin.'

'Yeah.'

'And you're going to take it.'

'Sure.'

She looks up at me. 'You've had several psychiatric diagnoses in the past – bipolar, depression, psychosis, even Asperger's at one point.'

She leaves a gap, like she's waitin for me ta fill it in.

I say nothin.

She waits.

'What?' But I know what she's waitin for and I'm not gointa give it to her. Why should she get ta hear what's goin on in me head when nobody else does? So I change tack, put on a cheerful face like I believed everythin the cunt said.

'Yeah, it's good news, isn't it? He seemed ta think this was the one. Said it explained a lot.'

You have had mild epileptic seizures in the past but it's not uncommon for epilepsy to be associated with your disorder. If you take the medication regularly, it will help with your extreme behaviour, the restlessness, mood swings, so on. It may also alleviate some of the visual symptoms, the flashing lights and so forth, although I can't guarantee that.

'So I suppose that's that.'

I get up ta go.

'I'd like to see you again in a fortnight.'

'Why? I got the pills. I'm fine now.' I knock on the glass for the screw ta unlock us.

'Lucy?'

I turn.

'Your medication is only one aspect of your mental health. I still need to carry out evaluations and assess your needs under your new treatment. That way we can ensure we're on the right track.'

Right track?

She taps the desk. 'For the appeal.'

Before I can say anythin else she's scribblin in her diary. 'I'm going back home for Thanksgiving so I'll put you down for three weeks' time. Okay?'

The door opens.

*

On me way back, I crash inta him. He's comin outta the artroom with his rake a books under one arm and his heavy cardboard box under the other. I'm vexed for some reason, don't know why, not lookin where I'm goin, so I walk straight inta him without even seein. He loses his balance and grabs the box. The books go everywhere. I think about leavin him there ta pick them up himself but then I think again and kneel down ta help.

'Careful,' he says. 'Don't bend them.'

On purpose I let the cover a one a the books bend backwards. 'Oh, sorry,' I say, like I only just noticed, and make a big deal a smoothin it out. 'Sorry about that.'

He shifts around, tryin ta move the box around under his arm so it's comfortable. His tweed jacket is all scrunched up, showin a white shirt tucked inta a pair a jeans. At least he's not in them beige yokes.

I hand him the books. He shifts again, tryin ta balance the weight a the box. 'Em . . .'

'D'ya want me ta carry them?' I spell it out like he's special.

'Please,' he says, a bit vexed.

We walk down the landin. His skin is fair, almost transparent, with a dustin a yella freckles across his nose. When we pass Lola Byrne's cell, some a the yokes inside start whistlin. I ignore them but he goes scarlet; a soft wash a red that sweeps over his skin. With each flush me own itchin gets worse. I scratch under me ear. He glances at me.

'Slasher's got a fella!' shouts Lola Byrne. More whistles.

He glances away, scarlet again. Light catches in his hair. It's fair, thick, hangin down over his forehead, longish at the back. His nose is a bit too big for him ta be proper good-lookin. He's got long hands with thin fingers.

'Here.' At the gate he beckons for the books. I hand them to him. He turns.

'Eh . . .' I say, surprisin meself.

He turns back. 'Yes?'

'I wanta join the class.'

'Oh.' He looks surprised. Then frowns, thinkin. 'Have you ever—'

'I'm a natural,' I tell him.

He stares at me and I think *Fuck this*. Then he smiles, a smile that comes outta nowhere. It makes him look different. Real young. 'Okay then.'

I smile back without meanin ta.

'I'm in on Tuesdays, this landing in the mornings.'

'I know. I'm Lucy, by the way.' I offer him me hand. 'Lucy Dolan.'

'Derek Jones,' he says, and shakes. His fingers are cool and light, stronger than I woulda expected. Must be from all the piana playin.

I watch as he makes his awkward way down the stairs, the gates hissin open and closed behind him like snakes' mouths.

The new pill works different ta the XYZs. It's not bad. A mellow feelin that . . . fuck, it's not bad.

Lovely Rita. They give it ta kids and all, kids as jiggy as me. They useta have it in speed.

I thinka Jimmy Marconi whizzin round sixties' Dublin and the fact they're givin me the very same thing ta calm me down makes me laugh.

Sharo Stokes uses every time she can. I hear her sigh as the gear shoots through her.

I am beyond all that, I tell meself. I don't need that shit any more.

I wake up with a dry throat.

'Piana lessons?' Ma raises her eyebrows. 'Whatcha wanta do that for?'

John Paul looks at her sideways. 'It's for the early release, Ma. They wanta see she's makin an effort.'

Slasher Teen Mends Her Ways.

'That right, Lucy?' says John Paul.

I nod. Who are they for me ta tell them the truth?

'The solicitor got the reports in,' says John Paul. 'Very happy with them, Lucy. He thinks he'll be able ta push for ya ta get out early, two years' time maybe, if ya keep on with the pills and stay off the . . . ya know. All they need is the headshrinker's reports ta confirm and ya should be happy as Larry.'

Two fuckin years? The rash on me legs flares. I scratch.

'That far away?' I ask.

'Jesus, Lucy.' John Paul looks round. 'Take it easy. Ya didn't just rob a purse.'

Ma laughs.

I wanta punch her. Then I think a Sam who isn't hangin off Ma's coat in dozens any more, just one picture in a locket round her neck, and I tell meself ta calm down.

'Did ya say Tara was thinkin a comin ta see me?' I ask.

John Paul looks at Ma. 'Well . . . maybe.'

'Will she bring the kids?'

I think about you that night, and Sam, but the thoughts feel different in me head than before. They are velvet-smooth, and cool and airy, like me head is a big open space instead a the usual cramped cupboard under the stairs. There's room ta work stuff out proper instead a bein caught up by the feelins. It's like the me, the see-er, is still at the bottom a the well even though I amn't focusin on everyday Lucy Dolan at the moment.

It's mad, bein so . . . calm about all that. I feel like one a them telly detectives.

I think about all the usual whys for killin Sam: the sacrifice, an accident, all that. Then I thinka somethin new. That maybe ya killed her because a the very thing that made all other reasons wrong – her innocence. When she came up dressed like that, like any other young wan, followin us up for the sake of a party, well . . . maybe ya seen she could be spoiled, like anyone else, and ya killed her because ya couldn't let that happen. Ya didn't want her havin that sorta life, bein used by . . . fellas or somethin, ya didn't think she deserved that, and at least your way she'd be . . . saved. Then I think am I just makin excuses for ya? Because how would that match up with the sheer sickness it took ta hide her? Only another new thought comes; maybe I gotcha wrong. Maybe ya took her away ta protect me. Because if I'd been caught with her they'd have banged me up for sure; for life even.

Then that vision I had the last night she was alive comes inta me head; the one where ya took the presents out from under her bed and gave her them and in return she told ya about the readin Ma done for Cindy Devlin and . . .

It surprises me, comin inta me head, because that vision was shite, wasn't it? Okay, so ya called her Little Hen when she came in the door, but I coulda picked that up anytime ya were goofin. As for her sellin secrets, there was no proof, no jewels under the carpet. No way was that vision a real *seein*, like Granny mighta had. It was just bollocks, me puttin together all sortsa shit; like them brassers comin ta Ma and Sam under the table and that jewellery she got and wouldn't say where it came from, like that little daisy necklace she coulda easily got off of anyone, even Lisa Gough –

Me thoughts stop, snaggin on somethin.

I try ta work out what it is for a while, but it won't come. And you're keepin yer peace tonight, neither helpin nor hinderin. So I just leave it there, that vision and all the other thoughts, leave them hangin ta rest untested till the day I meet ya.

If I meet ya, says another thought.

Whatcha mean if? I'm gettin out, amn't I? And then I'm gointa find ya.

Am I?

Are ya, Lucy? His neck is as twisted as ever, but he's not upta his usual tauntin. His question's serious like I haven't heard before. He seems almost ta care.

But as soon as he appears, the coolness starts ta break up and me mind collapses in on itself again, back ta bein a cupboard under the stairs, and I try ta think about other things, like me first piana lesson and what the fuck that Yank shrink wants outta me.

Sharo Stokes sighs. *Sick cunt.* Get outta me fuckin cell, bitch.

I sweated all the way through. Derek told me later it was because I'd been thinkin about it too much. I'd been wantin ta play, and was sure I could, but when push came ta shove I just didn't know if I was upta it. I looked very uncomfortable, he said later, like I was sittin on a bed a nails. I had that fuckin rash at the time, Derek, I said, not wantin ta give him an in. He shrugged and said, Well, that's what he seen, and we left it at that till the end a class when I owned up and told him he was right after all, I had been nervous.

'Can you read music?' he asked.

'No.'

Margo laughed. I felt like bootin her in the gee but I managed ta hold back.

'Can you play any other instrument?'

'No.'

The next question shoulda been, Then what do you want –? But he didn't ask it.

'Play me somethin,' I told him. 'And I'll folla.'

He played it twice and I listened till me ears were on stalks, fixin the notes in me mind so I could concentrate on the story behind the tune. It was simple enough. A bold beginnin, a sudden change, a build in the middle and then a tricky end. Somethin for beginners.

We swapped places. The chair was warm from where he'd been sittin. I put out me hands, feelin like a tosser but knowin at the same time it was too late ta turn back.

The room faded. All I could hear was me breathin, the bits a the tune runnin in me head, a bird chatterin outside. Dreary sunlight pushin down on the back a me shaved head. The stink a me sweat; as familiar and repulsive ta me as me past. The pricklin a the rash on me legs and arms, the scratchin nylon brush a me trackie bottoms. In me mouth the hot sweet remnants a me last cup a tea.

I concentrated and called up the memory a what I'd heard. The keys rose ta meet me, warm and cool and known and strange all at once. I fixed the first note in me mind and pressed. The key shook its reflection in me body. I listened, tryin ta match the pitch I remembered Derek makin with the one ringin through me skin. No. Not this not this not this but maybe . . . Me fingers paused, held, dipped, pressed. And . . . yes. The story began, wavin me ta folla.

Me hands came alive, I lifted up over them, watchin the jail-house tats, me three dots, me ACAB, me inked initials, dissolve inta movement.

Jesus, I was bad. Okay-ish at the beginnin, but then I fucked up. If I didn't have the notes from Derek's playin still in me head, I'da given up, what with me fingers slippin everywhere and Margo takin the piss. And it wasn't till the end, the twist, which surprised me, because I was sure I was gointa fuck that one up bigtime but it just sorta . . . kicked in, and I got it, was able ta forget the struggle, just ride on the tune, let the music play me like the weight a what had gone before was just pushin me on, this note that note and I didn't even hafta make an effort any more and . . . yeah. That was okay. That was worth it.

And all the way through, I could feel the ghost a you batterin dimly at the cage. Fuck off, old pal. This is none a your biz. This is my time, sunshine.

'Okay,' said Derek at the end. No more. No less. I liked that.

'I went wrong in the middle,' I said.

'Yeah,' he said, even as Margo butted in with her, 'That was fuckin brill Lucy wasn't it that sounded like the real thing—'

'Yeah.' He scratched his head. 'Okay. Margo, your turn.'

I sleep like a baby that night. No dreams. No visions. No you whisperin in me ear. Even the airport lad stays away. Sharo might sigh but I don't hear her either. In the mornin the rash is miles better, only peelin a bit round me elbows and knees.

In the cell a black bird sings, tellin us she's found the answer. Mahalia Jackson's her name, Derek tells me. She's gospel. She's found the answer. She loves ta pray.

He plays all sortsa music. Some is classical, like what Oscar-from-The-Odd-Couple played on his radio, but he's inta rock too, mainly fellas' bands I haven't hearda, from America and all. Jane's Addiction. Smashin Pumpkins. Flamin Lips. They sound like porno films ta me. He plays them ta me and Margo every so often, just for fun, he says. They're all guitars and spooky lyrics; kids thrashin

557

on about love and pain as if they actually know what it means.

'Jesus, Derek,' I say. 'Wouldn'a had ya for that sorta stuff.' He flushes, likin that, ta be thought hard.

We get a good buzz off of him too when he plays the gospel music.

'Are ya religious, Derek?' I ask.

He looks at me, blank. Then laughs. 'Jesus. No. I have beliefs, but . . .' He looks worried. 'Do I appear religious?'

'Yeah,' I say, just ta wind him up. Then, because he seems a bit serious, 'No, only messin. But if ya not, why d'ya listen ta all that stuff?'

'Derek's a Buddhist, Slasher,' says Margo.

'No, I'm not—'

'One a them Hare Krishnas,' she says. 'Oh hare, hare krishna, hare, hare krishna.'

I join in.

'Jesus!' says Derek, laughin.

'He believes in reincarnation, all that.' Margo winks.

'I don't, I—'

'Hare, hare krishna,' we both sing. 'Hare, hare krishna.'

He's a year older than me. He's engaged. He wanted ta be a concert pianist but he isn't good enough. Or so he says. I don't know, he sounds good enough ta me. I get all the info from Margo. He still doesn't speak much ta me except when I ask questions or he talks about the music.

'He'll relax,' says Margo. 'He was dead nervous with me too at the start.'

I wonder if he will. She still calls me Slasher in front a him.

I'm improvin. I'm still makin false starts and fuckin up the tricky bits but it's flowin better. Plus I'm startin ta remember the words a songs again and I'm gettin tunes playin in me head even when there's nothin on the radio. But for the most part Derek treats me just the same as Margo and sometimes I wonder if, in his ears, I'm as brutal as her.

I don't think so. The way she plonks away at them scales – that's the up and down notes – like she's diggin weeds outta a garden.

Plonk plonk plonk. She's even worse when she plays tunes.

'Fucksake!' I say, loud.

'What?'

'Ya tryin ta murder the thing?'

'No, Slasher, murder's not my bag. Leave that upta you.'

'Fuck off.'

I look over ta Derek, wary, checkin ta see if he got the dig, but he's starin out the winda, a dreamy far-away look in his eyes.

I click me fingers at him. 'Here, wake up, Derek. I know she's bad but—'

Margo stops playin. 'Jesus, Slasher, wouldya ever fuck off.'

'Sorry, Margo.' Derek shakes his head like he's tryin ta wake himself up. 'Okay. You show us how it's done, Lucy.'

I look over ta make sure he isn't buzzin off of me.

'Go on.' He sounds tired.

I sit, shake out me imaginary cuffs like they do on the telly, start playin.

He's not good-lookin. Like I said earlier, his nose is too big and his skin is too fair and his eyes even with the dark lashes are way too light.

I got a picture once, durin them weeks. It wasn't like me usual ones, bad. It was just his parents – his auld lad and auld wan. I recognized them from the trial. They seemed dead normal, and they were standin in the music class lookin on at me as I had the crack with Derek and Margo.

How can you laugh like that after what you've done?

I had easy answers on the tip a me tongue. Like: time passes. Life goes on. Nothin can be carried for ever. But when I looked in their eyes the words failed me.

'Ah.' She looks up like I'm a surprise.

'Ya wanted me ta come and see ya again.'

'Yes. Can you give me a moment?' She starts rummagin in her briefcase.

I sit down, wary. I don't see why I should see her now. Them pills are workin fine. Alright, I need her name on the reports ta get the early release, but we both know that's just a game. She gets paid no matter how I do, and as long as I stay off the gear and on them little poppers I'm fine.

Come on, Irene.

I start hummin that poxy song under me breath but she doesn't look up.

She digs out some folders and looks through them. Then she puts the folders back, rummages through the briefcase again, digs out another folder, looks through it, puts it back, digs again.

'Sorry,' she says at last. 'I thought I'd forgotten my notes. I just wanted to check . . .' She leafs through again. The rash on me legs rises onta me belly. I scratch.

'How are you physically, Lucy?' she asks without lookin up.

'Fine,' I say, scratchin.

'Good.' She smiles. 'No side-effects from the medication?'

'No.'

'Okay.' She taps her pencil. 'We need to clarify things. I've got the results of your psychometric tests here. Both Dr Greene and I have had a look. We think . . . well, owing to the severity of your sentence, you need to be able to show you've rehabilitated in a few areas before we can make any recommendations for early release. As I said before, your medication is only one aspect of the process.'

She looks up and gives me one a her smiles. I don't know what ta say, but before I can even open me mouth she's off again.

'Now. I don't know if you're aware of this but there was a recent review of the prison healthcare system. One recommendation was that the psychology service set up structures to address substance abuse, particularly for women. They've already started on a programme in Mountjoy and we've been given the green light to begin work here.'

I don't mean ta say it but it comes out. 'Ah, yeah. Yer speciality.'

She blinks. 'You do understand, Lucy, that your rehabilitation could be seriously compromised if you start using heroin again?'

I hesitate.

'Look, I've no desire to stand over you as a moral guardian. But on a medical basis, any psychoactive drug will affect your mood and behaviour, which is problematic . . . particularly for you, in terms of your history of assault charges. We also need to look at the fact that most of your convictions, including the assaults . . . and so on, have been drug-related.' She pauses, takes off her specs, wipes them, puts them on again. 'Basically, neither Dr Greene nor I will be able to help you if we don't know whether you are going to relapse or not.'

Relapse. I laugh. 'Ya make it sound like a sickness.'

'Isn't that what it is?'

Is it?

She says nothin.

Go. Stay. Go early.

'I'm clean,' I say. 'Clean six weeks tomorra.'

'Okay.' She sucks the pencil. 'Cravings.' She says it like it's not a question.

'Time ta time.'

'They're planning to bring a methadone programme into the prison. You may have heard?'

I don't answer.

'I'm sure you're aware of the benefits. Apart from reducing harm, it's far easier to manage. I know some women on maintenance programmes in the UK who've held down jobs for years. And because it's supervised we'd be able to work out the correct dosage and monitor it along with your other medication. The only problem is . . .' She pauses, eyein me. 'People who haven't registered for methadone with a clinic prior to their sentence will have to go on a waiting list.'

She looks at me, waitin.

'I don't want that shit. I'm clean. Totally clean.'

She waits for a minute before sayin 'Okay.' Then she looks down at her folder and writes somethin again. 'So we'll need to find a different approach.'

'Lookit, miss, I'm clean. I sorted this out already. I don't need yer help—'

'No?' Her voice is calm as ever. 'Well, you can leave now, Lucy, if you want.'

I thinka the report. I thinka stayin cooped up for another four years.

She told me we'd work on me attitudes and beliefs. If I got ta grips with them I could see what was goin underneath, and then I could tackle me behaviours and we could come up with practical strategies ta deal with me temper. And that way I wouldn't feel I'd hafta rely on the gear ta sort out me problems.

She told me we'd need ta speak about me family history and pals and all that because, as she put it, dependency didn't happen in a vacuum. It was a response, she said, ta particular events.

That was when the first warnin bell began ta go in me mind.

She said she understood there'd be painful stuff I mightn't wanta address, but the more honest I was with her, the better chance a me long-term recovery.

The first lie came the day we started. It wasn't planned, I swear. It's just she dumped me inta it, straightaway.

'When was the first time you used, Lucy?' She doesn't make a big deal of it; it's like a box just needs ta be ticked, and that almost gets me answerin, but then I stop meself just in time because I remember you.

She looks up. 'The police reports state you were found carrying when you were fifteen. The time your sister disappeared.'

Good. Off the hook.

'But there was a suspicion that wasn't the first time.'

Shit. Back on it.

For a second I think about it. I really do. I *could* tell her, about you and the squat. What's there ta lose? She's only tryin ta help, isn't she? And this stuff hasta be confidential, doesn't it? But then me mind recoils. Stupid, Lucy. Ya don't think she'll keep that sorta info to herself?

I see the rozzers diggin through their files, unearthin yer name, makin their calls, trackin ya down, robbin me of me last chance for freedom.

Too late now ta walk out.

562

'Yeah.' I nod, lean back in me chair. 'I been usin since I was fourteen but they didn't cop on.' I see her mouth pout, ready for the next question, the who, and I jump the gun. 'Me brother supplied me. The one that died.'

She frowns, leafs through her reports. 'The one who was imprisoned while you were hospitalized the first time.'

Fuck. Forgot about that. 'Well . . .' Hang on, Lucy. Think. Yes! Ping whap goes the pinball in me mind.

'Yeah. Actually, it was just before I set fire ta the school. I never thought about it that way before but Jesus . . .'

Ping whap. Blame everythin on the gear, Lucy Lu, why don'tcha? Oh, the lengths I've gone ta keep ya hidden, Nayler.

I play, pound, make ya go away, fight the itchin so it retreats outta me skin back ta wherever it came from. Get back in yer box, old buddy, I tell yer ghost, inventin notes I've never heard ta push ya away. I build the lines a music, repeat them, force ya down. Get back.

It works. But I'm startin ta get flashes a stupid stuff I never got before, snatches a speech and pictures and old songs, stuff from the seventies, even ads for mad shit, sportswear and all, stuff that comes and goes so fast in me mind I can't fix it, can't tell what it's doin there, what it means, and –

Sharo's makin me sick, swayin all over the gaff, her trackie bottoms pulled down so ya can see the gee hairs and the trackmarks riddlin her crotch. Her sighin booms in me head at nights. Die, ya sick cunt, I think at her. Overdose and fuckin die.

I put in a request ta be moved ta the new Drug Free Landin they're supposed ta be settin up for Christmas, ask Irene ta give me a recommendation and all.

The Governor has ta think about it.

And the boy with the twisted neck just watches me, not laughin nor tauntin any more.

'Not bad.' Derek nods as I find me way through a song. It's a country music number but it's still good. I like the words and the way they play with the tune. It's empty-soundin, but full a feelin.

About darkness, and seein through it and how much people love—

'Here, Derek,' I say, lookin over at Margo.

'Yeah?' He's flickin through the lyric sheet a the album, tryin ta find another song for me ta play.

'What do Buddhists believe in if they don't have a God?' I make the question sound like I really mean it.

'Well, I'm not a . . .' He pauses, thinkin. 'Em . . . enlightenment, I suppose.' He goes scarlet.

'What's that?'

'It's, eh . . .' He scratches his head. 'Jesus, I dunno.'

'The mystery card, yeah, Derek?'

Margo laughs, rememberin the spreads I useta do on the landins.

He looks blank, then his face clears. 'Well . . . yeah, I suppose. It's . . . well, it's a way as much as an end, Lucy. You try to . . . I suppose, experience the moment. Take each day as it comes.'

'Like in the ninja comics?' says Margo. 'Slasher knows all about them, don't ya, Slasher? Gets us ta read them ta her and all. Use the force, Luke.'

I kick her. 'That's fuckin *Star Wars*, Margo.'

'Okay, Lucy, can we just get this straight?'

'Jesus, Irene, did I not tell ya . . . ?'

'Lucy.'

I waited for her ta let up. But she didn't. She wanted me ta give her me life on a plate and she wouldn't let go till she had it all there. Lifestory, she called it. Piece together events and people, deduce beliefs and then – and only then – could she – we – she find the magic keys ta unlock me habit and guide me down that golden road ta pill-poppin health.

Fucksake, what did I need a lifestory for? They were all very well for sad loser junkies like Sharo Stokes who didn't know what they were doin or what their plans were. Who needed someone else ta guide them. But I was clean, I was well, I had me plans and me pills, and I didn't need that Yank interferin – fuck, no.

If there'da been a group, it woulda been easier. I'da been able ta slip away from the net; deflect onta other people. If I hadn'a needed that report, it woulda been easier still. I'da told her ta shove her poxy lifestory up her hole. But she hadn't got the group set up back then, bureaucracy, she said, and that report was the only thing givin me hope, so . . .

So in the end I done what anyone else in me shoes woulda. I made it up.

Now, it wasn't like it all came ta me in one go, readymade. I had ta work on it, find out what she wanted ta hear and fuck around with me memories and the other stuff in me mind so it would all take on the right shape. I had ta play her, make sure what I said matched the tests she'd set me, the ideas she hada me; sound convincin enough ta be the truth. But it wasn't like it was all lies neither. The best stories always have some truth in them, as Granny useta say. The rest is just decoration.

The pills slowed me down enough so's I could read the pattern and meanin of her little movements, the ones we all make but don't know we're doin. Lookin down ta the left meant she was listenin but not fully believin. Lookin up ta the right meant she believed but she was already makin her own ideas up. Chewin on her pencil meant she was tryin ta match what I was tellin her ta stuff she'd come across with other people. Twistin her legs meant she was gettin restless, she sorta knew what was comin next and was fightin with herself not ta let it out. Tappin on the desk meant it was time for her ta take charge. Rustlin her papers meant she was tryin ta think of a new question. Runnin her hand through her hair meant she was angry. She never let the signs inta her voice but her body couldn't help leakin somethin out.

Readin her made it easier but I still had ta be careful. I had ta make it look genuine, struggle a bit, pretend not ta understand, lead her up wrong tracks, show her I was still – what she put it – doin me manipulations. Otherwise I'd a come across too . . . compliant, the word is.

Fairly early on, I rumbled her. She thought it was all down ta family – and Ma in particular. Oh, she loved it when I talked about that auld waggon. Her head cocked ta the right, and she twisted her pencil around in her fingers, jumpin ta conclusions.

Ma? As if that cunt ever had that much power over me.

She liked me talkin about Sam too, so I had ta watch it that I wouldn't feed her too much, leak you inta me made-up life. And the day I told her about me Da she sprang alive, steppin over her own boundary, more or less tellin me that him goin away was the key ta everythin. All along I was searchin for me Da in the gear. I'd put him onta Micko and I'd put Micko onta the gear, and that was why I couldn't have functional relationships, because I was tryin ta make everythin turn out the same way again so I could save meself for me Da who I'd never find.

She didn't say all this, understand, but she set up her nods and maybes and do ya think that Lucys in a way that made it easy for me ta say it for her.

'Me Ma made him go,' I told her. This wasn't a lie; not a deliberate one in anyways. It just sorta jumped outta me mouth.

She stopped twiddlin the pencil and I knew I'd struck gold.

'Is that what you think?' she said.

I looked at her all dawnin realizin like *Aw, Irene, that's it*.

Understand, I'm not sayin she was thick. She was very good on some stuff; she got Greene ta pull in that specialist and give me them pills and she had some good tips on the behaviours, like what ta do when Ma came visitin or the screws vexed me, and she had some practical stuff about usin, and yeah . . . she was on the right track far as the gear was concerned, it wasn't it that was important but whatcha used it for. But she didn't know everythin and I was damned if she ever would.

I made you as small as I could; ya were like that midget in the films, a Mini-Me, down in the basement a me memory. Ya were me brother's dealer, I told her, and ya supplied me when he was gone. Ya were a pal but not that close. I fucked up once, let slip ya useta be like a brother ta me, and that made her all twitchy and eager, sniffin like a rabbit for dirt, but luckily I copped on and turned it round, best as I could, by stoppin in mid-sentence, all surprised, and sayin, 'It was Micko really, though, I was tryin ta get close ta, wasn't it?' She nodded.

566

I never told her we shared that room in the squat and I didn't go near what went on with Ma or Sash or Amanda, or any a the stuff in the basement, or Snags, a course, and I got around mosta the other shite by paintin yer bad deeds onta Micko, elevatin him inta the Numero Uno Rascal of all time. I even put it across that them times I was runnin for ya, it was him, givin ya instructions from jail on how ta mess with me head. She liked that, a lot.

Understand why I'm doin this, I told me brother's ghost. This is only so I can get ta him before anyone else does.

Bitter bitter bitter his ghost. I prayed it understood.

The weird thing was that it started workin. Between the lies I spun for Irene and the music Derek gave me that brung me somewhere else, ya began ta fade, becomin thinner, somehow, like the ghost a yerself. No, scratch that. Like the ghost a me memory of you.

I had more nights where me thoughts opened up, like a big wide room with white curtains, where I could take apart the events that happened and figure out the reasons why and put them together again.

Still holes, sure. Still questions needin answers. Still odd thoughts that snagged at me mind and couldn't be teased out. Still stupid meaninless flashes a sound and vision – probably shit from me childhood on accounta the therapy – though I didn't bother talkin ta Irene about it.

But I could ignore all that – the holes, the questions, the thoughts. Because it was workin. Because under the starin, silent, reproachful eyes a me victim even the question *Is it right, what I'm plannin?* was at last startin ta cool down, almost enough ta handle.

In December the Governor's reply comes through. Happy Christmas ta Lucy. I get moved ta the landin above, in with a young wan from Limerick convicted a beatin her sister-in-law near ta death with a fryin pan, and a serial shoplifter from Tallaght. Neither a them, nor the seven others on the landin, are users.

Ah, how the world works, what?

And I got me first Temporary Release, two days ta spend in John

Paul and Tara's lovely three-roomed gaff in Phibsboro.

I stayed in the house both days. Even if they hadn't been keepin such a close eye on me, I wouldn'a trusted meself ta go out on me own. Not ready yet.

'Last session you started telling me about the boy you attacked. In the airport.'

'Yeah,' I say.

She looks at me, patient.

This one's tricky but I hafta do it. This is the big one. If I can make her understand . . .

'He . . .' I stop. Me throat's clogged up and I don't think it's just actin. I cough ta clear it. 'He was somebody else when I stuck that knife in.'

She nods like she's been expectin it. And so she should. I been leadin upta this for ages.

'For a good while after, I useta think he was me dealer.'

A shada flickers over her face.

'But –'

Sorry, I tell the boy. I'm sorry, but I hafta do it this way.

'– I don't think that now. He was . . .'

She doesn't move a muscle but man, she's gearin up. I smell it off her.

'Me Ma.'

She nods.

'I couldn't . . . I had ta . . . ya know . . .'

I start cryin. It's what she wants, after all. Funny. Doesn't feel like I'm pretendin.

She hands me a tissue. 'Good, Lucy. Good.'

'We let fear use us in all kinds of ways,' she said ta me once. It was when we were talkin about me gettin clean and how I fucked up that time after I first went ta see her. She said I'd fucked up because I knew I was startin ta get better and I couldn't cope with that.

Maybe she was right. Maybe not.

Why couldn't she a left it after I talked about the killin? Why couldn't she a just let it go? She'd helped me enough by then. And it wasn't her job ta go further – I'm still convinced a that. She wasn't bein paid ta fix every last little broken bit a wirin, she was bein paid ta get us fit enough ta be shunted outta the pens and back inta the real world. So she coulda left it there. No problem. She'da got what she wanted. I'da got what I needed. But oh no, she didn't.

Then again, maybe it was my fault. Maybe it was me who invited her over that line.

It was the end of a session and we were just chattin idly, small-talk really, and I think I musta gone off me guard after landin the one about the airport. I was sayin somethin about Ma visitin later that week, and I let somethin out without meanin ta, like how she probably wouldn't come down, probably out ridin one of her fellas, disgustin auld bitch, ride anyone she would, and next thing I know there's a silence and Irene's lookin at me and I know the look means trouble.

'Disgusting.' It's one a them sentences a hers that sounds like a question.

Shit.

'Yeah. Sex, ya know.'

'Sex is disgusting.'

'No, fuck. I mean . . . fuck. What would I know . . . ?'

'What would you know . . . ?'

'I mean, what would I know about sex? I know nothin about it, right.'

She looks at me.

'I don't,' I say again. I breathe in, deep. 'I'm still a virgin.'

'A virgin.'

'Yeah.'

'After living on the streets all those years . . .' She can't help it. Her forehead furrows. Only a bit but it's enough.

'Ya think I'm lyin.'

'Why would I think that?'

Her voice is calm but fuck calmness any more.

'I'm not a fuckin liar, Irene.'

Ma's sweatin. The smell is awful. I wish there was some way I could block me nose the way I can do with me ears and me eyes. She's givin off about me gettin out early like it'll be some kinda disaster. I'm vexed and even though I try doin what Irene suggests – just observe, don't give inta the pattern that goes on between us, because that's all it is, a pattern – it's gettin harder by the minute.

At one stage she laughs at me, her usual laugh, thick and wheezy, a dirty laugh, 'All that headshrinkin workin for ya, is it, Lucy?' and I snap, can't hold back any more.

'What the fuck would you know, ya whore?' I say it proper, whore not hooer, and soon as it's out I know I shouldn'a.

She looks at me, cold, and in her pupils I see yer face, watchin me as ya fuck her.

'Some name-callin that,' she says. 'Takes one ta know one.'

I feel dirty after, like it was me not her that was after ridin strangers on her filthy bed, and in the shower I scrub meself so hard I'm red-raw afterwards.

I try ta push the dreams away, a you fuckin her on the kitchen table. A yer eyes watchin me, stayin glued on me even as ya end it early, way too soon for her. A yer hand reachin out across her flopped body with her burst balloon tits, grabbin the back a me head and jeerin – *come on come on Lucy come back don't* – as ya drag me closer ta yer sharp teeth, latch onta me mouth and don't let go.

Even when I manage ta get you outta the picture she's still there. Ridin. Ridin anyone, every man in the world, the good the bad and the ugly, and at the foot of her bed a beautiful-lookin young wan with long dark hair hidin her face is pissin herself laughin.

Some time after five or six I crash out.

Derek Jones.

'So where does the Jones come from?' I'm narked, God-awful restless, wound up from not sleepin. 'Are ya English or what?'

He's gettin used ta me. He looks at me, shrugs. 'Welsh,

probably, somewhere down the line. I'm a bit of a mongrel. Why?'
Fake-innocent. 'Do you have a problem with that, Lucy?'

'No.'

He smiles. There's a new glint in his eyes. 'No rabid Brit-bashers
in your family, then, who wouldn't approve of me?'

Margo shifts around.

'Jesus!' I say, for want a anythin better. 'You're fuckin mad.' I
laugh. Margo sniggers.

He keeps lookin at me. His eyes are light blue, made lighter
again by the dark lashes. Today they look nearly white, like little
suns. Sounds mad, but for a minute I feel them suns lookin right
through me, uncoverin the madness I've tucked away; the dirt on
me conscience overlyin me like a scum. Does he see ya too, Nayler,
under the bloody twisted face a the lad from the airport?

I stop laughin.

He loses the glint and flushes, one a them proper order big scarlet
jobs that makes his freckles turn inta sunburn. He looks away.

Margo makes a kissy face. I could kill that waggon.

I jut me chin out. 'So when are ya gointa teach me the scales,
Derek?'

He starts leafin through one a his books, distracted. 'You don't
need scales, Lucy.'

'Margo learns them.'

'Yeah, well . . .' He's uncomfortable.

'Am I not good enough?' I make me voice innocent as I can, but
still tauntin, so he can't tell if I mean it or not. 'Am I not good
enough ta learn things the right way, Derek?'

He doesn't answer. I sink me fingers down on the keys, let the
warm plastic slide inta me skin. I start playin, nothin in particular,
just doodlin. He reaches over, touches one a the keys beside me
fingertip, stoppin me.

'Okay. Scales.'

He takes his hand away, reaches in his bag, takes out some sheets
and puts them in fronta me. The black marks jump around on the
page like little flies.

Margo laughs. 'Didn't know ya could read, Slasher.'

'The name's fuckin Lucy, cunt!' I round on her. She jerks away from me.

'Lucy—' says Derek.

I feel suddenly sick. I push the sheet aside and walk out.

We let fear use us in all sorts a ways. Maybe we fuckin do, Irene. But I'm afraid a nothin. Me, Lucy Dolan, afraid? Ya got hold a the wrong end a the stick there, Irene.

I start seein people from me made-up lifestory in the faces a those on the landin. A scowl in me soup is me Granny on a bad day. Sam's hair on Avril Meagher, Micko's eyes lookin out from Derek's face. Me Da reflected in shinin things; a pretty boy, betrayed and edgy. It's unsettlin me. It shouldn't. I made the whole thing up, didn't I? I am in control.

Minutes pass. One a us shoulda spoken by now and accordin ta the rules a the game it should be me. But I don't fuckin feel like it.

'You've dropped the music lessons.' She whistles through her pursed mouth, reads me file for what must be the fortieth time.

'What are ya sayin, Irene?'

She looks up.

I don't mean ta let meself show like this. But I've got so used ta comin out with stuff that it's hard ta suddenly switch off.

'Ya sayin I dropped the class because I'm too stupid? Too lazy? Too much of a fuckin problem?'

She sucks her pencil. 'Is that what you think, Lucy?'

fuck fuck fuck fuck fuck fuck You

I have a dream that night that I'm back on the gear. I'm strung out, desperate, and I can't move. When I look down I see me feet are stuck in concrete; still wet but startin ta harden. The need fills me, thumpin through me skin. I wake up wringin wet, drippin with shame, relieved I'm clean, achin for a fix.

After breakfast I look at me pills in their little white beaker.

What the fuck use are youse ta me, ya poxy little bastards?

I think about fuckin them through the winda. There's a broken pane at the top corner and I could shoot them through there, be freed a them and poxy Irene's poxy ideas a what I am and what I should be, and give up the whole stupid idea a gettin out early.

I could do it.

I lift the cup, tilt it, swalla them. They're bitter as poison.

John Paul and Tara came in that afternoon with their youngest kid – Darren or Eamonn or Damien, somethin like that. He'd just gone five and was runnin all over the gaff. Reminded me a meself at that age.

'You'd wanta watch it he doesn't get the ADHD,' I told Tara just for the mess. 'It's genetic, ya know. He'll be fucked if he does, turn out like me.' Then I remembered he was the kid that was gointa die in the bath so I didn't say any more.

'Ya lookin good,' John Paul told me. 'Yer hair's nice growin out like that.' Liar.

I asked them where Ma was and John Paul shuffled around, lookin awkward. Tara tried ta lie, sayin Ma was sick, but I interrupted.

'No worries, Tara, I know she's gone ta ground. Terrified a seein me free. Ya never know what I might say.'

'Hmm.' Now it was Tara's turn ta look awkward. 'Eh . . . Damien, come back here!'

'How's the piana lessons goin, Lucy?' said John Paul.

'Okay. Still tinklin away.' I pretended ta play a tune in the air. Fucked if I was gointa give him any ammo Ma could use. *Shoulda known ya couldn'a kept them up, ya useless little bitch. If it was Samantha now . . .*

Just before they went, John Paul told me Marlene had died.

'We wanted ta tell ya sooner, but . . .'

'Lucy,' said Tara. 'Are ya alright?'

'Yeah, sure I am.' I got up. Me legs felt very shaky.

'Lucy?' called John Paul. I waved me hand, go away, John Paul, even as I could see the others look up from their chats – nosin in, any excuse for scandal – and pushed me way through ta the door.

★

It's not like Micko. It's not her dyin that's important. I've known she's been on her way out for ages. And it's not like I care, not really; she's hasn't been anythin ta me, not really, not since that Hallowe'en. But she's gone. And that means—

Fuck.

One less witness.

Shoulda been prepared. I knew this was comin. Yeah, but they said the chemo was workin and—

Makes no odds. Shoulda been prepared.

Ya tickle me sides. I turn ta catch ya, ta prove ya still you, not him any more, but when I look ya gone.

One less witness. Only Damo and Charlie and Amanda left ta prove that anythin happened at all. I still have them, remember. I still have—

Ah, cop on, Lucy Dolan. Ya not still hopin they'll come runnin back ta ya?

No, but . . .

Wake up, Lucy Dolan. Smell the coffee. Maybe everyone's right. Maybe nothin happened. Maybe ya did imagine it – the body, the mornin, even the night on the mountain.

No fuckin way—

But . . . maybe?

Ya tickle me again, but so soft I hardly feel it.

Maybe I did. Maybe the tales I been tellin Irene are true after all. I amn't lookin ta put things right. There was no murder. Sam disappeared off her own bat, pure and simple. She never came up that Club, never listened, never followed me. I never seen a body. I woke up all alone in that house on the mountain, deluded from the withdrawals, fucked outta me head, convinced I'd seen stuff the night before I hadn't. And I'm still deludin meself now because I'm frightened, oh yes, I, so-called fearless Lucy Dolan, am fuckin *terrified* there's nothin for me in that big wide future. Attitudes and beliefs. Attitudes and beliefs. And I, stupid bitch, believe I've nothin. Poor little lamb with nowhere ta go.

In front a me on the blue blanket rests the baggie I got off of Lola Byrne in the yard.

Oh yeah, the usual plan. That'll sort the future out. That'll help me run away, won't it? That'll fuck it all up, get the two year slapped back on the sentence so I won't hafta go out before I'm ready. And in the meantime I can lie on me bunk, rottin away, pallin out with loser Sharo Stokes and all the others. Maybe even get on the game when I get out, like fuckin Ma and that fuckin Irene think I done in anyways when I was on the streets, and die a fuckin AIDS like me loser fuckin brother, and before I die I might even kill someone else, why not, yeah? Except there'll be no good reason for that one, will there? No reason sound enough even for my sick little mind?

Is that the plan, Lucy? Is that whatcha wanta do, prove yer stupid auld Ma right?

No, I . . .

Is that what real is ta you, Lucy? That little bag a gear? That all?

No.

What, then?

I slump down on the blanket, me face an inch away from the baggie. It looks enormous ta me now, ten times bigger than Liberty Hall.

You're everywhere and nowhere. I can't put a face ta yer name. You've melted inta a dark stain on the ceilin, a pair a blazin eyes.

In the night it comes ta me. That thing Derek told me. It comes ta me as I'm lyin on the bed, fully dressed, facin the baggie that's on the pilla right beside me, so big it's all I see.

He'd said Buddhists don't have a God. They believe in enlightenment, whatever that is. In livin in the moment, takin each day as it comes. At the time it hadn't meant anythin ta me; like Margo said, just a sayin from a ninja comic.

But he'd meant it. I knew by the way he'd gone scarlet.

Live in the moment.

I slide me fingers up, touch the baggie.

I see meself fallin, slippin while the see-er at the bottom a the well yawns and spits. I see meself OD'in again, rushed ta hospital with a broken needle stickin outta me thigh, Sharo screamin at me, Go with them, go with them, Lucy, or you'll lose yer fuckin leg.

I see meself playin the piana in front of a room full a people, everyone cheerin. Even Ma's on her feet, cheerin.

You wish, Lucy Dolan.

Live in the moment.

Ya scream while I lock ya in. Ya scream and scream. But I pour concrete over the roof, wait till it's hardened, then pour more, then more, then more till I can't hear ya any more.

Okay? I ask the lad from the airport. Happy now?

But he doesn't say anythin and when I turn ta find out if there's an answer in his starin eyes I can't see him anywhere.

Once the choice is made it's easy enough. I put the past behind me. I forget what's ahead. I don't think a ya – and this isn't like before when I was gettin ready, still plannin. This time there's nothin ta get ready for. I don't think a ya one minute, one sec. Ya dead ta me, Nayler.

I ignore yer screamin.

On me way over ta Irene, I wait in the cage for the gate ta open onta the yard. The sun hurts me eyes. I feel empty inside.

The screw with me nods at the one in the box. The one in the box presses the green button. The gate opens.

When it does, I see Derek's on the other side.

'Lucy.' He smiles. He hasn't planned it. It just happens. He tries ta cover it over then, stops smilin and looks at me ta see what I feel, but I'm smilin too and I haven't planned mine either.

I think a that picture I had, a playin the piana with all the people watchin.

You fuckin wish, Lucy Dolan.

I am in the moment, I tell meself. The past is behind me.

'Go on in,' says the psycho screw.

The door is half-open but when I push it all the way she's not there. Instead, a pretty-lookin girl with dark hair is sittin behind the table, lookin at her nails. She jumps up soon as she sees me and holds out her hand.

'Hello,' she says. 'I'm Deborah, Irene's replacement.'

Up the pole and gone back ta the States ta be with the Da. I hafta laugh.

In fact I did, when I got back ta the cell. I laughed and fuckin laughed. The one time where I mighta needed, coulda started tellin her the truth –

'So,' says pretty Deborah, smilin. 'Irene says you'll be getting out next year.'

'Yeah,' I say.

'Now . . .' she says, leafin through the folder.

'Lookit,' I tell her. 'I've gone through all that with Irene. The addiction counsellin and the anger therapy and all. I just wanta . . .' I search for the right words, 'stay . . .'

'Focused?' she says helpfully.

'Yeah, that's it. Stay focused on the, ya know, moment.'

'Oh,' she says. She looks through the notes. 'Well, I suppose . . .'

Fresh outta college. They gave her the job because she knew the Governor's nephew. Jesus, the world works in mysterious ways.

She said the best thing for me would be a group. Narcotics Anonymous was comin inta the prison soon, under the Psychology Service, and maybe I could help chair some a the meetins.

I felt dirty after talkin ta her, like I'd cheated somehow and gotten away with it, but then I realized that was just guilt and I told meself I didn't need guilt any more. Like everythin else, it was behind me.

He's on his own when I go in, hunched over the keyboard, playin somethin that sounds like church music but way better.

He doesn't hear me at first. When he does he looks up and stops, embarrassed.

'Hey, Lucy,' he says at last.

'Hey.'

He looks back down, starts playin somethin soft.

'Okay,' I say. 'I'm sorry for losin the head that last class.'

He lets his fingers slide through the music, sewin a cloth a jewels between us.

'I still wanta learn the scales, Derek.'

He looks up ta speak but I keep goin. 'I can't read. There's somethin wrong with me eyes, me brain and all, and I can't do it. But if ya show me, I'll listen and I'll folla.'

He searches me ta see if I'm havin him on.

'I mean it, Derek. I wanta do it right.'

'You don't need to, Lucy. You're a natural.' He smiles.

'Natural, bollocks.'

He stops smilin. 'Look, Lucy—'

'I wanta know what I'm doin, Derek,' I say without thinkin, knowin only that I don't want him ta teach me without knowin the reason. 'I wanta know that the notes are right, not just in me head.'

He looks up at me. 'That's . . . well, Jesus, that's a lifetime's work.'

I look back at him. I don't nod, don't try ta hide the emptiness stretchin taut under me skin. Let him see it, if he can. Let him even pity me.

Ya may be bangin away, Nayler, on yer prison a concrete, but he won't hear ya. You're behind me now.

This time he doesn't go scarlet or look away. 'Okay,' he says, and nods.

C major is the first. It sounds like everyday. Like warm wood and a beach before it gets too hot. It sounds normal.

F is next. It's sharper. There's one black key in each eight and ya hafta work yer fingers round ta make sure ya get it in. Then G, with one black key too; then D with two, A with three, E with four and last but certainly not least B with five.

I go back ta the art class and on cardboard I draw up a keyboard for meself with the notes done as different colours. That way I can remember where each ABCD is on the keys without havin ta read the letters. That night I play me scales one after another, listenin ta the music in me head as me fingers dance on the black and brown cardboard.

I do them for him the next class. I fuck up a coupla times, but on the whole I'm not too bad. He's a good teacher, keeps tabs on what I do wrong. One or two lessons in he starts talkin serious ta me, usin big words, not simple ones just because he thinks I won't understand. When he's listenin ta me playin he gets real . . . concentrated, like Charlie useta when he was hatchin a plan. In them moments it's like all that matters is the music.

Suits me.

He's right; it is a lifetime's work. Even if I get the major scales down, I'll need ta learn minor ones, then other ones after that, with the long names.

Chromatic. Pentatonic. Diminished. Harmonic. Dorian. Lydian. Phrygian.

And that's only the start. I'll hafta learn ta read, sooner or later, if I wanta play like he does. At the worst, he says, I can get away with tablature – he shows me what it is, just letters one after another on a page – but ta do it proper, not just chords, I'll hafta be able ta read sheet music. That's the only way I'll learn where the notes really go, how they lead from one ta the next, how long I should hold me fingers down and when the left hand takes over from the right. He makes it sound awful.

'It's okay,' I tell him. 'I'll do it. The new girl's gettin a quack in ta test me optics.'

'Optics?'

'Seein.' I point ta me eyes. 'She thinks she can sort out me readin problems.'

'Well, don't get too hung up about it. You're doing fine as you are.'

I can tell he's gettin impatient. He's startin ta jig and he never does that.

'What?' I say, vexed, stoppin the scale.

'It's . . .' He sighs. 'Jesus, it's your bloody fingers, Lucy, okay. Look.' He scrunches his chair up next ta mine, plays a few notes. 'See?'

He holds his hands like they're cups, archin over from wrist ta fingertip.

'Now play something.' I try a scale but I can see what he means. Me fingers are flat, sprawled, awkward, ugly-lookin.

'Fuck,' I say, and start laughin. 'Fix them for me, Derek.'

He goes ta take me hand. Then pauses, awkward. 'Okay, look.' He puts his hand on his head and before I can slag him off – 'Hold your hand like this.' I do what he says, feelin like a spa. 'Now keep it like that and bring it down to the keys.'

I lift me hand off. It's a cup, curved over. Me fingers brush the plastic.

'See?' he says. 'It feels ready that way. Poised.'

I haven't heard the word before but I know what it means. He says it so it sounds like what it is; up in the air, waitin.

I play, CDEF and on, and on, the same notes over and over. They carve a rhythm through me mind. I lose meself in it. Behind me I feel him, watchin. At the end a the class, he touches me shoulder, real light, ta let me know it's over.

When I tell Derek about livin in the moment and all, he says one a the main things that's supposed ta help with that is forgiveness. Forgivin isn't the same as . . . what's the word? Condonin, he says. Sayin it's all okay. It's more like lettin go.

Not bein able ta let go can be as tricky as not facin upta things, says Derek. Means ya have an exaggerated sense a responsibility. Then he laughs; not like he's slaggin me, more regretful sorta, like he's thinkin maybe he's not too good at the lettin go himself. I don't ask him what he's holdin onta.

'I'm sorry, Ma,' I say the next time she comes. 'I been under stress and I shouldn'a said them things ta ya.'

She stares at me like I'm a piece a shite. Nothin new there.

'Just with the therapy and everythin, ya know . . .'

Forgive her, Lucy. 'I suppose I've never forgiven ya for tellin me Da ta get lost.'

She keeps starin.

★

I thought that woulda made me feel better straightaway, but instead I felt sorta . . . uneasy. Then I told meself ta cop on. Lucy, stop tryin ta sort out everythin at the same time. As Derek says, lettin go, it's not the easiest thing in the world. If there's somethin else I need ta forgive Ma for, it'll come lookin for me in time. Then I was able ta relax again.

Same thing happened after I asked the Limerick girl ta write a letter for me, ta the lad's parents. Started off okay but after a coupla sentences I told her not ta bother.

No reason. Just . . . uneasy again. Only I really didn't wanta feel it because seein as all that was ta do with him, and you, it made me think maybe things weren't finished, but they musta been because I couldn't see him anywhere, or hear him any more and . . .

Best ta keep things simple for the moment, I thought. I'll contact them when I get out. Plenty a time for forgiveness then.

At least them stupid flashes a rubbish have stopped. Thank Christ.

I pour two cups a tea inta the plastic beakers. The brown liquid sloshes, foams. 'Where's Margo?' he asks, swingin his foot under his chair like a kid.

'On the rag,' I say without thinkin.

He laughs.

'Nah,' I say. 'Only messin. She can't handle sharin the class with me. Me talent drives her mad.'

He opens his book, leafs through pages. With the central heatin it's swelterin. The back a me neck is damp and prickly from where me hair's growin out. Nearly two inches now. I should get it shaved again but . . .

'What we doin, Derek?'

He closes the book, sits back, sips his tea. 'Oh God,' he says lazily. 'I don't know, Lucy. You think of something. Entertain me.'

I start hummin the Robbie Williams song. He looks at me under his lashes. I stop hummin, doodle on the keys.

'Hard day, Derek, what?'

He raises an eyebrow, gives me a real *what's that ya sayin?* look.

I give him an innocent one back. He smiles, shakes his head, closes his eyes. I begin ta play.

'This is me own version a the one ya played us on the CD,' I say. 'The raindrops.'

He smiles again, eyes still closed, noddin his head as he recognizes the notes.

'Ya may notice I still haven't gotten round ta readin the sheets yet. That's why I'm sorta fuckin around with the tune a bit.' I speed it up. 'I've added a few things, a few . . . arpeggios –' I roll the new word around in me mouth, testin it '– that weren't on the CD. But I said ta meself, Derek will appreciate this, yeah.'

He nods, gettin serious as I move inta the slow bit, the . . . lente it's called. Like Lent but with an Eh! at the end. That's the bit that got me the other day when we listened ta it. There's an ache in it, a longin for what's gone.

Time's a whore, I think, as I stumble over the notes, savourin the beauty that's still there under me mistakes. I dip me hands over the board and it's like I'm dippin them in the wounds a the past and liftin the blood ta me face and it smells a –

Roses.

'Beautiful,' murmurs Derek.

Oh, the sweetness a bad things gone. That's why we hafta stick the past behind us, underground, where it belongs, where it won't bother us any more.

As the raindrops fall, I go out there, past the winda with its thirty panes a glass, out inta the fields and down that motorway ta the city, over the houses I fly, circlin me home town, that manky brasser Dublin, then I rise and flee down me old huntin grounds, the North Circular and across Dorset Street and down O'Connell Street, and rise higher again, over the sprawl and inta the suburbs and out inta the country and the houses thin out and the people get scarce and I fly over the hill and I circle it, a hawk.

Sam melts inta a dim white shape, blurrin inta brown ground.

The mountain fades, becomes nothin.

I can't hear ya. I can't hear ya.

*

'Beautiful, Lucy,' says Derek again at the enda the class.

I can't think a anythin ta say so I just rub the back a me neck.

Beads a sweat gleam on his pale forehead, his upper lip. His eyes are sleepy but clear at the same time, like blue glass the rain has washed clean.

'Derek . . .' I say at last. 'Ya know with the Zen stuff?'

'Yeah?'

'Does that say if all animals are born equal or not?'

He frowns, thinkin.

IV

Ten months ta go. In and around that. Deborah said she was very happy with me progress. Me psychometric tests were lookin good and I hadn't lost the head with anyone in ages. She sent me off ta Dr Proctor ta do more tests on me eyes and he gave me the coloured specs and fuckit, but I started seein things proper for the first time ever, was even able ta begin me ABCs.

I stopped boxin. Derek said it was bad for me hands. I started makin up me own tunes, some with words, some not, and played them for the jail at the Christmas concert. Everyone clapped. We were allowed two outside visitors but only John Paul turned up. Tara woulda come, he said, only she'd got sick. Expectin again. I didn't ask about Ma.

I got Temporary Release second year in a row and we ate turkey and pulled the crap jokes outta the crackers and even the kids seemed ta be enjoyin themselves round me.

I learnt the Italian names for fast, slow, soft, loud, build, fall and all them other words that ya can't translate proper because only the Italian makes them sound what they are. Con brio. Lente. Piano. Forte. Adagio. Allegro. Sonata. Concerto. Staccato. Andante. Diminuendo. And me favourite – Crescendo. I thought a Jimmy Marconi and his da Gianni and I whispered the words ta them both before I went ta sleep.

I done me best. Learnt fugues, nocturnes, preludes as well as the normal stuff, songs by bands and singers I liked or Derek brought in. And when I wasn't learnin, me and Derek talked, mainly about life and stuff. He told me about this thing I can't remember the name for, like Granny's Wheel a Fortune from the cards, and how it's supposed ta mean events come around again, but that made me a bit edgy, so I told him I just wanted ta stay in the moment, without thinkin a the future. A coupla months in he said he wasn't really a Buddhist, more a Taoist, and he wasn't really that either, it just . . . attracted him, that way a thinkin. I asked him what it meant, bein a Taoist, and he said, for him, tryin ta live his life just the way he lived it, honest as he could, although . . .

Then he laughed. I knew what he meant. Sometimes ya just don't hack it.

I asked him if his bird was one a them Taoists too. He got awkward at that, shrugged.

He never showed me a single photo of her. Not that I minded. She seemed borin. She musta been; if she was interestin, he'da talked about her.

We talked about Jesus too, and religion and how it fucks things up, and is there a God and whether things happen for a reason. I'd let things slip, time ta time, when I wasn't watchin meself, but he wouldn't catch on the way Irene woulda done. He asked me some questions about me past, but not about anythin I done – like robbin or dealin – more about what was goin on in me head, like the loony bin or the time I was on the streets. He never pushed me; he always let me do the talkin and only asked questions when he thought it was alright. Sometimes he told me about his world, his family and where he went ta school, and growin up a Prod in Dublin and how mad that was, lonely at times, and I talked a bit about me own family, but I could tell we were both holdin back.

On hot days I watched his skin gleam and smelt the salt and soap off his white shirts and felt me own sweat trickle down me back, prickle between me shoulder blades, collect in the dip a me chest, the fold a me belly, the base a me spine, the backs a me legs.

Once I asked him why he didn't make up his own tunes. 'If I can do it, you can.'

'It's not as easy as that,' he said.

'Yeah?' I said, pryin, but he shook his head, wouldn't say any more.

'Go on, Derek.' I was curious now.

'No. Come on. Try the new song, Lucy. Please.'

It was only near the end he told me he was workin on some-thin, a symphony, but he hadn't wanted ta talk about it in case he jinxed it.

'That's like me. Terrified everythin will all turn ta shit again.'

'Yeah.' He laughed.

When he swept back his hair his forehead lurched out, remindin me a some movie star – Jeff Bridges, maybe – even though Derek wasn't good-lookin, not that way.

'What do you think of when you play?' he said once, makin sure ta put the question real idle so I wouldn't suss he was interested. I trickled me finger down a scale.

'This and that.'

'Memories?' He stopped himself, pretended ta be shocked. 'Oh, sorry, Lucy, I forgot you don't do that.'

I let him away with it, mainly on account it was so hot and I wasn't bothered makin a big deal. So I just swivelled the chair and kicked at his ankle, not hard, and he laughed and shoved back at me with his foot, and then I began ta get restless so I swivelled the chair back round and started playin a tune.

He was only half-right. When I played me own tunes I closed me eyes and let the music wash through me, soothin the past, bringin it out inta a different light. I let half-seen shapes come ta life and die. The notes stumbled inta the forms a familiar voices, eyes, footsteps, but anytime they started hardenin inta somethin real, I changed key, tempo, beat, shovin the scraps a the past back in the rubbish bin where they belonged. And I told meself this wasn't cheatin, this was alright, because I wasn't thinkin this way. I wasn't rememberin. I wasn't dredgin anythin up. I was only feelin.

I grew me hair long, went ta the gym, started havin normal conversations with the wans on the landin. I chaired some Narcotics Anonymous meetins, and sat in on others, listenin while they banged on about the higher force that controls our lives, and thinkin, but not sayin, there is no higher force, bud, there's only me and you, bud, zonin out only when the other sob-stories became too hot ta handle, sharin the lessons a me made-up past only when it was safe ta do so. I avoided the growlin packs a the Wacker's women and Snags's molls. I tried ta blend inta the background.

Derek got me a kid's plastic keyboard that I could plug in and I used it in the cell ta hammer out the start a new tunes. It was only three octaves long, half the size a his, useless for proper scales, but grand for what I needed.

On the Drug Free Landin, inside one a the raised ridges a me old cardboard keyboard, I keep the baggie Lola Byrne sold me. A reminder ta stay in the present.

'There's a story in the paper about ya,' says me cellmate, the girl who nearly murdered her sister-in-law with a fryin pan. 'Do ya wanta see it?'

'No,' I say.

I picture the headline, in big black letters that I'm just about able ta read.

Slasher Back on Streets

'That has nothin ta do with me,' I tell fryin-pan girl. 'That's just lies ta sell papers.'

She understands, so she leaves me be.

But it rattles me, funnily enough, not on account a what's done but what's lyin ahead. So far I been very disciplined with the future. Deborah's sortin out a residential scheme for when I get out; there's therapy in it and all, but that should be a piece a cake after all I been through with Irene, plus the NA and the tips I got from Derek's Zen stuff, so I'm not worried. And when I get through that, Deborah says there might be a farm in Wexford that'll take me on for a year. Deborah set up the scheme for me and Irene gave me a very strong recommendation. I didn't hafta do a thing. But then that's what the Zen stuff says, ya let the universe look after ya, and it will.

But what happens next? What happens after Wexford? What happens if . . .

It's okay, I tell meself, walkin down the landin. It's okay, Lucy. Let the universe look after ya. Don't fuckin think about it.

*

He's late. He's in the jail alright, but not in our room. I pace around. I wish I'd brought me keyboard in with me so I could practise. I'm just about ta knock for the screw ta open the cell door so's I can get it when he comes in.

He looks dog-tired. He's got blue rings under his eyes and his shirt is all crumpled over his jeans. The neck's loose so I can see the points of his collarbones.

'Where were ya?' I don't mean it ta sound snappy but it does. He sighs like I'm a vexin kid and takes out the books.

'Lookit, we don't hafta, Derek.'

He glares at me. 'Okay, Lucy. Jesus, make my life even harder, why don't you?'

'Fucksake, who let the cat out?'

The tension crouches between us, unfamiliar.

'Sorry,' we both say at the same time.

I help him lift the keyboard outta its cardboard parcel. He plugs it in.

'Did ya read it?' I ask him.

'What?'

'The story about me.'

'Hmm?'

'In the paper last week.'

'Eh . . . no.' He says the no like it's not important.

'A real hatchet job and all it was.' I don't know why I'm doin this. I should shut up and just start playin, but I don't.

'Oh.'

'Oh,' I say, takin him off, real normal, real I-don't-give-a-fuck-what's-happenin-in-yer-life-Lucy. 'Shoulda known better than ta ask, I suppose, seein as ya never read the papers.'

He looks at me, and I see he's not really there.

'What's up, Derek?' I say it for real, not ta get a rise outta him.

He smiles, a false doctor's smile. 'Nothing, Lucy.'

'Oh, okay then,' I say, bright, smilin just as false as him, and plonk down behind the keyboard.

Be like that, Derek, I think as I go through the scales. Don't fuckin talk ta me like a normal person. Keep treatin me like a –

'Piano,' he says. He's lookin out the winda at the horizon, his eyes clouded over.

I'd keep jabbin but me fingers, outta habit, soften and glide over the notes.

'Good,' he says.

When I stop, I see he's been watchin me. His face is open now, more relaxed. His eyes are all there.

'You okay?' I say.

'Oh.' He shrugs. 'Yeah.' He smiles, but unlike normal it does nothin ta hide the tiredness. The skin under his eyes is bruised, tender-lookin. I get an idea.

'Here, tell ya what'll cheer ya up.' I stick me hand out. 'I'll read yer fortune.'

Avoid the past. Avoid the future, Lucy. But Jesus, what harm can it do? I'm only playin, after all. I only want things between us ta be back ta normal.

He looks puzzled. 'I didn't know you could do that.'

'Sure. I got the gift, got it handed down from me Ma and her Ma before that. Come on.'

I beckon him. He looks at me, then pushes his shirt cuff up. What I can see of his arm is a pale goldy colour. Smooth skin, like a kid's. Strong clean lines a muscle and bone. He leans forward, puts his hand on mine, palm ta palm. His fingers are steady, hard at the tips. His skin is cool, but there's a warm pulsin in the heart of his palm.

'This way up.' I turn his hand so his knuckles rest on me palm, and catch him by the wrist. With me other hand I start workin him, teasin open the fingers, pushin the little bones in his palm apart so I can get a better purchase on the lines. He shifts on his seat and one of his knees touches mine. Sharp, warm. Stays there a second, then he moves it.

He laughs. 'Maybe we shouldn't be doing this. What would Confucius say?'

'Fuck Confucius.'

A strand a me hair gets in me eyes so I push it away, then go back ta workin his palm. The lines twist and curl in spirals. His lifeline is long, broken near the end. I take it in, feel the cold risin around me.

'Come on, Lucy,' he says, teasin. 'Don't chicken out on me now.'

'Who's a fuckin chicken?'

We look at each other. His eyes are clear; the sea last thing at night before the sun sets. Behind him, shapes gather. I fall inta the cold. And see . . . a weddin ring, someone screamin, a basin filled with blood, the moon, a woman in a long dress at a windasill. A desert. A lizard.

The shapes melt inta nothin. I blink.

'Well?'

I hesitate. Then I tell him. 'Someone stole somethin off ya a while back and ya been lookin for it.'

He doesn't nod, like Irene woulda. His hand stays where it is.

'So will I find it?'

A key turns. We both look round. The door opens. I check the clock.

'We're not over,' I say. Then I realize I still got Derek's hand in mine so I let it go.

'Visit,' says the screw. 'Your sister.'

I musta made a sound, like an animal gruntin or moanin. Because they both looked at me odd. Then I got up, pushin the keyboard outta me way so Derek had ta dive ta stop it from crashin on the ground, and walked out the door.

Walk slowly, I tell meself as the gate ta the cage slides open. Take it easy. Wise up, wise up now, Lucy Dolan. This is a mistake. Fuckin Tara's come on her own even though I don't want her ta, what do we hafta say ta each other? Especially tellin the fuckin screws she's me sister, fuck that, what does that mean? Tryin ta wreck me head she is. A mistake. But I can't help me heart soarin and me blood racin and I'm tryin not ta cry because if it is her it proves fucksake it proves *it proves ya killed him for no good reason* but that aside and maybe I was mad back then but Jesus it proves . . .

★

'Hello,' says the woman in the green coat.

I stare at her straight blonde hair, blow-dried ta make her look like yer wan outta *Friends*, and her tanned face, the little lines webbin out at her eyes, the two stronger lines carvin down from her nose ta the corners a her mouth. Her face is too square, I tell meself then, No, sure plastic surgery can do anythin. But Sam's face was lovely the way it useta be, why would she wanta make it square? Her hands are tanned too, capped with bright red nail polish and gold rings.

'Ya don't remember me, do ya?' she says.

Somethin familiar in the eyes, in the rise a the chest. Her wrists are thinnish. She flicks her hair.

Fuck.

'Amanda?' I say, hardly believin.

Her name in me mouth feels wrong after all this time, too big, too strange.

She looks at me. Her eyes are wet and afraid.

'Why the . . .'

In the cement basement yer eyes grow, wink, snap open.

She'd read the paper, she told me.

Vicious Murder Junkie Let Loose

She'd been pregnant seven times in the last ten years, and each time she'd lost the baby. They'd taken her womb out four months ago and she had a breakdown after. She was bein punished, she felt, punished for runnin out on me, leavin me and me sister with ya on the mountain that night. It had taken her weeks ta make the decision, but once she read the newspaper report last week, she knew she had ta. She didn't wanta but she knew she had ta.

I said nothin. What was there ta say?

She was the one who got the others ta go. She couldn't stick bein round ya, bein jeered like that while I lay outta it upstairs, fucked up on the gear.

'I hated ya usin that stuff, Lucy. I always did.'

She said she didn't know I'd OD'd.

She told me youse had bantered for a spell after I went upstairs. Then she and Charlie started canoodlin and they were at it for a while, while you drank the hooch and chatted with Sam. Ya were a bit distracted, she said, kept lookin at them but lookin round too, like ya thought there was someone else in the room. Then ya got up a coupla times, like ya were gointa leave, but didn't. Once ya even picked up yer bag. Sam kept sippin at the hooch when ya weren't lookin and then she got up, said she wasn't feelin well, and went outside. It was then ya started throwin comments over ta Charlie about the abortion, not spellin it out but sly stuff, like what about that baby, Amanda? Have ya told Charlie who the real daddy was? – and then Charlie turned on her, tellin her she was a slut and couldn't be trusted, and he was so off his face on the acid she knew she couldn't argue with him.

Then ya said real mockin, Ah dear, looks like the two a youse aren't havin so much fun any more, and that ya were goin upstairs ta get me because maybe I'd like ta join in with her and Charlie? Kissin cousins, make a threesome, that'd be more Lucy's style, yeah? Then ya started making digs, she said, goin on how I always needed someone or somethin else ta get me kicks because I didn't know what I really wanted. It was then she decided ta go. Couldn't take the way ya were usin me just ta get a rise outta her, bitchin like that, like ya cared, after everythin ya done on me, puttin me on that filth and all. Let's go, Charlie, she said. Come on. But he was already headin upstairs, on that kissin cousins lark, and ya started laughin at her then, sayin she was fucked now because Charlie wasn't goin, she'd hafta stick around just like she always done and put up with things.

Then Sam came in and Amanda said, Okay, we're goin. Ready, Sam? but Sam just started hummin a song, that one, *where's your momma gone*, and sat down, rubbin her neck, sayin the tattoo was makin her sick. What tattoo? said Amanda, and Sam showed it – a lovely little daisy on her neck – said she'd got it through a pal a Lisa Gough's sister who was startin off and needed the practice. She hadn't told me nor Ma about it because we'da gone mad. Lisa got hers first; a love heart, Sam was a bit scared a the needles, but then

Lisa started jeerin her so she went ahead and done it only now she was worried it was making her sick. Amanda tried ta comfort her, sayin the tattoo looked lovely and the girl mustn'a needed that much practice. But Sam said the girl's fella had helped out, Mark or Marty or somethin. Amanda asked about this Mark just ta be sure there been no hanky-panky but Sam said no it was fine, he was very nice, big smile, cosy voice, didn't go near her nor Lisa, just gave the girl the ink and the needles and told her what ta do. Well, that sounds fine, said Amanda and Sam said yeah, but she knew she'd been awful sick since she got it. Then she conked out.

Amanda was stuck then because she still wanted ta go but she didn't wanta leave Sam not feelin too good and with you in that mood, even though ya weren't so restless any more, just standin at the winda, sippin the hooch. She couldn't tell if ya'd heard a word Sam said. So she told herself she'd give herself a while. The while passed and ya still seemed quiet enough so she thought maybe it'd be better if she did stay, wait for Sam ta wake up, then go. So she asked ya for some hooch, not because she wanted a drink, just it was just the two a youse now and youse hadn't chatted in ages and . . .

Ya looked up and it was like ya didn't know who she was or where ya were. Lost, sorta. She never seen ya look like that before and she was about ta say, Ya okay, Neil? but ya just started pushin past her towards the door, callin me name, *Lucy, Lucy Dolan*, excited sorta, and that really pissed her off. Like couldya not just let me be, God knows whatcha were plannin, probably aimin ta feed me more a that filth or make a fool outta me again like earlier – so she grabbed ya and told ya ta fuckin stop it, ya done nothin but bring shit ta me, it was better ya just let me be from now on, no good for me ya were ever. Then ya turned on her, angry sorta, and for a second she thought ya were gointa give her a slap. Only then ya got this real pityin look on yer face and ya started laughin, like there was some joke she couldn't get, sayin she knew nothin about you and me and what we really had goin, why'd she think I brung her upta the squat that time ta be rode by you? It wasn't outta the goodness a me heart. It was for the fuckin gear. That's how much of a friend I was ta her. Then ya said, still laughin, mad thing was, ya didn't even fuckin want—

But by then Amanda was over at Damo, slappin him ta wake him, haulin him on his feet, draggin him out past ya and that was how she left ya in the end, like she'd never had the courage ta leave ya all them times before.

It was tricky makin their way down the hill but they done the best they could. It took them ages without the torch or you leadin, way longer than the way up. Damo kept fallin and once or twice he even went for a kip in the bushes. Coulda been an hour nearly when they got ta the bottom. They were just on the path when they heard Charlie come tearin through the trees, racin after them, yellin, Wait, wait, he'd made a mistake, he loved Amanda, he really did, please don't leave him on his own, he thought he was invisible in the corner but all the monsters were comin for him.

'Monsters?' I said.

Oh, ya know, the usual, said Amanda. Rubbish. Zombies on the stairs and devils all over the place in doors and kissin blue vampires and in the flames a hell with swords. And angels, sleepin and fallen. And weird stuff, like secrets his Ma knew about the dawn. Kept goin on and on about the drugs too, sayin he wasn't a pusher but he had ta be a stoner, only way ta protect himself round the zombies, and then he kept lookin round and sayin if he didn't watch it he'd have soldiers comin after him.

It took a while ta calm him down but she managed ta get him and Damo through the last bit a the wood and onta the road. Damo kept askin where they'd been. The Phoenix Park, said Amanda.

'Why?' I said.

She shrugged. 'I said it and they believed me. I coulda told eithera them anythin and they'da believed me.'

'But—'

She looked at me. I stopped what I was gointa say.

They did believe her. Charlie was too fucked and Damo too pissed ta ask any different. When they got ta Rathfarnham – Amanda said it was Castleknock – Charlie took some money outta the bank with Marlene's card and they got in a taxi ta Damo's.

Damo's auld lad and auld wan were away – a weddin in Sligo – and his brother was out clubbin when they got back. He staggered in about an hour later. They heard him crashin around downstairs. He made a fry and then he went ta bed.

Charlie couldn't sleep and kept her awake, bangin on about his plans for the future, how nothin would stop him doin what he wanted, reelin off long speeches that were just numbers, code he called it. He got up early, he had ta get home, he said, see his Ma, and Amanda walked him ta the cab rank. While they waited for the jo, he said, 'Mad last night, wasn't it?' She said, 'Ya mean in Damo's?' He looked real scared for a second, then his face cleared and he said, 'Yeah. Damo's. That's where we were, weren't we? Can't remember it, really.' 'Me neither,' she said. Then they kissed and he got in the jo. 'See ya,' he said.

When the news broke that Sam was missin the first thing she thought was—

She stopped.

'Tell me,' I said.

'I thought ya'd killed her.' Her eyes got wet again but she brushed her finger under the lashes, takin care not ta smudge her mascara.

I said nothin.

'Oh, come on, Lucy,' she said. 'Ya were always in love with him. Ya tried ta hide it but . . .' She laughed again. 'And ya always had a vicious temper. If he'd started on Sam next, woke her up and started foolin round with her, and ya'd come down and seen them . . . Jesus, ya coulda done anythin on that stuff.'

Done anythin on that stuff? Fucksake. I nearly laughed at that, thinkin a how useless and noddy I get on the gear, only then she told me when they found the squat burnin she thought I'd done that too, what with it bein just like the fire in our school.

The boy is back again, starin silently at me over Amanda's head.

She tells her stories and the words come at me like machine-gun fire, punchin holes in the casket I've built for ya, coverin me with the rotten-rose smell a the past. I zone out, hearin, not hearin.

I ask a question, zone out again. And all I can think under the details she spews at me is, *It is not over*.

At me shoulder stands Sam's ghost, her face bloody, bone under flayed skin.

So many questions. They line up like skittles and I do me best ta shoot them down.

Was Charlie not worried about findin me OD'd like that? Did he not suggest maybe gettin hold of a doctor or somethin?

'He never said he seen ya.'

'What? But all that stuff . . . the zombies and vampires. That musta been me.'

'He said nothin about ya. Even if he seen ya, he probably didn't know it was you, the state his head was in.'

'But did ya not—'

She looks like I'm the one shouldn't be believed. 'Charlie'd been sayin things all night, Lucy. Ghosts and shite. It was no different.'

After, when the news came out, did she not think you'd planned it; that was what ya wanted, ta get rid of her and Damo and Charlie, that's why ya turned on her like that?

She takes a drag, says nothin.

And when Charlie came runnin down that mountain like his heels were on fire, did she not *fuckin think* ta go back and get Sam?

'Christ, Amanda. Ya knew what he was capable of.'

'I knew nothin, Lucy. Youse never told me what stuff went on, you and Charlie.'

'Ya knew how he was with women. Ya said it yerself, he could even a started foolin round with her. Ya shoulda—'

'Please don't tell me what I shoulda, Lucy.' She smiles one of her bitter smiles. 'She wasn't my little sister.'

We look at each other. I can't tell which of us looks away first. Then I ask it, the one I been storin thirteen year.

'So why did ya never say anythin, Amanda?'

She looks down at her nails. 'I thought you'd gone mad. With the fire and all—'

'Jesus. I was in a copshop all day, then the hospital. I couldn'a set fire ta a thing.'

She blinks. 'Yeah. That's what it said in the paper last week.'

'Why didn't ya say anythin ta Charlie that mornin? Why did ya pretend—?'

'I thought he'd blanked it out, a bad trip or somethin.'

'Fucksake, Amanda—'

She twists the strap of her leather bag between her fingers. She looks up. 'Oh, d'ya not get it, Lucy? I wanted outta whatever sick game the two a youse had goin.'

'What sick game? He was—'

'Lyin when he told me how youse used me?' She laughs a hard little laugh. 'Save me.'

Rat a tat tat tat tat.

She rang Charlie a coupla times after, but he was always out when she called, and he never rang back. She didn't know what he knew but there was nothin in the paper ta suggest he'd talked, so she left it at that. She called down ta Damo the next day and, while they were chattin, made sure he remembered they'd been in his gaff all night. He said somethin about the Phoeno Park and she said yeah, they went there, but only for a bit. She wasn't sure if he believed that, or if he was just playin along because he didn't wanta be involved either. But as long as he didn't speak up, she wouldn't. And that's why she kept ta her story when John Paul knocked on the door.

At times she questioned herself – was it right? Should she tell the truth, what she seen? But Sam stayed missin and over time the fuss in the papers died down and she thought, Jesus, why? Why rake up somethin like that when what did she know in anyways that would help? When I got done for the boy in the airport it made everythin alright. I'd been punished. But it made it not alright too.

'It made me think I'd been protectin ya, Lucy. If I'd come out with what I'd known they'd a put ya away sooner, and ya wouldn'a done what ya done, and that made me feel terrible guilty.'

I felt like spittin at her then.

Early that December she found out she was pregnant again.

'Whose was it this time?'

She goes scarlet. 'Jesus Christ, Lucy, grow up. Who d'ya think? Charlie's.'

She was only six week gone so she hooked up with a lad three year older than her, a pal of her cousin's who lived out in Blanchardstown. She rode him soon as she could. When she so-called found out about bein up the pole, the lad told her he loved her and he'd marry her soon as she was old enough. Right accordin ta plan.

It worked out – well, sorta; she lost the baby but kept the lad. He stuck by her, minded her through the miscarriage and after, and in time she grew fond a him. They married nine year ago. She was expectin again when I got banged up for the boy.

Her fella runs a car rental firm in Blanch, makes good money. She's in the tennis club. She does aerobics ta stay trim. They told her it would be a while after the operation till she could work out again. I look at her toned legs and think, Yeah. Oh yeah, Amanda.

'Whatcha want from me?'

She doesn't answer. That afraid look in her eyes again.

I shouldn't but I laugh. 'Ya wanta know what happened; if . . . ?'

She nods.

'Well, ya right on one count, Amanda. Sam's dead. I woke up on me own and found her there the next mornin. But ya wrong on the other. It wasn't me.'

I start cryin though I don't wanta. 'He'd stripped her, battered her face in, banged her up.'

'Jesus.' She twists the strap of her bag between her fingers. She sighs.

I force the tears back. 'Ya know, Amanda, before ya came along I'd more or less convinced meself I'd made the whole thing up.'

Deep inside me ya growl and tear, rippin open the last shreds a yer tomb. 'Do ya believe me?'

She shakes her head. She starts cryin too. 'Jesus, Lucy. I don't know what ta believe any more.'

I lean across. 'I didn't do it, Amanda. I done the other but I didn't do that. Ya think I'm some kinda monster?'

'I—'

'I didn't do it, for fucksake. Whatcha want – proof?'

She starts sayin somethin else but I wave her ta be quiet.

Before the visit was up I asked if she could remember anythin she mighta missed back then – a sign thatcha were plannin it, maybe; a sign ya weren't.

She looked wary at that, disbelievin again, and I felt like slappin her. Then I remembered.

'He said somethin when he seen her at the winda, Amanda. What did he say? I couldn't make it out from where I was.' Pushed ta the floor like a piece a shit.

She frowns, shakes her head. Then –

'Oh. Yeah. That. Didn't make sense at all. He asked who sent her.'

We sit for a bit in silence, not lookin at each other. I'm the first ta stand up. I don't bother stoppin at the door ta turn and wave goodbye.

Live in the moment. How fuckin stupid was I ta think I could get away with it?

Ya back and ya might as well never a been away. I don't even think a goin back ta Derek, but that afternoon I sit down in front a me plastic keyboard ta try and still me head that won't stop, the poison-oil thoughts bubblin behind me eyes.

I lift me hands but when I drop them I can't make them work. The notes are all wrong, ugly. No melody, no rhythm. I wish I had one a them lids like on real pianas so I could crash it down on me stupid fingers, but no such luck. So instead I rip the plug outta the wall and throw the stupid fuckin thing in the corner.

I go down the gym before the last lock-up. I strip down, tape up me knuckles, put on me gloves and batter the shit outta the punchbag. I'm outta condition, breathless, leakin sweat, but after twenty minutes I welcome the exhaustion. I punch and punch, knockin the life outta you, outta Amanda, outta everyone that matters. Sam spars with me, spreadin herself on the punchbag like an extra skin, and I punch her too, once, twice, too hard, in the mouth, the cheeks, the jaw.

He's laughin at me again.

Shut up you, I say. Shut the fuck up. Don't think ya can stop me any more.

It is not over. How could I a been so stupid?

The barber looks at me. Me hair is gone past me shoulders. The razor buzzes in her hand.

'No,' I say, changin me mind, rememberin the night we went up there, how the ends a me ponytail snaked round me neck, tanglin in me collar. 'Leave it.' I pull off the apron, get up.

I'll tie it up on top a me head like one a them Samurai soldiers in the ninja comics. I'll put feathers and beads in it so it'll scratch and sing when I find ya, so God help me, when I jump on ya like a demon from yer worst nightmares.

I start listenin ta gossip again. Snags is in trouble, say the rumours. Took on too much when he started barterin with the Bishop. He lost a consignment recently. They say one a his own men is involved, has gone on the run. They say this fella knows stuff on Snags, bad stuff Snags been keepin secret for years. They say he's dangerous.

I try not ta think too much about Amanda's story, nor worry through the ins and outs. There'll be plenty a time for thinkin when I find you.

But in the night the dreams come hard and fast. Ya sit on me chest, laughin yer sick heart out. Come on, Lucy, ya scream in me face. Wakey, wakey! Ya hold Sam's neck in yer hands and break it. A daisy tattoo leaks yella blood.

600

Ya sing songs, tuneful, in me ear.

A dark-haired woman laughs and laughs. She bends in two. Snaps.

Emmet Whelan's skeleton cracks his bony knuckles, throws his signet ring at me. It lands on me finger.

Come on, Lucy! ya scream, standin arms up in a V at a winda. Wake up!

'Where's the HellFire Club?' I ask Nicole Duffy. She useta be mad inta the hill-walkin, she told me, before her banker boss found she'd been siphonin money from the company account inta her own and had her banged up for fraud.

'Oh,' she says. 'That's out near Glencree, isn't it? Killakee Lodge?'

Kill a Key. 'Yeah, maybe. Don't know the names. Just gettin inta the history these days. Thought it might be somewhere ta visit when I get out.'

She laughs. 'I suppose it's colourful enough.'

'That's the word, yeah. Colourful.'

'You wouldn't want to believe all the stories you hear about it, though. There's an awful lot of rubbish in those folk tales.'

She does me a map. I look at it every night and memorize the routes. The green lenses in me specs make everythin clear, steady.

Funny how easy it is ta break down somethin that took so long ta build up.

'Lucy. Wait a second!'

I try ta split but it's too late. He's seen me and he's comin towards me, walkin fast down the gauntlet a the open cells each side.

I press me back against the wall.

'Where've you been?' He's a bit outta breath from carryin the keyboard.

'Busy,' I say, lookin round.

'That's . . . well . . .' He sets the keyboard down. 'Jesus, that's a shame. The class isn't the same without you.'

I look down at me fingers. I've a bruise on the back a me right knuckle from trainin bare-fisted.

'Boxing? Bad girl.' He's teasin. 'I told you . . .'

He sees I'm not joinin in and trails off. 'Are you coming back?'

'No.' I don't wanta meet his eyes.

'Oh.' He pauses. 'Shame.'

Shame indeed, Derek.

'When are you out?'

'Soon.'

'Oh.' He flushes, sudden like he useta when I first met him. 'Lucy, was it—'

I laugh, cuttin him off. No. Nothin ya done, Derek.

We stay like that a while. *Pox off*, I tell him with me mind. Pox off with yer stupid do-gooder ideas about life and death and fuckin God that don't mean nothin ta real people, least of all me. Go off and dream a skirtin round some other music class loser with fuckin small-talk because ya too afraid ta touch her. Go find some other so-called prodigy ya can entertain yer snobby dinner-party pals with. Go. Leave. Pox off ta yer empty house and yer cold bed and yer unfinished fuckin symphony and yer fiancée that ran off ta Australia without ya, takin yer stupid useless heart that's still fuckin broken over her. Sayonara buddy.

'Well,' he says, turnin ta go.

I watch him walk awkwardly over ta the piana room, his keyboard under his arm.

Shoulda known. He was never able ta answer me question about the animals.

Three days later I get an envelope from Margo Clarke. There's nothin inside only a bit a paper with the names a tunes written on it. Field. Nocturne no. 7. That sorta stuff.

'Derek says you're ta remember them tunes when ya get out,' says Margo. I can tell she's thrilled I'm not in the class any more.

'Thanks.' If she wasn't so fuckin gloatin I'da torn it up in fronta her, but I wanta torment her, so I fold it real slow, like it means somethin, and stick it in me pocket.

'He's a darlin, isn't he?' I say, givin her a big wet smile. 'Real carin. Ta, doll.'

She leaves, fumin.

I don't use. Nothin ta do with the Drug Free Landin. It's just I've no need of it . . . yet. Not while I got you in me sights at the bottom a the barrel.

The visions are back but now they're real as anythin else I'm seein. They hover beside the people they own, strings a the future and the past stretchin off inta the other world. I ignore them. They don't freak me out any more. They are nothin ta do with me.

Them stupid flashes are back. They don't seem so stupid any more but they're still movin too way fast for me ta catch them. They taunt me. They're changin shape, becomin yer jeerin, screamin voice. Yer crooked smile. Yer hell-hot breath. Yer thumpin fists.

I leave me pills in their beaker, grind them inta the tiles, feck them out the winda. Somedays I take them. Somedays it makes a difference. Mostly it doesn't. I am a bullet, sharpened for use.

I blank him out when we pass on the landin. He belongs ta another world now and that's fine by me. I tidy up with the wans, make sure there'll be nobody lookin for me blood when I get out. I build bridges, smoke joints, swap gossip. I get slapped on the back.

Snags's mob is splinterin, say the rumours. Snags will be okay, though, he's always okay. Got the Devil on his side, how else would he a kept himself outta the courts and the papers all this time? Story is he's it all worked out and plannin ta go straight. He's been clever with his money. He'll be fine, once he catches that lad on the run, the lad that has stuff on him. I ask which lad and get blank looks. Some fella's been away for a while. They call him the Executioner on accounta he does the dirty work. Knives? I ask. Yeah, guns too. But nobody knows him from roundabout. Plastic surgery is a wonderful thing, I think, wonderin what face you've built for yerself now.

It's harder with the family. John Paul doesn't suss it at all, thinks it's just gate fever, but She knows somethin's up. I can tell from the way her eyes rake me, like she's smellin ya off me skin. Or maybe it's Sam's ghost she sees, hoverin behind me, her hands playin with me hair, groomin me for the kill.

'Now,' says Deborah, enthusiastic.

I put on me good-girl face.

'Your application for the rehab programme has gone through. They're giving you two nights in a hostel before you move to the residential scheme. How does that make you feel?'

She shoulda asked it like Irene would, expressionless, not hintin, but she can't help the excitement showin through. Her first success story.

'Great,' I say. 'Real excited.'

'Well . . . good luck.' She shakes me hand. Then she tidies up her folder, closes it.

Open and shut, I think, watchin her. The thought nearly makes me laugh.

Before I left the cell, I picked up the cardboard keyboard and dug inta the groove where I hid the baggie, me useless reminder ta stay in the present. It was still there. I thought about takin it out and hidin it in me shoe, but then I thought again and folded the whole thing up, keyboard and all, and stuck it in me bag.

'Alright, Slasher,' says Lola, puttin her arms out for a hug. 'Dodger Burrowes,' she whispers inta me ear. 'Tell him I sent ya.'

They give me requests, whispered, on paper. I stick them in me shoes, me pants, anywhere.

John Paul and Tara collected me. The kids were with them and all, seemed happy ta see me. After we finished the grub Tara laid on, they said I could stay longer in theirs, but I told them I had ta sign inta the hostel. It was makin me nervous, havin them kids round.

'Sure,' said John Paul. 'I'll give ya a lift.'

'No. You're alright. I'll walk.'

He gave me a nosy look and I laughed. 'Fucksake, John Paul. Ya don't think I'm gointa fuck it up now, do ya?'

'No.' But I could tell he wasn't that sure.

'Hello? Anybody home?' I knock a coupla times. Overhead I hear a winda open.

I look up. 'It's alright, Missus Devlin. It's only me, Lucy Dolan. I'm back.'

'Jesus,' she says, squintin. 'I wouldn'a recognized ya.'

'Me neither.' I laugh but she doesn't get the joke.

She hasn't changed the keys. The door creaks open with a dirty scrape.

'Hello?'

The place smells foul. A piss and whiskey and worse. The wallpaper is fallin off the walls. I go inta her bedroom and she's lyin there, face down on the blanket, snorin. An empty bottle hangs from her hand. I take it off her and put it on the bedside locker.

Then I open her drawers and search for them.

It takes me a while but at last I find them. They're ragged at the edges, bent and worn. I shuffle them, lookin at her. I feel like I should say somethin and almost go ta shake her awake. But then I pull back because I'm not sure what I should tell her.

She mumbles in her sleep.

On the back a her door hangs the coat she useta wear before Micko died – the one with all the Missin posters a Sam hangin off it. I pull off one a the posters and fold it and put it in me pocket.

I walk through the rooms. Without the resta us, they're empty, dusty, screechin a memories. I go ta Sam's bed that hasn't been changed in thirteen year and sniff the pilla. It still smells a her. Her ghost pulls at the short hairs on the back a me arms, hurtin me.

Soon, Sam.

I go for a piss and as I crouch over the bog I think a dogs, sprayin their territory. I take out all the numbers and messages the headcases inside wrote for me ta pass onta their buddies and I wipe meself with them, scrap after scrap a prison paper till they're all soaked through. Then I drop them in and flush. I watch the pieces a paper swirl against the yella foam.

Goodnight, ladies.

The city screeches and hums and bellows below. Smoke risin, metal glintin. Somewhere in the distance I can see the blue curve a the sea, the dusty purple wedge a the mountains. I dig me hand inta the hole. It's still there, and so's that fuckin thorn branch.

That makes me laugh, more than anythin, but when I pull at the barrel in its canvas bag the thorn branch gives way and comes out too, and I see it's not thorns after all, it's a stick with stuff wrapped round it, tarnished metal stuff with spikes stickin out that dig inta me skin. I pull at one a the spikes and it comes loose. With the tarnish it coulda been anythin but I know what it is.

A brass necklace with daisies hangin off it that once useta be silver.

A ring with a green stone.

Gold bracelets black with time.

Ah, Mouse. Little hen.

Okay.

Where d'ya want me ta start, Nayler? With the feelins? The disappointment, the anger, the pity? The shock that's not really shock, just a dull knowin that me vision the night before Sam died had some truth in it after all; that in exchange for bits a tat, me sister let ya in on the secrets them poor girls shared with me Ma.

But it wasn't just the brassers' secrets ya wanted from Sam, was it? Ya wanted the guidance Ma gave them too. Was that what brung ya down the docks on the right night after Cindy Devlin? A beautiful woman in a love triangle waits by water for her sweetheart and the freedom he's bringin, the readin in me vision said.

Love triangle? Sweetheart? Bollocks. But when could Ma ever read the truth in them cards, or anythin else for that matter? Was that how ya knew Cindy'd be waitin by the river, Nayler, for Emmet Whelan and the boat ticket he was bringin, so she could get free a you and Snags and every other headcase in this gaff?

Ma told Cindy she'd find her freedom by the water. But she gave no meanins for the two other cards she'd seen; the Knight and the Ace a Swords. While Cindy waited, full a hope, you crept outta the shadas, yer knife in yer hand. And ten weeks later a lovely long-haired woman was found free alright; floatin naked, green and swollen in the stinkin water a the city's harbours, her throat slit. Number Twenty-Two, the World. Things women know.

I'm not sayin Ma seen ya do that murder in the cards and hid it from Cindy on purpse. All Ma probably read was her own igno-rant lines – you and Cindy and some other lad in a love triangle – and outta jealousy kept ya outta the picture. Nor am I sayin Sam seen the killin either, and tried but failed ta hide it from ya. I'm not even sayin the cards told ya exactly where or when. What I am sayin is that you, old pal, have always put way too much weight on signs. Wouldya still a killed Cindy that way, that night, Nayler, if Sam hadn'a told ya what Ma seen and didn't see? And how many other girls' bodies are lyin in saltwater or under cement thanks ta me little sister's –

What? Her weakness for pretty necklaces? Her need for comfort from someone, even if that someone was you? You tell me.

Is that why ya killed Sam? Because she leaked brassers' secrets without knowin fully what they were?

Is that why she . . . deserved it?

Fuck this. Let's start again. Back ta the feelins.

Standin on the roof, do I still pity her? Am I bitter with disap-pointment? Am I still ragin at her for havin dealins with ya, at meself for bein raged? Do I care any more why she even done it?

Or am I just bleedin for her tarnished innocence and failed wisdom, achin ta hold her in me arms again – the real her, not the flailin ghost ya turned her inta – and shakin, with a feelin I can't understand, that's leakin up through the ground, that's tellin me, *Ssh ladies, that's not it, Lucy, but ya closer, come on, come on, come on.*

Above me poor Cindy Devlin is twistin on her spit again.

Sorry, darlin, I tell her. I know I betrayed ya – and Ma and Sam

607

coulda too, with or without their knowledge – and I regret all that. Ya hafta see, though, there's nothin more I can do for ya. I've only enough will and spirit and room in me arsenal to avenge one killin, enough courage to atone for a second. And I'm sorry ta say, darlin, but neithera them is yours.

I don't know if she's heard. But it's the best I can do.

I shove the jewellery in me bag and stick Charlie's holdall on me shoulder and jump onta the ledge. I stand there, not botherin ta stick me hands out like poxy Leo in *Titanic*.

Just watch me, airport boy.

While I'm diggin in me pocket for the change for the bus I find Derek's scrap a paper. I'd never got round ta tearin it up after all. I could then, after payin the driver, but instead I wait till I'm sittin down. Then I unfold the page and look at his writin. He'd made the numbers of each tune and the first O way bigger than anythin else.

Still think I can't read, ya patronizin little fuck?

Chopin, Fantasie impromptu in C sharp minor, Op. 66

Grieg, *Peer Gynt*, Op. 46, 'In the Hall a the Mountain King'

John Field, Nocturne no. 7: Moderato

Mozart, Requiem, no. 8: Lacrimosa

Beethoven, Symphony no. 7

The Chopin starts playin in me head. I will it down as the houses flash past. Let the rage begin.

The first thing I do when I get inside is make the star. I draw it on the ground with chalk. A five-point star inside a circle. At each point I put somethin, me own pieces a magic; me baggie from inside, Sam's poster, Ma's cards, the gun Charlie robbed, loaded with the ammo I bought today off of Dodger Burrowes. The gear is earth, Coins. Sam is water, Cups. The cards are air, Swords. The gun is fire, Wands. At the last point I put me. I'm the Magician. Number One a the major arcana.

I put the jewellery ya bought me sister with in the centre, and over that I place the letter ta the airport lad's parents that I never finished writin. Then I light a candle for each point and then I call ya up.

Come ta me, Nayler, I say, wherever ya are. Then, ta be on the safe side, I ask yer master. Give him ta me, Buck ya auld fucker.

And I sit back and wait.

Show

This is it, Nayler. That's the story, done and dusted. No details left out, except what I still can't remember or make sense a.

And here I am, in the cold light a the dawn, still waitin.

I've let the past rise up through me – though I haven't wanted ta, fuck, no. Me history has sung itself through every cell a me body, torn me apart, a weave a lies and truth, forcin me ta see things the way I never done with Irene, see me own choices and fuck-ups, me own stupid sins, and still ya haven't come.

I've thrown me pills in the fireplace, willin the visions ta come. The ghosts have risen and me head has spun with flashin pictures, lost words, stupid songs, none a which makes sense, none a which stands still long enough for me ta fix it. None a which matters because it's not you.

I've begged yer master ta send ya ta me, so I can torture ya with questions and knives the way ya done so many others. I've willed meself ta see ya come in through that door and confess, cryin on yer knees, beggin for forgiveness. I don't care if ya come in braggin and struttin, like auld Buck himself, laughin as ya tell me every-thin ya done on Sam when ya raped and killed her and got rid a her body and how ya enjoyed every minute of it. If ya stagger in, ugly, shrivelled and spent, a renegade loser junkie on his last days. If ya healthy, sleek, uncarin. If ya don't even recognize me.

Just as long as ya come.

I've raged and pictured every cruel death in the world for ya. I've imagined knifin ya, chokin ya, shootin ya through the head, kickin ya in the balls and belly and face so hard yer own Aunt Joan wouldn't recognize ya. I've longed for the hot taste a yer blood in me mouth. I've smelt a long, cold death where I laugh and toy with ya like you're a kitten, slidin cool steel under yer fingernails and inta yer black eyes.

I've prayed for ya ta crouch on me chest, breathin inta me face, raisin a knife.

But ya still haven't come.

Around two-thirty, I dealt meself a hand ta see what would happen next. The Page a Swords. Me. The Empress. Powerful woman. The Five a Wands. A struggle. The Four a Cups. An offer refused. The Eight a Swords. Not knowin. The Devil. You. The World. Freedom; a girl with long hair; all the lost women in the world; Sasha, Cindy, Sam. The Wheel a Fortune. Fate. The Hanged Man. The mystery card.

Ya still didn't come.

Me visions spent, I crumpled back against the wall. The last a the candles guttered out.

At 5 a.m. I wake, disturbed by a sound upstairs. I've no watch but I'm grown so used ta countin time inside I know it ta the minute.

There's been a rustlin all night, a scrabblin on the roof that I've put down ta a rat or somethin.

No ghost, fuck no. I got all the ghosts I need right here – me family, the ones ya killed, me own bloody victim – they're still around me, breathin in me ears. I'm not afraid a them. Me, Lucy Dolan, afraid? No. Any ghost that's in here can come down and chat. No need ta stay cooped upstairs in the bricks.

This is no ghost, this thing upstairs. This is somethin livin. I've tried to ignore it, tried not ta let it interfere with me invocation. And for mosta the night, me strategy has worked. I was able ta blank it out, ignore its claws scrabblin on the floor over me head while I concentrated on the real business; waitin for you. Even when I fell asleep, I screened it out from whatever dark dream I had.

This sound, the one that's woken me, is new. It's a thud, like someone's landed on a roof or windasill. There are trees outside. Easy ta swing across and in through one a the gapped curved windas.

Is he here, Buck? Have ya brung him to me after all?

Another thud, directly overhead now. I look around, get me bearins. Thank God the candles are out. From the outside I'm invisible.

Whoever it is, is in the room up from this.

I look ta me left. The dark stairs yawn.

Me hands begin ta sweat.

Don't cop out now, Lucy.

I move as quiet as I can, tryin not ta jolt the empty beercans. I pick up Charlie's gun, cock it, cradle it in me arms.

Another sound from upstairs. A yawnin, human sound. A groan.

I stand at the dark openin ta the stairs, the stairs that leads ta the room where I fell all them years ago.

I hesitate.

I think a the years spent searchin. I think a the mistake.

Live in the moment.

I step forward.

As I climb, Derek's note comes inta me mind. All them scribbled numbers and the big O: O, 66, 46, 7, 8, 7. I shake me head, tryin ta lose them.

Now I'm closer, I hear more. An uneven thud. Like footsteps. They're interrupted by a groanin, then a scrapin, metal against earth. The noise a loose bar on a cell winda might make; or a chain dragged across the floor; or a sleepin bag zip gratin against the ground when it's moved, when someone, say, turns over in their sleep.

Me hands are so wet with sweat I'm afraid the gun will slip. I reach the top a the stairs, press close against the damp wall, peer along it.

The scrapin stops.

I hear breathin.

I step forward. Me breath is hot but I force it slow and steady.

Another rustle. I stop.

A shape moves in the darkness. I put the gun on me shoulder, flick the switch ta manual, aim.

Two eyes glint.

There's a scream and then ya come at me, rushin outta the dark and knockin me off balance. I shoot. The ammo explodes, the gun jerks back against me shoulder, wallopin me, and I drop it, howlin. Ya grab me hair, pullin me. Shoulda fuckin shaved it after all. I reach for it, but ya slash at me hands with yer knife. I grab somethin soft and warm, yer throat, and I squeeze.

Yer heartbeat quickens, yer knife slashes. I keep squeezin. Yer heart jerks, raw, awkward, staggers, slows.

I feel the life tickin away under me hands. Goin, goin . . .

And then his face is before me, purple, ugly, the stupid fringe floppin in front of his eyes. His eyes are full of terror. In his pupils – not his face, his pupils – I see you, Nayler.

Jesus sweet jesus no

Me hands stop squeezin.

The thing shudders, and falls, crashin inta me ribs. I yell, tryin ta get away from it, but it's grabbin onta me hair, clawin me skin, and won't let go. One big black wing lifts, tries ta spread, falls back. It shudders again, eases.

I stop movin, sink ta the ground. The bird sinks with me, its claws still tangled in me clothes and hair.

Its eyes look up at me. Dull. Barely alive. Its heart is still beatin, but only just; a flutter under black feathers.

I take it inta me arms.

And as I crouch there, hunkerin over it while it retreats inta death, I ask the question that boy's been goadin me ta wake up and answer ever since I killed him.

Was his death not the first? Did I kill her too, me baby sister? Is this what I been buryin? Is this the memory that waits inside the bad room – the monstrous beatin, the fists loosed on bone in the heat a unspent rage, the cold puncturin of her skin with fat blue needles?

616

I've toyed with this notion time ta time, I've dreamt of it even, but the toyin and dreams never held me fast. I've always been so sure I didn't. But what's sure any more?

Our minds are very good at playin tricks on us, Irene told me once. Is this why I could never make it up here, never find her body? Because I didn't wanta remember?

Is this why I told nobody? Is this why I could never find the Why, the reason strong enough to explain whatcha done?

Is this why I blanked out that word Derek told me, that word that means ya do things over and over – karma, it is, karma – because I didn't wanta remember the first time I killed?

Is this what them flashes were about, that I never let settle, because I was afraid a what I might see or hear?

Is this why ever since I left Ma's, I kept hearin that shushin? *Sshh*. Because all these years I been askin Sam's ghost ta stay quiet, not ta remind me a what I done?

Was Amanda right after all? Am I a monster?

There's a small rattlin whisper. I look down. The raven's heart flickers once under its chest. Its eyes grow dull.

No excuses any more. I do what I know I hafta.

Cradlin the bird, I stand up and walk over the threshold inta the bad room.

In the bricks I feel Buck's women screamin, worse than ever. Blood drenchin their hair, runnin in rivers down their beautiful faces. I push them aside. I'm only after the truth now.

Dawn may be risin over the city but it hasn't yet found its way inta this pit. Me eyes adjust, seekin out the corners.

Prove I didn't do it, I beg the room. Remind me. Give me a picture, a story, a word, a song, anythin. One a them flashes. Just give me a sign it wasn't me.

Nothin stirs in me memory. Outside, the sky grows grey.

Okay then. Forget about that. Prove it *was* me, then. I don't care any more. Just show me the truth. Because I can't stick this ignorance any longer.

A trickle a cold light creeps in through the winda, gleamin dull off the black ground. There's nothin in this place. No sign a you. No sleepin bag. No hidden cocaine stash stolen from Snags. Only rubbish, heaps of old cans and fags and broken glass, clingin ta the walls and floor like a second skin.

I push away the disappointment. No time for that now. All I want right now is me memory back. Please.

The light spreads, wormin itself onta the rubbish pile nearest me.

Come on. A sign.

Glass gleams, broken.

Broken.

And then –

I remember somethin. Staggerin up the next mornin, lungin at the wall. A crunch under me foot. Lookin down and seein somethin shiny; plastic or glass; me spike, I thought. Somethin feelin wrong about that thought. Because –

Because it wasn't me spike. Me spike was on the other side a the room. And the thing I stood on was more than one spike. It was two, three. Two or three that hadn't been there the night before. The floor had been clean. I'd noticed that; mad, such a manky gaff but a clean floor. So what was in –

But before I can finish the thought them flashes are back, wheelin round me head, catchin me up in them like clothes in a washin machine, mixin in with other stuff, things I seen, heard, knew, didn't know, thought I knew, thought I didn't know, knew I didn't want ta know, mixin in with what Amanda told me, and more, and I'm seein it now, what I been buryin all this time because I'd no way a makin sense of it, and hearin it too, though I still can't make sense, too much all at once and Buck's women are at it again, and –

Screamin. Shoutin. Screamin. Shoutin again, yellin, sobbin –

A mutterin, harsh and broken. *Lucy wake up wake up wake up wake fuckin sick cunt bastard own blood christ innocent kid fuckin wake jesus come on wake up—*

A snatch a music. The seventies. *Where's your momma gone? Where's your—*

A picture. I'm hangin from the blackened ceilin a the room, lookin down at what's happenin below, like they say on the telly people do when they—

That things that weren't me spike. The doctors found somethin in me blood. Said I coulda died, I'd so much shit in me, even with the – fuck, what was it? They found somethin, not hooch nor vallies. Somethin startin with a . . . neh. Na. Naxy? No. *Naa*—

Charlie's voice in me ear. Devils. Vampires. Zombies. Fallin angels. Stoner. Push –

A howl, animal. 'What the fuck have ya done, ya stupid cunt—'

Naa – Locks. Na – Locks – Na Locks – NaLocks—

Where's your momma gone? Where's your momma—

Sam sleepin by the fire. A tattoo on her neck, a tattoo a fella called Mark done – Mark or Marty or—

Christsake Jesus help me poor kid what kinda life I shouldn'a fuck doesn't deserve that I shoulda we coulda he's fucked can't let him win let him use—

Yer face when she walked across the grass. Yer mouth opens, slow motion. *Ah Christ, who sent her up here*—

Charlie, gabblin. A secret about the dawn.

In. NaLocks – In. Nalocks – in. Nalox—

A pressure on me chest, pushin down on me. Thumpin. Thumpin.

fuckin christ fuckin work ya cunt work ya fuckin don't you die on me don't—

A laugh. *Ya know nothin, Amanda, a what me and Lucy really have goin on*—

Suspicious, that detective was, when I kept tellin him I'd recovered on me own. Because in me blood they found—

A dark-haired woman laughin. Sasha. Laughin. At somethin I said.

I hafta see just do what you will what I do save protect die poor kid kind only thing just do it just do it just –

Where's your momma gone? Where's your momma gone?

Naloxone. Number one antidote for heroin ODs. *Keep it on ya all times and tell yer buddy*. Well, I never kept it but –

A howl. *WHAT THE FUCK HAVE YA DONE YA STUPID CUNT*
– you did.
Yer voice, real soft. 'Lucy, I—'
Stops.

Jesus.
What the fuck have ya done, Nayler?
What the fuck have I done?
And what haven't we—
Jesus.

Where do I start, Nayler? Where do I begin the unravellin?
At the beginnin, says Granny.
But the beginnin a what, Granny? There's too many stories, all
twistin up in me head, eatin each other's tails like a bed a snakes,
so I don't know where ta—
Start with the facts, Lucy, says Irene's voice, calm and steady.
But what facts, Irene? Shreds a memory? Tatters a stories could
be just more lies? Pictures I'm only seein now? Sounds I thought
were—
Facts when, Irene? Where? How? The facts keep changin. Day
ta day, year ta year, place ta place, person ta person—
Whose facts? Sam's? Amanda's? Charlie's?
Sasha's? Snags's?
Don Ryan's? Fred Mahon's? Emmet Whelan's? Rose Dolan's?
Mine? Yours, Nayler? Ours?
What facts? There's hundreds goin on here and I don't know
where ta—
Just start, Lucy. Start with what ya know.
This is crucifyin. I know noth—
Liar. Spit it out.
I know—
Spit it fuckin out.
Okay.

*

Okay.

I know who Sam's real da is. I've known for years – well, guessed. Ever since I seen him look at her like that durin Ma Mahon's funeral and I—

Spit it out.

I think ya knew too, Nayler. And I think I thought that's what but I couldn't and then it and I couldn't but now I—

Go on.

Fuckit. I think someone else knew too, that shouldn'a. That really shouldn'a. And—

Go fuckin on.

I think I was the one told that other person, Nayler. Not directly. I'd never a done that. But I told the one person who'da told him.

Where's your momma gone, where's your momma gone—

Shut up.

I seen him at Ma Mahon's funeral. He looked over at her. Not us. Her. Looked at her like he wanted ta eat her. Then he smiled, a lovely smile, like hers. He'd always wanted a kid, the stories said. Only had a nephew but was dyin for a kid of his own. And when he seen her at the funeral, he knew she was his. That's when I guessed. But it makes sense, see? Why Da sided with the Wacker and not him all them years ago.

Not that kinda brother, said Micko. He kept callin round when Da was off on that stretch. Gave us ice-creams in Fortes. A man with a lovely big winnin smile and dark brown eyes and long long legs. Just like Sam.

That song. *Where's your—*

Ma'd been hummin it all mornin. Sam picked it up, kept hummin it, all day. I laughed, on accounta the words. *Far far away.* Wished Ma was. Except Ma wasn't hummin that verse, about the momma. She was hummin the other one. About the poppa. The Da. The photo woulda put the song in Ma's head. The photo in the paper she seen stacked up outside the newsagent's on her way home from the early house. The photo of a man steppin inta a prison van. *Far far away.* Portlaoise's not that far but . . .

It was a secret. A secret about the . . .

Dawn, Charlie said.

Dawn? Don.

A secret Ma never told anyone. Except you and—

When did ya find out, Nayler? Did she tell ya after one a yer rides? That look on yer face the first time I let somethin slip. Sasha asked about me singin and I said about Da and us all gettin the rhythm off of him, only I said nothin about Sam. Then she asked me, What did Sam get off him? And I said, Sam? She's a different story. Laughed.

Ya looked over, warnin.

Warnin. But why? Why—

Jesus. Them fuckin snakes again, roilin round in me head. I can't concentrate. I should just leave. This is thick thick thick I can't—

Stick with what ya know, Lucy.

Okay.

She kept askin me, Nayler. Our lovely Dutch mermaid. All them chats we had about me family. Real interested, she was. Like Irene. Was I like me Da or Ma? And Micko and John Paul. Who did they take after? And Sam. Who was she like? And how was Ma round us? Different or the same? Blah blah blah. Kept changin the subject when you came in. But I didn't let it out, what I guessed. Until—

I can't.

Spit it out, Lucy. That's Sam now at me shoulder, face broke, eyes stern.

That day ya went after Snags I was startin ta withdraw. I'd gone ta Ma's and she'd been at me, sayin she never wanted me, and Sam was there, lookin for help, and I couldn't, and when I went back ta the squat ya'd taken me gear and I was crawlin the walls and heard ya come in and—

Started rantin.

'Fucksake!' I screamed, not carin whatcha heard, not even knowin what I was sayin. 'If all she ever wanted was Sam, Nayler, why'd she go ta the bother a marryin me Da when she coulda had

Don fuckin Ryan and given him more beautiful babies—'

But it wasn't you at the door. It was Sasha. She started ta laugh.

I'd told her, the last person in the world I shoulda. And that's parta what – *sssh, Lucy* – I been carryin round with me all these—

But—

No.

This is shit. Means nothin. This is just lies. Lies I'm tellin ta make sense a –

sick cunt ah lucy ya shouldn'a fuckin wake up I need fuck wake –

That vision I kept rememberin, a Sam tellin ya Cindy Devlin's secrets. That wasn't about Cindy or whatcha done on her, or even what Sam done, or Ma. Or me. That was about him. Only I wouldn't let meself go there. Me mind kept . . . snaggin on it, remember?

Yer face turnin inta Snags's, singin tuneful in me sister's ear as he sucked the blood outta her neck. *Tell me, little hen.*

NO. This is fuckin bollocks. This is—

After I let it slip, I told meself not ta think about it. Told meself? Didn't hafta. That little betrayal went sinkin down ta the Egyptian river-bed fast as a lead weight. And there was lots kept it sunk. I'd seen Sash with Whelan, thought she'd already jumped ship, would never pass it on. In anyways, we were in the shit. Snags might never come back.

Even after he did and Sash moved in with him, I didn't dwell on it. So what if she'd told him about Sam? He was doin well, makin the peace deal with the Don, gettin his mitts on that money – for what would he use information on me sister? Maybe he'd even told the Don already and that's why they were makin the peace. And when Sasha left him, that just meant she might never a told him. So there was no need for me ta even think about it.

Even – fucksake – even that vision a you turnin inta him and suckin Sam's neck I didn't dwell on overly, because it was you I was vexed with. You I didn't want ta see on me sister's bed, suckin her neck. You I didn't want ta think had secret dealins with her.

Even when – 'How's Sam?' ya asked the next mornin outside that shop – I was so vexed with ya for askin me that because it just made me think a that dream that I didn't hear one warnin bell, not once.

And oh boy, I blanked them bells that were screamin good-oh at the sighta yer shock when she came upta the Club because I was fuckin ragin, Nayler, at the way ya talked ta her after, puttin yer arm round her, like what happened between us was nothin and—

Stop.

Stop, Lucy. Sshh.

This is goin nowhere. This is . . . what's that word Derek has? Speculation. Noth—

But he—

I don't believe it. It's shit. Rubbish—

jesus christ Lucy wake up he's fuck Lucy he's fucked her up just a little kid—

Fucked her up?

Okay. Facts. The jury likes facts. Well I don't know if these are, but—

One. Snags Ryan was and is a sick vicious revenge-hungry cunt. True or false?

In the words a the man himself: *I'll fuck them up. I'll learn them a lesson. Poxhead uncle. I'll tear them open. I'll feed them the virus. I'll use every last chink in their armour. Ya know me, kiddo, I can take me time—*

Enough.

Two. Snags knew Sam was the Don's daughter. Thanks ta me and me big mouth and the lovely Sasha. True or false? More than likely, knowin Sasha.

Three. Nobody knows who whacked Emmet Whelan apart from me. I thought ya done it for yerself, ta find out for sure Sash was the rat. Everyone else thought Wacker ordered it outta spite. But

John Paul swore he didn't. And when that peace deal between the Don and Snags went sour, rumours said it was on accounta Whelo. Which means—

Steady. Four. Nobody knows for sure who wrecked Ma Mahon's grave that time. Story went it was the Don, gettin back at the Wacker for Whelan. But everyone said that was real vicious for Don Ryan, not his style at all. Vicious. Ring any bells?

This is stupid. This is thick. I should just—

Five. Wacker *loved* his Ma. After the grave, he was rippin, so mad he'da done anythin on the Don. Anythin? Like what? Well, he once laid a sick threat, sayin Don Ryan should thank his stars he didn't have a kid because he, the Wacker, would make its life so bad he, the Don, would wish it was dead.

Six. Just a point. The Wacker, for all his psycho shit, never hurt a kid in his life.

Seven. A rumour said someone in Snags's mob had somethin on him. A secret. Bad.

Any guesses what that secret could be, Nayler? How about this?

Snags stirred it up between the Wacker and the Don on purpose. Wreckin the grave, gettin you ta whack Whelan. So when somethin bad happened ta Sam, breakin the Don's heart, and news got out, fingers would point ta the Wacker. Two bits a revenge for the price a one. And Snags would be in the clear because he wasn't pickin fights with a soul.

Somethin bad? Like what? Like—

Ah. Fuck . . . ah, no. I can't. I hafta go. I just can't any more. I've had enough. I hafta—

What did I do, Nayler? Really? What did I—

Fucksake. Them snakes in me head are startin ta—

Settle, Lucy. One thing at a time. What I know.

I can't. I don't know—

We always know what we're afraid of, said Irene. But do we, Irene? Do we—

wake up lucy wake up wake up wake up—

Okay. Me sacrifice theory is wrong. Isn't it? Funny. It always seemed the best explanation. Not just on accounta how ya laid her out, but because – fucksake, even though I wasn't aware of it, deep down I thought I knew the Why. All these years I been kiddin meself I been searchin but all along I was convinced—

Say it.

I thought ya chose her because she was Snags's blood, ya see. Best currency is blood, ya always said, especially the blood that binds ya ta another. So I thought or believed in some fucked-up black magic way ya'd used her because a that. Even though I still wasn't sure if bein related ta him woulda been a good enough reason, what with it being so whacked-out, all them risks and mess and all. But I couldn't face lookin at it out in the open, because—

Say it.

I'd hafta admit I knew she was the Don's kid and there was a part a me that was still, yeah, a tiny bit worried about what I'd told Sasha. So I just . . . pushed it all ta one side.

Then I heard how the Don had fallen out with Snags over Whelan . . . But. Well. I mean . . . I was in such a state round then, gone inside for that lad, still on the gear, locked in the madness. So I couldn't even begin ta think about it. That if Snags wasn't so pally with the Don as everyone thought, well maybe he'd asked ya ta kill Whelan as parta his plan. That if he still hated his uncle, well maybe Sam would be useful ta him after all. That there musta been a reason why he'd called upta ya a week before Hallowe'en . . .

But there was no way me mind was goin there, that ya killed her for him, as a job, professional, because that was – no. Then Micko died and with the pills I started thinkin a other reasons, and then Irene messed with me mind and that thing with Sasha started creepin up, and thing was, if Irene hadn't left or Marlene died I mighta even a started talkin—

But I didn't. Then Amanda came and I . . . fuck. Didn't know what ta think any more.

I know. Hands up. I admit it. I wouldn'a had any a this head-wreck if I'd just asked ya that mornin, straight out. *So, Nayler, ya still in with Snags?* But I didn't. Because I was afraid ya were on accounta the gear. And I was hopin ya were on accounta the gear.

And I was prayin ya weren't on accounta – fuck, everythin else. And – fuck*sake*, I'd never asked ya any a that before, had I, whenever I'd the chance, so why should I a then?

But I'll ask ya now, Nayler. Ready?

Were ya still in with Snags? Did ya kill Whelan for him? Did ya kill Sasha for him too, ta keep her quiet? And then did he ask ya ta kill Sam?

Hello?

Hel-lo-o?

Heeelllll-llloo-oo.

Lucy Dolan callin Nayler Hayes. Come in, Nayler. I need some answers—

Fuck. This. Just. Go. Just fuckin go. Just fuckin—

Or do them answers even matter any more when what he done was so—

Look, whispers Sam, pointin ta the tattoo on her broken neck. *It's makin me sick.*

No. No. No. No. No. No.

Yes, Lucy. The facts.

Do I hafta? Can't I just—

The facts.

Okay.

Sam got that tattoo coupla days before Hallowe'en. She told Amanda she done it on the sly, with Lisa Gough. Lisa got a love heart. Sam got a daisy. Sam was scared at first but she was so anxious not ta get a slaggin from Lisa she went ahead and done it.

A girl done the tattoos, a pal a Lisa's sister, not from round us. Her fella – Mark or Marty; *Marty*? – helped out. Gave the girl the needles and the inks and told her what ta do. Nice he was, said Sam. Friendly. Big smile. Cosy-soundin voice.

Marty. Short for Martin. Snags's first name. We all know about Snagglepuss's friendly smile and cosy voice. He got a new mot after Sash, not from round us. And he useta work in a tattoo parlour in Amsterdam. That's where he met Sasha.

Wacker's threat on the Don way back was very . . . specific. Didn't say he'd kill Don Ryan's kid. Said he'd make its life so bad the Don would wish it was dead. Very risky ta kill a kid, no matter what kinda sick cunt ya are. Messy. Even harder ta get holda someone who'll do it for ya. Even the coldest professionals don't like it.

Lotta people think death is the worst thing ya can do ta someone. I don't. You neither. And I don't think Snags Ryan has ever thought that, not once.

Snags once told ya he fucked someone up in Amsterdam. Tore them apart and gave them the virus. True or false, Nayler?

Seven year ago, at the age a eighteen, Lisa Gough found out she was HIV. Can take years for the symptoms ta show. Four years later she'd full-blown AIDS. She's still alive. Just about. Lisa didn't use smack, Ma said, gettin a dig in at me. Musta been some bad yoke gave it ta her.

Bad? How bad?

Sam said, more than once, she'd been sick since she'd got that tattoo. Real sick.

So . . .

Is this what the invisible jury holds me guilty for, Nayler? Is this—

What the fuck have ya done, ya stupid cunt?

Not just bringin her up here, but leadin him—

Fuck. No. I can't . . . I just can't . . .

But this is . . . crap. Just ideas and . . . nobody would do that. Go ta them lengths—

He would. He fuckin—

But people would know. Lisa woulda seen him. And Sam. He—

Could cover his tracks. The mot wouldn'a known his history. Lisa's sister been in England for ages, wouldn'a known Snags ta see. As for Sam and Lisa, they were just little girls, never inta the gang stuff like me and the lads. And for all the rumours, Snags wasn't exactly Mr Visible round our area the last few years.

But how—

He never even thought a askin ya ta kill her. That was never it. He had his own—

No. No. This I can't believe. Ya guilty too, Nayler. I hear them flashin sounds now, only they're slowin down inta yer voice, harsh and broken, and from whatcha sayin I know ya got yer own jury judgin you and they're tellin me there's no way you're innocent in all a this. You're the one was Snags's creature. You're the one cut, dealt, hurt, killed for him. And ya were still his that night. Weren't ya?

I said, weren't ya?

I said, *fuckin weren't ya?*

Or is this some – fuck fuck fuck – some other stupid half-truth I couldn't even let meself face ta see if it was real or not?

Ya went . . . calm, Amanda said, after Sam conked out. Very quiet. Just stood at the winda lookin out. Calm because it was no surprise? Because ya'd known all along what was happenin, what Snags was gointa do ta her?

Bollocks.

Amanda could never read ya like I could. Calm, fuck. Ya were twitchin. Ya were panickin. Under that calm ya were in a fuckin state because ya'd only then sussed what he was plannin.

Only then? So what had ya thought up till then?

What does it matter? What does it fuckin—

jesus lucy come on wake up wake fuckin up jesus fuckin christ wake up wake up wake up Wake Up WAKE UP—

O K A Y.

Okay, Nayler.

Rewind.

Ya were edgy that Hallowe'en mornin. Lookin round. Like checkin who was watchin. Yer fingers weren't the steadiest, lightin me fag. Very good at the hidin, Nayler, but ya forget. I could always read ya. That mornin, under the cool, ya were nervous.

That bag on yer shoulder. The jacket. Like a mercenary ya looked, off on yer travels. All grown up. In the squat later on it was like ya were pretendin. Like ya didn't belong there any more. Like ya'd already left. So what were ya leavin – Dublin or him?

Forward.

That Manfred story always bothered me. Will I tell ya why? It was the bit at the end. The master fucked his servant over, set him on fire. Fine. That was Snags danglin ya on a hook, all that. But at the end ya said Manfred got away. The servant left the master. But if ya were still in with Snags, or desperate ta get back with him, why tell a story about gettin away?

Rewind, further.

Them rumours bothered me too, how ya'd kept leavin, that time I was gettin clean. Goin off, enda the world, England, whatever. Only then ya kept comin back. Why keep leavin if ya still wanted in with Snags? Why come back if ya didn't?

Rewind, further.

That batin ya got from Snags. For years I been tellin meself that was what cracked ya open, made ya go psycho. But what if it cracked ya open, but not the way I thought? What if it made ya see Snags for what he was, a sick vicious cunt? What if it made ya see yerself in a new light too? See, that other thing that bothered me. The way ya stood at that winda, yer arms in a V. Blazin. Pure, sorta. Pure – but not in a psycho way. Ya just looked . . . happy ta be alive. New. Was the newness in knowin that ya didn't hafta spend the resta yer life servin him after all? Was that why—

Forward.

Up here yer voice got real sharp when I challenged ya about the hurtin. Almost like ya didn't believe yer own rules any more, the rules kept ya happy workin for him—

No. No no.

This is fuckin . . . shit. Bollocks. Ya were still his, Nayler.

Ya killed Sasha for him. He couldn't have her know about Sam and live. He asked ya ta do it. That's why her hair was on yer chain. Ya killed Whelan for him too.

But the signet ring? Why'd ya keep that? Stupid, keepin evidence like that. Risky—

Okay. Ya kept the ring because killin Whelan meant somethin ta ya. Ya killed him not just because Snags asked ya but for yerself too, ta find out who the rat was—

Who did ya think it was?

Fuck. Ah, no – Ah, fuckin no. I'm not—

Rewind.

Ya gave yer bag ta Damo when we were leavin the squat. So it wouldn't look . . . obvious, that ya were doin a runner? On the street ya kept teasin Amanda, grabbin her, but up here ya stopped. Were ya doin it on purpose, that teasin? So ya'd look like a young fella on a jaunt, not goin anywhere, certainly not leggin it from his boss, just after his hole, messin round with a young wan he always said had lovely tits? So why—

Who did ya think the rat was, Nayler?

No no no no no.

Yes, yes, fuckin yes. Ya thought it mighta been me, didn't ya? But only after ya found me souvenirs. That's why ya looked at me like that. Because ya thought ya mighta got it wrong, if yer little errant girl could steal yer secrets well maybe could she rat on ya too—

Funny. I never once thought that, thatcha woulda—

Got it wrong? Did Snags think it was me? Was that why ya let him rip that beautiful horse off of yer arm? Ta protect me? Is that whatcha meant by *ya don't even know what a sacrifice is, Lucy*? Did he do more than destroy that tattoo? Was that why ya killed Whelan? Ta find out for sure I hadn't—

Shit this is shit this is shit this is

Facts.

Ya watched that bus after we got off. On the way up Amanda kept hearin things. *Nothin there*, ya said. Vexed. Because . . . maybe she was right? Maybe there was someone there. Someone comin after ya. Ya made us go quiet. Then . . . that chase. The rain. The wind. Noisy. Couldn't hear a thing. Ya know these woods, Nayler. Inside out. Been comin here since ya were a kid. Since yer da tied ya ta that tree at seven year old and left ya there all night on yer own. Ya knew once we were inside the trees, ya'd

lose whoever it was. But ya wouldn't lose me. Because I always—
Found ya.

Rewind.

Ya said ya came lookin for me the day after I left ya, and I believed ya. Why'd ya come lookin, Nayler? Ta say sorry, didn't mean ta hurt yer feelins, Lucy, nearly stranglin ya with that poxy chain? Or ta ask me upfront, no messin, had I betrayed ya or not?

What did ya feel, Nayler, when Emmet Whelan looked at ya from under all that blood and told ya it was Sasha been the rat, always her, never me? Is that why—

No. Shit this is shit this is shit this is

Facts. Facts. Forward.

That look on yer face when ya seen Sam out the winda. *Ah, Christ, who sent her up here?* Did ya think *he*'d sent her? But why?

Rewind.

Sasha. Did ya kill her just for Snags, Nayler? Was it ta punish her, or—

We both know there's things worse than dyin. Ya can be kind, ya told me once. Sasha was sick, the rumours said. In a bad way. Is that whatcha meant by kindness, Nayler? A mercy killin? Is that why ya killed her? Not just because he asked ya, but ta put her outta her misery? Did ya do it sweet, easy, with no hurtin? Did she appreciate yer mercy, Nayler? Is that why she told ya what she'd told Snags, about knowin who Sam was? Is that why ya took so bad, when ya seen Sam outside, because ya'd figured out he was upta somethin on her, but didn't know what, and when ya seen her ya thought he'd maybe got holda her and sent her after ya and was tryin ta rope ya in and—

Forward.

Ya kept quizzin Sam, how'd she folla us, how'd she know what we were upta? Just one a me feelins, she said. Ya relaxed. Because – Great, ya thought. Nobody'd sent her. Ya were okay. It was all gointa be okay. She was up here, safe –

Safe? Safe round you? Ya fuckin killer?

– he couldn't get at her. You were safe too, away from him and—

Shit this is shit this is shit this is

Mind playin games on me again. Bollocks. More lies—

Fast fuckin forward. Re fuckin wind.

I don't know how much ya were his, Nayler. I admit it. I don't know. How much killin them people was ta serve him, how much was ta play him, how much was for yerself. I don't know if he asked ya ta kill Sam. I'm sure he didn't—

Sure? How?

I don't know. Too risky. Too messy. Don't fuckin know, okay? But even so, Nayler, I don't think it even matters any more because there's still one big ugly question and don't you dare fuckin think ya can walk away from it squeaky clean.

If all this is true, if ya weren't psycho and ya weren't Snags's and ya guessed he was gointa use Sam, then why the fuck didn't ya tell me? And—

Oh . . . cunt. No. Don't lay this one on me. I'm not takin this. I swear I'm—

How's Sam? ya said that mornin. I got pissed off so I cut ya off. Were ya gointa warn me, only I didn't give ya—

Don't lay this on me. Ya coulda still told me. Ya shoulda. In the squat. Okay, the others were around, but in that back room—

Why didn't ya? What held ya back? Were ya—

Fuck. Scared I'd lose the head, start rantin? Bring down Snags on us so fast we'd all be fucked, give ya no chance ta make yer getaway?

But ya coulda still told me. On the bus. Insteada—

Thankin me. Thankin me for what?

Ya shoulda told me. I coulda just got off and gone back ta Sam or she'da followed me and we coulda got some help. John Paul, Marlene. And yeah—

Too late, Sam's voice in me ear

yeah, she'd got the tattoo by then, but you weren't ta know that
nor me so—

Why didn't ya tell me up here? Was that what all that slaggin
me off about bein too loud and not bein brave was? How d'ya think
I'da ever known—

Oh, for fucksake, Lucy Dolan. Ask the real question.

Why, Nayler, if ya suspected anythin at all, didn't ya come ta me
soon as ya could, them months I was gettin clean? We coulda done
somethin. We coulda saved her, maybe. Yeah. And don't tell me ya
were afraid.

Oh . . .

Ya were, ya cunt. This is what yer jury been booin ya for, isn't
it? Ya were afraid I wouldn't listen ta ya. That I wouldn't let ya in.
That John Paul would fuck ya out. Or Ma. That even if ya did tell
me I'd go nuts because I was the one told Sasha. And—

Yeah, yeah, yeah, I can understand all that and ya might even a
been right. But worse than all that, what isn't right, ya—

Spit it out.

Ya were afraid that if ya told me he'd know soon as ya did and
then ya'd hafta split but I'd hafta stay ta protect Sam and then
there'd be no chance for us ta—

Yer arm holdin me, beside the canal. Meltin inta—

Forward. When ya first seen the souvenirs. Ya fingered them,
like ya were fingerin a bird for the first time. Like ya wanted—

Forward. *I came lookin for ya, Lucy.* No black rage that mornin.
Just a spark. A dare. A plan bein hatched. But what plan? What
plan? A big fucked-up blood sacrifice? A plan ta tell me about Snags
and Sam, somewhere we'd be safe? Or somethin else?

No. I'm not doin this. This is crap. I never meant anythin ta ya,
Nayler, and don't start tellin me, and what's more ya can tell yer
fuckin jury ta shut their fuckin traps or—

A hindrance, that's all. A pack animal. An ugly little plain-as-the-
day gobshite geeless fuckin mascot good for a slaggin—

*

Man, the heat liftin from yer skin that mornin. We kept tryin ta walk away from each other. Go. Head. Leave. You as much as me. But we couldn't.

Let's do somethin real, ya said. Smiled when I asked ya what that meant. I know that smile. *You tell me*, is what it says.

You tell me, Nayler. What did ya mean?

Will ya come with me, Lucy? No questions.

Come where? The Club? But I was the one brung it up first. Come for what? The game? But ya only took them cards out after I taunted yer story, after I wouldn't tell me own in return.

The gear? Was that yer plan? Ta hook me in again? You were the one brung it out. Ya shouldn'a. That was low. And yeah I know I provoked ya with that Manfred dig but ya still didn't need—

No? Who was bangin on about it all night, lookin for somethin so-called real? Me. Not you. Who wanted coke—

Ah, fuck—

Who started bangin on about coke when they coulda—

Fuck this. The book, the five-point star—

Imaginins. Nothin real.

But the stake. I staked me life, Nayler, and ya let me do it. Why?

Will ya come with me? Come where, Nayler? As far as the HellFire Club or—

Why didn't ya tell me about Sam, Nayler? Why—

Why did ya pick that rose on the way up here, Nayler? The rose that left its sweet scent on ya? Why did ya pull off its petals and put them on the little bed a bracken in the side room, petals I thought were colouredy bits a paper the next mornin, petals kept comin inta me mind over and over all these years, on a bed a bracken ya put them, a bed in the side room, the side room ya were draggin me towards after we—

I was lucky, the doctors said. All that stuff in me system. Very slight chance a recovery, even with the amounta –

Naloxone, Lucy.

– antidote I'd been given. Why'd I blank it, Nayler? Why'd I blank that name? Naloxone? Why'd I blank what them doctors told me, that I'd been lucky, that I'd been—

Saved.

Saved?

I hang, poised, under the ceilin, and watch. I'm driftin. Gettin cold. Me face down there's a bit blue lookin. Blood down me front. That's me Da's jacket ruined. She'll be ragin. I'm lyin on me back. Thick. I'll choke on me blood. Me chest is only just movin. Me heart? God knows where that's at.

Charlie's in the corner, watchin me. Fascinated. Keeps wantin ta touch me because the blood makes me look beautiful, like a lovely blue vampire, but soon as he thinks that the acid turns his head around and I'm the ugliest thing in the world again. A monster—

No no no. I've had enough. Thick. This is not real what I'm seein. If it was real I'da seen it before. I'da remembered it before. I'm not—

Ya were still his. Ya were still—

Facts.

After Sam conked out, ya stood at the winda. Calm on the surface, twitchin underneath. Amanda let ya be a while, then asked ya for some hooch. Ya turned. Lost, ya looked. She never seen that look on ya before but I have, Nayler. Anytime Snags fucked ya over I seen it. It wasn't just Sam ya were twitchin about, was it? It was yerself.

So how had he fucked ya, Nayler? Will I take a guess?

The virus would keep it clean. No abduction car. No guns. No killers. No fingerprints. No hatchets holdin hair and cloth. No body parts. No trail. No press. The mot wouldn't know the stuff was infected. Sam wouldn't even hafta know what happened, long as the important people done. Like I said, takes years for the symptoms ta show. By then nobody'd remember a tattoo. Lisa Gough certainly didn't.

But Snagglepuss had a problem. He needed ta finger the Wacker. Ta pass on the virus ya need ta be round the other person, find a way a givin them the bad blood. But the Wacker'd never been seen round Sam – or, for that matter, bad blood. Everyone knew he hated junkies. Sacked any huzzy a his was on the gear or got sick.

Ooh, Snagglepuss, whatcha gointa do?

Snagglepuss had a think. Snagglepuss was good at thinkin. Snagglepuss came up with answers. All he needed was ta stick it on someone who ticked the four boxes. Means. Opportunity. Motive. Connection.

Who could that someone be? Someone close ta Sam; pal a the family maybe? Someone with access ta manky needles – needles any dealer could pick up if they knew the scene? Someone with a grudge against the Don and his family – someone been left danglin by Snags, maybe? Someone who'd been seen callin upta Fred Mahon. Cleaned-up seeminly, accordin ta me brother John Paul. Lookin for protection. Seeminly.

Some gear-lovin ruthless killin nineteen-year-old piece a street scum ditched by his boss and with nobody else in the world that cared what happened him.

Nobody?

Sshh, Lucy. Concentrate.

Tick tick tick. Tick.

Great word, *seeminly*. Did ya visit Wacker off yer own bat, or did Snags tell ya ta, sayin he'd a plan ta set him up? Was that what tipped ya over, made ya decide ta leg it?

Is this what went on in yer head, while Amanda was bidin her time, thinkin about stayin or goin? Ya realized the scope a the set-up. He was gointa name ya as the Wacker's pawn – killin ya first so ya couldn't deny it; probably even say he killed ya because ya'd confessed. Then he'd take the story ta Wacker and blackmail him for control over the north city.

If the Wacker bought it there and then, Snags would hafta keep quiet about Sam . . . for a bit. But he never minded waitin. Sooner or later she'd get sick. The Don would find out, have his heart broke, and Snags could blacken yer name and Wacker's as much as he liked. If Wacker played tough, he'd take a risk, spread the rumours earlier. Within weeks Fred Mahon's name would be mud, Snags could move in ta take over his territory and nobody would bat an eyelid.

Either ways old Snagglepuss would be lickin his lips at the sweet cold taste a revenge. Except—

Charlie, gabblin in me ear again. About vampires kissin devils and devils in doors and standin in the flames a hell holdin swords over sleepin angels and zombies on the stairs comin for him and stoners and pushers and—

Back, youse demons. Back. Back. Back.

So ya weren't his. Fine. Okay. Then why's yer jury still booin ya? And don't tell me—

Bitchin about me, Amanda said, after I went upstairs, how I didn't know what I wanted—

What did I want? Oh, you tell me, Nayler. You tell me.

Always needed somethin else ta get me kicks –

Else than what, Nayler?

– made her sick, she said, ta see ya actin like ya cared—

Actin?

Restless ya were, she said, kept gettin upta go, even picked up yer bag, then just sat down again. I know that feelin. Want ta leave, can't. Want ta walk out, forget the cunt. Can't. Wanta not have anythin ta do with them ever again because they're no fuckin use ta ya. Can't. Don't wanta think a how they've fucked themselves up because it's none a yer business. Can't. And even when it gets worse, when ya know ya've landed yerself in the shit, and them too, and what's precious ta them, and it's all fucked, way worse than ya thought, and there's no excuses any more and ya should just – Leave. Head. Go.

Ya can't.

Ya start towards the door, pushin past Amanda, callin me name.

Amanda grabs ya.

'Jesus Christ, stop it, Neil! Ya done nothin but bring shit ta her, just let her be. Ya been no good for her, not ever—'

True, Amanda, or false? Did she really want ta protect me? Was she really worried ya were gointa go up and mess more with me head? Or was she just a little bit jealous that for all yer flirtin and messin ya wouldn't tell *her* what was goin on?

Shit. The washin machine's started again, rollin me head round. Too many thoughts. Thumpin on me chest. Can't breathe. Won't. Iron grippin me heart. Can't beat. Won't—

It's sorta . . . interestin bein up here. If a bit cold. There's Charlie, still hidden in his corner. Still fascinated by the blood on me face and front. So fascinated he's . . .

Ungh. Get yer hands off me, kissin cousin

smeared some on his fingers.

Voices downstairs. Loud. That Amanda? Or—

Ya turn on Amanda, angry, because what does she, stupid cow—

But then ya see the look on her face and it makes ya feel real sorry for her and then ya start laughin. Because it's so fucked up. And yeah, in one way she's right, ya are no good ta me and never have been and this shit we're all in now is proof a that. But I'm no good for you neither. And that's what she can't see, poor stupid cow. There's always been two a us playin that game and she knows nothin a what we really had—

Ah ah. Stop.

What did we have goin on, Nayler? A one-sided usin? Master and dog? A fight a equals? A game a dares, risin stakes, called bluffs? Or a thing that crept in under the skin, an itch that wouldn't stop burnin, a big vexin pain in the hole that neither of us wanted but neither of us could live without?

Hello? Hell – oh?

Lucy callin—

*

Rewind. Fifteen year ago, a canal bank. A beautiful lad with a bleached Mohawk, sharp and swaggerin. Flicks his lazy insultin gaze onta me face and as he holds it there, one two three four five seconds too long, the insult leaks out and all that's left is pure . . .

You, said yer eyes glued ta me face. Ya pulled away – an effort – took in me body, owned it. *I want*. Back ta me face. Only a second. Enough. *You*.

Hunger? True or false? You tell me.

What did he want? A snotty-nosed kid? A plain-as-the-day gobshite mascot good for a laugh? Or his own Lucy Lu, buddin inta a girl version of her handsome da, pretty-boy Italian face, wiry body, skin burstin with hot thoughts after lyin beside sexy Amanda.

Ya glanced at Micko, went ta dig me. Dig me or yer first try at a—

Kiss.

Disgustin, I thought, pullin away. Disgustin? True or false?

Second try. Basement stairs. Ya grab me head, pull me towards yer mouth. I pull away. Ya grab harder. I pull harder. Stalemate. Ya ruffle me hair. Good dog.

Third. Days a the old HellFire Club. Yer room. Yer arm lands on me shoulder. Itched me, that arm, so fuckin hot. Couldn't stick bein close. Couldn't stick bein apart. Same for you? I don't know.

Forward.

Footsteps. Ya standin in the doorway. Ya see me on the ground. Ya look upset at that. Angry. Charlie's scared. Because he thinks ya the Devil. The Devil in the door. He's keepin quiet, pressin himself inta the corner so ya won't see him. Ssshh. He shouldn't be worried. Ya've forgotten he exists, let alone he's up here. Like ya've always forgotten Charlie.

Ya down on yer knees. Fast. Ya got me mouth open, head tilted—

Huhgh. Blood on me tongue. Am I down here again or am I—

Ya roll me over on me side. Very professional. Callin me name.

Hahgh. Hurts. That—

That's me chest ya thumpin, Nayler. Hard. Now ya puttin yer mouth on mine—

Ah. Salt. Spices too, under the iron a me blood. Yer breath is clean. Sweet and—

Not doin much good, pal. Afraid I'm still blue.

Charlie's eyes is very round, watchin the Devil kissin the vampire. But ya can't see him because he's bein quiet as a—

Did ya see him that day, Nayler, hidin in the basement? Or did ya just see me? Why didn't ya grab me, boot me up the stairs? Why did ya leave me there? Ta protect me? Test me? Punish me? Were ya ragin I'd found a way in? What did it feel like, Nayler, cuttin slices off of Mainser's face and knowin I was listenin? Did it feel . . . real? As real as Mainser's bloody eartips felt between me fingers? As real as they felt ta you the day ya found me souvenirs?

So. Why d'ya come up here, Lucy? Gave me enough chances before ya first offered me the gear. What built yer offer, Nayler? Yer hunger? Yer need ta call me bluff? Play me? Teach me a lesson? Hire me for Snags? Does it matter? I took the bait.

Safe that was, for both of us. Oh, yeah, much safer ta put our wantin on the gear; for you ta watch me suck, swoon, fall insteada—

For me ta watch ya ridin Ma insteada—

Rewind.

And ya keep laughin, crackin yerself up as – 'See the mad thing was, Amanda, I never fuckin wanted—'

Hang on. If this is whatcha sayin, if it wasn't her ya wanted, if it was me, then why did ya hold back, Nayler? I know I always batted ya off, butcha coulda had me easy, if ya were that desperate. Coulda stuck it in me when I was goofin. I wouldn't even a cared. But ya never done. Why? Manners, was it? Waitin for a yes? Did ya really think it'd be like ridin yer brother? Or did ya just not want me when I was off me head, stupid and useless on the gear?

Does it matter? Ya mightn'a been able or willin but ya were fucked if anyone else was either. Ragin, ya were, stormin after me down that street when I headed off ta buy from them other cunts. Ragin at what I might hafta sell. Ragin too when I started bangin up. Naggin me on about Snags, what he done ta make me do it, like he'da—

Bang bang, baby. Bang bang.

But—

No. Fuck this. See, we're forgettin, Nayler. Sasha. She was the one ya held, stroked, kissed. Remember? The one ya fuckin . . . idolized. Doesn't matter how good ya took care a me after I left Ma, how ya taught me yer knife tricks, read me yer books, how bored ya got with them other girls. Doesn't matter even that ya took that hammer for me or I stepped upta that axe for you—

No. Because once she was back I was stuck on the cold side a the triangle again while the two a youse mooned round each other. Yeah, I know ya couldn't fuck her, Nayler – scared a the virus, was it? or just Snags? – but still . . . call that real?

And yeah, okay, let's say ya still did . . . care, and protect me, not just her, and it cost ya that tattoo or worse, and on comin back from the beatin ya wanted ta be free a them both, her and him. Let's say ya even wanted ta rearrange that triangle . . .

Soft, yer arm was round me, warmin me up beside the canal. Fourth try?

And yeah, let's say findin them souvenirs was about you and me as much as anythin else, the shit that's between us and the—

And ya still laughin, even with all the other shit that's goin on in yer head, even though Amanda's racin over ta Damo and wakin him, ya laughin because what Amanda doesn't know – or only half-does, *Ya were always in love with him, Lucy* – but you do, now if ya never done, is that besides bein shit for each other, both of us believe, pain in the arse though it is, that we are maybe the realest thing for each other too and always will be, which is why even though ya thought I was the rat and despised me for that ya were still sure no I wasn't—

Which is why even though ya wanted out from Snags ya came

back ta Dublin because ya had ta talk ta Whelan and when ya done that it just made ya more sure—

Which is why ya risked stayin in Dublin all that time and in the end brung me up here ta ask me fuckin ridiculous and all as it was ta—

Fifth try. Micko's room. *Sick, Lucy? I thought ya were all better.*
Nayler, I . . .

We drove each other to it. Me because I wanted the gear and because ya'd maddened me with yer secrecy. You because I'd maddened ya too, battin ya off, over and over, actin so fuckin . . . smart. We wanted ta punish each other. Yeah. But we wanted ta test each other too. Ta see what we really wanted. The gear. Or you. Snags. Or me. I don't know if we even knew that was goin on. But we went ahead and played. Old habits die hard. And then I won. Lucky me. Big sour puss. And ya knew it wasn't the gear I was after.

That look came inta yer face after ya seen I was sickened by the win. Alive and laughin and somethin else. What was that somethin else, Nayler? Was that . . . hope? You, me cool-headed captain, lettin himself . . . hope? Was that what sent ya flyin across that room ta grab me and this time not let me bat ya off—

Sixth try. Yer mouth a hairsbreadth from me skin. A line a white fire, screamin.

Hope for what? That we could be together for a night: Number Six, The Lovers, bare and simple on a bed a bracken and roses? Or more? The hope ya'd been holdin since we'd met that mornin that, fucked up as it sounds, I'd agree ta run with ya, wherever ya were goin? Was that what ya were plannin? Why ya couldn't tell me about Sam? Because once ya did ya knew I'd never go anywhere? I'd hafta stay, ta mind her.

True or false? I don't know. The second yer mouth met me throat all I could say was yes.

Yes yes yes. Let's dance, sweetheart. Let's take a chance.

*

If if if.

The airport boy is laughin. Haven't heard him in ages but he's loud and clear now.

If ya hadn't gone ta Amsterdam. If I hadn't told Sasha. If it'd been you in that doorway. If I'd told ya sooner about seein Sash with Whelan. If ya hadn't found me souvenirs. If I'd stayed on that street till the mornin. If Sash hadn't wanted back in with Snags. If ya'd come ta me sooner. If you'd won the game. If Sam hadn't come up here. If her comin hadn't put that fear a Snags back inta ya. If ya hadn't pushed me off ya like I was a piece a shit. If I hadn't told ya ta fuck off ya sad cunt. If ya hadn't just let me go. If ya'd stormed up them stairs straight after me and grabbed the gear off of me and told me ta Cop on, Lucy. For fuck's sake. Cop on. It's you I fuckin—

Ah. If if if. Millions a them, stretchin endless inta the past and the future.

Keep laughin, airport boy. I don't blame ya.

Yeah. Sure. The realest thing in the world ta each other. Which is why why fuckin why, in spite a all the bad shit I know ya done, I walked off trustin me precious little sister ta ya. Was I the fool, Nayler? Can I ask yer jury that? Can I ask them ta take us both through this last dance? Are ya ready, now, me Knight a Swords?

It's gettin real cold.

Ya've given me two lots a the antidote already. It's supposed ta work fast. But there's too much shit in the way. The hooch. The vallies. The draw. The coke's okay, might even help, but—

Ya back doin the breathin, bangin me chest. Ya were yer usual self at first. Kept the head, done the job. But now yer hands are sweatin. Shakin. Ya talkin faster, harsher. Tellin me ta come on, wake up, ya need me.

I don't think I can come down from the ceilin, though. Me heart's too—

Ya take out the last phial, stick on a spike. Ya talk ta it. Sounds funny. Tell it ta come on and work ya beauty, work ya cunt. Ya shoot.

Charlie's terrified. Hasn't a clue what's goin on.

Ya beggin me now. Come on, wake up. Beggin the antidote too. Work ya cunt.

It's not listenin.

Ya take yer hands off me. Shakin. Start ta mutter, broken, not like you, about useless what the fuck are Jesus just a little kid that sick bastard own blood how could he. Then ya back again. Rubbin, thumpin, breathin, beggin. Ya tell me ta come on, come on, come back. Call me darlin, sweetheart. That's funny. Tell me we hafta—

What do we hafta, Nayler?

Ya don't finish. Pull away, mutterin again; angry, hopeless. How ya shoulda Jesus whatcha gointa that sick cunt settin ya up and fuckin her up and ya shoulda and I shouldn'a and we coulda and can't let him use and win this is fuckin useless and—

Ya jump up. Pace, fast, fists clenched. Charlie squeezes deeper inta the corner. He's only a few feet away but ya don't sense him. Must have yer radar off. You're in a state, edgier than I've ever seen ya, even strung-out. Ya tug yer hair. Stop, shake yer head. Pace. Stop. Hug yerself. Pace, gnawin yer knuckles. Stop. Rock on yer feet. Smash yer fist at the wall. Just miss Charlie. Pace again. Then—

Stop, sudden. Calm. Eyes hidden. Ya thinkin. Ya say somethin, soft. Sounds like *I could just* . . . Then shake yer head. Race back ta me, kneel. Start all over again. Pleadin. Come *on*, I'm beggin ya, come *on*, wake up darlin.

Stop. Jump up. Pace. Stop. Down. Plead. Up. Pace. Smash. Stop. Stand. Twitch.

The Devil's all over the place, said Charlie ta Amanda.

Back down. Angry yer hands are, shakin me. Ya cryin, Nayler? Don't think so.

Hittin me, angry, angry at him the cunt sick lowlife sayin ya'll smash him for what he's done. Hey, easy with me chest, Nayler. It's not me ya wanta smash. Ya commandin me now, come on, come on, wake up, Lucy Dolan. You're me captain, Nayler. I should obey ya. And I would. I'd come down from the ceilin. Only—

Can't. Too much stuff in the way.

Ya stop. Yer hands soften. Ya stroke me hair, me mouth, me

neck. Ya lift me head onta yer lap, hold it. Yer voice is gone quiet now, like when ya useta go ta Ma for the readins. Ya start askin me stuff, What sorta life would that be for her? Tell me, Lucy. Is that what she deserves. A little kid hasn't hurt – bein used like that. What kinda life. Sick. Ugly livin death. That's not better than dyin. Tell me, Lucy. What sorta. Ya only whisperin but it sounds—

Christ, ya say. Desperate. Now ya shakin me, callin me a stupid bitch for dyin on ya but ya huggin me too so tight sayin ya hafta it's the only thing that's what ya do do what ya will it's the only thing but ya can be kind yeah kind isn't that better Lucy savin kind than be left livin a sick bein used I hafta understand I'm the only one ya wish ya hada but it's what ya do only thing ya fuckin do and—

Then ya gone. Like that. The Devil's out the door.

He beat me. Yer voice was droney on the phy. Stripped me ta me skin, tied me ta a willa tree, took off his belt and whacked me so hard he cut me open. Then he kept whackin till I could see the rib. That'll teach ya ta be afraid, son.

Sins a the fathers, I said, and laughed, droney.

Ya touched me face. Fuck, no, Lucy. Things is never that simple.

Ya took me hand, pushed up yer tee-shirt, placed me palm across yer scar.

There. I seen ya look at it enough times, Lucy.

Four inches between our mouths. White space, blazin. Nothin between me palm, yer skin, only heat. The tattered curtains in the winda. Blowin in, blowin out.

He left me out there all night. Came back the next mornin. Hugged me. Cried, told me he'd always come back for me, he loved me. Ya laughed. Lyin cunt. Call that love? That's not real love.

So what is, Nayler? Me voice sounded very far away.

Ya smiled. You tell me.

Silence held between us. Then I started laughin again because all I could think was, *Not fuckin this.*

*

Not this, Nayler.

Sam sleeps, hand tucked under her cheek.

I know. I can't see that from here. All I can see is the room and Charlie sneakin up outta his corner, over me body, out the door and down the stairs where he—

Seen the Devil in the flames a hell holdin his sword over the angel.

Ya stand beside her, one hand reachin past the hilt a yer sword for the needle in yer jacket, the other reachin for the lethal dose a smack in yer back pocket.

Is this what yer jury hate ya for, Nayler?

Do it. Kill her. This is what you do. It would be kind. You could save her from him. He couldn't use her then. Let her die innocent. Beautiful. Make it kind, Nayler. Do what you will. And this is what you do. You kill. Save her.

True or false?

The tattoo coulda been nothin, Nayler. Coincidence. A man with the same name, smile, voice. Sam was feelin sick but – fucksake, she coulda been startin her periods. And so what if she had a bad feelin? What worth is that? A so-called gift a second sight? How real is that? What proof is that? And even if she was sick, even if he had got her, so what? There's drugs out there, good ones, and doctors. Her life wouldn't hafta be—

How could killin her protect her, Nayler? What gives you the right ta make that choice? Just because ya good with a knife or a gun? What did ya really want? Ta save her from Snags or ta get yer own back on him? That's not noble. Or kind. That's not protectin her. That's not savin. That's just—

Hah. The airport boy laughs. Revenge.

And what about yer own rules, about people deservin ta die? Did she deserve that? That's just—

Do it. One last death and ya can be free.

Free a what, Nayler? Free ta do what?

Charlie sees ya touchin the hilt a yer sword. Ya pull out the needle.

One last death. A kind one.

Kind? I was still alive, Nayler. Up here. Yes, barely. Dead, nearly—
Ya reach in the other pocket, take out the gear.

But long as there was a chance even the slightest that I would wake up and see her then how could ya betray that trust I'd always had in ya, no matter what ya—

Tick—

What happened, Nayler? Did all the reasons, the excuses, the noble and the not so noble, leak outta ya, along with any thought a me – us; whatever that was? What were ya left with? A hot twitchin under the skin? A curiosity, cool and hungry, at what it would be like ta—

Go on. Do it. Just for the sake of it. Ya've always wanted ta.

An intent, cold and natural ta ya as breathin?

Was there even a trace a yer iron will left ta fight it? Or—

Tick—

This I can't prove. This I've no memory a. All I have is what happened at the end and the *zombies on the stairs had ta protect meself didn't know she was the angel* shite—

So this is what I imagine.

Ya drop yer fists.

Tock.

Did ya blaze with white fire in that moment, Nayler? Were ya pure? Or were ya just . . . fallen? Bare? Lost? A skinny white-faced boy with shakin hands and no idea a who he was any more?

'Hey, little hen.' Ya bend down, shake her shoulder. Yer palms are clammy. Ya feel dazed, sick. Dirty. 'Wake up, sweetheart. Lucy's bad. We hafta—'

Get me ta the hospital, Nayler? Very responsible a ya. Her eyes flutter, open.

'Okay, darlin. Wait here. I'll be down in a bit.' Then ya get up, walk out, still in a daze, and . . .

Crash. Fall over Charlie who's scramblin away from ya back up the stairs.

And that's when all the shoutin starts.

Me body's still lyin on the ground. Faded. Breath slow. Heart too. That stuff ya gave me doesn't have much of a chance. I'm driftin higher. Colder. I can hear sounds below, like people talkin underwater. Hearin is the last sense ta go, Derek says . . .

'Get off me! No!' He scrabbles backwards. 'You're the Devil! Get away from me—'

'Jesus fuck! What the fuck you still doin here ya little—' Meanin, *what did ya see?*

Charlie lifts somethin. 'I'm warnin ya . . . stay away!'

'Fucksake, Charlie, relax, okay, relax. I'm tryin ta—'

'Don't kill me! I seen ya hurt Lucy! Keep away!'

'I didn't fuckin hurt—' What did he see? What did he hear? Ya rethink, put yer hands up. 'Look . . . Charlie, it's only me. Nayler.' Take a breath. Try ta keep calm. Take a step, slow. Smile. Mis-take.

Yer teeth are red with the blood from me mouth. Charlie screams, swings the brick at yer head. Ya twist, shove him off. He staggers down a coupla steps, knockin over a candle. Pitch black. Only a dim square a cloud-covered moonlight from a winda.

'Nayler?' says a thin voice. 'What's the . . . Charlie?'

Then the moon comes out and it all turns ta shit. He's screamin again, worse than before, he's already got another brick and even though ya racin down the steps ta get between him and her, the zombie he sees comin for him, callin his name, face sick blue in the moonlight, glitterin like Christmas lights, black blood down its cheeks, empty eyes, bony arms reachin out tryin ta protect herself, even though ya yellin no no Charlie, it's Sam, he can't hear ya because he's racin at her with that brick and screamin too and she is too and . . .

Ya get ta him, knock his arm. Too late. The brick misses her nose but glances off of her forehead. Her face sinks backwards. The moon disappears. Pitch again. Ya grab his wrist but his skin's slippy – blood. He twists himself free, swings his arm back for another swipe. Ya jerk yer head. Can't see. The brick misses yer face, swoops down, connects with yer ribs, bashin open that old

649

wound. Ya grunt, crumple, fall. He swings the other way. Sound a somethin shatterin. Stone on bone. A crunch. Her head inta the wall. Another shatter . . .

Ya tear yerself up, fly at him but he's kickin, wild, boots ya in the jaw. Swings the brick. Ya dodge it. Another crunch. Ya brave his kicks, grab his arm, knee him in the bollocks, slap his head. He loses balance, crashes against the wall just as the moon comes out again. And ya see . . .

He's knocked inta her. Her head jerks, her back jack-knifes, her scarred legs on them stupid red platforms totter. And then she falls, somersaultin head over heels through the moonlight, pale and beautiful, down the stairs. Blonde hair, battered face, long white arms flyin like wings.

'Oh, Jesus!' screams Charlie and starts ta cry. 'I didn't mean ta push her. I thought it was a zombie. I didn't know it was—'

An angel, fallin. There's a crack as her head smashes inta the ground.

Sounds real slow, the way I'm tellin it. I'd say it was fast, though.

A vision of a woman's face, beautiful, bleedin in the wall. From the past or the future?

Loose bricks on the stairs that I stumbled over on me way down that mornin. A wet patch on the wall. Mould? Or . . . her blood?

I wasn't the pusher, Charlie told Amanda. But I had ta be a stoner, only way ta protect meself round the zombies.

Wrong. I didn't push her, said Charlie. But I had ta stone her. Only way ta protect—

Ya scream, an animal howl from the bottom a yer soul.

'What the fuck have ya done ya stupid cunt?'

What the fuck has he done, Nayler?

What the fuck have we all done, stupid cunts that we are?

I only remember the shoutin and the screamin, the bashin and the wailin. After that it got quiet and I don't remember much till the end. But here's what I guess.

The next mornin he kept tellin Amanda about his plans for the future, code, all that, how nothin would ever stop him doin what he wanted. Nothin?

How long did it take him ta think of it? How long did it take for his sobbin ta cease and that cold, clever parta him ta kick in? Did it come ta him as he watched ya bend over her, try ta bring her back, smooth her hair off her ruined face? As ya stood, shakin, rememberin me, started walkin back up them stairs, thinkin, Fuck, Lucy, what can I—

It woulda made perfect sense ta him. He wasn't the one hurt, tortured, robbed, killed. He wasn't the one stood over people with a sword. Why should he take the flak when there was you? How did he do it? By tellin ya how much he knew on ya, the post office job, all that? How deep Stevo was in with the right people? How Marlene would fix it, like she fixed Amanda's baby, Stevo's money, the assault charge on the auld wan?

Was he nervous as he threatened ya? Gleeful ta get his own back on the arrogant stupid cunt who'd always underestimated him? Or was he just . . . cold?

What about you then, Nayler? Were ya still dazed, sick and ragin at him for what he'd done, and yerself too – wanted ta punish him, someone, anyone? Or was it just the animal in ya kickin in; survive, no matter what?

Was that why ya turned his threat back on him, told him – calm, were ya, on the surface again? – that if his Ma was so good at fixin stuff, maybe she should remember who Sam's real da was. And then maybe she should have a think about who that da would believe killed his daughter in that messy way. A professional like you – or him?

It was a bluff, a course. You were nowhere near the Don any more. But still . . .

A secret Marlene knew, Charlie told Amanda. *About the dawn.*

Not just you and me, then?

Marlene got real uneasy, at that party years ago when me Da's old enemy Morsey started bangin on about where Sam got her

651

brown eyes from. Ma'da told Marlene because she needed ta tell someone. I see the two a them, pissed in the kitchen, two young wans roarin laughin about the bold things they got upta behind their fellas' backs.

Did it sicken ya, Nayler, ta think maybe she coulda helped if ya'd told me about Snags and Sam sooner? Or were ya well gone beyond sickened then?

Soldiers comin after him, Charlie told Amanda.

Ya threatened him with more than the Don if he didn't get Marlene ta cover for youse. Didn't ya? Ya laid the Soldier on him, whose gun he'd robbed.

Ya bad cunt.

Facts, Irene? Evidence, jury?

See, I always wondered about them, that couple I seen the next mornin, barrellin up the path. Funny, I thought, even at the time, even me head the way it was, not yer typical relaxed Bank Hollyer walk. A fair-haired cunt and a skinny woman. They looked at me like they knew me, knew what had happened. I kept me head down. Runnin up that hill, they were. A woman, greyhound-skinny and fast.

Where's Marlene? I asked that bitchy twin on the phone. Gone on a walk.

A walk? Marlene never went on walks.

They seen me come outta that clearin. They'da found her in . . . fuck. Minutes.

Hung up every time I called. Sent Charlie off ta boardin school. Gates, security, broken glass, cleaners. Off ta England for university. Told the coppers nothin, John Paul neither. Nor Ma.

I can see why. Government contracts, nice big house, five kids they wanted ta send ta college, a young fella they were pushin as the next Bill Gates. A naked girl with her face battered ta pieces? Oh, yeah. I can see it.

I can see too how they thought it would be alright. Sam was dead; bein hid away wouldn't hurt her any more. I was a lost cause.

Micko, another. John Paul was fine, he'd survive Armageddon. And Ma? Ah well. Poor auld Rose. Someone had ta pay.

Besides, I'm sure they told themselves that I coulda always told Ma I seen the body. If I wanted ta. Why should it be them ta speak first?

Was that why Marlene never said a thing ta me in them visions I had a her dyin? What could she say after doin that?

Charlie's gone a good while. Hard ta see any more, even though I think it's gettin light outside. Ya sittin beside me, yer back against the wall, yer feet drawn up, huggin yer knees. Close as ya can get ta me without touchin. Ya not sayin anythin. Ya been like this for ages.

Now ya—

Aah. Curlin up round me. Still takin care not ta touch. Belly ta back. Chestbone ta shoulder blades. Knees ta knees. An inch a space. Makes no odds. I can still feel that heat that's always between us.

Ya hafta go. That's what it means, the curlin up. But not without—

Yer mouth opens. I think ya wanta say somethin but ya can't find the words.

Hurry up there, Nayler. I hafta go.

'Lucy, I—'

Ya stop. That's because ya still can't find a way a sayin it that wouldn't be false.

Come on, Nayler. I hafta—

Aah. Ya lift yer arm, cradle me waist, close the gap.

Then ya say it. Ya bring yer mouth in and ya kiss the back a me neck. A long, fierce kiss that's got all the care in the world in it.

The last warmth rips away from me.

Ya gone.

Real high up now. And cold.

Nothin.

Nothin.

★

Ten a Swords. Body lyin face down, ten big ones stuck in its back. It's got a lotta meanins, like all them cards.

The first is the most obvious. Death, desolation, ruin. *This is what I am.* Is that whatcha were sayin when ya eased the first spike inta her? *This is what I done. Doesn't matter I chose not. She still got killed. Because I was there. I willed it. This is what I am. A killer. Destroyer. Ruiner. This is what I do and nothin, least of all me own choices, can change it.*

The second spike. *This is what we all are. Me, Snags, You, Charlie, Sasha, Amanda. Killers, destroyers, ruiners.*

Another meanin is failure in battle, also sorta obvious with the swords and all, especially in Ma's pack.

The third spike. *This body is a casualty. Unknown soldier.*

The fourth. *This may a been a war crime. A sacrifice for power and territory.*

The card also means endgame, burnout, nowhere ta go.

Fifth spike. *This is all I have left. Nothin.*

Sixth. *I am nothin. I was born with nothin, I know nothin. I deserve nothin. I am scum.*

Thing is, the card can mean truth as well. As in, facin the truth of a situation.

I'd say with the seventh and eight spikes ya said nothin, Nayler. Because there was nothin left ta say. Because if there had a been, you'da said it ta me instead a just kissin me. But on the ninth I think ya seen the truth a what ya were tryin ta do with them needles.

I want this death ta have meanin. Is that whatcha were sayin? *I want this death ta be made beautiful. Ta be marked. Ta not go unseen. I want this death ta be remembered.*

And the tenth spike? Well, they say sometimes that card means a new start.

That spike was for me, though ya never meant me ta see it.

Price for everythin. A life for a life. A sacrifice. Means, I think, givin up somethin ya love for the greater good. Not sure how it fits inta our story, but . . .

Was the moment ya spiked her with the tenth the same the anti-

654

dote finally kicked in, joinin forces with the coke ta reef the smack away and send me thrashin back down ta livin hell? Nice ta think it, but I've never had yer faith in the power a symbols, old pal.

Do what you will. *I nail. I nail. I nail.* Ten swords ya put in her. I hope ya were kind. That when ya stripped her ya treated her respectful, like a little dead cat found on the road, not a young wan ya had any bad thoughts about. That when ya spiked her ya made sure not ta hurt the veins more than ya needed. That when ya washed the blood off her face ya were gentle as Granny was when she read inside Micko's broken mouth.

I go ta the winda and watch the pinka the eastern sky turn gold. The blades a grass where she lay that mornin shine silver with the dew.

I see ya in the fog. A grey ghost. Ya take off the chain with me souvenirs, leave it round her head. *Enough a this*, that says. Then I see ya go.

Ya hup yer bag on yer shoulder, and run. Through the foggy Wickla mountains ya race, in yer mercenary's jacket, down the sand and fields a the east coast, ta Wexford and a waitin ship, runnin fast as ya can ta get away from here; yer past, yer fall, yer ruin.

Ya turn ta face the city, invisible in the murk. And then ya walk, slow and considered, the long way round the hill, down the path and back ta Dublin, ta that stinkin squat and the ugly death Snags has lined up for ya.

Does it matter where ya went?

In me dreams I always heard ya sayin ya'd come back for me. But ya never will, will ya?

Ya gone, Nayler.

I stay in the room long enough ta own it; no denial, no exaggerated responsibility. I take hold a what I done, the betrayals, the rage, the abandonment.

I let go a what I didn't. The batterin. The . . . intent.

Proof? I may never prove what really happened here that night, no matter what blood tests I dig up, or what the experts find when I send them a-lookin. But I'll do me best. When I go visitin Charlie in that English jail, I'll dig whatever truth I can outta him, so help me God, and help you too. I'll talk ta John Paul, ask him ta cross the line and ask Fred Mahon did he get a phone call early one All Souls' mornin, that told him Snags Ryan had planned ta set him up, and if that's why Snags left the northside and in thirteen year has never once gone back? I might even round up Lisa Gough and ask her what she knew, dig out a picture a Snagglepuss, maybe, and see. And I'll try and find her. No matter what it takes, what I hafta lay on Stevo or Charlie or any a them, I'll try and find her.

Because I'm willin at last ta take me sentence from the invisible jury.

I am sorry, I tell her wounded ghost who's waitin ta walk alongside me the resta me life. I know the words will never be enough, but I turn away from the bad room and open me arms, lettin the bird fall.

And him? Oh, ladies and gentlemen a the jury, that twisted boy I owe big time for wakin me up ta the truth, whatever that is. Him I'm more than happy ta keep in me sights.

Downstairs the place is a shambles.

I put the raven in the middle a the star, on top a the jewellery ya bought Sam with. Then I pile me pills up and put them beside the bird. I scatter Ma's cards over them. Then I open Lola's baggie and – yeah, still takes an effort – I sprinkle the gear over everythin. I take out the piece a paper where Derek coded his phone number and think a tearin it up. But I can't. I know every one a them pieces a music and if I tore up the paper, they'd only start playin in me head, remindin me.

I put the gun on top a the heap, after wipin it down. I may be thick as pure shit at times but I'm fucked if I'm goin behind them bars again any longer than I need.

Then I unfold me keyboard and set it in front a the pile. I move me fingers over it, and in me head the tune starts, a lament for all the ones that are gone, a chorus a risin ugly arpeggios and sad diminuendos. I play. For lovely two-faced Sasha, for me broken brother, for long-legged Cindy, for crazy Betty, for me quick-talkin mirror, me Italian Da in his Swingin Sixties suits, for me maddened Ma with her ruined rosebud mouth, for me short-sighted Granny, me fortune-tellin great-grandda, his beautiful wife, for me diamond-hard aunt Marlene, me once-gorgeous Amanda, me sappy pal Damo and me frightened cousin Charlie who was never as clever as he thought he was. I play for the twisted boy whose life I stole tryin ta get ta you, or what I thought was you. For his parents, who may one day read a letter.

For Sam.

Then, even though the angels might hate me for doin it, I play for the bullyboys. For Mainser and the Soldier, and even old Emmet Whelan. Because what were they only animals, like me and you, animals that stopped at nothin ta make themselves more equal, and who knows if there is or ever been such a thing as an angel?

And last I play for you, Nayler, me one-time captain, me Knight a Swords, wherever ya are. Still roamin unforgiven round the world, or quiet ashes long since melted inta the ground. I play for yer angel-white skin, the bruised shadas under yer eyes, the softness of yer mouth, the hardness of yer bones. The knotted muscles in yer arms, the sharpness of yer teeth, yer child's bitten nails. Yer clever killer's hands they coulda hacked off in that stinkin basement. Yer thin white feet they coulda hacked off too. Yer cat's eyes they coulda put out with a knife. Yer fine hard body they coulda drenched in oil before Snags lit the match. I play for the gear ya fed me, for the life ya saved me that at times been no life at all, for everythin ya done that should be forgot. For what we never were together, bare and easy on a bed a bracken. And last I play me thanks that ya didn't tell me at the end that ya loved me, or cried, or hugged me, or promised ya'd come back ta me.

Because that's not real—

Love.

Then I strike a match.

As I do, I think I hear Buck laughin.

Don't be fooled, auld sod, I tell him. I'm not expectin some madey-up ritual fire ta burn it all away. I know some shit stains for life. Still . . .

I wonder what the fuck I'm gointa tell Ma.

I walk out onta the hill. The sun's risin. There's a mist up, fine, faint, beautiful. Skippin the hostel last night could land me in the Joy for a bit, but it's a small price, and after that me freedom will be waitin for me, stretchin before me like the sky.

I know I can't help fuckin up; it's part a me nature, part a what makes Lucy Dolan the animal she is. I'll do me best, sure. I may even risk phonin Derek, if I'm upta it, see if there's anythin real there, beyond pity or curiosity, and if there is, well . . . maybe. But . . .

No guarantees.

I shake me out me hair, run me fingers through it.

Behind me, Buck's house begins to burn.

Acknowledgements

Thanks to everyone I've worked with on the Artists in Prisons Scheme in Portlaoise Prison and the drama workshops at the Merchants Quay Rehabilitation Project. Also: Maureen Collender, Deirdre Kinahan, Rita Gray and Eileen Sheridan from Tall Tales Theatre Company, whose support was invaluable in kick-starting the process that led to this book; Ena May, Alice Barry, Billie Traynor, Sue Mythen, Judith Ryan for the company and inspiration; the Arts Council of Ireland for their Special Projects funding; and Jocelyn Clarke, Karin McAuley and Lynne Parker for their incisive comments at a very early stage.

While this story draws on a general sense of life in a particular part of Dublin from the late 1960s to the present, it is a work of fiction, with no intention to represent any real person – apart from a mythic version of Thomas 'Buck' Whaley. Any factual inaccuracies are mine.

For their patience in answering my questions about drug use, the law and young offenders in the 70s, 80s and 90s: Clive Burquett, Roger Killeen, Sgt Dave Watts, Tara Gray, Breda, Mary Kotsonouris, Cathal Holland, Martin Tansey, Dr Brian Nolan. Thanks to Mark Wale for providing some local history and Denis Mullins for the loan of Shane Butler's excellent book *Alcohol, Drugs and Health Promotion in Modern Ireland*. *Gangland* by Paul Williams helped give me a different perspective, as did Paul Reynolds' *King Scum*.

All my friends for their support and interest along the way, especially Emer MacDowell, Karen Hand, Una MacNulty and Rex Dunlop for taking the time to read and comment on the first draft. A big one to Ruth Meehan, not only for reading, commenting and listening but also for being at the end of the phone whenever I needed it.

A special thanks to my agent, Jonathan Williams, whose faith and clear-sightedness not only brought this to the right people but also helped keep me true to the original vision; to my editor, Patricia Deevy, for her commitment, passion, understanding, pragmatism, exactitude, insights . . . and above all, her very tricky questions; and to Michael McLoughlin, Ann Cooke, Helen Campbell, Cliona Lewis, Patricia McVeigh and everyone at Penguin Ireland.

To Mum for blazing the trail, Dad for introducing me to Buck Whaley and the HellFire Club, and both of you for your unquestioning support and love over the years.

And last but not least, Seán – for everything.

The author and publisher would like to thank the following for permission to reproduce copyright material:
Warner/Chappell Overseas Holdings Ltd, London w6 8bs for the extract from 'Chirpy Chirpy Cheep Cheep' (words by Giuseppe Cassia and Claudio Fabi, music by Harold Stott) © 1971 Gruppo Intersong S.r.l. and Warner/Chappell Italiana S.p.A., Italy; the National Safety Council of Ireland for the 'Safe Cross Code' jingle; and the artist Louise Bourgeois for the text from her 'Untitled' artwork (mixed media sewn on fabric handkerchief; collection Jerry Gorovoy, New York) used in the epigraph.